Tom Sharpe

Tom Sharpe was born in 1928 and educated at Lancing College and at Pembroke College, Cambridge. He did his National Service in the Marines before going to South Africa in 1951, where he did social work before teaching in Natal. He had a photographic studio in Pietermaritzburg from 1957 until 1961, when he was deported. From 1963 to 1972 he was a lecturer in History at the Cambridge College of Arts and Technology. In 1986 he was awarded the XXXIIIeme Grand Prix de L'Humour Noir Xavier Forneret. He is married and lives in Cambridge.

Tom Sharpe

Blott on the Landscape

The Wilt Alternative

The Great Pursuit

PAN BOOKS
IN ASSOCIATION WITH SECKER AND WARBURG

Blott on the Landscape First published 1975 by Martin Secker & Warburg Ltd
and first published by Pan Books 1977
The Wilt Alternative First published 1979 by Martin Secker & Warburg Ltd
and first published by Pan Books 1981
The Great Pursuit First published 1977 by Martin Secker & Warburg Ltd
and first published by Pan Books 1979

This combined edition published 1995 by Pan Books
an imprint of Macmillan General Books
25 Eccleston Place, London SW1W 9NF

Associated companies throughout the world

ISBN 0 330 34591 5

A CIP catalogue record for this book is available from
the British Library

Printed and bound in Great Britain

'Happy Birthday'. Copyright 1939, reproduced in *The Great Pursuit* by permission of Keith
Prowse Music Publishing Company Limited 138-140 Charing Cross Road, London WC2

Blott on the Landscape

to Geoff Millard

1

Sir Giles Lynchwood, Member of Parliament for South Worfordshire, sat in his study and lit a cigar. Outside his window tulips and primroses bloomed, a thrush pecked at the lawn and the sun shone down out of a cloudless sky. In the distance he could see the cliffs of the Cleene Gorge rising above the river.

But Sir Giles had no thoughts for the beauties of the landscape. His mind was occupied with other things; with money and Mrs Forthby and the disparity between things as they were and things as they might have been. Not that the view from his window was one of uninterrupted beauty. It held Lady Maud, and whatever else she might be, nobody in his right mind would ever have described her as beautiful. She was large and ponderous and possessed a shape that someone had once aptly called Rodinesque — certainly Sir Giles, viewing her as dispassionately as six years of marriage allowed, found her monumentally unattractive. Sir Giles was not particularly fussy about external appearances. His fortune had been made by recognizing potential advantage in unprepossessing properties and he could justly claim to have evicted more impecunious tenants than any other anonymous landlord in London. Maud's appearance was the least of his marital problems. It was rather the cast of her mind, her outspoken self-assurance, that infuriated him. That, and the fact that for once in his life he was lumbered with a wife he could not leave and a house he could not sell.

Maud was a Handyman and Handyman Hall had always been her family home. A vast rambling building with twenty bedrooms, a ballroom with a sprung floor, a plumbing system that held fascinations for industrial archaeologists but which kept Sir Giles awake at night, and a central heating system that had been designed to consume coke by the ton, and now seemed to gulp oil by the megagallon. Handyman Hall had been built in 1899 to make manifest in bricks, mortar and the more hideous furnishings of the period the fact that the Handyman family had arrived. Theirs had been a brief social season. Edward the Seventh had twice paid visits to the house, on each occasion seducing Mrs Handyman in the mistaken belief that she was a chambermaid (a result of the diffidence which left her speechless in the presence of Royalty). In recompense for this royal gaffe, and for services rendered, her husband Bulstrode was raised to the Peerage. From that brief moment of social acceptance the Handymans had sunk to their present obscurity. Borne to prominence on a tide of ale – Handyman Pale, Handyman Triple XXX and Handyman West Country had been famous in their time – they had succumbed to a taste for brandy. The first earl of Handyman had died, a suspicious husband and an understandably ardent republican, in time to achieve posthumous fame as the first cadaver to incur Lloyd George's exorbitant death duties. He had been followed almost immediately by his eldest son Bartholomew, whose reaction to the taxman's summons had been to drink himself to death on two bottles of his father's Trois Six de Montpellier.

The outbreak of the First World War had completed the decline in the family fortunes. Boothroyd, the second son, had returned from France with his taste buds so irreparably impaired by taking a swig from a bottle of battery acid to steady his nerves before going over the top that his efforts to restore Handyman Ale to its pre-war quality and popularity had quite the contrary effect. For the first time the title 'Brewers Extraordinary to his Majesty the King' accurately reflected the character of the beer dispensed by the Handyman Brewery. During the twenties and thirties sales dropped until they were confined to a dozen tied houses in Worfordshire whose patrons were forced to consume Boothroyd's appalling concoctions out of a sense of loyalty to the family and by the refusal of the local magistrates (Boothroyd among them) to grant licences to sell spirituous liquors to anyone else. By that time the Handymans had been reduced to living in one wing of the great house and had celebrated the outbreak of the Second World War by offering the rest of their home to the War Office. Boothroyd had died on Home Guard duty to be succeeded by his brother Busby, Maud's father, and the Hall had served first as a home for General de Gaulle's chief of staff and the entire Free French army of that time and later as an Italian prisoner-of-war camp. The fourth Earl had done what he could to restore Handyman Ale to its previous popularity by reverting to the original recipe, and to restore the family fortune by using his influence to see that the War Office paid a quite disproportionately high rent for a building they didn't want.

It had been that influence, the Handyman influence, which had persuaded Sir Giles that he could do worse than marry Lady Maud and through her acquire a seat in Parliament. Looking back over the years Sir Giles was inclined to think that he had paid too high a price for the Hall and social acceptance. A marriage of convenience he had called it at the time, but the term had proved singularly inappropriate. Nothing about Maud's appearance had suggested an unduly fastidious attitude to sex and Sir Giles had been surprised, not to say pained, by her too literal interpretation of his suggestion on their honeymoon that she should tie him to the bed and beat him. Sir Giles' screams had been audible a quarter of a mile along the Costa Brava and had led to an embarrassing interview with the hotel manager. Sir Giles had stood all the way home and ever since had sought refuge in a separate bedroom and in Mrs Forthby, in whose flat in St John's Wood he could at least be assured of moderation. To make matters worse there was no possibility of a divorce. Their marriage settlement included a reversionary clause whereby the Hall and the Estate, for which he had had to pay one hundred thousand pounds to Maud, would revert to her in the event of his death without heirs or of misconduct on his part leading to a divorce case. Sir Giles was a rich man but one hundred thousand pounds was too high a price to pay for freedom.

He sighed and glanced out of the window. Lady Maud had disappeared but the scene was no pleasanter for her going. Her place had been taken by Blott, the gardener, who was plodding across the lawn towards the kitchen garden. Sir Giles studied the squat figure with distaste. For a gardener, for an Italian gardener *and* an ex PoW, Blott had an air of contentment that grated on Sir Giles' nerves. He liked his servants to be obsequious and there was nothing obsequious about Blott. The wretched fellow seemed to think he owned the place. Sir Giles watched him disappear through the door in the wall of the kitchen garden and considered ways and means of getting rid of Blott, Lady Maud and Handyman Hall. He had just had an idea.

·

So had Lady Maud. As she lumbered about the garden, uprooting here a dandelion and there a chickweed, her mind was occupied with thoughts of maternity.

'It's now or never,' she murmured as she squashed a slug. Between her legs she could see Sir Giles in his study and wondered once again why it was that she should have married a man with so little sense of duty. In her view there was no higher virtue. It was out of duty to her family that she had married him. Left to herself she would have chosen a younger, more attractive man, but young attractive men with fortunes were in short supply in Worfordshire and Maud too plain to seek them out in London.

'Coming out?' she had shouted at her mother when Lady Handyman had suggested she should be presented at court. 'Coming out? But I've already been.'

And it was true. Lady Maud's moment of beauty had been premature. At fifteen she had been lovely. At twenty-one the Handyman features, the prominent nose in particular, had made themselves and her plain. At thirty-five she was a Handyman all over and only acceptable to someone with Sir Giles' depraved taste and eye for hidden advantage. She had accepted his proposal without illusions, only to discover too late that his long bachelorhood had left him with a set of habits and fantasies which made it impossible for him to fulfil his part of the bargain. Whatever else Sir Giles was cut out for it was not paternity. After the unfortunate experience of their honeymoon, Maud had attempted a reconciliation, but without result. She had resorted to drink, to spicy foods, to oysters and champagne, to hard-boiled eggs, but Sir Giles had remained obdurately impotent. Now on this bright spring day when everything about her was breaking out or sprouting or proclaiming the joys of parenthood from every corner of the estate, Lady Maud felt distinctly wanton. She would make one more effort to make Sir Giles see reason. Straightening her back she marched across the lawn to the house and went down the passage.

'Giles,' she said entering the study without knocking, 'it's time we had this thing out.'

Sir Giles looked up from his *Times*. 'What thing?' he asked.

'You know very well what I'm talking about. There's no need to beat about the bush.'

Sir Giles folded the paper. 'Bush, dear?' he said doubtfully.

'Don't prevaricate,' said Lady Maud.

'I'm not prevaricating,' Sir Giles protested, 'I simply don't know what you are talking about.'

Lady Maud put her hands on the desk and leant forward menacingly. 'Sex,' she snarled.

Sir Giles curdled in his chair. 'Oh that,' he murmured. 'What about it?'

'I'm not getting any younger.'

Sir Giles nodded sympathetically. It was one of the few things he was grateful for.

'In another year or two it will be too late.'

Thank God, thought Sir Giles, but the words remained unspoken. Instead he selected a Ramon Allones from his cigarbox. It was an unfortunate move. Lady Maud leant forward and twitched it from his fingers.

'Now you listen to me, Giles Lynchwood,' she said, 'I didn't marry you to be left a childless widow.'

'Widow?' said Sir Giles flinching.

'The operative word is childless. Whether you live or die is of no great moment to me. What is important is that I have an heir. When I married you it was on the clear understanding

11

that you would be a father to my children. We have been married six years now. It is time for you to do your duty.'

Sir Giles crossed his legs defiantly. 'We've been through all this before,' he muttered.

'We have never been through it at all. That is precisely what I am complaining about. You have steadfastly refused to act like a normal husband. You have—'

'We all have our little problems, dear,' Sir Giles said.

'Quite,' said Lady Maud, 'so we do. Unfortunately my problem is rather more pressing than yours. I am over forty and as I have already pointed out, in a year or two I will be past the childbearing age. My family has lived in the Gorge for five hundred years and I do not intend to go to my grave with the knowledge that I am the last of the Handymans.'

'I don't really see how you can avoid that whatever happens,' said Sir Giles. 'After all, in the unlikely event of our having any children, their name would be Lynchwood.'

'I have always intended,' said Lady Maud, 'changing the name by deed poll.'

'Have you indeed? Well then let me inform you that there will be no need,' said Sir Giles. 'There will be no children by our marriage and that's final.'

'In that case,' said Lady Maud, 'I shall take steps to get a divorce. You will be hearing from my solicitors.'

She left the room and slammed the door. Behind her Sir Giles sat in his chair shaken but content. The years of his misery were over. He would get his divorce and keep the Hall. He had nothing more to worry about. He reached for another cigar and lit it. Upstairs he could hear his wife's heavy movements in her bedroom. She was no doubt going out to see Mr Turnbull of Ganglion, Turnbull and Shrine, the family solicitors in Worford. Sir Giles unfolded *The Times* and read the letter about the cuckoo once again.

2

Mr Turnbull of Ganglion, Turnbull and Shrine was sympathetic but unhelpful. 'If you initiate proceedings on grounds as evidently insubstantial as those you have so vividly outlined,' he told Lady Maud, 'the reversionary clause becomes null and void. You might well end up losing the Hall and the Estate.'

'Do you mean to sit there and tell me that I cannot divorce my husband without losing my family home?' Lady Maud demanded.

Mr Turnbull nodded. 'Sir Giles has only to deny your allegations,' he explained, 'and frankly I can hardly see a man in his position admitting them. I'm afraid the Court would find for him. The difficulty about this sort of case is that you can't produce convincing proof.'

'I should have thought my virginity was proof enough,' Lady Maud told him bluntly. Mr Turnbull suppressed a shudder. The notion of Lady Maud presenting her maidenhead as Exhibit A was not one that appealed to him.

'I think we should need something a little more orthodox than that. After all, Sir Giles could claim that you had refused him his conjugal rights. It would simply be his word against yours. Of course, you could still get your divorce, but the Hall would remain legally his.'

'There must be something I can do,' Lady Maud protested. Looking at her, Mr Turnbull rather doubted it but he was tactful enough not to say so.

'And you say you have attempted a reconciliation?'

'I have told Giles that he must do his duty by me.'

'That's not quite what I meant,' Mr Turnbull told her. 'Marriage is after all a difficult relationship at the best of times. Perhaps a little tenderness on your part would . . .'

'Tenderness?' said Lady Maud. 'Tenderness? You seem to forget that my husband is a pervert. Do you imagine that a man who finds satisfaction in being—'

'No,' said Mr Turnbull hurriedly. 'I take your point. Perhaps tenderness is the wrong word. What I meant was ... well ... a little understanding.'

Lady Maud looked at him scornfully.

'After all *tout comprendre, c'est tout pardonner,*' continued Mr Turnbull, relapsing into the language he associated with sophistication in matters of the heart.

'I beg your pardon,' said Lady Maud.

'I was merely saying that to understand all is to pardon all,' Mr Turnbull explained.

'Coming from a legal man I find that remark astonishing,' said Lady Maud, 'and in any case I am not interested in either understanding or in pardon. I am simply interested in bearing a child. My family have lived in the Gorge for five hundred years and I have no intention of being responsible for their not living there for another five hundred. You may find my insistence on the importance of my family romantic. I can only say that I regard it as my duty to have an heir. If my husband refuses to do his duty by me I shall find someone who will.'

'My dear Lady Maud,' said Mr Turnbull, suddenly conscious that he might be in danger of becoming the first object of her extramarital attentions, 'I beg you not to do anything hasty. An act of adultery on your part would certainly allow Sir Giles to obtain a divorce on grounds which would invalidate the reversionary clause. Perhaps you would like me to have a word with him. It sometimes helps to have a third party, someone entirely impartial you understand, to bring about a reconciliation.'

Lady Maud shook her head. She was thinking about adultery.

'If Giles were to commit adultery,' she said finally, 'would I be right in supposing that the Estate would revert to me?'

Mr Turnbull beamed at the prospect. 'No difficulties at all in that case,' he said. 'You would have an absolute right to the Estate. It's in the settlement. No difficulties at all.'

'Good,' said Lady Maud, and stood up. She went downstairs, leaving Mr Turnbull with the distinct impression that Sir Giles Lynchwood was in for a nasty surprise and, better still, that the

14

firm of Ganglion, Turnbull and Shrine could look forward to a protracted case with substantial fees.

Outside Blott was waiting in the car.

'Blott,' said Lady Maud climbing into the back seat, 'what do you know about telephone tapping?'

Blott smiled and started the car. 'Easy,' he said, 'all you need is some wire and a pair of headphones.'

'In that case stop at the first radio shop you come to and buy the necessary equipment.'

By the time they returned to Handyman Hall, Lady Maud had laid her plans.

•

So had Sir Giles. The first moment of elation at the prospect of a divorce had worn off and Sir Giles, weighing the matter up in his mind, had recognized some ugly possibilities. For one thing he did not relish the thought of being cross-examined about his private life by some eminent barrister. The newspapers, particularly one or two of the Sundays, would have a ball with Lady Maud's description of their honeymoon. Worse still, he would be unable to issue writs for libel. The story could be verified by the hotel manager and while Sir Giles might well win the divorce case and retain the Hall he would certainly lose his public reputation. No, the matter would have to be handled in some less conspicuous manner. Sir Giles picked up a pencil and began to doodle.

The problem was a simple one. The divorce, if and when it came, must be on grounds of his own choosing. He must be free from any breath of scandal. It was too much to hope that Lady Maud would find a lover, but desperation might drive her to some act of folly. Sir Giles rather doubted it, and besides, her age, shape and general disposition made it seem unlikely. And then there was the Hall and the one hundred thousand pounds he had paid for it. He drew a cat and was just considering that there were more ways of making a profit from property than selling it or burning it to the ground when the shape of his drawing, an eight with ears and tail, put him in mind of something he had once seen from the air. A flyover, a spaghetti junction, a motorway.

A moment later he was unfolding an ordnance survey map and studying it with intense interest. Of course. Why hadn't he thought of it before? The Cleene Gorge was the ideal route. It lay directly between Sheffingham and Knighton. And with motorways there came compulsory purchase orders and large sums paid in compensation. The perfect solution. All it needed was a word or two in the right ear. Sir Giles picked up the phone and dialled. By the time Lady Maud returned from Worford he was in excellent humour. Hoskins at the Worfordshire Planning Authority had been most helpful, but then Hoskins had always been helpful. It paid him to be and it certainly paid for a rather larger house than his salary would have led one to expect. Sir Giles smiled to himself. Influence was a wonderful thing.

'I'm going down to London this afternoon,' he told Lady Maud as they sat down to lunch. 'One or two business things to fix up. I daresay I shall be tied up for a couple of days.'

'I shouldn't be at all surprised,' said Lady Maud.

'If you need me for anything, leave a message with my secretary.'

Lady Maud helped herself to cottage pie. She was in a good humour. She had no doubt whatsoever that Sir Giles indulged his taste for restrictive practices with someone in London. It might take time to find out the name of his mistress but she was prepared to wait.

●

'Extraordinary woman, Lady Maud,' Mr Turnbull said as he and Mr Ganglion sat in the bar of the Four Feathers in Worford.

'Extraordinary family,' Mr Ganglion agreed. 'I don't suppose you remember her grandmother, the old Countess. No, you wouldn't. Before your time. I remember drawing up her will in ... now when can it have been ... must have been in March 1936. Let's see, she died in June of that year so it must have been in March. Insisted on my inserting the fact that her son, Busby, was of partially royal parentage. I did point out that in that case he was not entitled to inherit but she was adamant. "Royal Blood," she kept saying. In the end I got her to sign several copies of the will but it was only in the top one that any mention was made of the royal bastardy.'

'Good Lord,' said Mr Turnbull, 'do you think there was anything in it?'

Mr Ganglion looked over the top of his glasses at him. 'Between ourselves, I must admit it was not outside the bounds of possibility. The dates did match. Busby was born in 1905 and the Royal visit took place in '04. Edward the Seventh had quite a reputation for that sort of thing.'

'It certainly goes some way to explain Lady Maud's looks,' Mr Turnbull admitted. 'And her arrogance, come to that.'

'These things are best forgotten,' said Mr Ganglion sadly. 'What did she want to see you about?'

'She's seeking a divorce. I dissuaded her, at least temporarily. Seems that Lynchwood has a taste for flagellation.'

'Extraordinary what some fellows like,' said Mr Ganglion. 'It's not as though he went to a public school either. Most peculiar. Still, I should have thought Maud could have satisfied him if anyone could. She's got a forearm like a navvy.'

'I got the impression that she had rather overdone it,' Mr Turnbull explained.

'Splendid. Splendid.'

'The main trouble seems to be non-consummation. She wants an heir before it's too late.'

'The perennial obsession of these old families. What did you advise? Artificial insemination?'

Mr Turnbull finished his drink. 'Certainly not,' he muttered. 'Apparently she's still a virgin.'

Mr Ganglion sniggered. 'There was an old virgin of forty, whose habits were fearfully naughty. She owned a giraffe whose terrible laugh . . . or was it distaff? I forget now.'

They went into lunch.

•

Blott finished his lunch in the greenhouse at the end of the kitchen garden. Around him early geraniums and chrysanthemums, pink and red, matched the colour of his complexion. This was the inner sanctum of Blott's world where he could sit surrounded by flowers whose beauty was proof to him that life was not entirely without meaning. Through the glass windows he could look down the kitchen garden at the lettuces, the peas and beans, the redcurrant bushes and the gooseberries of which he was so proud. And all around the old brick walls cut out the world he mistrusted. Blott emptied his thermos flask and stood up. Above his head he could see the telephone wires stretching from the house. He went outside and fetched a ladder and presently was busily engaged in attaching his wires to the line above. He was still there when Sir Giles left in the Bentley. Blott watched him pass without interest. He disliked Sir Giles intensely and it was one of the advantages of working in the kitchen garden that they seldom came into contact. He finished his work and fitted the headphones and bell. Then he went into the house. He found Lady Maud washing up in the kitchen.

'It's ready,' he said, 'we can test it.'

Lady Maud dried her hands. 'What do I do?'

'When the bell rings put the headphones on,' Blott explained.

'You go into the study and ring a number and I'll listen,' said Lady Maud. Blott went into the study and sat behind the desk. He picked up the phone and tried to think of someone to call. There wasn't anyone he knew to call. Finally his eye fell on a number written in pencil on the pad in front of him. Beside it there were some doodles and a drawing of a cat. Blott dialled the number. It was rather a long one and began with 01 and he had to wait for some time for an answer.

'Hullo, Felicia Forthby speaking,' said a woman's voice.

Blott tried to think of something to say. 'This is Blott,' he said finally.

'Blott?' said Mrs Forthby. 'Do I know you?'

'No,' said Blott.

'Is there anything I can do for you?'

'No,' said Blott.

There was an awkward silence and then Mrs Forthby spoke. 'What do you want?'

Blott tried to think of something he wanted. 'I want a ton of pig manure,' he said.

'You must have the wrong number.'

'Yes,' said Blott and put the phone down.

In the greenhouse Lady Maud was delighted with the experiment. 'I'll soon find out who's beating him now,' she thought and took the headphones off. She went back to the house.

'We shall take it in turns to monitor all telephone calls my husband makes,' she told Blott. 'I want to find out who he's visiting in London. You must write down the name of anyone he talks to. Do you understand?'

'Yes,' said Blott and went back to the kitchen garden happily. In the kitchen Lady Maud finished washing up. She'd meant to ask Blott who he had been talking to. Never mind, it wasn't important.

3

Sir Giles got back from London rather sooner than he had expected. Mrs Forthby's period had put her in a foul mood and Sir Giles had enough on his plate without having to put up with the side-effects of Mrs Forthby's menstrual tension. And besides, Mrs Forthby in the flesh was a different kettle of fish to Mrs Forthby in his fantasies. In the latter she had a multitude of perverse inclinations, which corresponded exactly with his own unfortunate requirements, while possessing a discretion that would have done credit to a Trappist nun. In the flesh she was disappointingly different. She seemed to think, and in Sir Giles' opinion there could be no greater fault in a woman, that he loved her for herself alone. It was a phrase that sent a shudder through him. If he loved her at all, and it was only in

19

her absence that his heart grew even approximately fonder, it was not for Mrs Forthby's self. It was precisely because as far as he could make out she lacked *any* self that he was attracted to her in the first place.

Externally Mrs Forthby had all the attributes of desirable womanhood, rather too many for more fastidious tastes, and all confined within corsets, panties, suspender belts and bras that inflamed Sir Giles' imagination and reminded him of the advertisements in women's magazines on which his sexual immaturity had first cut its teeth. Internally Mrs Forthby was a void if her inconsequential conversation was anything to go by and it was this void that Sir Giles, ever hopeful of finding a lover with needs as depraved as his own, sought to fill. And here he had to admit that Mrs Forthby fell far short of his expectations. Broad-minded she might be, though he sometimes doubted that she had a mind, but she still lacked enthusiasm for the intricate contortions and strangleholds that constituted Sir Giles' notions of foreplay. And besides she had an unfortunate habit of giggling at moments of his grossest concentration and of interjecting reminiscences of her Girl Guide training while tightening the granny knots which so affected him. Worst of all was her absent-mindedness (and here he had no quarrel with the term). She had been known to leave him trussed to the bed and gagged for several hours while she entertained friends to tea in the next room. It was at such moments of enforced contemplation that Sir Giles was most conscious of the discrepancies between his public and his private posture and hoped to hell the two wouldn't be brought closer together by some damned woman looking for the lavatory. Not that he wouldn't have welcomed some intervention into his fantasy world if only he could be certain that he wouldn't be the laughing-stock of Westminster. After one such episode he had threatened to murder Mrs Forthby and had only been restrained by his inability to stand upright even after she had untied him.

'Where the hell have you been?' he shouted when she returned at one o'clock in the morning.

'Covent Garden,' Mrs Forthby said. 'The Magic Flute. A divine performance.'

'You might have told me. I've been lying here in agony for six hours.'

'I thought you liked that,' Mrs Forthby said. 'I thought that's what you wanted.'

'Wanted?' Sir Giles screamed. 'Six hours? Nobody in his right mind wants to be trussed up like a spring chicken for six hours.'

'No, dear,' Mrs Forthby said agreeably. 'It's just that I forgot. Shall I get you your enema now?'

'Certainly not,' shouted Sir Giles, in whom some measure of self-respect had been induced by his confinement. 'And don't meddle with my leg.'

'But it shouldn't be there, dear. It looks unnatural.'

Sir Giles stared violently out of the corner of his right eye at his toes. 'I know it shouldn't be there,' he yelled. 'And it wouldn't be if you hadn't been so damned forgetful.'

Mrs Forthby had tidied up the straps and buckles and had made a pot of tea. 'I'll tie a knot in my handkerchief next time,' she said tactlessly, propping Sir Giles up on some pillows so that he could drink his tea.

'There won't be a next time,' he had snarled and had spent a sleepless night trying desperately to assume a less contorted posture. It had been an empty promise. There was always a next time. Mrs Forthby's absent shape and her ready acceptance of his revolting foibles made good the lapses of her memory and Sir Giles returned to her flat whenever he was in London, each time with the fervent prayer that she wouldn't leave him hooded and bound while she spent a month in the Bahamas.

•

But if Sir Giles had difficulties with Mrs Forthby there were remarkably few as far as the motorway was concerned. The thing was already on the drawing board.

'It's designated the Mid-Wales Motorway, the M101,' he was told when he made discreet enquiries of the Ministry of the

Environment. 'It has been sent up for Ministerial approval. I believe there have been some doubts on conservation grounds. For God's sake don't quote me.' Sir Giles put the phone down and considered his tactics. Ostensibly he would have to oppose the scheme if only to keep his seat as member for South Worfordshire but there was opposition and opposition. He invested heavily in Imperial Cement, who seemed likely to benefit from the demand for concrete. He had lunch with the Chairman of Imperial Motors, dinner with the Managing Director of Motorway Manufacturers Limited, drinks with the Secretary of the Amalgamated Union of Roadworkers, and he pointed out to the Chief Whip the need to do something to lower the rate of unemployment in his constituency.

In short he was the catalyst in the chemistry of progress. And with it all no money passed hands. Sir Giles was too old a dog for that. He passed information. What companies were on the way to making profits, what shares to buy, and what to sell, these were the tender of his influence. And to insure himself against future suspicions he made a speech at the annual dinner of the Countryside Conservation League in which he urged eternal vigilance against the depredations of the property speculator. He returned to Handyman Hall in time to be outraged by the news of the proposed motorway.

'I shall demand an immediate enquiry,' he told Lady Maud when the requisition order arrived. He reached for the phone.

In the greenhouse Blott had his time cut out listening to Sir Giles' telephone calls. He had no sooner settled down to deal with some aphids on the ornamental apple trees that grew against the wall than the bell rang. Blott dashed in and listened to General Burnett fulminating from the Grange about blackguards in Whitehall, red tape, green belts and blue-stockings, none of which he fully understood. He went back to his aphids when the phone rang again. This time it was Mr Bullett-Finch phoning to find out what Sir Giles intended to do about stopping the motorway.

'It's going to take half the garden,' he said. 'We have spent the last six years getting things shipshape and now for this to happen. It's too much. It's not as though Ivy's nerves can stand it.'

Sir Giles sympathized unctuously. He was, he said, organizing a protest committee. There was bound to be an Enquiry. Mr Bullett-Finch could rest assured that no stone would be left unturned. Blott returned to the aphids puzzled. The English language still retained its power to baffle him, and Blott occasionally found himself trapped in some idiom. Shipshape? There was nothing vaguely in the shape of a ship about Mr Bullett-Finch's garden. But then Blott had to admit that the English themselves remained a mystery to him. They paid people more when they were unemployed than when they had to work. They paid bricklayers more than teachers. They raised money for earthquake victims in Peru while old-age pensioners lived on a pittance. They refused Entry Permits to Australians and invited Russians to come and live in England. Finally they seemed to take particular pleasure in being shot at by the Irish. All in all they were a source of constant astonishment to him and of reassurance. They were only happy when something dreadful happened to them, be it flood, fire, war or some appalling disaster, and Blott, whose early life had been a chapter of disasters, took comfort from the fact that he was living in a community that actually enjoyed misfortunes.

Born when, of whom, where, he had no idea. The date of his discovery in the Ladies Room in the Dresden railway station was as near as he could get to a birthday and since the lady cleaner had disclaimed any responsibility for his appearance there, although hard pressed by the authorities to do so, he had no idea who his mother was – let alone his father. He couldn't even be sure his parents had been Germans. For all he and the authorities knew they might have been Jews, though even the Director of the Race Classification Bureau had had the illogical grace to admit that Jews did not make a habit of abandoning their offspring in railway cloakrooms. Still, the notion lent a further element of uncertainty to Blott's adolescence in the Third Reich and he had got no help from his appearance. Dark, hook-nosed pure Aryans there doubtless were, but Blott, who had taken an obsessive interest in the question, found few who were happy to discuss their pedigree with him. Certainly no one was prepared to adopt him, and even the orphanage tended to push him into the background when there were visitors. As for the Hitler Youth ... Blott preferred to forget his adolescence and even the memory of his arrival in England still filled him with uneasiness.

It had been a dark night and Blott, who had been put in to stiffen the resolve of the crew of an Italian bomber, had taken the opportunity to emigrate. Besides, he had a shrewd suspicion that his squadron leader had ordered him to volunteer as navigator to the Italians in the hope that he would not return. It seemed the only explanation for his choice and Blott, whose previous experience had been as a rear-gunner where his only contribution to the war effort had been to shoot down two Messerschmidt 109s that were supposed to be escorting his bomber squadron, had fulfilled his squadron leader's expectations to the letter. Even the Italian airmen, pusillanimous to a man, had been surprised by Blott's insistence that Margate was situated in the heart of Worcestershire. After a heated argument they dropped their bombs over Exmoor and headed back for the Pas de Calais across the Bristol Channel before running out of fuel over the mountains of North Wales. It was at this point that the Italians decided to bale out and were attempting to explain the urgency of the situation to Blott, whose knowledge of Italian was negligible, when they were saved the bother by the intervention of a mountain which, according to Blott's bump of direction, should not have been there. In the ensuing holocaust Blott was the sole survivor and since he was discovered naked in the wreckage of an Italian bomber by a search party next morning it was naturally assumed that he must be Italian. The fact that he couldn't speak a word of his native tongue deceived nobody, least of all the Major in charge of the prisoner-of-war camp to which Blott was sent, for the simple reason that he couldn't speak Italian either and Blott was his first prisoner. It was only much later, with the arrival of some genuine Italian prisoners from North Africa, that doubts were cast on his nationality, but by that time Blott had established his bona fides by displaying no interest in the course of the war and by resolutely demonstrating a reluctance to escape that was authentically Italian. Besides, his claim to have been born the son of a shepherd in the Tyrol explained his lack of Italian.

In 1942 the camp had been moved to Handyman Hall and Blott had made the place his home. The Hall and the Handyman family appealed to him. They were both the epitome of Englishness and in Blott's view there could be no higher praise. To be English was the supreme virtue and being a prisoner in England was better than being free anywhere else. If he had had his way the war would have continued indefinitely. He lived in a great house, he had a park to walk in, a river to fish in, a kitchen garden to grow things in, and the run of an idyllic countryside full of woods and hills and fair women whose husbands were away fighting to save the world from people like Blott. Even at night when the camp gates were closed it was perfectly easy to scale the walls and go where he liked. There were no air-raids, no sudden alarms and the whole question of earning a living was taken care of. Even the food was good, supplemented as it was by his poaching and his husbandry in the kitchen garden. To Blott the place was paradise and his only worry was that Germany might win the war. It was an eventuality he dreaded. It had been bad enough being a German in Germany. He couldn't imagine what it would be like to be an Italian who was a German who looked like a Jew in conquered Britain, and the notion of trying to explain how he came to be what he was where he was to the German occupying authorities appalled him. It was one of the nicest things about the English that they didn't seem to worry about such details, but he knew his own countrymen too well to imagine that they would be satisfied with his evasions. Layer by layer, they would peel off his equivocations until the nothing that was the essential Blott was revealed quite naked and then they would shoot what was left for desertion. Blott had no doubt about his fate, and what made matters worse was that as far as he could tell the British were quite incapable of winning the war. Half the time they seemed oblivious of the fact that there was a war on, and for the rest conducted it with an inefficiency that astonished him. Shortly after his arrival at the Hall, Western Command had conducted manoeuvres in the Cleene Forest and Blott had watched the chaos that ensued with horror. If these were the men on whose fighting qualities he had to depend for his captivity, he would have to look for his salvation elsewhere. He found it in a nearby ammunition dump which was, quite typically, unguarded and Blott, determined that if the English wouldn't defend him he would, slowly acquired a small arsenal which he buried in the forest. Two-inch mortars, Bren guns, rifles, boxes of ammunition, all disappeared without notice and were cached, carefully greased and watertight, under the bracken in the hills behind the Hall. By 1945 Blott was in a position to fight a guerrilla war in South Worfordshire. And then the war ended and new problems arose.

The prospect of being repatriated to Italy was not one that appealed to him and he couldn't see himself settling down in Naples after so many agreeable years in England. On the other hand he had no intention of returning to what remained of Dresden. It was in the Russian Zone and Blott had no desire to swop the comforts of life in Worfordshire for the rigours of existence in Siberia. Besides, he rather doubted if even a defeated Fatherland would welcome home a man who had spent five years masquerading as an Italian PoW. It seemed far wiser to stay where he was, and here his devotion to the Handyman family paid off.

Lord Handyman had been a man of enthusiasms. Long before it was generally fashionable he had conceived the notion that the world's resources were on the verge of extinction and had sought to avoid the personal consequences by saving everything. He had been particularly keen on compost and Blott had dug enormous pits in the kitchen garden into which all household refuse of an organic sort was thrown.

'Nothing must be wasted,' the Earl had declared, and nothing was. Under his direction the Hall's sewage system had been diverted to empty into the compost pits and Blott and the Earl had spent happy hours observing the layers of cabbage stalks, potato peelings, and excrement which made up the day's leavings. As each pit filled Blott dug another one and the process began again. The results were quite astonishing. Enormous cabbages and alarming marrows and cucumbers proliferated. So, in summer, did the flies until the situation became intolerable and Lady Handyman, who had lost her appetite since the recycling began, put her foot down and insisted that either the flies went or she would. Blott diverted the sewage system back to its proper place while the Earl, evidently inspired by the rate of reproduction of the flies, turned his attention to rabbits. Blott had constructed several dozen hutches built one above the other on the lines of apartment buildings in which the Earl installed the largest rabbits he could buy, a breed called Flemish Giants. Like all the Earl's schemes, the rabbits had not been an unqualified success. They consumed enormous quantities of vegetation and the family had developed an aversion for rabbit pie, roast rabbit, rabbit stew and lapin à l'orange, while Blott had been driven to distraction trying to keep pace with their voracious appetites. To add to his problems Maud, then ten, had identified her father with Mr McGregor and had aided and abetted the rabbits to escape. As peace broke out in Europe the Gorge was overrun with Flemish Giants. By then Lord Handyman's enthusiasm had waned. He turned to ducks and particularly to Khaki Campbells, a species which had the advantage that they were largely self-supporting and produced an abundance of eggs.

'Can't go wrong with ducks,' he had said cheerfully as the family switched from a diet of rabbit to duck eggs. As usual with his prophecies this one had proved unfounded. It was all too easy to go wrong with ducks, as the family found out when the Earl succumbed to a lethal egg that had been laid too close to one of his old compost pits. Passing away as peacefully as

27

ptomaine poisoning allowed, he had left Maud and her mother to manage alone. It was largely thanks to his death that Blott had been allowed to stay on at the Hall.

4

Over the next few weeks Lady Maud was intensely active. She took legal advice from Mr Turnbull daily. She canvassed opposition to the proposed motorway from every quarter of South Worfordshire and she sat almost continuously on committees. In particular she made her considerable presence felt on the Committee for the Preservation of the Cleene Gorge. General Burnett of the Grange, Guildstead Carbonell, was elected President but as Secretary Lady Maud was the driving force. Petitions were organized, protest meetings held, motions proposed, seconded and passed, money raised and posters printed.

'The price of justice is eternal publicity,' she said with an originality that startled her hearers, but which in fact she had found in *Bartlett's Familiar Quotations*. 'It is not enough to protest, we must make our protest known. If the Gorge is to be saved it will not be by words alone but by action.' On the platform beside her Sir Giles nodded his apparent approval, but inwardly he was alarmed. Publicity was all very well, and justice was fine when it applied to other people but he didn't want public attention focused too closely on his role in the affair. He had expected the motorway to upset Lady Maud; he had not foreseen that she would turn into a human tornado. He certainly hadn't supposed that his seat would be jeopardized by the uproar she seemed bent on provoking.

'If you don't see that the Hall is saved,' Lady Maud told him, 'I'll see to it that you don't sit for South Worfordshire at the next election.' Sir Giles took the threat seriously and consulted Hoskins at the Planning Authority in Worford.

'I thought you wanted the thing to go through the Gorge,' Hoskins told him as they sat in the bar of the Handyman Arms.

Sir Giles nodded unhappily. 'I do,' he admitted, 'but Maud has gone berserk. She's threatening . . . well, never mind.'

Hoskins was reassuring. 'She'll get over it. They always do. Got to give them time to get used to the idea.'

'It's all very well for you to talk,' said Sir Giles, 'but I have to live with the beastly woman. She's up half the night thundering about the bloody house and I'm having to cook for myself. Besides, I don't like the way she keeps cleaning her father's shotgun in the kitchen.'

'You know she took a potshot at one of the surveyors last week,' Hoskins said.

'Can't you have her charged?' Sir Giles asked eagerly. 'That would take the heat off for a bit. Haul her up before the local beaks.'

'She *is* a local magistrate,' Hoskins pointed out, 'and anyway there's no proof. She would just claim she was shooting rabbits.'

'And that's another thing. She's got the house full of bloody great Alsatians. Hired them from some damned security firm. I tell you I can't go down the passage for a pee in the night without running the risk of being bitten.' He ordered another two whiskies and considered the problem. 'There'll have to be an Enquiry,' he said finally. 'Promise them an Enquiry and they'll calm down a bit. Secondly, offer the Enquiry a totally unacceptable alternative. Like we did with the block of flats in Shrewton.'

'You mean give planning permission for a sewage farm?'

'That's what we did there. Worked like a charm,' Sir Giles said. 'Now if we could come up with an alternative route which nobody in his right mind would accept . . .'

'There's always Ottertown,' said Hoskins.

'What about Ottertown?'

'It's ten miles out of the way and you'd have to go through a council estate.'

Sir Giles smiled. 'Right through the middle?'

'Right through the middle.'

'It sounds promising,' Sir Giles agreed. 'I think I shall be the first to advocate the Ottertown route. You're quite sure it's unacceptable?'

'Quite sure,' said Hoskins. 'And, by the way, I'll take my fee in advance.'

Sir Giles looked round the bar. 'My advice is to buy ...' he began.

'Cash this time,' said Hoskins, 'I lost on United Oils.'

Sir Giles returned to Handyman Hall in a fairly good humour. He disliked parting with money but Hoskins was worth it and the Ottertown idea was the sort of strategy he liked. It would take Maud's mind off eternal publicity. Tempers would cool and the Enquiry would decide in favour of the Gorge. By then it would be too late to inflame public opinion once again. Enquiries were splendid soporifics. He ran the gauntlet of the guard dogs and spent the evening in his study writing a letter to the Minister of the Environment demanding the setting up of an Enquiry. No one could say that the Member of Parliament for South Worfordshire had not got the interests of his constituents at heart.

•

While Sir Giles connived and Lady Maud committed, Blott in the kitchen garden had his work cut out trying to do his conflicting duties. He would settle down to weed the lettuces only to be interrupted by the bell in the greenhouse. Blott spent hours listening to long conversations between Sir Giles and officials at the Ministry, between Sir Giles and members of his constituency or his stockbroker or his business partners, but never between Sir Giles and Mrs Forthby. Sir Giles had been forewarned. Mrs Forthby's remark that she had received a call from someone called Blott who had ordered a ton of pig manure had alarmed Sir Giles. There was obviously some mistake though how Blott could have got hold of the number in the first place he couldn't imagine. It wasn't in the telephone index on his desk. He kept it in his private diary and the diary was in his pocket. Sir Giles memorized the number and then erased it from the diary. There would be no more calls to Mrs Forthby from Handyman Hall.

When Sir Giles wasn't on the telephone, Lady Maud was, issuing orders, drumming up support or hurling defiance at the authorities with a self-assurance that amazed and delighted Blott. You knew where you were with her and Blott, who prized certainty above all else, emerged from the greenhouse after listening to her with the feeling that all was well with the world and would remain so. Handyman Hall, the Park, the Lodge, a great triumphal arch at the bottom of the drive where Blott lived, the kitchen garden, all those things to which he had grafted his own anonymity in a hostile world, would remain safe and secure if Lady Maud had anything to do with it. Sir Giles' calls left a different impression. His protests were muted, too polite and too equivocal to satisfy Blott, so that he came away with the feeling that something was wrong. He couldn't put his finger on it, but whenever he took the earphones off after listening to Sir Giles he felt uneasy. There was too much talk about money for Blott's liking, and in particular about ample compensation for the Hall. The sum most frequently mentioned was a quarter of a million pounds. As he went down the rows of lettuces with his hoe, Blott shook his head. 'Money talks,' Sir Giles had told his caller but it had said nothing to Blott. There were more important words in his vocabulary. On the other hand his hours of listening to Sir Giles had done wonders for his accent. With the headphones on Blott had sat practising Sir Giles' pronunciation. In his study Sir Giles said, 'Of course, my dear fellow, I absolutely agree with you ...' In the greenhouse Blott repeated the words. By the end of a week his imitation was so exact that Lady Maud, coming into the kitchen garden to collect some radishes and spring onions for lunch one day, had been astonished to hear Sir Giles' voice issuing from among the geraniums. 'I looked upon the whole thing as an infringement of the rules of conservation,' he was saying. 'My dear General, I shall do my damnedest to see that the matter is raised in the House.' Lady

Maud stood and gazed into the greenhouse and was just considering the possibility that Blott had rigged up a loudspeaker there when he emerged, beaming triumphantly.

'You like it, my pronunciation?' he asked.

'Good heavens, was that you? You gave me quite a start,' Lady Maud said.

Blott smirked proudly. 'I have been practising correct English,' he said.

'But you speak English perfectly.'

'I don't. Not like an Englishman.'

'Well, I'd be glad if you didn't go round speaking like my husband,' said Lady Maud. 'It's bad enough having one of him about the place.'

Blott smiled happily. These were his sentiments exactly.

'Which reminds me,' she continued, 'I must see that the TV people cover the Enquiry. We must get the maximum publicity.'

Blott collected his hoe and went back to his lettuces while Lady Maud, having collected her radishes, returned to the kitchen. He was rather pleased with himself. It wasn't often he got a chance to demonstrate his ability to mimic people. It was a skill that had developed from his earliest days at the orphanage. Not knowing who he was, Blott had tried out other people's personalities. It had come in handy poaching, too. More than one gamekeeper had been startled to hear his employer's voice issuing from the darkness to tell him to stop making an ass of himself while Blott made good his escape. Now as he worked away at the weeds he tried out Sir Giles again. 'I demand that there be an Enquiry into this whole business,' he said. Blott smiled to himself. It sounded quite authentic. And there was going to be an Enquiry too. Lady Maud had said so.

5

The Enquiry was held in the Old Courthouse in Worford. Everyone was there – everyone, that is, whose property stood on the proposed route through the Cleene Gorge. General Burnett, Mr and Mrs Bullett-Finch, Colonel and Mrs Chapman, Miss Percival, Mrs Thomas, the Dickinsons, all seven of them, and the Fullbrooks who rented a farm from the General. There were also a few other influential families who were quite unaffected by the motorway but who came to support Lady Maud. She sat in front with Sir Giles and Mr Turnbull and behind them the seats were all filled. Blott stood at the back. On the other side of the aisle the seats were empty except for a solicitor representing the Ottertown Town Council. It was quite clear that nobody seriously supposed that Lord Leakham would decide in favour of Ottertown. The thing was a foregone conclusion – or would have been but for the intervention of Lady Maud and the intransigence of Lord Leakham, whose previous career as a judge had been confined to criminal cases in the High Court. The choice of venue was unfortunate, too. The Old Courthouse resembled too closely the courtrooms of Lord Leakham's youth for the old man to deal at all moderately with Lady Maud's frequent interruption of the evidence.

'Madam, you are trying the court's patience,' he told her when she rose to her feet for the tenth time to protest that the scheme as outlined by Mr Hoskins for the Planning Board was an invasion of individual liberty and the rights of property. Lady Maud bristled in tweeds.

'My family has held land in the Cleene Gorge since 1472,' she shouted. 'It was entrusted to us by Edward the Fourth who designated the Handyman family custodians of the Gorge—'

'Whatever His Majesty Edward the Fourth may have done,' said Lord Leakham, 'in 1472 has no relevance to the evidence being presented by Mr Hoskins. Be so good as to sit down.'

Lady Maud sat down. 'Why don't you two men do something?' she demanded loudly. Sir Giles and Mr Turnbull shifted uncomfortably in their seats.

'You may continue, Mr Hoskins,' said the judge.

Mr Hoskins turned to a large relief model of the county which stood on a table. 'As you can see from this model South Worfordshire is a particularly beautiful county,' he began.

'Any fool with eyes in his head can see that,' Lady Maud commented loudly. 'It doesn't require a damnfool model.'

'Continue, Mr Hoskins, continue,' Lord Leakham said with a restraint that suggested he had in mind giving Lady Maud rope to hang herself with.

'Bearing this in mind the Ministry has attempted to preserve the natural amenities of the area to the greatest possible extent—'

'My foot,' said Lady Maud.

'We have here,' Mr Hoskins went on, pointing to a ridge of hills that ran north and south of the Gorge, 'the Cleene Forest, an area of designated natural beauty noted for its wild life . . .'

'Why is it,' Lady Maud enquired of Mr Turnbull, 'that the only species that doesn't seem to be protected is the human?'

By the time the Enquiry adjourned for lunch Mr Hoskins had presented the case for the Ministry. As they went downstairs Mr Turnbull had to admit that he was not optimistic.

'The snag as I see it lies in those seventy-five council houses in Ottertown. If it weren't for them I think we would stand a good chance, but quite frankly I can't see the Enquiry deciding in favour of demolishing them. The cost would be enormous and in any case there is the additional ten miles to be taken into account. Frankly, I am not hopeful.'

It was market day in Worford and the town was full. Outside the courtroom two TV cameras had been set up.

'I have no intention of being evicted from my home,' Lady Maud told the interviewer from the BBC. 'My family have lived in the Cleene Gorge for five hundred years and . . .'

Mr Turnbull turned away sadly. It was no good. Lady Maud might say what she liked, it would make no difference. The motorway would still come through the Gorge. In any case

Lady Maud had made a bad impression on Lord Leakham. He waited for her to finish and then they made their way through the market stalls to the Handyman Arms.

'I wonder where Giles has got to,' she said as they entered the hotel.

'I think he's gone over to the Four Feathers with Lord Leakham,' Mr Turnbull told her. 'He said something about putting him in a more mellow mood.'

Lady Maud looked at him furiously. 'Did he indeed? Well, I'll see about that,' she snapped and leaving Mr Turnbull in the foyer she went into the manager's office and phoned the Four Feathers. When she came out there was a new glint of malice in her eye.

They went into the dining-room and sat down.

·

At the Four Feathers Sir Giles ordered two large whiskies in the lounge before sending for the menu.

Lord Leakham took his whisky doubtfully.

'I really shouldn't at this time of the day,' he said. 'Peptic ulcer you know. Still, it's been a tiring morning. Who was that ghastly woman in the front row who kept interrupting?'

'I think I'll have prawns to start with,' said Sir Giles hurriedly.

'Reminded me of the assizes in Newbury in '28,' Lord Leakham continued. 'Had a lot of trouble with a woman there. Kept getting up in the dock and shouting. Now what was her name?' He scratched his head with a mottled hand.

'Lady Maud is rather outspoken,' Sir Giles agreed. 'She has something of a reputation in this part of the world.'

'I can well believe it,' said the Judge.

'She's a Handyman, you know.'

'Really?' said Lord Leakham indifferently. 'I should have thought she could have afforded to employ one.'

'The Handyman family have always been very influential,' Sir Giles explained. 'They own the brewery and a number of licensed premises. This is a Handyman House, as a matter of fact.'

'Elsie Watson,' said Lord Leakham abruptly. 'That's the name.' Sir Giles looked doubtful.

'Poisoned her husband. Kept shouting abuse from the dock. Didn't make the slightest difference. Hanged her just the same.' He smiled at the recollection. Sir Giles studied the menu wistfully and tried to think what to recommend for someone with a peptic ulcer. Oxtail à la Handyman or consommé? On the other hand, he was delighted at the way things had gone at the Enquiry. Maud's display had clinched the matter. Finally he ordered Tournedos Handyman for himself, and Lord Leakham ordered fish.

'Fish is off,' said the head waiter.

'Off?' said Sir Giles irritably.

'Not on, sir,' the man explained.

'What on earth is Bal de Boeuf Handyman?' asked the Judge.

'Faggot.'

'I beg your pardon.'

'Meatball.'

'And Brandade de Handyman?' Lord Leakham enquired.

'Cod balls.'

'Cod? That sounds all right. Yes I think I'll have that.'

'Cod's off,' said the waiter.

Lord Leakham looked desperately at the menu. 'Is anything on?'

'I can recommend the Poule au Pot Edward the Fourth,' said Sir Giles.

'Very appropriate,' said Lord Leakham grimly. 'Oh well I suppose I'd better have it.'

'And a bottle of Chambertin,' Sir Giles said indistinctly. He wasn't very happy with his French.

'Extraordinary way to run an hotel,' said Lord Leakham. Sir Giles ordered two more whiskies to hide his irritation.

•

In the kitchen the chef took their order. 'You can forget the chicken,' he said. 'He can have Lancashire hotpot or faggots à la me.'

'But it's Lord Leakham and he ordered chicken,' the waiter protested. 'Can't you do something?'

The chef took a bottle of chilli powder off the shelf. 'I'll fix something,' he said.

The wine waiter meanwhile was having difficulty finding a Chambertin. In the end he took the oldest bottle he could find. 'Are you sure you want me to serve him this?' he asked the manager, holding up a bottle filled with a purple cloudy fluid that looked like a post-mortem specimen.

'That's what her ladyship instructed,' said the manager. 'Just change the label.'

'It seems a bloody peculiar thing to do.'

The manager sighed. 'Don't blame me,' he muttered. 'If she wants to poison the old bugger that's her affair. I'm just paid to do what she tells me. What is it anyway?'

The wine waiter wiped the bottle. 'It says it's crusted port,' he said doubtfully.

'Crusted's about the word,' said the manager and went back to the kitchen, where the chef was crumbling some leftover faggots on to half a fried chicken. 'For God's sake don't let anyone else have a taste of that stuff,' he told the chef.

'Serve him right for poking his nose into our affairs,' said the chef, and poured sauce from the Lancashire hotpot on to the dish. The manager went upstairs and signalled to the head waiter. Sir Giles and Lord Leakham finished their whiskies and went through into the dining-room.

•

At the Handyman Arms Lady Maud finished her lunch and ordered coffee. 'One can place too much reliance on the law,' she said. 'My family didn't get where they did by appealing to the courts.'

'My dear Lady Maud,' said Mr Turnbull, 'I implore you not to do anything foolish. The situation is already fraught with difficulty and quite frankly your interruptions this morning didn't help. I'm afraid Lord Leakham may have been prejudiced against us.'

Lady Maud snorted. 'If he isn't he soon will be,' she said.

'You don't seriously suppose that I intend to accept his judgment? The man is a buffoon.'

'He is also a retired judge of considerable reputation,' said Mr Turnbull doubtfully.

'His reputation is only just beginning.' Lady Maud replied. 'It has been perfectly obvious from the beginning that he was going to decide to recommend that the motorway be put through the Gorge. The Ottertown route is not an alternative. It's a red herring. Well, I for one am not going to put up with that.'

'I don't really see what you can do.'

'That, Henry Turnbull, is because you are a lawyer and hold the law in high regard. I don't. And since the law is an ass I intend to see that everyone is aware of the fact.'

'I wish I could see some way out of the situation,' said Mr Turnbull sadly.

Lady Maud stood up. 'You will, Henry, you will,' she said. 'There are more ways of killing a cat than choking it with cream.' And leaving Mr Turnbull to meditate on the implications of this remark she stalked out of the dining-room.

•

At the Four Feathers Lord Leakham would have understood at once, though given the choice he would have chosen cream every time. The prawn cocktail which he had not ordered but which had been thrust on him by the head waiter appeared to have been marinated in tabasco, but it was as nothing to the Poule au Pot Edward the Fourth. His first mouthful left him speechless and with the absolute conviction that he had swallowed some appalling corrosive substance like caustic soda.

'That chicken looks good,' said Sir Giles as the Judge struggled to get his breath. 'It's a speciality of the maison, you know.'

Lord Leakham didn't know. With starting eyes he reached for his glass of wine and took a large swig. For a moment he cherished the illusion that the wine would help. His hope was short-lived. His palate, in spite of being cauterized by the Poule au Pot, was still sufficiently sensitive to recognize that whatever it was he was in the process of swallowing it most certainly wasn't Chambertin '64. For one thing it appeared to be filled with some sort of gravel which put him in mind of ground glass and for another what he could taste of the muck seemed to be nauseatingly sweet. Stifling the impulse to vomit he held the glass up to the light and stared into its opaque depths.

'Anything the matter?' asked Sir Giles.

'What did you say this was?' asked the Judge.

Sir Giles looked at the label on the bottle. 'Chambertin '64', he muttered. 'Is it corked or something?'

'It's certainly something,' said Lord Leakham who wished the stuff had never been bottled, let alone corked.

'I'll get another bottle,' said Sir Giles and signalled to the wine waiter.

'Not on my account I beg you.'

But it was too late. As the wine waiter hurried away Lord Leakham, distracted by the strange residue under his upper dentures, absent-mindedly took another mouthful of Poule au Pot.

'I thought it looked a bit dark myself,' said Sir Giles ignoring the desperate look in Lord Leakham's bloodshot eyes. 'Mind you I have to admit I'm not a connoisseur of wines.'

Still gasping for air, Lord Leakham pushed his plate away. For a moment he resisted the temptation to quench the flames with crusted port but the certain knowledge that unless he did something he would never speak again swept aside all considerations of taste. Lord Leakham drained his glass.

·

In the public bar of the Handyman Arms Lady Maud announced that drinks were on the house. Then she crossed the Market Square to the Goat and Goblet and repeated the order before making her way to the Red Cow. Behind her the bars filled with thirsty farmers and by two o'clock all Worford was drinking Lady Maud's health and damnation to the motorway. Outside the Old Courthouse she stopped to chat with the TV men. A crowd had assembled and Lady Maud was cheered as she went inside.

'I must say we do seem to have the public on our side,' said General Burnett as they went upstairs. 'Mind you I thought things looked pretty grim this morning.'

Lady Maud smiled to herself. 'I think you will find they liven up this afternoon,' she said and swept majestically into the courtroom where Colonel and Mrs Chapman were chattering with the Bullett-Finches.

'Leakham has a fine record as a judge,' Colonel Chapman was saying. 'I think we can rely on him to see our point of view.'

•

By the time he had finished his lunch Lord Leakham was incapable of seeing anyone's point of view but his own. What prawns tabasco and Poule au Pot had begun, the Chambertin '64 and its successor, a refined vinegar that Sir Giles chose to imagine was a Chablis, had completed. That and the Pêche Maud with which Lord Leakham had attempted to soothe the spasms of his peptic ulcer. The tinned peaches had been all right but the ice cream had been larded with a mixture of cloves and nutmeg, and as for the coffee . . .

As he hobbled down the steps of the Four Feathers in the vain hope of finding his car waiting for him – it had been moved on by a traffic warden – as he limped up Ferret Lane and across Abbey Close accompanied by his loathsome host, Lord Leakham's internal organs sounded the death knell of what little restraint he had shown before lunch. By the time he reached the Old Courthouse to be booed by a large crowd of farmers and their wives he was less a retired judge than an active incendiary device.

'Have those damned oafs moved on,' he snarled at Sir Giles. 'I will not be subject to hooliganism.'

Sir Giles phoned the police station and asked them to send some men over to the Courthouse. As he took his seat beside Lady Maud it was clear that things were not proceeding as he had expected. Lord Leakham's complexion was horribly mottled and his hand shook as he rapped the gavel on the bench.

'The hearing will resume,' he said huskily. 'Silence in court.' The courtroom was crowded and the Judge had to use his gavel a second time before the talking stopped. 'Next witness.'

Lady Maud rose to her feet. 'I wish to make a statement,' she said. Lord Leakham looked at her reluctantly. Lady Maud was not a sight for sore stomachs. She was large and her manner suggested something indigestible.

'We are here to take evidence,' said the Judge, 'not to listen to statements of opinion.'

Mr Turnbull stood up. 'My lord,' he said deferentially, 'my client's opinion is evidence before this Enquiry.'

'Opinion is not evidence,' said Lord Leakham. 'Your client whoever she may be . . .'

'Lady Maud Lynchwood of Handyman Hall, my lord,' Mr Turnbull informed him.

'. . . is entitled to hold what opinions she may choose,' Lord Leakham continued, staring at the author of Poule au Pot Edward the Fourth with undisguised loathing, 'but she may not express them in this court and expect them to be accepted as evidence. You should know the rules of evidence, sir.'

Mr Turnbull adjusted his glasses defiantly. 'The rules of evidence do not, with due deference to your lordship's opinion, apply in the present circumstances. My client is not under oath and—'

'Silence in court,' snarled the Judge, addressing himself to a drunken farmer from Guildstead Carbonell who was discussing swine fever with his neighbour. With a pathetic look at Lady Maud Mr Turnbull sat down.

'Next witness,' said Lord Leakham.

Lady Maud stood her ground. 'I wish to protest,' she said with a ring of authority that brought a hush to the courtroom. 'This Enquiry is a travesty . . .'

'Silence in court,' shouted the Judge.

'I will not be silenced,' Lady Maud shouted back. 'This is not a courtroom—'

'It most certainly is,' snarled the Judge.

Lady Maud hesitated. The courtroom was obviously a court-room. There was no denying the fact.

'What I meant to say . . .' she began.

'Silence in court,' screamed Lord Leakham whose peptic ulcer was in the throes of a new crisis.

Lady Maud echoed the Judge's private thoughts. 'You are not fit to conduct this Enquiry,' she shouted, and was supported by several members of the public. 'You are a senile old fool. I have a right to be heard.'

In his chair Lord Leakham's mottled head turned a plum colour and his hand reached for the gavel. 'I hold you in con-tempt of court,' he shouted banging the gavel. Lady Maud lurched towards him menacingly. 'Officer, arrest this woman.'

'My lord,' Mr Turnbull said, 'I beg you to . . .' but it was too late. As Lady Maud advanced two constables, evidently acting on the assumption that an ex-judge of the High Court knew his law better than they did, seized her arms. It was a terrible mistake. Even Sir Giles could see that. Beside him Mr Turnbull was shouting that this was an unlawful act, and behind him pandemonium had broken out as members of the public rose in their seats and surged forward. As his wife was frog-marched, still shouting abuse, from the courtroom, as Lord Leakham bellowed in vain for the court to be cleared, as fighting broke out and windows were broken, Sir Giles sat slumped in his seat and contemplated the ruin of his plans.

•

Downstairs the TV cameramen, alerted by the shouts and the fragments of broken glass raining on their heads from the windows above, aimed their cameras on the courtroom door as Lady Maud emerged dishevelled and suddenly surprisingly demure between two large policemen. Somewhere between the courtroom and the cameras her twinset had been quite ob-scenely disarranged, a shoe had been discarded, her skirt was torn suggestively and she appeared to have lost two front teeth. With a brave attempt at a smile she collapsed on the pavement, and was filmed being dragged across the market square to the police station. 'Help,' she screamed as the crowd parted. 'Please help.' And help was forthcoming. A small dark figure hurtled out of the Courthouse and on to the larger of the two policemen. Inspired by Blott's example several stallholders threw themselves into the fray. Hidden by the crowd from the cameras Lady Maud reasserted her authority. 'Blott,' she said sternly, 'let go of the constable's ears.' Blott dropped to the ground and the stallholders fell back obediently. 'Constables, do your duty,' said Lady Maud and led the way to the police station.

Behind her the crowd turned its attention to Lord Leakham's Rolls-Royce. Apples and tomatoes rained on the Old Courthouse. To roars of approval from the onlookers Blott attempted single-handed to turn the car over and was immediately joined by several dozen farmers. When Lord Leakham, escorted by a posse of policemen, emerged from the Courthouse it was to find his Rolls on its side. It took several baton charges to clear a way through the crowd and all the time the cameras recorded faithfully the public response to the proposed motorway through the Cleene Gorge. In Ferret Lane shop windows were broken. Outside the Goat and Goblet Lord Leakham was drenched with a pail of cold water. In the Abbey Close he was concussed by a portion of broken tombstone, and when he finally reached the Four Feathers the Fire Brigade had to be called to use their hoses to disperse the crowd that besieged the hotel. By that time the Rolls-Royce was on fire and groups of drunken youths roamed the streets demonstrating their loyalty to the Handyman family by smashing street lamps.

In her cell in the police station Lady Maud removed her dentures from her pocket and smiled at the sounds of revelry. If the price of justice was eternal publicity she was assured of a fair trial. She had done what she had set out to do.

6

In London the Cabinet, meeting to cope with yet another turn for the worse in the balance of payments crisis, greeted the news of the disturbances in Worford less enthusiastically. The evening papers had headlined the arrest of an MP's wife but it was left to the television news to convey to millions of homes the impression that Lady Maud was the victim of quite outrageous police brutality.

'Oh my God,' said the Prime Minister as he watched her on the screen. 'What the hell do they think they've been doing?'

'It rather looks as if she's lost a couple of teeth,' said the Secretary of State for Foreign Affairs. 'Is that a teat hanging out there?'

Lady Maud smiled bravely and collapsed on to the pavement.

'I shall institute a full investigation at once,' said the Home Secretary.

'Who the hell appointed Leakham in the first place?' snarled the Prime Minister.

'It seemed a suitably impartial appointment at the time,' murmured the Minister of the Environment. 'As I remember it was thought that an Enquiry would satisfy local opinion.'

'Satisfy . . .?' began the Prime Minister, only to be interrupted by a phone call from the Lord Chancellor who complained that the rule of law was breaking down and even after it was explained to him that Lord Leakham was a retired judge muttered mysteriously that the law was indivisible.

The Prime Minister put the phone down and turned on the Minister of the Environment. 'This is your pigeon. You got us into this mess. You get us out. Anyone would think we had an absolute majority.'

'I'll see what I can do,' said the Minister.

'You'll do better than that,' said the Prime Minister grimly. On the screen Lord Leakham's Rolls-Royce was burning brilliantly.

The Minister of the Environment hurried from the room and

phoned the home number of his Under-Secretary. 'I want a troubleshooter sent to Worford to sort this mess out,' he said.

'A troubleshooter?' Mr Rees, who was in bed with flu and whose temperature was 102, was in no fit state to deal with Ministerial requests for troubleshooters.

'Someone with a flair for public relations.'

'Public relations?' said Mr Rees, searching his mind for a subordinate who knew anything about public relations. 'Can I let you know by Wednesday?'

'No,' said the Minister, 'I need to be able to tell the Prime Minister that we have the situation in hand. I want someone despatched tomorrow morning by the latest. We need to have someone up there who will take charge of negotiations. I look to you to pick someone with initiative. None of your run-of-the-mill old fogies. Someone different.'

Mr Rees put the phone down with a sigh. 'Someone different indeed,' he muttered. 'Troubleshooters.' He felt aggrieved. He disliked being phoned at home, he disliked being ordered to make rapid decisions, he disliked the Minister and he particularly disliked the suggestion that his department consisted of run-of-the-mill old fogies.

He took another spoonful of cough mixture and considered a suitable candidate to send to Worford. Harrison was on leave. Beard was engaged on the Tanker Terminal at Scunthorpe. Then there was Dundridge. Dundridge was clearly unsuitable. But the Minister had specified someone different and Dundridge was decidedly different. There was no denying that. Mr Rees lay back in his bed, his head fuzzy with flu and recalled some of Dundridge's initiatives. There had been the one-way system for Central London, of an inflexibility that would have made it impossible to drive from Hyde Park Corner to Piccadilly except by way of Tower Bridge and Fleet Street. Then there was his pilot project for installing solid-state traffic lights in Clapham, a scheme so aptly named that it had isolated that suburb from the rest of London for almost a week. In practical terms Dundridge was clearly a disaster. On the other hand he did have a flair for public relations. His schemes sounded good and year by year Dundridge had been promoted, carried upward by an ineluctable wave of inefficiency and the need to save the public the practical consequences of his latest idea until he had reached that rarefied zone of administration where, thanks to the inertia of his subordinates, his projects could never be implemented.

Mr Rees, semi-delirious and drugged with cough medicine, decided on Dundridge. He went downstairs and dictated his instructions by phone to the tape recorder on his secretary's desk at the Ministry. Then he poured himself a large whisky and drank to the thought of Dundridge in Worford. 'Trouble-shooter,' he said and went back to bed.

•

Dundridge travelled to work by tube. It was in his opinion the rational way to travel and one that avoided the harsh confusion of reality. Seated in the train he was able to concentrate on essentials and to find some sense of order in the world above by studying the diagram of the Northern Line on the wall opposite. Far above him there was chaos. Streets, houses, shops, blocks of flats, bridges, cars, people, a welter of disparate and perverse phenomena which defied easy categorization. By looking at the diagram he could forget that confusion. Chalk Farm followed Belsize Park and was itself followed by Camden Town in a perfectly logical sequence so that he knew exactly where he was and where he was going. Then again, the diagram showed all the stations as equidistant from their neighbours and while he knew that in fact they weren't, the schematic arrangement suggested that they should be. If Dundridge had had anything to do with it they would have been. His life had been spent in pursuit of order, an abstract order that would have supplanted the perplexities of experience. As far as he was concerned variety was not the spice of life but gave it a very bitter flavour. In Dundridge's philosophy everything conformed to a norm. On one side there was chance, nature red in tooth and claw and everything haphazard; on the other science, logic and numeration.

Dundridge particularly favoured numeration and his flat in

Hendon conformed to his ideal. Everything he possessed was numbered and marked on a chart above his bed. His socks for instance were 01/7, the 01 referring to Dundridge himself and the 7 to the socks and were to be found in the top drawer left (1) of his chest of drawers 23 against the wall 4 of his bedroom 3. By referring to the chart and looking for 01/7/1/23/4/3 he could locate them almost immediately. Outside his flat things were less amenable and his attempts to introduce a similar system into his office at the Ministry had met with considerable – grade 10 on the Dundridge scale – resistance and contributed to his frequent transfers from one department to another.

He was therefore not in the least surprised to find that Mr Joynson wanted to see him in his office at 9.15. Dundridge arrived at 9.25.

'I got held up in the tube,' he explained bitterly. 'It's really most irritating. I should have got here by 9.10 but the train didn't arrive on time. It never does.'

'So I've noticed,' said Mr Joynson.

'It's the irregularity of the stops that does it,' said Dundridge. 'Sometimes it stops for half a minute and at other times for a minute and a half. Really, you know, I do think it's time we gave serious consideration to a system of continuous flow underground transportation.'

'I don't suppose it would make any difference,' said Mr Joynson wearily. 'Why don't you just catch an earlier train?'

'I'd be early.'

'It would make a change. Anyway I didn't ask you here to discuss the deficiencies of the Underground system.' He paused and studied Mr Rees' instructions. Quite apart from the incredible choice of Dundridge to handle a situation which demanded intelligence, flexibility and persuasiveness, there was an unusually garbled quality about the syntax that surprised him. Still, there was a lot to be said for getting Dundridge out of London for a while and he couldn't be held personally responsible for his appointment.

'I have here,' he said finally, 'details of your new job. Mr Rees wants you . . .'

'My new job?' said Dundridge. 'But I'm with Leisure Activities.'

'And very appropriate too,' said Mr Joynson. 'And now you are with Motorways Midlands. Next month I daresay we'll be able to find you a niche in Parks and Gardens.'

'I must say I find all this moving around very disturbing. I don't see how I can be expected to get anything constructive done when I'm being shifted from one Department to another all the time.'

'There is that to be said for it,' Mr Joynson agreed. 'However, in this case there is nothing constructive for you to do. You will merely be required to exercise a moderating influence.'

'A moderating influence?' Dundridge perked up.

Mr Joynson nodded. 'A moderating influence,' he said and consulted his instructions again. 'You have been appointed the Minister's troubleshooter in Worford.'

'What?' said Dundridge, now thoroughly alarmed. 'But there's just been a riot in Worford.'

Mr Joynson smiled. He was beginning to enjoy himself. 'So there has,' he said. 'Well now, your job is to see that there are no more riots in Worford. I'm told it is a charming little town.'

'It didn't look very charming on the news last night,' said Dundridge.

'Oh well, we mustn't go by appearances now, must we? Here is your letter of appointment. As you can see it gives you full powers to conduct negotiations—'

'But I thought Lord Leakham was heading the Enquiry,' said Dundridge.

'Well, yes he is. But I understand he's a little indisposed just at the moment and in any case he appears to be under some misapprehension as to his role.'

'You mean he is in hospital, don't you?' said Dundridge.

Mr Joynson ignored the question. He turned to a map on the wall behind him. 'The issue you will have to consider is really quite simple,' he said. 'The M101, as you can see here, has two possible routes. One through the Cleene Gorge here, the other through Ottertown. The Ottertown route is out of the question for a number of reasons. You will see to it that Leakham decides on the Cleene Gorge route.'

'Surely it's up to him to decide,' said Dundridge.

Mr Joynson sighed. 'My dear Dundridge, when you have been in public service as long as I have you will know that Enquiries, Royal Commissions and Boards of Arbitration are only set up to make recommendations that concur with decisions already taken by the experts. Your job is to see that Lord Leakham arrives at the correct decision.'

'What happens if he doesn't?'

'God alone knows. I suppose in the present climate of opinion we'll have to go ahead and build the bloody thing through Ottertown, and then there would be hell to pay. It is up to you to see it doesn't. You have full powers to negotiate with the parties involved and I daresay Leakham will cooperate.'

'I don't see how I can negotiate when I've got nothing to negotiate with,' Dundridge pointed out plaintively. 'And in any case what does it mean by troubleshooter?'

'Presumably whatever you choose to make it,' said Mr Joynson.

Dundridge took the file on the M101 back to his office. 'I'm the Minister's troubleshooter in the Midlands division,' he told his secretary grandly and phoned the transport pool for a car. Then he read his letter of authority once again. It was quite clear that his abilities had been recognized in high places. Dundridge had power, and he was determined to use it.

•

At Handyman Hall Lady Maud congratulated herself on her skill in disrupting the Enquiry. Released from custody against her own better judgment at the express command of the Chief Constable, she returned to the Hall to be deluged by messages of support. General Burnett called to offer her his congratulations. Mrs Bullett-Finch phoned to see if there was anything she needed after the ordeal of her confinement, a term Lady Maud found almost as offensive as Colonel Chapman's comment that she was full of spunk. Even Mrs Thomas wrote to thank her on behalf, as she modestly put it, of the common people. Lady Maud accepted these tributes abruptly. They were she felt quite unnecessary. She had only been doing her duty after all. As she put it to the reporter from the *Observer*, 'Local interests can only be looked after by local authorities,' a sufficiently ambiguous expression to satisfy the correspondent while stating very precisely Lady Maud's own view of her role in South Worfordshire.

'And do you intend to sue the police for unlawful arrest?' the reporter asked.

'Certainly not. I have the greatest respect for the police. They do a magnificent job. I hold Lord Leakham entirely responsible. I am taking legal counsel as to what action I should take against him.'

•

In the Worford Cottage Hospital Lord Leakham greeted the news that she was considering legal proceedings against him with a show of indifference. He had more immediate problems, the state of his digestive system for one thing, six stitches in his scalp for another, and besides he was suffering from concussion. In his lucid moments he prayed for death and in his delirium shouted obscenities.

•

But if Lord Leakham was too preoccupied with his own problems to think at all clearly about the disruption of the Enquiry, Sir Giles could think of little else.

'The whole situation is extremely awkward,' he told Hoskins when they conferred at the latter's office the next morning. 'That bloody woman has put the cat among the pigeons and no mistake. She's turned the whole thing into an issue of national interest. I've been inundated with calls from conservationists from all over the country, all supporting our stand. It's bloody infuriating. Why can't they mind their own confounded business?'

Hoskins lit his pipe moodily. 'That's not all,' he said, 'they're sending some bigwig up from the Ministry to take charge of the negotiations.'

'That's all we need, some damned bureaucrat to come poking his nose into our affairs.'

'Quite,' said Hoskins, 'so from now on no more phone calls to me here. I can't afford to be connected with you.'

'Do you think he's going to choose the Ottertown route?'

Hoskins shrugged. 'I've no idea. All I do know is that if I were in his shoes I'm damned if I'd recommend the Gorge.'

'Let me know what the blighter suggests,' said Sir Giles and went out to his car.

7

To Dundridge, travelling up the M1, the underlying complexities of the situation in South Worfordshire were quite unknown. For the first time in his life he was armed with authority and he intended to put it to good use. He would make a name for himself. The years of frustration were over. He would return to London with his reputation for swift, decisive action firmly established.

At Warwick he stopped for lunch, and while he ate he studied the file on the motorway. There was a map of the district, the outline of the alternative routes, and a list of those people through whose property the motorway would run and the sums they would receive as compensation. Dundridge concentrated his attention on the latter. A single glance was enough to explain the urgency of his appointment and the difficulty of his mission. The list read like a roll-call of the upper class in the county. Sir Giles Lynchwood, General Burnett, Colonel Chapman, Mr Bullett-Finch, Miss Percival. Dundridge peered uncomfortably at the names and incredulously at the sums they were being offered. A quarter of a million pounds for Sir Giles. One hundred and fifty thousand to General Burnett. One hundred and twenty thousand to Colonel Chapman. Even Miss Percival whose occupation was listed as schoolteacher was offered fifty-five thousand. Dundridge compared these sums with his own income and felt a surge of envy. There was no justice in the world and Dundridge (whose socialism was embodied in the maxim 'To each according to his abilities, from each according to his needs', the 'his' in both cases referring to Dundridge himself) found his thoughts wandering in the direction of money. It had been Dundridge's mother who had instilled in him the saying 'Don't marry money, go where money is' and since this had been easier said than done, Dundridge's sex life had been largely confined to his imagination. There, safe from the disagreeable complexities of real life, he had indulged his various passions. In his imagination Dundridge was rich, Dundridge was powerful and Dundridge was the possessor of an entourage of immaculate women – or to be precise of one woman, a composite creature made up of bits and pieces of real women who had once partially attracted him but without any of their concomitant disadvantages. Now for the first time he was going where money was. It was an alluring prospect. He finished his lunch and drove on.

And as he drove he became increasingly aware that the countryside had changed. He had left the motorway and was on a minor road that twisted and turned. The hedgerows grew taller and more rank. Hills rose up and fell away into empty valleys and woods took on a rougher, less domesticated air. Even the houses had lost the comfortable homogeneous look of the North London suburbs. They were either large and isolated, standing in their own grounds, or stone-built farmhouses surrounded by dark corrugated iron sheds and barns. Every now and again he passed through villages, strange conglomerations of cottages and shops, buildings that loomed misshapenly over the road or retreated behind hedges with an eccentricity of ornaments he found disturbing. And finally there were churches. Dundridge disliked churches most of all. They reminded him of death and burial, guilt and sin and the hereafter. Archaic reminders of a superstitious past. And since Dundridge lived if not for the present at least the immediate future, these memento mori held no attractions for him. They cast horrid doubts on the rational nature of existence. Not that Dundridge believed in reason. He placed his faith in science and numeration.

Now as he drove northwards he had to admit that he was entering a world far removed from his ideal. Even the sky had changed with the landscape and the shadows of large clouds slid erratically across the fields and hills. By the time he reached South Worfordshire he was distinctly perturbed. If Worford was anything like the surrounding countryside it must be a horrid place filled with violent, irrational creatures swayed by strange emotions. It was. As he drove over the bridge that spanned the Cleene he seemed to have moved out of the twentieth century into an earlier age. The houses below the town gate were huddled together higgledy-piggledy and only their scrubbed doorsteps redeemed their squalid lack of uniformity. The gate, a great stuccoed tower with a dark narrow entrance, loomed up before him. He drove nervously through and emerged into a street lined with eighteenth-century houses. Here he felt temporarily more at home but his relief evaporated when he reached the town centre. Dark narrow alleyways, half-timbered medieval houses jutting over the pavement, cobbled streets, and shopfronts which retained the format of an earlier age. Pots and pans, spades and sickles hung outside an ironmongers. Duffel coats, corduroy trousers and breeches were displayed outside an outfitters. A mackerel gleamed on a fishmonger's marble slab while a saddler's was adorned with bits and bridles and leather belts. Worford was in short a perfectly normal market town but to Dundridge, accustomed to the soothing anonymity of supermarkets, there was a disturbing, archaic quality about it. He drove into the Market Square and asked the car-park attendant for the Regional Planning Office. The attendant didn't know or if he did, Dundridge was none the wiser. The accents of Wales and England met in South Worfordshire, met and mingled incomprehensibly. Dundridge parked his car and went into a telephone kiosk. He looked in the Directory and found the Planning Office in Knacker's Yard.

'Where's Knacker's Yard?' he asked the car-park attendant.

'Down Giblet Walk.'

'Very informative,' said Dundridge with a shudder. 'And where's Giblet Walk?'

'Well now, let's see, you can go down past the Goat and Goblet or you can take a short cut through the Shambles,' said the old man and spat into the gutter.

Dundridge considered this unenticing alternative. 'Where are the Shambles?' he asked finally.

'Behind you,' said the attendant.

Dundridge turned round and looked into the shadow of a narrow alley. It was cobbled and led down the hill and out of sight. He walked down it uncomfortably. Several of the houses were boarded up and one or two had actually fallen down and the alleyway had a peculiar smell that he associated with footpaths and tunnels under railway lines. Dundridge held his breath and hurried on and came out into Knacker's Yard where a sign in front of a large red-brick building said Regional Planning Board. He opened an iron gate and went down a path to the door.

'Planning Board's on the second floor,' said a dentist's assistant who emerged from a room holding a metal bowl in which a pair of false teeth rested pinkly. 'You'll be lucky if you find it open though. You looking for anyone in particular?'

'Mr Hoskins,' said Dundridge.

'Try the Club,' said the woman. 'He's usually there this time of day. It's on the first floor.'

'Thank you,' said Dundridge and went upstairs. On the first landing there was a door marked Worford and District Gladstone Club. Dundridge looked at it doubtfully and went on up. As the woman had said, the Regional Planning Board was shut. Dundridge went downstairs and stood uncertainly on the landing. Then, reminding himself that he was the Minister's plenipotentiary and troubleshooter, he opened the door and looked inside.

'You looking for someone?' asked a large red-faced man who was standing beside a billiard table.

'I'm looking for Mr Hoskins, the Planning Officer,' said Dundridge. The red-faced man put down his cue and stepped forward.

'Then you've come to the right place,' he said. 'Bob, there's a bloke wants to see you.'

Another large red-faced man who was sitting at the bar in the corner turned round and stared at Dundridge. 'What can I do for you?' he asked.

'I'm from the Ministry of the Environment,' said Dundridge.

'Christ,' said Mr Hoskins and got down from his bar stool. 'You're early aren't you? Wasn't expecting you till tomorrow.'

'The Minister is most anxious that I should get down to work as rapidly as possible.'

'Quite right,' said Mr Hoskins more cheerfully now that he could see that Dundridge wasn't sixty, didn't wear gold-rimmed glasses and didn't carry an air of authority about him. 'What will you have?'

Dundridge hesitated. It wasn't his habit to drink in the middle of the afternoon. 'A half of bitter,' he said finally.

'Make it two pints,' Hoskins told the barman. They took their glasses across to a small table in the corner and sat down. At the billiard table the men resumed their game.

'Awkward business this,' said Mr Hoskins, 'I don't envy you your job. Local feeling's none too good.'

'So I've noticed,' said Dundridge sipping his beer. It tasted, as he had anticipated, both strong and unpleasantly organic. On the wall opposite a portrait of Mr Gladstone glared relentlessly down on this dereliction of the licensing laws. Spurred on by his example, Dundridge attempted to explain his mission. 'The Minister is particularly anxious that the negotiations should be handled tactfully. He has sent me to see that the outcome of these negotiations has the backing of all the parties involved.'

'Has he?' said Mr Hoskins. 'Well, all I can say is that you'll have your work cut out.'

'Now as I see it, the best approach would be to propose an alternative route,' Dundridge continued.

'We've done that already. Through Ottertown.'

'Out of the question,' said Dundridge.

'I couldn't agree more,' said Mr Hoskins. 'Which leaves the Cleene Gorge.'

'Or the hills to the south?' suggested Dundridge hopefully.

Mr Hoskins shook his head. 'Cleene Forest is an area of natural beauty, a designated area. Not a hope in hell.'

'Well that doesn't leave us with many alternatives, does it?'

'It doesn't leave us with any,' said Mr Hoskins.

Dundridge drank some more beer. The mood of optimism with which he had started the day had quite left him. It was all very well to talk about negotiating but there didn't seem any negotiations to conduct. He was faced with the unenviable task of enforcing a thoroughly unpopular decision on a group of extremely influential and hostile landowners. It was not a prospect he relished. 'I don't suppose there is any chance of persuading Sir Giles Lynchwood and General Burnett to drop their opposition,' he said without much hope.

'Not a hope in hell,' Hoskins told him, 'and anyway if they did it wouldn't make the slightest difference. It's Lady Maud you've got to worry about. And she isn't going to budge.'

'I must say you make it all sound extremely difficult,' said Dundridge and finished his beer. By the time he left the Gladstone Club he had a clear picture of the situation. The stumbling block was Handyman Hall and Lady Maud. He would explore the possibilities of that more fully in the morning. He walked back up the Shambles and Giblet Walk to the Market Square and booked in at the Handyman Arms.

•

At the Hall Sir Giles spent the day sequestered in his study. This seclusion was only partly to be explained by the presence in the house and grounds of half a dozen guard dogs who seemed to feel that he was an intruder in his own home. More to the point was the fact that Lady Maud had expressed herself very forcibly on the matter of his lunch with Lord Leakham. If the Judge regretted that lunch, and from the reports of the doctors at the Cottage Hospital he had cause to, so did Sir Giles.

'I was only trying to help,' he had explained. 'I thought if I gave him a good lunch he might be more prepared to see our side of the case.'

'Our side of the case?' Lady Maud snorted. 'If it comes to that we didn't have a case at all. It was perfectly obvious he was going to recommend the route through the Gorge.'

'There is the Ottertown alternative,' Sir Giles pointed out.

'Alternative my foot,' said Lady Maud. 'If you can't see a red herring when it's thrust under your nose, you're a bigger fool than I take you for.'

Sir Giles had retreated to his study cursing his wife for her perspicacity. There had been a very nasty look in her eye at the mention of Ottertown, and one or two unpleasant cracks about property speculators and their ways over breakfast had made him wonder if she had heard anything about Hoskins' new house. And now there was this damned official from Whitehall to poke his nose into the affair. Finally and most disturbing of all there had been the voices. Or rather one voice: his own. While putting the car away before lunch he had distinctly heard himself assuring nobody in particular that they could look to him to see that nothing was done that would in any way jeopardize ... Sir Giles had stared round the yard with a wild surmise. For a moment he had supposed that he had been talking to himself but the presence in his mouth of a cigar had ended that explanation. Besides the voice had been quite distinct. It had been a most disturbing experience and one for which there was no rational explanation. It had taken two stiff whiskies to convince him that he had imagined the whole thing. Now to take his mind off the occurrence he sat at his desk and concentrated on the motorway.

'Red herring indeed,' he muttered to himself. 'I wonder what she would have said if Leakham had decided in favour of

Ottertown.' It was an idle thought and quite out of the question. They would never build a motorway through Ottertown. Old Francis Puckerington would have another heart attack. Old Francis Puckerington ... Sir Giles stopped in his tracks, amazed at his own intuitive brilliance. Francis Puckerington, the Member for Ottertown, was a dying man. What had the doctors said? That he'd be lucky to live to the next general election. There had been rumours that he was going to resign his seat. And his majority at the last election had been a negligible one, somewhere in the region of fifty. If Leakham had decided on the Ottertown route it would have killed old Francis. And then there would have to be a bye-election. Sir Giles' devious mind catalogued the consequences. A bye-election fought on the issue of the motorway and the demolition of seventy-five council houses with a previous majority of fifty. It wasn't to be thought of. The Chief Whip would go berserk. Leakham's decision would be reversed. The motorway would come through the Cleene Gorge after all. And best of all not a shred of suspicion would rest on Sir Giles. It was a brilliant stratagem. It would put him in the clear. He was about to reach for the phone to call Hoskins when it occurred to him that he had better wait to hear what the man from the Ministry had to say. There was no point in rushing things now. He would go and see Hoskins in the morning. Imbued with a new spirit of defiance he left the study and selecting a large walking-stick from the rack in the hall he went out into the garden for a stroll.

It was a glorious afternoon. The sun shone down out of a cloudless sky. Birds sang. The flowering cherries by the kitchen garden flowered and Sir Giles himself blossomed with smug self-satisfaction. He paused for a moment to admire the goldfish in the ornamental pond and was just considering the possibility of pushing up the compensation to three hundred thousand when for the second time that day he heard himself speaking. 'I'm damned if I'm going to allow the countryside to be desecrated by a motorway. I shall take the earliest opportunity of raising the matter in the House.' Sir Giles stared round the garden panic-stricken, but there was no one in sight. He turned and looked at the Hall but the windows were all shut. To his right was the wall of the kitchen garden. Sir Giles hurried across the lawn to the door in the wall and peered inside. Blott was busy in a cucumber frame.

'Did you say anything?' Sir Giles asked.

'Me?' said Blott. 'I didn't say anything. Did you?'

Sir Giles hurried back to the house. It was no longer a glorious afternoon. It was a quite horrible afternoon. He went into his study and shut the door.

8

Dundridge spent a perfectly foul night at the Handyman Arms. His room there had a sloping floor, a yellowed ceiling, an ochre chest of drawers and a wardrobe whose door opened of its own accord ten minutes after he had shut it. It did so with a hideous wheeze and would then creak softly until he got out of bed and shut it again. He spent half the night trying to devise some method of keeping it closed and the other half listening to the noises coming from the next room. These were of a most disturbing sort and suggested an incompatibility of size and temperament that played havoc with his imagination. At two o'clock he managed to get to sleep, only to be woken at three by a sudden eruption in the drainpipe of his washbasin which appeared to be most unhygienically connected to the one next door. At half past three a dawn breeze rattled the signboard outside his window. At four the man next door asked if someone wanted it again. 'For God's sake,' Dundridge muttered and buried his head under the pillow to shut out this evidence of sexual excess. At ten past four the wardrobe door, responding to the seismic tremors from the next room, opened again and creaked softly. Dundridge let it creak and turned for relief to his composite woman. With her assistance he managed to get back to sleep to be woken at seven by a repulsive-looking girl with a tea-tray.

'Is there anything else you wanted?' she asked coyly.

'Certainly not,' said Dundridge wondering what there was about him that led only the most revolting females to offer him their venereal services. He got up and went along to the bathroom and wrestled with the intricacies of a gas-fired geyser which had evidently set its mind on asphyxiating him or blowing him up. In the end he had a cold wash.

By the time he had finished breakfast he was in a thoroughly bad mood. He had been unable to formulate any coherent strategy and had no idea what to do next. Hoskins had advised him to have a word with Sir Giles Lynchwood and Dundridge decided he would do that later. To begin with he would pay a call on Lord Leakham at the Cottage Hospital.

After wandering down narrow lanes and up a flight of steps behind the Worford Museum he found the hospital, a grey gaunt stone building that looked as though it had once been a workhouse. It fronted on to the Abbey and in the small front garden a number of geriatric patients were sitting around in dressing-gowns. Stifling his disgust, Dundridge went inside and asked for Lord Leakham.

'Visiting hours are two to three,' said the nurse at Admissions.

'I'm here on Government business,' said Dundridge feeling that it was about time someone understood he was not to be trifled with.

'I'll have to ask Matron,' said the nurse. Dundridge went outside into the sunshine to wait. He didn't like hospitals. They were not, he felt, his forte, particularly hospitals which overlooked graveyards, stank of disinfectant and had the gall to call themselves Cottage Hospitals when they were situated in the middle of towns. He was just considering the awful prospect of being treated for a serious complaint in such a dead-and-alive hole when the Matron appeared. She was gaunt, grey-haired and grim.

'I understand you want to see Lord Leakham,' she said.

'On Government business,' said Dundridge pompously.

'You can have five minutes,' said the Matron and led the way down the passage to a private room. 'He's still suffering from concussion and shock.' She opened the door and Dundridge went inside. 'Now nothing controversial,' said the Matron. 'We don't want to have a relapse, do we?'

On the bed, ashen-faced and with his head swathed in bandages, Lord Leakham regarded her venomously. 'There's nothing the matter with me apart from food poisoning,' he said. Dundridge sat down beside his bed.

'My name is Dundridge,' he said. 'The Minister of the Environment has asked me to come up to see if I can do something to ... er ... well to negotiate some sort of settlement in regard to the motorway.'

Lord Leakham looked at him vindictively over the top of his glasses. 'Has he indeed? Well let me tell you what I intend to do about the motorway first and then you can inform him,' he said. He raised himself on his pillows and leant towards Dundridge. 'I was appointed to head the Enquiry into the motorway and I do not intend to relinquish my responsibility.'

'Oh quite,' said Dundridge.

'Furthermore,' said the Judge, 'I have no intention whatsoever of allowing myself to be influenced by hooliganism and riot from doing my duty as I see it.'

'Oh definitely,' said Dundridge.

'As soon as these damnfool doctors get it into their thick heads that there is nothing wrong with me except a peptic ulcer, I shall re-open the Enquiry and announce my decision.' Dundridge nodded.

'Quite right too,' he said. 'And what will your decision be? Or is it too early to ask that?'

'It most certainly isn't,' shouted Lord Leakham. 'I intend to recommend that the motorway goes through the Cleene Gorge, plumb through it, you understand. I intend to see that that damned woman's home is levelled to the ground, brick by brick. I intend ...' He sank back on to the bed exhausted by his outburst.

'I see,' said Dundridge, wondering what possible use there was in trying to negotiate a compromise between an irresistible force and an immovable object.

'Oh no you don't,' said Lord Leakham. 'That woman deliberately sent her husband to poison me. She interrupted the proceedings. She insulted me in my own court. She incited to riot. She made a mockery of the legal process and she shall rue the day. The law shall not be mocked, sir.'

'Oh quite,' said Dundridge.

'So you go and negotiate all you want but just remember the decision to go through the Gorge is mine and I do not for one moment intend to forgo the pleasure of making it.'

Dundridge went out into the passage and conferred with the Matron.

'He seems to think someone tried to poison him,' he said carefully skirting the law of libel. The Matron smiled gently.

'That's the concussion,' she said. 'He'll get over that in a day or two.'

Dundridge went out into the Abbey Close past the geriatric patients and wandered disconsolately down the steps and out into Market Street. It didn't seem likely to him that Lord Leakham would get over his conviction that Lady Maud had tried to poison him and he had a shrewd suspicion that the Judge had in some perverse way enjoyed the contretemps in court and was looking forward to pursuing his vendetta as soon as he was up and about. He was just considering what to do next when he caught sight of his reflection in a shop window. It was not that of a man of authority. There was a sort of dispirited look about it, a hangdog look quite out of keeping with his role as the Minister's troubleshooter. It was time to take the bull by the horns. He straightened his back, marched across the road to the Post Office and telephoned Handyman Hall. He got Lady Maud and explained that he would like to see Sir Giles.

'I'm afraid Sir Giles is out just at present,' she said modulating her tone to suggest a secretary. 'He'll be back shortly. Would eleven o'clock be convenient?'

Dundridge said it would. He left the Post Office and threaded his way through the market stalls to the car park to collect his car.

•

At Handyman Hall Lady Maud congratulated herself on her performance. She was rather looking forward to a private chat with the man from the Ministry. Dundridge, he had said his name was. From the Ministry. Sir Giles had mentioned the fact that someone had been sent up from London on a fact-finding mission. And since Giles had said he would be out until late in the afternoon this seemed an ideal opportunity to provide this Mr Dundridge with facts that would suit her book. She went upstairs to change, and to consider her tactics. She had spiked Lord Leakham's guns by frontal assault but Dundridge on the phone had sounded far less self-assured than she had expected. It might be better to try persuasion, perhaps even a little charm. It would confuse the issue. Lady Maud selected a cotton frock and dabbed a little Lavender Water behind her ears. Mr Dundridge would get the meek treatment, the helpless little girl approach. If that didn't work she could always revert to sterner methods.

•

In the greenhouse Blott put down the earphones and went back to the broad beans. So an official was coming to see Sir Giles, was he? An official. Blott felt strongly about officials. They had made his early life a misery and he had no time for them. Still, Lady Maud had invited this one to the Hall so presumably she knew what she was doing. It was a pity. Blott would have liked to have been ordered to give this Dundridge the reception he deserved and he was just considering what sort of reception he would have organized for him when Lady Maud came into the garden. Blott straightened up and stared at her. She was wearing a cotton frock and to Blott at least she looked quite beautiful. It was not a notion anyone else would have shared but Blott's standards of beauty were not determined by fashion. Large breasts, enormous thighs and hips were attributes of a good or at least ample mother, and since Blott had never had a good, ample or even *any* mother in a post-natal sense he placed great emphasis on these outward signs of potential maternity. Now, standing among the broad beans, he was filled with a sudden sense of desire. Lady Maud in a cotton frock dappled with a floral pattern combined botany with biology. Blott goggled.

'Blott,' said Lady Maud, oblivious of the effect she was having, 'there's a man from the Ministry of the Environment coming to lunch. I want some flowers in the house. I want to make a good impression on him.'

Blott went into the greenhouse and looked for something suitable while Lady Maud bent low to select a lettuce for lunch. As she did so Blott glanced out of the greenhouse door. It was the turning point in his life. The silent devotion to the Handyman family which had been the passive mainspring of his existence for so long was gone, to be replaced by an active urgency of feeling.

Blott was in love.

9

Dundridge left Worford by the town gate, crossed the river and took the Ottertown road. On his left the Cleene wandered through meadows and on his right the Cleene Hills rose steeply to a wooded crest. He drove for three miles and turned up a side road that was signposted Guildstead Carbonell and found himself in evidently hostile territory. Every barn had the slogan 'Save the Gorge' whitewashed on it and there were similar sentiments painted on the road itself. At one point an avenue of beeches had been daubed with letters that spelt out 'No to the Motorway' so that as he drove down it Dundridge was left in no doubt that local feeling was against the scheme.

Even without the slogans Dundridge would have been alarmed. The Cleene Forest was nature undomesticated. There was none of that neatness that he found so reassuring in Middlesex. The hedges were rank, the few farmhouses he passed looked medieval, and the forest itself dense with large trees, humped and gnarled with bracken growing thickly underneath. He was relieved when the road ran into an open valley with hedges and little fields. The respite was brief. At the top of the next hill he came to a crossroads marked by nothing more informative than a decayed gibbet.

Dundridge stopped the car and consulted his map. According to his calculations Guildstead Carbonell lay to the left while in front was the Gorge and Handyman Hall. Dundridge wished it wasn't. Below him the forest lay thicker than before and the road less metalled, with moss and grass growing down the middle. He drove on for a mile and was beginning to wonder if the map had misled him when the trees thinned and he found himself looking down into the Gorge itself.

He stopped the car and got out. Below him the Cleene tumbled between cliffs overgrown with brambles, ivy and creepers. Ahead lay Handyman Hall. It stood, an amalgam in stone and brick, timber and tile and turret, a monument to all that was most eclectic and least attractive in English architecture. To Dundridge, himself a devotee of function, for whom simplicity was all, it was a nightmare. Ruskin and Morris, Gilbert Scott, Vanbrugh, Inigo Jones and Wren to name but a few had all lent their influence to a building that combined the utility of a water-tower with the homeliness of Wormwood Scrubs. Around it lay a few acres of parkland, a wall, and beyond the wall a circle of hills, heavily wooded. Over the whole scene there lay a sense of isolation. Somewhere to the west there were presumably towns and houses, shops and buses, but to Dundridge it seemed that he was standing on the very edge of civilization if not actually beyond it. With the sinking feeling that he was committing himself to the unknown he got back into the car and drove on, down the hill into the Gorge. Presently he came to a small iron suspension bridge across the river which rattled as he drove over. On the far side something large and strange loomed through the trees. It was the Lodge. Dundridge stopped the car and gaped at the building through the windshield.

Constructed in 1904 to mark the occasion of the visit of Edward the Seventh, the Lodge, in deference to the King's Francophilia, had been modelled on the Arc de Triomphe. There were differences. The Lodge was slightly smaller, its frieze did not depict scenes of battle, but for all that the resemblance was remarkable and to Dundridge its existence in the heart of Worfordshire came as final proof that whoever had built Handyman Hall had been an architectural kleptomaniac. Above all the Lodge bespoke a lofty arrogance which, coming so shortly after Lord Leakham's outburst, made a tactful approach all the more necessary. As he stood looking up at it Dundridge was recalled to his task. Some sort of compromise was clearly necessary to avoid his becoming embroiled in an extremely nasty situation. If the Ottertown route was out of the question and he had it on the highest authority that it was, and if the Gorge ... There was no if about the Gorge, Dundridge had seen enough to convince him of that, then a third route was imperative. But there was no third route. Dundridge got back into his car and drove thoughtfully through the great arch and as he did so a vision of the third route dawned upon him. A tunnel. A tunnel under the Cleene Hills. A tunnel had all the merits of simplicity, of straightness and, best of all, of leaving undisturbed the hideous landscape that so many irate and influential people inexplicably admired. There would be no more wrangles about property rights, no compensation, no trouble. Dundridge had discovered the ideal solution.

In the entrance hall Lady Maud, radiant in Tootal, lurked among the ferns. High above her head the stained-glass rooflight cast a reddish glow upon the marble staircase and lent a fresh air of apoplexy to the ruddy faces of her ancestors glowering down from the walls. Lady Maud patted her hair in readiness. She had laid her plans. Mr Dundridge would get the gracious treatment, at least to begin with. After that she would see how he responded. As his car crunched on the gravel outside she adjusted her step-in and gave a practice smile to a vase of snapdragons. Then she stepped forward and opened the door.

•

'Nincompoop? Nincompoop? Did you say nincompoop?' said Sir Giles. In his constituency office situated conveniently close to Hoskins' Regional Planning Board the word had a reassuring ring to it.

'A perfect nincompoop,' said Hoskins.

'Are you sure?'

'Positive. A first rate, Grade A nincompoop.'

'It sounds too good to be true,' said Sir Giles doubtfully. 'You can't always go by appearances. I've known some very slippery customers in my time who looked like idiots.'

'I'm not going by appearances,' Hoskins said. 'He doesn't look an idiot. He is one. Wouldn't know one end of a motorway from the other.'

Sir Giles considered the statement. 'I'm not sure I would come to that,' he said.

'You know what I mean,' said Hoskins. 'He's no more an expert on motorways than I am.'

Sir Giles pursed his lips. 'If he's such a dimwit why did the Minister send him up? He's given him full authority to negotiate.'

'Don't look a gift horse in the mouth, is what I say.'

'I daresay there's something in that,' said Sir Giles. 'So you don't think there's anything to worry about?'

Hoskins smiled. 'Not a thing in the world. He'll nosey around a bit and then he will do just what we want. I tell you this bloke takes the biscuit. Butter wouldn't melt in his mouth.'

Sir Giles considered this mixture of metaphors and found it to his taste. 'I hear Lord Leakham's still foaming at the mouth.'

'He can't wait to re-open the Enquiry. Says he's going to put the motorway through the Gorge if it's the last thing he does.'

'It probably will be if Maud has anything to do with it,' said Sir Giles. 'She's in a very nasty frame of mind.'

'There's nothing much she can do about it once the decision is taken,' said Hoskins.

'I wouldn't be too sure about that.'

Sir Giles got up and stared out of the window and considered his alternative plan. 'You don't think this fellow Dundridge will advise against the Gorge?' he asked finally.

'Lord Leakham wouldn't listen to him if he did. He's got it into his head you tried to poison him,' said Hoskins and went back to his office leaving Sir Giles to ponder on the best-laid plans of mice and men. It was all very well for Hoskins to talk confidently about nincompoops from the Ministry. He had nothing to lose. Sir Giles had. His seat in Parliament for one thing. Well, if the worst came to the worst and Maud carried out her threat he could always get another. It was worth the risk. Reassured by the thought that Lord Leakham had made up his mind to route the motorway through the Gorge Sir Giles went out to lunch.

•

At Handyman Hall Lady Maud's gracious approach had worked wonders. Like some delicate plant in need of water, Dundridge had blossomed out. He had come expecting to meet Sir Giles but, after the first shock of finding himself alone in a large house with a large woman had worn off, Dundridge began to enjoy himself. For the first time since he had arrived in Worfordshire he was being taken seriously. Lady Maud treated him as a person of consequence.

'It is so good to know that you have come to take over from Lord Leakham,' Lady Maud said as she led him down a corridor to the drawing-room.

Dundridge said he hadn't actually come to take over. 'I'm simply here in an advisory capacity,' he said modestly.

Lady Maud smiled knowingly. 'Oh quite, and we all know what that means, don't we?' she murmured, drawing Dunbridge into a warm complicity he found quite delightful.

Dundridge relaxed on the sofa. 'The Minister is most anxious that the proposed motorway should fit in with the needs of local residents as much as possible.'

Maud smothered a snarl with another smile. The notion that she was a local resident made her blood boil, but she had set out to humour this snivelling civil servant and humour him she would. 'And there is the landscape to consider too,' she said. 'The Cleene Forest is one of the few remaining examples of virgin woodland left in England. It would be a terrible shame to spoil it with a motorway, don't you think?'

Dundridge didn't think anything of the sort but he knew better than to say so, and besides this seemed as good an opportunity as any to test out his theory of a tunnel. 'I think I've found a solution to the problem,' he said. 'Of course it's only an idea, you understand, and it has no official standing, but it should be possible to build a tunnel under the Cleene Hills.' He stopped. Lady Maud was staring at him intently. 'Of course, as I say, it's only an idea . . .'

Lady Maud had risen and for one terrible moment Dundridge thought she was about to assault him. She lurched forward and took his hand. 'Oh how wonderful,' she said. 'How absolutely brilliant. You dear, dear man,' and she sat down beside him on the sofa and gazed into his face ecstatically. Dundridge blushed and looked down at his shoes. He was quite unused to married women taking his hand, gazing into his face ecstatically and calling him their dear, dear man. 'It's nothing. Only an idea.'

'A splendid idea,' said Lady Maud, engulfing him in a blast of Lavender Water. Out of the corner of his eye Dundridge could see her bosom quivering beneath a nosegay of marigolds. He shrank into the sofa.

'Of course, there would have to be a feasibility study . . .' he began but Lady Maud brushed his remark aside.

'Of course there would, but that would take time wouldn't it?'

'Months,' said Dundridge.

'Months!'

'Six months at least.'

'Six months!' Lady Maud relinquished his hand with a sigh and contemplated a respite of six months. In six months so much could happen and if she had anything to do with it a great deal would. Giles would throw his weight behind the tunnel or she would know the reason why. She would drum up support from conservationists across the country. In six months she would do wonders. And she owed it all to this insubstantial little man with plastic shoes. Now that she came to look at him she realized she had misjudged him. There was something almost appealing about his vulnerability. 'You'll stay to lunch,' she said.

'Well . . . er . . . I really . . .'

'Of course you will,' said Lady Maud. 'I insist. And you can tell Giles all about the tunnel when he gets back this afternoon.' She rose and, leaving Dundridge to wonder how it was that Sir Giles who had been coming back at eleven had delayed his return until the afternoon, Lady Maud swept from the room. Left to himself, Dundridge sat stunned by the enthusiasm his suggestion had unleashed. If Sir Giles' reaction was as favourable as that of his wife he would have made some influential friends. And rich ones. He ran his fingers appreciatively over the moulding of a rosewood table. So this was how the other half lived, he thought, before realizing that the cliché was inappropriate. The other two per cent. Useful people to know.

•

Sir Giles returned from Worford at four to find Lady Maud in a remarkably good mood.

'I had a visit from such a strange young man,' she told him when he enquired what the matter was.

'Oh really?'

'He was called Dundridge. He was from the Ministry of the—'

'Dundridge? Did you say Dundridge?'

'Yes. Such a very interesting man . . .'

'Interesting? I understood he was a nincom . . . oh never mind. What did he have to say for himself?'

'Oh, this and that,' said Lady Maud, gratified by her husband's agitation.

'What do you mean "this and that"?'

'We talked about the absurdity of putting a motorway through the Gorge,' said Lady Maud.

'I suppose he's in favour of the Ottertown route.'

Lady Maud shook her head. 'As a matter of fact he isn't.'

'He isn't?' said Sir Giles, now thoroughly alarmed. 'What the hell is he in favour of then?'

Lady Maud savoured his concern. 'He has in mind a third route,' she said. 'One that avoids both Ottertown and the Gorge.'

Sir Giles turned pale. 'A third route? But there isn't a third route. There can't be. He's not thinking of going through the Forest, is he? It's an area of designated public beauty.'

'Not through it. Under it,' said Lady Maud triumphantly.

'Under it?'

'A tunnel. A tunnel under the Cleene Hills. Don't you think that's a marvellous idea.'

Sir Giles sat down heavily. He was looking quite ill.

'I said "Don't you think that's a marvellous idea",' said Lady Maud.

Sir Giles pulled himself together. 'Er . . . What . . . oh yes . . . splendid,' he muttered. 'Quite splendid.'

'You don't sound very enthusiastic,' said Lady Maud.

'It's just that I wouldn't have thought it was financially viable,' Sir Giles said. 'The cost would be enormous. I can't see the Ministry taking to the idea at all readily.'

'I can,' said Lady Maud, 'with a little prodding.' She went out through the french windows on to the terrace and looked lovingly across the park. With Dundridge's help she had solved one problem. The house had been saved. There remained the question of an heir and it had just occurred to her that here again Dundridge might prove invaluable. Over lunch he had waxed quite eloquent about his work. Once or twice he had mentioned cementation. The word had struck a chord in her. Now as she leant over the balustrade and stared into the depths of the pinetum it returned to her insistently. 'Sementation,' she murmured, 'sementation.' It was a new word to her and strangely technical for such an intimate act, but Lady Maud was in no mood to quibble.

·

Sir Giles was. He waddled off to the study and phoned Hoskins. 'What's all this about that bastard Dundridge being a nincompoop?' he snarled. 'Do you know what he's come up with now? A tunnel. You heard me. A bloody tunnel under the Cleene Hills.'

'A tunnel?' said Hoskins. 'That's out of the question. They can't put a tunnel under the Forest.'

'Why not? They're putting one under the blasted Channel. They can put tunnels wherever they bloody well want to these days.'

'I know that, but it would be cost-prohibitive,' said Hoskins.

'Cost-prohibitive my arse. If this sod goes round bleating about tunnels he'll whip up support from every environmental crank in the country. He's got to be stopped.'

'I'll do my best,' said Hoskins doubtfully.

'You'll do better than that,' Sir Giles snarled. 'You get him on to the idea of Ottertown.'

'But what about the seventy-five council houses—'

'Bugger the seventy-five council houses. Just get him off the bloody tunnel.' Sir Giles put down the phone and stared out of the window vindictively. If he didn't do something drastic he would be saddled with Handyman Hall. And with Lady Maud to boot. He got up and kicked the wastepaper basket into the corner.

10

Dundridge drove back to Worford with no thought for the landscape. His encounter with Lady Maud had left him stunned and with his sense of self-importance greatly inflated. Lunch had been most enjoyable and Dundridge with two large gins inside him had found Lady Maud a most appreciative audience. She had listened to his exposition of the theory of non-interruptive constant-flow transportation with an evident fervour usually quite absent in his audience and Dundridge had found her enthusiasm extraordinarily refreshing. Moreover she exuded confidence, a supreme self-confidence which was contagious and which exerted an enormous fascination over him. In spite of her lack of symmetry, of beauty, in spite of the manifest discrepancy between her physique and that of the ideal woman of his imagination, he had to admit that she held charms for him. After lunch she had shown him over the house and garden and Dundridge had followed her from room to room with a quite inexplicable sense of weak-kneed excitement. Once when he had stumbled in the rockery Lady Maud had taken his arm and Dundridge had felt limp with pleasure. Again when he had squeezed past her in the doorway of the bathroom he had been conscious of a delicious passivity. By the time he left the house he felt quite childishly happy. He was appreciated. It made all the difference.

He got back to the Handyman Arms to find Hoskins waiting for him in the lounge.

'Just thought I'd drop in to see how you were getting on.'

'Fine. Fine. Just fine,' said Dundridge.

'Got on all right with Leakham?'

The warm glow in Dundridge cooled. 'I can't say I like his attitude,' he said. 'He seems determined to go ahead with the Gorge route. He has evidently developed a quite irrational hatred for Lady Maud. I must say I find his attitude inexplicable. She seems a perfectly charming woman to me.'

Hoskins stared at him incredulously. 'She does?'

'Delightful,' said Dundridge, the warm glow returning gently.

'Delightful?'

'Charming,' said Dundridge dreamily.

'Good God,' said Hoskins unable to contain his astonishment any longer. The notion that anyone could find Lady Maud charming and delightful was quite beyond him. He looked at

Dundridge with a new interest. 'She's a bit large, don't you think?' he suggested.

'Comely,' said Dundridge benevolently. 'Just comely.'

Hoskins shuddered and changed the subject. 'About this tunnel,' he began. Dundridge looked at him in surprise.

'How did you hear about that?'

'News travels fast in these parts.'

'It must,' said Dundridge, 'I only mentioned it this morning.'

'You're not seriously proposing to recommend the construction of a tunnel under the Cleene Hills, are you?'

'I don't see why not,' said Dundridge, 'it seems a sensible compromise.'

'A bloody expensive one,' said Hoskins, 'it would cost millions and take years to put through.'

'At least it would avoid another riot. I came up here to try to find a solution that would be acceptable to all parties. It seems to me that a tunnel would be a very sensible alternative. In any case the plan is still in the formative stage.'

'Yes, but ...' Hoskins began but Dundridge had risen and with an airy remark about the need for vision had gone up to his room. Hoskins went back to the Regional Planning Board in a pensive mood. He had been wrong about Dundridge. The man wasn't such a nincompoop after all. On the other hand he had found Lady Maud charming and delightful. 'Bloody pervert,' Hoskins muttered as he picked up the phone. Sir Giles wasn't going to like this.

•

Nor was Blott. He had had a relatively phone-free day in the kitchen garden. There had been Dundridge's call in the morning but for the most part he had been left in peace. At half past four he had heard Sir Giles call Hoskins and tell him about the tunnel. At half past five he was watering the tomatoes when Hoskins called back to say that Dundridge was serious about the tunnel.

'He can't be,' Sir Giles snarled. 'It's an outrageous idea. A gross waste of taxpayers' money.'

74

Blott shook his head. The tunnel sounded a very good idea to him.

'You try telling him that,' said Hoskins.

'What about Leakham?' Sir Giles asked. 'He's not going to buy it, is he?'

'I wouldn't like to say. Depends what sort of weight this fellow Dundridge carries in London. The Ministry may bring pressure to bear on Leakham.'

There was a silence while Sir Giles considered this. In the greenhouse Blott wrestled with the intricacies of the English language. Why should Lord Leakham buy the tunnel? How could Dundridge carry weight in London? And in any case why should Sir Giles dislike the idea of a tunnel? It was all very odd.

'I've got another bit of news for you,' Hoskins said finally. 'He's keen on your missus.'

There was a strangled sound from Sir Giles. 'He's what?' he shouted.

'He has taken a fancy to Maud,' Hoskins told him. 'He said he found her charming and delightful.'

'Charming and delightful?' said Sir Giles. 'Maud?'

'And comely.'

'Good God. No wonder she's looking like the cat that's swallowed the canary,' said Sir Giles.

'I just thought you ought to know,' said Hoskins. 'It might give us some sort of lever.'

'Kinky?'

'Could be,' said Hoskins.

'Meet me at the Club at nine,' said Sir Giles, suddenly making up his mind. 'This needs thinking about.' He rang off.

•

In the greenhouse Blott stared lividly into the geraniums. If Sir Giles had been surprised, Blott's reaction was stronger still. The sudden discovery that he was in love with Lady Maud had coloured his day. The thought of Dundridge sharing his feelings for her infuriated him. Sir Giles he discounted. It was quite clear that Lady Maud despised her husband and from what she had said Blott had gathered that there was another woman in London. Dundridge was another matter. Blott left the greenhouse, tidied up and went home.

Home for Blott was the Lodge. The architect of the arch had managed to combine monumentality with utility and at one time the Lodge had housed several families of estate workers in rather cramped and insanitary conditions. Blott had the place to himself and found it quite adequate. The arch had its little inconveniences; the windows were extremely small and hidden among the decorations on the exterior; there was only one door so that to get from one side of the arch to the other one had to climb the staircase to the top and then cross over, but Blott had made himself very comfortable in a large room that spanned the arch. Through a circular window on one side he could keep an eye on the Hall and through another he could inspect visitors crossing the bridge. He had converted one small room into a bathroom and another into a kitchen, while he stored apples in some of the others so that the whole place had a pleasant smell to it. And finally there was Blott's library filled with books that he had picked up on the market stalls in Worford or in the second-hand bookshop in Ferret Lane. There were no novels in Blott's library, no light reading, only books on English history. In its way it was a scholar's library born of an intense curiosity about the country of his adoption. If the secret of being an Englishman was to be found anywhere it was to be found, Blott thought, in the past. Through the long winter evenings he would sit in front of his fire absorbed in the romance of England. Certain figures loomed large in his imagination, Henry VIII, Drake, Cromwell, Edward I, and he tended to identify if not himself at least other people with the heroes and villains of history. Lady Maud, in spite of her marriage, he saw as the Virgin Queen, while Sir Giles seemed to have the less savoury aspects of Sir Robert Walpole.

But that was for winter. During the summer he was out and about. Twice a week he cycled over to Guildstead Carbonell to the Royal George and sat in the bar until it was time for bed, the bed in question belonging to Mrs Wynn who ran the pub and whose husband had obligingly left her a widow as a result of enemy action on D-Day. Mrs Wynn was the last of Blott's wartime customers and the affair had lingered on owing more to habit than to affection. Mrs Wynn found Blott useful, he dried glasses and carried bottles, and Blott found Mrs Wynn comfortable, undemanding and accommodating in the matter of beer. He had a weakness for Handyman Brown.

But now as he washed his neck – it was Friday night and Mrs Wynn was expecting him – he was conscious that he no longer felt the same way about her. Not that he had ever felt very much, but that little had been swept aside by his sudden surge of feeling for Maud. He was sensible enough not to entertain any expectations of being able to do anything about it. It just didn't seem right to go off to Mrs Wynn any more. In any case it was all most peculiar. He had always had a soft spot for Lady Maud but this was different and it occurred to him that he might be sickening for something. He stuck out his tongue and studied it in the bathroom mirror but it looked all right. It might be the weather. He had once heard someone say something about spring and young men's fancies but Blott wasn't a young man. He was fifty. Fifty and in love. Daft.

He went downstairs and got on his bicycle and cycled off across the bridge towards Guildstead Carbonell. He had just reached the crossroads when he heard a car coming up fast behind him. He got off the bike to let it go by. It was Sir Giles in the Bentley. 'Going to the Golf Club to see Hoskins,' he thought, and looked after the car suspiciously. 'He's up to something.' He got back on to his bike and freewheeled reluctantly down the hill towards the Royal George and Mrs Wynn. Perhaps he ought to tell Maud what he had heard. It didn't seem a good idea and in any case he wasn't going to let her know that Dundridge fancied her. 'He can sow his own row,' he said to himself and was pleased at his command of the idiom.

In the Worford Golf Club, Sir Giles and Hoskins discussed tactics.

'He's got to have a weakness,' said Sir Giles. 'Every man has his price.'

'Maud?' said Hoskins.

'Be your age,' said Sir Giles. 'She isn't going to fartarse around with some tinpot civil servant with that reversionary clause in the contract at stake. Besides, I don't believe it.'

'I distinctly heard him say he found her charming. And comely.'

'All right, so he likes fat women. What else does he like? Money?'

Hoskins shrugged. 'Hard to tell. You need time to find that out.'

'Time is what we haven't got. He's only got to start blabbing about that bleeding tunnel and the fat's in the fire. No, we've got to act fast.'

Hoskins looked at him suspiciously. 'What's all this "We" business?' he asked. 'It's your problem, not mine.'

Sir Giles gnawed a fingernail thoughtfully. 'How much?'

'Five thousand.'

'For what?'

'Whatever you decide.'

'Make it five per cent of the compensation. When it's paid.'

Hoskins did a quick calculation and made it twelve and a half thousand. 'Cash on the nail,' he said.

'You're a hard man, Hoskins, a hard man,' Sir Giles said sorrowfully.

'Anyway what do you want me to do? Sound him out?'

Sir Giles shook his head. His little eyes glittered. 'Kinky,' he said. 'Kinky. What made you say that?'

'I don't know. Just wondered,' said Hoskins.

'Boys, do you think?'

'Difficult to know,' said Hoskins. 'These things take time to find out.'

'Drink, drugs, boys, women, money. There's got to be some damned thing he's itching for.'

'Of course, we *could* frame him,' said Hoskins. 'It's been done before.'

Sir Giles nodded. 'The unsolicited gift. The anonymous donor. It's been done before all right. But it's too risky. What if he goes to the police?'

'Nothing ventured nothing gained,' said Hoskins. 'In any case there would be no indication where it came from. My bet is he'd take the bait.'

'If he didn't we would have lost him. No, it's got to be something foolproof.'

They sat in silence and considered a suitably compromising future for Dundridge.

'Ambitious would you say?' Sir Giles asked finally. Hoskins nodded.

'Very.'

'Know any queers?'

'In Worford? You've got to be joking,' said Hoskins.

'Anywhere.'

Hoskins shook his head. 'If you're thinking what I'm thinking . . .'

'I am.'

'Photos?'

'Photos,' Sir Giles agreed. 'Nice compromising photos.'

Hoskins gave the matter some thought. 'There's Bessie Williams,' he said. 'Used to be a model, if you know what I mean. Married a photographer in Bridgeminster. She'd do it if the money was right.' He smiled reminiscently. 'I can have a word with her.'

'You do that,' said Sir Giles. 'I'll pay up to five hundred for a decent set of photos.'

'Leave it to me,' Hoskins told him. 'Now then, about the cash.'

By the time Sir Giles left the Golf Club the matter was fixed. He drove home in a haze of whisky. 'The stick first and then the carrot,' he muttered. Tomorrow he would go to London and visit Mrs Forthby. It was just as well to be out of the way when things happened.

11

Dundridge spent the following morning at the Regional Planning Board with Hoskins poring over maps and discussing the tunnel. He was rather surprised to find that Hoskins had undergone a change of heart about the project and seemed to favour it. 'It's a brilliant idea. Pity we didn't think of it before. Would have saved no end of trouble,' he said, and while Dundridge was flattered he wasn't so sure. He had begun to have doubts about the feasibility of a tunnel. The Ministry wouldn't exactly like the cost, the delay would be considerable and there was still Lord Leakham to be persuaded. 'You don't think we could find an alternative route,' he asked but Hoskins shook his head.

'It's either the Cleene Gorge or Ottertown or your tunnel.' Dundridge, studying the maps, had to concede that there wasn't any other route. The Cleene Hills stretched unbroken save for the Gorge from Worford to Ottertown.

'Ridiculous fuss people make about a bit of forest,' Dundridge complained. 'Just trees. What's so special about trees?'

They had lunch at a restaurant in River Street. At the next table a couple in their thirties seemed to find Dundridge quite fascinating and more than once Dundridge looked up to find the woman looking at him with a quiet smile. She was rather attractive, with almond eyes.

In the afternoon Hoskins took him on a tour of the proposed route through Ottertown. They drove over and inspected the council houses and returned through Guildstead Carbonell, Hoskins stopping the car every now and again and insisting that they climb to the top of some hill to get a better view of the proposed route. By the time they got back to Worford Dundridge was exhausted. He was also rather drunk. They had stopped at several pubs along the way and, thanks to Hoskins' insistence that pints were for men and that only boys drank halves – he put rather a nasty inflection on boys – Dundridge had consumed rather more Handyman Triple XXX than he was used to.

'We're having a little celebration party at the Golf Club tonight,' Hoskins said as they drove through the town gate. 'If you'd care to come over . . .'

'I think I'll get an early night,' said Dundridge.

'Pity,' Hoskins said. 'You'd meet a number of influential local people. Doesn't do to give the locals the idea you're hoity-toity.'

'Oh all right,' said Dundridge grudgingly. 'I'll have a bath and something to eat and see how I feel.'

'See you later, old boy,' said Hoskins as Dundridge got out of the car and went up to his room in the Handyman Arms. A bath and a meal and he'd probably feel all right. He fetched a towel and went down the passage to the bathroom. When he returned having immersed himself briefly in a lukewarm bath – the geyser still refused to operate at all efficiently – he was feeling better. He had dinner and decided that Hoskins was probably right. It might be useful to meet some of the more influential local people. Dundridge went out to his car and drove over to the Golf Club.

'Delighted you could make it,' said Hoskins when Dundridge made his way through the crush to him. 'What's your poison?'

Dundridge said he'd have a gin and tonic. He'd had enough beer for one day. Around him large men shouted about doglegs on the third and water hazards on the fifth. Dundridge felt out of it. Hoskins brought him his drink and introduced him to a Mr Snell. 'Glad to meet you, squire,' said Mr Snell heartily from behind a large moustache. 'What's your handicap?' Suppressing his immediate reaction to tell him to mind his own damned business, Dundridge said that as far as he knew he didn't have one. 'A Beginner, eh? Well, never mind. Give it time. We've all got to start somewhere.' He drifted away and Dundridge wandered in the opposite direction. Looking round the room at the veined faces of the men and the hennaed hair of the women Dundridge cursed himself for coming. If this was

Hoskins' idea of local influence he could keep it. Presently he went out on to the terrace and stared resentfully down the eighteenth. He'd finish his drink and then go home. He drained his glass and was about to go inside when a voice at his elbow said, 'If you're going to the bar, you could get me another one.' It was a soft seductive voice. Dundridge turned and looked into a pair of almond eyes. Dundridge changed his mind about leaving. He went through to the bar and got two more drinks.

'These affairs are such a bore,' said the girl. 'Are you a great golfer?'

Dundridge said he wasn't a golfer at all.

'Nor am I. Such a boring game.' She sat down and crossed her legs. They were really very nice legs. 'And anyway I don't like sporty types. I prefer intellectuals.' She smiled at Dundridge. 'My name is Sally Boles. What's yours?'

'Dundridge,' said Dundridge and sat down where he could see more of her legs. Ten minutes later he got another two drinks. Twenty minutes later two more. He was enjoying himself at last.

Miss Boles, he learnt, was visiting her uncle. She came from London too. She worked for a firm of beauty consultants. Dundridge said he could well believe it. She found the country so boring. Dundridge said he did too. He waxed lyrical about the joys of living in London and all the time Miss Boles' almond eyes smiled seductively at him and her legs crossed and recrossed in the gathering dusk. When Dundridge suggested another drink Miss Boles insisted on getting it.

'It's my turn,' she said, 'and besides I want to powder my nose.' She left Dundridge sitting alone on the terrace in a happy stupor. When she returned with the drinks she was looking thoughtful.

'My uncle's gone without me,' she said, 'I suppose he thought I had gone home already. Would it be too much for you to give me a lift?'

'Of course not. I'd be delighted,' said Dundridge and sipped his drink. It tasted extraordinarily bitter.

'I'm so sorry, I got Campari,' Miss Boles said by way of

explanation. Dundridge said it was quite all right. He finished his drink and they wandered off the terrace towards the car park. 'It's been such a lovely evening,' Miss Boles said as she climbed into Dundridge's car. 'You must look me up in London.'

'I'd like to,' said Dundridge. 'I'd like to see a lot more of you.'

'That's a promise,' said Miss Boles.

'You really mean that?'

'Call me Sally,' said Miss Boles and leant against him.

'Oh Sally ...' Dundridge began, and suddenly felt quite extraordinarily tired, '... I do want to see so much more of you.'

'You will, my pet, you will,' said Miss Boles and took the car keys out of his inert fingers. Dundridge had passed out.

•

In London Sir Giles lay back supine on the bed while Mrs Forthby tightened the straps. Occasionally he struggled briefly for the look of the thing and whimpered hoarsely but Mrs Forthby was, at least superficially, implacable. The scenario of Sir Giles' fantasy called for a brutal implacability and Mrs Forthby did her best. She wasn't very good, being a kind-hearted soul and not given to tying people up and whipping them, and as a matter of fact she disapproved of corporal punishment on principle. It was largely because she was so progressive that she was prepared to indulge Sir Giles in the first place. 'If it gives the poor man pleasure who am I to say him nay,' she told herself. Certainly she had to say nay a great many times to Sir Giles in the throes of his ritual. But if Mrs Forthby wasn't naturally brutal, with the lights down low it was possible to imagine that she was and she had the merit of being strong and wearing her costume – there were several – most convincingly. Tonight she was Cat Woman, Miss Dracula, the Cruel Mistress Experimenting On Her Helpless Victim.

'No, no,' whimpered Sir Giles.

'Yes, yes,' insisted Mrs Forthby.

'No, no.'

'Yes, yes.'

Mrs Forthby's fingers forced his mouth open and inserted the gag. 'No . . .' It was too late. Mrs Forthby inflated the gag and smiled maliciously down at him. Her breasts loomed above him, heavy with menace. Her gloved hands . . .

Mrs Forthby went into the kitchen and made a pot of tea. While she waited for the kettle to boil she nibbled a digestive biscuit thoughtfully. There were times when she tired of Sir Giles' desultory attachment and longed for a more permanent arrangement. She would have to speak to him about it. She warmed the teapot, put in two teabags and then a third for the pot and poured the boiling water in. After all she was getting on and she rather fancied the idea of being Lady Lynchwood. She looked round the kitchen. Now where had she put the lid of the teapot?

On the bed Sir Giles struggled with his bonds and was still. He lay back happily exhausted and waited for his cruel mistress. He had to wait a long time. In between spasms of excitement his mind went back to Dundridge. He hoped Hoskins hadn't made a bloody mess of things. That was the trouble with subordinates, you couldn't trust them. Sir Giles preferred to attend to matters himself but he had too much to lose to be closely involved in the actual details of this particular operation. First the stick and then the carrot. He wondered how much the carrot would have to be. Two, three, four thousand pounds? Expensive. Add Hoskins' five thousand. Still, it was worth it. A profit of £150,000 was worth it. So was the prospect of Maud's fury when she realized that the motorway was coming through the Gorge. Teach the stupid bitch. But where was Mrs Forthby? Why didn't she come back?

Mrs Forthby finished her cup of tea and poured another. She was getting rather hot in her tight costume. Perhaps she would go and have a bath. She got up and went into the bathroom and turned on the tap before remembering that there was something she still had to do. 'Silly old me; talk about forgetful,' she said to herself and picked up the thin cane. The Cruel Mistress,

Miss Dracula, went through to the bedroom and closed the door.

•

In his library in the Lodge Blott sat reading Sir Arthur Bryant, but his mind wasn't on the Age of Elegance. It kept slipping away to Maud, Mrs Wynn, Dundridge, Sir Giles. Besides, he didn't much care for the Prince Regent. Nasty piece of goods in Blott's opinion. But then Blott had no time for any of the Georges. His sympathies were all with the Jacobites. The lost cause and Bonnie Prince Charlie. In his present mood of romantic devotion he felt a longing to kneel before Lady Maud and confess his love. It was an absurd notion. She would be furious with him. Worse still, she might laugh. The thought of her contemptuous laughter made him put the book down and go downstairs. It was a lovely evening. The sun had set over the hills to the west but the sky was still bright. Blott felt like a beer. He wasn't going over to Guildstead Carbonell for one. Mrs Wynn would expect him to spend the night and Blott didn't feel like another night with her. He had spent the previous evening wrestling with his conscience and trying to make up his mind to tell her it was all over between them. In the end his sense of realism had prevailed. Lady Maud wasn't for the likes of Blott. He would just have to dream about her. He had done so while making love to Mrs Wynn, who had been amazed at his renewed fervour. 'Just like the old days,' she had said wistfully as Blott got dressed to cycle back to the Lodge. No, he definitely didn't feel like another night at the Royal George. He would go for a walk. There were some rabbits over by the pinetum. Blott fetched his shotgun and set off across the Park. Beside him the river murmured gently and there was a smell of summer in the air. A blackbird called from a bush. Blott ignored his surroundings. He was dreaming of changed circumstances, of Lady Maud in peril, an act of heroism on his part that would reveal his true feelings for her and bring them together in love and happiness. By the time he reached the pinetum it was too dark to see any rabbits. But Blott wasn't interested in rabbits any more. A light had come on in Lady Maud's bedroom. Blott crept across the lawn and stood looking up at it until it went out. Then he walked home and went to bed.

12

Dundridge woke in a lay-by on the London road. He had a splitting headache, he was extremely cold and the gear lever was sticking into his ribs. He sat up, untangled his legs from under the steering wheel and wondered where the hell he was, how he had got there and what the devil had happened. He had an extremely clear memory of the party at the Golf Club. He could remember talking to Miss Boles on the terrace. He could even recall walking back to his car with her. After that nothing.

He got out of the car to try to get the circulation moving in his legs and discovered that his trousers were undone. He did them up hurriedly and reached up automatically to tighten the knot in his tie to hide his embarrassment only to find that he wasn't wearing a tie. He felt his open shirt collar and the vest underneath. It was on back to front. He pulled the vest out a bit and looked down at the label. St Michael Combed Cotton it said. It was definitely on back to front. Now he came to think of it, his Y-fronts felt peculiar too. He took a step forward and tripped over a shoelace. His shoes were untied. Dundridge staggered against the car, seriously alarmed. He was in the middle of nowhere at ... He looked at his watch. At six a.m. with his shoes untied, his vest and pants on back to front, and his trousers undone, and all he could remember was getting into the car with a girl with almond eyes and lovely legs.

And suddenly Dundridge had a horrid picture of the night's events. Perhaps he had raped the girl. A sudden brainstorm. That would explain the headache. The years of self-indulgence with his composite woman had come home to roost. He had gone mad and raped Miss Boles, possibly killed her. He looked down at his hands. At least there wasn't any blood on them. He could have strangled her. There was always that possibility. There were any number of awful possibilities. Dundridge bent over painfully and did up his shoes and then, having looked in the ditch to make sure that there was no body there, he got back into the car and wondered what to do. There was obviously no point in sitting in the lay-by. Dundridge started the car and drove on until he came to a signpost which told him he was going towards London. He turned the car round and drove back to Worford, parked in the yard of the Handyman Arms and went quietly up to his room. He was in bed when the girl brought him his tea.

'What time is it?' he asked sleepily. The girl looked at him with a nasty smile.

'You ought to know,' she said, 'you've only just come in. I saw you sneaking up the stairs. Been having a night on the tiles, have you?'

She put the tray down and went out, leaving Dundridge cursing himself for a fool. He drank some tea and felt worse. There was no point in doing anything until he felt better. He turned on his side and went to sleep. When he awoke it was midday. He washed and shaved, studying his face in the mirror for some sign of the sexual mania he suspected. The face that stared back at him was a perfectly ordinary face but Dundridge was not reassured. Murderers tended to have perfectly ordinary faces. Perhaps he had simply had a blackout or amnesia. But that wouldn't explain his vest being on back to front, nor his Y-fronts. At some time during the night he had undressed. Worse still, he had dressed in such a hurry that he hadn't noticed what he was doing. That suggested panic or at least an extraordinary urgency. He went downstairs and had lunch. After lunch he would get hold of a telephone directory and look up Boles. Of course her uncle might not be called Boles but it was worth a try. If that didn't work he would try Hoskins or the Golf Club. On second thoughts, that might not be such a good idea. There was no point in drawing attention to the fact that he had taken Miss Boles home. Or hadn't.

In the event there was no need to look in the telephone directory. As he passed the hotel desk, the clerk handed him a large envelope. It was addressed to Mr Dundridge and marked Private and Confidential. Dundridge took it up to his room before opening it and was extremely thankful that he hadn't opened it in the foyer. Dundridge knew now how he had spent the night.

He dropped the photographs on to the bed and slumped into a chair. A moment later he was up and locking the door. Then he turned back and stared at the pictures. They were 10 by 8 glossies and quite revolting. Taken with a flash, they were extremely clear and portrayed Dundridge with an unmistakable clarity, naked and all too evidently unashamed, engaged in a series of monstrous activities beyond his wildest imaginings with Miss Boles. At least he supposed it was Miss Boles. The fact that she seemed ... Not seemed, *was* wearing a mask, a sort of hood, made identification impossible. He thumbed through the pictures and came to the hooded man. Dundridge hurriedly put them back in the envelope and sat sweating on the edge of the bed. He'd been framed. The word seemed wholly inappropriate. Nothing on God's earth would get him to frame these pictures. Someone was trying to blackmail him.

Trying? They had bloody well succeeded, but Dundridge had no money. He couldn't pay anything. Dundridge opened the envelope again and stared at the evidence of his depravity. Miss Boles? Miss Boles? It obviously wasn't her real name. Sally Boles. He had heard that name before somewhere. Of course, Sally Bowles in *I am a Camera*. Dundridge didn't need telling. He'd been had in many more ways than one. In many more ways if the photos were anything to go by.

He was just wondering what to do next when the telephone rang. Dundridge grabbed it. 'Yes,' he said.

'Mr Dundridge?' said a woman's voice.

'Speaking,' said Dundridge shakily.

'I hope you like the proofs.'

'Proofs, you bitch?' Dundridge snarled.

'Call me Sally,' said the voice. 'There's no need to be formal with me now.'

'What do you want?'

'A thousand pounds . . . to be going on with.'

'A thousand pounds? I haven't got a thousand pounds.'

'Then you had better get it, hadn't you sweetie?'

'I'll tell you what I'm going to get,' shouted Dundridge, 'I'm going to get the police.'

'You do that,' said a man's voice roughly, 'and you'll end up with your face cut to ribbons. You're not playing with small fry, mate. We're bigtime, understand.'

Dundridge understood all too well. The woman's voice came back on the line. 'If you do go to the police remember we've had one or two customers there. We'll know. You just start looking for your thousand pounds.'

'I can't—'

'Don't call us. We'll call you,' said Miss Boles, and put the phone down. Dundridge replaced his receiver more slowly. Then he leant forward and held his head in his hands.

•

Sir Giles returned from London in excellent spirits. Mrs Forthby had excelled herself and he was still tingling with satisfaction. Best of all had been Hoskins' cryptic message over the phone. 'The fish is hooked,' he had said. All that was required now was to provide a net in which Mr Dundridge could flounder. Sir Giles parked his car and went up to his constituency office and sent for Hoskins.

'Here they are. As nice a set of prints as you could wish for,' Hoskins said, laying the photographs out on the desk.

Sir Giles studied them with an appreciative eye. 'Very nice,' he said finally. 'Very nice indeed. And what does lover-boy have to say for himself now?'

'They've asked him for a thousand pounds. He says he hasn't got it.'

'He'll have it, never fear,' said Sir Giles. 'He'll have his thousand pounds and we'll have him. There won't be any more talk about tunnels in future. From now on it's going to be Otter-town.'

'Ottertown?' said Hoskins, thoroughly puzzled. 'But I thought you wanted it through the Gorge. I thought—'

'The trouble with you, Hoskins,' said Sir Giles, putting the photographs back into the envelope and the envelope into his briefcase, 'is that you can't see further than the end of your nose. You don't really think I want to lose my lovely house and my beautiful wife, do you? You don't think I haven't got the interests of my constituents like General Burnett and Mr Bull-ett-Bloody-Finch at heart, do you? Of course I have. I'm honest Sir Giles, the poor man's friend,' and leaving Hoskins com-pletely confused by this strange change of tack, he went down-stairs.

There was nothing like throwing people off the scent. Killing two birds with one stone, he thought as he got into the Bent-ley. The decision to go through Ottertown would kill Puck-erington for sure. Sir Giles looked forward to his demise with relish. Puckerington was no friend of his. Snobby bastard. Well, he was bird number one. Then the bye-election in Ottertown and they would have to change the route to the Gorge and Handyman Hall would go. Bird number two. By that time he would be able to claim even more compensation and no one, least of all Maud, could say he hadn't done his damnedest. There was only one snag. That old fool Leakham might still insist on the Gorge route. It was hardly a snag. Maud would create a bit more. He might lose his seat in Parliament but he would be £150,000 richer and Mrs Forthby was waiting. Swings or roundabouts, Sir Giles couldn't lose. The main thing was to see that the tunnel scheme was scotched. Sir Giles parked out-side the Handyman Arms, went inside and sent a message up to Dundridge's room to say that Sir Giles Lynchwood was looking forward to his company in the lounge.

Dundridge went downstairs gloomily. The last person he wanted to see was the local MP. He could hardly consult him about blackmail. Sir Giles greeted him with a heartiness Dun-dridge no longer felt that his position warranted. 'My dear fellow, I'm delighted to see you,' he said shaking Dundridge's limp hand vigorously. 'Been meaning to look you up and have a chat about this motorway nonsense. Had to go to London unfortunately. Looking after you all right here? It's one of our houses, you know. Any complaints, just let me know and I'll see to it. We'll have tea in the private lounge.' He led the way up some steps into a small lounge with a TV set in the corner. Sir Giles plumped into a chair and took out a cigar. 'Smoke?'

Dundridge shook his head.

'Very wise of you. Still they do say cigars don't do one any harm and a fellow's entitled to one or two little vices, eh, what?' said Sir Giles and pierced the end of the cigar with a silver cutter. Dundridge winced. The cigar reminded him of something that had figured rather too largely in his activities with Miss Boles, and as for vices . . .

'Now then, about this business of the motorway,' said Sir Giles, 'I think it's as well to put our cards on the table. I'm a man who doesn't beat about the bush I can tell you. Call a spade a bloody shovel. I don't let the grass grow under my feet. Wouldn't be where I was if I did.' He paused briefly to allow Dundridge to savour this wealth of metaphors and the bluff dishonesty of his approach. 'And I don't mind telling you that I don't like this idea of your building a motorway through my damned land one little bit.'

'It was hardly my idea,' said Dundridge.

'Not yours personally,' said Sir Giles, 'but you fellows at the Ministry have made up your mind to slap the bloody thing smack through the Gorge. Don't tell me you haven't.'

'Well, as a matter of fact . . .' Dundridge began.

'There you are. What did I tell you? Told you so. Can't pull the wool over my eyes.'

'As a matter of fact I'm against the Gorge route,' Dundridge said when he got the opportunity. Sir Giles looked at him dubiously.

'You are?' he said. 'Damned glad to hear it. I suppose you favour Ottertown. Can't say I blame you. Best route by far.'

'No,' said Dundridge. 'Not through Ottertown. A tunnel under the Cleene Hills . . .'

Sir Giles feigned astonishment. 'Now wait a minute,' he said, 'the Cleene Forest is an area of designated public beauty. You can't start mucking around with that.' His accent, as variable as a weathercock, had veered round to Huddersfield.

'There's no question of mucking about . . .' Dundridge began but Sir Giles was leaning across the table towards him with a very nasty look on his face.

'You can say that again,' he said poking his forefinger into Dundridge's shirt front. 'Now you just listen to me, young man. You can forget all about tunnels and suchlike. I want a quick decision one way or t'other. I don't like to be kept hanging about while lads like you dither about talking a lot of airy twaddle about tunnels. That's all right for my missus, she being a gullible woman, but it won't wash with me. I want a straight answer. Yes or No. Yes to Ottertown and No to the Gorge.' He sat back and puffed his cigar.

'In that case,' said Dundridge stiffly, 'you had better have a word with Lord Leakham. He's the one who makes the final decision.'

'Leakham? Leakham? Makes the final decision?' said Sir Giles. 'Don't try to have me on, lad. The Minister didn't send you up so that that dry old stick could make decisions. He sent you up to tell him what to say. You can't fool me. I know an expert when I see one. He'll do what you tell him.'

Dundridge felt better. This was the recognition he had been waiting for. 'Well I suppose I do have some influence,' he conceded.

Sir Giles beamed. 'What did I say? Top men don't grow on trees and I've got a nose for talent. Well, you won't find me ungenerous. You pop round and see me when you've had your little chat with Lord Leakham. I'll see you right.'

Dundridge goggled at him. 'You don't mean—'

'Name your own charity,' said Sir Giles with a prodigious wink. 'Mind you, I always say "Charity begins at home". Eh? I'm not a mean man. I pays for what I gets.' He drew on his cigar and watched Dundridge through a cloud of smoke. This was the moment of truth. Dundridge swallowed nervously.

'That's very kind of you . . .' he began.

'Say no more,' said Sir Giles. 'Say no more. Any time you want me I'll be in my constituency office or out at the Hall. Best time to catch me is in the morning at the office.'

'But what am I going to say to Lord Leakham?' Dundridge said. 'He's adamant about the Gorge route.'

'You tell him from me that my good lady wife intends to take him to the cleaners about that unlawful arrest unless he decides for Ottertown. You tell him that.'

'I don't think Lord Leakham would appreciate that very much,' said Dundridge nervously. He didn't much like the idea of uttering threats against the old judge.

'You tell him I'll sue him for every brass farthing he's got. And I've got witnesses, remember. Influential witnesses who'll stand up in court and swear that he was drunk and disorderly at that Enquiry, and abusive too. You tell him he won't have a reputation and he won't have a penny by the time we've finished with him. I'll see to that.'

'I doubt if he'll like it,' said Dundridge, who certainly didn't.

'Don't suppose he will,' said Sir Giles, 'I'm not a man to run up against.'

Dundridge could see that. By the time Sir Giles left Dundridge had no doubts on that score at all. As Sir Giles drove away Dundridge went up to his room and looked at the photographs again. Spurred on by their obscenity he took an aspirin and went slowly round to the Cottage Hospital. He'd make Lord Leakham change his mind about the Gorge. Sir Giles had said he would pay for what he got and Dundridge intended to see that he got something to pay for. He didn't have any choice any longer. It was either that or ruin.

•

On the way back to Handyman Hall, Sir Giles stopped and unlocked his briefcase and took out the photographs. They were really very interesting. Mrs Williams was an imaginative woman. No doubt about it. And attractive. Most attractive. He might look her up one of these days. He put the photographs away and drove back to the Hall.

13

At the Cottage Hospital Dundridge had some difficulty in finding Lord Leakham. He wasn't in his room. 'It's very naughty of him to wander about like this,' said the Matron. 'You'll probably find him in the Abbey. He's taken to going over there when he shouldn't. Says he likes looking at the tombstones. Morbid, I call it.'

'You don't think his mind has been affected, do you?' Dundridge asked hopefully.

'Not so's you'd notice. All lords are potty in my experience,' the Matron told him.

In the end Dundridge found him in the garden discussing the merits of the cat o'nine tails with a retired vet who had the good fortune to be deaf.

'Well what do you want now?' Lord Leakham asked irritably when Dundridge interrupted.

'Just a word with you,' said Dundridge.

'Well, what is it?' said Lord Leakham.

'It's about the motorway,' Dundridge explained.

'What about it? I'm re-opening the Enquiry on Monday. Can't it wait till then?'

'I'm afraid not,' said Dundridge. 'The thing is that as a result of an in-depth on-the-spot investigative study of the socio-environmental and geognostic ancillary factors . . .'

'Good God,' said Lord Leakham, 'I thought you said you wanted a word . . .'

'It is our considered conclusion,' continued Dundridge, manfully devising a jargon to suit the occasion, 'that given the—'

'Which is it to be? Ottertown or the Cleene Gorge? Spit it out, man.'

'Ottertown,' said Dundridge.

'Over my dead body,' said Lord Leakham.

'I trust not,' said Dundridge, disguising his true feelings. 'There's just one other thing I think you ought to know. As you are probably aware the Government is most anxious to avoid any further adverse publicity about the motorway . . .'

'You can't expect to demolish seventy-five brand-new council houses without attracting adverse publicity,' Lord Leakham pointed out.

'And,' continued Dundridge, 'the civil action for damages which Lady Lynchwood intends to institute against you is bound—'

'Against *me*?' shouted the Judge. 'She intends to—'

'For unlawful arrest,' said Dundridge.

'That's a police matter. If she has any complaints let her sue those responsible. In any case no sane judge would find for her.'

'I understand she intends to call some rather eminent people as witnesses,' said Dundridge. 'Their testimony will be that you were drunk.'

Lord Leakham began to swell.

'And personally abusive,' said Dundridge gritting his teeth. 'And disorderly. In fact that you were not in a fit state . . .'

'WHAT?' yelled the Judge, with a violence that sent several elderly patients scurrying for cover and a number of pigeons fluttering off the hospital roof.

'In short,' said Dundridge as the echo died away across the Abbey Close, 'she intends to impugn your reputation. Naturally the Minister has to take all these things into account, you do see that?'

But it was doubtful if Lord Leakham could see anything. He had slumped on to a bench and was staring lividly at his bedroom slippers.

'Naturally too,' continued Dundridge, pursuing his advantage, 'there is a fairly widespread feeling that you might be biased against her in the matter of the Gorge.'

'Biased?' Lord Leakham snuffled. 'The Gorge is the logical route.'

'On the grounds of the civil action she intends to take. Now if you were to decide on Ottertown ...' Dundridge left the consequences hanging in the air.

'You think she might reconsider her decision?'

'I feel sure she would,' said Dundridge. 'In fact I'm positive she would.'

Dundridge walked back to the Handyman Arms rather pleased with his performance. Desperation had lent him a fluency he had never known before. In the morning he would go and see Sir Giles about a thousand pounds. He had an early dinner and went up to his room, locked the door and examined the photographs again. Then he turned out the light and considered several things he hadn't done to Miss Sally Boles but which on reflection he wished he had. Strangled the bitch for one thing.

•

At Handyman Hall Sir Giles and Lady Maud dined alone. Their conversation seldom sparkled and was usually limited to an exchange of acrimonious opinions but for once they were both in a good mood at the same time. Dundridge was the cause of their good humour.

'Such a sensible young man,' Lady Maud said helping herself to asparagus. 'I'm sure that tunnel is the right answer.'

Sir Giles rather doubted it. 'My bet is he'll go for Ottertown,' he said.

Lady Maud said she hoped not. 'It seems such a shame to turn those poor people out of their homes. I'm sure they would feel just as strongly as I do about the Hall.'

'They build them new houses,' said Sir Giles. 'It's not as if they turn them out into the street. Anyway, people who live on council estates deserve what they get. Sponging off public money.'

Lady Maud said some people couldn't help being poor. They were just built that way like Blott. 'Dear Blott,' she said. 'You know he did such a strange thing this morning, he brought me a present, a little figure he had carved out of wood.'

But Sir Giles wasn't listening. He was still thinking about

people who lived in council houses. 'What the man in the street doesn't seem to be able to get into his thick head is that the world doesn't owe him a living.'

'I thought it was rather sweet of him,' said Lady Maud.

Sir Giles helped himself to cheese soufflé. 'What people don't understand is that we're just animals,' he said. 'The world is a bloody jungle. It's dog eat dog in this life and no mistake.'

'Dog?' said Lady Maud, roused from her reverie by the word. 'That reminds me. I suppose I'll have to send all those Alsatians back now. Just when I was getting fond of them. You're quite sure Mr Dundridge is going to advise Ottertown?'

'Positive,' said Sir Giles, 'I'd stake my life on it.'

'Really,' said Lady Maud wistfully, 'I don't see how you can be so certain. Have you spoken to him?'

Sir Giles hesitated. 'I have it on the best authority,' he said.

'Hoskins,' said Lady Maud, 'that horrid man. I wouldn't trust him any further than I could throw him. He'd say anything.'

'He also says that this fellow Dundridge has taken a fancy to you,' Sir Giles said. 'It seems you had a considerable effect on him.'

Lady Maud considered the remark and found it intriguing. 'I'm sure that can't be true. Hoskins is making things up.'

'It might explain why he is in favour of the Ottertown route,' Sir Giles said. 'You bowled him over with your charm.'

'Very funny,' said Lady Maud.

But afterwards as she washed up in the kitchen she found herself thinking about Dundridge, if not fondly, at least with a renewed interest. There was something rather appealing about the little man, a vulnerability that she found preferable to Sir Giles' disgusting self-sufficiency . . . and Dundridge had taken a fancy to her. It was useful to know these things. She would have to cultivate him. She smiled to herself. If Sir Giles could have his little affairs in London, there was no reason why she shouldn't avail herself of his absence for her own purposes. But above all there was an anonymity about Dundridge that appealed to her. 'He'll do,' she said to herself and dried her hands.

•

Next morning Dundridge went round to Sir Giles' constituency office at eleven. 'I've had a word with Lord Leakham and I think he'll be amenable,' he said.

'Splendid, my dear fellow, splendid. Delighted to hear it. I knew you could do it. A great weight off my mind, I can tell you. Now then is there anything I can do for you?' Sir Giles leant back in his chair expansively. 'After all, one good turn deserves another.'

Dundridge braced himself for the request. 'As a matter of fact, there is,' he said, and hesitated before going on.

'I'll tell you what I'll do,' said Sir Giles coming to his rescue. 'I don't know if you're a betting man but I am. I'll bet you a thousand pounds to a penny that old Leakham says the motorway has to go through Ottertown. How about that? Couldn't ask for anything fairer, eh?'

'A thousand pounds to a penny?' said Dundridge, hardly able to believe his ears.

'That's right. A thousand pounds to a penny. Take it or leave it.'

'I'll take it,' said Dundridge.

'Good man. I thought you would,' said Sir Giles, 'and just to show my good faith I'll put the stake up now.' He reached down to a drawer in the desk and took out an envelope. 'You can count it at your leisure.' He put the envelope on the desk. 'No need for a receipt. Just don't spend it until Leakham gives his decision.'

'Of course not,' said Dundridge. He put the envelope in his pocket.

'Nice meeting you,' said Sir Giles. Dundridge went out and down the stairs. He had accepted a bare-faced bribe. It was the first time in his life. Behind him Sir Giles switched off the tape recorder. It was just as well to have a receipt. Once the Enquiry was over he would burn the tape but in the meantime better safe than sorry.

14

Lord Leakham's announcement that he was recommending the Ottertown route provoked mixed reactions. In Worford there was open rejoicing and the Handyman pubs dispensed free beer. In Ottertown the Member of Parliament, Francis Puckerington, was inundated with telephone calls and protest letters and suffered a relapse as a result. In London the Prime Minister, relieved that there hadn't been another riot in Worford, congratulated the Minister of the Environment on the adroit way his department had handled the matter, and the Minister congratulated Mr Rees on his choice of a troubleshooter. No one in the Ministry shared his enthusiasm.

'That bloody idiot Dundridge has dropped us in it this time,' said Mr Joynson. 'I knew it was a mistake to send him up there. The Ottertown route is going to cost an extra ten million.'

'In for a penny in for a pound,' said Rees. 'At least we've got rid of him.'

'Got rid of him? He'll be back tomorrow crowing about his success as a negotiator.'

'He won't you know,' Rees told him. 'He got us into this mess, he can damned well get us out. The Minister has approved his appointment as Controller Motorways Midlands.'

'Controller Motorways Midlands? I didn't know there was such a post.'

'There wasn't. It's been specially created for him. Don't ask me why. All I know is that Dundridge has found favour with one or two influential people in South Worfordshire. Wheels within wheels,' said Mr Rees.

In Worford Dundridge greeted the news of his appointment with consternation. He had spent an anxious weekend confined to his room at the Handyman Arms partly because he was afraid of missing the telephone call from Miss Boles and partly because he had no intention of leaving the money he had received from Sir Giles in his suitcase or of carrying it around on his person. But there had been no phone call. To add to his troubles, there was the knowledge that he had accepted a bribe. He tried to persuade himself that he had merely taken a bet on, but it was no use.

'I could get three years for this,' he said to himself, and seriously considered handing the money back. He was deterred by the photographs. He couldn't imagine how many years he could get for doing what they suggested he had done.

By the time the Enquiry re-opened on Monday, Dundridge's nerves were frayed to breaking point. He had taken his seat inconspicuously at the back of the courtroom and had hardly listened to the evidence. The presence of a large number of policemen, brought in to ensure that there was no further outbreak of violence, had done nothing to reassure him. Dundridge had misconstrued their role and had finally left the courtroom before Lord Leakham announced his decision. He was standing in the hall downstairs when a burst of cheering indicated that the Enquiry was over.

Sir Giles and Lady Maud were the first to congratulate him. They issued from the courtroom and down the stairs followed by General Burnett and Mr and Mrs Bullett-Finch.

'Splendid news,' said Sir Giles. Lady Maud seized Dundridge's hand.

'I feel we owe you a great debt of gratitude,' she said staring into his face significantly.

'It was nothing,' murmured Dundridge modestly.

'Nonsense,' said Lady Maud, 'you have made me very happy. You must come and see us before you leave.'

Sir Giles had winked prodigiously — Dundridge had come to loathe that wink — and had whispered something about a bet being a bet and Hoskins had insisted on their going to have a drink together to celebrate. Dundridge couldn't see anything to celebrate about.

'You've got friends at court,' Hoskins explained.

'Friends at court?' said Dundridge. 'What on earth do you mean?'

100

'A little bird has told me that someone has put in a good word for you. You wait and see.'

Dundridge had waited in the hope (though that was hardly the right word) that Miss Boles would call but instead of a demand for a thousand pounds he had received a letter of appointment. 'Controller Motorways Midlands with responsibility for co-ordinating . . . Good God!' he muttered. He made a number of frantic phone calls to the Ministry threatening to resign unless he was brought back to London, but the enthusiasm with which Mr Rees endorsed his decision was enough to make him retract it.

Even Hoskins, who might have been expected to resent Dundridge's appointment as his superior, seemed relieved. 'What did I tell you, old boy,' he said when Dundridge told him the news. 'Friends at court. Friends at court.'

'But I don't know anything about motorway construction. I'm an administrator not an engineer.'

'All you have to do is see that the contractors keep to schedule,' Hoskins explained. 'Nothing to it. You leave all the rest of it to me. Basically yours is a public-relations role.'

'But I'm responsible for coordinating construction work. It says so here,' Dundridge protested, waving his letter of appointment, ' "and in particular problems relating to environmental factors and human ecology". I suppose that means dealing with the tenants of those council houses in Ottertown.'

'That sort of thing,' said Hoskins. 'I shouldn't worry about that too much. Cross your bridges when you come to them is my motto.'

'Oh well, I suppose I'll just have to get used to the idea.'

'I'll fix you up an office here. You'd better set about finding somewhere to live.'

Dundridge had spent two days looking at flats in Worford before settling on an apartment overlooking Worford Castle. It wasn't a prospect he found particularly pleasing, but the flat had the merit of being comparatively modern and was certainly better than some of the squalid rooms he had looked at elsewhere. And besides it had a telephone and was partly furnished. Dundridge placed particular emphasis upon the telephone. He didn't want Miss Boles to get the false idea that he wasn't prepared to pay a thousand pounds for the photographs and negatives. But as the days passed and there was still no demand from her he began to relax. Perhaps the whole thing had been some sort of filthy practical joke. He even asked Hoskins if he knew anything about the girl at the party but Hoskins said he couldn't remember much about the evening and hadn't known half the people who were there.

'My mind's a blank on the whole evening, old chap,' he said. 'Had a good time, though. I do remember that. Why? Are you thinking of looking her up again?'

'Just wondered who she was,' said Dundridge and went back to his office to draw up plans for the opening ceremony to mark the start of the construction of the motorway. It was going to be a grand affair, he had decided.

*

So had Lady Maud, though the affair she had in mind was of quite a different sort. She waited until Sir Giles said he was going to spend a fortnight in London before inviting Dundridge to dinner. She sent a formal invitation.

Dundridge hired a dinner-jacket and expected to find a number of other guests. He was extremely nervous and had fortified himself in advance with two stiff gins. In the event he need not have bothered. He arrived to find Lady Maud dressed, if not to kill, at least to seriously endanger anyone who came near her.

'I'm so glad you could come,' she said taking his arm almost as soon as he had entered the front door. 'I'm afraid my husband has had to go to London on business. I hope you don't mind having to put up with me.'

'Not at all,' said Dundridge, conscious once again of that weakness in his legs that Lady Maud's presence seemed to induce in him. They went into the drawing-room and Lady Maud mixed drinks. 'I did think of inviting General Burnett and the Bullett-Finches but the General does tend to monopolize the conversation and Ivy Bullett-Finch is a bit of a wet blanket.'

Dundridge sipped his drink and wondered what the hell she had put into it. It looked innocuous, but clearly wasn't. Lady Maud's dress, on the other hand, practised no such deception. A thing of silk designed to emphasize the curvature of the female form, it had evidently been created with someone more lissom in mind. It bulged where it should have hung and wheezed when it should have rustled. Above all it was so clearly breathtaking in its constriction that Dundridge found himself almost panting in empathy. Besides Lady Maud's voice had undergone a strange alteration. It was curiously husky.

'How do you like your new flat?' she asked, sitting down beside him with a squeak of pre-stressed silk.

'Flat?' said Dundridge momentarily unable to make the transition between adjective and noun. 'Oh flat. Yes. Very pleasant.'

'You must let me come up and see it some time,' said Lady Maud. 'Unless you feel I might be compromising you.' She sighed, and her great bosom heaved like an approaching breaker.

'Compromising?' said Dundridge, who couldn't imagine that he was likely to be compromised by being alone in his flat with her any more than he was already by those beastly photographs. 'I'd be delighted to have you.'

Lady Maud tittered coyly. 'I'm afraid you're going to miss the excitement of life in London,' she murmured. 'We must do what we can to see that you don't get bored.'

It seemed a remote prospect to Dundridge. He sat rigid on the sofa and tried to keep his eyes averted from the incomprehensible fascinations of her body.

'Let me get you another drink,' she breathed softly, and once again he was conscious of a feeling of being overcome. It was partly the drink, partly the waft of perfume, but it was mostly the strength of her self-assurance that held him fascinated. In spite of her size, in spite of her assertiveness, in spite of everything about her that conflicted with his idea of a beautiful woman, Lady Maud was wholly confident. And Dundridge, who wasn't (or at best only partially and whose completeness, depending on achievement and money, lay in the future) was intoxicated by her presence. If the past could confer such assurance there was more to be said for it than Dundridge had previously admitted. Dundridge sipped his drink and smiled at her. Lady Maud smiled back.

By the time they went in to dinner, Dundridge was incongruously gay. He opened the door for her; he held her arm; he pulled back her chair and nudged it forward against her thighs meaningfully; he opened the champagne with a nonchalance that suggested he seldom drank anything else and laughed debonairly as the cork tinkled among the glass lustres of the chandelier. And through the meal, oysters followed by cold duck, Dundridge no longer cared what the world might think of him. Lady Maud's appreciative smile, half yawn and half abyss, beckoned him on to be himself. And Dundridge was. For the first time in his life he lived up to his own expectations, up to and far beyond. The champagne cork flew a second time into the upper reaches of the room, the duck disappeared to be followed by strawberries and cream, and Dundridge lost the last vestiges of inhibition or even the apprehension that there was anything at all unusual about dining alone with a married woman whose husband was away on business. All such considerations vanished in the bubble of his gaiety and in the light of Lady Maud's approval. Under the table her knee confirmed the implications of her smile; on top her hand lay heavily on his and traced the contours of his fingers; and when, their coffee finished, she took his arm and suggested that they dance Dundridge heard himself say he would be delighted to. Arm-in-arm they went down the passage to the ballroom with the sprung floor. Only then, with the chandeliers lighting the great room brilliantly and a record on the turntable, did he realize what he had let himself in for. Dundridge had never danced in his life.

•

Blott walked down the hill from Wilfrid's Castle. For a week he had been avoiding the Royal George in Guildstead Carbonell and Mrs Wynn's favours. He had taken to going over to a small pub on the lane leading from the church to the Ottertown Road. It wasn't up to the standard of the Royal George, merely a room with benches round the walls and a barrel of Handyman beer in one corner, but its dismal atmosphere suited Blott's mood. By the time he had silently consumed eight pints he was ready for bed. He wobbled up the hill past the church and stood gazing down at the Hall in amazement. The great ballroom lights were on. Blott couldn't remember when he had last seen them on, certainly not since Lady Maud's marriage. They cast yellow rectangles on to the lawn, and the conservatory which opened out of the ballroom glowed green with ferns and palms. He stumbled down the path and across the bridge into the pinetum. Here it was pitch-dark but Blott knew his way instinctively. He came out at the gate and crossed the lawn to the terrace. Music, old-fashioned music, floated out towards him. Blott went round the corner and peered through the window.

Inside Lady Maud was dancing. Or learning to dance. Or teaching someone to dance. Blott found difficulty in making up his mind. Under the great chandeliers she moved with a tender gracelessness that took his breath away. Up and down, round and about, in great sweeps and double turns she went, the floor moving visibly beneath her, and in her arms she held a small thin man with an expression of intense concentration on his face. Blott recognized him. He was the man from the Ministry who had stayed to lunch the previous week. Blott hadn't liked the look of him then and he liked it even less now. And Sir Giles was away. Sick with disgust Blott blundered off the flower bed and away from the window. He had half a mind to go in and say what he thought. It wouldn't do any good. He walked unsteadily round the front of the house. There was a car standing there. He peered at it. The man's car. Serve him right if he had to walk home, the bastard. Blott knelt by the front tyre and undid the valve. Then he went round to the boot and let the air out of the spare tyre. That would teach the swine to come messing about with other people's wives. Blott staggered off down the drive to the Lodge and climbed into bed. Through the circular window he could see the lights of the Hall. They were still on when he fell asleep and through the night air there came the faint sound of trombones.

15

What drinks, dinner and Lady Maud's assiduous coquetry had done for Dundridge, dancing had undone. In particular her interpretation of the hesitation waltz – Dundridge considered the probability of a slipped disc – while her tango had threatened hernia. All his attempts to get her to do something a little less complicated had been ignored.

'You're doing splendidly,' she said treading on his toes. 'All you need is a little practice.'

'What about something modern?' said Dundridge.

'Modern dancing is so unromantic,' said Maud, changing the record to a quickstep. 'There's no intimacy in it.'

Intimacy was not what Dundridge had in mind. 'I think I'll sit this one out,' he said limping to a chair. But Lady Maud wouldn't hear of it. She whirled him on to the floor and strode off through a series of half-turns clasping him to her bosom with a grip that brooked no argument. When the record stopped Dundridge put his foot down politely.

'I really think it is time I was off,' he said.

'What? So early? Just one more teeny weeny glass ōf champers,' said Lady Maud, relapsing rather prematurely into the language of the nursery.

'Oh all right,' said Dundridge choosing the devil of drink to the deep blue sea of the dance floor. They took their glasses through to the conservatory and stood for a moment among the ferns.

'What a wonderful night. Let's go out on the terrace,' said Lady Maud and took his arm. They leant on the stone balustrade and looked into the darkness of the pinetum.

'All we need now is a lovers' moon,' Lady Maud murmured and turned to face him. Dundridge looked up into the night sky. It was long past his bedtime and besides not even the champagne could disguise the fact that he was in an ambiguous situation. He had had enough of ambiguous situations lately to last him a lifetime and he certainly didn't relish the thought of Sir Giles returning home unexpectedly to find him on the terrace drinking champagne with his wife at one o'clock in the morning.

'It looks as if it's going to rain,' he said to change the topic from lovers' moons.

'Silly boy,' cooed Lady Maud. 'It's a lovely starlit night.'

'Yes. Well, I really do think I must be getting along,' Dundridge insisted. 'It's been a lovely evening.'

'Oh well if you must go . . .' They went indoors again.

'Just one more glass . . .?' Lady Maud said but Dundridge shook his head and limped on down the passage.

'You must look me up again,' said Lady Maud as he climbed into his car. 'The sooner the better. It's been ages since I had so much fun.' She waved goodbye and Dundridge drove off down the drive. He didn't get very far. There was something dreadfully wrong with the steering. The car seemed to veer to the left all the time and there was a thumping sound. Dundridge stopped and got out and went round to the front.

'Damn,' said Dundridge feeling the flat tyre. He went to the boot and got the jack out. By the time he had jacked the car up and taken the left front wheel off, the lights in the Hall had gone out. He fetched the spare wheel from the boot and bolted it into place. He let the jack down and stowed it away. Then he got back into the car and started the engine and drove off. There was a thumping noise and the car pulled to the left. Dundridge stopped with a curse.

'I must have put the flat tyre on again,' he muttered and got out the jack.

•

In the Hall Lady Maud switched off the ballroom lights sadly. She had enjoyed the evening and was sorry it had ended so tamely. There had been a moment earlier in the evening when she had thought Dundridge was going to prove amenable to her few charms.

'Men,' she said contemptuously as she undressed and stood looking at herself dispassionately in the mirror. She was not, and she was the first to admit it, a beautiful woman by contemporary standards of beauty but then she didn't pay much heed to contemporary standards of any sort. The world she lived for had admired substantial things, large women, heavy furniture, healthy appetites and strong feelings. She had no time for the present with its talk of sex, its girlish men and boyish women, and its reducing diets. She longed to be swept off her feet by a strong man who knew the value of bed, board and babies. She wasn't going to find him in Dundridge.

'Silly little goose doesn't know what he's missing,' she said, and climbed into bed.

*

Outside the silly little goose knew only too well what he was missing. An inflated tyre. He had changed the wheel again and had let down the jack only to find that his spare tyre had been flat after all. He got back into the car and tried to think what to do. Nearby something moved heavily through the grass and a night bird called. Dundridge shut the door. He couldn't sit there all night. He got out of the car and trudged back up the drive to the house and rang the doorbell.

Upstairs Lady Maud climbed out of bed and turned on the light. So the silly little goose had come back after all. He had caught her unprepared. She grabbed a lipstick and daubed her lips hastily, powdered her face and put a dollop of Chanel behind each ear. Finally she changed out of her pyjamas and slid into a see-through nightdress and went downstairs and opened the door.

'I'm sorry to bother you like this but I'm afraid I've had a puncture,' said Dundridge nervously. Lady Maud smiled knowingly.

'A puncture?'

'Yes, two as a matter of fact.'

'Two punctures?'

'Yes. Two,' said Dundridge conscious that there was something rather improbable about having two punctures at the same time.

'You had better come in,' said Lady Maud eagerly. Dundridge hesitated.

'If I could just use the phone to call a garage . . .'

But Lady Maud wouldn't hear of it. 'Of course you can't,' she said, 'it's far too late for anyone to come out now.' She took his arm and led him into the house and closed the door.

'I'm terribly sorry to be such a nuisance,' said Dundridge but Lady Maud shushed him.

'What a silly boy you are,' she cooed. 'Now come upstairs and we'll see about a bed.'

'Oh really . . .' Dundridge began but it was no good. She turned and led the way, a perfumed spinnaker, up the marble staircase. Dundridge followed miserably.

'You can have this room,' she said as they stood on the landing and she switched on the light. 'Now you go down to the bathroom and have a wash and I'll make the bed up.'

'The bathroom?' said Dundridge gazing at her astonished. In the dim light of the hall Lady Maud had been a mere if substantial shape but now he could see the full extent of her abundant charms. Her face was extraordinary too. Lady Maud smiled, a crimson gash with teeth. And the perfume!

'It's down the corridor on the left.'

Dundridge stumbled down the corridor and tried several doors before he found the bathroom. He went inside and locked the door. When he came out he found the corridor in darkness. He groped his way back to the landing and tried to remember which room she had given him. Finally he found one that was open. It was dark inside. Dundridge felt for the switch but it wasn't where he had expected.

'Is there anyone there?' he whispered but there was no reply. 'This must be the room,' he muttered and closed the door. He edged across the room and felt the end of the bed. A faint light came from the window. Dundridge undressed and noticed that Lady Maud's perfume still lingered heavily on the air. He went across to the window and opened it and then, moving carefully so as not to stub his toes, he went back and got into bed. As he did so he knew there was something terribly wrong. A blast of Chanel No. 5 issued from the bedclothes overpoweringly. So did Lady Maud. Her arms closed round him and with a husky, 'Oh you wicked boy,' her mouth descended on his. The next moment Dundridge was engulfed. Things seemed to fold round him, huge hot terrible things, legs, arms, breasts, lips, noses, thighs, bearing him up, entwining him, and bearing him down again in a frenzy of importunate flesh. He floundered frantically while the waves of Lady Maud's mistaken response broke over him. Only his mind remained untrammelled, his mind and his inhibitions. As he writhed in her arms his thoughts raced to a number of ghastly conclusions. He had chosen the wrong room; she was in love with him; he was in bed with a nymphomaniac; she was providing her husband with grounds for divorce; she was seducing him. There was no question about the last. She was seducing him. Her hands left him in no doubt about that, particularly her left hand. And Dundridge, accustomed to the wholly abstract stimulus of his composite woman, found the inexperience of a real woman – and Lady Maud was both real and inexperienced – hard to put up with.

'There's been a terr—' he managed to squeak as Lady Maud surfaced for air, but a moment later her mouth closed over his, silencing his protest while threatening him with suffocation. It was this last that gave him the desperation he needed. With a truly Herculean revulsion Dundridge hurled himself and Lady Maud, still clinging limpetlike to him, out of the bed. With a crash the bedside table fell to the floor as Dundridge broke free and leapt to his feet. The next moment he was through the door and running down the corridor. Behind him Lady Maud staggered to the bed and pulled the light cord. Stunned by the vigour of his rejection and by the bedside table which had caught her on the side of the head, she lumbered into the corridor and turned on the light but there was no sign of Dundridge.

'There's no need to be shy,' she called but there was no reply. She went into the next room and switched on the light. No Dundridge. The next room was empty too. She went from room to room switching on lights and calling his name, but Dundridge had vanished. Even the bathroom was unlocked and empty and she was just wondering where to look next when a sound from the landing drew her attention. She went back and switched on the hall light and caught him in the act of tiptoeing down the stairs. For an instant he stood there, a petrified satyr, and turned pathetic eyes towards her and then he was off down the stairs and across the marble floor, his slender legs and pale feet twinkling among the squares. Lady Maud leant over the balustrade and laughed. She was still laughing as she went down the staircase, laughing and holding on to the banister to keep herself from falling. Her laughter echoed in the emptiness of the hall and filtered down the corridors.

In the darkness by the kitchen Dundridge listened to it and shuddered. He had no idea where he was and there was a demented quality about that laughter that appalled him. He was just wondering what to do when, silhouetted against the hall light at the end of the passage he saw her bulky outline. She had stopped laughing and was peering into the gloom.

'It's all right, you can come out now,' she called, but Dundridge knew better. He understood now why his car had two flat tyres, why he had been invited to the Hall when Sir Giles was away. Lady Maud was a raving nymphomaniac. He was alone in a huge house in the middle of the back of beyond with no clothes on, a disabled car and an enormously powerful and naked female lunatic. Nothing on God's earth would induce him to come out now. As Lady Maud lumbered down the passage Dundridge turned and fled, collided with a table, lurched into some iron banisters and was off up the servants' stairs. Behind him a light went on. As he reached the landing he glanced back and saw Lady Maud's face staring up at him. One glance was enough to confirm his fears. The smudged lipstick, the patches of rouge, the disordered hair . . . mad as a hatter. Dundridge scampered down another corridor and behind him came the final proof of her madness.

'Tally ho,' shouted Lady Maud. 'Gone away.' Dundridge went away as fast as he could.

•

In the Lodge, Blott woke up and stared out through the circular window. Dimly below the rim of the hills he could see the dark shape of the Hall and he was about to turn over and go back to sleep when a light came on in an upstairs room to be followed almost immediately by another and then a third. Blott sat up in bed and watched as one room after another lit up. He glanced at his clock and saw it was ten past two. He looked back towards the house and saw the stained glass roof-light above the hall glowing. He got up and opened the window and stared out and as he did so there came the faint sound of hysterical laughter. Or crying. Lady Maud. Blott pulled on a pair of trousers, put on his slippers, took his twelve-bore and ran downstairs. There was something terribly wrong up at the house. He ran up the drive, almost colliding in the darkness with Dundridge's car. The bastard was still around. Probably chasing her from room to room. That would explain the lights going on and the hysterical laughter. He'd soon put a stop to that. Clutching his shotgun he went through the stable yard and in the kitchen door. The lights were on. Blott went across to the passage and listened. There was no sound now. He went down the passage to the hall and stood there. Must be upstairs. He was halfway up when Lady Maud emerged from a corridor on to the landing breathlessly. She ran across the landing to the top of the stairs and stood looking down at Blott naked as the day she was born. Blott gaped up at her open mouthed. There above him was the woman he loved. Clothed she had been splendid. Naked she was perfection. Her great breasts, her stomach, her magnificent thighs, she was everything Blott had ever dreamed of and, to make matters even better, she was clearly in distress. Tear-stains ran down her daubed cheeks. His moment of heroism on her behalf had arrived.

'Blott,' said Lady Maud, 'what on earth are you doing here? And what are you doing with that gun?'

'I am here at your service,' said Blott gallantly assuming the language of history.

'At my service?' said Lady Maud, oblivious of the fact that she wasn't exactly dressed for discussions about service with her gardener. 'What do you mean by my service? You're here to look after the garden, not to wander about the house in the middle of the night in your bedroom slippers armed with a shotgun.'

On the staircase Blott bowed before the storm. 'I came to protect your honour,' he murmured.

'My honour? You came to protect my honour? With a shotgun? Are you out of your mind?'

Blott was beginning to wonder. He had come up expecting to find her lying raped and murdered, or at least pleading for mercy, and here she was standing naked at the top of the stairs dressing him down. It didn't seem right. It didn't seem exactly right to Lady Maud now that she came to think of it. She turned and went into her bedroom and put on a dressing-gown.

'Now then,' she said with a renewed sense of authority, 'what's all this nonsense about my honour?'

'I thought I heard you call for help,' Blott mumbled.

'Call for help indeed,' she snorted. 'You heard nothing of the sort. You've been drinking. I've spoken to you about drinking before and I don't want to mention it again. And what's more when I need any help protecting my so-called honour, which God knows I most certainly don't, I won't ask you to come up here with a twelve-bore. Now then go back to the Lodge and go to bed. I don't want to hear any more about this nonsense, do you understand?'

Blott nodded and slunk down the staircase.

'And you can turn the lights off down there as you go.'

'Yes, ma'am,' said Blott and went down the passage to the kitchen filled with a new and terrible sense of injustice. He turned the kitchen light off and went back to the ballroom and switched off the chandeliers. Then he made his way through the conservatory to the terrace and was about to shut the door when he glimpsed a figure cowering among the ferns. It was the man from the Ministry, and like Lady Maud he was naked. Blott slammed the door and went off down the terrace steps, his mind seething with dreams of revenge. He had come up to the house with the best of intentions to protect his beloved mistress from the sexual depravity of that beastly little man and instead he had been blamed and abused and told he was drunk. It was all so unfair. In the middle of the park he paused and aimed the shotgun into the air and fired both barrels. That was what he thought of the bloody world. That was all that the bloody world understood. Force. He stamped off across the field to the Lodge and went upstairs to his room.

•

To Dundridge, still cowering in the conservatory, the sound of the shotgun came as final proof that Lady Maud's intentions towards him were homicidal. He had been lured to the Hall, his tyres had been punctured, he had suffered attempted rape, he had been chased naked around the house by a laughing and demented woman and now he was being hunted by a man with a gun. And finally he was in danger of freezing to death. He stayed in the conservatory for twenty minutes anxiously listening for any sounds that might indicate pursuit, but the house was silent. He crept out from his hiding-place and went through the door to the terrace and peered outside. There was no sign of the man with the gun. He would have to take a chance. There was a light look about the eastern sky which suggested the coming of dawn and he had to get away while it was still dark. He ran across the terrace and scampered down the steps towards his car.

Two minutes later he was in the driver's seat and had started the engine. He drove off as fast as the flat tyre would allow, crouching low and waiting for the blast of the shotgun. But nothing came and he passed under the Lodge and into the darkness of the wood. He switched on the headlights, negotiated the suspension bridge and headed up the hill, his flat tyre thumping on the road and the steering pulling violently to the left. Around him the Cleene Forest closed in, his headlights picked out monstrous shapes and weird shadows but Dundridge had lost his terror of the wild landscape. Anything was preferable to the human horrors he had left behind and even when two miles further on the tyre finally came away from the rim and he had to jack the car up and change it for the other flat spare he did so without hesitation. After that he drove more slowly and reached Worford as dawn broke. He parked his car on the double yellow line outside his flat, made sure there was nobody about and flitted across the pavement and down the alley to the outside stairs that led up to his apartment. Even here he was baulked. The key of his flat was in the pocket of his dinner-jacket.

Dundridge stood on the landing outside his door, naked, shivering and livid. Deprived of dignity, pretensions, authority and reason, Dundridge was almost human. For a moment he hesitated and then with a sudden ferocity he hurled himself against the door. At the second attempt the lock gave. He went inside slamming it to behind him. He had made up his mind. Come hell or high water he would do his damnedest to see that the route of the motorway was changed. They could bribe him and blackmail him for all they were worth but he'd get his own back. By the time he had finished that fat insane bitch would laugh on the other side of her filthy face.

16

His opportunity came sooner than he had expected and from an unforeseen quarter. Overwhelmed by the volume of complaints arriving at his office from the tenants of the seventy-five council houses due for demolition, harried by the Ottertown Town Council, infuriated by the refusal of the Minister of the

Environment to re-open the Enquiry, and warned by his doctors that unless he curtailed most of his activities his heart would end them all, Francis Puckerington resigned his seat in Parliament. Sir Giles was the first to congratulate him on the wisdom of his withdrawal from public life. 'Wish I could do the same myself,' he said, 'but you know how things are.'

Mr Puckerington didn't but he had a shrewd idea that lurking behind Sir Giles' benevolent concern there was financial advantage. Lady Maud shared his suspicion. Ever since the Enquiry there had been something strange about Giles' manner, an air of expectation and suppressed excitement about him which she found disturbing. Several times she had noticed him looking at her with a smile on his face and when Sir Giles smiled it usually meant that something unpleasant was about to happen. What it was she couldn't imagine and since she took no interest in politics the likely consequences of Mr Puckerington's resignation escaped her. Hoskins was understandably more informed. He realized at once why Sir Giles had agreed so readily to the Ottertown route. 'Brilliant,' he told him when he saw him at the Golf Club. Sir Giles looked mystified.

'I don't know what you're talking about. I had no idea the poor fellow was so ill. A great loss to the party.'

'My eye and Betty Martin,' said Hoskins.

'I'd rather have your Bessie Williams myself,' Sir Giles said, relaxing a little. 'I trust she is keeping well?'

'Very well. She and her husband took a holiday in Majorca I believe.'

'Sensible of them,' Sir Giles said. 'So our young friend Dundridge must be a little puzzled by now. No harm in keeping him hanging in the wind, as someone once put it.'

'He's probably blown that money you gave him.'

'I gave him?' said Sir Giles who preferred not to let his right hand know what his left was doing.

'Say no more,' said Hoskins. 'I'll tell you one thing though. He's lost all interest in your wife.'

Sir Giles sighed. 'Such a pity,' he said. 'There was a time

when I entertained the hope that he would . . . One can't expect miracles. Still, it was a nice thought.'

'He's got it in for her now, anyway. Hates her guts.'

'I wonder why,' said Sir Giles thoughtfully. 'Ah well, it happens to us all in the end. Still, it couldn't have come at a better time.'

'That's what I thought,' said Hoskins. 'He's already sent three memoranda to the Ministry asking for the motorway to be re-routed through the Gorge.'

'Quite the little weathercock, isn't he? I trust you tried to dissuade him.'

'Every time. Every time.'

'But not too hard, eh?'

Hoskins smiled. 'I try to keep an open mind on the matter.'

'Very wise of you,' said Sir Giles. 'No point in getting yourself involved. Well, things seem to be moving.'

•

Things certainly were. In London Francis Puckerington's resignation had immediate repercussions.

'Seventy-five council houses due for demolition in a constituency with a bye-election pending?' said the Prime Minister. 'And what did you say his last majority was?'

'Forty-five,' said the Chief Whip. 'A marginal seat.'

'Marginal be damned. It's lost.'

'It does rather look that way,' the Chief Whip agreed. 'Of course if the motorway could be re-routed . . .'

The Prime Minister reached for the phone.

•

Ten minutes later Mr Rees sent for Mr Joynson.

'Done it,' he said beaming delightedly.

'Done what?'

'Pulled the fat out of the fire. The Ottertown scheme is dead and buried. The M101 is going ahead through the Cleene Gorge.'

'Oh, that is good news,' said Mr Joynson. 'How on earth did you do it?'

'Just a question of patience and gentle persuasion. Ministers may come and Ministers may go but in the end they do tend to see the errors of their ways.'

'I suppose this means you'll be recalling Dundridge,' said Mr Joynson, who was inclined to look on the dark side of things.

'Not on your Nelly,' said Mr Rees, 'Dundridge is coping very well. I look forward to his perpetual absence.'

•

Dundridge received the news with mixed emotions. On the one hand here was his golden opportunity to teach that bitch Lady Maud a lesson. On the other the knowledge that he had accepted a bribe from Sir Giles bothered him. He looked forward to Lady Maud's misery when she learnt that Handyman Hall was going to be demolished after all but he didn't relish the thought of her husband's reaction. He need not have worried. Sir Giles, anxious to be out of the way when the storm broke, had taken the precaution of being tied up in London in advance of the announcement. In any case Hoskins was reassuring.

'You don't have to worry about Giles,' he told Dundridge. 'It's Maud who'll be out for blood.'

Dundridge knew exactly what he meant. 'If she calls I'm not in,' he told the girl on the switchboard. 'Remember that. I am never in to Lady Maud.'

While Hoskins concentrated on the actual details of the new route and arranged for the posting of advance notices of compulsory purchase, Dundridge spent much of his time on field work, which meant in fact sitting in his flat and not answering the telephone. To occupy his mind and to lend some sort of credence to his title of Controller Motorways Midlands, he set about devising a strategy for dealing with the campaign to stop construction which he was convinced Lady Maud would initiate.

'Surprise is of the essence,' he explained to Hoskins.

'She's had that already,' Hoskins pointed out. He had in his time supervised the eviction of too many obstinate householders to be daunted by the threat of Lady Maud, and besides he was relying on Sir Giles to undermine her efforts. 'She's not going to give us any trouble. You'll see. When it comes to the push she'll go. They all do. It's the law.' Dundridge wasn't convinced. From his personal experience he knew how little the law meant to Lady Maud.

'The thing is to move quickly,' he explained.

'Move quickly?' said Hoskins. 'You can't move quickly when you're building a motorway. It's a slow process.'

Dundridge waved his objections aside. 'We must hit at key objectives. Seize the commanding heights. Maintain the initiative,' he said grandly.

Hoskins looked at him doubtfully. He wasn't used to this sort of military language. 'Look, old boy, I know how you feel and all that but . . .'

'You don't,' said Dundridge vehemently.

'But what I was going to say was that there's no need to go in for anything complicated. Just let things take their natural course and you'll find people will get used to the idea. It's amazing how adaptable people are.'

'That's precisely what's worrying me,' said Dundridge. 'Now then the essence of my plan is to make random sorties.'

'Random sorties?' said Hoskins. 'What on earth with?'

'Bulldozers,' said Dundridge and spread out a map of the district.

'Bulldozers? You can't have bulldozers roaming the countryside making random sorties,' said Hoskins, now thoroughly alarmed. 'What the hell are they going to randomly sort?'

'Vital areas of control,' said Dundridge, 'lines of communication. Bridgeheads.'

'Bridgeheads? But—'

'As I see it,' Dundridge continued implacably, 'the main centre of resistance is going to be here.' He pointed to the Cleene Gorge. 'Strategically this is the vital area. Seize that and we've won.'

'Seize it? You can't suddenly go in and seize the Cleene Gorge!' shouted Hoskins. 'The motorway has to proceed by deliberate stages. Contractors work according to a schedule and we have to keep to that.'

'That is precisely the mistake you're making,' said Dundridge. 'Our tactics must be to alter the schedule just when the enemy least expects it.'

'But that's impossible,' Hoskins insisted. 'You can't go about knocking people's houses down without giving them fair warning.'

'Who said anything about knocking houses down?' said Dundridge indignantly. 'I certainly didn't. What I have in mind is something entirely different. Now then what we'll do is this.'

For the next half hour he outlined his grand strategy while Hoskins listened. When he had finished Hoskins was impressed in spite of himself. He had been quite wrong to call Dundridge a nincompoop. In his own peculiar way the man had flair.

'All the same I just hope it doesn't have to come to that,' he said finally.

'You'll see,' said Dundridge. 'That bitch isn't going to sit back and let us put a motorway through her wretched house without putting up a struggle. She's going to fight to the bitter end.'

Hoskins went back to his office thoughtfully. There was nothing illegal about Dundridge's plan in spite of the military jargon. In a way it was extremely shrewd.

•

The Committee for the Preservation of the Cleene Gorge met under the Presidency of General Burnett at Handyman Hall. Lady Maud was the first speaker.

'I intend to fight this project to the bitter end,' she said, fulfilling Dundridge's prediction. 'I have no intention of being driven from my own home simply because a lot of bureaucratic dunderheads in London take it into their thick skulls to ignore the recommendations of a properly constituted Enquiry. It's outrageous.'

'It's so unfair,' said Mrs Bullett-Finch, 'particularly after what Lord Leakham said about preserving the wildlife of the area. What I can't understand is why they changed their minds so suddenly.'

'As I see it,' said General Burnett, 'the change is a direct consequence of Puckerington's resignation. I have it on the highest authority that the Government felt that the new candidate was bound to lose the bye-election if they went ahead with the route through Ottertown.'

'Why did Puckerington resign?' asked Miss Percival.

'Ill-health,' said Colonel Chapman. 'He's got a dicky heart.'

Lady Maud said nothing. What she had just heard explained a great many things and suggested more. She knew now why Sir Giles had smiled so secretively at her and why he had had that air of expectation. Everything suddenly fell into place in her mind. She understood why he had been so alarmed about the possibility of a tunnel, why he had insisted on Ottertown, why he had been so pleased at Lord Leakham's decision. Above all, she realized for the first time the full enormity of his betrayal. Colonel Chapman put her thoughts into numbers.

'I suppose there is this to be said for it. I've heard a rumour that we are going to get increased compensation,' he said. 'The figure mentioned was twenty per cent. That makes your sum, Lady Maud, something in the region of three hundred thousand pounds.'

Lady Maud sat rigid in her chair. Three hundred thousand pounds. It was not her share. Sir Giles owned the Hall. Owned it and had put it up for sale in the only way legally available to him. Faced with such treachery there was nothing left for her to say. She shook her head wearily and while the discussion continued round her she stared out of the window to where Blott was mowing the lawn.

The meeting broke up without any decision being taken on the next move.

'Poor old Maud seems quite broken up about this dreadful business,' General Burnett said to Mrs Bullett-Finch as they walked across the drive to their cars. 'It's knocked all the spirit out of her. Bad business.'

'One does feel so terribly sorry for her,' Mrs Bullett-Finch agreed.

Lady Maud watched them leave and then went back into the

house to think. Committees would achieve nothing now. They would talk and pass resolutions but when the time for taking action came they would still be talking. Colonel Chapman had given the game away by talking about money. They would settle.

She went down the passage to the study and stood there looking round the room. It was here that Giles had thought the whole thing out, in this sanctum; at this desk where her father and grandfather had sat, and it was here that she would sit and think until she had planned some way of stopping the motorway and of destroying him. In her mind the two things were inextricably linked. Giles had conceived the idea of the motorway, he would be broken by it. There was no compunction left in her. She had been outwitted and betrayed by a man she had always despised. She had sold herself to him to preserve the house and the family and the knowledge of her own guilt added force to her determination. If need be she would sell herself to the devil to stop him now. Lady Maud sat down behind the desk and stared at the filigree of her grandfather's silver inkstand for inspiration. It was shaped like a lion's head. An hour later she had found the solution she was looking for. She reached for the phone and was about to pick it up when it rang. It was Sir Giles calling from London.

'I just thought I had better let you know I shan't be back this weekend,' he said. 'I know it is a damned inconvenient time for me to be away with all this motorway business going on, but I really can't get away.'

'That's all right,' said Lady Maud, feigning her usual degree of indifference, 'I daresay I'll be able to cope without you.'

'How are things going?'

'We've just had a committee meeting to discuss the next move. We are thinking of organizing protest meetings round the county.'

'That's the sort of thing we need,' said Sir Giles. 'I'm doing my damnedest down here to get the Ministry to reconsider. Keep up the good work at your end.' He rang off. Lady Maud smiled grimly. She would keep up the good work all right. And he could go on doing his damnedest. She picked up the phone and dialled. In the next two hours she spoke to her bank manager, the Head Keeper at Whipsnade Zoo, the Game Warden at Woburn Wildlife Park, the managers of five small private zoos and a firm of fencing experts in Birmingham. Finally she went outside to look for Blott.

Ever since the night of Dundridge's visit she had been worried by Blott's attitude. It hadn't been like him to behave like that and she had been alarmed by the sound of the shotgun going off outside. She rather regretted what she had said about his drinking too. It certainly hadn't had any good effect. If anything he had taken to going off to the Royal George more often and late one night she had heard him singing in the pinetum. 'Typically Italian,' she thought, confusing 'Wir Fahren Gegen England' with *La Traviata*. 'Probably pining for Naples.' But Blott stumbling through the park was merely drunk and if he was pining for anything it was for her innocence which Dundridge's visit had destroyed.

She found him, as she had expected, in the kitchen garden. 'Blott,' she said, 'I want you to do something for me.'

Blott grunted morosely. 'What?'

'You know the wall safe in the study?' Blott nodded. 'I want you to open it for me.'

Blott shook his head and went on weeding the onion bed. 'Not possible without the combination,' he said.

'If I had the combination I wouldn't have to ask you to open it,' Lady Maud said tartly. Blott shrugged. 'If I don't know the combination,' he said, 'how do I open it?'

'You blow it open,' said Lady Maud. Blott straightened up and looked at her.

'Blow it open?'

'With explosive. Use a . . . what are those things with flames . . . oxy . . .'

'Acetylene torch,' said Blott. 'It wouldn't work.'

'I don't mind how you do it. You can pull it out of the wall

123

and drop it from the roof for all I care but I want that safe opened. I've got to know what is inside it.'

Blott pushed back his hat and scratched his head. This was a new Lady Maud speaking. 'Why don't you ask him for the combination?' he said.

'Him?' said Lady Maud with a new contempt. 'Because I don't want him to know. That's why.'

'He'll know it if we blow it open,' Blott pointed out.

Lady Maud thought for a moment. 'We can always say it was burglars,' she said finally.

Blott considered the implications of this remark and found them to his liking. 'Yes, we could do that. Let's go and have a look at it.'

They went into the house and stood in the study examining the safe which was set into the wall behind some books.

'Difficult,' said Blott. He went into the dining-room next door and looked at the wall on that side. 'It's going to do a lot of damage,' he said when he came back.

'Do whatever damage you have to. The house is coming down if we don't do something. What does it matter if we do some damage to it now? It can always be repaired.'

'Ah,' said Blott, who had begun to understand. 'Then I'll use a sledgehammer.' He went round to the workshop in the yard and returned with a sledgehammer, a metal wedge and a crowbar.

'You're quite sure?' he asked. Lady Maud nodded. Blott swung the sledgehammer against the dining-room wall. Half an hour later the safe was out of the wall. Together they carried it outside and laid it on the drive. It was quite small. Blott twiddled the knob idly and tried to think what next to do.

'What we need is some high-explosive,' he said. 'Dynamite would do it.'

'We haven't got any dynamite,' Lady Maud pointed out. 'And you can't go into a shop and buy it. You couldn't bore a hole in it and hoik things out with a wire?'

'Too thick and the steel is too hard,' said Blott. 'It's like armour-plate on a tank.' He stopped. Like a tank. Somewhere among the armoury of weapons he had collected during the war there was a rocket-launcher. It was in a long wooden box and labelled PIAT. Projectile Infantry Anti-Tank. Now where had he buried it?

17

As dusk fell over the Cleene Gorge Blott left the Lodge with a spade. He had had his supper, sausages and mashed potatoes, and was comfortably full. Above all he was happy. As he followed the park wall round to the west and found the exact spot where he had climbed over as a prisoner of war he was boyishly excited. There had been a piece of iron fencing which he had propped against the wall to give himself a leg-up. It was still there, rusting in a patch of stinging-nettles. Blott dragged it out and leant it against the wall and climbed up. The barbed-wire had gone but as he straddled the top of the wall and dropped down on the other side he had the same feeling of freedom he had experienced night after night over thirty years before. Not that he had disliked life in the camp. He had felt freer then than at any time before. To sneak out at night and roam the woods on his own was to escape from the orphanage in Dresden and all the petty restrictions of his dreadful childhood. It had been to cock a snook at authority and to be himself.

And so it was now as he pushed through the bracken and began to climb through the trees. He was doing the forbidden thing again and he exulted in it. Half a mile up the hillside he came to a clearing. You turned left here. Blott turned left, following the old instinct as surely as if there had been a path there, and came out into the setting sunlight behind a mound of stones that had once been a cottage. Here he turned up the hill again until he found the tree he was looking for. It was a large old oak. Blott went round the trunk and found the slash he had made in the bark. He walked away from the tree, counting his paces. Then he took off his jacket and began to dig. It took him an hour to get down to the cache but it was there exactly where he had recalled. He pulled out a box and prised the lid open with a hammer. Inside caked in grease and wrapped in oilskin was a two-inch mortar. He dragged out another box. Mortar bombs. Finally he found what he was looking for. The long box and the four cases of armour-piercing rockets. He sat down on the box and wondered what to do next. Now that he came to think about it, all he needed were the rockets. All he had to do was to tie a piece of string to the fin and drop it from a height on to the safe. That would do the trick just as well as firing the rocket at the safe.

Still, he had come so far, he might as well take the PIAT home with him and clean it up. It would make an interesting souvenir. Blott put the mortar back with the cases of bombs, and covered them with earth. Then he went back down the hill with the long box. It was very heavy and he had to stop fairly frequently to rest. By the time he got back to the Lodge it was dark. He humped the box up to his room and went back for the rockets. He didn't take those up to his room but left them in the grass outside. He didn't feel like sleeping beside some rockets that were thirty years old.

In the morning he was up early and busy in the Gorge. He fetched the safe down on a wheelbarrow and stood it upright at the bottom of the cliff. Then he took a long piece of twine and tied it to the knob of the combination lock before going back up the cliff with it and attaching it to an overhanging branch so that it ran in a straight line some fifty feet down to the safe. Finally he fetched two of the finned projectiles and tied a short length of string to the fin of the first. At the other end of the string he tied a small ring, undid the twine and fitted the ring over it and tied it back on to the branch. Then he lay down at the top of the cliff and removed the cap from the detonator on the nose of the rocket. Blott peered over the edge. There was the safe directly below. He held the PIAT bomb out and let go and watched as it plummeted down the twine. The next moment there was a flash and a roar. Blott shut his eyes and pulled his head back and as he did so something hurtled past him into the air above. He looked up. The fin of the rocket reached its peak, curved over and fell into the road behind him. Blott got up and went down to the safe. The bomb had missed the combination lock but it had done its job. A small hole the size of a pencil was blown in the front of the safe and the door was loose.

Lady Maud was having breakfast when the blast came. For a moment she thought Blott was out shooting rabbits but there had been a concussion and an echo about the explosion that had suggested something more powerful than a shotgun. She went outside and saw Blott coming down the cliff path on the other side of the river. Of course, the safe. He had sworn he would blow it open and that's what he had done. She ran across the lawn and through the pinetum and over the footbridge.

Blott was bending over the safe when she came up.

'Have you done it?' she asked.

'Yes, it's open,' said Blott, 'but there's nothing much in it.' Lady Maud could see that. The safe was much smaller inside than she had expected and it appeared to be filled with burnt, charred and torn fragments of paper. She reached in and picked one out. It was a portion of what had once been a photograph. She held it up and looked at it. It appeared to be the legs of a naked man. She reached in and took out another piece, this time an arm, a bare arm and what looked like a woman's breast. She peered into the safe again but apart from the shreds of photographs there was nothing inside.

'I'll go and get an envelope,' Lady Maud said. 'Don't touch anything until I get back.' She walked off thoughtfully towards the Hall while Blott went back to the top of the cliff and collected the unused PIAT bomb. At least he knew now that they worked. 'Might come in handy,' he said to himself and took it back to the Lodge.

An hour later the safe was buried under some bushes at the base of the cliff and Blott had gone back to the kitchen garden. In the study Lady Maud sat at the desk and examined the fragments of photographs, trying to sort out which portion of anatomy fitted the next. It was a difficult task and an unedifying one. The photographs were too charred and torn to be reassembled properly and besides the force of the explosion had decapitated the participants in what even on this slender evidence appeared to be a series of extremely unnatural acts. And slender was the word. Certainly in the case of the man. That ruled out Sir Giles. It was a pity. She could have done with some photographic proof of his obscene habits. She picked up another fragment and was about to look for the appropriate place in the jigsaw puzzle where it would fit when she suddenly realized where she had seen those slender legs and pale feet. Of course. Twinkling across the marble floor of the hall. She looked again at the portion of leg, at the arm. She was certain now. Dundridge. Dundridge engaged in . . . It was unthinkable. She was just trying to work out what this extraordinary idea implied when the front doorbell rang. She went out and opened the door. It was the manager of the high-security fencing company.

'Ah, good,' said Lady Maud. 'Now then, to business. I'll show you exactly what I want.' They went inside to the billiard room and Lady Maud unrolled a map of the estate. 'I am opening a wildlife park,' she explained. 'I want a fence extending the entire perimeter of the park. It must be absolutely secure and proof against any sort of animal.'

'But I understood . . .' the manager began.

'Never mind what you understood,' said Lady Maud. 'Just understand that I am opening a wildlife park in three weeks' time.'

'In three weeks? That's out of the question.'

Lady Maud rolled up the map. 'In that case I shall employ someone else,' she said. 'Some enterprising firm that can erect a suitable fence . . .'

'You won't get any firm to do it in three weeks,' said the manager. 'Not unless you pay a fortune.'

'I am prepared to pay a fortune,' said Lady Maud.

The manager looked at her and rubbed his jaw. 'Three weeks?' he said.

'Three weeks,' said Lady Maud.

The manager took out a notebook and made some calculations. 'This is simply a rough estimate,' he said finally, 'but I would say somewhere in the region of twenty-five thousand pounds.'

'Say thirty and be done with it,' said Lady Maud. 'Thirty thousand pounds for the fence to be completed in three weeks from today with a bonus of one thousand a day for every day under three weeks and a penalty clause of two thousand pounds for every day after three weeks.'

The manager gaped at her. 'I suppose you know what you're doing,' he muttered.

'I know precisely what I'm doing, thank you very much,' said Lady Maud. 'What is more you will work day and night. You will bring your materials in at night. I don't want any lorries coming here during the day and you will house your men here. I will provide accommodation. You will see to their bedding and their food. This whole operation must be done in the strictest secrecy.'

'If you don't mind,' said the manager and sat down in a chair. Lady Maud sat down opposite him.

'Well?'

'I don't know,' said the manager. 'It *can* be done . . .

'It will be,' Lady Maud assured him. 'Either by you or someone else.'

'You realize that if we were to finish the job in a fortnight the cost would have risen to thirty-seven thousand pounds.'

'And I should be delighted. And if you can finish in a week I shall be happy to pay forty-two thousand pounds,' she said. 'Are we agreed?' The manager nodded. 'Right, in that case I shall make out a cheque to you for ten thousand now and two post-dated cheques for the same amount. I trust that will be a sufficient earnest of my good faith.' She went through to the study and wrote out the cheques. 'I shall expect the arrival of materials tonight and work to begin at once. You can bring the contract tomorrow for me to sign.'

The manager went out and got into his car in a state of

shock. 'Mad as a March bloody hare,' he muttered as he drove down the drive.

Behind him Lady Maud went back to the study and sat down. It was costing more than she had anticipated but it was worth every penny. And then there was the price of the animals. Lions didn't come cheap. Nor did a rhinoceros. And finally there was the puzzle of the photographs. What were obscene pictures of Mr Dundridge doing in Giles' safe? She got up and went out into the garden and walked up and down the path by the wall of the kitchen garden. And suddenly it dawned on her. It explained everything and in particular why Dundridge had changed his mind about the tunnel. The wretched little man had been blackmailed. Well, two could play at that game. By God they could. She went through the door into the kitchen garden.

'Has my husband ever put through a call to a woman in London?' she asked Blott.

'His secretary,' said Blott. Lady Maud shook her head. Sir Giles' secretary wasn't the sort of woman who would take kindly to the suggestion that she should tie her employer to a bed and beat him and in any case she was happily married.

'Anyone else?'

'No.'

'Has he ever mentioned a woman in any of his conversations on the phone?'

Blott tried to remember. 'No, I don't think so.'

'In that case, Blott,' she said, 'you and I are going to London tomorrow.'

Blott gazed at her in astonishment. 'To London?' He had never been to London.

'To London. We shall be away for a few days.'

'But what shall I wear?' said Blott.

'A suit of course.'

'I haven't got one,' said Blott.

'Well then,' said Lady Maud, 'we had better go into Worford and get you one. And while we're about it we'll get a camera as well. I'll pick you up in ten minutes.'

She went back into the house and put the photographs into an envelope and hid it behind a set of Jorrocks on the bookshelf. It might be worth paying Mr Dundridge a visit while she was in Worford.

18

But Dundridge was not to be found in Worford. 'He's out,' said the girl at the Regional Planning Board.

'Where?' said Lady Maud.

'Inspecting the site,' said the girl.

'Well, kindly tell him when he comes back that I have some sights I would like him to inspect.'

The girl looked at her. 'I'm sure I don't know what you mean,' she said nastily. Lady Maud suppressed the reaction to tell the little hussy exactly what she did mean.

'Tell Mr Dundridge that I have a number of photographs in which I feel sure he will take a particular interest. You had better write it down before you forget it. Tell him that. He knows where he can find me.'

She went back to the outfitters where Blott was trying on a salmon-pink suit of Harris Tweed. 'If you think I'm going to be seen with you in London in that revolting article of menswear, you've got another think coming,' she snorted. She ran an eye over a number of less conspicuous suits and finally selected a dark grey pinstripe. 'That'll do.' By the time they left the shop Blott was fitted out with shirts, socks, underwear and ties. They called at a shoe shop and bought a pair of black shoes.

'And now all we need is a camera,' said Lady Maud as they stowed Blott's new clothes in the back of the Land-Rover. They went into a camera shop.

'I want a camera with an excellent lens,' she told the assistant, 'one that can be operated by a complete idiot.'

'You need an automatic camera,' said the man.

'No, she doesn't,' said Blott who resented being called a complete idiot in front of strangers. 'She means a Leica.'

'A Leica?' said the man. 'But that's not a camera for a novice. That's a . . .'

'Blott,' said Lady Maud, taking him out on to the pavement, 'do you mean to say that you know how to take photographs?'

'In the Luft . . . before the war I was trained in photography. I was . . .'

Lady Maud beamed at him. 'Oh Blott,' she said, 'you're a godsend. An absolute godsend. Go and buy whatever you need to take good clear photographs.'

'What of?' asked Blott. Lady Maud hesitated. Oh well, he would have to know sooner or later. She took the plunge. 'Him in bed with another woman.'

'Him?'

'Yes.'

It was Blott's turn to beam now. 'We'll need flash and a wide-angle lens.' They went back into the shop and came out with a second-hand Leica, an enlarger, a developing tank, an electronic flash, and everything they needed. As they drove back to Handyman Hall Blott was in his seventh heaven.

•

Dundridge, on the other hand, was in the other place. The girl at the switchboard had phoned him as soon as Lady Maud had left.

'Lady Maud's been,' she told him. 'She left a message for you.'

'Oh yes,' said Dundridge. 'I hope you didn't tell her where I was.'

'No, I didn't,' said the girl. 'She's a horrid old bag isn't she? I wouldn't wish her on my worst enemy.'

'You can say that again,' Dundridge agreed. 'What was the message?'

'She said "Tell Mr Dundridge that I have a number of photographs in which I feel sure he will take a particular interest". She made me write it down. Hullo, are you still there? Mr Dundridge. Hullo. Hullo. Mr Dundridge, are you there?' But there was no reply. She put the phone down.

In his flat Dundridge sat in a state of shock. He still clutched the phone but he was no longer listening. His thoughts were concentrated on one terrible fact, Lady Maud had those ghastly photographs. She could destroy him. There was nothing he could do about it. She would use them if the motorway went ahead and there was absolutely no way he could stop it now. The fucking bitch had arranged the whole thing. First the photographs, then the bribe, and finally the attempt to murder him. The woman was insane. There could be no doubt about it now. Dundridge put down the phone and tried desperately to think what to do. He couldn't even go to the police. In the first place they would never believe him. Lady Maud was a Justice of the Peace, a respected figure in the community and what had that Miss Boles told him? 'We'll know if you tell the police. We've had customers in the police.' And in any case he had no proof that she was involved. Only the word of the girl at the Planning Board and Lady Maud would claim she had been talking about photographs of the Hall or something like that. He needed proof but above all he needed legal advice. A good lawyer.

He picked up the telephone directory and looked in the yellow pages under Solicitors. 'Ganglion, Turnbull and Shrine.' Dundridge dialled and asked to speak to Mr Ganglion. Mr Ganglion would see him in the morning at ten o'clock. Dundridge spent the evening and most of the night pacing his room in an agony of doubt and suspense. Several times he picked up the phone to call Lady Maud only to put it down again. There was nothing he could say to her that would have the slightest effect and he dreaded what she would have to say to him. Towards dawn he fell into a restless sleep and awoke exhausted at seven.

•

At Handyman Hall Lady Maud and Blott slept fitfully too; Blott because he was kept awake by the rumble of lorries through the arch; Lady Maud because she was superintending the whole operation and explaining where she wanted things put.

'Your men can sleep in the servants' quarters,' she told the manager. 'I shall be away for a week. Here is the key to the back door.'

When she finally got to bed in the early hours Handyman Hall had assumed the aspect of a construction camp. Concrete mixers, posts, lorries, fencing wire, bags of cement and gravel were arranged in the park and work had already begun by the light of lamps and a portable generator.

She lay in bed listening to the voices and the rumble of the machines and was well satisfied. When money was no object you could still get things done quickly even in England. 'Money no object,' she thought and smiled to herself at the oddity of the phrase. She would have to do something about money before very long. She would think about it in the morning.

At seven she was up and had breakfasted. Through the window of the kitchen she was pleased to note that several concrete posts had already been installed and that a strange machine that looked like a giant corkscrew was boring holes for some more. She went along to the study and spent an hour going through Sir Giles' filing-cabinets. She paid particular attention to a file marked Investments and took down the details of his shareholdings and the correspondence with his stock-broker. Then she went carefully through his personal correspondence, but there was no indication to be found there of any mistress with a penchant for whips and handcuffs.

At nine she signed the contract and went up to her room to pack and at ten she and Blott, now dressed in his pinstripe suit and wearing a blue polka-dot tie, drove off in the Land-Rover for Hereford and the train to London. Behind them in the study the phone was off the stand. There would be no phone calls to Handyman Hall from Sir Giles.

•

Dundridge arrived promptly at the offices of Ganglion, Turnbull and Shrine and was kept waiting for ten minutes. He sat in an outer office clutching his briefcase and looking miserably at the sporting prints on the walls. They didn't suggest the sophisticated modern approach to life that he felt an understanding of his particular case required. Nor did Mr Ganglion, who finally deigned to see him. He was an elderly man with gold-rimmed glasses over which he looked at Dundridge critically. Dundridge sat down in front of his desk and tried to think how to begin.

'And what did you wish to consult me about, Mr Dundridge?' Mr Ganglion enquired. 'I think you should know in advance that if this has anything to do with the motorway we are not prepared to handle it.'

Dundridge shook his head. 'It hasn't got anything to do with the motorway, well not exactly,' he said. 'The thing is that I'm being blackmailed.'

Mr Ganglion put the tips of his fingers together and tapped them. 'Blackmailed? Indeed. An unusual crime in this part of the world. I can't remember when we last had a case of blackmail. Still it does make a change, I must say. Yes, blackmail. You interest me, Mr Dundridge. Do go on.'

Dundridge swallowed nervously. He hadn't come to interest Mr Ganglion or at least not in the way his smile suggested. 'It's like this,' he said. 'I went to a party at the Golf Club and I met this girl . . .'

'A girl, eh?' said Mr Ganglion and drew his chair up to the desk. 'An attractive girl I daresay.'

'Yes,' said Dundridge.

'And you went home with her, I suppose,' said Mr Ganglion, his eyes alight with a very genuine interest now.

'No,' said Dundridge. 'At least I don't think so.'

'You don't think so?' said Mr Ganglion. 'Surely you know what you did?'

'That's the whole point,' Dundridge said, 'I don't know what I did.' He stopped. He did know what he had done. The photographs proclaimed his actions all too clearly. 'Well actually . . . I know what I did and all that . . .'

'Yes,' Mr Ganglion said encouragingly.

'The thing is I don't know where I did it.'

'In a field perhaps?'

Dundridge shook his head. 'Not in a field.'

'In the back of a car?'

'No,' said Dundridge. 'The thing is that I was unconscious.'

'Were you really? Extraordinary. Unconscious?'

'You see, I had a Campari before we left. It tasted bitter but then Campari does, doesn't it?'

'I have no idea,' said Mr Ganglion, 'what Campari tastes like but I'll take your word for it.'

'Very bitter,' said Dundridge, 'and we got into the car and that's the last thing I remember.'

'How very unfortunate,' said Mr Ganglion, clearly disappointed that he wasn't going to hear the more intimate details of the encounter.

'The next thing I knew I was sitting in my car in a lay-by.'

'A lay-by. Very appropriate. And what happened next?'

Dundridge shifted nervously in his chair. This was the part he had been dreading. 'I got some photographs.'

Mr Ganglion's flagging interest revived immediately. 'Did you really? Splendid. Photographs indeed.'

'And a demand for a thousand pounds.'

'A thousand pounds? Did you pay it?'

'No,' said Dundridge. 'No I didn't.'

'You mean they weren't worth it?'

Dundridge chewed his lip. 'I don't know what they're worth,' he muttered bitterly.

'Then you've still got them,' said Mr Ganglion. 'Good. Good. Well I'll soon tell you what I think of them.'

'I'd rather . . .' Dundridge began but Mr Ganglion insisted.

'The evidence,' he said, 'let's have a look at the evidence of blackmail. Most important.'

'They're pretty awful,' said Dundridge.

'Bound to be,' said Mr Ganglion. 'For a thousand pounds they must be quite revolting.'

'They are,' said Dundridge. Encouraged by Mr Ganglion's broad-mindedness, he opened his briefcase and took out the envelope. 'The thing is you've got to remember I was unconscious at the time.'

Mr Ganglion nodded understandingly. 'Of course, my dear fellow, of course.' He reached out and took the envelope and opened it. 'Good God,' he muttered as he looked at the first one. Dundridge squirmed in his chair and stared at the ceiling, and listened while Mr Ganglion thumbed through the photographs, grunting in an ecstasy of disgust and astonishment.

'Well?' he asked when Mr Ganglion sat back exhausted in his chair. The solicitor was staring at him incredulously.

'A thousand pounds? Is that really all they asked?' he said. Dundridge nodded. 'Well, all I can say is that you got off damned lightly.'

'But I didn't pay,' Dundridge reminded him. Mr Ganglion goggled at him.

'You didn't? You mean to tell me you baulked at a mere thousand pounds after having . . .' he stopped at a loss for words while his finger wavered over a particularly revolting photograph.

'I couldn't,' said Dundridge feeling hard done by.

'Couldn't?'

'They never called me back. I had one phone call and I've been waiting for another.'

'I see,' said Mr Ganglion. He looked back at the photograph. 'And you've no idea who this remarkable woman is?'

'None at all. I only met her the once.'

'Once is enough by the look of things,' Mr Ganglion said. 'And no more phone calls? No letters?'

'Not until last night,' said Dundridge, 'and then I got a message from the girl at the desk at the Regional Planning Board.'

'The girl at the desk at the Regional Planning Board,' said Mr Ganglion, eagerly reaching for a pencil. 'And what's her name?'

'She's got nothing to do with it,' Dundridge said, 'she was simply phoning to give me the message. It said Lady Maud Lynchwood had called and wanted me to know that she had some photographs of particular interest to me . . .' He stopped. Mr Ganglion had half-risen from his seat and was glaring at him furiously.

'Lady Maud?' he yelled. 'You come in here with this set of the most revolting photographs I've ever set eyes on and have the audacity to tell me that Lady Maud Lynchwood has something to do with them. My God, sir, I've half a mind to horse-whip you. Lady Maud Lynchwood is one of our most respected clients, a dear sweet lady, a woman of the highest virtues, a member of one of the best families ...' He fell back into his chair, speechless.

'But—' Dundridge began.

'But me no buts,' said Mr Ganglion, trembling with rage. 'Get out of my office. If I have one more word out of you, sir, I shall institute proceedings for slander immediately. Do you hear me? One more word here or anywhere else. One breath of rumour from you and I won't hesitate, do you hear me?'

Dundridge could still hear him fulminating as he dashed downstairs and into the street clutching his briefcase. It was only when he got back to his apartment that he realized he had left his photographs on Mr Ganglion's desk. They could stay there for all he cared. He wasn't going back for the beastly things.

Behind him Mr Ganglion simmered down. On the desk in front of him Dundridge and the masked woman lay frozen in two-dimensional contortions. Mr Ganglion adjusted his bi-focals and studied them with interest. Then he put the photo-graphs into the envelope and the envelope into his safe. The good name of the Handymans was safe with him. Mind you, come to think of it, he wouldn't put anything past her. Remark-able woman, Maud, quite remarkable.

*

By the time they reached London Lady Maud had explained Blott's new duties to him.

'You will hire a taxi and wait outside his flat until he comes out and then you will follow him wherever he goes. Particularly in the evening. I want to know where he spends his nights. If he goes into a block of flats, go in after him and make a note of the floor the lift stops at. Do you understand?'

Blott said he did.

'And on no account let him catch sight of you.' She studied him critically. In his dark grey suit Blott was practically unrec-ognizable anyway. Still, it was best to be careful. She would buy him a bowler at Harrods. 'If you see him with a woman follow them wherever they go and if they separate follow the woman. We have got to find out who she is and where she lives.'

'And then we break in and take the photographs of them?' said Blott eagerly.

'Certainly not,' said Lady Maud. 'When we find out who the woman is we'll decide what we're going to do.'

They took a taxi to an hotel in Kensington, stopping on the way to buy Blott's bowler, and at five o'clock Blott was sitting in a taxi outside Sir Giles' flat in Victoria.

'I suppose you know what you're doing,' said the driver when they had been sitting there for an hour with the meter running. 'This is costing you a packet.' Blott, with a hundred pounds in his pocket, said he knew what he was doing. He was enjoying himself watching the traffic go by and studying the pedestrians. He was in London, the capital of Great Britain, the heart of what had been the world's greatest Empire, the seat of those great Kings and Queens he had read so much about and all the romance in Blott's nature thrilled at the thought. What was even better he was tracking down him – Blott had never deigned to call him anything else – him and his mistress. He was doing Lady Maud a service after all.

At seven Sir Giles came out and drove to his Club for dinner. Behind him Blott's taxi followed relentlessly. At eight he came out and drove across to St John's Wood, Blott's taxi still behind. He parked in Elm Road and went into a house while Blott stared out of the taxi and noticed that he pressed the second bell. As soon as Sir Giles had gone inside, Blott got out and walked across the road and took a note of the name on the doorbell. It read Mrs Forthby. Blott went back to the taxi.

'Mrs Forthby, Mrs Forthby,' said Lady Maud when Blott reported to her. 'Elm Road.' She looked Mrs Forthby up in the telephone directory. 'That's very clever of you, Blott. Very clever indeed. And you say he didn't come out?'

'No. But the taxi-driver wouldn't wait any longer. He said it was time for his supper.'

'Never mind. You've done very well. Now the only thing to do is to find out what sort of woman she is. I would like to get to know Mrs Forthby a little better. I wonder how I can do that.'

'I can follow her,' said Blott.

'I don't see what good that would do,' said Lady Maud. 'And in any case how would you know her to follow?'

'She's the only woman living in the house,' Blott said. 'There's a Mr Sykes on the top floor and a Mr Billington on the ground floor.'

'Excellent,' said Lady Maud. 'You are an observant man. Now then how can I get to know her? There must be some way of arranging a meeting.'

'I could,' said Blott, adopting the voice of Sir Giles, 'ring her up and pretend I was him and ask her to meet me somewhere . . .' he said.

Lady Maud gazed at him. 'Of course. Oh Blott what would I do without you?' Blott blushed. 'But no, that wouldn't do,' Lady Maud continued. 'She would tell him. I'll have to think of something else.'

Blott went up to his room and went to bed. He was tired and very hungry but these little inconveniences counted for nothing beside the knowledge that Lady Maud was pleased with him. Blott fell asleep blissfully happy.

So did Lady Maud, though her happiness was more practical and centred on the solution to a problem that had been worrying her. Money. The fence for the Wildlife Park was going to cost at least thirty thousand pounds and the animals she had ordered came to another twenty. Fifty thousand pounds was a lot of money to pay to save the Hall and besides there was no guarantee that it would work. If anybody should be paying it was Giles, who was responsible for the whole wretched business. And she had found a way of making him pay. She would ruin him yet.

*

Next morning at eight o'clock she and Blott were sitting in a taxi at the end of Elm Road. At nine they saw Sir Giles leave.

Lady Maud paid the taxi-driver and with Blott at her heels strode down to number six.

'Now remember what to say,' Lady Maud told Blott as she pressed the bell. There was a buzz.

'Who is it?' Mrs Forthby asked.

'It's me. I've left my car keys,' said Blott in the accents of Sir Giles.

'And I thought I was the forgetful one,' said Mrs Forthby.

The door opened. Blott and Lady Maud went upstairs. Mrs Forthby opened the door of her flat. She was dressed in a housecoat and was holding a yellow duster.

'Good morning,' said Lady Maud and walked past her into the flat.

'But I thought . . .' Mrs Forthby began.

'Do let me introduce myself,' said Lady Maud. 'I am Lady Maud Lynchwood and you must be Mrs Forthby.' She took Mrs Forthby's hand. 'I've been looking forward to meeting you. Giles has told me so much about you.'

'Oh dear,' said Mrs Forthby. 'How frightfully embarrassing.' Behind her Blott closed the door. Lady Maud took stock of the furniture, including Mrs Forthby in the process, and then sat down in an armchair.

'Quite the little love nest,' she said finally. Mrs Forthby stood plumply in front of her wringing the duster.

'Oh this is awful,' she said, 'simply awful.'

'Nonsense. It's nothing of the sort. And do stop twisting that duster. You make me nervous.'

'I'm so sorry,' said Mrs Forthby. 'It's just that I feel . . . well . . . just that I owe you an apology.'

'An apology? What on earth for?' said Lady Maud.

'Well . . . you know . . .' Mrs Forthby shook her head helplessly.

'If you imagine for one moment that I have anything against you, you're mightily mistaken. As far as I am concerned you have been a positive godsend.'

'A godsend?' Mrs Forthby mumbled and sat down on the sofa.

'Of course,' said Lady Maud. 'I have always found my husband a positively disgusting man with the very vilest of personal habits. The fact that you appear to be prepared, presumably out of the goodness of your heart, to satisfy his obscene requirements leaves me very much in your debt.'

'It does?' said Mrs Forthby, her world being stood on its head by this extraordinary woman who sat in her armchair and addressed her in her own flat as if she were a servant.

'Very much so,' Lady Maud continued. 'And where do these absurdities take place? In the bedroom I suppose.' Mrs Forthby nodded. 'Blott, have a look in the bedroom.'

'Yes, ma'am,' said Blott and went through first one door and then another. Mrs Forthby sat and stared at Lady Maud, hypnotized.

'Now then, you and I are going to have a little chat,' Lady Maud continued. 'You seem to be a sensible sort of woman with a head on your shoulders. I'm sure we can come to some mutually advantageous arrangement.'

'Arrangement?'

'Yes,' said Lady Maud, 'arrangement. Tell me, have you ever been a co-respondent in a divorce case?'

'No, never,' said Mrs Forthby.

'Well my dear,' Lady Maud went on, 'unless you are prepared to do exactly what I tell you down to the finest detail I'm afraid you are going to find yourself involved in quite the most sordid divorce case this country has seen for a very long time.'

'Oh dear,' Mrs Forthby whimpered, 'how simply awful. What would Cedric think of me?'

'Cedric?'

'My first husband. My late husband I should say. The poor dear would be absolutely furious. He'd never speak to me again. He was very particular, you know. Doctors have to be.'

'Well, we wouldn't want to upset Cedric, would we?' said Lady Maud. 'And there will be absolutely no need to if you do what I say. First of all I want you to tell me what Giles likes you to do.'

'Well . . .' Mrs Forthby began only to be interrupted by Blott

142

who emerged from the bedroom with the Miss Dracula, the Cruel Mistress, costume.

'I found this,' he announced.

'Oh dear, how frightfully embarrassing,' said Mrs Forthby.

'Not half as embarrassing, my dear, as it will be when we produce that in court as an exhibit. Now then, the details.'

Mrs Forthby got up. 'It's all written down,' she said. 'He writes it all down for me. You see I'm terribly forgetful and I do tend to get things wrong. I'll get you the game plan.' She went through to the bedroom and returned with a notebook. 'It's all there.'

Lady Maud took the book and studied a page. 'And what were you last night?' she asked finally. 'Miss Catheter, the Wicked Nurse, or Sister Florinda, the Nymphomaniac Nun?'

Mrs Forthby blushed. 'Doris, the Schoolgirl Sexpot,' she tittered.

Lady Maud looked at her doubtfully. 'My husband must have a truly remarkable imagination,' she said, 'but I find his literary style rather limited. And what are you going to be tonight?'

'Oh he doesn't come tonight. He's had to go to Plymouth for a business conference. He's coming again the day after tomorrow. That's Nanny Whip's night.'

Lady Maud put the book down. 'Now then, this is the arrangement,' she said. 'In return for your co-operation I will settle for a divorce on the grounds of incompatibility. There will be no mention of you at all and Sir Giles need know nothing about the help you have given me. All I want you to do is to go out for a little while on Thursday night so that I can have a little chat with him.'

Mrs Forthby hesitated. 'He'll be awfully cross,' she said.

'With me,' Lady Maud assured her. 'I don't think he'll worry about you by the time I've had my say. He'll have other things on his mind.'

'You won't do anything nasty to him, will you?' said Mrs Forthby. 'I wouldn't want him to be hurt or anything. I know he's not very nice but I'm really quite fond of him.'

'I won't touch him,' Lady Maud said. 'I give you my word of

honour I won't so much as lift a little finger to him. And let me say I think your feelings do you great credit.'

Mrs Forthby began to weep. 'You're very kind,' she said.

Lady Maud stood up. 'Not at all,' she said truthfully. 'And now if you'll be so good as to give me the key of the flat I'll send Blott to get a duplicate cut.'

By the time they left the flat Mrs Forthby was feeling better. 'It's been so nice meeting you and getting things straightened out,' she said. 'It's taken a great weight off my mind. I do hate deception so.'

'Quite,' said Lady Maud. 'Unfortunately men seem to live in a fantasy world and as the weaker sex we have to follow suit.'

'That's what I keep telling myself,' Mrs Forthby said. 'Felicia, I say, you may find it peculiar but if it makes him happy you can't afford to be choosey.'

'My sentiments exactly,' said Lady Maud. She and Blott went downstairs. They took a taxi across London to Sir Giles' flat in Victoria. On the way Lady Maud coached Blott in his new role.

19

In Worford Dundridge asserted himself. Now that he came to think about it, he could see that he had been wise to visit Mr Ganglion. The old man's reaction might have been violent but at least it had been genuine and served to indicate that the solicitor was far too respectable to be a party to a blackmail attempt by one of his clients no matter how influential she might be. And Mr Ganglion could do one of two things: he could let Lady Maud know that Dundridge had visited him and had accused her of blackmail, or, more likely, since it was unprofessional to disclose one client's business to another, he could keep silent. In either case Dundridge was in a fairly strong position. If Ganglion spoke to Lady Maud she would not dare to repeat her threat. If he kept silent . . . Dundridge considered the most likely consequence. There would be another message from her. Dundridge got up and went out and bought himself a tape recorder. The next time he visited Mr Ganglion he would tape evidence, solid evidence that Lady Maud was involved. That was the thing to do.

Having arrived at that conclusion he felt better. He had spiked the bitch's guns. Operation Overland could proceed. He went round to the Regional Planning Board and sent for Hoskins.

'We are going ahead,' he told him.

'Of course we are,' said Hoskins. 'Work has already started at Bunnington.'

'Never mind that,' said Dundridge, 'I want a task force to begin work in the Gorge.'

Hoskins consulted his schedule. 'We're not due there until October.'

'I know that but all the same I want work to begin there at once. Just a token force, you understand.'

'At Handyman Hall? A token force?'

'Not at the Hall. In the Gorge itself,' said Dundridge.

'But we haven't even served a compulsory purchase order on the Lynchwoods yet,' Hoskins protested.

'In that case it is about time we did. I want orders out to Miss Percival, General Burnett, and the Lynchwoods at once. We've got to bring pressure to bear on them as quickly as possible. Do you understand?'

'Well, I understand that,' said Hoskins who was beginning to resent Dundridge's authoritarian manner, 'but quite frankly I can't see what all the hurry is about.'

'You wouldn't,' said Dundridge, 'but I'm telling you to do it so get it done. In any case we don't need a compulsory purchase order for the entrance to the Gorge. It's common land. Move men in there tomorrow.'

'And what the hell do you expect them to do? Storm the bloody Hall under cover of darkness?'

'Hoskins,' said Dundridge, 'I'm getting a little tired of your sarcasm. You seem to forget that I am Controller Motorways Midlands and what I say goes.'

'Oh all right,' said Hoskins. 'Just remember that if anything goes wrong you'll have to take the can back. What do you want the task force to do?'

Dundridge looked at the plans for construction. 'It says here that the cliffs have to be cleared and the Gorge widened. They can start work on that.'

'That means dynamiting,' Hoskins pointed out.

'Excellent,' said Dundridge, 'that ought to serve notice on the old bag that we mean business.'

'It will do that all right,' said Hoskins. 'She'll probably be round here like a flash.'

'And I shall be only too glad to see her,' Dundridge said. Hoskins went back to his office puzzled. The more he saw of the Controller Motorways Midlands the odder he found him.

'I never thought he would stand up to Lady Maud like this,' he muttered. 'Well, better him than me.'

In his office Dundridge smiled to himself. Dynamite. That was just the thing to bring Lady Maud rushing into the trap he had set. He took the tape recorder out of his briefcase and tested it. The thing worked perfectly.

•

In Sir Giles' flat in Victoria, Lady Maud and Blott sat down by the desk. In front of her were the details of Sir Giles' shareholdings. In front of Blott the telephone and the script of his part.

'Ready?' said Lady Maud.

'Ready,' said Blott and dialled.

'Schaeffer, Blodger and Vaizey,' said the girl at the stockbrokers.

'Mr Blodger please,' said Blott.

'Sir Giles Lynchwood on the line for you, Mr Blodger,' he heard the girl say.

'Ah Lynchwood,' said Blodger, 'good morning.'

'Good morning Blodger,' said Blott. 'Now then, I want to sell the following at best. Four thousand President Rand. One thousand five hundred ICM. Ten thousand Rio Pinto. All my Zinc and Copper . . .'

At the other end of the line there was a choking sound. Mr Blodger was evidently having some difficulty coming to terms with Sir Giles' orders. 'I say, Lynchwood,' he muttered, 'are you all right?'

'All right? What the devil do you mean? Of course I'm all right,' snarled Blott.

'It's just that . . . well . . . I mean the market's rock bottom just at the moment. Wouldn't it be better to wait . . .'

'Listen Blodger,' said Blott, 'I know what I'm doing and when I say sell I mean sell. And if you'll take my advice you'll get out now too.'

'You really think . . .' Mr Blodger began.

'Think?' said Blott. 'I know. Now then see what you can get and call me back. I'll be here at the flat for the next twenty minutes.'

'Well if you say so,' said Mr Blodger.

Blott put the phone down.

'Brilliant, Blott, absolutely brilliant. For a moment even I thought it was Giles talking,' said Lady Maud. 'Well that should put the cat among the pigeons. Or the bulls among the bears. Now, when he calls back give him the second list.'

•

At the offices of Schaeffer, Blodger and Vaizey there was consternation. Blodger consulted Schaeffer and together they sent for Vaizey.

'Either he's gone out of his mind or he knows something,' shouted Blodger. 'He's dropping eighty thousand on the President Rand.'

'What about Rio Pinto?' Schaeffer yelled. 'He bought in at twenty-five and he's selling at ten.'

'He's usually right,' said Vaizey. 'In all the years we've handled his account he hasn't put a foot wrong.'

'A foot! He's putting his whole damned body wrong if you ask me.'

'Unless he knows something,' said Vaizey.

They looked at one another. 'He must know something,' said Schaeffer.

'Do you want to speak to him?' asked Blodger.

Schaeffer shook his head. 'My nerves couldn't stand it,' he muttered.

Blodger picked up the phone. 'Get me Sir Giles Lynchwood,' he told the girl on the switchboard. 'No, come to think of it, don't. I'll use the outside line.' He dialled Sir Giles' number.

Ten minutes later he staggered through to Schaeffer's office whitefaced.

'He wants out,' he said and slumped into a chair.

'Out?'

'Everything. The whole damned lot. And today. He knows something all right.'

•

'Well,' said Lady Maud, 'that's taken care of that. We had better spend another hour or two here in case they phone back. It's a great pity we can't do the same thing with some of his property. Still, there's no point in overdoing things.'

At two o'clock Blodger phoned again to say that Sir Giles' instructions had been carried out.

'Good,' said Blott. 'Send the transfers round tomorrow. I'm going to Paris overnight. And by the way, I want the money transferred to my current account at Westlands in Worford.'

•

Sir Giles returned from Plymouth the following afternoon by car. He was in a good humour. The conference had gone well and he was looking forward to an evening with Nanny Whip. He went to his flat, had a bath, dined in a restaurant and drove round to Elm Road to find Mrs Forthby already dressed for the part.

'Now then you naughty boy,' she said with just that touch of benign menace he found most affecting, 'off with your clothes.'

'No, no,' said Sir Giles.

'Yes, yes,' said Nanny Whip.

'No, no.'

'Yes, yes.'

Sir Giles succumbed to the allure of her apron. It smelt of

childhood. Nanny Whip's breath, on the other hand, suggested something more mature but Sir Giles was too intoxicated with her insistence that he behave himself while she fixed his nappy that he took no notice. It was only when he was finally strapped down and was having his bonnet adjusted that he caught a full whiff. It was brandy.

'You've been drinking,' he spluttered.

'Yes, yes,' said Mrs Forthby and stuffed a dummy into his mouth. Sir Giles stared up at her incredulously. Mrs Forthby never drank. The bloody woman was a teetotaller. It was one of the things he liked about her. She didn't cost much to entertain. She might be absent-minded but she was ... My God, if she was absent-minded sober what the hell was she going to be like drunk? Sir Giles writhed on the bed and realized that he was tied down rather more firmly than he had expected. Nanny Whip had excelled herself. He could hardly move.

'I'm just going to pop downstairs for some fish fingers,' she said, 'I won't be a moment.'

Sir Giles stared lividly at her while she took off her cap and put on a coat over her costume. What in God's name did the bloody woman want with fish fingers at this time of night? A moment? Sir Giles knew her moments. He was liable to be left strapped up in baby clothes and with a dummy in his mouth until the small hours while she went to some fucking concert. Sir Giles gnawed frantically at the dummy but the damned thing was tied on too tightly.

'Now you be a good boy while I'm away,' said Nanny Whip, 'and don't do anything I wouldn't do. Ta, ta.'

She went out and shut the door. Sir Giles subsided. There was no point in worrying now. He might as well enjoy his impotence while he could. There would probably be plenty of time later on for genuine concern. With the necessarily silent prayer that she hadn't been given tickets for the Ring Cycle he settled down to be Naughty Boy and he was just beginning to get into the role when the front doorbell rang. Sir Giles assumed an even greater rigidity. A moment later he was petrified.

'Is anyone at home?' a voice called. Sir Giles knew that voice. It was the voice of hell itself. It was Lady Maud.

'Oh well, the key's in the door,' he heard her say, 'so we might as well go in and wait.'

On the bed Sir Giles had palpitations. The thought of being discovered in this ghastly position by Lady Maud was bad enough but the fact that she had somebody with her was utterly appalling. He could hear them moving about the next room. If only they would stay there. And what the hell was Lady Maud doing there anyway? How on earth had she discovered about Mrs Forthby? And just at that moment the door opened and Lady Maud stood framed in it.

'Ah there you are,' she said cheerfully, 'I had an idea we'd find you here. How very convenient.'

From under his frilled bonnet Sir Giles peered up at her venomously, his face the colour of the sheet on which he was lying and his legs jerking convulsively in the air. Convenient! Convenient! The fucking woman was out of her mind. The next moment he was certain of it.

'You can come in, Blott,' she said, 'Giles won't mind.' Blott came into the room. He was carrying a camera and a flash gun.

'And now,' said Lady Maud, 'we're going to have a little chat.'

'What about the pictures?' said Blott. 'Shouldn't we take them first?'

'Do you think he would prefer the pictures first?' she asked. Blott nodded his head vigorously while Sir Giles shook his. For the next five minutes Blott went round the room taking photographs from every conceivable angle. Then he changed the film and took some close-ups. 'That will do for now,' he announced finally. 'We should have enough.'

'I'm sure we have,' said Lady Maud and drew up a chair beside the bed. 'Now then we are going to have our little chat about your future, my dear.' She bent over and took out the comforter.

'Don't touch me,' squealed Sir Giles.

'I have no intention of touching you,' said Lady Maud with evident disgust. 'It has been one of the few compensations for our wholly unsatisfactory marriage that I don't have to. I am simply here to arrange terms.'

'Terms? What terms?' squawked Sir Giles. Lady Maud rummaged in her handbag.

'The terms of our divorce,' she said and produced a document. 'You will simply append your signature here.'

Sir Giles stared up at it blankly. 'I need my reading-glasses,' he muttered.

Lady Maud perched them on his nose. Sir Giles read the document. 'You expect me to sign that?' he yelled. 'You really think I'm going to—'

Lady Maud replaced the dummy. 'You unspeakable creature,' she snarled, 'you'll sign this document if it's the last thing you do. And this.' She waved another piece of paper in front of him. 'And this.' Another. 'And this.'

On the bed Sir Giles struggled with the straps convulsively. Nothing on God's earth would make him sign a document that was an open confession that he had made a habit of deceiving his lawful wife, had denied her her conjugal rights, had committed adultery on countless occasions and had subjected her for six years to mental and physical cruelty. Lady Maud read his thoughts.

'In return for your signature I will not distribute copies of the photographs we have just taken to the Prime Minister, the Chief Whip, the members of your constituency party or the press. You will sign that document, Giles, and you will see that the motorway is stopped within a month. A month, do you hear me? Those are my terms. What do you say to that?' She removed the dummy.

'You filthy bitch.'

'Quite,' said Lady Maud, 'so you agree to sign?'

'I do not,' screamed Sir Giles and was promptly silenced.

'I don't know if you know your Shakespeare,' she said, 'but in *Edward the Second* . . .'

Sir Giles didn't know his Marlowe either but he did know about Edward the Second.

'Blott,' said Lady Maud, 'go into the kitchen and see if you can find—'

But already Sir Giles was nodding his head. He would sign anything now.

While Blott untied his right hand Lady Maud took a fountain pen out of her handbag. 'Here,' she said pointing to a dotted line. Sir Giles signed. 'Here,' and 'Here.' Sir Giles signed and signed. When he had finished Blott witnessed his signatures. Then he was tied down again.

'Good,' said Lady Maud, 'I will institute proceedings for divorce at once and you will stop the motorway or face the consequences. And don't you dare to set foot on my property again. I will have your things sent down to you.' She took out the dummy. 'Have you anything to say?'

'If I do manage to stop the motorway will you guarantee to let me have the photographs and negatives back?'

'Of course,' said Lady Maud, 'we Handymans may have our faults, but breaking our promises isn't one of them.' She stuffed the dummy back into his mouth and tied it behind his head. Then, having removed his glasses, she adjusted his bonnet and left the room.

On the staircase they met Mrs Forthby in a dither. 'You didn't do anything horrid, did you?' she asked.

'Of course not,' Lady Maud assured her, 'just got him to sign a document consenting to divorce.'

'Oh dear, I do hope he isn't too cross. He gets into such terrible tantrums.'

'Come, come, Nanny Whip, be your true self,' said Lady Maud. 'You must be firm.'

'Yes, you're quite right,' said Mrs Forthby. 'But it's very difficult. It's not in my nature to be unkind.'

'And before I forget, here's a little honorarium for your assistance.' Lady Maud produced a cheque from her bag but Mrs Forthby shook her head.

'I may be a silly woman and not very nice but I do have my

standards,' she said. 'And besides I'd probably forget to cash it.' She went upstairs a little wistfully.

•

'That woman,' said Lady Maud as they drove to Paddington to catch the train to Worford, 'is far too good for Giles. She deserves something better.' On the way they stopped to post the share transfers to Messrs Schaeffer, Blodger and Vaizey.

20

By the time they reached Handyman Hall it was two o'clock in the morning but the park was well lit. Under the floodlights men were busily engaged in erecting the fencing posts and already one side of the park was fenced in. Lady Maud drove round to have a look and congratulated Mr Firkin, the manager, on the progress.

'I'm afraid you're going to have to pay the bonus,' he told her. 'At this rate we'll be finished in ten days.'

'Make it a week,' said Lady Maud. 'Money's no problem.' She went into the house and up to bed well content. Money was no object now. In the morning she would withdraw every penny from their joint account at Westland Bank in Worford and deposit it in her own private account at the Northern. Sir Giles would scream blue murder but there was nothing he could do. He had signed the share transfer certificates if not of his own free will at least in circumstances which made it impossible for him to argue otherwise. And besides she still held one card up her sleeve, the photographs of Dundridge. She would call on the little goose and force him to admit that he had been blackmailed by Giles. Once she had proof of that there would be no question of the motorway continuing. She wouldn't even have to bother with her own awful photographs. Giles would be in jail, his seat in Parliament empty, a bye-election, and the whole wretched business finished.

Whatever happened now she was safe and so was the Hall. 'Fight fire with fire,' she thought and lay in bed considering the strange set of circumstances that had turned her from a plain, simple home-loving woman, a Justice of the Peace and a respectable member of the community, into a blackmailer dealing in obscene photographs and extorting signatures under threat of torture. Evidently the blood of her ancestors who had held the Gorge (by fair means and foul) against all comers still ran in her veins.

'You can't make omelettes without breaking eggs,' she murmured, and fell asleep.

*

In Mrs Forthby's flat one of the eggs in question lay in his frilly bonnet desperately trying to think of some way out of both his predicaments and promising himself that he would murder Nanny Fucking Whip as soon as he got free. Not that there seemed much chance of that before morning. Nanny Whip was snoring loudly on the sofa in the sitting-room. One look at Sir Giles' suffused face had been enough to persuade her that Naughty Boy's naughtiness had not diminished during her absence. A policy of continued restraint seemed called for. Nanny Whip went into the kitchen and hit the bottle of cooking brandy. 'A drop will give me some Dutch courage,' she thought and poured herself a large glass. By the time she had finished it she had forgotten what she had been taking it for. 'A little of what you fancy does you good,' she murmured, and collapsed on to the sofa.

A little of what Sir Giles fancied wasn't doing him any good at all. Besides, eight hours wasn't a little. As the clock on the mantelpiece chimed the hours Sir Giles' thoughts turned from murder to the more lurid forms of slow torture and in between he tried to think what the hell to do about Maud. There didn't seem anything he could do short of applying for the Chiltern Hundreds, resigning from all his clubs, realizing his assets and taking a quick trip to Brazil where the extradition laws didn't apply. And even then he wasn't sure he had any assets to realize. At about four in the morning it dawned on him that some of those pieces of paper he had signed had looked remarkably like share transfer certificates. At the time he hadn't been in any shape to consider them at all carefully. Not that he was in any better shape now but at least the threat of following Edward the Second to an agonizing death had been removed. Finally exhausted by his ordeal he fell into a semi-coma, waking every now and then to consider new and more awful fates for that absent-minded old sot in the next room.

Mrs Forthby woke with a hangover. She staggered off the sofa and ran a bath and it was only when she was drying herself that she remembered Sir Giles.

'Oh dear, he will be cross,' she thought, and went through to the kitchen to make a pot of tea. She carried the tray through to the bedroom and put it down on the bedside table. 'Wakey, wakey, rise and shine,' she said cheerfully and untied the straps. Sir Giles spat the dummy out of his mouth. This was the moment he had been waiting twelve hours for but there was no rising and shining for Sir Giles. He slithered sideways off the bed and crawled towards Mrs Forthby like a crab with rheumatoid arthritis.

'No, no, you naughty boy,' said Mrs Forthby horrified at his colour. She rushed out of the room and locked herself in the bathroom. There was no need to hurry. Behind her Sir Giles was stuck in the bedroom door and one of his legs had attached itself inextricably to a standard lamp.

•

In his office at the Regional Planning Board the Controller Motorways Midlands was having second thoughts about his plan for proving that Lady Maud was a blackmailer. The wretched woman had phoned the switchboard to say that she was coming in to Worford and wanted a word in private with him. Dundridge could well understand her desire for privacy but he did not share it. He had seen more than enough of Lady Maud in private and he had no intention of seeing any more. On the other hand she was hardly likely to threaten him with blackmail in front of a large audience. Dundridge paced up and down his office trying to find some way out of the quandary. In the end he decided to use Hoskins as a bodyguard. He sent for him.

'We've flushed the old cow out with that dynamiting,' he said.

'We've done what?' said Hoskins.

'She's coming to see me this morning. I want you to be present.'

Hoskins had his doubts. 'I don't know about that,' he muttered. 'And anyway, we haven't started dynamiting yet.'

'But the task force has moved in, hasn't it?'

'Yes, though I do wish you wouldn't call it a task force. All this military jargon is getting on my nerves.'

'Never mind that,' said Dundridge. 'The point is that she's coming. I want you to conceal yourself somewhere where you can hear what she has to say and make an appearance if she turns nasty.'

'*Turns* nasty?' said Hoskins. 'The bloody woman *is* nasty. She doesn't have to turn it.'

'I mean if she becomes violent,' Dundridge explained. 'Now then, we've got to find somewhere for you to hide.' He looked hopefully at a filing cabinet but Hoskins was adamant.

'Why can't I just sit in the corner?' he asked.

'Because she wants to see me in private.'

'Well then see her in private for God's sake,' said Hoskins. 'She isn't likely to assault you.'

'That's what you think,' said Dundridge. 'And in any case I want you as a witness. I have reason to believe that she is going to make an attempt to blackmail me.'

'Blackmail you?' said Hoskins turning pale. He didn't like that 'reason to believe'. It smacked of a policeman giving evidence.

'With photographs,' said Dundridge.

'With photographs?' echoed Hoskins, now thoroughly alarmed.

'Obscene photographs,' said Dundridge, with a deal more confidence than Hoskins happened to know was called for.

'What are you going to do?' he asked.

'I'm going to tell her to go jump in a lake,' said Dundridge.

Hoskins looked at him incredulously. To think that he had once described this extraordinary man as a nincompoop. The bastard was as tough as nails.

'I'll tell you what I'll do,' he said finally, 'I'll stand outside the door and listen to what she says. Will that do?'

Dundridge said it would have to and Hoskins hurried back to his office and phoned Mrs Williams.

'Sally,' he said, 'this is you-know-who.'

'I don't, you know,' said Mrs Williams, who had had a hard night.

'It's me. Horsey, horsey catkins,' snarled Hoskins desperately searching for a pseudonym that would deceive anyone listening in on the switchboard.

'Horsey horsey catkins?'

'Hoskins, for God's sake,' whispered Hoskins.

'Oh, Hoskins, why didn't you say so in the first place?'

Hoskins controlled his frayed temper. 'Listen carefully,' he said, 'the gaff's blown. The gaff. Gee for Gifuckingraffe. A for Animal. F for Freddie.'

'What's it mean?' interrupted Mrs Williams.

'The fuzz,' said Hoskins. 'It means the balloon's going to go up. Burn the lot, you understand. Negatives, prints, the tootee. You've never heard of me and I've never heard of you. Get it. No names, no pack drill. And you've never been near the Golf Club.'

By the time he had put the phone down Mrs Williams had got the message. So had Hoskins. If Mrs Williams was going to be nabbed, he could be sure that he would be standing in the dock beside her. She had left him in no doubt about that.

He went back to Dundridge's office and was there to open the door for Lady Maud when she arrived. Then he stationed himself outside and listened.

Inside Dundridge nerved himself for the ordeal. At least with Hoskins outside the door he could always call for help and in any case Lady Maud seemed to be rather better disposed towards him than he had expected.

'Mr Dundridge,' she said, taking a seat in front of his desk, 'I would like to make it quite clear that I have come here this morning in no spirit of animosity. I know we've had our little contretemps in the past but as far as I am concerned all is forgiven and forgotten.'

Dundridge looked at her balefully and said nothing. As far as he was concerned nothing was ever likely to be forgotten and certainly he wasn't in a forgiving mood.

'No, I have come here to ask for your co-operation,' she went on, 'and I want to assure you that what I am about to say will go no further.'

Dundridge glanced at the door and said he was glad to hear it.

'Yes, I rather thought you might,' said Lady Maud. 'You see I have reason to believe that you have been the subject of a blackmail attempt.'

Dundridge stared at her. She knew damned well he had been subject to blackmail.

'What makes you think that?'

'These photographs,' said Lady Maud and, producing an envelope from her handbag, she spread the torn and charred fragments of the photographs out on the desk. Dundridge studied them carefully. Why the hell were they torn and charred? He sorted through them looking for his face. It wasn't there. If she thought she was going to blackmail him with this lot she was very much mistaken.

'What about them?' he asked.

'You know nothing about them?'

'Certainly not,' said Dundridge, thoroughly confident now. He knew what had happened. He had left these photographs on Mr Ganglion's desk. Ganglion had torn them up and thrown them in the fire and had then changed his mind. He had taken them out and had visited Lady Maud and explained that he, Dundridge, had accused her of blackmail. And here she was trying to wriggle out of it. Her next remark confirmed this theory.

'Then my husband has never tried to influence you in any of your decisions by using these photographs,' she said.

'Your husband? Your husband?' said Dundridge indignantly. 'Are you suggesting that your husband has attempted to blackmail me with these . . . obscene photographs?'

'Yes,' said Lady Maud, 'that is exactly what I am suggesting.'

'Then all I can say is that you are mistaken. Sir Giles has always treated me with the greatest consideration and courtesy, which is,' he glanced at the door before continuing courageously, 'more than I can say for you.'

Lady Maud looked at him, mystified. 'Is that all you have to say?'

'Yes,' said Dundridge, 'except this. Why don't you take those photographs to the police?'

Lady Maud hesitated. She hadn't bargained on this attitude from Dundridge. 'I don't think that would be very sensible, do you?'

'Yes,' said Dundridge, 'as a matter of fact I do. Now then I am a busy man and you are wasting my time. You know your way out.'

Lady Maud rose from her chair wrathfully. 'How dare you speak to me like that?' she shouted.

Dundridge leapt out of his chair and opened the door. 'Hoskins,' he said, 'show Lady Maud Lynchwood out.'

'I will find my own way,' said Lady Maud, and stormed past them and down the corridor. Dundridge went back into his office and collapsed into his chair. He had called her bluff. He had shown her the door. Nobody could say the Controller Motorways Midlands wasn't master in his own house. He was astonished at his own performance.

So was Hoskins. He stared at Dundridge for a moment and staggered back to his own office shaken by what he had just heard. She had confronted Dundridge with those awful photographs and he had had the nerve to tell her to take them to the police. My God, a man who could do that was capable of doing anything. The fat was really in the fire now. On the other hand she had said it wouldn't be sensible. Hoskins agreed with her wholeheartedly. 'She must be protecting Sir Giles,' he thought and wondered how the hell she had got hold of the photographs in the first place. For a moment he thought of phoning Sir Giles but decided against it. The best thing to do was to sit tight and keep his mouth shut and hope that things would blow over.

He had just reached this comforting conclusion when the bell rang. It was Dundridge again. Hoskins went back down the corridor and found the Controller in a jubilant mood.

'Well that's put paid to that little scheme,' he said. 'You heard her threatening me with filthy photographs. She thought she was going to get me to use my influence to change the route of the motorway. I told her.'

'You most certainly did,' said Hoskins deferentially.

'Right,' said Dundridge turning to a map he had pinned on the wall, 'we must strike while the iron is hot. Operation Overland will proceed immediately. Have the compulsory purchase orders been served?'

'Yes,' said Hoskins.

'And the task force has begun demolition work in the Gorge?'

'Demolition work?'

'Dynamiting.'

'Not yet. They've only just moved in.'

'They must start at once,' said Dundridge. 'We must keep the initiative and maintain the pressure. I intend to establish a mobile HQ here.' He pointed to a spot on the map two miles east of Guildstead Carbonell.

'A mobile HQ?' said Hoskins.

'Arrange for a caravan to be set up there. I intend to supervise this operation personally. You and I will move our offices out there.'

'That's going to be frightfully inconvenient,' Hoskins pointed out.

'Damn the inconvenience,' said Dundridge, 'I mean to have that bitch out of Handyman Hall before Christmas come hell or high water. She's on the run now and by God I mean to see she stays there.'

'Oh all right,' said Hoskins gloomily. He knew better than to argue with Dundridge now.

●

Lady Maud drove back to the Hall pensively. She could have sworn that the thin legs in the photographs were the legs she had seen twinkling across the marble floor but evidently she had been wrong. Dundridge's self-righteous indignation had been wholly convincing. She had expected the wretched little man to blush and stammer and make excuses but instead he had stood up to her and ordered her out of his office. He had even suggested she should take the photographs to the police and, considering his pusillanimity in other less threatening circumstances, it was impossible to suppose he had been bluffing. No, she had been wrong. It was a pity. She would have liked to have seen Sir Giles in court, but it hardly mattered. She had enough to be going on with. Sir Giles would move heaven and earth to see that the motorway was stopped now and if he failed she would force him to resign his seat. There would have to be another bye-election and what had worked in the case of Ottertown would work again in the case of the Gorge. The Government would cancel the motorway. And finally if that too failed there was always the Wildlife Park. It was one thing to demolish half a dozen houses and evict the families that lived there, but it was quite a different kettle of fish to deprive ten lions, four giraffes, a rhinoceros and a dozen ostriches of their livelihood. The British public would never stand for cruelty to animals. She arrived at the Hall to find Blott busy washing his films in the kitchen.

'I've turned the boiler-room into a darkroom,' he explained, and held up a film for her to look at. Lady Maud studied it inexpertly.

'Have they come out all right?' she asked.

'Very nicely,' said Blott. 'Quite lovely.'

'I doubt if Giles would share your opinion,' said Lady Maud and went out into the garden to pick a lettuce for lunch. Blott finished washing his films in the sink and took them down to the boiler-room and hung them up to dry. When he came back lunch was ready on the kitchen table.

'You'll eat in here with me,' said Lady Maud. 'I'm very pleased with you, Blott, and besides, it's nice to have a man about the house.'

Blott hesitated. It seemed an illogical remark. There appeared to be a great many men about the house, tramping up and down the servants' stairs to their bedrooms and working day and night on the fencing. Still, if Lady Maud wanted him to eat with her, he was not going to argue. Things were looking up. She was going to get a divorce from her husband. He was in love and while he had no hope of ever being able to do anything about it, he was happy just to sit and eat with her. And then there was the fence. Blott was delighted by the fence. It brought back memories of the war and his happiness as a prisoner. It would shut out the world and he and Maud would live singly but happily ever after.

They had just finished lunch and were washing-up when there was a dull boom in the distance and the windows rattled.

'I wonder what that was,' said Lady Maud.

'Sounds like blasting,' said Blott.

'Blasting?'

'In a quarry.'

'But there aren't any quarries round here,' said Lady Maud. They went out on to the lawn and stood looking at a cloud of dust rising slowly into the sky a mile or two to the east.

Operation Overland had begun.

21

And Operation Overland continued. Day after day the silence of the Gorge was broken by the rumbling of bulldozers and the dull thump of explosions as the cliffs were blasted and the rocks cleared. Day after day the contractors complained to Hoskins that the way to build a motorway was to start at the beginning and go on to the end, or at least to stick to some sort of predetermined schedule and not go jumping all over the place digging up a field here and rooting out a wood there, starting a bridge and then abandoning construction to begin a flyover. And day after day Hoskins took their complaints and some of his own to Dundridge, and was overruled.

'The essential feature of Operation Overland lies in the random nature of our movements,' Dundridge explained. 'The enemy never knows where we are going to be next.'

'Nor do I, come to that,' said Hoskins bitterly. 'I had a job finding this place this morning. You might have warned me you were going to move it before I went home last night.'

Dundridge looked round the Mobile Headquarters. 'That's odd,' he said, 'I thought *you* had it moved.'

'Me? Why should I do that?'

'I don't know. To be nearer the front line I suppose.'

'Nearer the front line?' said Hoskins. 'All I want is to be back in my bloody office, not traipsing round the countryside in a fucking caravan.'

'Well anyway, whoever had it moved had a good idea,' said Dundridge. 'We are nearer the scene of action.'

Hoskins looked out of the window as a giant dumper rumbled past.

'Nearer?' he shouted above the din. 'We're bloody well in it if you ask me.' As if to confirm his words there was a deafening roar and two hundred yards away a portion of cliff collapsed. As the dust settled Dundridge surveyed the scene with satisfaction. This was nature as man, and in particular Dundridge, intended. Nature conquered, nature subdued, nature disciplined. This was progress, slow progress but inexorable. Behind them cuttings and embankments, concrete and steel, ahead the Gorge and Handyman Hall.

'By the way,' said Hoskins when he could hear himself speak, 'we've had a complaint from General Burnett. He says one of our trucks damaged his garden wall.'

'So what?' said Dundridge. 'He won't have a garden or a wall in two months' time. What's he complaining about?'

'And Mr Bullett-Finch phoned to say—'

But Dundridge wasn't interested. 'File all complaints,' he said dismissively, 'I haven't got time for details.'

●

In London Sir Giles didn't share his opinion. He was obsessed with details, particularly those concerned with the sale of his shares and what Lady Maud was going to do with those damned photographs.

'I lost half a million on those shares,' he yelled at Blodger. 'Half a bleeding million.'

Blodger commiserated. 'I said at the time I thought you were being a little hasty,' he said.

'You thought? You didn't think at all,' Sir Giles screamed. 'If you'd thought you would have known that wasn't me on the phone.'

'But it sounded like you. And you asked me to call you back at your flat.'

'I did nothing of the sort. You don't seriously imagine I would sell four thousand President Rand when the market was at rock bottom. I'm not fucking insane you know.'

Blodger looked at him appraisingly. The thought had crossed his mind. It was Schaeffer who brought the altercation to an end.

'If you must swear,' he said, 'I can only suggest that you would do so more profitably before a Commissioner of Oaths.'

'And what would I want with a Commissioner of Fucking Oaths?'

'A sworn statement that the signatures on the share transfer certificates were forgeries,' said Schaeffer coldly.

Sir Giles picked up his hat. 'Don't think this is the end of the fucking matter,' he snarled. 'You'll be hearing from me again.'

Schaeffer opened the door for him. 'I can only hope fucking not,' he said.

●

But if his stockbrokers were not sympathetic, Mrs Forthby was.

'It's all my fault,' she wailed squinting at him through the two black eyes he had given her for her pains. 'If only I hadn't gone out for those fish fingers this would never have happened.'

'Fish fucking . . .' he began and pulled himself up. He had to keep a grip on his sanity and Mrs Forthby's self-denunciations didn't help. 'Never mind about that. I've got to think what to do. That bloody wife of mine isn't going to get away with this if I can help it.'

'Well, if all she wants is a divorce . . .'

'A divorce? A divorce? If you think that's all she wants . . .' He stopped again. Mrs Forthby mustn't hear anything about those photographs. Nobody must hear about them. The moment that information got out he would be a ruined man and he had just three weeks to do something about them. He went back to his flat and sat there trying to think of some way of stopping the motorway. There wasn't much he could do in London. His request to discuss the matter with the Minister of the Environment had been turned down, his demand for a further Enquiry denied. And his private source in the Ministry had been adamant that it was too late to do anything now.

'The thing is under construction already. Barring accidents nothing can stop it.'

Sir Giles put down the phone and thought about accidents, nasty accidents, like Maud falling downstairs and breaking her neck or having a fatal car crash. It didn't seem very likely somehow. Finally he thought about Dundridge. If Maud had something on him, he had something on the Controller Motorways Midlands. He telephoned Hoskins at the Regional Planning Board.

'He's out at SHMOCON,' said the girl on the switchboard.

'Shmocon?' said Sir Giles desperately trying to think of a village by that name in South Worfordshire.

'Supreme Headquarters Motorway Construction,' said the girl. 'He's Deputy Field Commander.'

'What?' said Sir Giles. 'What the hell's going on up there?'

'Don't ask me,' said the girl, 'I'm only a field telegraphist. Shall I put you through?'

'Yes,' said Sir Giles. 'It sounds batty to me.'

'It is,' said the girl. 'It's a wonder I don't have to use morse code.'

Certainly Hoskins sounded peculiar when Sir Giles finally got through to him. 'Deputy Field—' he began but Sir Giles interrupted.

'Don't give me that crap, Hoskins,' he shouted. 'What the hell do you think you're playing at? Some sort of war game?'

'Yes,' said Hoskins looking nervously out of the window. There was a deafening roar as a charge of dynamite went off.

'What the hell was that?' yelled Sir Giles.

'Just a near miss,' said Hoskins as small fragments of rock rattled on the roof of the caravan.

'You can cut the wisecracks,' said Sir Giles, 'I didn't call you to talk nonsense. There's been a change of plan. The motorway has got to be stopped. I've decided . . .'

'Stopped?' Hoskins interrupted him. 'You haven't a celluloid rat's hope in hell of stopping this little lot now. We're advancing into the Gorge at the rate of a hundred yards a day.'

'Into the Gorge?'

'You heard me,' said Hoskins.

'Good God,' said Sir Giles. 'What the hell's been going on? Has Dundridge gone off his head or something?'

'You could put it like that,' said Hoskins hesitantly. The Controller Motorways Midlands had just come into the caravan covered in dust and was taking off his helmet.

'Well, stop him,' shouted Sir Giles.

'I'm afraid that is impossible, sir,' said Hoskins modulating his tone to indicate that he was no longer alone. 'I will make a note of your complaint, and forward it to the appropriate authorities.'

'You'll do more than that,' bawled Sir Giles, 'you'll use those photographs. You will—'

'I understand the police deal with these matters, sir,' said Hoskins. 'As far as we are concerned I can only suggest that you use an incinerator.'

'An *incinerator*? What the hell do I want with an incinerator?'

'I have found that the best method is to burn that sort of rubbish. The answer is in the negative.'

'In the negative?'

'Quite, sir,' said Hoskins. 'I have found that it avoids the health risk to incinerate inflammable material. And now if you'll excuse me, I have someone with me.' Hoskins rang off and Sir Giles sat back and deciphered his message.

'Incinerators. Police. Negative. Health risks.' These were the words Hoskins had emphasized and it dawned on Sir Giles that all hope of influencing Dundridge had gone up in flames. He was particularly alarmed by the mention of the police. 'Good God, that little bastard Dundridge has been to the cops,' he muttered, and suddenly recalled that his safe at Handyman Hall contained evidence that hadn't been incinerated. Maud was sitting on a safe containing photographs that could send him to prison. 'Inflammable material. That bitch can get me five years,' he thought. 'I'd like to incinerate her.' Incinerate her? Sir Giles stared into space. He had suddenly seen a way out of all his problems.

He picked up a pencil and detailed the advantages. Number One, he would destroy the evidence of his attempt to blackmail Dundridge. Number Two, he would get rid of those photographs Blott had taken of him in Mrs Forthby's flat. Number Three, by acting before Maud could divorce him he would still be the owner of the ashes of Handyman Hall and liable for the insurance money and possibly the compensation from the motorway. Number Four, if Maud were to die . . . Number Four was a particularly attractive prospect and just the sort of accident he had been hoping for.

He picked up the sheet of paper and carried it across to the fireplace and lit a match. As the paper flared up Sir Giles watched it with immense satisfaction. There was nothing like a good fire for cleansing the past. All he needed now was a perfect alibi.

At Handyman Hall Lady Maud surveyed her handiwork with equal satisfaction. The fence had been finished in ten days, the lions, giraffes, and the rhinoceros had been installed and the ostriches were accommodated in the old tennis court. It was really very pleasant to wander round the house and watch the lions padding across the park or lying under the trees.

'It gives one a certain sense of security,' she told Blott, whose movements had been restricted to the kitchen garden and who complained that the rhinoceros was mucking up the lawn.

'It may give you a sense of security,' said Blott, 'but the postman has other ideas. He won't come further than the Lodge and the milkman won't either.'

'What nonsense,' said Lady Maud. 'The way to deal with lions is to put a bold front on and look them squarely in the eyes.'

'That's as maybe,' said Blott, 'but that rhino needs spectacles.'

'The thing with rhinos,' said Lady Maud, 'is to move at right angles to their line of approach.'

'That didn't work with the butcher's van. You've no idea what it did to his back mudguard.'

'I have a very precise idea. Sixty pounds worth of damage but it didn't charge the van.'

'No,' said Blott, 'it just leant up again it and scratched its backside.'

'Well at least the giraffes are behaving themselves,' said Lady Maud.

'What's left of them,' said Blott.

'What do you mean "What's left of them"?'

'Well, there's only two left.'

'Two? But there were four. Where have the other two got to?'

'You had better ask the lions about that,' Blott told her. 'I have an idea they rather like giraffes for dinner.'

'In that case we had better order another hundredweight of meat from the butchers. We can't have them eating one another.'

She strode off across the lawn imperiously, stopping to prod the rhinoceros with her shooting stick. 'I won't have you in the rockery,' she told it. Outside the kitchen door a lion was snoozing in the sun. 'Be off with you, you lazy beast.' The lion got up and slunk away.

Blott watched with admiration and then shut the door of the kitchen garden. 'What a woman,' he murmured and went back to the tomatoes. He was interrupted five minutes later by a dull thump from the Gorge. Blott looked up. They were getting nearer. It was about time he did something about that business. So far his efforts had been confined to moving Dundridge's mobile headquarters about the countryside at night and altering the position of the pegs that marked the route so that had the motorway proceeded as the contractors desired it would have been several degrees off course. Unfortunately Dundridge's insistence on random construction had defeated Blott's efforts. His only success had been the felling of all the trees in Colonel Chapman's orchard which was a quarter of a mile away from the supposed route of the motorway. Blott was rather proud of that. The Colonel had raised Cain with the authorities and had been promised additional compensation. A few more miscalculations like that and there would be a public outcry. Blott applied his mind to the problem.

•

That night Blott visited the Royal George at Guildstead Carbonell for the first time in several weeks.

Mrs Wynn greeted him enthusiastically. 'I'm so glad you've come,' she said, 'I thought you'd given me up for good.'

Blott said he had been busy. 'Busy?' said Mrs Wynn. 'You're one to talk. I've been rushed off my feet with all the men from the motorway. They come in here at lunch and they're back at night. I tell you, I can't remember anything like it.'

Blott looked round the bar and could see what she meant. The pub was filled with construction workers. He helped himself to a pint of Handyman Brown and went to a table in the corner. An hour later he was deep in conversation with the driver of a bulldozer.

'Must be interesting work knocking things down,' said Blott.

'The pay's good,' said the driver.

'I imagine you've got to be a real expert to demolish a big building like Handyman Hall.'

'I don't know. The bigger they is the harder they falls is what I say,' said the driver, flattered by Blott's interest.

'Let me get you another pint,' said Blott.

Three pints later the driver was explaining the niceties of demolition to a fascinated Blott.

'It's a question of hitting the corner stone,' he said. 'Find that, swing the ball back and let it go and Bob's your uncle, the whole house is down like a pack of cards. I tell you I've done that more times than you've had hot dinners.'

Blott said he could well believe it. By closing time he knew a great deal about demolition work and the driver said he looked forward to meeting him again. Blott helped Mrs Wynn with washing the glasses and then did his duty by her but his heart wasn't in it. Mrs Wynn noticed it.

'You're not your usual self tonight,' she said when they had finished. Blott grunted. 'Mind you I can't say I'm any great shakes myself. My legs are killing me. What I need is a holiday.'

'Why don't you take a day off?' said Blott.

'How can I? Who would look after the customers?'

'I would,' said Blott.

•

At five he was up and cycling down the main street of Guildstead Carbonell towards Handyman Hall. At seven he had fed the lions and when Lady Maud came down to breakfast Blott was waiting for her.

'I'm taking the day off,' he announced.

'You're what?' said Lady Maud. Blott didn't take days off.

'Taking the day off. And I'll need the Land-Rover.'

'What for?' said Lady Maud who wasn't used to being told by her gardener that he needed her Land-Rover.

'Never you mind,' said Blott. 'No names, no pack drill.'

'No names, no pack drill? Are you feeling all right?'

'And a note for Mr Wilkes at the Brewery to say he's to give me Very Special Brew.'

Lady Maud sat down at the kitchen table and looked at him doubtfully. 'I don't like the sound of this, Blott. You're up to something.'

'And I don't like the sound of that,' said Blott as a dull thump came from the Gorge. Lady Maud nodded. She didn't like the sound of it either.

'Has it got anything to do with that?' she asked. Blott nodded. 'In that case you can have what you want but I don't want you getting into any trouble on my account, you understand.'

She went through to the study and wrote a note to Mr Wilkes, the manager of the Handyman Brewery in Worford, telling him to give Blott whatever he asked for.

At ten Blott was in the manager's office.

'Very Special?' said Mr Wilkes. 'But Very Special is for special occasions. Coronations and suchlike.'

'This is a special occasion,' said Blott.

Mr Wilkes looked at the letter again. 'If Lady Maud says so, I suppose I must, but it's strictly against the law to sell Very Special. It's twenty per cent proof.'

'And ten bottles of vodka,' said Blott. They went down to the cellar and loaded the Land-Rover.

'Forget you've seen me,' Blott said when they had finished.

'I'll do my best,' said the manager, 'this is all bloody irregular.'

•

Blott drove to the Royal George and saw Mrs Wynn on to the bus. Then he went back into the pub and set to work. By lunchtime he had emptied one barrel of Handyman Bitter down the drain and had refilled it with bottles of Very Special and five bottles of vodka. He tried it out on a couple of customers and was delighted with the result. During the afternoon he had a nap and then took a stroll through the village and up past the Bullett-Finches' house. It was a large house in mock Tudor set back from the road and with a very fine garden. Outside the gates a sign announced that Finch Grove was For Sale. The Bullett-Finches didn't fancy living within a hundred yards of a motorway. Blott didn't blame them. Then he walked back through the village and looked at Miss Percival's cottage. That wasn't for sale. It was due for demolition and Miss Percival had already vacated it. A large crane with a steel ball on the end of its arm stood nearby. Blott climbed into the driver's seat and played with the controls. Then he walked back to the pub and sat behind the bar, waiting for opening time.

22

Sir Giles busied himself in Mrs Forthby's flat. He altered the date on the clock on the mantelpiece. He turned the pages of the *Radio Times* to the following day and hid the newspaper. Several times he asserted that today was Wednesday.

'That just goes to show what a muddlehead I am,' said Mrs Forthby, who was busy making supper in the kitchen, 'I could have sworn it was Tuesday.'

'Tomorrow's Thursday,' said Sir Giles.

'If you say so, dear,' said Mrs Forthby. 'I'm sure I don't know what day of the week it is. My memory is simply shocking.'

Sir Giles nodded approvingly. It was on Mrs Forthby's appalling memory that his alibi depended, that and sleeping pills. 'Silly old bitch won't miss a day in her life,' he thought as he crunched six tablets up in the bottom of a glass with the handle of a toothbrush before adding a large tot of whisky. According to his doctor the lethal dose was twelve. 'Six would probably put you out for twenty-four hours,' the doctor had told him and twenty-four hours was all Sir Giles needed. He went through to the kitchen and had supper.

'What about a nightcap?' he said when they had finished.

'You know I never drink,' said Mrs Forthby.

'You did the other night. You finished half a bottle of cooking brandy.'

'That was different. I wasn't feeling myself.'

It was on the tip of Sir Giles' tongue to tell her that she wouldn't feel anything let alone herself by the time she had finished that little lot but he restrained himself. 'Cheers,' he said, and finished his glass.

'Cheers,' said Mrs Forthby doubtfully and sipped her whisky.

Sir Giles poured himself another glass. 'Down the hatch,' he said.

Mrs Forthby took another sip. 'You know I could have sworn today was Tuesday,' she said.

Sir Giles could have sworn, period. 'Today is Wednesday.'

'But I've got a hair appointment on Wednesday. If today is Wednesday I must have missed it.'

'You have,' said Sir Giles truthfully. Whatever happened, Mrs Forthby had missed her hair appointment. He raised his glass. 'Mud in your eye.'

'Mud in your eye,' said Mrs Forthby and sipped again. 'If today is Wednesday, tomorrow must be Thursday in which case I've got a pottery class in the afternoon.'

Sir Giles poured himself another whisky hurriedly. It was on just such insignificant details that the best plans foundered. 'I was thinking of going down to Brighton for the weekend,' he improvised. 'I thought you would like that.'

'With me?' said Mrs Forthby, her eyes shining.

'Just us two together,' said Sir Giles.

'Oh, you are thoughtful.'

'A votre santé,' said Sir Giles.

Mrs Forthby finished her drink and got to her feet. 'It's Nurse Catheter tonight, isn't it?' she said moving unsteadily towards him.

'Forget it,' said Sir Giles, 'I'm not in the mood.' Nor was Mrs Forthby. He carried her through to the bedroom and put her to bed. When he left the flat five minutes later she was snoring soundly. By the time she woke up he would be back and in bed beside her. He got into his car and began the drive north.

•

At the Royal George in Guildstead Carbonell Blott's experiment in induced narcosis proceeded more slowly but with gayer results. By nine o'clock the pub was filled with singing dumper drivers, two fights had erupted and died down before they could get well under way, a darts match had had to be cancelled when a non-participant had been pinned by his ear to last year's calendar, and two consenting adults had been ejected from the Gents by Blott and Mrs Wynn's Alsatian. By ten o'clock Blott's promise that the Very Special was needed for a special occasion had been fulfilled to the letter. Two more fights, this time between locals and the men from the motorway, had started and had not died down but had spread to the Saloon Bar where the operator of a piledriver was attempting to demonstrate his craft to the fiancée of the secretary of the Young Conservatives, the darts match had been resumed using a portrait of Sir Winston Churchill as a dartboard, and half a dozen bulldozer drivers were giving an exhibition of clog dancing on the bar-billiards table. In between whiles Blott had coaxed Mr Edwards, who claimed to have knocked down more houses than Blott had had hot dinners, into a nicely belligerent mood.

'I can knock any damned house you like to show me down with one bloody blow,' he shouted.

Blott raised an eyebrow. 'Tell me another one.'

'I tell you I can,' Mr Edwards asserted. 'One knock in the right place and Bob's your uncle.'

'I'll believe it when I see it,' said Blott and poured him another pint of Very Special.

'I'll show you. I'll bloody show you,' said Mr Edwards and took a swig.

By closing time Very Special had cast if not a healing balm at least a soporific one on the whole proceedings. As the motorway men stumbled off to their cars and the Young Conservatives drove off nursing their wounds, Blott shut up shop and helped Mr Edwards to his feet.

'I tell you I can,' he mumbled.

'Never,' said Blott.

Together they staggered off down the street towards Miss Percival's cottage, Blott clutching a bottle of vodka and Mr Edwards' arm.

'I'll show you,' said Mr Edwards as they crossed the field to the cottage. 'I'll fucking show you.'

He climbed into the crane and started it up. Blott stood behind him and watched.

'Oh what a pity she's only one titty to bang against the wall,' Mr Edwards sang as the crane jerked forward through the hedge and into the garden. Behind them the iron ball wobbled and swung. Mr Edwards stopped the crane and adjusted the controls. The arm of the crane swung round and the ball followed. It went wide.

'I thought you said you could do it in one,' said Blott.

'That,' said Mr Edwards, 'was just a practice swing.' He lowered the crane and a sundial disintegrated. Mr Edwards raised it again.

'Never been laid, never been made, Queen of all the Fairies,' he bawled. The crane swung round and Blott darted out of the way as the iron ball lolloped past him. The next moment it hurtled into the side of the cottage. There was a roar of falling bricks, tiles, breaking glass and a great cloud of dust momentarily obscured what had once been Miss Percival's attractive home. When the dust finally cleared what remained of the cottage held few attractions. On the other hand it was not entirely demolished. A chimney still stood and the roof while hanging at a disreputable angle was still recognizably the roof. Blott regarded the result sceptically.

'I don't think much of that,' he said superciliously. 'Still I suppose there's always a first time.'

'Whadja mean always a first time?' said Mr Edwards. 'I knocked it down, didn't I?'

'No,' said Blott, 'not with one blow.'

Mr Edwards consoled himself with vodka. ''sonly a fucking cottage. Can't expect much with a cottage. Got no bulk to it.

Gotta have bulk, got to have weight. Show me a house, a proper house, a big bulky house and I'll ...' He slumped over the controls. Blott climbed up into the cab and shook him.

'Wake up,' he shouted. Mr Edwards woke up.

'Show me a proper house ...'

'All right, I will,' said Blott. 'Show me how to drive this thing and I'll show you a proper house.'

Mr Edwards did his best to show him. 'You pull that lever and you press that 'celerator.' Five minutes later Guildstead Carbonell, already disturbed by the eruption of violence at the Royal George, was convulsed a second time as Blott with Mr Edwards' assistance attempted to negotiate the High Street at something over the statutory speed limit. As the mobile crane hurtled into the first of several corners at forty miles per hour Blott struggled to keep it on the road. He wasn't helped by Mr Edwards' inertia nor by that of the iron ball which, swinging behind, tended to demonstrate the attractions of centrifugal force. On the first corner it gave a glancing blow to the plate-glass window of a newly opened mini-market, bounced off the roof of a parked car, entered the front parlour of Mrs Tate's house and came out through Mr and Mrs Williams' sitting-room, decapitated the War Memorial and took a telegraph pole and fifty yards of wire in tow. On the second it took a short cut through the forecourt of Mr Dugdale's garage neatly severing the stanchions that had formerly supported the roof and de-molishing four petrol pumps and a sign advertising free tumblers. By the time they had traversed the rest of the High Street, the ball had left its imprint on seven more cars and the façades of twelve splendid examples of eighteenth-century domestic architecture while the telegraph pole, not to be left out of things, had vaulted through every third window before disentangling itself from the crane and coming to rest in the vestry of the Primitive Methodist Chapel taking with it a large sign announcing the Coming of the Lord. As they left the vil-lage, the iron ball made its last contribution to the peace and tranquillity of the place by nudging an electricity transformer which exploded with a galaxy of blue sparks and plunged the entire district into darkness. At this point Mr Edwards woke up.

'Where are we?' he mumbled.

'Almost there,' said Blott, managing to slow the crane down. Mr Edwards took another swig of vodka.

'Show me the way to go home,' he sang, 'I'm tired and I want to go to bed.'

'Not yet,' said Blott and turned the crane up the drive towards the Bullett-Finches' house.

•

It was one of Mrs Bullett-Finch's pleasanter qualities from her husband's point of view that she went to bed early. 'It's the early bird that catches the worm,' she would say at nine o'clock every night and take herself upstairs, leaving Mr Bullett-Finch to sit up by himself and read about lawns in peace and quiet. And lawns interested him. They held a charm for him that Ivy Bullett-Finch had long since relinquished. Lawns improved with age, which was more than could be said for wives and what Mr Bullett-Finch didn't know about browntop and chewing fescue and velvet bent was not worth knowing. And the lawns around Finch Grove were in his opinion among the finest in the country. They stretched immaculately in front of the house down to the stream at the bottom of the garden. Not a dandelion scarred their surface, not a plantain, not a daisy. For six years Mr Bullett-Finch had nurtured his lawns, sanding, mowing, spiking, fertilizing, weedkilling, even going so far as to prohibit visitors with high heels from walking on them. And when Ivy wanted to go down to the orchard she had to wear her bedroom slippers. It may have been this insistence on his part that the front garden was sacrosanct that had contributed to her nervous disposition and sense of guilt. What the garden was to her husband, the house was to Ivy, a source of obsessive concern in which everything had its place, was dusted twice a day and polished three times a week so that she went to bed early less out of indolence than from sheer exhaustion and lay there wondering if she had turned everything off.

On this particular night Mr Bullett-Finch was deep in a chapter on hormone weedkillers when the lights went out. He got up and stumbled through to the fusebox only to find that the fuses were intact.

'Must be a power failure,' he thought and went up to bed in the dark. He had just undressed and was putting on his pyjamas when he became aware that something extremely large and powered by an enormous diesel engine appeared to be making its way up his drive. He rushed to the window and peered out into two powerful headlights. Temporarily blinded, he groped for his dressing-gown and slippers, found them and put them on and looked out of the window again. What looked like a gigantic crane had stopped on the gravel forecourt and was backing on to his lawn. With a scream of rage Mr Bullett-Finch told it to stop but it was too late. A moment later there was a winching noise and the crane began to swing. Mr Bullett-Finch pulled his head in the window and raced for the stairs. He was halfway down them when all concern for his precious lawn disappeared, to be replaced by the absolute conviction that Finch Grove was at the very centre of some gigantic earthquake. As the house disintegrated around him – Mr Edwards' claim to be a demolition expert entirely vindicated – Mr Bullett-Finch clung to the banisters and peered through a dust-storm of plaster and powdered brick while the furnishings of which his wife had been so rightly proud hurtled past him from the upstairs rooms. Among them came Mrs Bullett-Finch herself, screaming and hysterically proclaiming her innocence, which had until then never been in doubt, and he was just debating why she should assume responsibility for what was obviously a natural cataclysm when he was saved the trouble by the roof collapsing on top of him and the staircase collapsing underneath. Mr Bullett-Finch descended into the cellar and lay unconscious, surrounded by his small stock of claret. Mrs Bullett-Finch, still clinging to her mattress and the conviction that she had left the gas on, had meanwhile been catapulted into the herb-garden where she sobbed convulsively among the thyme.

From the cab of his crane Mr Edwards regarded his handiwork with pride.

'Told you I could do it,' he said and seized the bottle of vodka from Blott who had been steadying his nerves with it. Blott let him finish it. Then dragged him down from the cab and climbed back to wipe any fingerprints from the controls. Finally, hoisting Mr Edwards over his shoulder, he set off down the drive.

By the time he reached the Royal George Mrs Wynn was back from Worford, and washing glasses by candlelight.

'Look at all this mess,' she said irately, 'I leave you to look after the place for one day and what do I find when I get back. Anyone would think there had been an orgy here. And what's been going on in the village, I'd like to know? The place looks like it's been bombed.'

Blott helped with the glasses and then went out to the Land-Rover. Mr Edwards was still sleeping soundly in the back. He drove slowly out of the yard and turned towards Ottertown. It was a longer way round but Blott didn't want to be seen in the High Street. He stopped at the caravan site where the motorway workers lived and deposited Mr Edwards on the grass. Then he drove on towards the Gorge and Handyman Hall. At two o'clock he was in bed in the Lodge. All in all it had been a good day's work.

•

In Dundridge's flat the phone rang. He groped for it sleepily and switched on the light. It was Hoskins. 'What the hell do you want? Do you realize what time it is?'

'Yes,' said Hoskins, 'as a matter of fact I do. I just wanted to tell you that you've gone too far this time.'

'Gone too far?' said Dundridge. 'I haven't gone anywhere.'

'Don't give me that,' said Hoskins. 'You and your random sorties and your task forces and assault groups. Well you've certainly landed us in it this time. There were people living in that fucking house, you know, and it wasn't even scheduled for demolition in the first place and as for what you've done to Guildstead Carbonell . . . I hope you realize that the motorway wasn't supposed to go within a mile of that village. It's a historical monument, Guildstead Carbonell is ... was. It's a fucking ruin now, a disaster area.'

'A disaster area?' said Dundridge. 'What do you mean a disaster area?'

'You know very well what I mean,' shouted Hoskins hysterically. 'I always thought you were mad but now I know it.' He slammed the phone down, leaving Dundridge mystified. He sat on the edge of his bed and wondered what to do. Clearly something had gone wrong with Operation Overland. He was just about to call Hoskins back when the phone rang again. This time it was the police.

'Is that Mr Dundridge?'

'Yes, speaking.'

'This is the Chief Constable. I wonder if I could have a word with you. It's about this business at Guildstead Carbonell ...'

Dundridge got dressed.

•

Sir Giles parked his car outside Wilfrid's Castle Church. It was an unfrequented spot and nobody was likely to be out and about at two o'clock in the morning. It was one of the great advantages of a Bentley that it was not a noisy car. For the last five miles Sir Giles had driven without lights, coasting past farmhouses and keeping to back roads. He had seen no other vehicles and, so far as he could tell, had been seen by nobody. So far so good. Leaving the car he made his way down the footpath to the bridge. It was dark down there under the trees and he had some difficulty in finding his way. On the far side of the bridge he came to a wire-mesh gate. Using his torch briefly he unlatched it and went through into the pinetum. The gate puzzled Sir Giles. It was a long time since he had been over the bridge, not since the day of his wedding in fact, but he felt sure there had been no gate there then. Still he hadn't time to worry about little things like that. He had to move quickly. It wasn't easy. The pinetum was dark enough by daylight. At night it was pitch black. Sir Giles shone his torch on the ground and moved forward cautiously grateful to the carpet of pine needles that deadened his footsteps. He was halfway through the wood when he became conscious that he was not alone. Something was breathing nearby.

He switched off his torch and listened. Above him the pine trees sighed in a light breeze and for a moment Sir Giles hoped he had been mistaken. The next moment he knew he hadn't. An extraordinary whistling, wheezing noise issued from the wood. 'Must be a cow with asthma,' he thought though how an asthmatic cow had got into the pinetum he couldn't imagine. A moment later he was disabused of the notion of a cow. With a horrible snort whatever it was got to its feet, a process that involved breaking a number of branches, large branches by the sound of things, and lumbered off with a singlemindedness of purpose that seemed to bring it into contact with a great many trees. Sir Giles stood and quaked, partly from fear and partly because the ground beneath his feet was also quaking, and when finally the creature smashed through the iron fence at the edge of the wood with as little regard for property as for its own health and welfare he was in two minds about going on. In the end he forced himself to continue, though more cautiously. After all, whatever he had disturbed, it *had* run away.

Sir Giles came to the gate and stared at the house. The place was in darkness. He walked quickly across the lawn and round to the front door. Then taking off his shoes he unlocked the door and stepped inside. Silence. He went down the corridor to his study and shut the door. Then he switched on his torch and shone it on the safe – or rather on the hole in the wall where the safe had been. Sir Giles stared at it in horror. No wonder Hoskins had talked so insistently about incinerators and inflammable material and health risks. It hadn't been Dundridge who had been threatening to go to the police. It was Maud. But had she been already? There was no way of telling. He switched off the torch and stood in the darkness thinking. There was certainly one way of ensuring that if she hadn't been already she wasn't going to in future. Any doubts he had had, and they were few, about the wisdom of disposing of Handyman Hall and Maud disappeared. He would make certain of the bitch. He opened the door of the study and listened for a moment before tiptoeing down the passage towards the kitchen. Kitchens were the logical place for fires to start of their own accord and besides there were the oil tanks that fed the Aga cooker. On the way he stopped to put on his Wellington boots in the cloakroom under the stairs.

•

The twang of the iron fence woke Lady Maud. She sat up in bed and wondered what it portended. Iron fences didn't twang of their own accord and rhinoceroses didn't go charging across rockeries in the small hours of the morning without good reason. She switched on the bedside lamp to see what time it was but thanks to the power failure at Guildstead Carbonell the light didn't come on. Peculiar. She got out of bed and went to the window and was just in time to see a shadow slip across the lawn and disappear round the side of the house. It was a distinctly furtive shadow and it came from the pinetum. For a moment she supposed it to be Blott, but there was no reason for Blott to be running furtively about the park at ... she looked at her watch ... half past two in the morning. Anyway she could always check. She picked up the phone and dialled the Lodge.

'Blott,' she whispered, 'are you there?'

'Yes,' said Blott.

'Are the gates locked?'

'Yes,' said Blott, 'why?'

'I just wanted to make sure.' She put the phone down gently and got dressed. Then she went downstairs quietly and tried the front door. It was unlocked. Lady Maud looked around. A pair of shoes on the doorstep. She picked them up and sniffed. Giles. Unmistakably Giles. Then she put the shoes down again and shutting the front door behind her went round to the workshop. So the little beast had come back. She could imagine what for. Well, come back he might but he wouldn't get away so easily. A moment later she was running, remarkably swiftly for so large a woman and so dark a night, across the lawn towards the pinetum. Even there in the pitch darkness her pace did not slacken. A life-time's familiarity with the path gave her an unerring sense of when to twist or turn through the trees. Five minutes later she was at the gate to the footbridge. She reached into her pocket and took out a large lock, fitted it to the bolt and closed the hasp. Then, having tested it to see that it was firmly fastened, she turned and made her way back towards the Hall.

•

In the kitchen Sir Giles took his time. The essence of successful arson lay in simplicity, and murder was best when it looked like natural death. The Aga cooker was self-igniting. It came on automatically at intervals during the night. Sir Giles shone his torch on the time switch and saw that it was set for four o'clock. Plenty of time. He took an adjustable spanner out of his pocket and undid the nut that secured the feedpipe from the oil tanks to the stove. Oil began to pour out over the floor. Sir Giles sat down on a chair and listened to it. It slurped out steadily and spread under the table. Presently it would begin to run down the passage into the hall. There were a thousand gallons of heating oil in those tanks and as Sir Giles knew they had recently been filled. He would wait until they were empty and then replace the feedpipe but not tightly. To the police and the insurance investigators it would look as though there had been a simple leak. Yes, a thousand gallons of heating oil would certainly do the trick. Handyman Hall would turn into a raging furnace in seconds. The fire brigade would take at least half an hour to come from Worford and by that time the place would be in ashes. So would Maud. Sir Giles knew her too well to suppose that she would be sensible enough to jump from her bedroom window even if she had time. She might not even wake before the flames reached the first floor and if she did her first thought would be to rush out on to the landing and try to save her precious family home. It would be Blott in the Lodge who would raise the alarm. It was a pity about Blott. Sir Giles would have liked him to be cremated too.

•

Outside in the garden Lady Maud stood looking at the house.

Giles had come back to look for the negatives of the pictures they had taken of him. Well, he was hardly likely to find them. Blott had cut them into strips of six and had taken them back to the Lodge with him. Or perhaps he had come to get those photographs from his safe. He was going to be disappointed there too. Whichever way she looked at it he was going to be in for a nasty surprise. She went round to the front door and picked up his shoes. It might not be a bad idea to remove those while she was about it. She took them round to the garage and put them in an empty bucket and she was just coming out again when it struck her that there might be a more sinister purpose in Giles' visit. Six years of cohabitation with the brute had taught her that he was as ruthless as he was devious. It would pay her to be careful.

'I had better watch my step,' she thought, and went round to the kitchen door. She was just about to unlock it when she stepped in something slippery. She steadied herself and reached down. Oil. It was seeping out from under the kitchen door and down the steps into the yard. A moment later she understood the purpose of his visit. He was going to burn the Hall. By God, he wasn't. With a howl of rage Lady Maud hurled herself at the door, unlocked it and charged into the kitchen. For a moment she remained upright, the next she was flat on her back and sliding across the floor. So was Sir Giles though in a different direction. As Lady Maud's great bulk swept under him carrying his chair with her, Sir Giles catapulted through the air, landed on his face and slid irresistibly down the corridor and across the marble floor of the great hall. As he floundered about trying to get to his feet in a sea of oil he could hear Maud ricocheting about the kitchen. By the sound of things she had been joined by the entire complement of pots, pans, and kitchen utensils. Sir Giles slithered to the front door and managed to get to his feet on the mat. He grasped the handle and tried to turn it. The fucking thing wouldn't turn. He groped in his pocket for a handkerchief and wiped his hands and the doorknob and an instant later he was outside and reaching for his shoes. The bloody things weren't there.

There wasn't time to look for them. Behind him Maud had finally overcome the combined forces of grease and gravity and was coming down the passage promising to strangle him with her own bare hands. Sir Giles waited no longer. He galumphed off in his gumboots down the drive and across the lawn towards the pinetum. Behind him Lady Maud slithered into the downstairs lavatory and emerged with a shotgun. She went to the front door and opened it. Sir Giles was still visible across the lawn. Lady Maud raised the gun and fired. He was out of range but at least she had the satisfaction of knowing that he wouldn't come near the house again in a hurry. She put the gun back and began to clean up the mess.

23

In the Lodge Blott heard the shot and leapt out of bed. Lady Maud's telephone call had disturbed him. Why should she want to know if the gates were locked? And why had she whispered? Something was up. And with the sound of the shotgun Blott was certain. He dressed and went downstairs with his twelve-bore to the Land-Rover which he had parked just inside the archway. Before getting in he checked the lock on the gate. It was quite secure. Then he drove off up to the Hall and parked outside the front door and went inside.

'It's me, Blott,' he called into the darkness. 'Are you all right?'

From the kitchen there came the sound of someone sliding about and a muffled curse.

'Don't move,' Lady Maud shouted. 'There's oil everywhere.'

'Oil?' said Blott. Now that he came to think of it there was a stench of oil in the house.

'He's tried to burn the house down.'

Blott stared into the darkness and promised that if he got the chance he would kill him. 'The bastard,' he muttered. Lady Maud slithered down the passage with a squeegee.

'Now listen carefully, Blott,' she said. 'I want you to do something for me.'

'Anything,' said Blott gallantly.

'He came in through the pinetum. I've locked the gate there so he can't get out but his car must be up at Wilfrid's Castle. I want you to drive round there and remove the dis . . . the thing that goes round.'

'The rotor arm,' said Blott.

'Right,' said Lady Maud. 'And while you are about it you might as well put extra locks on both the gates. We must make quite sure that innocent people don't get into the park. Do you understand?'

Blott smiled in the darkness. He understood.

'I'll take the rotor arm off the Land-Rover too,' he said.

'A wise precaution,' Lady Maud agreed. 'And when you have finished come back here. I don't think he'll return tonight but it might be as well to take precautions.'

Blott turned to the door.

'There's just one other thing,' said Lady Maud. 'I don't think we'll feed the lions in the morning. They'll just have to fend for themselves for a day or two.'

'I didn't intend to,' said Blott and went outside.

Lady Maud sighed happily. It was so nice to have a real man about the house.

•

At Finch Grove Ivy Bullett-Finch's feelings were quite the reverse. What was left of the house seemed to be about the man and in any case what was left of Mr Bullett-Finch was real only in a material sense. He had died, as he had lived, concerned for the welfare of his lawn. Dundridge arrived with the Chief Constable in time to pay his last respects. As firemen carried her husband's remains out of the cellar, Mrs Bullett-Finch, relieved of the burden of guilt about the oven, vented her feelings on the Controller Motorways Midlands.

'You murderer,' she screamed, 'you killed him. You killed him with your awful ball.' She was led away by a policewoman. Dundridge looked balefully at the ball and crane.

'Nonsense,' he said, 'I had nothing to do with it.'

'We have been led to understand by your deputy, Mr Hoskins, that you gave orders for random sorties to be made by task forces of demolition experts,' said the Chief Constable. 'It would rather appear that they've carried out your instructions to the letter.'

'My instructions?' said Dundridge. 'I gave no instructions for this house to be demolished. Why should I?'

'We were rather hoping you would be able to tell us,' said the Chief Constable.

'But it's not even scheduled for demolition.'

'Quite. Nor to the best of my knowledge was the High Street. But since your equipment was used in both cases—'

'It's not my equipment,' shouted Dundridge, 'it belongs to the contractors. If anyone is fucking responsible—'

'I'd be glad if you didn't use offensive language,' said the Chief Constable. 'The situation is unpleasant enough as it is. Local feeling is running high. I think it would be best if you accompanied us to the station.'

'The station? Do you mean the police station?' said Dundridge.

'It's just for your own protection,' said the Chief Constable. 'We don't want any more accidents tonight, now do we?'

'This is monstrous,' said Dundridge.

'Quite so,' said the Chief Constable. 'And now if you'll just step this way.'

•

As the police car wound its way slowly through the rubble that littered the High Street, Dundridge could see that Hoskins had been telling the truth when he called Guildstead Carbonell a disaster area. The transformer still smouldered in the grey dawn, the Primitive Methodist Chapel lived up to at least part of its name, while the horribly mis-shapen relics of a dozen cars crouched beside the glass-strewn pavement. What the iron ball hadn't done with the aid of the telegraph pole to end Guild-stead Carbonell's reputation for old-world charm, the conflagration at Mr Dugdale's garage had. Ignited by some un-identifiable public-spirited person who had brought out a paraffin lamp to warn passers-by to watch out for the debris, the blast from the petrol storage tanks had blown in what few windows remained unbroken after Blott's passing and had set fire to the thatched roofs of several delightful cottages. The fire had spread to a row of almshouses. The simultaneous arrival of fire engines from Worford and Ottertown had added to the chaos. Working with high-pressure hoses in total darkness they had swept a number of inadequately clothed old-age pensioners who had escaped from the almshouses down the street before turning their attention to the Public Library which they had filled with foam. To Dundridge, staring miserably out of the window of the police car, the knowledge that he was held responsible for the catastrophe was intolerable. He wished now that he had never set eyes on South Worfordshire.

'I must have been mad to have come up here,' he thought.

The same thought had already occurred to Sir Giles though in his case the madness he had in mind was in no way meta-phorical. As dawn broke over the Park, Sir Giles wrestled with the lock on the gate to the footbridge and tried to imagine how it had got there. It had not been on the gate when he arrived. He wouldn't have been able to enter if it had. But if the exist-ence of the lock was bad enough, that of the fence was worse and it certainly hadn't been there when he had last been at the Hall. It was an extremely high fence with large metal brackets at the top and four strands of heavy barbed-wire overhanging the Park so that it was evidently designed to stop people get-ting out rather than trespassers getting in.

It was at this point that Sir Giles gave up the struggle with the lock and decided to look for some other way out. He fol-lowed the fence along the edge of the pinetum and was about to clamber over the iron railings when the sense of unreality that had come over him with the sudden appearance of a large lock where no lock had previously been took a decided turn for the worse. Against the grey dawn sky he saw a head, a small head with a long nose and knobs on it. Below the head there was a neck, a long neck, a very long neck indeed. Sir Giles shut his eyes and hoped to hell that when he opened them he wouldn't see what he thought he had seen. He opened them but the giraffe was still there. 'Oh my God,' he murmured and was about to move away when his eye caught sight of something even more terrifying. In the long grass fifty yards behind the giraffe there was another face, a large face with a mane and whiskers.

Sir Giles gave up all thought of looking for a way out in that direction. He turned and stumbled back into the pinetum. Either he had gone mad or he was in the middle of some fucking zoo. Giraffes? Lions? And what the hell was it that he had almost stumbled across during the night? An elephant? He got back to the gate and looked at the lock hopefully. But instead of one lock there were now two and the second was even larger than the first. He was just trying to think what this meant when he heard a noise on the path across the river. Sir Giles looked up. Blott was standing there with a shotgun, smiling down at him. It was a horrible smile, a smile of quiet satisfaction. Sir Giles turned and ran into the pinetum. He knew death when he saw it.

•

By the time Blott got back to the Hall Lady Maud was down and making breakfast in the kitchen.

'What took you so long?' she asked.

'I moved the Bentley,' Blott told her. 'I brought it round and put it in the garage. I thought it would look more natural.'

Lady Maud nodded. 'You are probably right,' she said. 'People might have started asking questions if they found it left up by the church. Besides if he did get out he might have telephoned the AA for assistance.'

'He isn't going to get out,' said Blott, 'I saw him. He's in the pinetum.'

'Well it's his own fault. He came up here to burn the house down and whatever happens now he has only himself to blame.' She handed Blott a plate of cereal. 'I'm afraid I can't give you a cooked breakfast. The electricity has been cut off. I telephoned the electricity office in Worford but they say there has been a power failure.'

Blott ate his cereal in silence. There didn't seem much point in telling her about his part in the power failure and besides she seemed in a talkative mood herself.

'The trouble with Giles was,' she said using the past tense in a way that Blott found most agreeable, 'that he liked to think of himself as a self-made man. I have always thought it an extremely presumptuous phrase and in his case particularly inappropriate. I suppose he had some right to call himself a man, though from my experience of him I wouldn't have said virility was his strong point, but as for being self-made, he was nothing of the kind. He made his money, and of course that's what he meant by self, by speculating in property, by evicting people from their homes and by obtaining planning permission to put up office blocks. At least my family made its money selling beer, and very good beer at that. And it took them generations to do it. There's nothing so splendid about that but at least they were honest men.' She was still talking and doing the washing-up when Blott left to go out to the kitchen garden.

'Is there anything else you want done about him?' he asked as he left.

Lady Maud shook her head. 'I think we can just leave nature to take its course,' she told him. 'He was a great believer in the law of the jungle.'

•

In Worford Police Station Dundridge was having difficulty with the law of the land. Hoskins had been no great help.

'According to him,' said the Superintendent in charge of the case, 'you gave specific orders for random sorties to be made by bulldozers on various properties. Now you say you didn't.'

'I was speaking figuratively,' Dundridge explained. 'I certainly didn't give any instructions that could lead anyone but a complete idiot to suppose that I wanted the late Mr Bullett-Finch's house demolished.'

'Nevertheless it was demolished.'

'By some lunatic. You don't seriously imagine I went out there and smashed the house up myself?'

'If you'll just keep calm, sir,' said the Superintendent, 'all I am trying to do is to establish the chain of circumstances that led up to this murder.'

'Murder?' mumbled Dundridge.

'You're not claiming it was an accident, are you? A person or persons unknown deliberately take a large crane and use it to pulverize a house in which two innocent people are sleeping. You can call that all sorts of things but not an accident. No sir, we are treating this as a case of murder.'

Dundridge thought for a moment. 'If that's the case there must have been a motive. Have you given any thought to that?'

'I'm glad you mentioned motive, sir,' said the Superintendent. 'Now I understand that Mr Bullett-Finch was an active member of the Save the Gorge Committee. Would you say that your relations with him were marked by an unusual degree of animosity?'

'Relations?' shouted Dundridge. 'I didn't have any relations with him. I never met the man in my life.'

'But you did speak to him over the telephone on a number of occasions.'

'I may have done,' said Dundridge. 'I seem to remember his phoning once to complain about something or other.'

'Would that have been the occasion on which you told him that quote "If you don't stop pestering me I'll see to it that you'll lose a bloody sight more than a quarter of an acre of your bleeding garden" unquote?'

'Who told you that?' snarled Dundridge.

'The identity of our informant is irrelevant, sir. The question is did you or did you not say that.'

'I may have done,' Dundridge admitted, promising himself that he would make Hoskins' life difficult for him in future.

'And wouldn't you agree that the late Mr Bullett-Finch has in fact lost more than a quarter of an acre of his bleeding garden?'

Dundridge had to admit that he had.

As the morning wore on the Controller Motorways Midlands had the definite impression that a trap was closing in around him.

•

In Sir Giles' case there was the absolute conviction. His attempts to scale the wire fence had failed miserably. Oily gumboots were not ideal for the purpose and Sir Giles' physical activities had been of too passive a nature to prepare him at all adequately for scrambling up wire mesh or coping with barbed-wire overhangs. What he needed was a ladder, but his only attempt to leave the pinetum to look for one had been foiled by the sight of a rhinoceros browsing in the rockery and of a lion sunning itself outside the kitchen door. Sir Giles stuck to the pinetum and waited for an opportunity. He waited a long time.

By three o'clock in the afternoon he was exceedingly hungry. So were the lions. From the lower branches of a tree overlooking the park Sir Giles watched as four lionesses stalked a giraffe, one moving upwind while the other three lay in the grass downwind. The giraffe moved off and a moment later was thrashing around in its death throes. From his eyrie Sir Giles watched in horror as the lionesses finished it off and were presently joined by the lions. Stifling his disgust and fear Sir Giles climbed down from the branch. This was his opportunity. Ignoring the rhinoceros which had its back to him he raced across the lawn towards the house as fast as his gumboots would allow. He reached the terrace and hurried round past the conservatory where Lady Maud was watering a castor-oil plant. As he ran past she looked up and for a moment he had an impulse to stop and beg her to let him in but the look on her face was enough to tell him he would be wasting his time. It expressed an indifference to his fate, almost an ignorance of his existence, which was in its way even more frightening than Blott's terrible smile. As far as Maud was concerned he simply wasn't there. She had married him to save the Hall and preserve the family. And now she was prepared to murder him by proxy for the same purpose. Sir Giles had no doubt about that.

He ran on into the yard and opened the garage door. Inside stood the Bentley. He could get away at last. He pushed the doors back and got into the car. The keys were still in the ignition. He turned them and the starter whirred. He tried again but the car wouldn't start.

•

In the kitchen garden Blott listened to the engine turning over. He was wasting his time. He could go on till Doomsday and the car wouldn't start. Blott had no sympathy for him. 'Nature must take its course,' Lady Maud had said and Blott agreed. Sir Giles meant nothing to him. He was like the pests in the garden, the slugs or the greenfly. No that wasn't true. He was worse. He was a traitor to the England that Blott revered, the old England, the upstanding England, the England that had carved an Empire by foolhardiness and accident, the England that had built this garden and planted the great oaks and elms not for its own immediate satisfaction but for the future. What had Sir Giles done for the future? Nothing. He had desecrated the past and betrayed the future. He deserved to die. Blott took his shotgun and went round to the garage.

•

Lady Maud in the conservatory was having second thoughts. The look on Sir Giles' face as he hesitated outside had awakened a slight feeling of pity in her. The man was afraid, desperately afraid, and Lady Maud had no time for cruelty. It was one thing to talk in the abstract about the law of the jungle, but it was another to participate in it.

'He's learnt his lesson by now,' she thought, 'I had better let him go.' And she was about to go out and look for him when the phone rang. It was General Burnett.

'It's about this business of poor old Bertie,' said the General. 'The committee would like to come over and have a chat with you.'

'Bertie?' said Lady Maud. 'Bertie Bullett-Finch?'

'You know he's dead, of course,' said the General.

'Dead?' said Lady Maud. 'I had no idea. When did this happen?'

'Last night. House was knocked down by the motorway swine. Bertie was inside at the time.'

Lady Maud sat down, stunned by the news. 'How absolutely dreadful. Do they know who did it?'

'They've taken that fellow Dundridge in for questioning,' said the General. Lady Maud could think of nothing to say. 'Knocked half Guildstead down too. The Colonel and I thought we ought to come over and have a talk to you about it. Puts a very different complexion on the whole business of the motorway, don't you know.'

'Of course,' said Lady Maud. 'Come over at once.' She put the phone down and tried to imagine what had happened. Dundridge taken in for questioning. Mr Bullett-Finch dead. Finch Grove demolished. Guildstead Carbonell . . . It was such astonishing news that it drove all thoughts of Giles from her mind.

'I must phone poor dear Ivy,' she muttered and dialled Finch Grove. Not surprisingly, she got no reply.

•

In the garage Sir Giles was doing his best to persuade Blott to stop pointing the twelve-bore at his chest.

'Five thousand pounds,' he said. 'Five thousand pounds. All you've got to do is open the gates.'

'You get out of here,' said Blott.

'What do you think I want to do? Stay here?'

'Out of the garage,' said Blott.

'Ten thousand. Twenty thousand. Anything you ask . . .'

'I'll count to ten,' said Blott. 'One.'

'Fifty thousand pounds.'

'Two,' said Blott.

'A hundred thousand. You can't ask better than that.'

'Three,' said Blott.

'I'll make it—'

'Four,' said Blott.

Sir Giles turned and ran. There was no mistaking the look on Blott's face. Sir Giles stumbled round the house and across the lawn to the pinetum. He scrambled over the iron railings and climbed back into his tree. The lions had finished the giraffe and were licking their paws and wiping their whiskers. Sir Giles wiped the sweat off his face with an oily handkerchief and tried to think what to do next.

•

Dundridge was saved that trouble by the discovery of an empty vodka bottle in the cab of the crane and by eye-witnesses who testified that one of the two men seen driving the crane up the High Street had been singing bawdy songs and was very clearly intoxicated.

'There seems to have been some mistake,' the Super-intendent told him apologetically. 'You're free to go.'

'But you told me you were treating the case as one of murder,' shouted Dundridge indignantly. 'Now you turn round and say it was simply drunken driving.'

'Murder in my view implies premeditation,' explained the Superintendent. 'Now, two blokes go out and have one too many. They get a bit merry and pinch a crane and knock a few houses down, well you can't feel the same about it, can you? There's no premeditation there. Just a bit of fun, that's all. Now I'm not saying I approve. Don't get me wrong. I'm as hard on vandalism and drunkenness as the next man, but there are mitigating circumstances to be taken into account.'

Dundridge left the police station unconvinced, and as far as Hoskins' behaviour was concerned he could find no mitigating circumstances whatsoever.

'You deliberately led the police to believe that I had given orders for the Bullett-Finches' house to be demolished,' he shouted at him in the Mobile HQ. 'You gave them to under-stand that I set out to murder Mr Bullett-Finch.'

'I only told them that you had had a row with him on the phone. I'd have said the same thing about Lady Maud if they had asked me,' Hoskins protested.

'Lady Maud doesn't happen to have been murdered,' yelled Dundridge. 'Nor does General Burnett or the Colonel and I've had rows with them too. I suppose if any of them get run over by a bus or die of food poisoning you'll tell the police I'm responsible.'

Hoskins said he didn't think that was being fair.

'Fair,' yelled Dundridge, 'fair? Now you just listen to what I've had to put up with since I've been up here. I've been threatened. I've been given doctored drinks. I've been . . . Well never mind about that. I've been shot at. I've been subject to abuse. I've had my car tyres slashed. I've been accused of murder and you have the fucking gall to stand there and talk to me about fairness. My God, I've fought clean up to now but not any longer. From now on anything goes and the first thing to go is you. Get out of here and don't come back.'

'There's just one thing I think I ought to know,' said Hoskins edging towards the door. 'You've got a new problem on your hands. Lady Maud Lynchwood is opening a Wildlife Park at Handyman Hall on Sunday.'

Dundridge sat down slowly and stared at him.

'She is what?'

Hoskins edged back into the office. 'Opening a Wildlife Park. She's had the whole place wired in and she's got lions and rhinoceroses and . . .'

'But she can't do that. She's had a compulsory purchase order served on her,' said Dundridge stunned by this latest example of opposition.

'She's done it all the same,' said Hoskins. 'There are signs up along the Ottertown Road and there was an advertisement in last night's *Worford Advertiser*. I've got a copy here.' He went through to his office and returned with a full-page advertisement announcing Open Day at Handyman Hall Wildlife Park. 'What are you going to do about that?'

Dundridge reached for the phone. 'I'm going to get on to the legal department and tell them to apply for an injunction to stop her,' he said. 'In the meantime you can see that work resumes in the Gorge immediately.'

'Don't you think we should hold off for a day or two,' said Hoskins, 'and wait for this fuss over the Bullett-Finches' house and Guildstead Carbonell to die down a bit.'

'Certainly not,' said Dundridge. 'If the police choose to

regard the whole thing as a trivial matter, I see no reason why we shouldn't. Work will proceed as before. If anything, faster.'

24

At Handyman Hall what was left of the Save the Gorge Committee met in the sitting-room lamenting the passing of Mr Bullett-Finch and seeking to take advantage from his sacrifice.

'The whole thing is an outrage against humanity,' said Colonel Chapman. 'A more inoffensive fellow than poor old Bertie you couldn't imagine. Never a harsh word from him.'

Lady Maud could remember several harsh words from Mr Bullett-Finch when she had taken the liberty of walking across his lawn, but she kept her thoughts to herself. Whatever his faults in life, Mr Bullett-Finch dead had been canonized. General Burnett put her thoughts into words.

'Terrible way to go,' he said, 'having a dashed great iron ball smash you to smithereens like that. Rather like a gigantic cannonball.'

'He probably didn't feel a thing,' said Colonel Chapman. 'It was late at night and he was in bed . . .'

'He wasn't you know. They found him in his dressing-gown. Must have heard it coming.'

'In the midst of life we are . . .' Miss Percival began but Lady Maud interrupted her.

'There is no point in dwelling on the past,' she said. 'We must concentrate our mind on the future. I have invited Ivy to come and stay here.'

'I rather doubt if she will accept,' said Colonel Chapman looking nervously out of the window. 'Her nerves were never up to much and this latest shock hasn't done them any good and those lions . . .'

'Nonsense,' said Lady Maud briskly. 'Perfectly harmless

creatures provided you know how to handle them. The main thing is to show you're not afraid of them. The moment they smell fear they become dangerous.'

'I'm sure I'd be no good at all,' said Miss Percival. General Burnett nodded.

'I remember once in the Punjab . . .' he began.

'I think we should keep to the matter in hand,' said Lady Maud. 'Much as I regret what has happened to poor Mr Bullett-Finch and indeed to Guildstead Carbonell, there is this to be said for it, it does put us all in a much stronger position vis-à-vis the Ministry of the Environment and this infernal motorway. I think you said, General, that the police were questioning that man Dundridge.'

General Burnett shook his head. 'The Chief Constable has been keeping me abreast of events,' he said. 'I'm afraid they've dropped that line of enquiry. It appears that there was some sort of shindig at the Royal George last night. Seems they're working on the theory that a couple of navvies had a bit too much beer and . . .'

'Beer?' said Lady Maud with a strange look on her face. 'Did I hear you say "Beer"?'

'My dear lady,' said the General apologetically, 'I only mentioned beer because I believe that is what these fellows drink. I wasn't for one moment imputing . . .'

'As a matter of fact I believe it was vodka,' said Colonel Chapman tactfully. 'In fact I'm sure it was. They found a bottle.'

But the damage had already been done. Lady Maud was looking quite distraught.

•

In the pinetum Sir Giles was desperately trying to make up his mind. From his tree he had watched General Burnett and Colonel Chapman and Miss Percival arrive. They had come in one car – Miss Percival had left her car outside the main gates and had joined the General in his – and their coming seemed to offer Sir Giles an opportunity to escape if only he could reach the house. Maud could hardly shoot him down in cold blood in front of her neighbours. There might be a nasty scene. She might accuse him of arson, of blackmail and bribery. She might expose him to ridicule but he was prepared to run these risks to get out of the Park alive. On the other hand he wasn't sure that he was prepared to run the gauntlet of the lions who had sauntered away from their last meal and were lying about on the lawn in front of the terrace. Then again he was now extremely hungry and the lions on the contrary weren't. They had just eaten their fill of giraffe.

At least Sir Giles hoped they had. It was a risk he had to take. If he stayed in the tree he would starve to death and sooner or later he would have to come down. Better sooner, he thought, than later. Sir Giles climbed down and got over the railings. Perhaps if he walked confidently . . . He didn't feel confident. He hesitated and then moved cautiously forward. If only he could reach the terrace. And as he moved across the grass he was conscious that he was increasing the distance between himself and the safety of the tree while decreasing that between himself and the lions. He reached the point of no return.

•

In the sitting-room General Burnett was lamenting Sir Giles' absence. 'I've tried ringing his flat in London and his office but nobody seems to know where he's got to,' he said. 'If only we could get in touch with him, I'm convinced we could bring pressure to bear on the Minister to call a halt to the motorway. I'm the last one to complain, but it's at a time like this that a constituency needs its MP.'

'I'm afraid my husband tends to let his business interests get in the way of his Parliamentary duties,' Lady Maud agreed.

'Of course, of course,' said Colonel Chapman. 'He's bound to have a lot of irons in the fire. Wouldn't have got where he has if he hadn't.'

'I think . . .' said Miss Percival nervously staring out of the window.

'All I'm saying is that it's about time he made his presence felt,' said the General.

'I really do think you ought to . . .' Miss Percival began.

'It's at times like this he ought to raise his voice . . . Good God! What the hell was that?'

There was a ghastly scream from the garden.

'I think it was Sir Giles raising his voice,' said Miss Percival, and fainted. The General and Colonel Chapman turned and looked out of the window in horror. Sir Giles was visible for a moment and then he disappeared beneath a lion. Lady Maud seized a poker and opened the french windows.

'How dare you?' she shouted charging across the terrace. 'Shoo, Shoo.'

But it was too late. The General and Colonel Chapman rushed out and dragged her back still waving the poker and shooing.

•

'Damned plucky little woman,' said the General as they drove home. Colonel Chapman said nothing. He was trying to rid his mind of the memory of those gumboots, and besides, he found the General's description of Lady Maud a little inappropriate even in these distressing circumstances. His left ear was still ringing from the blow she had given him for telling her she mustn't blame herself for what had happened.

'Mind you, I'm afraid it's put an end to the Wildlife Park,' continued the General. 'Pity really.'

'It's also put an end to Sir Giles,' said Colonel Chapman, who felt that General Burnett was taking the whole affair too calmly.

'There is that to be said for it,' said the General. 'Never could stomach the fellow.'

In the back seat Miss Percival fainted for the sixth time.

•

At Handyman Hall the Superintendent explained to Lady Maud as tactfully as possible that there would have to be a coroner's inquest.

'An inquest? But it's perfectly obvious what happened. General Burnett and Colonel Chapman were here.'

'Just a formality, I assure you,' said the Superintendent. 'And now I'll be getting along.'

He went out to his car with the gumboots and drove off. In the Park the lions were licking their paws and wiping their whiskers. Lady Maud stared out of the window at them. They would have to go of course. Sir Giles might not have been a nice man but Lady Maud's sense of social propriety wouldn't allow her to keep animals that couldn't be trusted not to eat people. And then there was Blott. Blott and the events of the previous evening in Guildstead Carbonell. It was all too obvious what he had wanted Very Special for and it was all her fault. And to think she had invited Ivy Bullett-Finch to come and stay. Well, at least she had a good excuse for cancelling the invitation now. She went through the kitchen and was about to go out when it occurred to her that having tasted human flesh once the lions might not succumb quite so readily to her fearlessness. She ought really to carry some sort of weapon. Lady Maud hesitated and then went on regardless. She owed it to her conscience to take some risks. She went down the path and into the kitchen garden.

'Blott,' she said, 'I want a word with you. Do you realize what you have done?'

Blott shrugged. 'He got what was coming to him,' he said.

'I'm not talking about him,' said Lady Maud, 'I'm talking about Mr Bullett-Finch.'

'What about him?'

'He's dead. He was killed last night when his house was demolished.'

Blott took off his hat and scratched his head. 'That's a pity,' he said thoughtfully.

'A pity? Is that all you've got to say?' said Lady Maud sternly.

'I don't know what else I can say. I didn't know he was in the house any more than you knew he was going to go and get eaten by those lions.' He picked a caterpillar off a cabbage and squashed it absent-mindedly.

'I must say if I had known what you were going to do I would never have given you the day off,' said Lady Maud and went back into the house.

Blott went on with his weeding. Women were odd things, he thought. You did what they wanted and all the thanks you got for it was a telling off. A telling off. That was an odd expression too, come to think of it. But then the world was full of mysteries.

•

In London Mrs Forthby woke with a vague sense that something was missing. She rolled over in bed, switched on the light and looked at the clock. It said eleven forty-eight and since it was dark it must be nearly midnight. On the other hand it didn't feel like midnight. She felt as though she had been asleep a lot longer than four hours, and where was Giles? She got out of bed and looked in the kitchen, the bathroom, but he wasn't in the flat. Oh well, he had probably gone out. She went back to the kitchen and made herself some tea. She was feeling very hungry too. That was strange because she had had a big dinner. She made some toast and boiled an egg. And all the time she had the nagging feeling that something was wrong. She had gone to bed at eight o'clock and here she was at midnight wide awake and famished. To while away the time she picked up a book but she didn't feel like reading. She turned on the radio and caught the news headlines. '. . . Lynchwood, Member of Parliament for South Worfordshire, who was killed at his home Handyman Hall near Worford by a lion. In Arizona a freak whirlwind destroyed . . .' Mrs Forthby switched off the radio and poured herself another cup of tea before remembering what the announcer had just said. 'Oh dear,' she said, 'this afternoon? But . . .' She went through to the sitting-room and looked at the date on the clock. It read Friday the 20th. But yesterday was Wednesday. Giles had said so. She had said it was Tuesday and he had said Wednesday. And now it was Friday morning and Giles had been killed by a lion. What was a lion doing at Handyman Hall? What was Sir Giles doing there, come to that? They had been going to Brighton together for the weekend. It was all too awfully perplexing and horrible. It couldn't be true. Mrs Forthby dialled the nice lady who told the time. 'At the third stroke it will be twelve ten and twenty seconds.'

'But what's the date? What day is it?' Mrs Forthby asked.

'At the third stroke it will be twelve ten and thirty seconds.'

'Oh dear, you really aren't being very helpful,' said Mrs Forthby, and began to cry. Giles hadn't been a very nice man but she had been fond of him and it was all her fault.

'If I hadn't been so forgetful and had remembered to wake up he would still be alive,' she murmured.

•

At his Mobile HQ Dundridge greeted the news next morning jubilantly.

'That'll teach the stupid bitch to build a bloody Wildlife Park,' he told Hoskins.

'I don't see how you can say that,' said Hoskins. 'All it's done is to create another vacancy in Parliament. There will have to be a bye-election and you know what happened last time.'

'All the more reason for pressing ahead as quickly as possible.'

'What? With Maud Lynchwood in mourning? The poor woman has just lost her husband under the most tragic circumstances and you—'

'Don't give me that bull,' said Dundridge. 'If you ask me she's probably delighted. Wouldn't surprise me to learn she'd arranged the whole thing just to stop us.'

'That's bloody libel, that is,' said Hoskins. 'She may be a bit of a tartar but . . .'

'Listen,' said Dundridge, 'she didn't give a tuppenny damn about her husband, I know.'

'You know?'

'Yes I do know as a matter of fact. I'll tell you something. That old cow tried to seduce me one night and when I wouldn't play ball she took a potshot at me with a twelve-bore. So don't come that crap about a sorrowing widow. We're going ahead, and fast.'

'Well all I can say is that you're flying in the face of public opinion,' said Hoskins, stunned by Dundridge's story of his attempted seduction. 'There's Bullett-Finch dead and now Sir Giles. There's bound to be a public outcry. I should have thought now was the time to lie doggo.'

'Now is the time to establish ourselves at the Park itself,' said Dundridge. 'I'm going to move two bulldozers and a base camp up by that arch of hers. If she wants to squawk let her squawk.'

•

But Lady Maud didn't squawk. She had been more shocked by Sir Giles' death than she would have expected and she felt personally responsible for what had happened to Mr Bullett-Finch. She went about her duties automatically but with an abstracted air, occupied with the moral dilemma in which she found herself. On the one hand she was faced with the destruction of everything she loved, the Hall, the Gorge, the wild landscape, the garden, the world her ancestors had fought for and created. All this would go, to be replaced by a motorway which would be a useless, obsolescent eyesore in fifty years when fossil fuel ran out. It wasn't as if the motorway was needed. It had been concocted by Giles to make himself a paltry sum of money, a mean, cruel gesture to hurt her. Well Giles had got his comeuppance but the legacy of the motorway remained and the methods she had had to use had degraded her. She had fought fire with fire and other people had been burnt, Bertie Bullett-Finch and — quite literally — the poor man who had put the paraffin lamp in front of Mr Dugdale's garage.

It was in this mood of self-recrimination that she attended the coroner's inquest which returned a verdict of accidental death on Sir Giles Lynchwood and commended his widow on her bravery while pointing out the unforeseen dangers of keeping undomesticated animals on domestic premises. It was in the same mood that she superintended the removal of the lions, the last giraffe and the ostriches, before going off to a Memorial Service at Worford Abbey. All this time she avoided Blott, who stuck to the kitchen garden in low dudgeon. It was only when, on her return from the Abbey, she saw the bulldozers parked near the iron suspension bridge opposite the Lodge that she felt a pang of remorse for the way she had upbraided him. She found him sulking among the blackcurrants.

'Blott, I'm sorry,' she said. 'I feel I owe you an apology. We all make mistakes from time to time and I've come to say how grateful I am to you for all the sacrifices you've made on my behalf.'

Blott blushed under his tanned complexion. 'It was nothing,' he mumbled.

'That's just not true,' said Lady Maud graciously, 'I don't know how I would have managed without you.'

'You don't have to thank me,' said Blott.

'I just wanted you to know that I appreciate it,' said Lady Maud. 'By the way as I came in I noticed the bulldozers by the Lodge ...'

'You want them stopped, I suppose?'

'Well, now that you come to mention it ...' Lady Maud began.

'Leave it to me,' said Blott, 'I'll stop them.'

Lady Maud hesitated. This was the moment of decision. She chose her words carefully.

'I wouldn't like to think that you were going to do anything violent.'

'Violent? Me?' said Blott sounding almost convincingly aggrieved at the suggestion.

'Yes, you,' said Lady Maud. 'Now, I don't mind spending money if it's needed. You can have what you want but I won't have anyone else getting hurt. There's been quite enough of that already.'

'Your forefathers fought for ...'

'I think I'm a rather better authority on what my ancestors did than you are,' said Lady Maud. 'I don't need telling. That was quite different. For one thing they were agents of the Crown and acting within the law and for another the only people to get hurt were the Welsh and they were savages.

Besides, I'm a Justice of the Peace and I can't condone anything illegal. Whatever you do must be lawful.'

'But . . .' began Blott.

Lady Maud interrupted him. 'I don't want to hear any more. What you do is your own affair. I want no part of it.'

She strode away and left Blott to consider her words.

'No violence,' he muttered. It was going to make things a little difficult but he would think of something. Women, even the best of them, were illogical creatures. He walked out of the garden and down the drive to the Lodge. On the far side of the suspension bridge two bulldozers, symbols of Dundridge's task force, stood under the trees. It would have been so easy to disable them with the PIAT or even to put sugar in their fuel tanks but if Maud said he must stay within the law . . . Stay within the law? That was another strange expression. As if the law was some sort of fortress. Blott looked up at the great arch towering above him.

He had just had an idea.

25

In spite of his intention to act swiftly the Controller Motorways Midlands found it difficult to act at all. Work on the motorway came to a virtual standstill while the various authorities responsible for the preservation of Guildstead Carbonell and law and order on the one hand wrangled with those responsible for the construction of the motorway and the destruction of the village on the other. To make matters worse there was a walk-out by dumper drivers who claimed they were being victimized by being barred from the Royal George for the damage done to the bar-billiards table by the clog-dancing of the bulldozer men, and a work-to-rule by the demolition experts who asserted that the arrest of Mr Edwards constituted a threat to their basic rights as Trade Unionists. To end the dispute Dundridge paid for the bar-billiards table out of incidental expenses and interceded with the police to release Mr Edwards on bail pending a psychiatrist's report. In the middle of the confusion he was summoned to London to explain remarks he had made in a television interview filmed in front of the ruins of Finch Grove.

'Couldn't you have thought of something better than "That is the way the cookie crumbles"?' Mr Rees demanded. 'And what in God's name did you mean by "There's many a slip twixt cup and lip"?'

'All I meant was that accidents do happen,' Dundridge explained. 'I was being bombarded with—'

'Bombarded? What do you think we've been since then? How many letters have we had?'

Mr Joynson consulted his list. 'Three thousand four hundred and eighty-two to date, not including postcards.'

'And what about "We all have to make sacrifices"? What sort of impression do you think that makes on three million viewers?' shouted Mr Rees. 'A man living peacefully in a quiet corner of rural England minding his own business is battered to death in the middle of the night by some fucking idiot with an iron ball weighing two tons and you talk about making sacrifices!'

'As a matter of fact he wasn't minding his own business,' Dundridge protested, 'he was continually ringing up to—'

'And I suppose you think that justifies . . . I give up.'

'I think we have to look at it from the point of view of the potential housebuyer,' said Mr Joynson tactfully. 'It's difficult enough for the average wage-earner to get a mortgage these days. We don't want to give people the idea that they run the risk of having their houses demolished without the slightest warning.'

'But the house wasn't even scheduled for demolition,' Mr Rees pointed out.

'Quite,' said Mr Joynson. 'The point I'm trying to make is that Dundridge here must adopt a more tactful approach. He should use persuasion.'

But Dundridge had had enough. 'Persuasion?' he snarled. 'You don't seem to understand what I'm up against. You seem to think all I've got to do is serve a compulsory purchase order and people simply get out of their houses and everything is hunky-dory. Well let me tell you it isn't that simple. I'm supposed to be in charge of building a motorway through a house and park belonging to a woman whose idea of persuasion is to take potshots at me with a twelve-bore.'

'And evidently missing,' sighed Mr Rees.

'Why didn't you inform the police?' Mr Joynson asked more practically.

'The police? She *is* the police,' said Dundridge. 'They eat out of her hand.'

'Like those lions I suppose,' said Mr Rees.

'And what do you think she built that Wildlife Park for?' Dundridge asked.

'I suppose you're going to tell us next that she wanted to find a way of disposing of her husband,' Mr Rees said wearily.

'To stop the motorway. She intended to whip up public support, gain sympathy and generally cause as much confusion as possible.'

'I should have thought she could have safely left that to you,' said Mr Rees.

Dundridge looked at him balefully. It was obvious that he did not enjoy the confidence of his superiors.

'If that's the way you feel I can only resign my position as Controller Motorways Midlands and return to London,' he said. Mr Rees looked at Mr Joynson. This was the ultimatum they had feared. Mr Joynson shook his head.

'My dear Dundridge, there is absolutely no need for you to do that,' said Mr Rees with forced affability. 'All we ask is that you try to avoid any more unfavourable publicity.'

'In that case I look to you to give me your full support,' said Dundridge. 'I can't be expected to overcome the sort of opposition I'm faced with unless the Ministry is prepared to throw its weight behind my efforts.'

'Anything we can do,' said Mr Rees, 'to help, we will certainly do.'

Dundridge left the office mollified and with the feeling that his authority had been enhanced after all.

'Give the swine enough rope and I daresay he'll hang himself,' said Mr Rees when he had gone. 'And frankly I wish Lady Maud the best of British luck.'

'Must be a terrible thing to lose a husband like that,' said Mr Joynson. 'No wonder the poor woman is upset.'

·

But it was less the loss of her husband that was upsetting Lady Maud than the bills she was receiving from various shops in Worford.

'One hundred and fifty tins of frankfurters? One thousand candles? Sixty tons of cement? Two hundred yards of barbed-wire? Forty six-foot reinforcing rods?' she muttered as she went through the bills. 'What on earth can Blott be thinking of?' But she paid the bills without question and kept herself to herself. Whatever Blott was up to she wanted to know as little about it as possible. 'Ignorance is bliss,' she thought, demonstrating a lack of understanding of the law which did her little credit as a magistrate.

·

And Blott was busy. He had spent the lull provided by Dundridge's troubles in preparing his defence. Lady Maud had specified that there must be no violence on his part and as far as he was concerned there would be no necessity for it. The Lodge was practically impregnable to anything short of a full-scale assault by tanks and artillery. He had filled all the rooms on either side of the archway with bits of old iron and cement and had sealed the stairway with concrete. He had covered the roof with sharpened iron rods embedded in concrete and entangled with barbed-wire. To secure an independent water supply he had run a plastic pipe down to the river before the concrete was poured into the rooms below and to ensure that he could withstand a prolonged siege he had laid in enough foodstuffs to last him for two years. If his electricity was cut off he had a thousand candles and several dozen containers of bottled gas and finally, to prevent any attempt to drive him out with tear gas, he had unearthed an old army gas-mask from his cache in the forest. Just in case the mask was no longer proof against the latest gases he had turned his library into an air-tight room to which he could retreat. All in all he had converted the Lodge from a very large ornamental arch into a fortress. The only entrance was through a hatch in the roof under the barbed-wire and spikes, and to enable him to leave when he wanted Blott had constructed a rope ladder which he could let down. Finally and just in case things did get violent he had collected a rifle, a Bren gun, a two-inch mortar, several cases of ammunition and hand-grenades with which to deter boarders. 'Of course, I'll only fire over their heads,' he told himself. But there would be no need. Blott knew the British too well to suppose they would do anything to endanger life. And yet without endangering life, and Blott's life in particular, there was no way of building the motorway on through the Park and Handyman Hall. The Lodge, now Festung Blott, stood directly in the path of the motorway. On either side the cliffs rose steeply. Before anything could be done the Lodge would have to be demolished and since Blott was encased within it, demolishing the arch would mean demolishing him. They couldn't even use dynamite to blast the cliffs on either side without seriously risking his life and threatening the collapse of the arch. Finally to ensure that no one could even drive through the gateway he erected a series of concrete blocks in the middle of the archway. It was this last that forced Lady Maud to ask him what the hell he thought he was doing.

'How do you expect me to do my shopping if I can't drive in and out?' she demanded.

Blott pointed to the Bentley and the Land-Rover parked beside the two bulldozers on the other side of the suspension bridge.

'Good Lord,' said Lady Maud, 'do you mean to say you moved them without my permission?'

'You said you didn't want to know what I was doing so I

didn't tell you,' Blott told her. Lady Maud had to admit the logic of the answer.

'It's going to be very inconvenient,' she said. She looked up at the Lodge. Apart from the spikes and the barbed-wire on the roof it looked as it had always looked. 'I just hope you know what you're doing,' she said and made her way through the concrete blocks and across the bridge to her car. She drove into Worford to see Mr Ganglion about Sir Giles' will. From what she had been able to ascertain she had been left a widow of very considerable means, and Lady Maud intended to put those means to good use.

•

'A fortune, my dear lady,' said Mr Ganglion, 'an absolute fortune even by today's standards. Properly invested, you should be able to live quite royally.' He looked at her appreciatively. Now that he came to think of it she had every right to live royally. There was that business of Edward the Seventh. 'And as a widower myself . . .' He looked at her even more appreciatively. She might not be to every man's taste but then he wasn't up to much himself and he was getting on in years. And ten million pounds in property was an inducement. So too were those photographs of Mr Dundridge.

'I intend to re-marry as soon as possible,' said Lady Maud. 'Sir Giles may have left me well provided for but he did not fulfil his proper functions as a husband.'

'Quite so. Quite so,' said Mr Ganglion, his mind busily considering Dundridge's accusation of blackmail. It might be worth his while to try a little expeditious blackmail himself. He turned to his safe and twiddled the knob.

'Besides, it's not good for you to have to live alone in that great house,' he continued. 'You need company. Someone to look after you.'

'I have already seen to that,' said Lady Maud. 'I have invited Mrs Forthby to come and make it her home.'

'Mrs Forthby? Mrs Forthby? Do I know her?'

'No,' said Lady Maud, 'I don't suppose you do. She was Giles' . . . er . . . governess in London.'

'Really?' said Mr Ganglion glancing at her over the top of his glasses. 'Now that you come to mention it I did hear something . . .'

'Well never mind that,' said Lady Maud, 'there's no point in flogging a dead horse. The thing is that from what I have seen of the will he had made no provision for the poor woman. I intend to make good the deficiency.'

'Very generous of you. Magnanimous,' said Mr Ganglion and took an envelope from the safe. 'And while we're on the subject of human frailties, I wonder if you would mind glancing at these photographs and telling me if you have seen them before.' He opened the envelope and spread them out before her. Lady Maud stared at them intently. It was obvious she had seen them before.

'Where did you get those?' she shouted.

'Ah,' said Mr Ganglion, 'now I'm afraid that would be telling.'

'Of course it would,' snarled Lady Maud, 'what do you think I asked you for?'

'Well,' said Mr Ganglion, putting the photographs back into the envelope, 'a certain person, let us say a prospective client, consulted me . . .'

'Dundridge. I knew it. Dundridge,' said Lady Maud.

'Your guess is as good as mine, my dear Lady Maud,' said Mr Ganglion. 'Well this client did suggest that you had been using these . . . er . . . rather revealing pictures to . . . er . . . blackmail him.'

'My God,' shouted Lady Maud, 'the filthy little beast!'

'Of course I did my best to assure him that such a thing was out of the question. However he remained unconvinced . . .' But Lady Maud had heard enough. She rose to her feet and seized the envelope. 'Now if you feel that we should institute proceedings for slander . . .'

'Accused me of blackmail? By God I'll make him regret the day he was born,' Lady Maud snarled and stumped out of the room with the photographs.

Dundridge was in his Mobile HQ drawing up plans for his next move against Handyman Hall when Lady Maud drove up. Now that he was assured that the Ministry would throw their full weight behind his efforts he viewed the future with renewed confidence. He had spoken to the Chief Constable and had demanded full police co-operation should Lady Maud refuse to comply with the order to move out of Handyman Hall and the Chief Constable had reluctantly agreed. He was just giving Hoskins his instructions to move into the Park when Lady Maud stormed through the door.

'You filthy little swine,' she shouted and tossed the photographs on to his desk. 'Take a good look at yourself.' Dundridge did. So did Hoskins.

'Well?' continued Lady Maud. 'And what have you got to say now?'

Dundridge stared up at her and tried to think of words to match his feelings. It was impossible.

'If you think you can get away with this you're mistaken,' bawled Lady Maud.

Dundridge clutched the telephone. The filthy bitch had come back to haunt him with those horrible photographs and this time there was no mistaking who was playing the main role in these obscene contortions and this time too Hoskins was present. The look of horror on Hoskins' face decided him. There was no way of avoiding a scandal. Dundridge dialled the police.

'Don't think you can wriggle out of this by calling a lawyer,' Lady Maud yelled.

'I'm not,' said Dundridge finding his voice at last, 'I am calling the police.'

'The police?' said Lady Maud.

'The police?' whispered Hoskins.

'I intend to have you charged with attempted blackmail,' said Dundridge.

Lady Maud launched herself across the desk at him. 'Why, you filthy little bastard,' she screamed. Dundridge lurched off his chair and ran for the door. Lady Maud turned and raced after him. Behind them Hoskins replaced the telephone and picked up the photographs. He went into the lavatory and shut the door. When he came out Dundridge was cowering behind a bulldozer, Lady Maud was being restrained by six bulldozer drivers and the photographs had been reduced to ashes and flushed down the pan. Hoskins sat down and wiped his face with a handkerchief. It had been a near thing.

'Don't think you're going to get away with this,' Lady Maud shouted as she was escorted back to her car. 'I'll sue you for slander. I'll take every penny you've got.' She drove away and Dundridge staggered back to the caravan.

'You heard her,' he said to Hoskins slumping into his chair. 'You heard her attempt to blackmail me.' He looked around for the photographs.

'I burnt them,' said Hoskins. 'I didn't think you'd want them lying around.'

Dundridge looked at him gratefully. He certainly didn't want them lying around. On the other hand the evidence of an attempted crime had been destroyed. There was no point in calling in the police now.

'Well at least if she does sue me you were a witness,' he said finally.

'Definitely,' said Hoskins. 'But she'll never dare.'

'I wouldn't put anything past that bitch,' said Dundridge recovering his confidence now that both Lady Maud and the photographs were out of the way. 'But I'll tell you one thing. We're going to move into Handyman Hall now. I'll teach her to threaten me.'

•

'Without the photographs I'm afraid you would have no case,' said Mr Ganglion when Lady Maud returned to his office.

'But he told you that I was blackmailing him. You told me so yourself,' said Lady Maud.

Mr Ganglion shook his head sadly. 'What he said to me, my dear Lady Maud, was by way of being a confidential communication. He was after all consulting me as a solicitor and since I represent you in any case my evidence would never be accepted by a court. Now if we could get Hoskins to testify that he had heard him accuse you of blackmail . . .' He phoned the Regional Planning Board and was put through to Hoskins at the Mobile HQ.

'Certainly not. I never heard anything of the sort,' said Hoskins. 'Photographs? I don't know what you're talking about.' The last thing he wanted to do was to appear in court to testify about those bloody photographs.

'Peculiar,' said Mr Ganglion. 'Most peculiar, but there it is. Hoskins won't testify.'

'That just goes to show you can't trust anyone these days,' said Lady Maud.

She drove home in a filthy temper which wasn't improved by having to park the Bentley outside the Lodge and walk up the drive.

26

If her temper was bad when she returned to the Hall that afternoon it was ten times worse the next morning. She woke to the sound of lorries driving down the Gorge road and men shouting outside the Lodge. Lady Maud picked up the phone and called Blott.

'What the devil is going on down there?' she asked.

'It's started,' said Blott.

'Started? What's started?'

'They've come to begin work.'

Lady Maud dressed and hurried down the drive to find Dundridge, Hoskins and the Chief Constable and a group of policemen standing looking at the concrete blocks under the archway.

'What's the meaning of this?' she demanded.

'We have come to begin work here,' said Dundridge keeping close to the Chief Constable. 'You are in receipt of a compulsory purchase order served on you on the 25th of June and . . .'

'This is private property,' said Lady Maud. 'Kindly leave.'

'My dear Lady Maud,' said the Chief Constable, 'I'm afraid these gentlemen are within their rights . . .'

'They are within my property,' said Lady Maud. 'And I want them off it.'

The Chief Constable shook his head sorrowfully. 'I'm sorry to have to say this . . .'

'Then don't,' said Lady Maud.

'But they are fully entitled to act in accordance with their instructions and begin work on the motorway through the Park. I am here to see that they are not hindered in any way. Now if you would be so good as to order your gardener to vacate these . . . er . . . premises.'

'Order him yourself.'

'We have attempted to serve an eviction order on him but he refuses to come down. He appears to have barricaded the door. Now we don't want to have to use force but unless he is prepared to come out I'm afraid we will have to make a forcible entry.'

'Well, I'm not stopping you,' said Lady Maud. 'If that's what you have to do, go ahead and do it.'

She stood to one side while the policemen went round the side of the Lodge and hammered at the door. Lady Maud sat on a concrete block and watched them.

The police battered at the door for ten minutes and finally broke it down only to find themselves confronted by a wall of concrete. Dundridge sent for a sledgehammer but it was quite clear that something more than a sledgehammer would be required to make an entry.

'The bastard has cemented himself in,' said Dundridge.

'I can see that for myself,' said the Chief Constable. 'What are you going to do now?'

Dundridge considered the problem and consulted Hoskins. Together they walked back to the bridge and looked up at the arch. In the circumstances it had assumed a new and quite daunting stature.

'There's no way round it,' said Hoskins, indicating the cliffs. 'We would have to move thousands of tons of rock.'

'Can't we blast a way round?'

Hoskins looked up at the cliffs and shook his head. 'Could do but we'd probably kill the stupid bugger in that arch in the process.'

'So what?' said Dundridge. 'If he won't come down it's his own fault if he gets hurt.' He didn't say it very convincingly. It was quite clear that killing Blott would come under the heading of very unfavourable publicity at the Ministry of the Environment.

'In any case,' Hoskins pointed out, 'the authorized route runs through the Gorge, not round it.'

'What about the blasting we did back at the entrance?'

'We were authorized to widen the Gorge there because of the river and besides that section doesn't come within the area designated as of natural beauty.'

'Fuck,' said Dundridge. 'I knew that old bitch would come up with something like this.'

They went back to the arch where the Chief Constable was arguing with Lady Maud.

'Are you seriously suggesting that I ordered my gardener to cement himself into the Lodge?'

'Yes,' said the Chief Constable.

'In that case, Percival Henry,' said Lady Maud, 'you're a bigger fool than I took you for.'

The Chief Constable winced. 'Listen, Maud,' he said, 'you know as well as I do he wouldn't have done this without your permission.'

'Nonsense,' said Lady Maud, 'I told him he could do what he wanted with the Lodge. He's been living there for thirty years. It's his home. If he chooses to fill the place with cement that's his business. I refuse to accept any responsibility for his actions.'

'In that case I shall have no option but to arrest you,' said the Chief Constable.

'On what grounds?'

'For obstruction.'

'Codswallop,' said Lady Maud. She got down from the block and walked round to the back of the arch and looked up at the window.

'Blott,' she called. Blott's head appeared at the circular window.

'Yes.'

'Blott, come down this instant and let these men get on with their work.'

'Won't,' said Blott.

'Blott,' shouted Lady Maud, 'I am ordering you to come down.'

'No,' said Blott and shut the window.

Lady Maud turned to the Chief Constable. 'There you are. I have told him to come down and he won't. Now then, are you still going to have me arrested for obstruction?'

The Chief Constable shook his head. He knew when he was beaten. Lady Maud strode back up the drive to the Hall. He turned to Dundridge. 'Well, what do you suggest now?'

'There must be something we can do,' said Dundridge.

'If you've got any bright ideas, just let me know,' said the Chief Constable.

'What happens if we just go ahead and demolish the arch with him in it?'

'The question is,' said the Chief Constable, 'what would happen to him if you did that?'

'That's his problem,' said Dundridge. 'We've got a legal right to remove that arch and if he's in it when we do we're not responsible for what happens to him.'

The Chief Constable shook his head. 'You try telling that to the judge when they try you for manslaughter. I should have thought you'd have learnt your lesson from what happened at Guildstead Carbonell.' He got into his car and drove away.

Dundridge walked back across the bridge and spoke to the foreman of the demolition gang.

'Is there any way of taking that arch down without injuring the man inside?' he asked.

The foreman looked at him doubtfully. 'Not if he doesn't want us to.'

As if to give added weight to his argument Blott appeared on the roof. He was carrying a shotgun.

'You see what I mean,' said the foreman.

Blott looked expectantly over their heads, raised his gun and fired. A wood pigeon plummeted out of the sky. Dundridge could see exactly what he meant.

'There's nothing in our contract to say we've got to take unnecessary risks,' said the foreman, 'and a bloke who cements himself into an arch and shoots pigeons on the wing constitutes more than an unnecessary risk. He's a bloody loony, and a crack shot into the bargain.'

Dundridge thought wistfully of Mr Edwards. He turned to Hoskins.

'I think,' said Hoskins, 'that we ought to contact the Ministry in London. This thing's too big for us.'

•

At the Hall Lady Maud heard the shot and picked up a pair of binoculars. Through them she could see Blott on the roof with the shotgun. She telephoned the Lodge.

'They're not shooting at you, are they?' she asked hopefully.

'No,' said Blott, 'I was just shooting a pigeon. They're still talking.'

'Remember what I said about violence,' Lady Maud told him. 'We must keep public sympathy on our side. I am going to get in touch with the BBC and ITV and all the national newspapers. I think we can make a big song and dance about this business.'

Blott put down the phone. Song and dance. The English language was *most* expressive. Song and dance.

•

At his Mobile HQ Dundridge was on the phone to London.

'Are you seriously trying to tell me that Lady Lynchwood's

gardener has cemented himself into an ornamental arch?' said Mr Rees incredulously. 'It doesn't sound possible.'

'The arch in question happens to be eighty feet high,' Dundridge explained. 'It has rooms inside. He's filled all the bottom ones with concrete. There's barbed-wire on the roof and short of blowing the place up there's no way of getting him out.'

'I should try the local fire brigade,' Mr Rees suggested. 'They use them to get cats out of trees.'

'I have tried the fire brigade,' said Dundridge.

'Well, what do they say?'

'They say their business is putting out fires, not storming fortresses.'

Mr Rees considered the problem. 'I imagine he'll have to come out sometime,' he said finally.

'Why?'

'Well, to eat for one thing.'

'Eat?' shouted Dundridge. 'Eat? He doesn't have to come out to eat. I've got a list here of the things he ordered from the local supermarket. Four hundred tins of baked beans, seven hundred cans of corned beef, one hundred and fifty tins of frankfurters. Need I go on?'

'No,' said Mr Rees hastily, 'the fellow must have a constitution like an ox. You would have thought he would have chosen something a little more appetizing.'

'Is that all you've got to say?' said Dundridge.

'Well I must admit that it does sound as if he intends to make a long stay of it,' Mr Rees agreed.

'And what are we going to do? Cancel the motorway for a couple of years while he munches his way through that little lot?'

Mr Rees tried to think. 'Can't you talk him down?' he asked. 'That's what they usually do with people threatening to commit suicide.'

'But he isn't threatening suicide,' Dundridge pointed out.

'It amounts to the same thing,' said Mr Rees. 'A diet of corned beef, baked beans and frankfurters in the quantities you've mentioned would certainly kill me. Still, I see what you mean. A man who can even contemplate living off that muck obviously means business. Have you any ideas on the subject?'

'As a matter of fact I have,' said Dundridge.

'Not another ball and crane job I hope,' said Mr Rees anxiously. 'We can't have another little episode of that sort so shortly after the last one.'

'I was thinking of using the army,' said Dundridge.

'The army? My dear fellow, this is a free country. We can't possibly ask the army to blast a perfectly innocent Englishman out of his own home with tanks and artillery.'

'To be precise,' said Dundridge, 'he doesn't happen to be an Englishman and I wasn't thinking of blasting him out with tanks and artillery.'

'I should think not. The public would never stand for it,' Mr Rees said. 'But if he's not an Englishman what is he?'

'An Italian.'

'An Italian? Are you sure? It doesn't sound like them to go in for this sort of thing,' said Mr Rees.

'He's naturalized,' said Dundridge.

'That explains it,' said Mr Rees. 'In that case I can't see any objection to using the army. They're used to dealing with foreigners. What precisely did you have in mind?'

Dundridge explained his plan.

'Well I'll see what I can do,' said Mr Rees. 'I'll call you back when I've had a word with the Minister.'

In Whitehall the wires buzzed. Mr Rees spoke to the Minister of the Environment and the Minister spoke to Defence. By five o'clock Army Command had agreed to supply a team of commandos trained in rock climbing on the explicit understanding that they were to be used simply in a police support role and would not use firearms. As the Minister of the Environment explained, the essence of the operation was to occupy the Lodge and hold Blott until the police could evict him in a lawful fashion. 'The great thing is that the media haven't got on to the story yet. If we can get him out of there before the newsmen start nosing around we can hush the whole thing up. The essence of the thing must be speed.'

·

It was a point that Dundridge made to the commandos when they arrived for briefing that night at his Mobile HQ. 'I have here a number of photographs taken this afternoon of the target,' he said handing them round. 'As you can see it is amply provided with handholds and there are two means of access. The two circular windows on either side and the hatch in the roof. I should have thought the best method of attack would be a diversionary move to the rear and a frontal assault—'

'I think you can leave the tactical details of the exercise to us,' said the Major in charge who didn't like being told his business by a civvy.

'I was only trying to help,' said Dundridge.

'Now then,' said the Major. 'We'll rendezvous at the Gibbet at twenty-four hundred hours and proceed on foot ...' Dundridge left them to it and went into the other office.

'Well, for once we're getting things done,' he told Hoskins. 'That old bitch isn't going to know what's hit her.'

Hoskins nodded doubtfully. He had been in the army himself and he didn't have Dundridge's faith in the efficiency of the military machine.

•

Blott spent the evening reading Sir Arthur Bryant but his mind was not on the past. He was considering the immediate future. They would either act quickly or try to wear him down psychologically by sending a succession of well-meaning people to talk to him. Blott had seen the sort of visitor he could expect on the television. Social workers, psychiatrists, priests and policemen, all of them imbued with an invincible faith in the possibility of compromise. They would argue and cajole (Blott looked the word up in his dictionary to see if it meant what he thought and found he was right) and do their best to make him see the error of his ways and they would fail, fail hopelessly because their assumptions were all wrong. They would assume he was an Italian whereas he wasn't. They would think he was acting on instructions or that he was simply being loyal, whereas he was in love. They would think a compromise was possible ... With a motorway? Blott smiled to himself at the stupidity of the idea. The motorway would either go through the Park and Handyman Hall or it wouldn't. Nothing they could tell him would alter that fact. But above all the people who came to talk to him would be city-dwellers for whom talk was currency and words were coins. An Englishman's word is his bond, Blott thought, but then he had never had much time for stocks and shares. 'Word merchants' old Lord Handyman had called such people, with contempt in his voice, and Blott agreed with him. Well they could talk themselves blue in the face but they wouldn't shift him. Everything that he cared for and loved and was lay there in the Park and the Garden and the Hall. Handyman Hall. And Blott was the handyman. He would die rather than give up the right to be needed. He undressed and climbed into bed and lay listening to the river tumbling by and the wind in the trees. Through his window he could see the light on in Lady Maud's bedroom. Blott watched it until it went out and then he fell asleep.

•

He was woken at one o'clock by a noise outside. It was a very slight noise but it awoke in him some instinct, an early-warning system that told him that there were people outside. He got out of bed and went to the window and peered into the darkness below. There was someone at the foot of the left-hand column. Blott went across the room to the other window. There was someone in the Park too. They must have climbed the fence to get in. Blott listened and presently he heard someone moving below. They were climbing up the side of the Lodge. Climbing? In the dark? Interesting.

He crossed to a cupboard and took out the Leica and the flash gun and went back to the window and leant out. The next moment the entire side of the Lodge was a brilliant white. There was a cry and a thud. Blott went to the other window and took another photograph. This time whoever it was who was clinging to the side of the arch shut his eyes and clung on. Blott put the camera down. Something stronger was needed. What would make climbing difficult? Something greasy. He went into his kitchen and came out with

223

a gallon can of cooking oil and climbed the ladder in the corner of the room to the hatch in the roof. Then he crawled to the edge and began pouring the oil down the wall. There was a curse from below, the sound of slithering and another thud followed by a cry. Blott emptied the rest of the can down the back wall and went down the ladder into his room and shone a torch out of the window. There was no one on the side of the arch now. At the foot a number of men in army uniforms stared up at him angrily. They had blackened faces and one of them was lying on the ground.

'Is there anything I can do for you?' Blott asked.

'Wait till we get hold of you, you bastard,' shouted the Major. 'You've broken his leg.'

'Not me,' said Blott, 'I never touched him. He broke it himself. I didn't ask him to climb up my wall in the middle of the night.'

He was interrupted by a sound from the other side of the Lodge. The sods were coming up there too. He went into the kitchen and fetched two cans of cooking oil and repeated the process. By the time he was finished the sides of the Lodge were streaked with oil and two more climbers had fallen.

Down below there was a muttered conference.

'We'll use the grappling irons,' said the Major.

Blott peered out of the window and shone his torch on them. There was an explosion and a three-pronged hook shot past him on to the roof and stuck in the barbed-wire. It was followed by another. Blott raced into the kitchen and grabbed a knife. A moment later he was on the roof and had cut through one rope. He crawled under the wire and cut another. There was another thud and a yell. Blott peered over.

'Anyone else coming up?' he asked. But the army was already in retreat. As they carried their wounded back across the suspension bridge and up the road Blott watched them wistfully. He rather regretted their going. A full-scale battle would have been marvellous publicity. A full-scale battle? Blott went to the cupboard where he kept his armoury. He would have to act quickly. Then he climbed up on the roof and let down the rope ladder. Ten minutes later he was standing on the suspension bridge with the Bren gun.

As the commandos trudged back up the road towards their transport at the Gibbet they were startled to hear the sound of automatic fire behind them. It lasted for several seconds and was repeated again and again. They stood still and listened. It stopped. A few moments later there was a much larger thump and it was followed by a second. Blott had tried out the PIAT and it still worked.

•

At the Hall Lady Maud sat up in bed and struggled to find the light switch. She was used to the occasional shot in the night but this was something entirely different. A positive bombardment. She reached for the phone and rang the Lodge. There was no reply.

'Oh my God,' she moaned, 'they've killed him.' She got out of bed and dressed hurriedly. The firing had stopped now. She phoned the Lodge again and still there was no reply. She put the phone down and called the Chief Constable.

'They've murdered him,' she shouted, 'they've attacked the Lodge and killed him!'

'Killed who?' asked the Chief Constable.

'Blott,' yelled Lady Maud.

'No?' said the Chief Constable.

'I tell you they have. They've been using machine-guns and something much bigger.'

'Oh my goodness gracious me,' said the Chief Constable. 'Are you sure? I mean couldn't there be some mistake?'

'Percival Henry,' screamed Lady Maud, 'you know me well enough to know that when I say something I mean it. Remember what happened to Bertie Bullett-Finch.'

The Chief Constable remembered all too well. Midnight assassinations were becoming a commonplace occurrence in South Worfordshire and besides Lady Maud's tone had the ring of sincere hysteria about it. And Lady Maud, whatever else she might be was not a woman who got hysterical for nothing.

'I'll get every available patrol car there as soon as possible,' he promised.

'And an ambulance too,' screamed Lady Maud.

Within minutes every police car in South Worfordshire was converging on the Gorge. At the Gibbet twelve men of the 41st Marine Commando, two of them with broken legs, were detained for questioning as they were about to leave in their transport. They were driven to Worford Police Station loudly protesting that they had been acting under the orders of the Area Commander and that the police had no legal authority to hold them.

'We'll see about that in the morning,' said the Inspector as they were herded into their cells.

•

At the Lodge Blott climbed up his rope ladder and hauled it up behind him. He was delighted with his experiment. All the weapons had worked splendidly and, while it was impossible in the darkness to tell what damage they had done to the Lodge, the sound of splintering stonework had suggested that there was plenty of evidence to show that the army had carried out its assault with undue force and quite unwarranted violence. It was only when he was back in his room that he could see how effective the Projectiles Infantry Anti-Tank had been. They had blown two substantial holes in the frieze and the room was littered with bits of stone. Both windows had been blown out by the blast and there were holes in the ceiling. He was just wondering what to do next when he heard footsteps running down the drive. Blott switched off his torch and went to the window. It was Lady Maud.

'Don't come any nearer,' he shouted, to lend verisimilitude to his recent ordeal and to tell her that he was unhurt. 'Lie down. They may start firing again.'

Lady Maud stopped in her tracks. 'Oh thank Heavens, you're all right, Blott,' she shouted. 'I thought you'd been killed.'

'Me? Killed?' said Blott. 'It would take more than that to kill me.'

'Who was it? Did you get a good look at them?'

'It was the army,' Blott told her. 'I've got photographs to prove it.'

27

By next morning Blott was famous. The news of the attack came too late to be carried by the early editions but the later ones all bore his name in their headlines. The BBC broadcast news of the atrocity and its legal implications were discussed on the *Today* programme. At one o'clock there were further developments when it was announced that twelve Marine Commandos were helping the police in their enquiries. During the afternoon questions were asked in the House and the Home Secretary promised a full Enquiry. And all day reporters and cameramen swarmed into the Gorge to interview Blott and Lady Maud and to photograph the damage. It was clearly visible and extensive. Bullet holes pockmarked the entire arch, suggesting that the army's fire had been quite extraordinarily wild. The heads of several figures in the frieze were missing and the PIATs had torn gaping holes in the wall. Even hardened correspondents used to the tactics adopted against the urban guerrillas in Belfast were astonished by the extent of the damage.

'I've never seen anything like this,' the BBC correspondent told his audience from the top of a ladder before interviewing Blott at the window. 'This might be Vietnam or the Lebanon but this is a quiet corner of rural England. I can only say that I am horrified that this could happen. And now Mr Blott, could you tell us first what you know about this attack?'

Blott looked out of the window into the camera.

'It must have been about one o'clock in the morning. I was asleep and I heard a noise outside. I got up and went to the window and looked out. There appeared to be men climbing up the wall. Well I didn't want that so I poured oil down the wall.'

'You poured oil down the wall to stop them?'

'Yes,' said Blott, 'olive oil. They slipped down and then the firing began.'

'The firing?'

'It sounded like machine-gun fire,' said Blott, 'so I ran into the kitchen and lay on the floor. Then a minute or two later there was an explosion and things flew around the room and a few seconds afterwards there came another explosion. After that there was nothing.'

'I see,' said the interviewer. 'Now at any time during the attack did you fire back? I understand you have a shotgun.'

Blott shook his head. 'It all happened too suddenly,' he said. 'I was all shook up.'

'Quite understandably. It must have been a terrifying experience for you. Just one more question. Was the oil you poured down the wall hot?'

'Hot?' said Blott. 'How could it be hot? I poured it out of the can. I hadn't got time to heat it up.'

'Well thank you very much,' said the interviewer and climbed down the ladder. 'I think we'll cut that last remark out,' he told the sound man. 'It made him sound as if he would have liked to have poured hot oil on them.'

'I can't say I blame him after what he's been through,' said the sound man. 'The buggers deserve boiling oil.'

•

It was an opinion shared by the Chief Constable.

'What do you mean, a police support role?' he shouted at the Colonel from the Commando Base who came up to explain that he had been ordered by the Ministry of Defence to send a team of rock-climbers to assist the police. 'There weren't any of my men within miles of the place. You send your killers in armed with rockets and machine-guns and blow hell out of . . .'

'My men were without any weapons,' said the Colonel.

The Chief Constable looked at him incredulously. 'Your men were without weapons? You can stand there and tell me to my face that your men were unarmed when I've seen what they did to that building. You'll be telling me next that they had nothing to do with the incident.'

'That's what they say,' said the Colonel. 'They all swear blue they had left and were on their way back to their transport when the firing occurred.'

'I'm not bloody surprised,' said the Chief Constable. 'If I had just bombarded somebody's private house in the middle of the night I'd say I hadn't been near the place. That doesn't mean anyone with any sense is going to believe them.'

'They weren't carrying weapons when you arrested them.'

'Probably ditched the damned things,' said the Chief Constable. 'And in any case for all I know there were others who got away before my men arrived.'

'I can assure you—' the Colonel began.

'Damn your assurances!' shouted the Chief Constable. 'I don't want assurances. I've got the evidence of the attack itself and I have twelve men trained in the use of the weapons needed for that attack who admit that they attempted to force an entry into the Lodge last night. What more do I need? They'll appear before a magistrate in the morning.'

The Colonel had to admit that the circumstantial evidence . . .

'Circumstantial evidence, my foot,' snarled the Chief Constable, 'they're as guilty as hell and you know it.'

'I still think you ought to look into the business of the civil servant who gave them their instructions,' said the Colonel despondently as he left. 'I believe his name is Dundridge.'

'I have already attended to that,' the Chief Constable told him. 'He is in London at the moment but I have sent two officers down to bring him back for questioning.'

•

But Dundridge had already spent five hours being questioned by Mr Rees and Mr Joynson and finally by the Minister himself.

'All I did was tell them to climb into the arch and hold Blott till the police could come and evict him legally,' he explained over and over again. 'I didn't know they were going to use guns and things.'

Neither Mr Rees nor the Minister was impressed.

'Let us just look at your record,' said the Minister as calmly as he could. 'You were appointed Controller Motorways Midlands with specific instructions to insure that the construction of the M101 went through with the minimum of fuss and bother, that local opinion felt that local interests were being looked after and that the environment was being protected. Now can you honestly say that the terms of reference of your appointment have been fulfilled in any single particular?'

'Well . . .' said Dundridge.

'No you can't,' snarled the Minister. 'Since you went to Worford there have been a series of appalling disasters. A Rotarian has been beaten to a pulp in his own house by a demented demolition expert who claims he was incited . . .'

'I didn't know Mr Bullett-Finch was a Rotarian,' said Dundridge desperately trying to divert the floodwaters of the Minister's mounting fury.

'You didn't know . . .' The Minister counted to ten and took a sip of water. 'Next, an entire village has been wrecked . . .'

'Not an entire village,' said Dundridge. 'It was only the High Street.'

The Minister stared at him maniacally. 'Mr Dundridge,' he said finally, 'you may be able to make these fine distinctions between Rotarians and human beings and entire villages which consist only of High Streets and the High Streets themselves but I am not prepared to. An entire village was wrecked, a pedestrian was incinerated and twenty persons injured, some of them seriously. And this village, mark you, was over a mile away from the route of the proposed motorway. A Member of Parliament has been devoured by lions . . .'

'That had absolutely nothing to do with me,' Dundridge protested. 'I didn't suggest he fill his ruddy garden with lions.'

'I wonder,' said the Minister, 'I wonder. Still, I shall reserve judgement on that question until the full facts have been ascertained. And finally at your instigation the army has been called in to evict an Italian gardener . . . No, don't say it . . . an Italian gardener from his home by bombarding it with machine-guns and anti-tank weapons.'

'But I didn't tell them—'

'Shut up,' roared the Minister. 'You're fired, you're sacked . . .'

•

'You're under arrest,' said the detective who was waiting outside Mr Rees' office when Dundridge finally staggered out. Dundridge went down in the lift between two police officers.

Mr Rees sat down at his desk with a sigh.

'I told you that stupid bastard would hang himself,' he said with quiet satisfaction.

'What about the motorway?' asked Mr Hoskins.

'What about it?'

'Do you think we can continue with it?'

'God alone knows,' said Mr Rees, 'but frankly I doubt it. You seem to forget there's another bye-election due in South Worfordshire.'

•

It was not a point that had escaped Lady Maud's attention. While the reporters and cameramen still swarmed about the Lodge, photographing it from all angles and interviewing Blott from the tops of ladders hired for the purpose, she had been applying her mind to the question of a successor to Sir Giles. A meeting of the Save the Gorge Committee was held at General Burnett's house to discuss the next move.

'Stout fellow, Blott,' said the General, 'for an Eyetie. Remarkable, standing up to a bombardment like that. They used to run like rabbits in the desert.'

'I think we all owe him a debt of gratitude for his sense of duty and self-sacrifice,' Colonel Chapman agreed. 'Frankly I think this latest episode has put the kybosh on the motorway. They'll never be able to carry on with it now. I hear there's a proposal for a sit-in of conservationists from all over the country outside the Lodge to see that there's no repetition of this disgraceful action.'

'I must say I was most impressed by Mr Blott's command of the English language on television the other night,' said Miss Percival. 'He handled the interview quite wonderfully. I particularly liked what he had to say about English traditions.'

'That bit about an Englishman's home being his castle. Couldn't agree with him more,' the General said.

'I was thinking rather about what he said about England being the home of freedom and the need for Englishmen to stand up for their traditional values.'

Lady Maud looked at them all contemptuously. 'I must say I think it is a poor show when we have to rely on Italians to look after our interests for us,' she said.

The General shifted in his seat. 'I wouldn't go so far as to say that,' he murmured.

'I would,' said Lady Maud. 'Without him we would have all lost our homes.'

'As it is Miss Percival's lost hers already,' said Colonel Chapman.

'You can hardly blame Blott for that.'

Miss Percival took out a handkerchief and wiped her eyes. 'It was such a pretty cottage,' she sighed.

'The point I am trying to make,' Lady Maud continued, 'is that I think the best way we can demonstrate our gratitude and support for Blott is by proposing him as the candidate for South Worfordshire in the forthcoming bye-election.'

The Committee stared at her in astonishment.

'An Italian standing for South Worfordshire?' said the General. 'I hardly think . . .'

'So I've noticed,' said Lady Maud brusquely. 'And Blott is not an Italian. He is a nationalized Englishman.'

'Surely you mean naturalized,' said Colonel Chapman. 'Nationalized means state-controlled. I would have thought he was the exact opposite.'

'I stand corrected,' said Lady Maud magnanimously. 'Then we are agreed that Blott should represent the party at the bye-election?'

She looked round the table. Miss Percival was the first to agree. 'I second the proposal,' she murmured.

'Motion,' Lady Maud corrected her, 'the motion. The proposal comes later. All those in favour.'

The General and Colonel Chapman raised their hands in surrender, and since the Save the Gorge Committee was the party in South Worfordshire Blott's candidacy was ensured.

•

Lady Maud announced their decision to the press outside the Lodge. As the newsmen dispersed to their cars she climbed the ladder to the window in the Lodge.

'Blott,' she called through the broken panes, 'I have something to tell you.'

Blott opened the window and leant out. 'Yes,' he said.

'I want you to prepare yourself for a shock,' she told him. Blott looked at her uncertainly. He had been prepared for a shock for some time. The British army didn't use 303 ammunition nowadays and PIATs had been scrapped years ago. It was a point he had overlooked at the time.

'I have decided that you are to succeed Sir Giles,' said Lady Maud gazing into his face.

Blott gaped at her. 'Succeed Sir Giles? Gott in Himmel,' he muttered.

'I very much doubt it,' said Lady Maud.

'You mean . . .'

'Yes,' said Lady Maud, 'from now on you will be the master of Handyman Hall. You can come out now.'

'But . . .' Blott began.

'If you'll hand me the machine-gun and whatever else it was you used I'll take them down with me and we'll bury them in the pinetum.'

As they walked back up the drive with the PIAT and the Bren gun, Blott's mind was in a state of confusion. 'How did you know?' he asked.

'How did I know? I telephoned you of course as soon as I heard the firing,' said Lady Maud with a smile. 'I'm not as green as I'm cabbage-looking.'

'Meine Liebling,' said Blott and took what he could of her in his arms.

•

At Worford magistrates court Dundridge was charged with being party to a conspiracy to commit a breach of the peace, attempted murder, malicious damage to property, and obstruction of the police in the course of their duty.

It was the last charge that particularly infuriated him.

'Obstruction?' he shouted at the bench. 'Obstruction? Who's talking about obstruction?'

'Remanded in custody for a week,' said Colonel Chapman. Dundridge was still shouting abuse as he was dragged out to the Black Maria. In the cells he was interviewed by Mr Ganglion, who had been appointed by the court to conduct his defence.

'I should plead guilty to all charges,' he advised him.

'Guilty? I haven't done anything wrong. It's all a pack of lies!' Dundridge shouted.

'I understand how you feel,' Mr Ganglion said, 'but I understand the police are considering additional charges.'

'Additional charges? But they've charged me with everything under the sun already.'

'There's just that little business of blackmail to be attended to. Now I know you wouldn't want those photographs to be produced in court. You could get life for that, you know.'

Dundridge stared at him despairingly. 'For blackmail?' he asked. 'But I was the one being blackmailed.'

'For what you were doing in those photographs.'

Dundridge considered the prospect and shook his head. Life for something that had been done to him. He had been blackmailed, obstructed, shot at and here he was being charged with these offences. If there was any conspiracy it was directed against him.

'I don't know what to say,' he mumbled.

'Just stick to "Guilty",' Mr Ganglion advised. 'It will save a lot of time and the court will appreciate it.'

'Time?' said Dundridge. 'How long do you think I'll get?'

'Difficult to say really. Seven or eight years I should imagine, but you'll probably be out in five.'

He gathered up his papers and left the cell. As he walked back to his chambers he smiled to himself. It was always nice to combine business with pleasure. He found Lady Maud and Blott waiting for him to discuss the marriage settlement.

'My fiancé has decided to change his name,' Lady Maud announced. 'From now on he wants to be known as Handyman. I want you to make the necessary arrangements.'

'I see,' said Mr Ganglion. 'Well there shouldn't be any difficulties. And what Christian name would he like?'

'I think we'll just stick to Blott. I'm used to it and all the men in the family have been Bs.'

'True,' said Mr Ganglion, with the private thought that some of the women had been too. 'And when is the happy day?'

'We are going to wait until after the election. I wouldn't want it to be thought that I was trying to influence the outcome.'

•

Mr Ganglion went out to lunch with Mr Turnbull.

'Amazing woman, Maud Lynchwood,' he said as they walked across to the Handyman Arms. 'I wouldn't put anything past her. Marrying her damned gardener and putting him up for Parliament.'

They went into the bar.

'What'll you have?' said Mr Turnbull.

'I feel like a large whisky,' said Mr Ganglion. 'I know it's prohibitively expensive but I need it.'

'Have you heard, sir?' said the barman. 'There's fivepence off a tot of whisky and tuppence off a pint of beer. Lady Maud's instructions. Seems she can afford to be generous now.'

'Good Lord,' said Mr Turnbull, 'you don't think it has anything to do with this election, do you?'

But Mr Ganglion wasn't listening. He was thinking how little things had changed since he was a boy. What was it his father had said? Something about Mr Gladstone being swept out of office on a tide of ale. And that was in '74.

28

It was a white wedding. Lady Maud with her customary frankness had prevailed over the Vicar.

'I can damned well prove it if you insist,' she had told him when he had raised one or two minor objections but the Vicar had surrendered meekly. Wilfrid's Castle Church was packed. Half the county was there as Lady Maud strode through the pinetum with Mrs Forthby as her bridesmaid. Blott, now Blott Handyman, MP, was waiting at the church in top-hat and tails. As the organist broke into 'Rule Britannia', which Blott had chosen, Lady Maud Lynchwood went down the aisle beside General Burnett, emerging half an hour later Lady Maud Handyman. They posed for photographs and then led the way down the path and across the footbridge to the Hall. The place was resplendent. Flags flew from the turrets; there was a striped marquee on the lawn and the conservatory was a blaze of colour. Everything that Sir Giles' fortune afforded had been provided. Champagne, caviar, smoked salmon, jellied eels for those that liked them, cucumber sandwiches, trifle. Mrs Forthby had seen to them all. Only the cake was missing. 'I knew I had forgotten something,' she wept but even that was found eventually in the pantry. It was a perfect replica of the Lodge.

'It seems a pity to spoil it,' said Blott as he and Maud stood poised with Busby Handyman's old sword.

'You should have thought of that before,' Maud whispered in his ear. They cut the cake and the photographs were taken. Even Blott's speech, authentically English in its inarticulacy, went down well. He thanked everyone for coming and Mrs Forthby for her catering and made everyone laugh and Lady Maud blush by saying that it wasn't every man who had either the opportunity or the good fortune to be able to marry his mistress.

'Extraordinary fellow,' General Burnett told Mrs Forthby, who rather appealed to him, 'got a multitude of talents. They say there's talk of him becoming a Whip.'

Mrs Forthby shook her head. 'I do hope not,' she said. 'It's so degrading.'

•

Mr Ganglion and Mr Turnbull took a bottle of champagne into the garden.

'They say that the occasion produces the man,' said Mr Turnbull philosophically. 'I must admit he's turned out better than I ever expected. Talk about silk purses out of sows' ears.'

'My dear fellow, you've got it quite wrong,' said Mr Ganglion. 'It takes a sow's ear to know a silk purse when she's got one.'

'What on earth do you mean by that?'

Mr Ganglion sat down on a wrought-iron bench. 'I was just considering Sir Giles. Remarkable how conveniently he timed his death. Have you ever thought about that? I have. What do you suppose he was doing in gumboots in August? It hadn't rained for weeks. Driest summer we've had for years and he dies with his gumboots on.'

'You're surely not suggesting . . .'

Mr Ganglion chuckled. 'I'm not suggesting anything. Merely cogitating. These old families. They haven't survived by relying on chance. They know their onions.'

'You're just being cynical,' said Mr Turnbull.

'Nonsense, I'm being realistic. They survive, my God, how they survive, and thank Heavens they do. Where would we be without them?' His head nodded. Mr Ganglion fell asleep.

•

In bed that night the Handymans lay in one another's arms, blissfully happy. Blott was himself at last, the possessor of a new past and a perfect present. There was no railway station waiting-room in Dresden, no orphanage, no youth, no uncertainties or doubts. Above all no motorway. He was an Englishman whose family had lived in the Gorge for five hundred years and if Blott had anything to do with it they would be living there still five hundred years hence. He had said as much in his maiden speech in the House on membership of the Common Market.

'What do we need Europe for?' he had asked. 'Ah, but you say "Europe needs us". And so she does. As an example, as a pole-star, as a haven. I speak from experience . . .'

It was a remarkable speech and too reminiscent of Churchill and the younger Pitt and of Burke to give the front bench much comfort.

'We've got to shut him up,' said the Prime Minister and Blott had been offered the Whip.

'You're not going to take it, are you?' Lady Maud had asked anxiously.

'Certainly not,' said Blott. 'There is a tide in the affairs of men . . .'

'Oh darling,' said Maud, 'how wonderful you are.'

'Which taken at its flood leads on to families.'

Lady Maud sighed with happiness. It was so good to be married to a man who had his priorities right.

•

In Ottertown Prison Dundridge began his sentence.

'Behave yourself properly and you'll be transferred to an open prison,' the Governor told him. 'With remission for good behaviour you should be out in nine months.'

'I don't want to go to an open prison,' said Dundridge. 'I like it here.'

And it was true. There was a logic about prison life that appealed to him. Everything was in its place and there were no unforeseen occurrences to upset him. Each day was exactly the same as the day before and each cell identical to its neighbour. Best of all, Dundridge had a number. It was what he had always wanted. He was 58295 and perfectly satisfied with it. Working in the prison library he felt safe. Nature played no part in prison life. Trees, woods, and all the gross aberrations of the landscape lay beyond the prison walls. Dundridge had no time for them. He was too busy cataloguing the prison library. He had discovered a far more numerate system than the Dewey Decimal.

It was called the Dundridge Digit.

The Wilt Alternative

to Bill and Tina Baker

1

It was Enrolment Week at the Tech. Henry Wilt sat at a table in Room 467 and stared into the face of the earnest woman opposite him and tried to look interested.

'Well, there is a vacancy in Rapid Reading on Monday evenings,' he said. 'If you'll just fill in the form over there . . .' He waved vaguely in the direction of the window but the woman was not to be fobbed off.

'I would like to know a little more about it. I mean it does help, doesn't it?'

'Help?' said Wilt refusing to be drawn into sharing her enthusiasm for self-improvement. 'It depends what you mean by help.'

'My problem has always been that I'm such a slow reader I can't remember what the beginning of a book was about by the time I've finished it,' said the woman. 'My husband says I'm practically illiterate.'

She smiled forlornly and implied a breaking marriage which Wilt could save by encouraging her to spend her Monday evenings away from home and the rest of the week reading books rapidly. Wilt doubted the therapy and tried to shift the burden of counselling somewhere else.

'Perhaps you would be better off taking Literary Appreciation,' he suggested.

'I did that last year and Mr Fogerty was wonderful. He said I had potential.'

Stifling the impulse to tell her that Mr Fogerty's notion of potential had nothing to do with literature and was more physical in its emphasis – though what the hell he could see in this earnest creature was a mystery – Wilt surrendered.

'The purpose of Rapid Reading,' he said going into the patter, 'is to improve your reading skills both in speed and retention of what you have read. You will find that you concentrate more the faster you go and that . . .'

He went on for five minutes delivering the set speech he had learnt by heart over four years of enrolling potential Rapid

Readers. In front of him the woman changed visibly. This was what she had come to hear, the gospel of evening-class improvement. By the time Wilt had finished and she had filled in the form there was a new buoyancy about her.

There was less about Wilt. He sat on for the rest of the two hours listening to other similar conversations at other tables and wondering how the devil Bill Paschendaele managed to maintain his proselytizing fervour for An Introduction To Fenland Sub-Culture after twenty years. The fellow positively glowed with enthusiasm. Wilt shuddered and enrolled six more Rapid Readers with a lack of interest that was calculated to dishearten all but the most fanatical. In the intervals he thanked God he didn't have to teach the subject any longer and was simply there to lead the sheep into the fold. As Head of Liberal Studies Wilt had passed beyond the Evening Classes into the realm of timetables, committees, memoranda, wondering which of his staff was going to have a nervous breakdown next, and the occasional lecture to Foreign Students. He had Mayfield to thank for the latter. While the rest of the Tech had been badly affected by financial cuts the Foreign Students paid for themselves and Dr Mayfield, now Head of Academic Development, had created an empire of Arabs, Swedes, Germans, South Americans and even several Japanese who marched from one lecture room to another pursuing an understanding of the English language and, more impossibly, English Culture and Customs, a hodge-podge of lectures which came under the heading of Advanced English For Foreigners. Wilt's contribution was a weekly discourse on British Family Life which afforded him the opportunity to discuss his own family life with a freedom and frankness which would have infuriated Eva and embarrassed Wilt himself had he not known that his students lacked the insight to understand what he was telling them. The discrepancy between Wilt's appearance and the facts had baffled even his closest friends. In front of eighty foreigners he was assured of anonymity. He was assured of anonymity, period. Sitting in Room 467 Wilt could while away the time speculating on the ironies of life.

In room after room, on floor above floor, in departments all over the Tech, lecturers sat at tables, people asked questions, received concerned answers and finally filled in the forms that ensured that lecturers would keep their jobs for at least another year. Wilt would keep his for ever. Liberal Studies couldn't fail for lack of students. The Education Act saw to that. Day Release Apprentices had to have their weekly hour of progressive opinions whether they liked it or not. Wilt was safe, and if it hadn't been for the boredom he would have been a happy man. The boredom and Eva.

Not that Eva was boring. Now that she had the quads to look after Eva Wilt's enthusiasms had widened to include every 'Alternative' under the sun. Alternative Medicine alternated with Alternative Gardening and Alternative Nutrition and even various Alternative Religions so that Wilt, coming home from each day's lack of choice at the Tech, could never be sure what was in store for him except that it was not what it had been the night before. About the only constant was the din made by the quads. Wilt's four daughters had taken after their mother. Where Eva was enthusiastic and energetic they were inexhaustible and quadrupled her multiple enthusiasms. To avoid arriving home before they were in bed Wilt had taken to walking to and from the Tech and was resolutely unselfish about using the car. To add to his problems, Eva had inherited a legacy from an aunt and since Wilt's salary had doubled they had moved from Parkview Avenue to Willington Road and a large house in a large garden. The Wilts had moved up the social scale. It was not an improvement, in Wilt's opinion, and there were days when he hankered for the old times when Eva's enthusiasms had been slightly muted by what the neighbours might think. Now, as the mother of four and the matron of a mansion, she no longer cared. A dreadful self-confidence had been born.

And so at the end of his two hours Wilt took his register of new students to the office and wandered along the corridor of the Administration Block towards the stairs. He was going down when Peter Braintree joined him.

'I've just enrolled fifteen landlubbers for Nautical Navigation. What about that to start the year off with a bang?'

'The bang starts tomorrow with Mayfield's bloody course board meeting,' said Wilt. 'Tonight was as nothing. I tried to dissuade several insistent women and four pimply youths from taking Rapid Reading and failed. I wonder we don't run a course on how to solve *The Times* crossword puzzle in fifteen minutes flat. It would probably boost their confidence more than beating the track record for *Paradise Lost.*'

They went downstairs and crossed the hall where Miss Pansak was still recruiting for Beginners' Badminton.

'Makes me feel like a beer,' said Braintree. Wilt nodded. Anything to delay going home. Outside, stragglers were still coming in and cars were parked densely along Post Road.

'What sort of time did you have in France?' asked Braintree.

'The sort of time you would expect with Eva and the brood in a tent. We were asked to leave the first camp site after Samantha had let down the guy ropes on two tents. It wouldn't have been so bad if the woman inside one hadn't had asthma. That was on the Loire. In La Vendée we were stuck next to a German who had fought on the Russian front and was suffering from shell-shock. I don't know if you've ever been woken in the night by a man screaming about *Flammenwerfern* but I can tell you it's unnerving. That time we moved on without being asked.'

'I thought you were going down to the Dordogne. Eva told Betty she'd been reading a book about three rivers and it was simply enthralling.'

'The reading may have been but the rivers weren't,' said Wilt, 'not the one we were next to. It rained and of course Eva had to have the tent in what amounted to a tributary. It was bad enough putting the thing up dry. Weighed a ton then, but moving it out of a flashflood up a hundred yards of bramble banks at twelve o'clock at night when the damned thing was sodden . . .' Wilt stopped. The memory was too much for him.

'And I suppose it went on raining,' said Braintree sympathetically. 'That's been our experience, anyway.'

'It did,' said Wilt. 'For five whole days. After that we moved into a hotel.'

'Best thing to do. You can eat decent meals and sleep in comfort.'

'You can perhaps. We couldn't. Not after Samantha shat in the bidet. I wondered what the stench was sometime around 2 a.m. Anyway let's talk about something civilized.'

They went went into The Pig In A Poke and ordered pints.

'Of course all men are selfish,' said Mavis Mottram as she and Eva sat in the kitchen at Willington Road. 'Patrick hardly ever gets home until after eight and he always has an excuse about the Open University. It's nothing of the sort, or if it is it's some divorcee student who wants extra coition. Not that I mind any longer. I said to him the other night, "If you want to make a fool of yourself running after other women that's your affair but don't think I'm going to take it lying down. You can go your way and I'll go mine." '

'What did he say to that?' Eva asked, testing the steam iron and starting on the quads' dresses.

'Oh just something stupid about not wanting it standing up anyway. Men are so coarse. I can't think why we bother with them.'

'I sometimes wish Henry was a bit coarser,' said Eva pensively. 'He always was lethargic but now he claims he's too tired because he walks to the Tech every day. It's six miles so I suppose he could be.'

'I can think of another reason,' said Mavis bitterly. 'Still waters etcetera . . .'

'Not with Henry. I'd know. Besides, ever since the quads were born he's been very thoughtful.'

'Yes, but what's he been thoughtful about? That's what you have to ask yourself, Eva.'

'I meant he's been considerate to me. He gets up at seven and brings me tea in bed and at night he always makes me Horlicks.'

'If Patrick started acting like that I'd be very suspicious,' said Mavis. 'It doesn't sound natural.'

'It doesn't, does it, but that's Henry all over. He's really kind. The only thing is he isn't very masterful. He says it's because he's surrounded by five women and he knows when he's beaten.'

'If you go ahead with this au pair girl plan that will make six,' said Mavis.

'Irmgard isn't a proper au pair girl. She's renting the top-floor flat and says she'll help around the house whenever she can.'

'Which, if the Everards' experience with their Finn is anything to go by, will be never. She stayed in bed till twelve and practically ate them out of house and home.'

'Finns are different,' said Eva. 'Irmgard is German. I met her at the Van Donkens' World Cup Protest Party. You know they raised nearly a hundred and twenty pounds for the Tortured Tupamaros.'

'I didn't think there were any Tupamaros in Argentina any more. I thought they had all been killed off by the army.'

'These are the ones who escaped,' said Eva. 'Anyway I met Miss Mueller and mentioned that we had this top flat and she was ever so eager to have it. She'll do all her own cooking and things.'

'Things? Did you ask her what things she had in mind?'

'Well, not exactly, but she says she wants to study a lot and she's very keen on physical fitness.'

'And what does Henry have to say about her?' asked Mavis moving closer to her real concern.

'I haven't told him yet. You know what he's like about having other people in the house, but I thought if she stays in the flat in the evenings and keeps out of his way . . .'

'Eva dear,' said Mavis with advanced sincerity, 'I know this is none of my business but aren't you tempting fate just a little?'

'I can't see how. I mean it's such a good arrangement. She can baby-sit when we want to go out, and the house is far too big for us and nobody ever goes up to the flat.'

'They will with her up there. You'll have all sorts of people coming through the house and she's bound to have a record player. They all do.'

'Even if she does we won't hear it. I've ordered rush matting

12

from Soales and I went up the other day with the transistor and you can hardly hear a thing.'

'Well, it's your affair, dear, but if I had an au pair girl in the house with Patrick around I'd want to be able to hear some things.'

'I thought you said you'd told Patrick he could do what he liked?'

'I didn't say in my house,' said Mavis. 'He can do what he likes elsewhere but if I ever caught him playing Casanova at home he'd live to regret it.'

'Well, Henry is different. I don't suppose he will even notice her,' said Eva complacently. 'I've told her he's very quiet and home-loving and she says all she wants is peace and quiet herself.'

With the private thought that Miss Irmgard Mueller was going to find living in the same house as Eva and the quads neither peaceful nor quiet, Mavis finished her coffee and got up to go. 'All the same I would keep an eye on Henry,' she said. 'He may be different but I wouldn't trust a man further than I could throw him. And my experience of foreign students is that they come over here to do a lot more than learn the English language.'

She went out to her car and drove home wondering what there was about Eva's simplicity that was so sinister. The Wilts were an odd couple, but since their move to Willington Road Mavis Mottram's dominance had diminished. The days when Eva had been her protégée in flower-arranging were over and Mavis was frankly jealous. On the other hand Willington Road was definitely in one of the best neighbourhoods in Ipford and there were social advantages to be gained from knowing the Wilts.

At the corner of Regal Gardens her headlights picked Wilt out as he walked slowly home and she called out to him. But he was deep in thought and didn't hear her.

As usual Wilt's thoughts were dark and mysterious and made the more so by the fact that he didn't understand why he had them. They had to do with strange violent fantasies that welled

13

up inside him, with dissatisfactions which could only be partly explained by his job, his marriage to a human dynamo, the dislike he felt for the atmosphere of Willington Road where everyone else was something important in high-energy physics or low-temperature conductivity and made more money than he did. And after all these explicable grounds for grumbling there was the feeling that his life was largely meaningless and that beyond the personal there was a universe which was random, chaotic and yet had some weird coherence about it which he would never fathom. Wilt speculated on the paradox of material progress and spiritual decadence and as usual came to no conclusion except that beer on an empty stomach didn't agree with him. One consolation was that now Eva was into Alternative Gardening he was likely to get a good supper and the quads would be fast asleep. If only the little buggers didn't wake in the night. Wilt had had his fill of broken sleep in the early years of breast-feeding and bottle-warming. Those days were largely over now and, apart from Samantha's occasional bout of sleepwalking and Penelope's bladder problem, his nights were undisturbed. And so he made his way along the trees that lined Willington Road and was greeted by the smell of casserole from the kitchen. Wilt felt relatively cheerful.

2

He left the house next morning in a far more despondent mood. 'I should have been warned by that casserole that she had some bloody ominous message to impart,' he muttered as he set off for the Tech. And Eva's announcement that she had found a lodger for the top flat had been ominous indeed. Wilt had been alert to the possibility ever since they had bought the house but Eva's immediate enthusiasms – gardening, herbalism, progressive playgrouping for the quads, redecorating the house and designing the ultimate kitchen – had postponed any decision about the top flat. Wilt had hoped that the matter would be forgotten. Now she had let the rooms without even bothering to tell him Wilt felt distinctly aggrieved. Worse still, he had been outwitted by the decoy of that splendid stew. When Eva wanted to cook she could, and Wilt had finished his second helping and a bottle of his better Spanish burgundy before she had announced this latest disaster. It had taken Wilt several seconds before he could focus on the problem.

'You've done what?' he said.

'Let it to a very nice young German girl,' said Eva. 'She's paying fifteen pounds a week and promises to be very quiet. You won't even know she's there.'

'I bloody well will. She'll have lovers fumbling their lascivious way up and down stairs all night and the house will reek of sauerkraut.'

'It won't. There's an extractor fan in the kitchenette up there and she's entitled to have boyfriends so long as they behave themselves nicely.'

'Nicely! Show me some loutish lover behaving nicely and I'll show you a camel with four humps . . .'

'They're called dromedaries,' said Eva using the tactic of muddled information that usually distracted Wilt and lured him into correcting her. But Wilt was too distracted already to bother.

'They're not. They're called fucking foreigners and I'm using fucking properly for once and if you think I want to lie in bed every night listening to some ruddy Latin prove his virility by imitating Popocatepetl in eruption on an inner sprung mattress eight feet above my head—'

'Dunlopillo,' said Eva. 'You never get things right.'

'Oh yes I do,' snarled Wilt. 'I knew this was in the wind ever since your bloody aunt had to die and leave you a legacy and you had to buy this miniature hotel. I knew then that you would turn it into some foul commune.'

'It's not a commune and anyway Mavis says the extended family was one of the good things about the old days.'

'She'd know all about extended families, Mavis would. Patrick has been extending his family for as long as I can remember, and into other people's.'

'Mavis has given him an ultimatum,' said Eva. 'She's not putting up with his carryings on any longer.'

'And I'm giving you an ultimatum,' said Wilt. 'One squeak out of those bedsprings up there, one whiff of pot, one twang of a guitar, one giggle on the stairs and I'll extend this family by finding digs in town until Miss Schickelgruber has moved out.'

'Her name isn't Schickelwhatchamacallit. It's Mueller. Irmgard Mueller.'

'So was one of Hitler's nastier Obergruppenführers and all I'm saying is—'

'You're just jealous,' said Eva. 'If you were a proper man and hadn't got hang-ups about sex from your parents you wouldn't get so hot under the collar about what other people do.'

Wilt regarded her balefully. Whenever Eva wanted to subdue him she launched a sexual offensive. Wilt retired to bed defeated. Discussions of his sexual inadequacies tended to result in his having to prove Eva wrong practically and after that stew he didn't feel up to it.

He didn't feel up to much by the time he reached the Tech next morning. The quads had fought their usual intersororial war about who was going to wear what dress before being dragged off to playgroup and there had been another letter in *The Times* from Lord Longford demanding the release of Myra Hindley, the Moors murderess, from prison on the grounds that she was now thoroughly reformed, a convinced Christian and a socially valuable citizen. 'In which case she can prove her social value and Christian charity by staying in prison and helping her fellow-convicts,' had been Wilt's infuriated reaction. The other news was just as depressing. Inflation was up again. Sterling down. North Sea gas would run out in five years. All in all the world was in its usual filthy mess and now he had to listen to Dr Mayfield extol the virtues of the Advanced English For Foreigners course for several intolerably boring hours before dealing with complaints from his

Liberal Studies lecturers about the way he had done the time-table.

One of the worst things about being Head of Liberal Studies was that he had to spend a large part of his summer vacation fitting classes into rooms and lecturers into classes, and when he had finished and had defeated the Head of Art who wanted Room 607 for Life Studies while Wilt needed it for Meat Three, he was still faced with a hassle at the beginning of the year and had to readjust the timetable because Mrs Fyfe couldn't make Tuesday at two with DMT One because her husband . . . It was on such occasions that Wilt wished he was back teaching *The Lord of the Flies* to Gasfitters instead of running the department. But his salary was good, the rates on Willington Road were exorbitant, and for the rest of the year he could spend much of his time sitting in his office dreaming.

He could sit through most committee meetings in a coma too, but Dr Mayfield's course board was the one exception. Wilt had to stay awake to prevent Mayfield lumbering him with several more lectures in his relative absence. Besides, Dr Board would start the term off with a row.

He did. Mayfield had only just begun to stress the need for a more student-oriented curriculum with special emphasis on socio-economic awareness when Dr Board intervened.

'Codswallop,' he said. 'The business of my department is to teach English students how to speak German, French, Spanish and Italian, not to explain the origins of their own languages to a whole lot of aliens, and as for socio-economic awareness, I suggest that Dr Mayfield has his priorities wrong. If the Arabs I had last year were anything to go by they were econo-mically aware to the nth degree about the purchasing power of oil and so socially backward that it will take more than a three-year course to persuade the sods that stoning women to death for being unfaithful isn't cricket. Perhaps if we had three hundred years . . .'

'Dr Board, this meeting may well last as long if you keep interrupting,' said the Vice-Principal. 'Now if Dr Mayfield will just continue . . '

The Head of Academic Development continued for another hour, and was all set for the entire morning when the Head of Engineering objected.

'I see that several of my staff are scheduled to deliver lectures on British Engineering Achievements in the Nineteenth Century. Now I would like to inform Dr Mayfield and this board that my department consists of engineers, not historians, and quite frankly they see no reason why they should be asked to lecture on topics outside their field.'

'Hear, hear,' said Dr Board.

'What is more, I would like to be informed why so much emphasis is being placed on a course for foreigners at the expense of our own British students.'

'I think I can answer that,' said the Vice-Principal. 'Thanks to the cuts that have been imposed on us by the local authority we have been forced to subsidize our existing non-paying courses and staff numbers by expanding the foreign sector where students pay substantial fees. If you want the figures of the profit we made last year . . .'

But no one took up the invitation. Even Dr Board was momentarily silenced.

'Until such time as the economy improves,' continued the Vice-Principal, 'a great many lecturers are only going to keep their jobs because we are running this course. What is more, it may well be possible to expand Advanced English for Foreigners into a degree course approved by the CNAA. I think you will all agree that anything which increases our chances of becoming a Polytechnic is to everyone's advantage.' The Vice-Principal stopped and looked round the rooom but nobody demurred. 'In which case all that remains is for Dr Mayfield to allocate the new lectures to the various departmental heads.'

Dr Mayfield distributed xeroxed lists. Wilt studied his new burden and found that it included The Development of Liberal and Progressive Social Attitudes in English Society, 1688 to 1978, and was just about to protest when the Head of Zoology got in first.

'I see here that I am down for Animal Husbandry and Agriculture with special reference to Intensive Farming of Pigs, Hens, and Stock-Rearing.'

'The subject has ecological significance—'

'And is student-oriented,' said Dr Board. 'Battery Education or possibly Hog Raising by Continuous Assessment. Perhaps we could even run a course on Composting.'

'Don't,' said Wilt with a shudder. Dr Board looked at him with interest.

'Your magnificent wife?' he enquired.

Wilt nodded dolefully. 'Yes, she has taken up—'

'If I may just get back to my original objection instead of hearing about Mr Wilt's matrimonial problems,' said the Head of Zoology. 'I want to make it absolutely clear now that I am not qualified to lecture on Animal Husbandry. I am a zoologist not a farmer and what I know about Stock-Rearing is zero.'

'We must all extend ourselves,' said Dr Board. 'After all if we are to acquire the doubtful privilege of calling ourselves a Polytechnic we must put the College before personal interest.'

'Perhaps you haven't seen what you're down to teach, Board,' Zoology continued, 'Sementic Influences . . . shouldn't that be Semantic, Mayfield?'

'Must be the typist's error,' said Mayfield. 'Yes it should read Semantic Influences on Current Sociological Theories. The bibliography includes Wittgenstein, Chomsky and Wilkes . . .'

'It doesn't include me,' said Board. 'You can count me out. I don't care if we descend to the level of a primary school but I am not going to mug up Wittgenstein or Chomsky for the benefit of anyone.'

'Well then, don't talk about my having to extend myself,' said the Head of Zoology. 'I am not going into a lecture room filled with Moslems to explain, even with my limited knowledge of the subject, the advantages of raising pigs in the Persian Gulf.'

'Gentlemen, while recognizing that there are one or two minor amendments necessary to the lecture titles I think they can be ironed out—'

'Wiped out more likely,' said Dr Board. The Vice-Principal

19

ignored his interruption. '—and the main thing is to keep the lectures in their present format while presenting them at a level suitable for the individual students.'

'I'm still not mentioning pigs,' said Zoology.

'You don't have to. You can do an elementary series of talks on plants,' said the Vice-Principal wearily.

'Great. And will someone tell me how in God's name I can even begin to talk in an elementary way about Wittgenstein? I had an Iraqi last year who couldn't even spell his own name, so what's the poor bugger going to do with Wittgenstein?' said Dr Board.

'And if I may just bring another subject up,' said a lecturer from the English department rather diffidently, 'I think we are going to have something of a communications problem with the eighteen Japanese and the young man from Tibet.'

'Oh really,' said Dr Mayfield. 'A communications problem. You know, it might be as well to add a lecture or two on Inter-communicational Discourse. It's the sort of subject which is likely to appeal to the Council for National Academic Awards.'

'It may appeal to them but it certainly doesn't appeal to me,' said Board. 'I've always said they were the scourings of the Academic world.'

'Yes, and we've already heard you on the subject,' said the Vice-Principal. 'And now to get back to the Japanese and the young man from Tibet. You did say Tibet, didn't you?'

'Well, I said it, but I can't be too sure,' answered the English lecturer. 'That's what I meant about a communications problem. He doesn't speak a word of English and my Tibet-anese isn't exactly fluent. It's the same with the Japanese.'

The Vice-Principal looked round the room. 'I suppose it is too much to expect anyone here to have a smattering of Japanese?'

'I've got a bit,' said the Head of Art, 'but I'm damned if I'm going to use it. When you've spent four years in a Nip prisoner-of-war camp the last thing you want is to have to talk to the bastards in later life. My digestive system is still in a hell of a mess.'

'Perhaps you could tutor our Chinese student instead. Tibet

is part of China now and if we include him with the four girls from Hong Kong . . .'

'We'll be able to advertise Take-Away Degrees,' said Dr Board and provoked another acrimonious exchange which lasted until lunchtime.

Wilt returned to his office to find that Mrs Fyfe couldn't take Mechanical Technicians at two on Tuesday because her husband had . . . It was exactly as he had anticipated. The Tech's year had begun as it always did. It continued in the same trying vein for the next four days. Wilt attended meetings on Interdepartmental Course Collaboration, gave a seminar to student teachers from the local training college on The Meaning of Liberal Studies, which was a contradiction in terms as far as he was concerned, was lectured by a sergeant from the Drug Squad on Pot Plant Recognition and Heroin Addiction and finally managed to fit Mrs Fyfe into Room 29 with Bread Two on Monday at 10 a.m. And all the time he brooded over Eva and her wretched lodger.

While Wilt busied himself lethargically at the Tech, Eva put her own plans implacably into operation. Miss Mueller arrived two mornings later and installed herself inconspicuously in the flat; so inconspicuously that it took Wilt two more days to realize she was there, and then only the delivery of nine milk bottles where there were usually eight gave him the clue. Wilt said nothing but waited for the first hint of gaiety upstairs before launching his counter-offensive of complaints.

But Miss Mueller lived up to Eva's promise. She was exceedingly quiet, came in unobtrusively when Wilt was still at the Tech and left in the morning after he had begun his daily walk. By the end of a fortnight he was beginning to think his worst fears were unjustified. In any case, he had his lectures to foreign students to prepare and the teaching term had finally started. The question of the lodger receded into the background as he tried to think what the hell to tell Mayfield's Empire, as Dr Board called it, about Progressive Social Attitudes in English Society since 1688. If Gasfitters were any indication there had been a regression, not a progressive development. The bastards had graduated to queer-bashing.

3

But if Wilt's fears were premature they were not long being realized. He was sitting one Saturday evening in the Piagetory, the purpose-built summerhouse at the bottom of the garden in which Eva had originally tried to play conceptual games with the 'wee ones', a phrase Wilt particularly detested, when the first blow fell.

It was less a blow than a revelation. The summerhouse was nicely secluded, set back among old apple trees with an arbour of clematis and climbing roses to hide it from the world and Wilt's consumption of homemade beer from Eva. Inside, it was hung with dried herbs. Wilt didn't approve of the herbs but he preferred them in their hung form rather than in the frightful infusions Eva sometimes tried to inflict on him, and they seemed to have the added advantage of keeping the flies from the compost heap at bay. He could sit there with the sun dappling the grass around and feel at relative peace with the world, and the more beer he drank the greater that peace became. Wilt prided himself on the effect of his beer. He brewed it in a plastic dustbin and occasionally fortified it with vodka before bottling it in the garage. After three bottles even the quads' din somehow receded and became almost natural, a chorus of whines, squeals and laughter, usually malicious when someone fell off the swing, but at least distant. And even that distraction was absent this evening. Eva had taken them to the ballet in the hope that early exposure to Stravinsky would turn Samantha into a second Margot Fonteyn. Wilt had his doubts about Samantha and Stravinsky. As far as he was concerned his daughter's talents were more suitable for an all-in wrestler, and Stravinsky's genius was overrated. It had to be if Eva approved it. Wilt's own taste ran to Mozart and Mugsy Spanier, an eclecticism Eva couldn't understand but which allowed him to annoy her by switching from a piano sonata she was enjoying to twenties jazz which she didn't.

Anyway, this evening there was no need to play his tape-recorder. It was sufficient to sit in the summerhouse and know that even if the quads woke him at five next morning he could still stay in bed until ten, and he was just uncorking his fourth bottle of fortified lager when his eye caught sight of a figure on the wooden balcony outside the dormer window of the top-floor flat. Wilt's hand on the bottle loosened and a moment later he was groping for the binoculars Eva had bought for bird-watching. He focused on the figure through a gap in the roses and forgot about beer. All his attention was riveted on Miss Irmgard Mueller.

She was standing looking out over the trees to the open country beyond, and from where Wilt sat and focused he had a particularly interesting view of her legs. There was no denying that they were shapely legs. In fact they were startlingly shapely legs and her thighs . . . Wilt moved up, found her breasts beneath a cream blouse entrancing, and finally reached her face. He stayed there. It wasn't that Irmgard – Miss Mueller and that bloody lodger were instantaneously words of the past – was an attractive young woman. Wilt had been faced by attractive young women at the Tech for too many years, young women who ogled him and sat with their legs distractingly apart, not to have built up sufficient sexual antibodies to deflect their juvenile charms. But Irmgard was not a juvenile. She was a woman, a woman of around twenty-eight, a beautiful woman with glorious legs, discreet and tight breasts, 'unsullied by suckling' was the phrase that sprang to Wilt's mind, with firm neat hips, even her hands grasping the balcony rail were some-how delicately strong with tapering fingers, lightly tanned as by some midnight sun. Wilt's mind spun into meaningless metaphors far removed from Eva's washing-up mitts, the can-yon wrinkles of her birth-pocked belly, the dugs that haunched her flaccid hips and all the physical erosion of twenty years of married life. He was swept into fancy by this splendid creature, but above all by her face.

Irmgard's face was not simply beautiful. In spite of the beer Wilt might have withstood the magnetism of mere beauty. He was defeated by the intelligence of her face. In fact there were imperfections in that face from a purely physical point of view. It was too strong for one thing, the nose was a shade retroussé to be commercially perfect, and the mouth too generous but it was individual, individual and intelligent and sensitive and mature and thoughtful and . . . Wilt gave up the addition in despair and as he did so it seemed to him that Irmgard was gazing down into his two adoring eyes, or anyway into the binoculars, and that a subtle smile played about her gorgeous lips. Then she turned away and went back into the flat. Wilt dropped the binoculars and reached trancelike for the beer bottle. What he had just seen had changed his view of life.

He was no longer Head of Liberal Studies, married to Eva, the father of four quarrelsome repulsive daughters, and thirty-eight. He was twenty-one again, a bright, lithe young man who wrote poetry and swam on summer mornings in the river and whose future was alight with achieved promise. He was already a great writer. The fact that being a writer involved writing was wholly irrelevant. It was being a writer that mattered and Wilt at twenty-one had long since settled his future in advance by reading Proust and Gide, and then books on Proust and Gide and books about books on Proust and Gide, until he could visualize himself at thirty-eight with a delightful anguish of anticipation. Looking back on those moments he could only compare them to the feeling he now had when he came out of the dentist's surgery without the need for any fillings. On an intellectual plane, of course. Spiritual, with smoke-filled, cork-lined rooms and pages of illegible but beautiful prose littering, almost fluttering from, his desk in some deliciously nondescript street in Paris. Or in a white-walled bedroom on white sheets entwined with a tanned woman with the sun shining through the shutters and shimmering on the ceiling from the azure sea somewhere near Hyères. Wilt had tasted all these pleasures in advance at twenty-one. Fame, fortune, the modesty of greatness, *bons mots* drifting effortlessly from his tongue over absinthe, allusions tossed and caught, tossed back again like intellectual shuttlecocks, and the intense walk home through dawn-deserted streets in Montparnasse.

About the only thing Wilt had eschewed from his borrowings off Proust and Gide had been small boys. Small boys and plastic dustbins. Not that he could see Gide buggering about brewing beer anyway, let alone in plastic dustbins. The sod was probably a teetotaller. There had to be some deficit to make up for the small boys. So Wilt had lifted Frieda from Lawrence while hoping to hell he didn't get TB, and had endowed her with a milder temperament. Together they had lain on the sand making love while the ripples of the azure sea broke over them on an empty beach. Come to think of it, that must have been about the time he saw *From Here to Eternity* and Frieda had looked like Deborah Kerr. The main thing was she had been strong and firm and in tune, if not with the infinite as such, with the infinite variations of Wilt's particular lusts. Only they hadn't been lusts. Lust was too insensitive a word for the sublime contortions Wilt had had in mind. Anyway, she had been a sort of sexual muse, more sex than muse, but someone to whom he could confide his deepest perceptions without being asked who Rochefou . . . what's-his-name was which was about as near being a blasted muse as Eva ever got. And now look at him, lurking in a bleeding Spockery drinking himself into a beer belly and temporary oblivion on something pretending to be lager that he'd brewed in a plastic dustbin. It was the plastic that got Wilt. At least a dustbin was appropriate for the muck but it could have had the dignity of being a metal one. But no, even that slight consolation had been denied him. He'd tried one and had damned near poisoned himself. Never mind that. Dustbins weren't important and what he had just seen had been his Muse. Wilt endowed the word with a capital M for the first time in seventeen disillusioning years and then promptly blamed the bloody lager for this lapse. Irmgard wasn't a muse. She was probably some dumb, handsome bitch whose Vater was Lagermeister of Cologne and owned five Mercedes. He got up and went into the house.

When Eva and the quads returned from the theatre he was sitting morosely in front of the television ostensibly watching football but inwardly seething with indignation at the dirty tricks life played on him.

'Now then you show Daddy how the lady danced,' said Eva, 'and I'll put the supper on.'

'She was ever so beautiful, Daddy,' Penelope told him. 'She went like this and there was this man and he . . .' Wilt had to sit through a replay of *The Rite of Spring* by four small lumpish girls who hadn't been able to follow the story anyway and who took turns to try to do a pas de chat off the arm of his chair.

'Yes, well, I can see she must have been brilliant from your performance,' said Wilt. 'Now if you don't mind I want to see who wins . . .'

But the quads took no notice and continued to hurl themselves about the room until Wilt was driven to take refuge in the kitchen.

'They'll never get anywhere if you don't take an interest in their dancing,' said Eva.

'They won't get anywhere anyway if you ask me and if you call that dancing I don't. It's like watching hippos trying to fly. They'll bring the bloody ceiling down if you don't look out.'

Instead Emmeline banged her head on the fireguard and Wilt had to put a blob of Savlon on the scratch. To complete the evening's miseries Eva announced that she had asked the Nyes round after supper.

'I want to talk to him about the Organic Toilet. It's not working properly.'

'I don't suppose it's meant to,' said Wilt. 'The bloody thing is a glorified earth closet and all earth closets stink.'

'It doesn't stink. It has a composty smell, that's all, but it doesn't give off enough gas to cook with and John said it would.'

'It gives off enough gas to turn the downstairs loo into a death-chamber if you ask me. One of these days some poor bugger is going to light a cigarette in there and blow us all to Kingdom Come.'

'You're just biased against the Alternative Society in general,' said Eva. 'And who was it who was always complaining about my using chemical toilet cleaner? You were. And don't say you didn't.'

'I have enough trouble with society as it is without being bunged into an alternative one, and, while we are on the subject, there must be an alternative to poisoning the atmosphere with methane and sterilizing it with Harpic. Frankly I'd say Harpic had something to recommend it. At least you could flush the bloody stuff down the drain. I defy anyone to flush Nye's filthy crap-digester with anything short of dynamite. It's a turd-encrusted drainpipe with a barrel at the bottom.'

'It has to be like that if you're going to put natural goodness back into the earth.'

'And get food poisoning,' said Wilt.

'Not if you compost it properly. The heat kills all the germs before you empty it.'

'I don't intend to empty it. You had the beastly thing installed and you can risk your life in the cellar disgorging it when it's good and ready. And don't blame me if the neighbours complain to the Health Department again.'

They argued on until supper and Wilt took the quads up to bed and read them *Mr Gumpy* for the umpteenth time. By the time he came down the Nyes had arrived and were opening a bottle of stinging-nettle wine with an alternative corkscrew John Nye had fashioned from an old bedspring.

'Ah, hullo Henry,' he said with that bright, almost religious goodwill which all Eva's friends in the Self-Sufficiency world seemed to affect. 'Not a bad vintage, 1976, though I say it myself.'

'Wasn't that the year of the drought?' asked Wilt.

'Yes, but it takes more than a drought to kill stinging-nettles. Hardy little fellows.'

'Grow them yourself?'

'No need to. They grow wild everywhere. We just gathered them from the wayside.'

Wilt looked doubtful. 'Mind telling which side of the way you harvested this particular *cru*?'

'As far as I remember it was between Ballingbourne and Umpston. In fact, I'm sure of it.' He poured a glass and handed it to Wilt.

'In that case I wouldn't touch the stuff myself,' said Wilt handing it back. 'I saw them cropspraying there in 1976. These nettles weren't grown organically. They've been contaminated.'

'But we've drunk gallons of the wine,' said Nye. 'It hasn't done us any harm.'

'Probably won't feel the effects until you're sixty,' said Wilt, 'and then it will be too late. It's the same with fluoride, you know.'

And having delivered himself of this dire warning he went through to the lounge, now rechristened by Eva the 'Being Room', and found her deep in conversation with Bertha Nye about the joys and deep responsibilities of motherhood. Since the Nyes were childless and lavished their affection on humus, two pigs, a dozen chickens and a goat, Bertha was receiving Eva's glowing account with a stoical smile. Wilt smiled stoically back and wandered out through the french windows to the summerhouse and stood in the darkness looking hopefully up at the dormer window. But the curtains were drawn. Wilt sighed, thought about what might have been and went back to hear what John Nye had to say about his Organic Toilet.

'To make the methane you have to maintain a steady temperature, and of course it would help if you had a cow.'

'Oh, I don't think we could keep a cow here,' said Eva. 'I mean we haven't the ground and . . .'

'I can't see you getting up at five every morning to milk it,' said Wilt, determined to put a stop to the awful possibility that 9 Willington Road might be turned into a smallholding. But Eva was back on the problem of the methane conversion.

'How do you go about heating it?' she asked.

'You could always install solar panels,' said Nye. 'All you need are several old radiators painted black and surrounded with straw and you pump water through them . . .'

'Wouldn't want to do that,' said Wilt. 'We'd need an electric pump and with the energy crisis what it is I have moral scruples about using electricity.'

'You don't need to use a significant amount,' said Bertha. 'And you could always work a pump off a Savonius rotor. All you require are two large drums . . .'

Wilt drifted off into his private reverie, awakening from it only to ask if there was some way of getting rid of the filthy smell from the downstairs loo, a question calculated to divert Eva's attention away from Savonius rotors, whatever they were.

'You can't have it every way, Henry,' said Nye. 'Waste not want not is an old motto, but it still applies.'

'I don't want that smell,' said Wilt. 'And if we can't produce enough methane to burn the pilot light on the gas stove without turning the garden into a stockyard, I don't see much point in wasting time stinking the house out.'

The problem was still unresolved when the Nyes left.

'Well, I must say you weren't very constructive,' said Eva as Wilt began undressing. 'I think those solar radiators sound very sensible. We could save all our hot water bills in the summer and if all you need are some old radiators and paint . . .'

'And some damned fool on the roof fixing them there. You can forget it. Knowing Nye, if he stuck them up there they'd fall off in the first gale and flatten someone underneath, and anyway with the summers we've had lately we'd be lucky to get away without having to run hot water up to them to stop them freezing and bursting and flooding the top flat.'

'You're just a pessimist,' said Eva, 'you always look on the worst side of things. Why can't you be positive for once in your life.'

'I'm a ruddy realist,' said Wilt, 'I've come to expect the worst from experience. And when the best happens I'm delighted.'

He climbed into bed and turned out the bedside lamp. By the time Eva bounced in beside him he was pretending to be asleep. Saturday nights tended to be what Eva called Nights of Togetherness, but Wilt was in love and his thoughts were all about Irmgard. Eva read another chapter on Composting and then turned her light out with a sigh. Why couldn't Henry be adventurous and enterprising like John Nye? Oh well, they could always make love in the morning.

But when she woke it was to find the bed beside her empty. For the first time since she could remember Henry had got up at seven on a Sunday morning without being driven out of bed by the quads. He was probably downstairs making her a pot of tea. Eva turned over and went back to sleep.

•

Wilt was not in the kitchen. He was walking along the path by the river. The morning was bright with autumn sunlight and the river sparkled. A light wind ruffled the willows and Wilt was alone with his thoughts and his feelings. As usual his thoughts were dark while his feelings were expressing themselves in verse. Unlike most modern poets Wilt's verse was not free. It scanned and rhymed. Or would have done if he could think of something that rhymed with Irmgard. About the only word that sprang to mind was Lifeguard. After that there was yard, sparred, barred and lard. None of them seemed to match the sensitivity of his feelings. After three fruitless miles he turned back and trudged towards his responsibilities as a married man. Wilt didn't want them.

4

He didn't much want what he found on his desk on Monday morning. It was a note from the Vice-Principal asking Wilt to come and see him at, rather sinisterly, 'your earliest, repeat earliest, convenience'.

'Bugger my convenience,' muttered Wilt. 'Why can't he say "immediately" and be done with it?'

With the thought that something was amiss and that he might as well get the bad news over and done with as quickly as possible, he went down two floors and along the corridor to the Vice-Principal's office.

'Ah Henry, I'm sorry to bother you like this,' said the Vice-Principal, 'but I'm afraid we've had some rather disturbing news about your department.'

'Disturbing?' said Wilt suspiciously.

'Distinctly disturbing. In fact all hell has been let loose up at County Hall.'

'What are they poking their noses into this time? If they think they can send any more advisers like the last one we had who wanted to know why we didn't have combined classes of bricklayers and nursery nurses so that there was sexual equality you can tell them from me . . .'

The Vice-Principal held up a protesting hand. 'That has nothing to do with what they want this time. It's what they don't want. And, quite frankly, if you had listened to their advice about multi-sexed classes this wouldn't have happened.'

'I know what would have,' said Wilt. 'We'd have been landed with a lot of pregnant nannies and—'

'If you would just listen a moment. Never mind nursery nurses. What do you know about buggering crocodiles?'

'What do I know about . . . did I hear you right?'

The Vice-Principal nodded. 'I'm afraid so.'

'Well if you want a frank answer I shouldn't have thought it was possible. And if you're suggesting . . .'

'What I am telling you, Henry, is that someone in your department has been doing it. They've even made a film of it.'

'Film of it?' said Wilt, still grappling with the appalling zoological implications of even approaching a crocodile, let alone buggering the brute.

'With some apprentice class,' continued the Vice-Principal, 'and the Education Committee have heard about it and want to know why.'

'I can't say I blame them,' said Wilt, 'I mean you'd have to be a suicidal candidate for Krafft-Ebing to proposition a fucking crocodile and while I know I've got some demented sods as part-timers I'd have noticed if any of them had been eaten. Where the hell did he get the crocodile from?'

'No use asking me,' said the Vice-Principal. 'All I know is that the Committee insist on seeing the film before passing judgement.'

'Well they can pass what judgements they like,' said Wilt, 'just so long as they leave me out of it. I accept no responsibility for any filming that's done in my department and if some maniac chooses to screw a crocodile, that's his business, not mine. I never wanted all those TV cameras and cines they foisted on to us. They cost a fortune to run and some damned fool is always breaking the things.'

'Whoever made this film should have been broken first if you ask me,' said the Vice-Principal. 'Anyway, the Committee want to see you in Room 80 at six and I'd advise you to find out what the hell has been going on before they start asking you questions.'

Wilt went wearily back to his office desperately trying to think which of the lecturers in his department was a reptile-lover, a follower of *nouvelle vague* brutalism in films and clean off his rocker. Pasco was undoubtedly insane, the result, in Wilt's opinion, of fourteen years continuous effort to get Gas-fitters to appreciate the linguistic subtleties of *Finnegans Wake*, but although he had twice spent a year's medical sabbatical in the local mental hospital he was relatively amiable and too hamfisted to use a cine-camera, and as for crocodiles . . . Wilt gave up and went along to the Audio-Visual Aid room to consult the register.

'I'm looking for some blithering idiot who's made a film about crocodiles,' he told Mr Dobble, the AVA caretaker. Mr Dobble snorted.

'You're a bit late. The Principal's got that film and he's carrying on something horrible. Mind you, I don't blame him. I said to Mr Macaulay when it came back from processing, "Blooming pornography and they pass that through the labs. Well I'm not letting that film out of here until it's been vetted." That's what I said and I meant it.'

'Vetted being the operative word,' said Wilt caustically. 'And I don't suppose it occurred to you to let me see it first before it went to the Principal?'

'Well, you don't have no control over the buggers in your department, do you Mr Wilt?'

'And which particular bugger made this film?'

'I'm not one for naming names but I will say this, Mr Bilger knows more about it than meets the eye.'

'Bilger? That bastard. I knew he was punch-drunk politically but what the hell's he want to make a film like this for?'

'No names, no packdrill,' said Mr Dobble, 'I don't want any trouble.'

'I do,' said Wilt and went out in pursuit of Bill Bilger. He found him in the staff-room drinking coffee and deep in dialectics with his acolyte, Joe Stoley, from the History Department. Bilger was arguing that a truly proletarian consciousness could only be achieved by destabilizing the fucking linguistic infrastructure of a fucking fascist state fucking hegemony.

'That's fucking Marcuse,' said Stoley rather hesitantly following Bilger into the semantic sewer of destabilization.

'And this is Wilt,' said Wilt. 'If you've got a moment to spare from discussing the millennium I'd like a word with you.'

'I'm buggered if I'm taking anyone else's class,' said Bilger adopting a sound trade-union stance. 'It's not my stand-in period you know.'

'I'm not asking you to do any extra work. I am simply asking you to have a private word with me. I realize this is infringing your inalienable right as a free individual in a fascist state to pursue happiness by stating your opinions but I'm afraid duty calls.'

'Not my bloody duty, mate,' said Bilger.

'No. Mine,' said Wilt. 'I'll be in my office in five minutes.'

'More than I will,' Wilt heard Bilger say as he headed towards the door but Wilt knew better. The man might swagger and pose to impress Stoley but Wilt still had the sanction of altering the timetable so that Bilger started the week at nine on Monday morning with Printers Three and ended it at eight on Friday evening with part-time Cooks Four. It was about the only sanction he possessed, but it was remarkably effective. While he waited he considered tactics and the composition of the Education Committee. Mrs Chatterway was bound to be there defending to the last her progressive opinion that teenage muggers were warm human beings who only needed a few sympathetic words to stop them from beating old ladies over the head. On her right there was Councillor Blighte-Smythe who would, given half a chance, have brought back hanging for poaching and probably the cat o' nine tails for the unemployed. In between these two extremes there were the Principal who hated anything or anyone who upset his leisurely schedule, the Chief Education Officer, who hated the Principal, and finally Mr Squidley, a local builder, for whom

Liberal Studies was an anathema and a bloody waste of time when the little blighters ought to have been putting in a good day's work carrying hods of bricks up blooming ladders. All in all the prospect of coping with the Education Committee was a grim one. He would have to handle them tactfully.

But first there was Bilger. He arrived after ten minutes and entered without knocking. 'Well?' he asked sitting down and staring at Wilt angrily.

'I thought we had better have this chat in private,' said Wilt. 'I just wanted to enquire about the film you made with a crocodile. I must say it sounds most enterprising. If only all Liberal Studies lecturers would use the facilities provided by the local authority to such effect . . .' He left the sentence with a tag end of unspoken approval. Bilger's hostility softened.

'The only way the working classes are going to understand how they're being manipulated by the media is to get them to make films themselves. That's all I do.'

'Quite so,' said Wilt, 'and getting them to film someone buggering a crocodile helps them to develop a proletarian consciousness transcending the false values they've been inculcated with by a capitalist hierarchy?'

'Right, mate,' said Bilger enthusiastically. 'Those fucking things are symbols of exploitation.'

'The bourgeoisie biting its conscience off, so to speak.'

'You've said it,' said Bilger, snapping at the bait.

Wilt looked at him in bewilderment. 'And what classes have you done this . . . er . . . fieldwork with?'

'Fitters and Turners Two. We got this croc thing in Nott Road and . . .'

'In Nott Road?' said Wilt, trying to square his knowledge of the street with docile and presumably homosexual crocodiles.

'Well, it's street theatre as well,' said Bilger, warming to his task. 'Half the people who live there need liberating too.'

'I daresay they do, but I wouldn't have thought encouraging them to screw crocodiles was exactly a liberating experience. I suppose as an example of the class struggle . . .'

'Here,' said Bilger, 'I thought you said you'd seen the film?'

'Not exactly. But news of its controversial content has

reached me. Someone said it was almost sub-Buñuel.'

'Really? Well, what we did is we got this toy crocodile, you know, the ones kiddies put pennies in and they get the privilege of a ride on them . . .'

'A *toy* crocodile? You mean you didn't actually use a real live one?'

'Of course we bloody didn't. I mean who'd be loony enough to rivet a real fucking crocodile? He might have been bitten.'

'Might?' said Wilt. 'I'd have said the odds on any self-respecting crocodile . . . Anyway, do go on.'

'So one of the lads gets on this plastic toy thing and we film him doing it.'

'Doing it? Let's get this quite straight. Don't you mean buggering it?'

'Sort of,' said Bilger. 'He didn't have his prick out or anything like that. There was nowhere he could have put it. No, all he did was simulate buggering the thing. That way he was symbolically screwing the whole reformist welfare statism of the capitalist system.'

'In the shape of a rocking crocodile?' said Wilt. He leant back in his chair and wondered yet again how it was that a supposedly intelligent man like Bilger, who had after all been to university and was a graduate, could still believe the world would be a better place once all the middle classes had been put up against a wall and shot. Nobody ever seemed to learn anything from the past. Well, Mr Bloody Bilger was going to learn something from the present. Wilt put his elbows on the desk.

'Let's get the record clear once and for all,' he said. 'You definitely consider it part of your duties as a Liberal Studies lecturer to teach apprentices Marxist-Leninist-Maoist-crocodile-buggerism and any other -Ism you care to mention?'

Bilger's hostility returned. 'It's a free country and I've a right to express my own personal opinions. You can't stop me.'

Wilt smiled at these splendid contradictions. 'Am I trying to?' he asked innocently. 'In fact you may not believe this, but I am willing to provide you with a platform on which to state them fully and clearly.'

'That'll be the day,' said Bilger.

'It is, Comrade Bilger, believe me it is. The Education Committee is meeting at six. The Chief Education Officer, the Principal, Councillor Blighte-Smythe—'

'That militaristic shit. What's he know about education? Just because they gave him the MC in the war he thinks he can go about trampling on the faces of the working classes.'

'Which, considering he has a wooden leg, doesn't say much for your opinion of the proletariat, does it?' said Wilt warming to his task. 'First you praise the working class for their intelligence and solidarity, then you reckon they are so dumb they can't tell their own interests from a soap advert on TV and have to be forcibly politicized, and now you tell me that a man who lost his leg can trample all over them. The way you talk they sound like morons.'

'I didn't say that,' said Bilger.

'No, but that seems to be your attitude and if you want to express yourself on the subject more lucidly you may do so to the Committee at six. I am sure they will be most interested.'

'I'm not going before any fucking Committee. I know my rights and—'

'This is a free country, as you keep telling me. Another splendid contradiction, and considering the country allows you to go around getting teenage apprentices to simulate fucking toy crocodiles I'd say a free fucking society just about sums it up. I just wish sometimes we were living in Russia.'

'They'd know what to do with blokes like you, Wilt,' said Bilger. 'You're just a deviationist reformist swine.'

'Deviationist, coming from you, is great,' shouted Wilt, 'and with their draconian laws anyone who went about filming Russian fitters buggering crocodiles would end up smartly in the Lubianka and wouldn't come out until they had put a bullet in the back of his mindless head. Either that or they would lock you up in some nuthouse and you'd probably be the only inmate who wasn't sane.'

'Right, Wilt,' Bilger shouted back, leaping from his chair, 'that does it. You may be Head of Department but if you think you can insult lecturers I know what I'm going to do. Lodge a complaint with the union.' He headed for the door.

'That's right,' yelled Wilt, 'run for your collective mummy and while you're about it tell the secretary you called me a deviationist swine. They'll appreciate the term.'

But Bilger was already out of the office and Wilt was left with the problem of finding some plausible excuse to offer the Committee. Not that he would have minded getting rid of Bilger but the idiot had a wife and three children and certainly couldn't expect help from his father, Rear-Admiral Bilger. It was typical of that kind of intellectual radical buffoon that he came from what was known as 'a good family'.

In the meantime he had to finish preparing his lecture to the Advanced Foreigners. Liberal and Progressive attitudes be damned, From 1688 to 1978, almost three hundred years of English history compressed into eight lectures, and all with Dr Mayfield's bland assumption that progress was continuous and that liberal attitudes were somehow independent of time and place. What about Ulster? A fat lot of liberal attitudes applied there in 1978. And the Empire hadn't exactly been a model of liberalism. The most you could say about it was that it hadn't been as bloody awful as the Belgian Congo or Angola. But then Mayfield was a sociologist and what he knew about history was dangerous. Not that Wilt knew much himself. And why English Liberalism? Mayfield seemed to think that the Welsh and Scots and Irish didn't exist, or if they did that they weren't progressive and liberal too.

Wilt got out a ballpoint and jotted down notes. They had nothing at all to do with Mayfield's proposed course. He was still rambling speculatively on when lunchtime came. He went down to the canteen and ate what was called curry and rice at a table by himself and returned to his office with fresh ideas. This time they concerned the influence of the Empire on England. Curry, baksheesh, pukka, posh, polo, thug – words that had infiltrated the English language from farflung outposts where the Wilts of a previous age had lorded it with an arrogance and authority he found it hard to imagine. He was interrupted in these pleasantly nostalgic speculations by Mrs Rosery, the Department secretary, who came to say that Mr Germiston was sick and couldn't take Electronic Technicians Three and that Mr Laxton, his stand-in, had done a swop with Mrs Vaugard without telling anyone and she wasn't available because she had previously made an appointment at the dentist and . . .

Wilt went downstairs and crossed to the hut where Electronic Technicians were sitting in a stupor of pub-lunch beer. 'Right,' he said sitting down behind the table, 'Now what have you been doing with Mr Germiston?'

'Haven't done a bloody thing with him,' said a red-headed youth in the front. 'He isn't worth it. One punch up the snout and . . .'

'What I meant,' said Wilt before redhead could go into the details of what would happen to Germiston in a fight, 'was what has he been talking to you about so far this term?'

'Fucking darkies,' said another technician.

'Not literally, I trust,' said Wilt hoping that his irony would not lead to a discussion of interracial sex. 'You mean race relations?'

'I mean spades. That's what I mean. Nignogs, wogs, foreigners, all them buggers what come in here and take jobs away from decent white blokes. What I say is . . .'

But he was interrupted by another ET 3. 'You don't want to listen to what he says. Joe's a member of the National Front—'

'What's so wrong with that?' demanded Joe. 'Our policy is to keep—'

'Out of politics,' said Wilt. 'That's my policy and I mean to stick with it. What you say outside is your affair but in the classroom we'll discuss something else.'

'Yeah, well you ought to tell old Germ-Piston that. He spends his bloody life telling us we got to be Christians and love our neighbours like ourselves. Well if he lived in our street he'd know different. We got a load of Jamrags two doors off and they play bongo drums and dustbins till four in the ruddy morning. If old Germy knows a way of loving that din all fucking night he must be blooming deaf.'

'You could always ask them to quieten down a bit or stop at eleven,' said Wilt.

'What, and get a knife in the guts for the privilege? You must be joking.'

'Then the police . . .'

Joe looked at him incredulously. 'A bloke four doors down went to the fuzz and you know what happened to him?'

'No,' said Wilt.

'Had his car tyres slashed two days later. That's what. And did the cops want to know? Did they fuck.'

'Well I can see you've got a problem,' Wilt had to admit.

'Yeah, and we know how to solve it too,' said Joe.

'You're not going to solve it by sending them back to Jamaica,' said the Technician who was anti the National Front. 'The ones in your street didn't come from there anyway. They were born in Brixton.'

'Brixton Nick if you ask me.'

'You're just prejudiced.'

'So would you be if you didn't get a night's kip in a month.' The battle raged on while Wilt sat contemplating the class. It was just as he had remembered it from his old days. You got the apprentices going and then left them to it, only prodding them into further controversy with a provocative comment when the argument flagged. And these were the selfsame apprentices the Bilgers of this world wanted to instil with political consciousness as if they were proletarian geese to be force-fed to produce a totalitarian pâté de foie gras.

But already Electronic Technicians Three had veered away from race and were arguing about last year's Cup Final. They seemed to have stronger feelings about football than politics. At the end of the hour Wilt left them and made his way across to the auditorium to deliver his lecture to Advanced Foreigners. To his horror he found the place packed. Dr Mayfield had been right in saying that the course was popular and immensely profitable. Looking up the rows, Wilt made a mental note that he was probably about to address several million poundsworth of oil wells, steelworks, shipyards and chemical industries scattered from Stockholm to Tokyo via Saudi Arabia and the Persian Gulf. Well, the blighters had come to learn about England and the English attitudes and he might as well give them their money's worth.

Wilt stepped up to the rostrum, arranged his few notes, tapped the microphone so that several loud booms issued from the loudspeakers at the back of the auditorium and began his lecture.

'It may come as something of a surprise to those of you who come from more authoritarian societies that I intend to ignore the title of the course of lectures I am supposed to be giving, namely The Development of Liberal and Progressive Social Attitudes in English Society from 1688 to the present day, and to concentrate on the more essential problem, not to say the enigma, of what constitutes the nature of being English. It is a problem that has baffled the finest foreign minds for centuries and I have no doubt that it will baffle you. I have to admit that I myself, although English, remain bewildered by the subject and I have no reason to suppose that I will be any clearer in my mind at the end of these lectures than I am now.'

Wilt paused and looked at his audience. Their heads were bent over notebooks and their ballpoints scribbled away. It was what he had come to expect. They would dutifully write down everything he had to tell them as unthinkingly as previous groups he had lectured, but somewhere among them there might be one person who would puzzle over what he had to say. He would give them all something to puzzle over this time.

'I will start with a list of books which are essential reading, but before I do so I will draw your attention to an example of the Englishness I hope to explore. It is that I have chosen to ignore the subject I am supposed to be teaching and have taken a topic of my own choice. I am also confining myself to England and ignoring Wales, Scotland, and what is popularly known as Great Britain. I know less about Glasgow than I do about New Delhi, and the inhabitants of those parts would feel insulted were I to include them among the English. In particular I shall avoid discussing the Irish. They are wholly beyond my comprehension as an Englishman and their methods of settling disputes are not ones that appeal to me. I will only repeat what Metternich, I believe, had to say about Ireland, that it is England's Poland.' Wilt paused again and allowed the class to make another wholly inconsequential note. If the Saudis had ever heard of Metternich he would be very surprised.

'And now the book list. The first is *The Wind in the Willows* by Kenneth Grahame. This gives the finest description of English middle-class aspirations and attitudes to be found in English literature. You will find that it deals entirely with animals, and that these animals are all male. The only women in the book are minor characters, one a bargewoman and the others a jailer's daughter and her aunt, and strictly speaking they are irrelevant. The main characters are a Water Rat, a Mole, a Badger and a Toad, none of whom is married or evinces the slightest interest in the opposite sex. Those of you who come from more torrid climates, or have sauntered through Soho, may find this lack of sexual motif surprising. I can only say that its absence is entirely in keeping with the values of middle-class family life in England. For those students who are not content with aspirations and attitudes but wish to study the subject in greater, if prurient, depth I can recommend certain of the daily newspapers, and in particular the Sunday ones. The number of choirboys indecently assaulted annually by vicars and churchwardens may lead you to suppose that England is a deeply religious country. I incline to the view held by some that . . .'

But whatever view Wilt was about to incline to, the class never learnt. He stopped in mid-sentence and stared down at a face in the third row. Irmgard Mueller was one of his students. Worse still, she was looking at him with a curious intensity and had not bothered to take any notes. Wilt gazed back and then looked down at his own notes and tried to think what to say next. But all the ideas he had so ironically rehearsed had disintegrated. For the first time in a long career of improvisation, Wilt dried up. He stood at the rostrum with sweating hands and looked at the clock. He had to say something for the next forty minutes, something intense and serious and . . . yes, even significant. That dread word of his sensitive youth burped to the surface. Wilt steeled himself.

'As I was saying,' he stammered just as his audience began to whisper among themselves, 'none of the books I have recommended will do more than scratch the surface of the problem of being English . . . or rather of knowing the nature of the English.' For the next half an hour he strung disjointed sentences together and finally muttering something about pragmaticism gathered his notes together and ended the lecture. He was just climbing down from the stage when Irmgard left her seat and approached him.

'Mr Wilt,' she said, 'I want to say how interesting I found your lecture.'

'Very good of you to say so,' said Wilt dissembling his passion.

'I was particularly interested in what you said about the parliamentary system only seeming to be democratic. You are the first lecturer we have had who has put the problem of England in the context of social reality and popular culture. You were very illuminating.'

It was an illuminated Wilt who floated out of the auditorium and up the steps to his office. There could be no doubt about it now. Irmgard was not simply beautiful. She was also radiantly intelligent. And Wilt had met the perfect woman twenty years too late.

5

He was so preoccupied with this new and exhilarating problem that he was twenty minutes late for the meeting of the Education Committee and arrived as Mr Dobble was leaving with the film projector and the air of a man who has done his duty by putting the cat among the pigeons.

'Don't blame me, Mr Wilt,' he said as Wilt scowled, 'I'm only here to . . .'

Wilt ignored him and entered the room to find the Committee arranging themselves around a long table. A solitary chair was placed conspicuously at the far end and, as Wilt had foreseen, they were all there, the Principal, the Vice-Principal, Councillor Blighte-Smythe, Mrs Chatterway, Mr Squidley and the Chief Education Officer.

'Ah, Wilt,' said the Principal by way of unenthusiastic greeting. 'Take a seat.'

Wilt steeled himself to avoid the solitary chair and sat down beside the Education Officer. 'I gather you want to see me about the anti-pornographic film made by a member of the Liberal Studies Department,' he said, trying to take the initiative.

The Committee glared at him.

'You can cut the anti for a start,' said Councillor Blighte-Smythe, 'what we have just seen buggers . . . er . . . beggars belief. The thing is downright pornography.'

'I suppose it might be to someone with a fetish about crocodiles,' said Wilt. 'Personally, since I haven't had the chance to see the film, I can't say how it would affect me.'

'But you did say it was anti-pornographic,' said Mrs Chatterway whose progressive opinions invariably put her at odds with the Councillor and Mr Squidley, 'and as Head of Liberal Studies you must have sanctioned it. I'm sure the Committee would like to hear your reasons.'

Wilt smiled wryly. 'I think the title of Head of Department needs some explaining, Mrs Chatterway,' he began, only to be interrupted by Blighte-Smythe.

'So does this fuc . . . filthy film we've just had to see. Let's stick to the issue,' he snapped.

'It happens to be the issue,' said Wilt. 'The mere fact that I am called Head of Liberal Studies doesn't mean I am in a position to control what the members of my so-called staff do.'

'We know what they ruddy well do,' said Mr Squidley, 'and if any man on my workforce started doing what we've watched I'd soon give him the boot.'

'Well, it's rather different in education,' said Wilt. 'I can lay down guidelines in regard to teaching policy, but I think the

43

Principal will agree that no Head of Department can sack a lecturer for failing to follow them.' Wilt looked at the Principal for confirmation. It came regretfully. The Principal would happily have sacked Wilt years ago. 'True,' he muttered.

'You mean to tell us you can't get rid of the pervert who made this film?' demanded Blighte-Smythe.

'Not unless he continually fails to turn up for his teaching periods, is habitually drunk, or openly cohabits with students, no,' said Wilt.

'Is that true?' Mr Squidley asked the Education Officer.

'I'm afraid so. Unless we can prove blatant incompetence or sexual immorality involving a student, there's no way of removing a full-time lecturer.'

'If getting a student to bugger a crocodile isn't sexual immorality I'd like to know what is,' said Councillor Blighte-Smythe.

'As I understand it the object in question was not a proper crocodile and there was no actual intercourse,' said Wilt, 'and in any case the lecturer merely recorded the event on film. He didn't participate himself.'

'He'd have been arrested if he had,' said Mr Squidley. 'It's a wonder the sod wasn't lynched.'

'Aren't we in danger of losing the central theme of this meeting?' asked the Principal. 'I believe Mr Ranlon has some other questions to raise.'

The Education Officer shuffled his notes. 'I would like to ask Mr Wilt what his policy guidelines are in regard to Liberal Studies. They may have some bearing on a number of complaints we have received from members of the public.' He glared at Wilt and waited.

'It might help if I knew what those complaints were,' said Wilt stalling for time but Mrs Chatterway intervened.

'Surely the purpose of Liberal Studies has always been to inculcate a sense of social responsibility and concern for others in the young people in our care, many of whom have themselves been deprived of a progressive education.'

'Depraved would be a better word if you ask me,' said Councillor Blighte-Smythe.

'Nobody did,' barked Mrs Chatterway. 'We all know very well what your views are.'

'Perhaps if we heard what Mr Wilt's views are . . .' suggested the Education Officer.

'Well, in the past Liberal Studies consisted largely of keeping day-release apprentices quiet for an hour by getting them to read books,' said Wilt. 'In my opinion they didn't learn anything and the system was a waste of time.' He halted in the hope that the Councillor would say something to infuriate Mrs Chatterway. Mr Squidley squashed the hope by agreeing with him.

'Always was and always will be. I've said it before and I'll say it again. They'd be better employed doing a proper day's work instead of wasting ratepayers' money loafing in classrooms.'

'Well at least we have some measure of agreement,' said the Principal pacifically. 'As I understand it Mr Wilt's guideline has been a more practical one. Am I right, Wilt?'

'The policy of the department has been to teach apprentices how to do things. I believe in interesting them in . . .'

'Crocodiles?' enquired Councillor Blighte-Smythe.

'No,' said Wilt.

The Education Officer looked down the list in front of him. 'I see here that your notion of practical education includes home brewing.'

Wilt nodded.

'May one ask why? I shouldn't have thought encouraging adolescents to become alcoholics served any educational purpose.'

'It serves to keep them out of pubs for a start,' said Wilt. 'And in any case Gas Engineers Four are not adolescents. Half of them are married men with children.'

'And does the course in home brewing extend to the manufacture of illicit stills?'

'Stills?' said Wilt.

'For making spirit.'

'I don't think anyone in my department would have the expertise. As it is the stuff they brew is . . .'

45

'According to Customs and Excise almost pure alcohol,' said the Education Officer. 'Certainly the forty-gallon drum they unearthed from the basement of the Engineering block had to be burnt. In the words of one Excise officer, you could run a car on the muck.'

'Perhaps that's what they intended it for,' said Wilt.

'In which case,' continued the Education Officer, 'it hardly seemed appropriate to have labelled several bottles Chateau Tech VSOP.'

The Principal looked at the ceiling and prayed but the Education Officer hadn't finished.

'Would you mind telling us about the class you have organized for Caterers on Self Sufficiency?'

'Well, actually it's called Living Off The Land,' said Wilt.

'Quite so. The land in question being Lord Podnorton's.'

'Never heard of him.'

'He has heard of this institution. His head gamekeeper caught two apprentice cooks in the act of decapitating a pheasant with the aid of a ten-foot length of plastic tubing through which had been looped a strand of piano wire stolen from the Music Department, which probably accounts for the fact that fourteen pianos have had to be restrung in the past two terms.'

'Good Lord, I thought they had been vandalized,' muttered the Principal.

'Lord Podnorton was under the same misapprehension about his greenhouses, four cold frames, a currant cage . . .'

'Well, all I can say,' interrupted Wilt, 'is that breaking into greenhouses wasn't part of the syllabus for Living Off The Land. I can assure you of that. I got the idea from my wife who is very keen on composting . . .'

'No doubt you got the next course from her too. I have here a letter from Mrs Tothingford complaining that we conduct classes in karate for nannies. Perhaps you would like to explain that.'

'We do have a course called Rape Retaliation for Nursery Nurses. We thought it wise in the light of the rising tide of violence.'

'Very sensible too,' said Mrs Chatterway, 'I heartily approve.'

'Perhaps you do,' said the Education Officer looking at her critically over his glasses, 'Mrs Tothingford doesn't. Her letter is addressed from the hospital where she is being treated for a broken collar-bone, a dislocated Adam's apple, and internal injuries inflicted on her by her nanny last Saturday night. You're not going to tell me that Mrs Tothingford is a rapist?'

'She might be,' said Wilt. 'Have you asked her if she is a lesbian? It's been known for—'

'Mrs Tothingford happens to be the mother of five and wife of . . .' He consulted the letter.

'Three?' asked Wilt.

'Judge Tothingford, Wilt,' snarled the Education Officer. 'And if you're suggesting that a judge's wife is a lesbian I would remind you that there is such a thing as slander.'

'There's such a thing as a married lesbian too,' said Wilt. 'I knew one once. She lived down our . . .'

'We are not here to discuss your deplorable acquaintances.'

'I thought you were. After all you asked me here to talk about a film made by a lecturer in my department and while I would not call him a friend I am vaguely acquainted . . .'

He was silenced by a kick under the table from the V-P.

'Is that the end of the casualty list?' asked the Principal hopefully.

'I could go on almost indefinitely, but I won't,' said the Education Officer. 'What it all adds up to is that the Liberal Studies Department is not only failing in its supposed function of instilling a sense of social responsibility in day-release apprentices but is actively fostering anti-social behaviour . . .'

'That's not my fault,' said Wilt angrily.

'You are responsible for the way your department is run, and as such answerable to the Local Authority.'

Wilt snorted. 'Local Authority, my foot. If I had any authority at all this film would never have been made. Instead of that I am lumbered with lecturers I didn't appoint and can't fire, half of whom are raving revolutionaries or anarchists, and the other half couldn't keep order if the students were in strait-jackets and you expect me to be answerable for everything that happens.'

Wilt looked at the members of the Committee and shook his head. Even the Education Officer was looking somewhat abashed.

'The problem is clearly a very complex one,' said Mrs Chatterway, who had swung round to Wilt's defence since hearing about the Rape Retaliation Course for Nursery Nurses. 'I think I can speak for the entire Committee when I say we appreciate the difficulties Mr Wilt faces.'

'Never mind what Mr Wilt faces,' intervened Blighte-Smythe. 'We are going to face a few difficulties ourselves if this thing ever gets out. If the press got wind of the story . . .'

Mrs Chatterway blanched at the prospect while the Principal covered his eyes. Wilt noted their reactions with interest.

'I don't know,' he said cheerfully. 'I'm all in favour of public debates on issues of educational importance. Parents ought to know the way their children are being taught. I've got four daughters and . . .'

'Wilt,' said the Principal violently, 'the Committee has generously agreed that you cannot be held wholly responsible for these deplorable incidents. I don't think we need detain you further.'

But Wilt remained seated and pursued his advantage. 'I take it then that you're not willing to bring this regrettable affair to the attention of the media. Well, if that is your decision . . .'

'Listen, Wilt,' snarled the Education Officer, 'if one word of this is leaked to the press or is discussed in any public form I'll see . . . Well, I wouldn't like to be in your shoes.'

Wilt stood up. 'I don't like being in them at the moment,' he said. 'You call me in here and cross-examine me about something I can't prevent because you refuse to give me any real authority and then when I propose making this disgraceful state of affairs a public issue you start threatening me. I've half a mind to complain to the union.' And having delivered this terrible threat he headed for the door.

'Wilt,' shouted the Principal, 'we haven't finished yet.'

'Nor have I,' said Wilt and opened the door. 'I find this whole attempt to cover up a matter of serious public concern most reprehensible. I do indeed.'

'Christ,' said Mrs Chatterway uncharacteristically calling for Divine guidance. 'You don't think he means it, do you?'

'I have long since given up trying to think what Wilt means,' said the Principal miserably. 'All I can be certain about is that I wish to God we'd never employed him.'

6

'You'd be committing promotional suicide,' Peter Braintree told Wilt as they sat over pints in The Glassblower's Arms later that evening.

'I feel like committing real suicide,' said Wilt, ignoring the pork pie Braintree had just bought him. 'And it's no use trying to tempt me with pork pies.'

'You've got to have some supper. In your condition it's vital.'

'In my condition, nothing is vital. On the one hand I am forced to fight battles with the Principal, the Chief Education Officer and his foul Committee on behalf of lunatics like Bilger who want a bloody revolution, and on the other, after I have spent years thrusting down predatory lusts for Senior Secretaries, Miss Trott and the occasional Nursery Nurse, Eva has to introduce into the house the most splendid, the most ravishing woman she can find. You may not believe me . . . remember that summer and the Swedes?'

'The ones you had to teach *Sons and Lovers* to?'

'Yes,' said Wilt, 'four weeks of D. H. Lawrence and thirty delectable Swedish girls. Well, if that wasn't a baptism of lust I don't know what is. And I came through unscathed. I went home to Eva every evening unblemished. If the sex war was openly declared I'd have won the Marital Medal for chastity beyond the call of duty.'

'Well we've all had to go through that phase,' said Braintree.

'And what exactly do you mean by "that phase"?' asked Wilt stiffly.

'The body beautiful, boobs, bottoms, the occasional glimpse of thigh. I remember once . . .'

'I prefer not to hear your loathsome fantasies,' said Wilt. 'Some other time perhaps. With Irmgard it's different. I am not talking about the merely physical. We relate.'

'Good God, Henry . . .' said Braintree, flabbergasted.

'Exactly. When did you hear me use that dreaded word before?'

'Never.'

'You're hearing it now. And if that doesn't indicate the fearful predicament I'm in, nothing will.'

'It does,' said Braintree. 'You're . . .'

'In love,' said Wilt.

'I was going to say out of your mind.'

'It amounts to the same thing. I am caught in the horns of a dilemma. I use that cliché advisedly, though to be perfectly frank horns don't come into it. I am married to a formidable, frenetic and basically insensitive wife . . .'

'Who doesn't understand you. We've heard all this before.'

'Who does understand me. And you haven't,' said Wilt and drank some more beer bitterly.

'Henry, someone has been putting stuff in your tea,' said Braintree.

'Yes, and we all know who that is. Mrs Crippen.'

'Mrs Crippen? What the hell are you talking about?'

'Has it ever occurred to you,' said Wilt pointedly shoving the pork pie down the counter, 'what would have happened if Mrs Crippen, instead of being childless and bullying her husband and generally being in the way, had had quads? I can see it hasn't. Well, it has to me. Ever since I taught that course on Orwell and the Art of the English Murder, I have gone into the subject deeply on my way home to an Alternative Supper consisting of uncooked soya sausage and homegrown sorrel washed down with dandelion coffee and I've come to certain conclusions.'

'Henry, this is verging on paranoia,' said Braintree sternly.

'Is it? Then answer my question. If Mrs Crippen had had quads who would have ended up under the cellar floor? Dr Crippen. No, don't interrupt. You are not aware of the change that maternity has brought to Eva. I am. I live in an oversize house with an oversize mother and four daughters and I can tell you that I have had an insight into the female of the species which is denied more fortunate men and I know when I'm not wanted.'

'What the hell are you on about now?'

'Two more pints please,' Wilt told the barman, 'and kindly return that pie to its cage.'

'Now look here, Henry, you're letting your imagination run away with you,' said Braintree. 'You're not seriously suggesting that Eva is setting out to poison you?'

'I won't go quite that far,' said Wilt, 'though the thought did cross my mind when Eva moved into Alternative Fungi. I soon put a stop to that by getting Samantha to taste them first. I may be redundant but the quads aren't. Not in Eva's opinion anyway. She sees her litter as being potential geniuses. Samantha is Einstein, Penelope's handiwork with a felt-pen on the sitting-room wall suggested she was a feminine Michelangelo, Josephine hardly needs an introduction with a name like that. Need I go on?'

Braintree shook his head.

'Right,' continued Wilt, despondently helping himself to the fresh beer. 'As a male I have performed my biological function and just when I was settling down relatively happily to premature senility Eva, with an infallible intuition, which I might add I never suspected, brings to live under the same roof a woman who possesses all those remarkable qualities, intelligence, beauty, a spiritual sensitivity and a radiance . . . all I can say is that Irmgard is the epitome of the woman I should have married.'

'And didn't,' said Braintree emerging from the beer-mug where he had taken refuge from Wilt's ghastly catalogue. 'You are lumbered with Eva and . . .'

'Lumbered is exact,' said Wilt. 'When Eva gets into bed . . . I'll spare you the sordid details. Suffice it to say that she's twice the man I am.' He relapsed into silence and finished his pint.

'Anyway, I still say you'd be making a hell of a mistake if

you brought the Tech any more bad publicity,' said Braintree, to change a distressing subject. 'Let sleeping dogs lie is my motto.'

'Mine too if people didn't sleep with crocs on film,' said Wilt. 'As it is that bastard Bilger has the gall to tell me I'm a deviationist swine and a lackey of capitalistic fascism . . . thank you, I will have another pint . . . and all the time I'm protecting the sod. I've half a mind to make a public issue of the whole damned thing. Only half a mind, because Toxted and his gang of National Front thugs are just waiting for a chance to have a punch-up and I'm not going to be their hero thank you very much.'

'I saw our little Hitler pinning up a poster in the canteen this morning,' said Braintree.

'Oh really, what's he advocating this time? Castration for coolies or bring back the rack?'

'Something to do with Zionism,' said Braintree. 'I'd have ripped the thing down if he hadn't had a bodyguard of Bedouins. He's moved in with the Arabs now, you know.'

'Brilliant,' said Wilt, 'absolutely brilliant. That's what I like about these maniacs of the right and left, they're so bloody inconsistent. There's Bilger who sends his children to a private school and lives in a ruddy great house his father bought him and he goes round advocating world revolution from the driving seat of a Porsche that must have cost six thousand if it cost a penny and he calls me a fascist pig. I'm just recovering from that one when I bang into Toxted who is a genuine fascist and lives in a council house and wants to send anyone with a pigmentation problem back to Islamabad even though they were actually born in Clapham and haven't been out of England since, and who does he team up with? A bunch of ruddy sheikhs with more oil dollars under their burnouses than he's had hot dinners, can't speak more than three words of English, and own half Mayfair. Add the fact that they're semites and he's so anti-semitic he makes Eichmann look like a Friend of Israel, and then tell me how his bloody mind ticks. I'm damned if I know. It's enough to drive a rational man to drink.'

As if to give point to this remark Wilt ordered two more pints.

'You've had six already,' said Braintree doubtfully. 'Eva will give you hell when you get home.'

'Eva gives me hell, period,' said Wilt. 'When I consider how my life is spent . . .'

'Yes, well I'd just as soon you didn't,' said Braintree, 'there's nothing worse than an introspective drunk.'

'I was quoting from the first line of "Testament of Beauty" by Robert Bridges,' said Wilt. 'Not that it's relevant. And I may be introspective but I am not introspectively drunk. I am merely pissed. If you'd had the sort of day I've had and were faced with the prospect of climbing into bed with Eva in a foul temper you would seek oblivion in beer too. Added to which is the knowledge that ten feet above my head, separated only by a ceiling, a floor and some wall-to-wall rush matting, will be lying the most beautiful, intelligent, radiant, sensitive creature . . .'

'If you mention the word Muse again, Henry . . .' said Braintree threateningly.

'I don't intend to,' said Wilt. 'Such ears as yours are far too coarse. Come to think of it, that almost rhymes. Has it ever occurred to you that English is a language most naturally fitted for poetry which rhymes?'

Wilt launched into this more agreeable topic and finished more beers. By the time they left The Glassblower's Arms Braintree was too drunk to drive home.

'I'll leave the car here and fetch it in the morning,' he told Wilt, who was propping up a telegraph pole, 'and if I were you I'd ring for a taxi. You're not even fit to walk.'

'I shall commune with nature,' said Wilt, 'I have no intention of hastening the time between now and reality. With any luck it'll be asleep by the time I get back.'

And he wobbled off in the direction of Willington Road, stopping occasionally to steady himself against a gatepost and twice to pee into someone else's garden. On the second occasion he mistook a rosebush for a hydrangea and scratched himself rather badly and was sitting on the grass verge attempting to use a handkerchief as a tourniquet when a police car pulled up beside him. Wilt blinked into the flashlight which shone in his face before travelling down to the bloodstained handkerchief.

'Are you all right?' asked the voice behind the flashlight, rather too obsequiously for Wilt's taste.

'Does it look like it?' he asked truculently. 'You find a bloke sitting on the kerb tying a handkerchief round the remains of his once-proud manhood and you ask a bloody fool question like that?'

'If you don't mind, sir, I'd lay off the abusive language,' said the policeman. 'There's a law against using it on the public highway.'

'There ought to be a law about planting ruddy rosebushes next to the fucking pavement,' said Wilt.

'And may one ask what you were doing to the rose, sir?'

'One may,' said Wilt, 'if one can't bloody well surmise for one's ruddy self, one may indeed.'

'Mind telling me, then?' said the policeman taking out a notebook. Wilt told him with a wealth of description and a volubility that brought the lights on in several houses down the road. Ten minutes later he was helped out of the police car into the station. 'Drunk and disorderly, using abusive language, disturbing the peace . . .'

Wilt intervened. 'Peace my bloody foot,' he shouted. 'That was no Peace. We've got a Peace in our front garden and it hasn't got thorns a foot long. And anyway I wasn't disturbing it. You want to try partial circumcision on flaming floribunda to find out what disturbs what. All I was doing was quietly relieving myself or in plain language having a slash when that infernal thicket of climbing cat's claws took it into its vegetable head to have a slash at me and if you don't believe me, go back and try for yourselves . . .'

'Take him down to the cells,' said the desk sergeant to prevent Wilt upsetting an elderly woman who had come in to report the loss of her Pekinese. But before the two constables could drag Wilt away to a cell they were interrupted by a shout from Inspector Flint's office. The Inspector had been called back to the station by the arrest of a long-suspected burglar and was happily interrogating him when the sound of a familiar voice reached him. He erupted from his office and stared lividly at Wilt.

'What the hell is he doing here?' he demanded.

'Well, sir . . .' one constable began but Wilt broke loose.

'According to your goons I was attempting to rape a rose-bush. According to me I was having a quiet pee . . .'

'Wilt,' yelled the Inspector, 'if you've come down here to make my life a misery again, forget it. And as for you two, take a good look at this bastard, a very good, long look and unless you catch him in the act of actually murdering someone, or better still wait until you've seen him do it, don't lay a finger on the brute. Now get him out of here.'

'But, sir—'

'I said out,' shouted Flint. 'I meant out. That thing you've just brought in is a human virus of infective insanity. Get him out of here before he turns this station into a madhouse.'

'Well, I like that,' Wilt protested. 'I get dragged down here on a trumped-up charge . . .'

He was dragged out again while Flint went back to his office and sat abstractedly thinking about Wilt. Visions of that damned doll still haunted his mind and he would never forget the hours he had spent interrogating the little sod. And then there was Mrs Eva Wilt whose corpse he had supposed to be buried under thirty tons of concrete while all the time the wretched woman was drifting down the river on a motor cruiser. Together the Wilts had made him look an idiot and there were jokes in the canteen about inflatable dolls. One of these days he would get his revenge. Yes, one of these days . . He turned back to the burglar with a new sense of purpose.

On the doorstep of his house in Willington Road Wilt sat staring up at the clouds and meditating on love and life and the differing impressions he made on people. What had Flint called him? An infective virus . . . a human virus of infective . . . The word recalled Wilt to his own injury.

'Might get tetanus or something,' he muttered and fumbled in his pocket for the doorkey. Ten minutes later, still wearing his jacket but without trousers and pants, Wilt was in the bathroom soaking his manhood in a toothmug filled with warm water and Dettol when Eva came in.

'Have you any idea what time it is? It's—' She stopped and stared in horror at the toothmug.

'Three o'clock,' said Wilt, trying to steer the conversation back to less controversial matters, but Eva's interest in the time had vanished.

'What on earth are doing with that thing?' she gasped. Wilt looked down at the toothmug.

'Well, now that you come to mention it, and despite all circum . . . circumstantial evidence to the contrary, I am not . . . well, actually I am trying to disinfect myself. You see—'

'Disinfect yourself?'

'Yes . . . well,' said Wilt conscious that there was an element of ambiguity about the explanation, 'the thing is . . .'

'In my toothmug,' shouted Eva. 'You stand there with your thingamajig in my toothmug and admit you're disinfecting yourself? And who was the woman, or didn't you bother to ask her name?'

'It wasn't a woman. It was . . .'

'Don't tell me. I don't want to know. Mavis was right about you. She said you didn't just walk home. She said you spent your evenings with some other woman.'

'It wasn't another woman. It was . . .'

'Don't lie to me. To think that after all these years of married life you have to resort to whores and prostitutes . . .'

'It wasn't a whore in that sense,' said Wilt. 'I suppose you could say hips and haws but it's spelt differently and . . .'

'That's right, try to wriggle out of it . . .'

'I'm not wriggling out of anything. I got caught in a rose-bush . . .'

'Is that what they call themselves nowadays? Rosebushes?' Eva stopped and stared at Wilt with fresh horror.

'As far as I know they've always called themselves rose-bushes,' said Wilt, unaware that Eva's suspicions had hit a new low. 'I don't see what else you can call them.'

'Gays? Faggots? How about them for a start?'

'What?' shouted Wilt, but Eva was not to be stopped.

'I always knew there was something wrong with you, Henry Wilt,' she bawled, 'and now I know what. And to think that you come back and use my toothmug to disinfect yourself. How low can you get?'

'Listen,' said Wilt, suddenly conscious that his Muse was privy to Eva's appalling innuendos, 'I can prove it was a rosebush. Take a look if you don't believe me.'

But Eva didn't wait. 'Don't think you're spending another night in my house,' she shouted from the passage. 'Never again! You can take yourself back to your boyfriend and . . .'

'I have had about as much as I can take from you,' yelled Wilt emerging in hot pursuit. He was brought up short by the sight of Penelope standing wide-eyed in the passage.

'Oh, shit,' said Wilt and retreated to the bathroom again. Outside he could hear Penelope sobbing and Eva hysterically pretending to calm her. A bedroom door opened and closed. Wilt sat on the edge of the bath and cursed. Then he emptied the toothmug down the toilet, dried himself distractedly on a towel and used the Elastoplast. Finally he squeezed toothpaste on to the electric toothbrush and was busily brushing his teeth when the bedroom door opened again and Eva rushed out.

'Henry Wilt, if you're using that toothbrush to . . .'

'Once and for all,' yelled Wilt with a mouthful of foam, 'I am sick and tired of your vile insinuations. I have had a long and tiring day and—'

'I can believe that,' bawled Eva.

'For your information I am simply brushing my teeth prior to climbing into bed and if you think I am doing anything else . . .' He was interrupted by the toothbrush. The end jumped off and fell into the washbasin.

'Now what are you doing?' Eva demanded.

'Trying to get the brush out of the plughole,' said Wilt, an explanation that led to further recriminations, a brief and uneven encounter at the top of the stairs and finally a disgruntled Wilt being shoved out through the kitchen door with a sleep-

ing-bag and told to spend the rest of the night in the summerhouse.

'I won't have you perverting the minds of the wee ones,' Eva
shouted through the door, 'and tomorrow I'm seeing a lawyer.'

'As if I bloody care,' Wilt shouted back and wove down the
garden to the summerhouse. For a while he stumbled about in
the darkness trying to find the zip in the sleeping-bag. It didn't
appear to have one. Wilt sat down on the floor and got his feet
into the thing and was just wriggling his way down it when a
sound from behind the summerhouse startled him into silence.
Someone was making his way through the orchard from the
field beyond. Wilt sat still in the darkness and listened. There
could be no doubt about it. There was a rustle of grass, and a
twig broke. Silence again. Wilt peered over the edge of the
window and as he did so the lights in the house went out. Eva
had gone to bed again. The sound of someone walking cautiously through the orchard began once more. In the summerhouse Wilt's imagination was toying with burglars and what he
would do if someone tried to break into the house, when he
saw close outside the window a dark figure. It was joined by a
second. Wilt crouched lower in the summerhouse and cursed
Eva for leaving him without his trousers and . . .

But a moment later his fears had gone. The two figures were
moving confidently across the lawn and one of them had spoken
in German. It was Irmgard's voice that reached Wilt and reassured him. And as the figures disappeared round the side of
the house Wilt wriggled down into the sleeping-bag with the
relatively comfortable thought that at least his Muse had been
spared that insight into English family life which Eva's denunciations would have revealed. On the other hand, what was
Irmgard doing out at this time of night and who was the other
person? A wave of self-pitying jealousy swept over Wilt before
being dislodged by more practical considerations. The summerhouse floor was hard, he had no pillow and the night had suddenly become extremely chilly. He was damned if he was going
to spend the rest of it outside. And anyway the keys to the front
door were still in his jacket pocket. Wilt climbed out of the
sleeping-bag and fumbled for his shoes. Then dragging the

sleeping-bag behind him he made his way across the lawn and round to the front door. Once inside he took off his shoes and crossed the hall to the sitting-room and ten minutes later was fast asleep on the sofa.

When he awoke Eva was banging things about in the kitchen while the quads, evidently gathered round the breakfast table, were discussing the events of the night. Wilt stared at the curtains and listened to the muffled questions of his daughters and Eva's evasive answers. As usual she was garnishing downright lies with mawkish sentimentality.

'Your father wasn't very well last night, darling,' he heard her say. 'He had the collywobbles in his tummy that's all and when he gets like that he says things . . . Yes, I know mumsy said things too, Hennypenny. I was . . . What did you say, Samantha? . . . I said that? . . . Well he can't have had it in the toothmug because tummies won't go in little things like that . . . Tummies, darling . . . You can't get collywobbles anywhere else . . . Where did you learn that word, Samantha? . . . No he didn't and if you go to playgroup and tell Miss Oates that Daddy had his . . .'

Wilt buried his head under the cushions to shut out the conversation. The bloody woman was doing it again, lying through her teeth to four damned girls who spent so much of their time trying to deceive one another they could spot a lie a mile off. And harping on about Miss Oates was calculated to make them compete to see who could be the first to tell the old bag and twenty-five other toddlers that daddy spent the night with his penis in a toothmug. By the time that story had been disseminated through the neighbourhood it would be common knowledge that the notorious Mr Wilt was some sort of toothmug fetishist.

He was just cursing Eva for her stupidity and himself for having drunk too much beer when the further consequences of too much beer made themselves felt. He needed a pee and badly. Wilt clambered out of the sleeping-bag. In the hall Eva could be heard hustling the quads into their coats. Wilt waited until the front door had closed behind them and then hobbled across the hall to the downstairs toilet. It was only then that full magnitude of his predicament became apparent. Wilt stared down at a large and extremely tenacious piece of sticking-plaster.

'Damn,' said Wilt, 'I must have been drunker than I thought. When the hell did I put that on?' There was a gap in his memory. He sat down on the toilet and wondered how on earth to get the bloody thing off without doing himself any more injury. From past experience of sticking-plaster he knew the best method was to wrench the stuff off with one jerk. It didn't seem advisable now.

'Might pull the whole bloody lot off,' he muttered. The safest thing would be to find a pair of scissors. Wilt emerged cautiously from the toilet and peered over the banisters. Just so long as he didn't meet Irmgard coming down from the flat in the attic. Considering the hour she had got back it was extremely unlikely. She was probably still in bed with some beastly boyfriend. Wilt went upstairs and into the bedroom. Eva kept some nail-scissors in the dressing table. He found them and was sitting on the edge of the bed when Eva returned. She headed upstairs, hesitated a moment on the landing and then entered the bedroom.

'I thought I'd find you here,' she said crossing the room to the curtains. 'I knew the moment my back was turned you'd sneak into the house. Well don't think you can worm your way out of this one because you can't. I've made up my mind.'

'What mind?' said Wilt.

'That's right. Insult me,' said Eva, pulling the curtains back and flooding the room with sunshine.

'I am not insulting you,' snarled Wilt, 'I am merely asking a question. Since I can't get it into your empty head that I am not a raving arse-bandit—'

'Language, language,' said Eva.

'Yes, language. It's a means of communication, not just a series of moos, coos and bleats the way you use it.'

But Eva was no longer listening. Her attention was riveted on the scissors. 'That's right. Cut the horrid thing off,' she squawked and promptly burst into tears. 'To think that you had to go and . . .'

'Shut up,' yelled Wilt. 'Here I am in imminent danger of bursting and you have to start howling like a banshee If you had used your bloody head instead of a perverted imagination last night I wouldn't have been in this predicament.'

'What predicament?' asked Eva between sobs.

'This,' shouted Wilt waving his agonized organ.

Eva glanced at it curiously. 'What did you do that for?' she asked.

'To stop the damned thing from bleeding. I have told you repeatedly that I caught it on a rosebush but you had to jump to idiotic conclusions. Now I can't get this bloody sticking-plaster off and I've got a gallon of beer backed up behind it.'

'You really meant it about the rose bush then?'

'Of course I did. I spend my life telling the truth and nothing but the truth and nobody ever believes me. For the last time I was having a pee next to a rosebush and I got snagged in the fucking thing. That is the simple truth, unembroidered, ungarnished and unexaggerated.'

'And you want the sticking-plaster off?'

'What the hell have I been saying for the last five minutes? I not only want it off. I need it off before I burst.'

'That's easy,' said Eva. 'All you've got to do . . .'

7

Twenty-five minutes later Wilt hobbled through the door of the Accident Centre at the Ipford Hospital, pale, pained and horribly embarrassed. He made his way to the desk and looked into the unsympathetic and obviously unimaginative eyes of the admissions clerk.

'I'd like to see a doctor,' he said with some difficulty.

'Have you broken something?' asked the woman.

'Sort of,' said Wilt, conscious that his conversation was being monitored by a dozen other patients with more obvious but less distressing injuries.

'What do you mean, sort of?'

Wilt eyed the woman and tried to convey wordlessly that his was a condition that required discretion. The woman was clearly extraordinarily obtuse.

'If it's not a break, cut or wound requiring immediate attention, or a case of poisoning you should consult your own doctor.' Wilt considered these options and decided that 'wound requiring immediate attention' fitted the bill.

'Wound,' he said.

'Where?' asked the woman picking up a ballpen and a pad of forms.

'Well . . .' said Wilt even more hoarsely than before. Half the other patients seemed to have brought their wives or mothers.

'I said where?' said the woman impatiently.

'I know you did,' whispered Wilt. 'The thing is . . .'

'I haven't got all day, you know.'

'I realize that,' said Wilt, 'it's just that . . . well I . . . Look, would you mind if I explained the situation to a doctor? You see . . .' But the woman didn't. In Wilt's opinion she was either a sadist or mentally deficient.

'I have to fill in this form and if you won't tell me where the wound is . . .' She hesitated and looked at Wilt suspiciously, 'I thought you said it was a break. Now you say it's a wound. You'd better make up your mind. I haven't got all day, you know.'

'Nor, at this rate, have I,' said Wilt irritated by the repetition. 'In fact if something isn't done almost immediately I may well pass out in front of you.'

The woman shrugged. People passing out in front of her were evidently part of her daily routine. 'I still have to state whether it is a wound or a break and its location and if you won't tell me what it is and where it is I can't admit you.'

Wilt glanced over his shoulder and was about to say that he had had his penis practically scalped by his bloody wife when

62

he caught the eyes of several middle-aged women who were paying close attention to the exchange. He changed his tactic hastily.

'Poison,' he muttered.

'Are you quite sure?'

'Of course I'm sure,' said Wilt. 'I took the stuff, didn't I?'

'You also claimed you had a break and then a wound. Now you say you've taken all three . . . I mean you've taken poison. And it's no good looking at me like that. I'm only doing my job, you know.'

'At the speed you're doing it I wonder anyone gets in here at all before they're actually dead,' snapped Wilt, and instantly regretted it. The woman was staring at him with open hostility. The look on her face suggested that as far as Wilt was concerned he had just expressed her most ardent hope.

'Look,' said Wilt trying to pacify the bitch, 'I'm sorry if I seem agitated . . .'

'Rude, more like.'

'Have it your own way. Rude then. I apologize but if you had just swallowed poison, fallen on your arm and broken it and suffered a wound in your posterior you'd be a bit agitated.'

To lend some sort of credibility to this list of catastrophes he raised his left arm limply and supported it with his right hand. The woman regarded it doubtfully and took up the ballpen again.

'Did you bring the bottle with you?' she asked.

'Bottle?'

'The bottle containing the poison you claim to have taken.'

'What would I do that for?'

'We can't help you unless we know what sort of poison you took.'

'It didn't say what sort of poison it was on the bottle,' said Wilt. 'It was in a lemonade bottle in the garage. All I know is that it was poison.'

'How?'

'How what?'

'How do you know it was poison?'

'Because it didn't taste like lemonade,' said Wilt frantically, aware that he was getting deeper and deeper into a morass of diagnostic confusion.

'Because something doesn't taste like lemonade it doesn't necessarily mean it's poisonous,' said the woman, exercising an indefatigable logic. 'Only lemonade tastes like lemonade. Nothing else does.'

'Of course it doesn't. But this stuff didn't simply not taste like lemonade. It tasted like deadly poison. Probably cyanide.'

'Nobody knows what cyanide tastes like,' said the woman continuing to batter Wilt's defences. 'Death is instantaneous.'

Wilt glared at her bleakly. 'All right,' he said finally, 'forget the poison. I've still got a broken arm and a wound that requires immediate attention. I demand to see a doctor.'

'Then you'll have to wait your turn. Now where did you say this wound was?'

'On my backside,' said Wilt, and spent the next hour regretting it. To substantiate his claim he had to stand while the other patients were treated and the admissions clerk continued to eye him with a mixture of outright suspicion and dislike. In an effort to avoid her eye Wilt tried to read the paper over the shoulder of a man whose only apparent claim to be in need of urgent attention was a bandaged toe. Wilt envied him and, not for the first time, considered the perversity of circumstances which rendered him incapable of being believed.

It wasn't as simple as Byron had suggested with his 'Truth is stranger than fiction'. If his own experience was anything to go by, truth and fiction were equally unacceptable. Some element of ambiguity in his own character, perhaps the ability to see every side of every problem, created an aura of insincerity around him and made it impossible for anyone to believe what he was saying. The truth, to be believed, had first to be plausible and probable, to fall into some easy category of predigested opinion. If it didn't conform to the expected, people refused to believe it. But Wilt's mind did not conform. It followed possibilities wherever they led in labyrinths of speculation beyond most people's ken. Certainly beyond Eva's. Not that Eva ever speculated. She leapt from one opinion to another without that intermediate stage of bewilderment which was Wilt's perpetual condition. In her world, every problem had an answer; in Wilt's, every problem had about ten, each of them in direct contradiction to all the others. Even now in this bleak waiting-room where his own immediate misery might have been expected to spare him concern for the rest of the world, Wilt's febrile intelligence found material to speculate upon.

The headlines in the paper OIL DISASTER: SEA BIRDS THREATENED dominated a page filled with apparently minor horrors. Apparently because they occupied such little space. There had been another terrorist raid on a security truck. The driver had been threatened with a rocket launcher and a guard had been callously shot through the head. The murderers had got away with £250,000 but this was of less importance than the plight of seagulls threatened by an oil slick off the coast. Wilt noted this distinction and wondered how the widow of the shot guard felt about her late husband's relegation to second place in public concern compared to the sea birds. What was it about the modern world that wildlife took precedence over personal misery? Perhaps the human species was so fearful of extinction that it no longer cared what happened to individuals, but closed collective ranks and saw the collision of two supertankers as a foretaste of its own eventual fate. Or perhaps . . .

Wilt was interrupted from this reverie by the sound of his name and looking up from the paper his eyes met those of a hatchet-faced nurse who was talking to the admissions clerk. The nurse disappeared and a moment later the admissions clerk was joined by an elderly and evidently important specialist, if his retinue of young doctors, a Sister and two nurses was anything to go by. Wilt watched unhappily while the man studied his record of injuries, looked over his spectacles at Wilt as at some specimen beneath his dignity to treat, nodded to one of the housemen and, smiling sardonically, departed.

'Mr Wilt,' called the young doctor. Wilt stepped cautiously forward.

'If you'll just go through to a cubicle and wait,' said the doctor.

'Excuse me, doctor,' said Wilt, 'I would like a word with you in private.'

'In due course, Mr Wilt, we will have words in private and now if you have nothing better to do kindly go through to a cubicle.' He turned on his heel and walked down the corridor. Wilt was about to hobble after him when the admissions clerk stopped him.

'Accident cubicles are that way,' she said pointing to curtains down another corridor. Wilt grimaced at her and went down to a cubicle.

At Willington Road Eva was on the telephone. She had called the Tech to say that Wilt was unavoidably detained at home by sickness and was now in conference with Mavis Mottram.

'I don't know what to think,' said Eva miserably. 'I mean it seemed so unlikely and when I found out he was really hurt I felt so awful.'

'My dear Eva,' said Mavis, who knew exactly what to think, 'you are far too ready to blame yourself and of course Henry exploits that. I mean that doll business must have given you some indication that he was peculiar.'

'I don't like to think about that,' said Eva. 'It was so long ago and Henry has changed since then.'

'Men don't change fundamentally and Henry is at a dangerous age. I warned you when you insisted on taking that German au pair girl.'

'That's another thing. She's not an au pair. She's paying much more rent than I asked for the flat but she won't help in the house. She has enrolled in the Foreigners' Course at the Tech and she speaks perfect English already.'

'What did I tell you, Eva? She never mentioned anything about the Tech when she came to you for a room, did she?'

'No,' said Eva.

'It wouldn't surprise me to find that Henry knew her already and told her you were letting the attic.'

'But how could he? He seemed very surprised and angry when I told him.'

'My dear, I hate to say this but you always look on the good side of Henry. Of course he would pretend to be surprised and angry. He knows exactly how to manipulate you and if he had seemed pleased you'd have known there was something wrong.'

'I suppose so,' said Eva doubtfully.

'And as for knowing her before,' continued Mavis, waging war vicariously against her Patrick by way of Wilt, 'I seem to remember he spent a lot of time at the Tech at the beginning of the summer vac and that's when the foreign students enrol.'

'But Henry doesn't have anything to do with that department. He was busy on the timetable.'

'He doesn't have to belong to the department to meet the slut, and for all you know when he was supposed to be doing the timetable the two of them were doing something quite different in his office.'

Eva considered this possibility only to dismiss it. 'Henry isn't like that, and anyway I would have noticed the change in him,' she said.

'My dear, what you have got to realize is that all men are like that. And I didn't notice any change in Patrick until it was too late. He'd been having an affair with his secretary for over a year before I knew anything about it,' said Mavis. 'And then it was only when he blew his nose on her panties that I got an inkling what was going on.'

'Blew his nose on her *what*?' said Eva, intrigued by the extraordinary perversion the statement conjured up.

'He had a streaming cold and at breakfast one morning he took out a pair of red panties and blew his nose on them,' said Mavis. 'Of course I knew then what he had been up to.'

'Yes, well you would, wouldn't you?' said Eva. 'What did he say when you asked him?'

'I didn't ask him. I knew. I told him that if he thought he could provoke me into divorcing him he was quite mistaken because . . .'

Mavis chattered on about her Patrick while Eva's mind turned slowly as she listened. There was something in her memory of the night that was coming to the surface. Something to do with Irmgard Mueller. After that awful row with Henry she hadn't been able to sleep. She had lain awake in the darkness wondering why Henry had to . . . well of course now she knew he hadn't but at the time . . . Yes, that was it, the time.

At four o'clock she had heard someone come upstairs very quietly and she had been sure it was Henry and then there had been sounds of creaking from the steps up to the attic and she had known it was Irmgard coming home. She remembered looking at the luminous dial of the alarm clock and seeing the hands at four and twelve and for a moment she had thought they pointed to twenty past twelve only Henry had come in at three and . . She had drifted off to sleep with a question half-formed in her mind. Now, against Mavis' chatter, the question completed itself. Had Henry been out with Irmgard? It wasn't like Henry to come in so late. She couldn't remember when he had done it before. And Irmgard certainly didn't behave like an au pair girl. She was too old for one thing, and she had so much money. But Mavis Mottram interrupted this slow train of thought by stating the conclusion Eva was moving towards.

'I know I'd keep an eye on that German girl,' she said. 'And if you take my advice you'll get rid of her at the end of the month.'

'Yes,' said Eva. 'Yes, I'll think about that, Mavis. Thank you for being so sympathetic.'

Eva put the phone down and stared out of the bedroom window at the beech tree that stood on the front lawn. It had been one of the first things to attract her to the house, the copper beech in the front garden, a large comfortable solid tree with roots that stretched as far underground as the branches did above. She had read that somewhere, and the balance between branches seeking the light and roots searching for water had seemed so right and so, somehow, organic, as to explain what she wanted from the house and could give it in return.

And the house had seemed right too. A big house with high ceilings and thick walls and a garden and orchard in which the quads could grow up happily and at a further remove from unsettling reality than Parkview Road would have allowed. But Henry hadn't like the move. She had had to force it on him and he had never succumbed to the call of the domesticated wildness of the orchard or the sense of social invulnerability she had found in the house and Willington Road. Not that Eva was a snob but she didn't like anyone to look down on her and now they couldn't. Even Mavis didn't patronize her any longer and that story about Patrick and the panties was something Mavis would never have told her if she had still been living two streets away. Anyway, Mavis was a bitch. She was always running Patrick down and if he was unfaithful physically Mavis was morally disloyal. Henry had said she committed adultery by gossip, and there was something in what he said. But there was also something in what Mavis said about Irmgard Mueller. She would keep an eye on her. There was a strange coldness about her – and what did she mean by saying she would help around the house and then suddenly enrolling at the Tech?

With an unusual sense of depression Eva made herself some coffee and then polished the hall floor and Hoovered the stair-carpet and tidied the living-room and put the dirty clothes in the washing-machine and brushed the rim of the Organic Toilet and did all those jobs which had to be done before she collected the quads from playschool. She had just finished and was brushing her hair in the bedroom when she heard the front door open and close and footsteps on the stairs. That couldn't be Henry. He never came up two at a time and anyway with his dooda in bandages he probably wouldn't come up at all. Eva crossed to the bedroom door and looked out at a startled young man on the landing.

'What do you think you're doing?' she asked in some alarm.

The young man raised his hands. 'Please, I am here for Miss Mueller,' he said with a thick foreign accent. 'She has borrowed me the key.' He held it up in front of him as evidence.

'She had no right to,' said Eva annoyed at herself for being so alarmed, 'I don't want people walking in and out without knocking.'

'Yes,' said the young man, 'I understand you. But Miss Mueller have told me I can work on my studies in her rooms. Where I am living too much noise.'

'All right, I don't mind you working here but I don't want any noise either,' said Eva and went back into the bedroom. The young man went on up the narrow steps to the attic while Eva finished brushing her hair with a suddenly lighter mind. If Irmgard invited rather good-looking young men to her room, she was unlikely to be interested in Henry. And the young man had been decidedly handsome. With a sigh which combined regret that she was not younger and more attractive herself, and relief that her marriage wasn't threatened, she went downstairs.

8

At the Tech Wilt's absence from the weekly meeting of Heads of Departments met with mixed reactions. The Principal was particularly alarmed.

'What with?' he asked the secretary who brought Eva's message that Wilt was sick.

'She didn't make that clear. She just said he would be incapacitated for a few days.'

'Would it were years,' murmured the Principal, and called the meeting to order. 'I have no doubt you have all heard the distressing news about the . . . er . . . film made by a Liberal Studies lecturer,' he said. 'I can't see there's much to be gained from discussing its implications for the College.'

He looked cheerlessly around the room. Only Dr Board seemed inclined to disagree. 'What I haven't been able to make out is whether it was a male or a female crocodile,' he said.

The Principal regarded him with disgust. 'In actual fact it was a toy one. As far as I know, they are not noticeably differentiated by sex.'

'No, I suppose not,' said Dr Board. 'Still it raises an interesting point—'

'Which, I feel sure, the rest of us would prefer not to discuss,' said the Principal.

'On the grounds of least said, soonest mended?' said Board. 'Though for the life of me I can't understand how the star of this film could be induced to—'

'Board,' said the Principal with dangerous patience, 'we are here to discuss academic matters, not the obscene aberrations of lecturers in the Liberal Studies Department.'

'Hear, hear,' said the Head of Catering. 'When I think that some of my girls are exposed to the influence of such disgusting perverts I can only say that I think we should consider very seriously the possibility of doing away with Liberal Studies altogether.'

There was a general murmur of approval. Dr Board was the exception.

'I can't see why you should blame Liberal Studies as a whole,' he said, 'and having had a look at some of your girls I should say—'

'Don't, Board, don't,' said the Principal.

Dr Mayfield took up the issue. 'This deplorable incident only reinforces my opinion that we should extend the parameters of our academic content to include courses of wider intellectual significance.'

For once Dr Board agreed with him. 'I suppose we could run an evening class in Reptile Sodomy,' he said. 'It might have the side-effect, if that is the right expression, of attracting a number of crocophiliacs, and on a more theoretical level doubtless a course on Bestiality Down The Ages might have a certain eclectic appeal. Have I said something wrong, Principal?'

But the Principal was beyond speech. The V-P stepped into the breach.

'The first essential is to see that this regrettable affair doesn't become public knowledge.'

'Well, considering that it took place in Nott Road—'

'Shut up, Board,' shouted the Principal, 'I have stood just about all I can stand of your infernal digressions. One more word out of you and I shall demand either your resignation or my own from the Education Committee. And if need be both. You can make your choice. Shut up or get out.'

Dr Board shut up.

At the Accident Centre Wilt was finding he had no choice at all. The doctor who finally arrived at his cubicle to attend to him was accompanied by a formidable Sister and two male nurses. Wilt regarded him balefully from the couch on which he had been told to lie.

'You've taken your time,' he grumbled. 'I've been lying here in agony for the last hour and . . .'

'Then we must get a move on,' said the doctor. 'We'll start with the poison first. A stomach wash-out will . . .'

'What?' said Wilt, sitting up on the couch in horror.

'It won't take more than a minute,' said the doctor. 'Just lie back while Sister inserts the tube.'

'Oh no! Nothing doing,' said Wilt, bolting from the couch into a corner of the cubicle as the nurse closed in with a length of rubber pipe. 'I haven't taken poison.'

'It says on your admittance sheet that you have,' said the doctor. 'You are Mr Henry Wilt, I take it?'

'Yes,' said Wilt, 'but you needn't take it that I have taken poison. I can assure you . . .' He dodged round the couch to avoid the Sister, only to find himself grabbed from behind by the two male nurses.

'I swear that—' Wilt's denial died on his lips as he was pushed back on to the couch. The pipe hovered over his mouth. Wilt stared villainously at the doctor. The man seemed to be smiling in a singularly sadistic manner.

'Now then, Mr Wilt, you will kindly cooperate.'

'Won't,' grunted Wilt through clenched teeth. Behind him the Sister held his head and waited.

'Mr Wilt,' said the doctor, 'you arrived here this morning and stated quite adamantly and of your own free will that you had swallowed poison, broken your arm and had suffered a wound that required immediate attention. Is that not so?'

Wilt debated how to answer. It seemed safest not to open his mouth. He nodded and then tried to shake his head.

'Thank you. Not only that but you were impolite, to put it mildly, to the lady at the desk.'

'Wasn't,' said Wilt only to regret both his rudeness and this attempt to state his case. Two hands attempted to insert the tube. Wilt bit the thing.

'Have to use the left nostril,' said the doctor.

'No you fucking don't,' yelled Wilt, but it was too late. As

72

the pipe slid up his nose and, by the feel of it, expanded in his throat, Wilt's protests came to an unintelligible end. He writhed and gurgled.

'You may find the next part slightly uncomfortable,' said the doctor with evident pleasure. Wilt stared at the man murderously and would, had the infernal pipe not prevented him, have stated forcibly that he found the present part bloody terrible. He was just burbling his protest when the curtains parted and the admissions clerk came in.

'I thought you might want to see this, Mrs Clemence,' said the doctor. 'Go ahead, Sister.' The Sister went ahead while Wilt silently promised himself that if he didn't suffocate first or burst he would wipe the smile off that sadistic doctor's face just as soon as this ghastly experience was over. By the time it was Wilt's condition prevented him from doing anything except moan feebly. Only the Sister's suggestion that perhaps to be on the safe side they ought to give him an oil enema into the bargain provided him with the strength to state his case.

'I came here to have my penis attended to,' he whispered hoarsely.

The doctor consulted his record sheet. 'It doesn't make any mention of your penis here,' he said. 'It states quite clearly that . . .'

'I know what it states,' squeaked Wilt. 'I also know that if you were forced to go into a waiting-room filled with middle-class mothers and their skateboard-suicidal sons and had to announce at the top of your voice to that harridan there that you needed stitches in the top of your prick you'd have been less than reluctant to do it.'

'I'm not standing here listening to a lunatic call me a harridan,' said the clerk.

'And I wasn't standing out there shouting the odds about what had happened to my penis for all the bloody world to hear. I asked to see a doctor but you wouldn't let me. Deny that if you can.'

'I asked you if you had broken a limb, suffered a wound that required—'

'I know what you asked me,' yelled Wilt, 'don't I just. I can quote it word for word. Well, for your information a penis is not a limb, not in my case anyway. I suppose it comes into the category of an appendage and if I'd said I had damaged my appendage you'd have asked me which one and where and how and on what occasion and with whom and then sent me round to the VD clinic and . . .'

'Mr Wilt,' interrupted the doctor, 'we are extremely busy here and if you come and refuse to state exactly what is wrong with you . . .'

'I get a fucking stomach-pump stuffed down my gullet for my pains,' shouted Wilt. 'And what happens if some poor bugger who is deaf and dumb comes in? I suppose you let him die on the waiting-room floor or whip his tonsils out to teach him to speak up for himself in future. And they call this the National Health Service. It's a fucking bureaucratic dictatorship. That's what I call it.'

'Never mind what it's called, Mr Wilt. If there is something really the matter with your penis we're quite prepared to look at it.'

'I'm not,' said the admissions clerk firmly, and disappeared through the curtains. Wilt lay back on the couch and removed his pants.

The doctor observed him cautiously.

'Mind telling me what you've got wound round it?' he asked.

'Bloody handkerchief,' said Wilt and slowly untied the makeshift bandage.

'Good God,' said the doctor, 'I see what you mean about an appendage. Would it be asking too much to enquire how you got your penis into this condition?'

'Yes,' said Wilt, 'it would. Everyone I've told so far hasn't believed me and I'd rather not go through that drill again.'

'Drill?' asked the doctor pensively. 'You're surely not implying that this injury was inflicted by a drill? I don't know what you think, Sister, but from where I stand it looks as though our friend here had a rather too intimate relationship with a mincing machine.'

'And from where I lie it feels like it,' said Wilt. 'And if it

74

will help to cut the badinage let me tell you that my wife was largely responsible.'

'Your wife?'

'Listen, doctor,' said Wilt, 'if it's all the same to you I'd just as soon not go into details.'

'Can't say I blame you,' said the doctor scrubbing his hands. 'If my wife did that to me I'd divorce the bitch. Were you having intercourse at the time?'

'No comment,' said Wilt deciding that silence was the best policy. The doctor donned surgical gloves and drew his own ghastly conclusions. He loaded a hypodermic.

'After what you've already been through,' he said approaching the couch, 'this isn't going to hurt at all.'

Wilt bounded off the couch again. 'Hold it,' he shouted. 'If you imagine for one moment that you're going to stick that surgical hornet into my private fucking parts you can think again. And what's that for?'

The Sister had picked up an aerosol can.

'Just a mild disinfectant and freezer. I'll spray it on first and you won't feel the little prick.'

'Won't I? Well let me tell you that I want to feel it. If I'd wanted anything else I'd have let nature take its course and I wouldn't be here now. And what's she doing with that razor?'

'Sterilizing it. We've got to shave you.'

'Have you just? I've heard that one before, and while we're on the subject of sterilizing I'd like to hear your views on vasectomy.'

'I'm pretty neutral on the subject,' said the doctor.

'Well I'm not,' snarled Wilt from the corner. 'In fact I am distinctly biased not to say prejudiced. What are you laughing about?' The muscular Sister was smiling. 'You're not some damned women's libber, are you?'

'I'm a working woman,' said the Sister, 'and my politics are my own affair. They don't enter into the matter.'

'And I'm a working man and I want to remain that way and politics do enter into the matter. I've heard what they get up to in India and if I walk out of here with a transistor, no balls and jabbering like an incipient mezzo-soprano I warn you I shall return with a meat cleaver and you'll both learn what social genetics are all about.'

'Well, if that is your attitude,' said the doctor, 'I suggest you try private medicine, Mr Wilt. You get what you pay for that way. I can only assure you . . .'

It took ten minutes to lure Wilt back on to the couch and five seconds to get him off again clutching his scrotum.

'Freezer,' he squealed. 'My God, you meant it too. What the hell do you think I've got down there, a packet of freezable peas?'

'We'll just wait until the anaesthetic takes effect,' said the doctor. 'It shouldn't be long now.'

'It isn't,' squawked Wilt peering down. 'It's bloody disappearing. I came in here to have minor medication, not a sexchange operation, and if you think my wife is going to be happy having a husband with a clitoris you sorely misjudge the woman.'

'I'd say you had already misjudged her,' said the doctor cheerfully. 'Any woman who can inflict that sort of damage on her husband deserves what she gets.'

'She may but I don't,' said Wilt frantically. 'I happen . . What's she doing with that tube?'

The Sister was unwrapping a catheter.

'Mr Wilt,' said the doctor, 'we are going to insert this . . .'

'No, you're not,' shouted Wilt. 'I may be shrinking rapidly in parts but I'm not Alice in Wonderland or a fucking dwarf with chronic constipation. I heard what she said about an oil enema and I'm not having one.'

'No one intends giving you an enema. This will simply enable you to pass water through the bandages. Now kindly get back on the couch before I have to call for assistance.'

'What do you mean pass water simply?' asked Wilt cautiously, climbing on to the couch. The doctor explained, and this time it took four male nurses to hold Wilt down. Throughout the operation he kept up a barrage of obscene observations and it was only the threat of a general anaesthetic that caused him to lower his voice. Even then his remark that the doctor and the Sister were less fitted for medicine than for off-shore oil drilling could be heard in the waiting-room.

'That's right, send me out into the world like a bleeding petrol pump,' he said when he was finally allowed to go. 'There's such a thing as the dignity of man, you know.'

The doctor looked at him sceptically. 'In the light of your behaviour I'll reserve my opinion on the matter. Call in again next week and we'll see how you're coming along.'

'The only reason I'll be back is if I don't come again,' said Wilt bitterly. 'From now on I'll see the family doctor.' He hobbled out to a telephone and called for a taxi.

By the time he got home the anaesthetic was beginning to wear off. He went wearily upstairs and climbed into bed. He was lying there staring at the ceiling and wondering why he was not as other men presumably were when it came to bearing pain manfully, and wishing he was, when Eva returned with the quads.

'You do look awful,' she said encouragingly as she stood by the bed.

'I am awful,' said Wilt. 'Why I should be married to a female circumcisionist, God alone knows.'

'Perhaps it will teach you not to drink so much in future.'

'It's already taught me not to let you get your mitts near my waterworks,' said Wilt. 'And I mean waterworks.'

Even Samantha had to contribute to his misery. 'When I grow up I'm going to be a nurse, daddy.'

'Bounce on the bed like that again and you won't grow up to be anything,' snarled Wilt on the recoil.

Downstairs the telephone rang.

'If it's the Tech again, what shall I tell them?' asked Eva.

'Again? I thought I told you to say I was sick.'

'I did but they've phoned back several times.'

'Tell them I'm still sick,' said Wilt. 'Just don't mention what with.'

'They probably know anyway by now. I saw Rowena Blackthorn at playschool and she said she was sorry to hear about your accident,' said Eva, going downstairs.

'And which of you quadraphonic loudspeakers blurted the good news about daddy's whatsit to Mrs Blackthorn's little prodigy?' asked Wilt, turning a terrible eye on the quads.

'I didn't,' said Samantha smugly.

'You just egged Penelope on to, I suppose. I know that look on your mug.'

'It wasn't Penny. It was Josephine. She played with Robin and they were playing mummies and daddies . . .'

'Well when you get a little older you'll learn that there's no such thing as playing mummies and daddies. You will find instead that there is a war between the sexes and that you, my sweethearts, being females of the species, invariably win.'

The quads retreated from the bedroom and could be heard conferring on the landing. Wilt edged his way out of bed in search of a book and was just getting back with *Nightmare Abbey*, which was sufficiently unromantic to suit his mood, when Emmeline was pushed into the room.

'What do you want now? Can't you see I'm ill?'

'Please Daddy,' said Emmeline, 'Samantha wants to know why you've got that bag tied to your leg.'

'Oh she does, does she?' said Wilt with dangerous calmness. 'Well you can tell Samantha and through her Miss Oates and her animal minders that your daddy wears a bag on his leg and a pipe up his prick because your mummsyfuckingwumsy took it into her empty head to try to rip off daddywaddy's genitalia on the end of a strip of fucking sticking-plaster. And if Miss Oates doesn't know what genitalia are tell her from me that they're the adult equivalent of a male stork only its spelt with a fucking L. Now get out of my sight before I add hernia, hypertension and multiple infanticide to my other infernal problems.'

The children fled. Downstairs Eva slammed the phone down and shouted.

'Henry Wilt . . .'

'Shut up,' yelled Wilt. 'One more comment out of anybody in this house and I won't be responsible for my actions.'

And for once he was obeyed. Eva went through to the kitchen .and put the kettle on for tea. If only Henry would be more masterful when he was up and about and well.

9

For the next three days Wilt was off work. He mooched about the house, sat in the Spockery and speculated on the nature of a world in which Progress with a capital P conflicted with Chaos and man with a small M was continually at loggerheads with Nature. In Wilt's view it was one of life's great paradoxes that Eva, who was forever accusing him of being cynical and non-progressive, should succumb so readily to the recessive call of nature in the shape of compost heaps, Organic Toilets, home weaving and anything that smacked of the primitive while at the same time maintaining an unshakable optimism in the future. For Wilt there was only the eternal present, a succession of present moments, not so much moving forward as aggregating behind him like a reputation. And if in the past his reputation had suffered some nasty blows, his latest misfortune had already added to his legend. From Mavis Mottram the ripples of gossip had spread out across Ipford's educational suburbia, gaining fresh credence and additional attributes with each retelling. By the time the story reached the Braintrees it had already incorporated the crocodile film by way of the Tech, Blighte-Smythe, and Mrs Chatterway, and rumour had it that Wilt was about to be arrested for grossly indecent behaviour with a circus alligator which had only managed to preserve its virginity by biting Wilt's member.

'That's typical of this bloody town,' Peter Braintree told his wife, Betty, when she brought this version home. 'Henry has merely to take a few days off from the Tech and the grapevine is buzzing with absolute lies.'

'Grapevines don't buzz,' said Betty. 'There's no smoke—'

'Without some evil-minded moron adding two and two together and coming up with fifty-nine. There's a bloke called Bilger in Liberal Studies who did make a film in which a plastic crocodile figures largely as a rape victim. Point one. Henry has to give some explanation to the Education Committee that will prevent Comrade Bilger's numerous offspring having to leave their private school because daddy is on the dole. Point two. Point three is that Wilt is taken ill next day . . .'

'Not according to Rowena Braintree. It's common knowledge Henry's penis has been mauled.'

'Where?'

'Where what?'

'Where is it common knowledge?'

'At the playgroup. The quads have been reporting progress on papa's dingaling daily.'

'Great,' said Braintree. 'For once common knowledge about sums it up. Henry's dutiful daughters wouldn't know a penis from a marrow-bone. Eva sees to that. She may be into self-sufficiency but it doesn't extend to sex. Not after the Prings-heims, and I can't see Henry in the role of Flash Harry. If anything, he's a bit of a prude.'

'Not where his language is concerned,' said Betty.

'His use of "fucking" as an adjective is the simple consequence of years of teaching apprentices. In the average bloke's sentence it serves as a sort of hyphen. If you listened to me more carefully you'd hear it at least twenty times in an average day. As I was saying, whatever's the matter with Henry he is *not* into crocodiles. Anyway, I'll pop round this evening and see what is up.'

But when he arrived at Willington Road that evening there was no sign of Wilt. Several cars were parked in the driveway, among them an Aston-Martin which looked out of place in the company of the Nyes' methane-converted Ford and Mavis Mottram's battered Minor. Braintree made his way across the obstacle course of cast-off clothing and the quads' toys that cluttered the hall and found Eva in the conservatory, chairing what appeared to be a committee on the problems of the Third World.

'The issue that seems to be overlooked is that Marangan medicine has an important part to play in providing an alternative to chemically derived drug treatment in the West,' Roberta Smott was saying as Braintree hesitated behind the bean flyscreen, 'I don't think we should forget that in helping the Marangans we are also helping ourselves in the long term.'

Braintree tiptoed away as John Nye launched into an impassioned plea for the preservation of Marangan agricultural methods and particularly the use of human excreta as fertilizer. 'It has all the natural goodness of . . .'

Braintree slipped through the kitchen door, skirted the Fertility Retainer or compost bin outside, and went down the Bio-dynamic kitchen garden to the summerhouse where he found Wilt lurking behind a cascade of dried herbs. He was reclining on a deckchair and wearing what looked suspiciously like a muslin bell-tent.

'As a matter of fact it's one of Eva's maternity gowns,' he said when Braintree enquired. 'In its time it has doubled as a wigwam, the interior sheet of a kingsize sleeping-bag, and the canopy of the camping loo. I rescued it from the mountain of clothing Eva's inflicting on her equatorial village.'

'I wondered what they were on about in there. Is this some sort of Oxfam exercise?'

'You're out of date. Eva's into Alternative Oxfam. Personal Assistance for Primitive People. Appropriately PAPP for short. You adopt some tribe in Africa or New Guinea and then load them with overcoats which would be unsuitably hot on a windy day in February here, write letters to the local witch-doctor asking his advice about herbal cures for chilblains, or better still frostbite, and generally twin Willington Road and the Ipford Brigade of the Anti-Male Chauvinist League with a cannibal community who go in for female circumcision with a rusty flint.'

'I didn't know you could circumcise females and anyway a rusty flint is out,' said Braintree.

'So are clitorises in Maranga,' said Wilt. 'I've tried to tell Eva but you know what she is. The noble savage is the latest vogue and it's nature worship run riot. If the Nyes had their way they'd import cobras to keep down rats in central London.'

'He was on about human faeces as a substitute for Growmore when I passed through. The man's an anal fanatic.'

'Religious,' said Wilt, 'I swear they sing Nearer My Turd to Thee before taking herbal communion at the compost heap every Sunday morning.'

'On a more personal note,' said Braintree, 'just exactly what is the matter with you?'

'I'd prefer not to discuss it,' said Wilt.

'All right, but why the ... er ... maternity drag?'

'Because it has none of the inconvenience of trousers,' said Wilt. 'There are depths of suffering you have yet to plumb. I use the word advisedly.'

'What, suffering?'

'Plumb,' said Wilt. 'If it hadn't been for all that beer we drank the other night I wouldn't be in this awful condition.'

'I notice you're not drinking your usual foul home-brewed lager.'

'I am not drinking anything in large quantities. In fact I am rationing myself to a thimble every four hours in the hope that I can sweat it out instead of peeing razor blades.'

Braintree smiled. 'Then there is some truth in the rumour,' he said.

'I don't know about the rumour,' said Wilt, 'but there's certainly truth in the description. Razor blades is exact.'

'Well, you'll be interested to hear that the gossip-mongers are thinking of awarding a medal to the croc that took the bit between its teeth. That's the version that's going the rounds.'

'Let it,' said Wilt. 'Nothing could be further from the truth.'

'Christ, you haven't got syphilis or something ghastly like that, have you?'

'Unfortunately not. I understand the modern treatment for syphilis is relatively painless. My condition isn't. And I've had all the fucking treatment I can stand. There are a number of people in this town I could cheerfully murder.'

'Oh dear,' said Braintree, 'things do sound grim.'

'They are,' said Wilt. 'They reached their nadir of grimness at four o'clock this morning when that little bitch Emmeline climbed into bed and stepped on my septic tank. It's bad enough being a human hose pipe but to be awakened in the dead hours of the night to find yourself peeing backwards is an experience that throws a new and terrible light on the human condition. Have you ever had a non-euphemistically wet dream in reverse?'

'Certainly not,' said Braintree with a shudder.

'Well I have,' said Wilt. 'And I can tell you that it destroys what few paternal feelings a father has. If I hadn't been in convulsions I'd have been charged with quadricide by now. Instead I have added volumes to Emmeline's vile vocabulary and Miss Mueller must be under the impression that English sex life is sado-masochistic in the extreme. God alone knows what she thought of the din we made last night.'

'And how is our Inspiration these days? Still musing?' asked Braintree.

'Evasive. Distinctly evasive. Mind you in my present condition I try not to be too conspicuous myself.'

'If you will go around in Eva's maternity gowns I can't say I'm surprised. It's enough to make anyone wonder.'

'Well, I'm puzzled too,' said Wilt. 'I can't make the woman out. Do you know she has a succession of disgustingly rich young men traipsing through the house?'

'That accounts for the Aston-Martin,' said Braintree. 'I wondered who had inherited a fortune.'

'Yes, but it doesn't account for the wig.'

'What wig?'

'The car belongs to some Casanova from Mexico. He wears a walrus moustache, Chanel Number something or other, and worst of all a wig. I have observed it closely through the binoculars. He takes it off when he gets up there.'

Wilt handed Braintree the binoculars and indicated the attic flat.

'I can't see anything. The venetian blinds are down,' said Braintree after a minute's observation.

'Well I can tell you he does wear a wig and I'd like to know why.'

'Probably because he's bald. That's the usual reason.'

'Which is precisely why I ask the question. Lothario Zapata isn't. He has a perfectly good head of hair, and yet when he gets up to the flat he takes his wig off.'

'What sort of wig?'

'Oh, a black shaggy thing,' said Wilt. 'Underneath he's blond. You've got to admit it's peculiar.'

'Why don't you ask your Irmgard? Could be she has a penchant for blond young men with wigs.'

But Wilt shook his head. 'In the first place because she leaves the house before I'm up and relatively about, and secondly because my sense of self-preservation tells me that anything in the way of sexual stimulation could have the most dire and possibly irreversible consequences. No, I prefer to speculate from afar.'

'Very wise,' said Braintree. 'I hate to think what Eva would do if she found you knew you were passionately in love with the au pair.'

'If what she has done for lesser reasons is anything to go by so do I,' said Wilt and left it at that.

'Any message for the Tech?' asked Braintree.

'Yes,' said Wilt, 'just tell them that I'll be back in circulation . . . Christ, what a word . . . when it's safe for me to sit down without back-firing.'

'I doubt if they'll understand what you mean.'

'I don't expect them to. I have emerged from this ordeal with the firm conviction that the last thing anyone will believe is the truth. It is far safer to lie in this vile world. Just say I am suffering from a virus. Nobody knows what a virus is but it covers a multitude of ailments.'

Braintree went back to the house leaving Wilt thinking dark thoughts about the truth. In a godless, credulous, violent and random world it was the only touchstone he had ever possessed and the only weapon. But like all his weapons it was double-edged and, from recent experience, served as much to harm him as to enlighten others. It was something best kept to oneself, a personal truth, probably meaningless in the long run but at least providing a moral self-sufficiency more effective than Eva's practical attempts to the same end in the garden. Having reached that conclusion and condemned Eva's world concern and PAPP, Wilt turned these findings on their head and accused himself of a quietism and passivity in the face of an underfed and deprived world. Eva's actions might not be more than sops to a liberal conscience but for all that they helped to sustain conscience and set an example to the quads which his own apathy denied. Somewhere there had to be a golden mean between charity beginning at home and improving the lot of starving millions. Wilt was damned if he knew where that mean was. It certainly wasn't to be found in doctrinaire shits like Bilger. Even John and Bertha Nye were trying to make a better world, not destroy a bad one. And what was he, Henry Wilt, doing? Nothing. Or rather, turning into a beer-swilling, self-pitying Peeping Tom without a worthwhile achievement to his credit. As if to prove that he had at least the courage of his garb, Wilt left the summerhouse and walked back to the house in full view of the conservatory, only to discover that the meeting had ended and Eva was putting the quads to bed.

When she came downstairs she found Wilt sitting at the kitchen table stringing runner beans.

'Wonders never cease,' she said. 'After all these years you're actually helping in the kitchen. You're not feeling ill or something?'

'I wasn't,' said Wilt, 'but now you mention it . . .'

'Don't go. There's something I want to discuss with you.'

'What?' said Wilt, stopping in the doorway.

'Upstairs,' said Eva, raising her eyes to the ceiling meaningfully.

'Upstairs?'

'You know what,' said Eva, increasing the circumspection.

'I don't,' said Wilt. 'At least I don't think I do, and if your tone of voice means anything, I don't want to. If you suppose for one moment I'm mechanically capable of . . .'

'I don't mean us. I mean them.'

'Them?'

'Miss Mueller and her friends.'

'Oh, them,' said Wilt and sat down again. 'What about them?'

'You must have heard,' said Eva.

'Heard what?' said Wilt.

'Oh, you know. You're just being difficult.'

'Lord,' said Wilt, 'we're back in Winnie-The-Pooh language. If you mean has it dawned on my semi-consciousness that they occasionally copulate, why don't you say so?'

'It's the children I'm thinking of,' said Eva. 'I'm not sure it's good for them to live in an environment where there's so much of what you just said going on.'

'If it didn't they wouldn't be here at all. And anyway your primitive penfriends are great ones for a bit of icketyboo, to use an expression that will suitably baffle Josephine. She usually comes straight out with—'

'Henry,' said Eva warningly.

'Well she does. Frequently. I heard her only yesterday tell Penelope to go—'

'I don't want to hear,' said Eva.

'I didn't either, come to that,' said Wilt, 'but the fact remains that the younger generation mature rather more rapidly in words and deeds than we did. When I was ten I still thought fuck was something father did with a hammer when he hit his thumb instead of the nail. Now it's common parlance at four . . .'

'Never mind that,' said Eva. 'Your father's language left much to be desired.'

'At least in my father's case it was his language. In your old man it was the whole person. I've often wondered how your mother could bring herself . . .'

'Henry Wilt, you'll leave my family out of this. I want to know what you think we should do about Miss Mueller.'

'Why ask me? You invited her to come and live here. You didn't consult me. And I certainly didn't want the damned woman. Now that she's turned out to be some sort of international sex fiend, according to you, who's likely to infect the children with premature nymphomania, I get dragged in . . .'

'All I want is your advice,' said Eva.

'Then here it is,' said Wilt. 'Tell her to get the hell out.'

'But that's the difficulty. She's given a month's rent in advance. I haven't put it in the bank yet, but still . . .'

'Well, give it back to her for Christ's sake. If you don't want the bag give her the boot.'

'It seems so inhospitable really,' said Eva. 'I mean she's foreign and far from home.'

'Not far enough from my home,' said Wilt, 'and all her boyfriends seem to be Croesus Juniors. She can shack up with them or stay at Claridges. My advice is to give her money back and bung her out.' And Wilt went through to the living-room and sat in front of the television until supper was ready.

In the kitchen Eva made up her mind. Mavis Mottram had been wrong again. Henry wasn't in the least interested in Miss Mueller and she could give the money to PAPP. So there was no need to ask the lodger to leave. Perhaps if she just suggested that things could be heard through the ceiling or . . . Anyway it was nice to know Henry hadn't been up to anything nasty. Which only went to show that she shouldn't listen to what Mavis had to say. Henry was a good husband in spite of his funny ways. It was a happy Eva who called Wilt to his supper that evening.

10

It was a surprisingly happy Wilt who left Dr Scally's surgery the following Wednesday. After an initial bout of jocularity about Wilt's injuries the removal of the bandages and the pipeline had proceeded comparatively painlessly.

'Absolutely no need for all this in my opinion,' said the doctor, 'but those young fellows up at the hospital like to make a thorough job of things while they're about it.'

A remark that almost persuaded Wilt to lodge an official complaint with the Health Ombudsman. Dr Scally was against it.

'Think of the scandal, my dear fellow, and strictly speaking they were within their rights. If you will go round saying you've been poisoned . . .'

It was a persuasive argument and with the doctor's promise that he'd soon be as right as rain again provided he didn't overdo things with his missus, Wilt emerged into the street feeling, if not on top of the world, at least half-way up it. The sun was shining on autumnal leaves, small boys were collecting conkers underneath the chestnuts in the park, and Dr Scally had given him a doctor's certificate keeping him away from the Tech for another week. Wilt strolled into town, spent an hour browsing in the second-hand bookshop, and was about to go home when he remembered he had to deposit Miss Mueller's advance in the bank. Wilt turned bankwards and felt even better. His brief infatuation for her had evaporated. Irmgard was just another silly foreign student with more money than sense, a taste for expensive cars and young men of every nationality.

And so he walked up the bank steps airily and went to the counter where he wrote out a deposit slip and handed it to the cashier. 'My wife has a special account,' he explained. 'It's a deposit account in the name of Wilt. Mrs H. Wilt. I've forgotten the number but it's for an African tribe and I think it's called . . .' But the cashier was clearly not listening. He was busy counting the notes and while Wilt watched he stopped several times. Finally with a brief 'Excuse me, sir,' he opened the hatch at the back of his cubicle and disappeared through it. Several customers behind Wilt moved to the next cashier, leaving him with that vague sense of unease he always felt when he had cashed a cheque and the clerk before stamping the back glanced at a list of customers who were presumably grossly overdrawn. But this time he was paying money in, not taking it out, and it wasn't possible for notes to bounce.

It was. Wilt was just beginning to work up some resentment at being kept waiting when a bank messenger approached him.

'If you wouldn't mind stepping into the manager's office, sir,' he said with a slightly threatening politeness. Wilt followed him across the foyer and into the manager's office.

'Mr Wilt?' said the manager. Wilt nodded. 'Do take a seat.' Wilt sat and glared at the cashier who was standing beside the manager's desk. The notes and the deposit slip lay on the blotting pad in front of him.

'I'd be glad if you would tell me what this is all about,' said Wilt with growing alarm. Behind him the bank messenger had taken up a position by the door.

'I think we'll reserve any comment until the police arrive,' said the manager.

'What do you mean "the police arrive"?'

The manager said nothing. He stared at Wilt with a look that managed to combine sorrow and suspicion.

'Now look here,' said Wilt. 'I don't know what's going on but I demand . . .'

Wilt's protest died away as the manager eyed the pile of notes on the desk.

'Good Lord, you're not suggesting they're forged?'

'Not forged, Mr Wilt, but as I said before when the police arrive you'll have a chance to explain matters. I'm sure there's some perfectly reasonable explanation. Nobody for one moment suspects you . . .'

'Of what?' said Wilt.

But again the bank manager said nothing. Apart from the noise of traffic outside there was silence and the day which only a few minutes before had seemed full of good cheer and hope suddenly became grey and horrid. Wilt searched his mind frantically for an explanation but could think of nothing, and he was about to protest that they had no right to keeep him there when there was a knock on the door and the bank messenger opened it cautiously. Inspector Flint, Sergeant Yates and two sinister plainclothes men entered.

'At last,' said the manager. 'This is really very awkward. Mr Wilt here is an old and respected customer . . .'

His defence died out. Flint was staring at Wilt.

'I didn't think there could be two Wilts in the same town,' he said triumphantly. 'Now then—'

But he was interrupted by the older of the two plainclothes men. 'If you don't mind, Inspector, we'll handle this,' he said with a brisk authority and almost a charm of manner that was even more alarming than the bank manager's previous coolness. He moved to the desk, picked up some of the notes and studied them. Wilt watched him with increasing concern.

'Would you mind telling us how you came by these five-pound notes, sir?' said the man. 'By the way, my name is Misterson.'

'They're a month's rent in advance from our lodger,' said Wilt. 'I came here to deposit them in my wife's PAPP account . . .'

'Pap, sir? Pap account?' said the smooth Mr Misterson.

'It stands for Personal Assistance for Primitive People,' said Wilt. 'My wife is the treasurer of the local branch. She's adopted a tribe in Africa and . . .'

'I understand, Mr Wilt,' said Misterson, casting a cold eye on Inspector Flint who had just muttered 'Typical'. He sat down and hitched his chair closer to Wilt. 'You were saying that this money came from the lodger and was destined for your wife's deposit account. What sort of lodger is this?'

'Female,' said Wilt slipping into cross-examination brevity.

'And her name, sir?'

'Irmgard Mueller.'

The two plainclothes men exchanged a look. Wilt followed it and said hastily, 'She's German.'

'Yes sir. And would you be able to identify her?'

'Identify her?' said Wilt. 'I'd be hard put not to. She's been living in the attic for the last month.'

'In which case if you'll kindly come to the station we'd be glad if you would look at some photographs,' said Misterson pushing back his chair.

'Now wait a moment. I want to know what this is all about,' said Wilt. 'I've been to that police station and frankly I don't want to go there again.' He stayed resolutely in his chair.

Mr Misterson reached in his pocket and took out a plastic licence which he opened.

'If you'll take a good look at this.'

Wilt did and felt sick. It stated that Superintendent Misterson of the Anti-Terrorist Branch was empowered . . . Wilt got up unsteadily and moved towards the door. Behind him the Superintendent was giving Inspector Flint, Sergeant Yates and the bank manager their orders. No one was to leave the office, there were to be no outgoing phone calls, maximum security and business as usual. Even the bank messenger was to remain where he was.

'And now Mr Wilt if you'll just walk out quite normally and follow me. We don't want to attract attention.'

Wilt followed him out and across the bank to the door and was hesitating there wondering what to do when a car drew up. The Superintendent opened the door and Wilt got in. Five minutes later he was sitting at a table being handed photographs of young women. It was twenty past twelve when he finally picked Miss Irmgard Mueller out.

'Are you absolutely certain?' asked the Superintendent.

'Of course I am,' said Wilt irritably. 'Now I don't know who she is or what the wretched woman has done but I'd be glad if you would go and arrest her or something. I want to get home to my lunch.'

'Quite so, sir. And is your wife in the house?'

Wilt looked at his watch. 'I don't see what that's got to do with it. As a matter of fact she will now be on her way back from playschool with the children and . . .'

The Superintendent sighed. It was a long ominous sigh. 'In that case I'm afraid there won't be any question of an arrest just yet,' he said. 'I take it that Miss . . . er . . . Mueller is in the house.'

'I don't know,' said Wilt, 'she was when I left this morning, and today being Wednesday she doesn't have any lectures, so she probably is. Why don't you go round and find out?'

'Because, sir, your lodger just happens to be one of the most dangerous woman terrorists in the world. I think that is self-explanatory.'

'Oh my God,' said Wilt, suddenly feeling very weak.

Superintendent Misterson leant across the desk. 'She has at least eight killings to her credit and she's suspected of being the mastermind . . . I'm sorry to use such melodramatic terms but in the event they happen to fit. As I was saying she has organized several bombings and we now know she's been involved in the hijacking of a security van in Gantrey last Tuesday. A man died in the attack. You may have read about the case.'

Wilt had. In the waiting-room at the Accident Centre. It had seemed then one of those remote and disgusting acts of gratuitous violence which made the morning paper such depressing reading. And yet because he read about it the murder of a security guard had been invested with a reality which it lacked in the present circumstances. Mastermind, terrorist, killings – words spoken casually in an office by a bland man with a paisley tie and a brown tweed suit. Like some country solicitor, Superintendent Misterson, was the last person he would have expected to use such words and it was this incongruity which was so alarming. Wilt stared at the man and shook his head.

'I'm afraid it's true,' said the Superintendent.

'But the money . . .'

'Marked sir. Marked and numbered. Bait in a trap.'

Wilt shook his head again. The truth was unbearable. 'What are you going to do? My wife and children are at home by now and if she's there . . . and there are all those other foreigners in the house too.'

'Would you mind telling us how many other . . . er . . . foreigners are there, sir?'

'I don't know,' said Wilt, 'it varies from day to day. There's a stream of them coming and going. Jesus wept.'

'Now, sir,' said the Superintendent briskly, 'what's your usual routine? Do you normally go home for lunch?'

'No. I usually have it at the Tech but just at the moment I'm off work and yes, I suppose I do.'

'So your wife will be surprised if you don't come home?'

'I doubt it,' said Wilt. 'Sometimes I drop into a pub for sandwiches.'

'And you don't telephone first?'

'Not always.'

'What I am trying to ascertain, sir, is whether your wife will

92

evince any alarm were you not to come home now or contact her.'

'She won't,' said Wilt. 'The only time she'll be alarmed is when she knows we've been providing accommodation for . . . What is the name of this bloody woman anyway?'

'Gudrun Schautz. And now, sir, I'll have some lunch sent up from the canteen and we'll make preparations.'

'What preparations?' asked Wilt but the Superintendent had left the room and the other plainclothes man seemed disinclined to talk. Wilt regarded the slight bulge under the man's right armpit and tried to stifle his growing feeling of insanity.

In the kitchen at Willington Road Eva was busy giving the quads their lunch.

'We won't wait for Daddy,' she said, 'he'll probably be back a little later.'

'Will he bring his bagpipe home?' asked Josephine.

'Bagpipe, dear? Daddy doesn't have a bagpipe.'

'He's been wearing one,' said Penelope.

'Yes, but not the sort you play.'

'I saw some men in dresses playing bagpipes at the show,' said Emmeline.

'Kilts, dear.'

'I saw Daddy playing with his pipe in the summerhouse,' said Penelope, 'and he was wearing Mummy's dress too.'

'Well he wasn't playing with it in the same way, Penny,' argued Eva, wondering privately what way Wilt had been playing with it.

'Bagpipes make a horrid noise anyway,' maintained Emmeline.

'And Daddy made a horrid noise when you got into bed . . .'

'Yes, dear, he was having a bad dream.'

'He called it a wet dream, Mummy. I heard him.'

'Well that's a bad dream too,' said Eva. 'Now then, what did you do at school today?'

But the quads were not to be diverted from the absorbing topic of their father's recent misfortune. 'Roger's mummy told him Daddy must have something wrong with his bladder to

93

have a pipe,' said Penelope. 'What's a bladder, Mummy?'

'I know,' shouted Emmeline, 'it's a pig's tummy and that's what they make bagpipes out of because Sally told me.'

'Daddy's not a pig . . .'

'That's enough of that,' said Eva firmly, 'we won't talk about Daddy any more. Now eat your cod's roe.'

'Roger says cod's roe is baby fishes,' said Penelope. 'I don't like it.'

'Well it's not. Fishes don't have babies. They lay eggs.'

'Do sausages lay eggs, mummy?' asked Josephine.

'Of course they don't, darling. Sausages aren't alive.'

'Roger says his daddy's sausage lays eggs and his mummy wears something . . .'

'I don't care to hear what Roger says any more,' said Eva torn between curiosity about the Rawstons and revulsion at her offsprings' encyclopedic knowledge. 'It's not nice to talk about such things.'

'Why not, Mummy?'

'Because it isn't,' said Eva unable to think of a suitably progressive argument to silence them. Caught between her own indoctrinated sense of niceness and her opinion that children's innate curiosity should never be thwarted, Eva struggled through lunch wishing that Henry were there to put a stop to their questions with a taciturn growl. But Henry still wasn't there at two o'clock when Mavis phoned to remind her that she had promised to pick her up on the way to the Symposium on Alternative Painting in Thailand.

'I'm sorry but Henry isn't back,' said Eva. 'He went to the doctor's this morning and I expected him home for lunch. I can't leave the children.'

'Patrick's got the car today,' said Mavis, 'his own is in for a service and I was relying on you.'

'Oh well, I'll go and ask Mrs de Frackas to baby-sit for half an hour,' said Eva, 'she's always volunteering to sit and Henry's bound to be back shortly.'

She went next door and presently old Mrs de Frackas was sitting in the summerhouse surrounded by the quads reading them the story of Rikki Tikki Tavi. The widow of Major-

General de Frackas, at eighty-two her memories of girlhood days in India were rather better than on topics of more recent occurrence. Eva drove off happily to pick up Mavis.

By the time Wilt had finished his lunch he had picked out two more terrorists from the mug shots as being frequent visitors to the house, and the police station had seen the arrival of several large vans containing a large number of surprisingly agile men in a motley of plain clothes. The canteen had been turned into a briefing centre and Superintendent Misterson's authority had been superseded by a Major (name undisclosed) of Special Ground Services.

'The Superintendent here will explain the initial stages of the operation,' said the Major condescendingly, 'but before he does I want to stress that we are dealing with some of the most ruthless killers in Europe. They must on no account escape. At the same time we naturally want to avoid bloodshed if at all possible. However, it has to be said that in the circumstances we are entitled to shoot first and ask questions afterwards if the target is able to answer. I have that authority from the Minister.' He smiled bleakly and sat down.

'After the house has been surrounded,' said the Superintendent, 'Mr Wilt will enter and hopefully effect the exit of his family. I want nothing done to prevent that first essential requirement. The second factor to take into account is that we have a unique opportunity to arrest at least three leading terrorists and possibly more, and again, hopefully, Mr Wilt will enable us to know how many members of the group are in the house at the moment of time of his exit. I'll go ahead with my side and leave the rest to the Major.'

He left the canteen and went up to the office where Wilt was finishing his Queen's pudding with the help of mouthfuls of coffee. Outside the door he met the SGS surgeon and para-psychologist who had been studying Wilt covertly.

'Nervous type,' he said gloomily. 'Couldn't be worse material. Sort of blighter who'd funk a jump from a tethered balloon.'

'Fortunately he doesn't have to jump from a tethered balloon,' said the Superintendent. 'All he has to do is enter the house and find an excuse for taking his family out.'

'All the same I think he ought to have a shot of something to stiffen his backbone. We don't want him dithering on the doorstep. Give the game away.'

He marched off to fetch his bag while the Superintendent went in to Wilt. 'Now then,' he said with alarming cheerfulness, 'all you've got to do . . .'

'Is enter a house filled with killers and ask my wife to come out. I know,' said Wilt.

'Nothing very difficult about that.'

Wilt looked at him incredulously. 'Nothing difficult?' said Wilt in a vaguely soprano voice. 'You don't know my bloody wife.'

'I haven't had the privilege yet,' admitted the Superintendent.

'Precisely,' said Wilt. 'Well, when and if you do you'll discover that if I go home and ask her to come out she'll think of a thousand reasons for staying in.'

'Difficult woman, sir?'

'Oh no, nothing difficult about Eva. Not at all. She's just bloody awkward, that's all.'

'I see, sir, and if you suggested she didn't go out you think she might in fact do so?'

'If you want my opinion,' said Wilt, 'if I do that she'll think I'm off my rocker. I mean what would you do if you were sitting peacefully at home and your wife came in and suggested out of the blue that you didn't go out when it had never occurred to you to go out in the first place? You'd think there was something fucking odd going on, wouldn't you?'

'I suppose I would,' said the Superintendent. 'Never thought of it like that before.'

'Well you'd better start now,' said Wilt, 'I'm not going . . .'

He was interrupted by the entrance of the Major and two other officers wearing jeans, T-shirts with UP THE IRA printed on them, and carrying rather large handbags.

'If we might just interrupt a moment,' said the Major, 'we would like Mr Wilt to draw a detailed plan of the house, vertical section and then horizontal.'

'What for?' said Wilt unable to take his eyes off the T-shirts.

'In the event that we have to storm the house, sir,' said the Major, 'we need to get the killing angles right. Don't want to go in and find the loo's in the wrong place and what not.'

'Listen, mate,' said Wilt, 'you go down Willington Road with those T-shirts and handbags you won't reach my house. You'll be bloody lynched by the neighbours. Mrs Fogin's nephew was blown up in Belfast and Professor Ball's got a thing about gays. His wife married one.'

'Better change into the KEEP CLAPHAM WHITE shirts, chaps,' said the Major.

'Better not,' said Wilt. 'Mr and Mrs Bokani at Number 11 would be on to Race Relations like the clappers. Can't you think of something neutral?'

'Mickey Mouse, sir?' suggested one of the officers.

'Oh, all right,' said the Major grumpily, 'one Mickey Mouse and the rest Donald Ducks.'

'Christ,' said Wilt, 'I don't know how many men you've got but if you're going to flood the neighbourhood with Donald Ducks armed to the teeth with whatever you have in those gigantic handbags you'll have a whole lot of schizophrenic infants on your conscience.'

'Never mind that,' said the Major, 'you leave the tactical angle to us. We've had experience before of this sort of operation and all we want from you is a detailed plan of the domestic terrain.'

'Talk about calling a spade an earth-inverting horticultural implement,' said Wilt. 'I never thought I'd live to hear my home called a domestic terrain.'

He picked up a pencil but the Superintendent intervened. 'Look, if we don't get Mr Wilt back to the house soon, some-one may begin wondering where he is,' he protested.

As if to reinforce this argument the phone rang.

'It's for you,' said the Major. 'Some bugger called Flint who says he's holed up in the bank.'

'I thought I told you not to make any outgoing calls,' the Superintendent said angrily into the phone. 'Relieve themselves? Of course they can . . . An appointment at three with Mr Daniles? Who's he? . . . Oh shit . . . Where? . . . Well, empty the wastepaper basket for Chrissake . . . I don't have to tell you where. I should have thought that was patently obvious . . . What do you mean it's going to look peculiar? . . . Do they have to cross the entire bank? . . . I know all about the smell. Get hold of an aerosol or something . . . Well if he objects detain the sod. And Flint, see if someone has a bucket and use that in future.'

He slammed down the phone and turned back to the Major. 'Things are steaming up at the bank and if we don't move swiftly—'

'Someone's going to smell a rat?' suggested Wilt. 'Now, do you want me to draw my house or not?'

'Yes,' said the Major, 'and fast.'

'There's no need to adopt that tone,' said Wilt. 'You may be eager to have a battle on my property but I want to know who's going to pay for the damage. My wife's a very particular woman and if you start killing people all over the carpet in the living-room . . .'

'Mr Wilt,' said the Major with determined patience, 'we shall do everything we can to avoid any violence on your property. It is for precisely that reason we need a detailed plan of the domestic . . . er . . . the house.'

'I think if we leave Mr Wilt to draw the plan . . .' said the Superintendent and nodded towards the door. The Major followed him out and they conferred in the corridor.

'Listen,' said the Superintendent, 'I've already had a report from your trick-cyclist that the little bastard's a mass of nerves and if you're going to start bullying him . . .'

'Superintendent,' said the Major, 'it may interest you to know that I have a casualty allowance of ten on this op and if he's one of them I shan't be sorry. War Office approval.'

'And if we don't get him in there, and his wife and children out, you'll have used up six of your quota,' snapped the Superintendent.

'All I can say is that a man who puts his living-room carpet before his country and the Western World . . .' He would have said a lot more had it not been for the arrival of the para-psychologist with a cup of coffee.

'Fixed him a spot of nervebracer,' he said cheerfully. 'Should see him through.'

'I certainly hope so,' said the Superintendent. 'I could do with something myself.'

'No need to worry about it working,' said the Major. 'Used it myself once in County Armagh when I had to defuse a bloody great bomb. Bugger went off before I could get to it but by God I felt good all the same.'

The medic went into the office and presently reappeared with the empty cup. 'In like a lamb, out like a lion,' he said. 'No trouble at all.'

11

Ten minutes later Wilt lived up to the prediction. He left the police station of his own free will and entered the Superintendent's car quite cheerfully.

'Just drop me off at the bottom of the road and I'll find my own way home,' he said. 'No need for you to bother to drive right up to the house.'

The Superintendent looked at him doubtfully. 'I hadn't intended to. The object of the exercise is for you to go into the house without arousing suspicion and persuade your wife to come out by telling her you've met this herbalist in a pub and he's invited you all round to look at his collection of plants. You've got that straight?'

'Wilco,' said Wilt.

'Wilco?'

'And what's more,' continued Wilt, 'if that doesn't flush the bitch out I'll take the children and leave her to stew in her own juice.'

'Stop the car, driver,' said the Superintendent hastily.

'What for?' said Wilt. 'You don't expect me to walk two

miles? When I said you could drop me off I didn't mean here.'

'Mr Wilt,' said the Superintendent, 'I must impress on you the seriousness of the situation. Gudrun Schautz is undoubtedly armed and she won't hesitate to shoot. The woman is a professional killer.'

'So what? Bloody woman comes into my house having killed people all over the place and expects me to give her bed and board. Like hell I will. Driver, drive on.'

'Oh God,' said the Superintendent, 'trust the army to cock this one up.'

'Want me to turn back, sir?' asked the driver.

'Certainly not,' said Wilt. 'The sooner I can get my family out and the army in the better. No need to look like that. Everything's going to be roger over and out.'

'I wouldn't be at all surprised,' said the Superintendent despondently. 'All right, drive on. Now then, Mr Wilt, for God's sake stick to your story about the herbalist. The fellow's name is . . .'

'Falkirk,' said Wilt automatically. 'He lives at Number 45 Barrabas Road. He has recently returned from South America with a collection of plants including tropical herbs previously uncultivated in this country . . .'

'At least he knows his lines,' muttered the Superintendent as they turned into Farringdon Avenue and pulled into the kerb. Wilt got out, slammed the car door with unnecessary violence and marched off down Willington Road. Behind him the Superintendent watched miserably and cursed the parapsychologist.

'Must have given him some sort of chemical kamikaze mixture,' he told the driver.

'There's still time to stop him, sir,' said the driver. But there wasn't. Wilt had dived into the gate of his house and disappeared. As soon as he had gone a head popped out of the hedge beside the car.

'Don't want to give the game away, old boy,' said an officer wearing the uniform of a Gas Inspector. 'If you'll just toddle along I'll call HQ and tell them the subject has entered the danger zone . . .'

'Oh no you won't,' snarled the Superintendent as the officer twiddled with the knobs of his walkie-talkie, 'there's to be strict radio silence until the family are safely out.'

'My orders are . . .'

'Countermanded as of now,' said the Superintendent. 'Innocent lives are at stake and I'm not having them jeopardized.'

'Oh all right,' said the officer. 'Anyway we've got the area sealed off. Not even a rabbit could get out of there now.'

'It's not simply a question of anyone getting out. We want as many to get in before we move.'

'Rightho, want to bag the lot of them eh? Nothing like going the whole hog, what!'

The officer disappeared into the hedge and the Superintendent drove on.

'Lions, lambs, and now fucking rabbits and hogs,' he told the driver, 'I wish to heaven the Special Ground Services hadn't been called in. They seem to have animals on the brain.'

'Comes of recruiting them from the huntin' an' shootin' set, I expect, sir,' said the driver. 'Wouldn't like to be in that bloke Wilt's shoes.'

In the garden of Number 9 Willington Road Wilt did not share his apprehensions. Stiffened by the parapsychologist's nerve-bracer he was in no mood to be trifled with. Bloody terrorists coming into his house without so much as a by-your-leave. Well, he'd soon show them the door. He marched resolutely up to the house and opened the front door before realizing that the car wasn't outside. Eva must be out with the quads. In which case there was no need for him to go in. 'To hell with that,' said Wilt to himself, 'this is my house and I'm entitled to do what I damned well please in it.' He went into the hall and shut the door. The house was silent and the living-room empty. Wilt went through the kitchen and wondered what to do next. In normal circumstances he would have left, but circumstances were not normal. To Wilt's intoxicated way of thinking they called for stern measures. The bloody army wanted a battle on his domestic terrain, did they? Well, he'd soon put a stop to that. Domestic terrain indeed! If people wanted to kill one another they could jolly well do it somewhere else. Which was all very fine, but how to persuade them? Well, the simplest way was to go up to the attic and heave Miss Bloody Schautz/Mueller's suitcases and clobber out into the front garden. That way when she came home she'd get the message and take herself off to someone else's domestic terrain.

With this simple solution in mind Wilt went upstairs and climbed the steps to the attic door only to find it locked. He went down to the kitchen, found the spare key and went back. For a moment he hesitated outside the door before knocking. There was no reply. Wilt unlocked the door and went inside.

The attic flat consisted of three rooms, a large bedsitter with the balcony looking down on to the garden, a kitchenette and beyond it a bathroom. Wilt shut the door behind him and looked around. The bedsitter which had occupied his former Muse was unexpectedly tidy. Gudrun Schautz might be a ruthless terrorist but she was also house-proud. Clothes hung neatly in a wall closet and the cups and saucers in the kitchen were all washed and set on shelves. Now, where would she have put her suitcases? Wilt looked round and tried another cupboard before remembering that Eva had moved the cold-water cistern to a higher position under the roof when the bathroom had been put in. There was a door to it somewhere.

He found it beside the stove in the kitchenette and crawled through only to discover that he had to stoop along under the eaves on a narrow plank to reach the storage space. He groped about in the darkness and found the lightswitch. The suitcases were in a row beside the cistern. Wilt made his way along and grabbed the handle of the first bag. It felt incredibly heavy. Also distinctly lumpy. Wilt dragged it down from the shelf and it dropped with a metallic thud on to the plank at his feet. He wasn't going to lug that back across the rafters. Wilt fumbled with the catches and finally opened the bag.

All his doubts about Miss Schautz/Mueller's profession vanished. He was looking down on some sort of sub-machine gun, a mound of revolvers, boxes of ammunition, a typewriter and what appeared to be grenades. And as he looked he heard the sound of a car outside. It had pulled into the drive and even to his untrained ear it sounded like the Aston-Martin. Cursing himself for not listening to his innate cowardice, Wilt struggled to get back along the plank to the door but the bag was in the way. He banged his head on the rafters above and was about to crawl over the bag when it occurred to him that the sub-machine gun might be loaded and could well go off if he prodded it in the wrong place. Best get the damned thing out. Again, that was easier said than done. The barrel got caught in the end of the bag and by the time he had disentangled it he could hear footsteps on the wooden stairs below. Too late to do anything now except switch the light off. Leaning forward across the bag and holding the machine gun at arm's length Wilt joggled the switch up with the muzzle before crouching down in the darkness.

Outside in the garden the quads had had a marvellous afternoon with old Mrs de Frackas. She had read them the story about Rikki Tikki Tavi, the mongoose, and the two cobras, and had then taken them into her house to show them what a stuffed cobra looked like (she had one in a glass case and it bared its fangs most realistically) and had told them about her own childhood in India before sitting them down to tea in her conservatory. For once the quads had behaved themselves. They had picked up from Eva a proper sense of Mrs de Frackas' social standing and in any case the old lady's voice had a distinctly firm ring to it – or as Wilt had once put it, if at eighty-two she could no longer break a sherry glass at fifty paces she could still make a guard dog whimper at forty. It was certainly true that the milkman had long since given up trying to collect his payment on a weekly basis. Mrs de Frackas belonged to a generation that had paid when it felt so inclined; the old lady sent her cheque only twice a year, and then it was wrong. The milk company did not dispute it. The widow of the late Major-General de Frackas, DSO etc. was a personage to whom people deferred and it was one of Eva's proudest boasts that she and the old lady got on like a house on fire. Nobody else in Willington Road did and it was almost entirely because Mrs de Frackas loved children and considered Eva, in spite of her obvious lack of breeding, to be an excellent mother that she smiled on the Wilts. To be precise, she seldom smiled on Wilt, evidently regarding him as an accident in the family process and one that, if her observation of his activities in the summerhouse of an evening was correct, drank. Since the Major-General had died of cirrhosis or as she bluntly said, hob-nailed liver, Wilt's solitary communion with the bottle only increased her regard for Eva and concern for the children. Being also rather deaf she thought them delightful girls, an opinion that was shared by no one else in the district.

And so this bright sunny afternoon Mrs de Frackas sat the quads in her conservatory and served tea, happily unaware of the gathering drama next door. Then she allowed them to play with the tiger rug in her drawing-room and even to knock over a potted palm before deciding it was time to go home. The little procession went out of the front gate and into Number 9 just as Wilt began his search in the attic. In the bushes on the opposite side of the road the officer whom the Superintendent had warned not to use the radio watched them enter the house and was desperately praying that they would come out again straightaway when the Aston-Martin drove up. Gudrun Schautz and two young men got out, opened the boot and took out several suitcases while the officer dithered but before he could make up his mind to tackle them in the open they had hurried in the front door. Only then did he break radio silence.

'Female target and two males have entered the zone,' he told the Major who was making a round of the SGS men posted at the bottom of the Wilts' garden. 'No present withdrawal of civilian occupants. Request instructions.'

In response the Major threaded his way through the gardens of Numbers 4 and 2 and accompanied by two privates carrying a theodolite and a striped pole promptly set this up on the pavement and began to take sightings down Willington Road while carrying on a conversation with the officer in the hedge.

'What do you mean you couldn't stop them?' demanded the Major when he learnt that the quads and an old lady had left the house next door and gone into the Wilts'. But before the officer could think of an answer they were interrupted by Professor Ball.

'What's the meaning of all this?' he demanded, regarding the two long-haired privates and the theodolite with equal distaste.

'Just making a survey for the new road extension,' said the Major improvising hastily.

'Road extension? What road extension?' said the Professor transferring his disgust to the handbag the Major had over his shoulder.

'The proposed road extension to the by-pass,' said the Major.

Professor Ball's voice rose. 'By-pass? Did I hear you say there's a proposal to put a road through here to the by-pass?'

'Only doing my job, sir,' said the Major, wishing to hell the old fool would get lost.

'And what job is that?' demanded the Professor, taking a notebook from his pocket.

'Surveyor's Department, Borough Engineering.'

'Really? And your name?' asked the Professor with a nasty glint in his eye. He wetted the end of his ballpen with his tongue while the Major hesitated.

'Palliser, sir,' said the Major. 'And now, sir, if you don't mind, we've got to get on.'

'Don't let me disturb you, Mr Palliser.' The Professor turned and stalked into his house. He returned a moment later with a heavy stick.

'It may interest you to know, Mr Palliser,' he said brandishing the stick, 'that I happen to sit on the Highways and Planning Committee of the City Council. Note the word "city", Mr Palliser. And we don't have a Borough Engineering Department. We have a City one.'

'Slip of the tongue, sir,' said the Major trying to keep one eye on the Wilts' house while conscious of the threat of the stick.

'And I suppose it was another slip of the tongue that you said that the City of Ipford was proposing to build an extension of this road to the by-pass . . .'

105

'It's just a vague idea, sir,' said the Major.

Professor Ball laughed dryly. 'It must indeed be vague considering we don't yet have a by-pass and that as Chairman of the Highways and Planning Committee I would be the first to hear of any proposed alterations to the existing roads. What's more, I happen to know a great deal about the use of theodolites and you don't look through the wrong end. Now then, you will kindly remain where you are until the police arrive. My housekeeper has already phoned . . .'

'If I could have a word with you in private,' said the Major fumbling frantically in his handbag for his credentials. But Professor Ball knew an imposter when he saw one and, as Wilt had predicted, his reaction to men who carried handbags was violent. With the descent of his stick the Major's credentials tipped from his handbag and clattered on the ground. They included one walkie-talkie, two revolvers and a teargas grenade.

'Fuck,' said the Major, stooping to retrieve his armoury, but Professor Ball's stick was in action again. This time it caught the Major on the back of the neck and sent him sprawling in the gutter. Behind him the private in charge of the theodolite moved swiftly. Throwing himself on the Professor he pinned his left arm behind his back and with a karate chop knocked the stick from his right hand.

'If you'll just come quietly, sir,' he said, but that was the last thing Professor Ball intended to do. Safety, from men pretending to be surveyors who carried revolvers and grenades, lay in making as much noise as he could and Willington Road was aroused from its suburban torpor by yells of 'Help! Murder! Call the police!'

'For God's sake gag the old bastard,' shouted the Major still scrabbling for his revolvers but it was too late. Across the road a face appeared at the attic skylight, was followed by a second, and before the Professor could be removed in silence they had disappeared.

Squatting in the darkness beside the water tank Wilt was only dimly aware that something odd was happening in the street.

Gudrun Schautz had decided to take a bath and the tank was rumbling and hissing but he could hear the reactions of her companions clearly enough.

'Police!' one of them yelled. 'Gudrun, the police are here.'

Another voice shouted from the balcony room. 'There are more in the garden with rifles.'

'Downstairs quickly. We take them on the ground.'

Footsteps clattered down the wooden staircase while Gudrun Schautz from the bathroom shouted instructions in German and then remembered to bawl them in English.

'The children,' she shouted, 'hold the children.'

It was too much for Wilt. Disregarding the bag and the machine gun he was holding he hurled himself at the door, fell through it into the kitchen and promptly sprayed the ceiling with bullets by accidentally pulling the trigger. The effect was quite remarkable. In the bathroom Gudrun Schautz screamed, downstairs the terrorists began firing into the back garden and at the little group including Professor Ball across the street, and from both the street and the back garden the SGS returned their fire fourfold, smashing windows, adding new holes in the leaves of Eva's Swiss Cheese plant and generally pock-marking the walls of the living-room where Mrs de Frackas and the quads were enjoying a Western on TV until the Mexican rug on the wall behind them was dislodged and covered their heads.

'Now then, children,' she said calmly, 'there's no need to be alarmed. We'll just lie on the floor until whatever's happening stops.' But the quads were not in the least alarmed. Inured by continual gunfights on television they were perfectly at home in the middle of a real one.

The same could hardly be said for Wilt. As the plaster from the perforated ceiling drifted down on to him he scrambled to his feet and was making for the stairs when a burst of small-arms fire heading through the back windows of the landing and out the front deterred him. Still clutching the sub-machine gun he stumbled back into the kitchen and then realized that the infernal Fräulein Schautz was behind him in the bathroom. She had stopped screaming and might at any moment emerge with a gun. 'Lock the bitch in,' was his first thought but since the key was on the inside . . . Wilt looked round for an alternative and found it in a kitchen chair which he jammed under the door handle. To make this doubly secure he tore the flex from a table-lamp in the main room and dragged it through before tying a loop to the handle and attaching the other end to the leg of the electric stove. Then having secured his rear he made another sortie to the stairs, but the battle below still raged. He was just about to risk going down when a head appeared on the landing, a head and shoulders carrying the same sort of weapon he had just used. Wilt didn't hesitate. He slammed the door of the flat, pushed up the safety lock and then dragged a bed from the wall and lodged it against the door. Finally he picked up his own gun and waited. If anyone tried to come through the door he would pull the trigger. But then just as suddenly as the battle had begun it ceased.

Silence reigned in Willington Road, a short, blissful, healthy silence. Wilt stood in the attic and listened breathlessly, wondering what to do next. It was decided for him by Gudrun Schautz trying the door of the bathroom. He edged into the kitchen and pointed the gun at the door.

'One more move in there and I fire,' he said, and even to Wilt his voice had a strange and unnaturally menacing, almost unrecognizable sound to it. To Gudrun Schautz it held the authentic tone of a man behind a gun. The door handle stopped wriggling. On the other hand there was someone at the top of the stairs trying to get into the flat. With a facility that astonished him Wilt turned and pulled the trigger and once more the flat resounded to a burst of gunfire. None of the bullets hit the door. They spattered the wall of the bedsitter while the submachine gun juddered in Wilt's hands. The bloody thing seemed to have a will of its own and it was a horrified Wilt who finally took his finger off the trigger and put the gun gingerly down on the kitchen table. Outside someone descended the stairs with remarkable rapidity but there was no other sound.

Wilt sat down and wondered what the hell was going to happen next.

12

Much the same question was occupying Superintendent Misterson's mind.

'What's the hell's going on?' he demanded of the dishevelled Major who arrived with Professor Ball and the two pseudo-surveyors at the corner of Willington Road and Farringdon Avenue. 'I thought I told you nothing must be done until the children were safely out of the house.'

'Don't look at me,' said the Major. 'This old fool had to poke his fucking nose in.'

He fingered the back of his neck and eyed the Professor with loathing.

'And who might you be?' Professor Ball asked the Superintendent.

'A police officer.'

'Then kindly do your duty and arrest these bandits. Come down the road with a damned theodolite and handbags filled with guns and tell me they're from the Roads Department and indulge in gun battles . . .'

'Anti-Terrorist Squad, sir,' said the Superintendent and showed him his pass. Professor Ball regarded it bleakly.

'A likely story. First I'm assaulted by . . .'

'Oh, get the old bugger out of here,' snarled the Major. 'If he hadn't interfered we'd have—'

'Interfered? Interfered indeed! I was exercising my right to make a citizen's arrest of these imposters when they start shooting into a perfectly ordinary house across the street and . . .' Two uniformed constables arrived to escort the Professor, still protesting angrily, to a waiting police car.

'You heard the damned man,' said the Major in response to the Superintendent's reiterated request for someone to please tell him what the hell had gone wrong. 'We were waiting for the children to come out when he arrives on the scene and blows the gaff. That's what happened. The next thing you know the sods were firing from the house, and by the sound of it using some damnably powerful weapons.'

'Right, so what you are saying is that the children are still in the house, Mr Wilt is still there, and so are a number of terrorists. Is that correct?'

'Yes,' said the Major.

'And all this in spite of your guarantee that you wouldn't do anything to jeopardize the lives of innocent civilians?'

'I didn't do a damned thing. I happened to be lying in the gutter when the balloon went up. And if you expect my men to sit quietly and let themselves be shot at by thugs using automatic weapons you're asking too much of human nature.'

'I suppose so,' the Superintendent conceded. 'Oh well, we'll just have to go into the usual siege routine. Any idea how many terrorists were in there?'

'Too bloody many for my liking,' said the Major looking to his men for confirmation.

'One of them was firing through the roof, sir,' said one of the privates. 'A burst of fire came through the tiles right at the beginning.'

'And I wouldn't say they were short of ammo. Not the way they were loosing off.'

'All right. First thing is to evacuate the street,' said the Superintendent. 'Don't want any more people involved than we can help.'

'Sounds as if someone else is already involved,' said the Major as the muffled burst of Wilt's second experiment with the machine gun echoed from Number 9. 'What the hell are they doing firing inside the house?'

'Probably started on the hostages,' said the Superintendent gloomily.

'Hardly likely, old chap. Not unless one of them tried to escape. Oh by the way I don't know if I mentioned it but there's a little old lady in there too. Went in with the four girls.'

'Went in with the four—' the Superintendent began lividly before being interrupted by his driver with the message that Inspector Flint had called from the bank to know if it was all right for him to leave now as it was closing time and the bank staff . . .

The Superintendent unleashed his fury on Flint via the

driver, and the Major made good his escape. Presently little groups of refugees from Willington Road were making their way circuitously out of the area while more armed men moved in to take their place. An armoured car with the Major perched safely on its turret rumbled past.

'HQ and Communications Centre are at Number 7,' he shouted. 'My signal chappies have rigged you up with a direct line in.'

He drove on before the Superintendent could think of a suitable retort. 'Damned military getting in the way all the time,' he grumbled and gave orders for parabolic listening devices to be brought up and for tape recorders and voiceprint analysers to be installed at the Communications Centre. In the meantime Farringdon Avenue was cordoned off by uniformed police at road blocks and a Press Briefing Room established at the Police Station.

'Got to give the public their pound of vicarious flesh,' he told his men, 'but I don't want any TV cameramen inside the area. The sods inside the house will be watching and frankly if I had my way there would be press and TV silence. These swine thrive on publicity.'

Only then did he make his way down Willington Road to Number 7 to begin the dialogue with the terrorists.

Eva drove home from Mavis Mottram's in a bad temper. The Symposium on Alternative Painting in Thailand had been cancelled because the artist-cum-lecturer had been arrested and was awaiting extradition proceedings for drug smuggling and instead Eva had had to sit through two hours of discussion on Alternative Childbirth about which, since she had given birth to four overweight infants in the course of forty minutes, she considered she knew more than the lecturer. To add to her irritation, several ardent advocates of abortion had used the occasion to promote their views and Eva had violent feelings about abortion.

'It's unnatural,' she told Mavis afterwards in the Coffee House with that simplicity her friends found so infuriating. 'If people don't want children they shouldn't have them.'

'Yes, dear,' said Mavis, 'but it's not as easy as all that.'

'It is. They can have their babies adopted by parents who can't have any. There are thousands of couples like that.'

'Yes, but in the case of teenage girls . . .'

'Teenage girls shouldn't have sex. I didn't.'

Mavis looked at her thoughtfully. 'No, but you're the exception, Eva. The modern generation is much more demanding than we were. They're physically more mature.'

'Perhaps they are, but Henry says they're mentally retarded.'

'Of course, he would know,' said Mavis but Eva was impervious to such slights.

'If they weren't they would take precautions.'

'But you're the one who is always going on about the pill being unnatural.'

'And so it is. I just meant they wouldn't allow boys to go so far. After all once they're married they can have as much as they like.'

'That's the first time I've heard you say that, dear. You're always complaining that Henry is too tired to bother.'

In the end Eva had had to riposte with a reference to Patrick Mottram and Mavis had seized the opportunity to catalogue his latest infidelities.

'Anyone would think the whole world revolved round Patrick,' Eva grumbled to herself as she drove away from Ms Mottram's house. 'And I don't care what anyone thinks, I still say abortion is wrong.' She turned into Farringdon Avenue and was immediately stopped by a policeman. A barrier had been erected across the road and several police cars were parked against the kerb.

'Sorry, ma'am, but you'll have to go back. No one is allowed through,' a uniformed constable told her.

'But I live here,' said Eva. 'I'm only going as far as Willington Road.'

'That's where the trouble is.'

'What trouble?' asked Eva, her instincts suddenly alert. 'Why have they got that barbed wire across the road?'

A sergeant walked across as Eva opened the door of the car and got out.

'Now then, if you'll kindly turn round and drive back the way you came,' he said.

'Says she lives in Willington Road,' the constable told him. At that moment two SGS men armed with automatic weapons came round the corner and entered Mrs Granberry's garden by way of her flowerbed of prize begonias. If anything was needed to confirm Eva's worst fears this was it.

'Those men have got guns,' she said. 'Oh my God, my children! Where are my children?'

'You'll find everyone from Willington Road in the Memorial Hall. Now what number do you live at?'

'Number 9. I left the quads with Mrs de Frackas and—'

'If you'll just come this way, Mrs Wilt,' said the sergeant gently and started to take her arm.

'How did you know my name?' Eva asked, staring at the sergeant with growing horror. 'You called me Mrs Wilt.'

'Now please keep calm. Everything is going to be all right.'

'No, it isn't.' And Eva threw his hand aside and began running down the road before being stopped by four policemen and dragged back to a car.

'Get the medic and a policewoman,' said the sergeant. 'Now you just sit in the back, Mrs Wilt.' Eva was forced into a police car.

'What's happened to the children? Somebody tell me what's happened.'

'The Superintendent will explain. They're quite safe so don't worry.'

'If they're safe why can't I go to them? Where's Henry? I want my Henry.'

But instead of Wilt she got the Superintendent who arrived with two policemen and a doctor.

'Now then, Mrs Wilt,' said the Superintendent, 'I'm afraid I've got some bad news for you. Not that it couldn't be worse. Your children are alive and quite safe, but they're in the hands of several armed men and we're trying to get them out of the house safely.'

Eva stared at him wildly. 'Armed men? What armed men?'

'Some foreigners.'

'You mean they're being held *hostage*?'

'We can't be too sure just yet. Your husband is with them.'

The doctor intervened. 'I'm just going to give you a sedative, Mrs Wilt,' he began but Eva recoiled in the back seat.

'No you aren't. I'm not taking anything. You can't make me.'

'If you'll just calm down . . .'

But Eva was adamant, and too strong to be easily given an injection in the confined space. After the doctor had had the hypodermic syringe knocked from his hand for the second time he gave up.

'All right, Mrs Wilt, you needn't take anything,' said the Superintendent. 'If you'll just sit still we'll drive you back to the police station and keep you fully informed of any developments.'

And in spite of Eva's protests that she wanted to stay where she was or even go down to the house she was driven away with an escort of two policewomen.

'Next time you want me to sedate that damned woman I'll get a tranquillizer gun from the Zoo,' said the doctor, nursing his wrist. 'And if you're sensible you'll keep her in a cell. If she gets loose she could foul things up properly.'

'As if they weren't already,' said the Superintendent and made his way back to the Communications Centre. It was situated in Mrs de Frackas' drawing-room and there incongruously, set among mementos of life in Imperial India, antimacassars, potted plants and beneath the ferocious portrait of the late Major-General, the SGS and the Anti-Terrorist Squad had collaborated to install a switchboard, a telephone amplifier, tape recorders and the voiceprint analyser.

'All ready to go, sir,' said the detective in charge of the apparatus. 'We've hooked into the line next door.'

'Have you got the listening devices in position?'

'Can't do that yet,' said the Major. 'No windows on this side and we can't move in across the lawn. Have a shot after dark, provided those buggers haven't got night sights.'

'Oh well, put me through,' said the Superintendent. 'The sooner we begin the dialogue the sooner everyone will be able to go home. If I know my job they'll start with a stream of abuse. So everyone stand by to be called a fascist shit.'

In the event he was mistaken. It was Mrs de Frackas who answered.

'This is Ipford 23 . . . I'm afraid I haven't got my glasses with me but I think it's . . . Now, young man . . .'

There was a brief pause during which Mrs de Frackas was evidently relieved of the phone.

'My name is Misterson, Superintendent Misterson,' said the Superintendent finally.

'Lying pig of a fascist shit,' shouted a voice, at last fulfilling his prediction. 'You think we are going to surrender, shit face, but you are wrong. We die first, you understand. Do you hear me, pig?'

The Superintendent sighed and said he did.

'Right. Get that straight in your pigshit fascist head. No way we surrender. If you want us you come in and kill us and you know what that means.'

'I don't think anyone wants . . .'

'What you want, pig, you don't get. You do what we want or people get hurt.'

'That's what I'm waiting to hear, what you want,' said the Superintendent, but the terrorists were evidently in consultation and after a minute the phone in the house was slammed down.

'Well, at least we know the little old lady hasn't been hurt and by the sound of things the children are all right.'

The Superintendent crossed to a coffee-dispenser and poured himself a cup.

'Bit of a bore being called a pig all the time,' said the Major sympathetically. 'You'd think they could come up with something slightly more original.'

'Don't you believe it. They're on a Marxist millennium ego-trip, kamikaze style, and what few brains they have they laundered years ago. That sounded like Chinanda, the Mexican.'

'Intonation and accent was right,' said the sergeant on the tape recorder.

'What's his record?' asked the Major.

'The usual. Rich parents, good education, flunked University and decided to save the world by knocking people off. To date, five. Specializes in car bombs, and crude ones at that. Not a very sophisticated laddie, our Miguel. Better get that tape through to the analysts. I want to hear their verdict on his stress pattern. And now we settle down to the long slog.'

'You expect him to call back with demands?'

'No. Next time we'll have the charming Fräulein Schautz. She's the one with the brains up top.'

It was an unintentionally apt description. Trapped in the bathroom, Gudrun Schautz had spent much of the afternoon wondering what had happened and why no one had either killed her or come to arrest her. She had also considered methods of escape but was hampered by the lack of her clothes, which she had left in the bedsitter, and by Wilt's threat that if she made one more move he would fire. Not that she knew it was Wilt who had made it. What she had heard of his domestic life through the floor above his bedroom had done nothing to suggest he was capable of any sort of heroism. He was simply an effete, degenerate and cowardly little Englishman who was bullied by his stupid wife.

Fräulein Schautz might speak English fluently but her understanding of the English was hopelessly deficient. Given the chance Wilt would have agreed in large measure with this assessment of his character but he was too preoccupied to waste time on introspection. He was trying to guess what had happened downstairs during the shooting. He had no way of knowing if the quads were still in the house, and only the presence of armed men at the bottom of the garden and across the road in front of the house told him that the terrorists were still on the ground floor. From the balcony window he could look down at the summerhouse where he had spent so many idle evenings regretting his wasted gifts and longing for a woman

116

who turned out in reality to be less a Muse than a private executioner. Now the summerhouse was occupied by men with guns while the field beyond was ringed with coils of barbed wire. The view from the skylight over the kitchen was even less encouraging. An armoured car had stationed itself outside the front gate with its gun turret turned towards the house, and there were more armed men in Professor Ball's garden.

Wilt climbed down and was wondering rather hysterically what the hell to do next when the telephone rang. He went into the main room and picked the extension up in time to hear Mrs de Frackas end her brief statement. Wilt listened to the tide of abuse wash over the uncomplaining Superintendent and felt briefly for the man. It sounded just like Bilger in one of his tirades, only this time the men downstairs had guns. They probably had the quads too. Wilt couldn't be certain but Mrs de Frackas' presence suggested as much. Wilt listened to see if his own name was mentioned and was relieved that it wasn't. When the one-sided conversation ended Wilt replaced his receiver very cautiously and with a slight feeling of optimism. It was very slight, a mere reaction from the tension and from a sudden sense of power. It wasn't the power of the gun but rather that of knowledge, what he knew and what nobody else apparently knew; that the attic was occupied by a man whose killing capacity was limited to flies and whose skill with firearms was less murderous than suicidal. About the only thing Wilt knew about machine guns and revolvers was that bullets came out the barrel when you pulled the trigger. But if he knew nothing about the workings of firearms the terrorists clearly had no idea what had happened in the attic. For all they knew the place was filled with armed policemen and the shots he had fired so accidentally could have killed Fräulein Bloody Schautz. If that were the case they would make no attempt to rescue her. Anyway, the illusion that the flat was held by desperate men who could kill without a moment's hesitation seemed definitely worth maintaining. He was just congratulating himself when the opposite thought occurred to him. What the hell would happen if they *did* discover he was up there?

117

Wilt slumped into a chair and considered this frightful possibility. If the quads were downstairs . . . Oh God . . . and all it needed was that blasted Superintendent to get on the phone and ask if Mr Wilt was all right. The mere mention of his name would be enough. The moment the swine downstairs realized he was up there they would kill the children. And even if they didn't they would threaten to unless he came down, which was much the same thing. Wilt's only answer to such an ultimatum would be to threaten to kill the Schautz bitch if they touched the children. That would be no sort of threat. He was incapable of killing anyone and even if he were it wouldn't save the children. Lunatics who supposed that they were adding to the sum total of human happiness by kidnapping, torturing and killing politicians and businessmen and who, when cornered, sheltered behind women and children, wouldn't listen to reason. All they wanted was maximum publicity for their cause and the murder of the quads would guarantee they got it. And then there was the theory of terrorism. Wilt had heard Bilger expound it in the staff-room and had been sickened by it then. Now he was panic-stricken. There had to be something he could do.

Well, first he could get the rest of the guns out of the bag in the storeroom and try to find out how to use them. He got up and went through the kitchen to the cupboard door and dragged the bag down. Inside were two revolvers, an automatic, four spare magazines for the sub-machine gun, several boxes of ammunition and three hand grenades. Wilt put the collection on the table, decided he didn't like the look of the hand grenades and put them back in the bag. It was then that he spotted a scrap of paper in the side pocket of the bag. He pulled it out and saw that he was holding what purported to be a COMMUNIQUE OF THE PEOPLE'S ARMY GROUP 4. That at least was the title but the space underneath was blank. Evidently no one had bothered to fill in the details. Probably nothing to communicate.

All the same it was interesting, very interesting. If this bunch were Group 4 it suggested that Groups 1, 2 and 3 were somewhere else and that there were possibly Groups 5, 6 and 7. Even more perhaps. On the other hand there might not be. The tactics of self-aggrandizement were not lost on Wilt. It was typical of tiny minorities to claim they were part of a much larger organization. It boosted their morale and helped to confuse the authorities. Then again it was just possible that a great many other groups did exist. How many? Ten, twenty? And with this sort of cell structure, one group would not know the members of another group. That was the whole point about cells. If one was captured and questioned there was no way of betraying anyone else. And with this realization Wilt lost interest in the arsenal on the table. There were more effective weapons than guns.

Wilt took out a pen and began to write. Presently he closed the kitchen door and picked up the phone.

13

Superintendent Misterson was enjoying a moment of quiet and comfortable relaxation on the mahogany seat of Mrs de Frackas' toilet when the telephone rang in the drawing-room and the sergeant came through to say that the terrorists were back on the line.

'Well, that's a good sign,' said the Superintendent, emerging hurriedly. 'They don't usually start the dialogue quite so quickly. With any luck we'll get them to listen to reason.'

But his illusions on that score were quickly dispersed. The squawk that issued from the amplifier was strange in the extreme. Even the Major's face, usually a blank mask of calculated inanity, registered bewilderment. Made weirdly falsetto by fear and guttural by the need to sound foreign, and preferably German, Wilt's voice alternately whimpered and snarled a series of extraordinary demands.

'Zis is communiqué Number Vun of ze People's Alternative

Army. Ve demand ze immediate release of all comrades held illegally in British prisons vizout trial. You understand?'

'No,' said the Superintendent, 'I certainly don't.'

'Fascistic schweinfleisch,' shouted Wilt. 'Zecond, ve demand . . .'

'Now hold on,' said the Superintendent, 'we don't have any of your . . . er . . . comrades in prison. We can't possibly meet your . . .'

'Lying pigdog,' yelled Wilt, 'Günther Jong, Erica Grass, Friederich Böll, Heinrich Musil to namen eine few. All in British prisons. You release wizin funf hours. Zecond, ve demand ze immediate halting of all false reportings on television, transistor radios und der newspapers financed by capitalistic-militarische-liberalistic-pseudo-democratische-multi-nazionalistische und finanzialistische conspirationialistische about our fightings here for freedom, ja. Dritte, ve demand ze immediate withdrawal of alles militaristic truppen aus der garden unter linden und die strasse Villington Road. Vierte, ve demand ze safe conduct for ze People's Alternative Army cadres and ze exposing of ze deviationist and reformist class treachery of ze CIA-Zionist-nihilistische murderers naming zemselves falsely People's Army Group Four who are threatening ze lives of women and children in ze propaganda attempt to deceive ze proletarian consciousness for ze true liberationist struggle for world freedom. End of communiqué.'

The line went dead.

'What the fuck was all that about?' asked the Major.

'I'm buggered if I know,' said the Superintendent with a glazed look in his eyes. 'Something's definitely screwy. If my ears and that sod's ghastly accent didn't deceive me he seemed to think Chinanda and the Schautz crowd are CIA agents working for Israel. Isn't that what he seemed to be saying?'

'It's what he said, sir,' said the sergeant. 'People's Army Group Four are the Schautz brigade and this bloke was blasting off at them. Could be we've got a splinter group in the People's Alternative Army.'

'Could be we've got a raving nut,' said the Superintendent. 'Are you positive that little lot came from the house?'

'Can't have come from anywhere else, sir. There's only one line in and we're hooked to it.'

'Somebody's got their wires crossed if you ask me,' said the Major, 'unless the Schautz crowd have come up with something new.'

'It's certainly new for a terrorist group to demand no TV or press coverage. That's one thing I do know,' muttered the Superintendent. 'What I don't know is where the hell he got that list of prisoners we're supposed to release. To the best of my knowledge we're not holding anyone called Günther Jong.'

'Might be worth checking that out, old boy. Some of these things are kept hush-hush.'

'If it's that top secret I can't see the Home Office blurting the fact out now. Anyway, let's hear that gobbledygook again.'

But for once the sophisticated electronic equipment failed them.

'I can't think what's wrong with the recorder, sir,' said the sergeant, 'I could have sworn I had it on.'

'Probably blew a fuse when that maniac came on the line,' said the Major, 'I know I damned near did.'

'Well, see the bloody thing works next time,' snapped the Superintendent, 'I want to get a voiceprint of this other bunch.' He poured himself another cup of coffee and sat waiting.

If there was confusion among the Anti-Terrorist Squad and the SGS following Wilt's extraordinary intervention, there was chaos in the house. On the ground floor Chinanda and Baggish had barricaded themselves into the kitchen and the front hall while the children and Mrs de Frackas had been bundled down into the cellar. The telephone in the kitchen was on the floor out of the line of fire and it had been Baggish who had picked it up and listened to the first part. Alarmed by the look on Baggish's face, Chinanda had grabbed the receiver and had heard himself described as an Israeli nihilistic murderer working for the CIA in a propaganda attempt to deceive proletarian consciousness.

'It's a lie,' he shouted at Baggish who was still trying to square a demand by the People's Alternative Army for the release of comrades held in British prisons with his previous belief that the attic flat was occupied by men from the Anti-Terrorist Squad.

'How do you mean a lie?'

'What they say. That we are CIA Zionists.'

'A lie?' yelled Baggish, desperately searching for a more extreme word to describe such a gross distortion of the truth. 'It's . . . Who said that?'

'Someone saying he was the People's Alternative Army.'

'But the People's Alternative Army demanded the release of prisoners held illegally by the British imperialists.'

'They did?'

'I heard them. First they say that and then they attack the false reporting on TV and then they demand all troops to be withdrawn.'

'Then why call us CIA-Zionist murderers?' demanded Chinanda. 'And where are these people?'

They looked suspiciously at the ceiling.

'They're up there, you think?' asked Baggish.

But, like the Superintendent, Chinanda didn't know what to think.

'Gudrun is up there. When we came down there was shooting.'

'So maybe Gudrun is dead,' said Baggish. 'Is a trick to fool us.'

'Could be,' said Chinanda, 'British intelligence is clever. They know how to use psycho-warfare.'

'So what we do now?'

'We make our own demands. We show them we are not fooled.'

'If I might just interrupt for a moment,' said Mrs de Frackas, emerging from the cellar, 'it's time I gave the quadruplets their supper.'

The two terrorists looked at her lividly. It was bad enough having the house ringed with troops and police, but when to add to their troubles they had to cope with incomprehensible demands from someone representing the People's Alternative

Army and at the same time were confronted by Mrs de Frackas' imperturbable self-assurance, they felt the need to assert their superior authority.

'Listen, old woman,' said Chinanda waving an automatic under her nose for emphasis, 'we give the orders here and you do what we say. You don't we kill you.'

But Mrs de Frackas was not to be so easily deterred. Over a long lifetime in which she had been bullied by governesses, shot at by Afghans, bombed out of two houses in two World Wars and had had to face an exceedingly liverish husband across the breakfast table for several decades, she had developed a truly remarkable resilience and, more usefully, a diplomatic deafness.

'I'm sure you will,' she said cheerfully, 'and now I'll see where Mrs Wilt keeps the eggs. I always think that children can't have enough eggs, don't you? So good for the digestive system.' And ignoring the automatic she bustled about the kitchen peering into cupboards. Chinanda and Baggish conferred in undertones.

'I kill the old bitch now,' said Baggish. 'That way she learns we're not bluffing.'

'That way we don't get out of here. We keep her and the children we got a chance and we keep up the propaganda war.'

'Without TV we got no propaganda war to keep up,' said Baggish. 'That was one of the demands of People's Alternative Army. No TV, no radio, no newspapers.'

'So we demand the opposite, full publicity,' said Chinanda, and picked up the phone. Upstairs Wilt who had been lying on the floor with the telephone to his ear answered it.

'Zis is People's Alternative Army. Communiqué Two. Ve demand . . .'

'No you don't. We do the demanding,' shouted Chinanda, 'Ve know British psycho-warfare.'

'Zionist pigs. Ve know CIA murderers,' countered Wilt. 'Ve are fighting for ze liberation of all peoples.'

'We are fighting for the liberation of Palestine . . .'

'So are ve. All peoples ve fight for.'

'If you would kindly make up your minds who is fighting for what,' intervened the Superintendent, 'we might be able to talk more reasonably.'

'Fascist police pig,' bellowed Wilt. 'Ve no discuss viz you. Ve know who ve are dealing viz.'

'I wish to God I did,' said the Superintendent, only to be told by Chinanda that the People's Army Group was—

'Revisionistic-deviationist lumpen schwein,' interjected Wilt. 'Ze revolutionary army of ze people rejects fascistic holding of hostages und . . .' He was interrupted by bangs from the bathroom which tended to contradict his argument and gave Chinanda the opportunity to state his demands. They included five million pounds, a jumbo jet and the use of an armoured car to take them to the airport. Wilt, having shut the kitchen door to drown out Gudrun Schautz's activities, came back in time to up the ante.

'Six million pounds and two armoured cars . . .'

'You can make it a round ten million for all I care,' said the Superintendent, 'it won't make any difference. I'm not bargaining.'

'Seven million or we kill the hostages. You have till eight in the morning to agree or we die with the hostages,' shouted Chinanda, and slammed down the phone before Wilt could make a further bid. Wilt replaced his own receiver with a sigh and tried to think what on earth to do now. There was no doubt in his mind that the terrorists downstairs would carry out their threat unless the police gave way. And it was just as certain that the police had no intention of providing an armoured car or a jet. They would simply play for time in the hope of breaking the terrorists' morale. If they didn't succeed and the children died along with their captors it would hardly matter to the authorities. Public policy dictated that terrorists' demands must never be met. In the past Wilt had agreed. But now private policy dictated anything that would save his family. To reinforce the need for some new plan, Fräulein Schautz sounded as though she was ripping up the linoleum in the bathroom. For a moment Wilt considered threatening to fire through the doorway if she didn't stop, but decided against it. It was no damned use. He was incapable of killing anyone except by accident. There had to be some other way.

In the Communications Centre ideas were in short supply too. As the echo of the last conflicting demands died away the Superintendent shook his head wearily.

'I said this was a bag of maggots and by God it is. Will someone kindly tell me what the hell is going on in there?'

'No use looking at me, old boy,' said the Major, 'I'm simply here to hold the ring while you Anti-Terrorist chappies establish rapport with the blighters. That's the drill.'

'It may be the drill but considering we seem to be dealing with two competing sets of world-changers it's fucking near impossible. Isn't there some way we can get a separate line to each group?'

'Don't see how, sir,' said the sergeant. 'The People's Alternative Army seem to be using the extension phone from upstairs and the only way would be to get into the house.'

The Major studied Wilt's clumsy map. 'I could call a chopper up and land some of my lads on the roof to take the bastards out.'

Superintendent Misterson looked at him suspiciously. 'By "take out" I don't suppose you mean literally?'

'Literally? Oh, see what you mean. No. Doubt it. Bound to be a bit of schemozzle, what!'

'Which is precisely what we've got to avoid. Now, if someone can come up with a scheme whereby I can talk to one group without being drowned out by the other I'd be grateful.'

But instead there was a buzz on the intercom. The sergeant listened and then spoke. 'The psychos and the idiot brigade on the line, sir. Want to know if it's OK to move in.'

'I suppose so,' said the Superintendent.

'Idiot brigade?' said the Major.

'Ideological Warfare Analysis and the Psychological Advisers. Home Office insists we use them and sometimes they come up with a sensible suggestion.'

'Christ,' said the Major. 'Damned if I know what the world is coming to. First they call the army a peace-keeping force and now Scotland Yard has to have psychoanalysts to do their sleuthing for them. Rum.'

'The People's Alternative Army are back on the line,' said the sergeant. Once more a barrage of abuse issued from the telephone amplifier but this time Wilt had changed his tactics. His guttural German had been doing things to his vocal cords and his new accent was a less demanding but equally less convincing Irish brogue.

'Bejasus it will be nobody's fault but your own if we have to shoot the poor innocent creature Irmgard Mueller herself before eight in the morning if the wee babies are not returned to their mam, look you.'

'What?' said the Superintendent baffled by this new threat.

'I wouldn't want to be repeating meself for the likes of reactionary pigs like yourself but if you're deaf I'll say it again.'

'Don't,' said the Superintendent firmly, 'We got the message first time.'

'Well I'll be hoping those Zionist spalpeens will have got the message too begorrah.'

A muffled flow of Spanish seemed to indicate that Chinanda had heard.

'Well then that'll be all. I wouldn't want to be running up too big a telephone bill now would I?' And Wilt slammed the phone down. It was left to the Superintendent to interpret this ultimatum to Chinanda as best he could, a difficult process made almost impossible by the terrorist's insistence that the People's Alternative Army was a gang of fascist police pigs under the Superintendent's command.

'We know you British use psychological warfare. You are experts,' he shouted, 'we are not to be so easily deceived.'

'But I assure you, Miguel . . .'

'Don't try bluffing me by calling me Miguel so I think you are my friend. We understand your tactics. First you threaten and then you keep us talking . . .'

'Well as a matter of fact I'm not keeping . . .'

'Shut your mouth, pig. I'm doing the talking now.'

'That's all I was going to say,' protested the Superintendent. 'But I want you to know there are no police . . .'

'Bullshit. You tried to trap us and now you threaten to kill Gudrun. Right, we do not respond to your threats. You kill Gudrun, we kill the hostages.'

'I'm not in a position to stop whoever is holding Fräulein Schautz...'

'You keep trying the bluff but it doesn't work. We know how clever you British imperialists are.' And Chinanda too slammed the phone down.

'I must say he seems to have a rather higher opinion of the British Empire than I have,' said the Major. 'I mean I can't actually see where we've got one, unless you count Gibraltar.'

But the Superintendent was in no mood to discuss the extent of the Empire. 'There's something demented about this bloody siege,' he muttered. 'First we need to get a separate telephone link through to the lunatics in that top flat. That's number one priority. If they shoot ... What on earth did he call the Schautz woman, sergeant?'

'I think the expression was "the poor innocent creature Irmgard Mueller",' sir? Do you want me to play the tape back?'

'No,' said the Superintendent, 'we'll wait for the analysts. In the meantime request use of helicopter to drop a field telephone on to the balcony of the flat. That way we'll at least get some idea who's up there.'

'Field telephone incorporating TV camera, sir?' asked the sergeant.

The Superintendent nodded. 'Second priority is to move the listening devices into position.'

'Can't do that until it gets dark,' said the Major. 'Not having my chaps shot down unless they're allowed to shoot back.'

'Well, we'll just have to wait,' said the Superintendent. 'That's always the way with these beastly sieges. Just a question of sitting and waiting. Though I must say this is the first time I've had to deal with two lots of terrorists at once.'

'Makes you feel sorry for those poor children,' said the Major. 'What they must be going through doesn't bear thinking about.'

But for once his sympathy was wasted. The quads were having a wonderful time. After the initial excitement of windows being shattered by bullets and the terrorists firing from the kitchen and the front hall, they had been bundled down into the cellar with Mrs de Frackas. Since the old lady refused to be flustered and seemed to regard the events upstairs as perfectly normal, the quads had taken the same attitude. Besides the cellar was usually forbidden territory, Wilt objecting to their visiting it on the ostensible grounds that the Organic Toilet was insanitary and dangerously explosive, while Eva barred the quads because she kept her stock of preserved fruit down there and the chest freezer was filled with homemade ice cream. The quads had made a bee-line for the ice cream and had finished a large carton before Mrs de Frackas' eyes had got accustomed to the dim light. By then the quads had found other interesting things to occupy their attention. A large coal bunker and a pile of logs gave them the opportunity to get thoroughly filthy. Eva's store of organically grown apples provided them with a second course after the ice cream, and they would undoubtedly have drunk themselves into a stupor on Wilt's homebrew if Mrs de Frackas hadn't put her foot down on a broken bottle first.

'You're not to go into that part of the cellar,' she said looking severely at the evidence of Wilt's inexpert brewing in the shape of several exploded bottles. 'It isn't safe.'

'Then why does Daddy drink it?' asked Penelope.

'When you get a little older you'll learn that men do a great many things that aren't very sensible or safe,' said Mrs de Frackas.

'Like wearing a bag on the end of their wigwags?' asked Josephine.

'Well I wouldn't quite know about that, dear,' said Mrs de Frackas evidently torn between curiosity and a desire not to enquire too closely into the Wilts' private life.

'Mummy said the doctor made him wear it,' continued Josephine adding an unmentionable disease to the old lady's dossier of Wilt's faults.

'And I stepped on it and Daddy screamed,' said Emmeline proudly. 'He screamed ever so loudly.'

'I'm sure he did, dear,' said Mrs de Frackas, trying to imagine the reaction of her late and liverish husband had any child been so unwise as to step on his penis. 'Now let's talk about something nice.'

The distinction was wasted on the quads. 'When daddy comes home from the doctor mummy says his wigwag will be better and he won't say "Fuck" when he goes weewee.'

'Say what, dear?' asked Mrs de Frackas, adjusting her hearing aid in the hope that it rather than Samantha had been at fault. The quads in unison disillusioned her.

'Fuck, fuck, fuck,' they squealed. Mrs de Frackas turned her hearing aid down.

'Well, really,' she said, 'I don't think you should use that word.'

'Mummy says we mustn't too but Michael's daddy told him . . .'

'I don't want to hear,' said Mrs de Frackas hastily. 'In my young days children didn't talk about such things.'

'How did babies get born then?' asked Penelope.

'In the usual way, dear, only we were brought up not to mention such things.'

'What things?' demanded Penelope.

Mrs de Frackas regarded her dubiously. It was beginning to dawn on her that the Wilt quads were not quite such nice children as she had supposed. In fact they were distinctly unnerving. 'Just things,' she said finally.

'Like cocks and cunts?' asked Emmeline.

Mrs de Frackas eyed her with disgust. 'You could put it like that, I suppose,' she said stiffly. 'Though frankly I'd prefer it if you didn't.'

'If you don't put it like that how do you put it?' asked the indefatigable Penelope.

Mrs de Frackas searched her mind in vain for an alternative. 'I don't quite know,' she said, surprised at her own ignorance. 'I suppose the matter never arose.'

'Daddy's does,' said Josephine, 'I saw it once.'

Mrs de Frackas turned her disgusted attention on the child and tried to stifle her own curiosity. 'You did?' she said involuntarily.

'He was in the bathroom with mummy and I looked through the keyhole and daddy's . . .'

'It's time you had baths too,' said Mrs de Frackas, getting to her feet before Josephine could divulge any further details of the Wilts' sexual life.

'We haven't had supper yet,' said Samantha.

'Then I'll get you some,' said Mrs de Frackas and went up the cellar steps to hunt for eggs. By the time she returned with a tray the quads were no longer hungry. They had finished a jar of pickled onions and were halfway through their second packet of dried figs.

'You've still got to have scrambled eggs,' said the old lady resolutely. 'I didn't go to the trouble of making them to have them wasted, you know.'

'You didn't make them,' said Penelope. 'Mummy hens made them.'

'And daddy hens are called cocks,' squealed Josephine but Mrs de Frackas, having just outfaced two armed bandits, was in no mood to be defied by four foul-minded girls.

'We won't discuss that any further, thank you,' she said, 'I've had quite enough.'

It was shortly apparent that the quads had too. As she shooed them up the cellar steps Emmeline was complaining that her tummy hurt.

'It will soon stop, dear,' said Mrs de Frackas, 'and it doesn't help to hiccup like that.'

'Not hiccuping,' retorted Emmeline, and promptly vomited on the kitchen floor. Mrs de Frackas looked around in the semi-darkness for the light switch and had just found it and turned it on when Chinanda cannoned into her and switched it off.

'What are you trying to do? Get us all killed?' he yelled.

'Not all of us,' said Mrs de Frackas, 'and if you don't look where you're going . . .'

A crash as the terrorist slid across the kitchen floor on a mixture of half-digested pickled onions and dried figs indicated that Chinanda hadn't.

'It's no use blaming me,' said Mrs de Frackas, 'and you shouldn't use language like that in front of children. It sets a very bad example.'

'I set an example all right,' shouted Chinanda, 'I spill your guts.'

'I rather think somebody is doing that already,' retorted the old lady as the other three quads, evidently sharing Emmeline's inability to cope with quite so eclectic a diet, followed her example. Presently the kitchen was filled with four howling and vomit-stained small girls, a very unappetizing smell, two demented terrorists and Mrs de Frackas at her most imperious. To add to the confusion Baggish had deserted his post in the front hall and had dashed in threatening to kill the first person who moved.

'I have no intention of moving,' said Mrs de Frackas, 'and since the only person who is happens to be that creature grovelling in the corner I suggest you put him out of his misery.'

From the direction of the sink Chinanda could be heard disentangling himself from Eva's Kenwood mixer which had joined him on the floor.

Mrs de Frackas turned the light on again. This time no one objected, Chinanda because he had been momentarily stunned and Baggish because he was too dismayed by the state of the kitchen.

'And now,' said the old lady, 'if you've quite finished I'll take the children up for their bath before putting them to bed.'

'Bed?' yelled Chinanda getting unsteadily to his feet. 'Nobody goes upstairs. You all sleep down in the cellar. Go down there now.'

'If you really suppose for one moment that I am going to allow these poor children to go down that cellar again in their present condition and without being thoroughly washed you're very much mistaken.'

Chinanda jerked the cord on the venetian blind and cut out the view from the garden.

'Then you wash them in here,' he said pointing to the sink.

'And where do you propose to be?'

'Where we can see what you are doing.'

Mrs de Frackas snorted derisively. 'I know your sort, and if you think I am going to expose their pure little bodies to your lascivious gaze . . .'

'What the hell is she saying?' demanded Baggish.

Mrs de Frackas turned her contempt on him. 'And yours too, don't I just. I haven't been through the Suez Canal and Port Said for nothing you know.'

Baggish stared at her. 'Port Said? The Suez Canal? I never been to Egypt in my life.'

'Well I have. And I know what I know.'

'So what are we talking about? You know what you know. I don't know what you know.'

'Postcards,' said Mrs de Frackas. 'I don't think I need say any more.'

'You haven't said anything yet. First the Suez Canal, then Port Said and now postcards. Will someone tell me what the hell these things have to do with washing children?'

'Well if you must know, I mean dirty postcards. I might also mention donkeys but I won't. And now if you'll both leave the room . . .'

But the implications of Mrs de Frackas' imperial prejudices had slowly dawned on Baggish.

'You mean pornography? What century you think you're living in? You want pornography you go to London. Soho is full—'

'I don't want pornography and I don't intend to discuss the matter further.'

'Then you go down the cellar before I kill you,' yelled the enraged Baggish. But Mrs de Frackas was too old to be persuaded by mere threats and it took bodily pressure to shove her through the cellar door with the quads. As they went down the steps Emmeline could be heard asking why the nasty man didn't like donkeys.

'I tell you the English are mad,' said Baggish. 'Why did we have to choose this crazy house?'

'It chose us,' said Chinanda miserably, and switched out the light.

But if Mrs de Frackas had decided to ignore the fact that her life was in danger, upstairs in the flat Wilt was now acutely aware that his previous tactics had backfired on him. To have invented the People's Alternative Army had served to confuse things for a while, but his threat to execute, or more accurately to murder Gudrun Schautz had been a terrific mistake. It put a time limit on his bluff. Looking back over forty years Wilt's record of violence was limited to the occasional and usually unsuccessful bout with flies and mosquitoes. No, to have issued that ultimatum had been almost as stupid as not getting out of the house when the going was good. Now it was distinctly bad, and the sounds coming from the bathroom suggested that Gudrun Schautz had torn up the lino and was busy on the floorboards. If she escaped and joined the men below she would add an intellectual fervour to their evidently stupid fanaticism. On the other hand he could think of no way of stopping her short of threatening to fire through the bathroom door, and if that didn't work . . . There had to be an alternative method. What if he opened the door himself and somehow persuaded her that it wasn't safe to go downstairs? In that way he could keep the two groups separate and provided they couldn't communicate with one another Fräulein Schautz would be hard put to it to influence her blood-brothers down below. Well, that was easy enough to do.

Wilt crossed to the telephone and jerked the cord from the wall. So far so good but there was still the little matter of the guns. The notion of sharing the flat with a woman who had cold-bloodedly murdered eight people was not an attractive one in any circumstances, but when that flat contained enough firearms to eliminate several hundred it became positively suicidal. The guns would have to go too. But where? He could hardly drop the damned things out of the window. The effect of a shower of revolvers, grenades and a sub-machine gun on the terrorists was likely to encourage them to come up and find out what the hell was going on. Anyway, the grenades might go off and there were enough misunderstandings floating around already without adding exploding grenades. The best thing would be to hide them. Very gingerly Wilt put his armoury back into the flight bag and went through the kitchen to the attic space. Gudrun Schautz was now definitely busy on the floorboards and under cover of the noise Wilt climbed up and edged his way along to the water cistern. There he lowered the bag into the water before replacing the cover. Then, having checked to make quite sure that he hadn't missed a gun, he steeled himself for the next move. It was, he considered, about as safe as opening the cage of a tiger at the zoo and inviting the thing to come out, but it had to be done and in an insane situation only an act of total lunacy could save the children. Wilt went through the kitchen to the bathroom door.

'Irmgard,' he whispered. Miss Schautz went on with her work of demolishing the bathroom floor. Wilt took another deep breath and whispered more loudly. Inside work ceased and there was silence.

'Irmgard,' said Wilt, 'is that you?'

There was a movement and then a quiet voice spoke. 'Who is there?'

'It's me,' said Wilt, sticking to the obvious and wishing to hell it wasn't, 'Henry Wilt.'

'Henry Wilt?'

'Yes. They've gone.'

'Who have gone?'

'I don't know. Whoever they were. You can come out now.'

'Come out?' asked Gudrun Schautz in a tone of voice that suggested the total bewilderment Wilt wanted.

'I'll undo the door.'

Wilt began to remove the flex from the doorhandle. It was difficult in the growing darkness but after several minutes he had undone the wire and removed the chair.

'It's OK now,' he said. 'You can come out.'

But Gudrun Schautz made no move. 'How do I know it's you?' she asked.

'I don't know,' said Wilt, glad of this opportunity to delay matters, 'it just is.'

'Who is with you?'

'No one. They've gone downstairs.'

'You keep saying "They". Who are these "They"?'

'I've no idea. Men with guns. The whole house is filled with men with guns.'

'So why are you here?' asked Miss Schautz.

'Because I can't be somewhere else,' said Wilt truthfully. 'You don't think I want to be here? They've been shooting at one another. I could have been killed. I don't know what the hell's going on.'

There was a silence from the bathroom. Gudrun Schautz was having difficulty working out what was going on too. In the darkness of the kitchen Wilt smiled to himself. Keep this up and he'd have the bitch bombed out of her mind.

'And no one is with you?' she asked.

'Of course not.'

'Then how did you know I was in the bathroom?'

'I heard you having a bath,' said Wilt, 'and then all these people started shouting and shooting and . . .'

'Where were you?'

'Look,' said Wilt deciding to change his tactics, 'I don't see why you keep asking me these questions. I mean I've taken the trouble to come up here and undo the door and you won't come out and you keep on about who they are and where I was and all that as if I knew. As a matter of fact I was having a nap in the bedroom and . . .'

'A nap? What is a nap?'

'A nap? Oh, a nap. Well it's a sort of after-lunch snooze. Sleep, you know. Anyway when all the hullabaloo started, the shooting and so on, and I heard you shout "Get the children," and I thought how jolly kind of you that was . . .'

'Kind of me? You thought that kind of me?' asked Miss Schautz with a distinctly strangulated disbelief.

'I mean putting the children first instead of your own safety. Most people wouldn't have thought of saving the children, would they?'

A gurgling noise from the bathroom indicated that Gudrun Schautz hadn't thought of this interpretation of her orders and was having to make readjustments in her attitude to Wilt's intelligence.

'No, that is so,' she said finally.

'Well naturally after that I couldn't leave you locked up here could I?' continued Wilt, realizing that talking like some idiotic chinless wonder had its advantages. 'Noblesse oblige and all that, what!'

'Noblesse oblige?'

'You know, one good turn deserves another and whatnot,' said Wilt. 'So as soon as the coast was clear I sort of came out from under the bed and hopped up here.'

'What coast?' demanded Miss Schautz suspiciously.

'When the blighters up here decided to go downstairs,' said Wilt. 'Seemed the safest place to be. Anyway, why don't you come out and have a chair. It must be jolly uncomfortable in there.'

Miss Schautz considered this proposition and the fact that Wilt sounded like a congenital idiot and took the risk.

'I haven't any clothes on,' she said opening the door an inch.

'Gosh,' said Wilt, 'I'm awfully sorry. Hadn't thought of that. I'll go and get you something.'

He went into the bedroom and rummaged in a cupboard and having found what felt like a raincoat in the darkness took it back.

'Here's a coat,' he said handing it through the doorway. 'Don't like to turn the bedroom light on in case those blokes downstairs see it and start pooping off again with their guns. Mind you I've locked the door and barricaded it so they'd have a job getting in.'

In the bathroom Miss Schautz put on the raincoat and cautiously came out to find Wilt pouring boiling water from the electric kettle into a teapot.

'Thought you'd like a nice cup of tea,' he said. 'Know I would.'

Behind him Gudrun Schautz tried to comprehend what had happened. From the moment she had been locked in the bathroom she had been convinced that the flat was occupied by

136

policemen. Now it seemed whoever had been there had gone and this weak and stupid Englishman was making tea as if nothing was wrong. Wilt's admission that he had spent the afternoon cowering under the bed in the room below had been convincingly ignominious and had helped to confirm the impression she had gathered from his previous nocturnal exchanges with Frau Wilt that he was no sort of threat. On the other hand she had to find out how much he knew.

'These men with guns,' she said, 'what sort of men are they?'

'Well I wasn't really in a very good position to see them,' said Wilt, 'being under the bed and so on. Some of them were wearing boots and some weren't, if you see what I mean.'

Gudrun Schautz didn't. 'Boots?'

'Not shoes. Do you take sugar, by the way?'

'No.'

'Very wise,' said Wilt, 'awfully bad for the teeth. Anyway here's your cup. Oh I am sorry. Here, let me get a cloth and wipe you down.'

And in the close confines of the little kitchen Wilt groped for a cloth and presently was mopping Gudrun Schautz's coat down where he had deliberately spilt the tea.

'You can stop now,' she said as Wilt transferred the attentions of the towel from her breasts to lower areas.

'Righto, and I'll pour another cup.'

She squeezed past him into the bedroom while Wilt considered what other domestic accidents he could provoke to distract her attention. There was always sex, of course, but in the circumstances it hardly seemed likely that the bitch would be particularly interested in it and, even if she were, the notion of making love with a professional murderess would make arousal extremely difficult. Whisky droop was bad enough, terror droop was infinitely worse. Still, flattery might help, and she certainly had nice boobs. Wilt took another cup of tea through to the bedroom and found her looking out of the balcony window into the garden.

'I shouldn't go over there,' he said, 'there are more maniacs outside with Donald Duck shirts on.'

'Donald Duck shirts?'

'And guns,' said Wilt. 'If you ask me the whole bloody place has gone loony.'

'And you have no idea what is happening?'

'Well I heard somebody shouting about Israelis, but it doesn't seem likely somehow, does it? I mean what on earth would Israelis want to come swarming all over Willington Road for?'

'Oh my God,' said Gudrun Schautz. 'So what do we do?'

'Do?' said Wilt. 'I don't see there is much we can do really. Except drink tea and make ourselves inconspicuous. It's all probably some ghastly mistake or other. I can't think what else it can be, can you?'

Gudrun Schautz could, and did, but to admit it to this idiot before she had the power to terrify him into doing what she wanted didn't seem a good idea. She headed for the kitchen and began to climb into the attic space. Wilt followed, sipping his tea. 'Of course I did try phoning the police,' he said, dropping his chin even more gormlessly.

Miss Schautz stopped in her tracks. 'The police? You phoned the police?'

'Couldn't actually,' said Wilt, 'some blighter had pulled the phone out of the wall. Can't think why. I mean with all that shooting going on . . .'

But Gudrun Schautz was no longer listening. She was clambering along the plank towards the luggage and Wilt could hear her rummaging among the suitcases. So long as the bitch didn't look in the water tank. To distract her attention Wilt poked his head through the door and switched off the light.

'Better not show a light,' he explained as she stumbled about in the pitch darkness cursing, 'don't want anyone to know we're up here. Best just to lie low until they go away.'

A stream of incomprehensible but evidently malevolent German greeted this suggestion, and after fruitlessly groping about for the bag for several more minutes Gudrun Schautz climbed down into the kitchen, breathing heavily.

Wilt decided to strike again. 'No need to be so upset, my dear. After all, this is England and nothing nasty can happen to you here.'

He placed a comforting arm round her shoulders. 'And anyway you've got me to look after you. Nothing to worry about.'

'Oh my God,' she said and suddenly began to shake with silent laughter. The thought that she had only this weak and stupid little coward to look after her was too much for the murderess. Nothing to worry about! The phrase suddenly took on a new and horribly inverted meaning and like a revelation she saw its truth, a truth she had been fighting against all her life. The only thing she had to worry about was nothing. Gudrun Schautz looked into oblivion, an infinity of nothingness and was filled with terror. With a desperate need to escape the vision she clung to Wilt and her raincoat hung open.

'I say . . .' Wilt began, realizing this new threat but Gudrun Schautz's mouth closed over his, her tongue flickering, while her hand dragged his fingers up to a breast. The creature who had brought only death into the world was now turning in her panic to the most ancient instinct of all.

15

Gudrun Schautz was not the only person in Ipford to look oblivion in the face. The manager of Wilt's bank had spent an exceedingly disturbing afternoon with Inspector Flint who kept assuring him that it was of national importance that he shouldn't phone his wife to cancel their dinner engagement and refusing to allow him to communicate with his staff and several clients who had made appointments to see him. The manager had found these aspersions on his discretion insulting and Flint's presence positively lethal to his reputation for financial probity.

'What the hell do you imagine the staff are thinking with three damned policemen closeted in my office all day?' he demanded, dropping the diplomatic language of banking for more earthy forms of address. He had been particularly put

139

out by having to choose between urinating in a bucket procured from the caretaker or suffer the indignity of being accompanied by a policeman every time he went to the toilet.

'If a man can't pee in his own bank without having some bloody gendarme breathing down his neck all I can say is that things have come to a pretty pass.'

'Very aptly put, sir,' said Flint, 'but I'm only acting under orders and if the Anti-Terrorist Squad say a thing's in the national interest then it is.'

'I can't see how it's in the national interest to stop me relieving myself in private,' said the manager. 'I shall see that a complaint goes to the Home Office.'

'You do that small thing,' said Flint, who had his own reasons for feeling disgruntled. The intrusion of the Anti-Terrorist Squad into his patch had undermined his authority. The fact that Wilt was responsible only maddened him still further and he was just speculating on Wilt's capacity for disrupting his life when the phone rang.

'I'll take it if you don't mind,' he said and lifted the receiver.

'Mr Fildroyd of Central Investment on the line, sir,' said the telephonist.

Flint looked at the bank manager. 'Some bloke called Fildroyd. Know anyone of that name?'

'Fildroyd? Of course I do.'

'Is he to be trusted?'

'Good Lord, man, Fildroyd to be trusted? He's in charge of the entire bank's investment policy.'

'Stocks and shares, eh?' asked Flint who had once had a little flutter in Australian bauxite and wasn't likely to forget the experience. 'In that case I wouldn't trust him further than I could throw him.'

He relayed this opinion in only slightly less offensive terms to the girl on the switchboard. A distant rumble suggested that Mr Fildroyd was on the line.

'Mr Fildroyd wants to know who's speaking,' said the girl.

'Well you just tell Mr Fildroyd that it's Inspector Flint of the Fenland Constabulary and if he knows what's good for him he'll keep his trap shut.'

He put the phone down and turned to the manager who was looking distinctly seedy. 'What's the matter with you?' Flint asked.

'Matter? Nothing, nothing at all. Only that you've just led the entire Central Investment Division to suppose I'm suspected of some serious crime.'

'Landing me with Mr Henry Wilt is a serious crime,' said Flint bitterly, 'and if you want my opinion this whole thing's a put-up job on Wilt's part to get himself another slice of publicity.'

'As I understood it Mr Wilt was the innocent victim of—'

'Innocent victim my foot. The day that sod's innocent I'll stop being a copper and take holy fucking orders.'

'Charming way of expressing yourself, I must say,' said the bank manager.

But Flint was too engrossed in a private line of speculation to note the sarcasm. He was recalling those hideous days and nights during which he and Wilt had been engaged in a dialogue on the subject of Mrs Wilt's disappearance. There were still dark hours before dawn when Flint would wake sweating at the memory of Wilt's extraordinary behaviour and swearing that one day he would catch the little sod out in a serious crime. And today had seemed the ideal opportunity, or would have done if the Anti-Terrorist Squad hadn't intervened. Well, at least they were having to cope with the situation but if Flint had had his way he would have discounted all that talk about German au pairs as so much hogwash and remanded Wilt in custody on a charge of being in possession of stolen money, never mind where he said he had got it from.

But when at five he left the bank and returned to the police station it was to discover that Wilt's account seemed yet again to correspond, however implausibly, with the facts.

'A siege?' he said to the desk sergeant. 'A siege at Willington Road? At Wilt's house?'

'Proof of the pudding's in there, sir,' said the sergeant indicating an office. Flint crossed to the window and glanced in.

Like some monolith to maternity Eva Wilt sat motionless on a chair staring into space, her mind evidently absent and with her children in the house in Willington Road. Flint turned away and for the umpteenth time wondered what it was about this woman and her apparently insignificant husband that had brought them together and by some strange fusion of incompatibility had turned them into a catalyst for disaster. It was a recurring enigma, this marriage between a woman whom Wilt had once described as a centrifugal force and a man whose imagination fostered bestial fantasies involving murder, rape, and those bizarre dreams that had come to light during the hours of his interrogation. Since Flint's own marriage was as conventionally happy as he could wish, the Wilts' was less a marriage in his eyes than some rather sinister symbiotic arrangement of almost vegetable origin, like mistletoe growing on an oak tree. There was certainly a vegetable-looking quality about Mrs Wilt sitting there in silence in the office and Inspector Flint shook his head sadly.

'Poor woman's in shock,' he said, and hurried away to discover for himself what was actually happening at Willington Road.

But as usual his diagnosis was wrong. Eva was not in a state of shock. She had long since realized that it was pointless telling the policewomen who were sitting with her that she wanted to go home, and now her mind was calmly and rather menacingly working on practical things. Out there in the gathering darkness her children were at the mercy of murderers and Henry was probably dead. Nothing was going to stop her from joining the quads and saving them. Beyond that goal she had not looked, but a brooding violence seeped through her.

'Perhaps you would like some friend to come and sit with you,' one of the policewomen suggested. 'Or we could come with you to a friend's house.'

But Eva shook her head. She didn't want sympathy. She had her own reserves of strength to cope with her misery. In the end a social worker arrived from the welfare hostel.

'We've got a nice warm room for you,' she said with an extruded cheerfulness that had served in the past to irritate a number of battered wives, 'and you needn't worry about nighties and toothbrushes and things like that. Everything you want will be provided for you.'

'It won't,' thought Eva but she thanked the policewomen and followed the social worker out to her car and sat docilely beside her as they drove away. And all the time the woman chattered on, asking questions about the quads and how old they were and saying how difficult it must be bringing up four girls at the same time as if the continually repeated assumption that nothing extraordinary had happened would somehow re-create the happy, humdrum world Eva had seen disintegrate round her that afternoon. Eva hardly heard her. The trite words were so grotesquely at odds with the instincts moving within her that they merely added anger to her terrible resolve. No silly woman who didn't have children could know what it meant to have them threatened and she wasn't going to be lulled into a passive acceptance of the situation.

At the corner of Dill Road and Persimmon Street she caught sight of a billboard outside a newsagent's shop. TERRORIST SIEGE LATEST.

'I want a newspaper,' said Eva abruptly and the woman pulled to the kerb.

'It won't tell you anything you don't know already,' she said.

'I know that. I just want to see what they're saying,' said Eva and opened the door of the car. But the woman stopped her.

'You just sit here and I'll get one for you. Would you like a magazine too?'

'Just the paper.'

And with the sad thought that even in terrible tragedies some people found solace by seeing their names in print the social worker crossed the pavement to the shop and went in. Three minutes later she came out and had opened the car door before she realized that the seat beside her was empty. Eva Wilt had disappeared into the night.

By the time Inspector Flint had made his way past the road blocks in Farrington Avenue and with the help of an SGS man had clambered across several gardens to the Communications Centre he had begun to have doubts about his theory that the whole business was yet another hoax on Wilt's part. If it was it had gone too far this time. The armoured car in the road and the spotlights that had been set up round Number 9 indicated how seriously the Anti-Terrorist Squad and Special Ground Services were taking the siege. In the conservatory at the back of Mrs de Frackas' house men were assembling strange looking equipment.

'Parabolic listening devices. PLDs for short,' explained a technician. 'Once we've installed them we'll be able to hear a cockroach fart in any room in the house.'

'Really? I had no idea cockroaches farted,' said Flint. 'One lives and learns.'

'We'll learn what those bastards are saying and just where they are.'

Flint went through the conservatory into the drawing-room and found the Superintendent and the Major listening to the adviser on International Terrorist Ideology who was discussing the tapes.

'If you want my opinion,' said Professor Maerlis gratuitously, 'I would have to say that the People's Alternative Army represents a sub-fraction or splinter group of the original cadre known as the People's Army Group. I think I would go so far.'

Flint took a seat in a corner and was pleased to note that the Superintendent and Major seemed to share his bewilderment.

'Are you saying that they're actually part of the same group?' asked the Superintendent.

'Specifically, no,' said the Professor. 'I can only surmise from the inherent contradictions expressed in their communiqués that there is a strong difference of opinion as to the tactical approach while at the same time the two groups share the same underlying ideological assumptions. Owing, however, to the molecular structure of terrorist organizations the actual identification of a member of one group by another member of another group or sub-faction of the same group remains extremely problematical.'

'The whole fucking situation is extremely problematical,

come to that,' said the Superintendent. 'So far we've had two communiqués from what sounds like a partially castrated German, one from an asthmatic Irishman, demands from a Mexican for a jumbo jet and six million quid, a counter-demand from the Kraut for seven millions, not to mention a stream of abuse from an Arab and everyone accusing everyone else of being a CIA agent working for Israel and who's fighting for whose freedom.'

'Beats me how they can begin to talk about freedom when they're holding innocent children and an old lady hostage and threatening to kill them,' said the Major.

'There I must disagree with you,' said the Professor. 'In terms of Neo-Hegelian post-Marxist political philosophy the freedom of the individual can only reside within the parameters of a collectively free society. The People's Army Groups regard themselves as in the forefront of total freedom and equality and as such are not bound to observe the moral norms which restrict the actions of lackeys of imperialist, fascist and neo-colonialist oppression'

'Listen, old boy,' said the Major angrily removing his Afro wig, 'just whose side are you on anyway?'

'I am merely stating the theory. If you want a more precise analysis . . .' began the Professor nervously, only to be interrupted by the Head of the Psychological Warfare team who had been working on the voiceprints.

'From our analysis of the stress factors revealed in these tape recordings we are of the opinion that the group holding Fräulein Schautz are emotionally more disturbed than the two other terrorists,' he announced, 'and frankly I think we should concentrate on reducing their anxiety level.'

'Are you saying the Schautz woman is likely to be shot?' asked the Superintendent.

The psychologist nodded. 'It's rather baffling actually. We've hit something rather odd with that lot, a variation from the normal pattern of speech reactions and I must admit I think she's the one who's most likely to get it in the neck.'

'No skin off my nose if she does,' said the Major, 'she's had it coming to her.'

'There'll be skin off everyone's nose if that happens,' said the Superintendent. 'My instructions are to keep this thing cool and if they start killing their hostages all hell will be let loose.'

'Yes,' said the Professor, 'a very interesting dialectical situation. You must understand that the theory of terrorism as a progressive force in world history demands the exacerbation of class warfare and the polarizing of political opinion. Now in terms of simple effectiveness we must say that the advantage lies with People's Army Group Four and not with the People's Alternative Army.'

'Say that again,' said the Major.

The Professor obliged. 'Put quite simply it is politically better to kill these children than eliminate Fräulein Schautz.'

'That may be your opinion,' said the Major, his fingers twitching on the butt of his revolver, 'but if you know what's good for you you won't express it round here again.'

'I was talking only in terms of political polarization,' said the Professor nervously. 'Only a very small minority will be perturbed if Fräulein Schautz dies but the effect of liquidating four small children, and coterminously conceived female siblings at that, would be considerable.'

'Thank you, Professor,' said the Superintendent hastily. And before the Major could decipher this sinister pronouncement he had ushered the adviser on Terrorist Ideologies out of the room.

'It's blasted eggheads like him who've ruined this country,' said the Major. 'To hear him talk you'd think there were two sides to every damned question.'

'Which is exactly the opposite of what we're getting on the voiceprints,' said the psychologist. 'Our analysis seems to indicate that there's only one spokesman for the People's Alternative Army.'

'One man?' said the Superintendent increduously. 'Didn't sound like one man to me. More like half-a-dozen insane ventriloquists.'

'Precisely. Which is why we think you should try to lower the anxiety level of that group. We may well be dealing with a

146

split personality. I'll play the tapes again and perhaps you'll see what I mean.'

'Must you? Oh well . . .'

But the sergeant had switched the recorder on and once again the cluttered drawing-room echoed to guttural snarls and whimpers of Wilt's communiqués. In a dark corner Inspector Flint who had been on the point of dozing off suddenly sprang to his feet.

'I knew it,' he shouted triumphantly, 'I knew it. I just knew it had to be and by God it is!'

'Had to be what?' asked the Superintendent.

'Henry Fucking Wilt who was behind this foul-up. And there's the proof on those tapes.'

'Are you sure, Inspector?'

'I'm more than that. I'm positive. I'd know that little sod's voice if he imitated an Eskimo in labour.'

'I don't think we have to go that far,' said the psychological adviser. 'Are you telling us you know the man we've just heard?'

'Know him?' said Flint. 'Of course I know the bastard. I ought to after what he did for me. And now he's having you lot on.'

'I must say I find it hard to believe,' said the Superintendent. 'A more inoffensive little man you couldn't wish to meet.'

'I could,' said Flint with feeling.

'But he had to be drugged up to the eyeballs before we could get him to go back in,' said the Major.

'Drugged? What with?' said the psychologist.

'No idea. Some concoction our medic brews up for blighters with a streak of yellow. Works wonders with the bomb-disposal chappies.'

'Well it wouldn't appear to have worked quite so well in this case,' said the psychologist nervously, 'but it certainly accounts for the remarkable readings we've been getting. We could well have a case of chemically induced schizophrenia on our hands.'

'I wouldn't bother too much about the "chemically induced" if I were you,' said Flint. 'Wilt's a nutter anyway. I'll give a hundred to one he set this thing up from the start.'

'You can't seriously be suggesting that Mr Wilt deliberately went out of his way to put his own children in the hands of a bunch of international terrorists,' said the Superintendent. 'When I discussed the matter with him he seemed genuinely astonished and disturbed.'

'What Wilt seems and what Wilt is are two entirely separate things. I can tell you this much though. Any man who can dress an inflatable doll up in his wife's clothes and ditch the thing at the bottom of a pile hole under thirty tons of quick-set concrete isn't—'

'Excuse me, sir,' interrupted the sergeant, 'message just come through from the station that Mrs Wilt has flown the coop.'

The four men looked at him in despair.

'She's what?' said the Superintendent.

'Escaped from custody, sir. Nobody seems to know where she is.'

'It fits,' said Flint, 'it fits and no mistake.'

'Fits? What fits for Chrissake?' asked the Superintendent, who was beginning to feel distinctly peculiar himself.

'The pattern, sir. Next thing we'll hear is that she was last seen on a motor cruiser going down the river, only she won't be.'

The Superintendent stared at him dementedly. 'And you call that a pattern? Oh, my God.'

'Well, it's the sort of thing Wilt would come up with, believe me. That little bugger can think up more ways of taking a perfectly sane and sensible situation and turning it into a raving nightmare than any villain I've ever met.'

'But there's got to be some motive for his actions.'

Flint laughed abruptly. 'Motive? With Henry Wilt? Not on your life. You can think of a thousand good motives, ten thousand if you like, for what he does but at the end of the day he'll come up with the one explanation you never even dreamt of. Wilt's the nearest thing to Ernie you could wish to meet.'

'Ernie?' said the Superintendent. 'Who the hell is Ernie?'

'That ruddy computer they use for the premium bonds, sir. You know, the one that picks numbers out at random. Well, Wilt's a random man, if you know what I mean.'

'I don't think I want to,' said the Superintendent. 'I thought all I had to cope with was a nice simple ordinary siege, instead of which this thing is developing into a madhouse.'

'While we're on that subject,' said the psychologist, 'I really do think it's very important to resume communications with the people in the top flat. Whoever is up there and holding the Schautz woman is in a highly disturbed state. She could be in grave danger.'

'No "could" about it,' said Flint. 'Is.'

'All right. I suppose we'll have to risk it,' said the Superintendent. 'Give the go-ahead for the helicopter to move in with a field telephone, sergeant.'

'Any orders regarding Mrs Wilt, sir?'

'You'd better ask the Inspector here. He seems to be the expert on the Wilt family. What sort of woman is Mrs Wilt? And don't say she's a random one.'

'I wouldn't really like to say,' said Flint, 'except that she's a very powerful woman.'

'What do you think she plans to do then? She obviously didn't leave the police station without some aim in mind.'

'Well, knowing Wilt as well as I do, sir, I have to admit I've grave doubts about her having a mind at all. Any normal woman would have been in a nut-house years ago living with a man like that.'

'You're not suggesting she's some sort of psychopath as well?'

'No, sir,' said Flint, 'all I'm saying is that she can't have any nerves worth speaking about.'

'That's a big help. So we've got a bunch of terrorists armed to the teeth, some sort of nutter in the shape of Wilt and a woman on the loose with a hide like a rhino. Put that little lot together and we've got ourselves one hell of a combination. All right, sergeant, put out an alert for Mrs Wilt and see that they take her into custody before anyone else gets hurt.'

The Superintendent crossed to the window and looked at the Wilts' house. Under the glare of the floodlights it stood out against the night sky like a monument erected to commemorate the stolidity and unswerving devotion to boredom of English middle-class life. Even the Major was moved to comment.

'Sort of suburban *son-et-lumière*, what?' he murmured.

'*Lumière* perhaps,' said the Superintendent, 'but at least we're spared the *son*.'

But not for long. From somewhere seemingly close at hand there came a series of terrible wails. The Wilt quads were giving tongue.

16

A mile away Eva Wilt moved towards her home with a fixed resolve that was wholly at variance with her appearance. The few people who noticed her as she bustled down narrow streets saw only an ordinary housewife in a hurry to fix her husband's supper and put the children to bed. But beneath her homely look Eva Wilt had changed. She had shed her cheerful silliness and her borrowed opinions and had only one thought in mind. She was going home and no one was going to stop her. What she would do when she got there she had no idea, and in a vague way she was aware that home was not simply a place. It was also what she was, the wife of Henry Wilt and mother of the quads, a working woman descended from a line of working women who had scrubbed floors, cooked meals and held families together in spite of illnesses and deaths and the vagaries of men. It wasn't a clearly defined thought but it was there driving her forward almost by instinct. But with instinct there came thought.

They would be waiting for her in Farringdon Avenue so she would avoid it. Instead of she would cross the river by the iron footbridge and go round by Barnaby Road and then across the fields where she had taken the children blackberrying only two months ago and enter the garden at the back. And then? She would have to wait and see. If there was any way of entering the house and joining the children she would take it. And if the terrorists killed her it was better than losing the quads. The main thing was that she would be there to protect them. Beneath this uncertain logic there was rage. Like her thoughts it was vague and diffuse and focused as much on the police as on the terrorists. If anything she blamed the police more. To her the terrorists were criminals and murderers and the police were there to save the public from such people. That was their job, and they hadn't done it properly. Instead they had allowed her children to be taken hostage and were now playing a sort of game in which the quads were merely pieces. It was a simple view but Eva's mind saw things simply and straightforwardly. Well, if the police wouldn't act she would.

It was only when she reached the footbridge over the river that she saw the full magnitude of the problem facing her. Half a mile away the house in Willington Road stood in an aura of white light. Around it the street lamps glimmered dimly and the other houses were black shadows. For a moment she paused, gripping the handrail and wondering what to do, but there was no point in hesitating. She had to go on. She went down the iron steps and along Barnaby Road until she came to the footpath across the field. She went through and followed it until she reached the muddy patch by the next gate. A group of bullocks stirred in the darkness near her but Eva had no fear of cattle. They were part of the natural world to which she felt she properly belonged.

But on the far side of the gate everything was unnatural. Against the sinister white glare of the floodlights she could see men with guns and when she had climbed the gate she stooped down and spotted the coils of barbed wire. They ran right across the field from Farringdon Avenue. Willington Road had been sealed off. Again instinct provoked cunning. There was a ditch to her left and if she made her way along it . . . But there would be a man there to stop her. She needed something to divert his attention. The bullocks would do. Eva opened the gate and then trudging through the mud shooed the beasts into the next field before closing the gate again. She shooed them still further and the bullocks scattered and were presently moving slowly forward in their usual inquisitive way. Eva scrambled down into the ditch and began to wade along it. It was a muddy ditch, half filled with water and as she went weeds gathered around her knees and the occasional bramble scratched her face. Twice she put her hand into clumps of stinging-nettles but Eva hardly felt them. Her mind was too occupied with other problems. Mainly the lights. They glared at the house with a brilliance that made it seem unreal and almost like looking at a photographic negative where all the tones were reversed and windows which should have shone with light were black squares against a lighter background. And all the time from somewhere across the field there came the incessant beat of an engine. Eva peered over the edge of the ditch and made out the dark shape of a generator. She knew what it was because John Nye had once explained how electricity was made when he had been trying to persuade her to install a Savonius rotor which ran off windpower. So that was how they were lighting the house. Not that it helped her. The generator was out in the middle of the field and she couldn't possibly reach it. Anyway, the bullocks were proving a useful distraction. They had gathered in a group round one of the armed men and he was trying to get rid of them. Eva went back into the ditch and stumbling along came to the barbed wire.

As she had expected it coiled down into the water and it was only by reaching down the full length of her arm that she could find the bottom strand. She pulled it up and then stooping down so that she was almost submerged managed to wriggle her way underneath. By the time she reached the hedge that ran along the backs of all the gardens she was soaked to the skin and her hands and legs were covered with mud, but the cold didn't affect her. Nothing mattered except the fear that she would be stopped before she reached the house. And there were bound to be more armed men in the garden.

Eva stood knee-deep in the mud and waited and watched. Noises came to her out of the night. There was certainly someone in Mrs Haslop's garden. The smell of cigarette smoke told her so, but her main attention was fixed on her own back garden and the lights that blazed her home into a fearful isolation. A man moved from the back of the summerhouse and crossed to the gate into the field. Eva watched him stroll away towards the generator. And still she waited with the cunning that sprang from some deep instinct. Another man moved behind the summerhouse, a match flared in the darkness as he lit a cigarette, and Eva, like some primeval amphibian, climbed slowly from the ditch and on her hands and knees crawled forward along the hedge. All the time her eyes were fixed on the glowing tip of the cigarette. By the time she reached the gate she could see the man's face each time he took a deep puff, and the gate was open. It swung slightly in the breeze, never quite shutting. Eva began to crawl through it when her knee touched something cylindrical and slippery. She felt down with a hand and found a thick plastic-coated cable. It ran through the gateway to the three floodlights stationed on the lawn. All she had to do was cut it and the lights would go off. And there were secateurs in the greenhouse. But if she used them she might electrocute herself. Better to take the axe with the long handle and that was by the woodpile on the far side of the summerhouse. If only the man with the cigarette would go she could reach it in no time. But what would make him move? If she threw a stone at the greenhouse he would certainly investigate.

Eva felt around on the path and had just found a piece of flint when the need for throwing it ended. A loud chattering noise was coming from behind her and turning her head she could make out the shape of a helicopter coming low over the field. And the man had moved. He was on his feet and had walked round the summerhouse so that his back was towards her. Eva crawled through the gate, got to her feet and ran for the woodpile. On the other side of the summerhouse the man didn't hear her. The helicopter was nearer now and its rotors drowned her movements. Already Eva had the axe and had returned to the cable and as the helicopter passed overhead she swung the axe down. A moment later the house had disappeared and the night had become intensely dark. She stumbled forward, trampled across the herb garden and reached the lawn before she realized that she seemed to be in the middle of a tornado. Above her the helicopter blades thrashed the air, the machine veered sideways, something swung past her head and a moment later there came the sound of breaking glass. Mrs de Frackas' conservatory was being demolished. Eva stopped in her tracks and threw herself flat on the lawn. From inside the house there came the rattle of automatic fire, and bullets riddled the summerhouse. She was in the middle of some awful battle and everything had suddenly gone horribly wrong.

In Mrs de Frackas' conservatory Superintendent Misterson had been watching the helicopter moving in towards the balcony window with the field telephone dangling beneath it, when the world had suddenly vanished. After the brilliance of the floodlights he could see nothing but he could still feel and hear and before he could grope his way back into the drawing-room he both felt and heard. He certainly felt the field telephone on the side of his head and he vaguely heard the sound of breaking glass. A second later he was on the tiled floor and the whole damned place seemed to be cascading glass, potted geraniums, *begonia semperflorens* and soilless compost. It was the latter that prevented him from expressing his true feelings.

'You bleeding maniac . . .' he began before choking in the dust storm. The Superintendent rolled on to his side and tried to avoid the debris but things were still falling from the shelves and Mrs de Frackas' treasured Cathedral Bell plant had detached itself from the wall and had draped him with tendrils. Finally as he tried to fight his way out of this home-grown jungle a large Camellia 'Donation' in a heavy clay pot toppled from its pedestal and put an end to his misery. The head of the Anti-Terrorist Squad lay comfortably unconscious on the tiles and made no comment.

But in the Communications Centre comments flew thick and fast. The Major yelled orders to the helicopter pilot while two operators wearing headphones were clutching their ears and screaming that some fucking lunatic was bouncing on the parabolic listening devices. Only Flint remained cool and comparatively detached. Ever since he had first learnt that Wilt was involved in the case he had known that something appalling was bound to happen. In Flint's mind the name Wilt spelt chaos, a sort of cosmic doom against which there was no protection, except possibly prayer, and now that catastrophe had struck he was secretly pleased. It proved his premonition right and the Superintendent's optimism entirely wrong. And so while the Major ordered the helicopter pilot to get the hell out, Flint picked his way through the rubble in the conservatory and disentangled his unconscious superior from the foliage.

'Better call an ambulance,' he told the Major as he dragged the injured man into the Communications Centre, 'the Super looks as if he's bought it.'

The Major was too busy to be concerned. 'That's your business, Inspector,' he said. 'I've got to see those swine don't get away.'

'Sounds as though they're still in the house,' said Flint as the sporadic firing continued from Number 9, but the Major shook his head.

'Doubt it. Could have left a suicide squad to cover their retreat, or rigged up a machine gun with a timing device to fire at intervals. Can't trust the buggers an inch.'

Flint radioed for medical help and ordered two constables to carry the Superintendent through the neighbouring gardens to Farringdon Avenue, a process that was impeded by the SGS men searching for escaping terrorists. It was half an hour before silence descended on Willington Road and the listening devices had confirmed that there was still human presence in the house.

There was also apparently something vertebrate lying on the Wilts' lawn. Flint, returning from the ambulance, found the Major grasping a revolver and preparing to make a sortie.

'Got one of the bastards by the sound of things,' he said as a massive heartbeat issued from an amplifier linked to a listening device. 'Going out to bring him in. Probably wounded in the cross-fire.'

He dashed out into the darkness and a few minutes later there was a yell, the sound of a violent struggle involving an extremely vigorous object and sections of the fence between the two gardens. Flint switched the amplifier off. Now that the massive heartbeat had gone there were other even more disturbing sounds coming from the machine. But what was finally dragged through the shattered conservatory was worst of all. Never the most attractive of women in Flint's eyes, Eva Wilt daubed in mud, weeds and soaked to the skin which showed through her torn dress in several places, now presented a positively prehistoric appearance. She was still struggling as the six SGS men bundled her into the room. The Major followed with a black eye.

'Well at least we've got one of the swine,' he said.

'I'm not one of the swine,' shouted Eva, 'I'm Mrs Wilt. You've no right to treat me like this.'

Inspector Flint retreated behind a chair. 'It's certainly Mrs Wilt,' he said. 'Mind telling us what you were trying to do?'

From the carpet Eva regarded him with loathing.

'I was trying to join my children. I've got a right to.'

'I've heard that one before,' said Flint. 'You and your rights. I suppose Henry put you up to this?'

'He did nothing of the sort. I don't even know what's happened to him. For all I know he's dead.' And she promptly burst into tears.

'All right, you can let her go now, chaps,' said the Major at last convinced that his captive was not one of the terrorists. 'You could have got yourself killed, you know.'

Eva ignored him and got to her feet. 'Inspector Flint, you're a father yourself. You must know what it means to be separated from your loved ones in their hour of need.'

'Yes, well . . .' said the Inspector awkwardly. Weeping Neanderthal women aroused mixed emotions in him and in any case his particular loved ones were two teenage louts with an embarrassing taste for vandalism. He was grateful for an interruption from one of the technicians in charge of the listening devices.

'Getting something peculiar, Inspector,' he said. 'Want to hear it?'

Flint nodded. Anything was better than appeals for sympathy from Eva Wilt. It wasn't. The technician switched the amplifier on.

'That's coming from Boom Number 4,' he explained as a series of grunts, groans, ecstatic cries and the insistent creaking of bedsprings issued from the loudspeaker.

'Boom Number 4? That's not a boom, that's a . . .'

'Sounds like a fucking sex maniac, begging the lady's pardon,' said the Major. But Eva was listening too intently to care.

'Where's it coming from?'

'Attic flat, sir. The one where you-know-who is.'

But the subterfuge was wasted on Eva. 'Yes, I do,' she shrieked, 'that's my Henry. I'd know that moan anywhere.'

A dozen disgusted eyes turned on her but Eva was unabashed. After all she had been through in so short a time this new revelation destroyed the last vestiges of her social discretion.

'He's making love to some other woman. Just wait till I lay my hands on him,' she screamed in fury and would have dashed out into the night again if she hadn't been seized.

'Handcuff the bitch,' shouted the Inspector, 'and take her back to the station and see she doesn't get out again. I want maximum security this time and I don't mean maybe.'

'Doesn't sound as if her husband does either, come to that,' said the Major as Eva was dragged off and the unequivocal evidence of Wilt's first affair continued to pulsate through the Communications Centre. Flint emerged from behind the chair and sat down.

'Well at least she's proved me right. I said the little bastard was in this thing up to his eyeballs.'

The Major shuddered. 'I can think of pleasanter ways of putting it, but it rather sounds as if you're right.'

'Of course I am,' said Flint smugly. 'I know friend Wilt's little tricks.'

'I'm glad I don't,' said the Major. 'If you ask me we ought to get the psycho to analyse this little lot.'

'It's all going down on the tape, sir,' said the radio man.

'In that case turn that filthy din off,' said Flint. 'I've got enough on my hands without having to listen to Wilt having it off.'

'Couldn't agree more,' said the Major, struck by the accuracy of the term, 'the fellow must have nerves of steel. Dashed if I could get it up in the circumstances.'

'You'd be surprised what that little bugger can get up to in any circumstances,' said Flint, 'and married to that maternal mastodon of his, is it any wonder? I'd just as soon go to bed with a giant clam as climb in with Eva Wilt.'

'I suppose there's something in that,' said the Major fingering his black eye cautiously. 'She certainly packs one hell of a punch. Can't stay around. Got to go and get those floodlights going again.'

He wandered out and Flint sat on wondering what to do. Now that the Superintendent was out of action he supposed he must be in charge of the case. It was not a promotion he wanted. About the only consolation he could find was the thought that Henry Wilt was about to get his final come-uppance.

In fact Wilt was concentrating his mind on just the opposite. The state of his manhood, so recently repaired, demanded it. Besides, adultery was not his forte and he had never found the process of making love when he didn't feel up to it at all appealing. And since when he felt like it Eva usually didn't, reserving her moments of passion until the quads were safely asleep and Wilt would have been given half a chance, he had become accustomed to a sort of split sexuality in which he did one thing while thinking about another. Not that Eva was satisfied with one thing. Her interest, while more single-minded than his, was infinitely eclectic in matters of procedure and Wilt had learnt to accept being bent, crushed, twisted and generally contorted along lines suggested by the manuals Eva consulted. They had titles like *How to Keep your Marriage Young* or *Making Love the Natural Way*. Wilt had objected that their marriage wasn't young and that there was nothing

158

natural about risking strangulated hernia by using the coitus position advocated by Dr Eugene van Yonk. Not that his arguments ever did any good. Eva replied by making unpleasant references to his adolescence and unwarranted accusations about what he did in the bathroom when she wasn't there and in the end he had been driven to prove his normality by doing what he considered thoroughly abnormal. But if Eva had been vigorously experimental in bed Gudrun Schautz was a demented carnivore.

From the moment in the kitchen when she had first latched on to him in a frenzy of blatant lust, Wilt had been bitten, scratched, licked, chewed and sucked with a violence and lack of discrimination that was frankly insulting, not to say dangerous, and which had led him to wonder why the bitch bothered to shoot people when she could just as easily have done them to death in more lawful and decidedly nastier ways. Anyway, nobody in his right mind could sensibly accuse him of being an unfaithful husband. If anything, quite the opposite; only the most dutiful and conscientious family man would have put himself so much at risk as to get voluntarily into bed with a wanted murderess. Wilt found the adjective singularly inappropriate and it was only by concentrating his imagination on Eva when he had first met her that he could evoke a modicum of desire. It was this flaccid response that provoked Gudrun Schautz. The bitch was not only a murderess; she managed to combine political terror with the expectation that Wilt was a male chauvinist pig who would launch himself into her without a second thought.

Wilt's views on the matter were different. It was one of the tenets of his confused philosophy that you didn't mess about with other women once you were married. And bouncing up and down on an extremely nubile young woman undoubtedly came into the category of messing about. On the other hand there was the interesting paradox that he was spiritually closer to Eva now than when he was actually making love to her and thinking about something else. More practically there wasn't a hope in hell of having an orgasm. The catheter had put paid to that for the time being. He could bounce away until the cows came home, but he was no more going to put his penis to the test of a genuine erection than fly. To prevent this dreadful possibility he alternated his vision of a youthful Eva with images of himself and the execrable Schautz lying on the autopsy table in a terminal coitus interruptus. Considering the din they were making it seemed all too likely and it was certainly a most effective anti-aphrodisiac. Besides, it had the additional advantage of confusing the Schautz woman. She was evidently accustomed to more committed lovers and Wilt's erratic fervour threw her.

'You like it some other way, Liebling?' she asked as Wilt receded for the umpteenth time.

'In the bath,' said Wilt who had suddenly become conscious that the terrorists below might decide to take a hand and that baths were more bulletproof than beds. Gudrun Schautz laughed. 'So funny, ja. In the bath!'

At that moment the floodlights went out and the roar of the helicopter could be heard. The noise seemed to spur her to a new frenzy of lust.

'Quick, quick,' she moaned, 'they're coming.'

'Buggered if I am,' muttered Wilt but the murderess was too busy trying to exorcise oblivion to hear him and as Mrs de Frackas' conservatory disintegrated and rapid gunfire sounded below he was hurtled once more into a maelstrom of lust that had nothing to do with real sex at all. Death was going through the motions of life and Wilt, unaware that his part in this grisly performance was being monitored for posterity, did his best to play his role. He tried thinking about Eva again.

17

Downstairs in the kitchen Chinanda and Baggish were having a hard time thinking at all. All the complexities of life from which they had tried to escape into the idiotic and murderous

160

fanaticism of terror seemed suddenly to have combined against them. They fired frantically into the darkness, and for one proud moment imagined they had hit the helicopter. Instead, the thing had apparently bombed the house next door. When they finally stopped shooting they were assailed by the yells of quads in the cellar. To make matters worse, the kitchen had become a health hazard. Eva's highly polished tiles were a slick of vomit and after Baggish had twice landed on his backside they had retreated to the hall to consider their next move. It was then that they heard the extraordinary noises emanating from the attic.

'They're raping Gudrun,' said Baggish and would have gone to her rescue if Chinanda hadn't stopped him.

'It's a trap the police pigs are setting. They want to get us upstairs and then they rush the house and rescue the hostages. We stay down here.'

'With that noise? How long do you think we can go on with all that yelling? We each need to sleep by turns and with them crying is impossible.'

'So we stop them,' said Chinanda and led the way down to the cellar where Mrs de Frackas was sitting on a wooden chair while the quads demanded mummy.

'Shut up, you hear me! You want to see your mummy you stop that noise,' Baggish shouted. But the quads only yelled the louder.

'I should have thought coping with small children would have been an essential part of your training,' said Mrs de Frackas unsympathetically. Baggish rounded on her. He still hadn't got over her suggestion that his proper métier was selling dirty postcards in Port Said.

'You make them quiet yourself,' he told her, waving his automatic in her face, 'or else we—'

'My dear boy, there are some things you have yet to learn,' said the old lady. 'By the time you reach my age dying is so imminent that I can't be bothered to worry about it. In any case I have always been an advocate of euthanasia. So much more sensible, don't you think, than putting one on a drip or one of those life-support machines or whatever they call them. I mean, who wants to keep a senile old person alive when she's no use to anyone?'

'I don't,' said Baggish fervently. Mrs de Frackas looked at him with interest.

'Besides, being a Moslem, you'd be doing me a favour. I've always understood that death in battle was a guarantee of salvation according to the Prophet, and while I can't say I'm actually battling I should have thought being shot by a murderer amounts to the same thing.'

'We are not murderers,' shouted Baggish, 'we are freedom fighters against international imperialism!'

'Which serves to prove my point,' continued Mrs de Frackas imperturbably. 'You're fighting and I am self-evidently a product of the Empire. If you kill me I should, according to your philosophy, go straight to heaven.'

'We are not here to discuss philosophy,' said Chinanda. 'You stupid old woman, what do you know about the suffering of the workers?'

Mrs de Frackas turned her attention to his clothes. 'Rather more than you do by the cut of your coat, young man. It may not be obvious but I spent several years working in a children's hospital in the slums of Calcutta and I think I know what misery means. Have you ever done a hard day's work in your life?'

Chinanda evaded the question. 'But what did you do about this misery?' he yelled, poking his face close to hers. 'You washed your conscience in the hospital and then went back and lived in luxury.'

'I had three square meals a day if that's what you mean by luxury. I certainly couldn't have afforded the sort of expensive car you drive around in,' riposted the old lady. 'And while we're on the subject of washing, I think it might help to quieten the children if you allowed me to bath them.'

The terrorists looked at the quads and tended to agree. The quads were not a pleasant sight.

'OK, we bring you water down and you can wash them here,' said Chinanda, who went up to the darkened kitchen and finally found a plastic bucket under the sink. He filled it with water and brought it down with a bar of soap. Mrs de Frackas looked into the bucket doubtfully.

'I said "Wash them". Not dye them.'

'Die them? What do you mean die them?'

'Take a look for yourself,' said Mrs de Frackas. The two terrorists did, and were appalled. The bucket was filled with dark blue water.

'Now they're trying to poison us,' yelled Baggish and headed up the stairs to register this fresh complaint against the Anti-Terrorist Squad.

Inspector Flint took the call. 'Poison you? By putting something in the water supply? I can assure you I know nothing about it.'

'Then how come it's blue?'

'I've no idea. Are you sure the water's blue?'

'I know fucking well it's blue,' shouted Baggish. 'We turn the tap and the water comes out blue. You think we're idiots or something.'

Flint hesitated but suppressed his true opinion in the interest of the hostages. 'Never mind what I think,' he said, 'all I'm saying is that we have done absolutely nothing to the water supply and—'

'Lying pig,' shouted Baggish. 'First you try trapping us by raping Gudrun and now you poison the water. We don't wait any longer. The water is clean in one hour and you let Gudrun go or we execute the old woman.'

He slammed the phone down, leaving Flint more mystified than ever. 'Raping Gudrun? The man's off his head. I wouldn't touch the bitch with a bargepole and how I can be in two places at the same time defeats me. And now he's saying the water's gone blue.'

'Could be they're on drugs,' said the sergeant. 'Gets them hallucinating sometimes, especially when they're under stress.'

'Stress? Don't talk to me about stress,' said Flint and turned his anger on a PLD operator. 'And what the hell are you smirking about?'

'They're trying it out in the bath now, sir. Wilt's idea. Randy little sod.'

'If you're seriously suggesting that a couple copulating in a bath can turn the rest of the water in the house blue, think again,' snapped Flint.

He leant his head back against an antimacassar and shut his eyes. His mind was churning with opinions. Wilt was mad. Wilt was a terrorist. Wilt was a mad terrorist. Wilt was possessed. Wilt was a bloody enigma. Only the last was certain, that and the Inspector's fervent wish that Wilt was a thousand miles away and that he had never heard of the bastard. Finally he roused himself.

'All right, I want that helicopter back and this time no balls-ups. The house is floodlit and it's going to stay that way. All they have to do is land that telephone through the balcony window and considering what they've done here that should be child's play. Tell the pilot he can rip the roof off if he wants to but I want a line through to that flat and fast. That's the only way we're going to find out exactly what Wilt's playing at.'

'Will do,' said the Major, and began issuing fresh instructions.

'He's playing politics now, sir,' said the operator. 'Makes Marx sound like a right-winger. Want to hear?'

'I suppose I'd better,' said Flint miserably, and the loud-speaker was switched on. Through the crackle Wilt could be heard expounding violently.

'We must annihilate the capitalist system lock stock and barrel. There must be no hesitation in exterminating the last vestiges of the ruling class and instilling a proletarian consciousness into the minds of the workers. This can best be achieved by exposing the fascistic nature of pseudo-democracy through the praxis of terror against the police and the lumpen executives of international finance. Only by demonstrating the fundamental antithesis between . . .'

'Christ, he sounds like a bloody textbook,' said Flint with unintentional accuracy. 'We've got a pocket Mao in the attic. Right, get these tapes through to the Idiot Brigade. Perhaps they can tell us what a lumpen executive is.'

'Helicopter's on its way,' said the Major. 'The telephone's

fitted with a micro-television camera. If all goes well we'll soon see what's going on up there.'

'As if I wanted to,' said Flint and retreated to the safety of the downstairs toilet.

Five minutes later the helicopter swirled across the orchard at the bottom of the garden, poised for a moment over Number 9, and a field telephone swung through the balcony window into the flat. As the pilot lifted the machine away a trail of wire spun out behind it like the thread of a mechanical spider.

Flint emerged from the toilet to find that Chinanda was back on the phone.

'Wants to know why we haven't cleared the water, sir,' said the operator.

Inspector Flint sat down with a sigh and took the call. 'Now listen, Miguel,' he began, imitating the friendly approach of the Superintendent, 'you may not believe this—'

A stream of abuse indicated all too clearly that the terrorist didn't.

'All right, I accept all that,' said Flint when the epithets dried up. 'But what I'm saying is that we aren't in the attic. We haven't put anything in the water.'

'Then why are you supplying them with weapons by helicopter?'

'That wasn't a weapon. It happened to be a telephone so we can talk to them . . . Yes, I daresay it doesn't sound likely. I'm the first to agree . . . No, we haven't. If anyone has it's the . . .'

'People's Alternative Army,' prompted the sergeant.

'The People's Alternative Army,' repeated Flint. 'They must have put something in the water, Miguel . . . What? . . . You don't like being called Miguel . . . Well as a matter of fact I don't particularly like being called fuzzpig . . . Yes, I heard you. I heard you the first time. And if you'll get off the line I'll talk to the bastards up there.'

And Flint slammed down the phone. 'All right, now get me through to the attic. And make it snappy. Time's running out.'

•

It was to run out for a further quarter of an hour. The sudden reappearance of the helicopter just when the Wilt alternative had switched from sex to politics had thrown Wilt's tactics out of joint. Having softened his victim up on the physical level he had begun confusing her still more by quoting the egregious Bilger at his most Marcusian. It hadn't been too difficult, and in any case Wilt had speculated on the injustice of human existence over many years. His dealings with Plasterers Four had taught him that he belonged to a relatively privileged society. Plasterers earned more than he did, and Printers were positively rich, but allowing for these discrepancies it was still true that he had been born into an affluent country with a favoured climate and sophisticated political institutions developed over the centuries. Above all an industrial society. The vast majority of mankind lived in abject poverty, were riddled with curable disease which went uncured, were subject to despotic governments and lived in terror and in danger of dying by starvation. To the extent that anyone tried to change this inequity, Wilt sympathized. Eva's Personal Assistance for Primitive People might be ineffectual but it had at least the merit of being personal and moving in the right direction. Terrorizing the innocent and murdering men, women and children was both ineffectual and barbaric. What difference was there between the terrorists and their victims? Only one of opinion. Chinanda and Gudrun Schautz came from wealthy families and Baggish, whose father had been a shopkeeper in Beirut, could hardly be called poor. None of these self-appointed executioners had been driven to murder by the desperation of poverty, and as far as Wilt could tell their fanaticism had its roots in no specific cause. They weren't trying to drive the British from Ulster, the Israelis from the Golan Heights or even the Turks from Cyprus. They were political poseurs whose enemy was life. In short they were murderers by personal choice, psychopaths who camouflaged their motives behind a screen of utopian theory. Power was their kick, the power to inflict pain and to terrify. Even their own readiness to die was a sort of power, some sick and infantile form of masochism and expiation of guilt, not for their filthy crimes, but for being alive at all. Beyond that there were doubtless other motives concerned with parents or toilet training. Wilt didn't care. It was enough that they were carriers of the same political rabies that had driven Hitler to construct Auschwitz and kill himself in the bunker, or the Cambodians to murder one another by the million. As such they were beyond the pale of sympathy. Wilt had his children to protect and only his wits to help him.

And so, in a desperate attempt to keep Gudrun Schautz isolated and uncertain, he mouthed Marcusian dogma until the helicopter interrupted his recital. As the telephone encased in a wooden box swung through the window Wilt hurled himself to the floor in the kitchen.

'Back into the bathroom,' he yelled convinced that the thing was some sort of tear-gas bomb. But Gudrun Schautz was already there. Wilt crawled through to her.

'They know we're here,' she whispered.

'They know I'm here,' said Wilt, grateful to the police for seeming to provide proof that he was a wanted man. 'What would they want with you?'

'They locked me in the bathroom. Why would they do that if they didn't want me?'

'Why would they do it if they did?' asked Wilt. 'They'd have dragged you out straightaway.' He paused and looked hard at her in the light reflected from the ceiling. 'But how did they get on to me? I ask myself that question. Who told them?'

Gudrun Schautz looked back and asked herself a great many questions. 'Why do you look at me? I don't know what you are talking about.'

'No?' said Wilt, deciding the time was ripe to switch to full-scale mania. 'That's what you say now. You come to my house when everything is going so good with the plan and now suddenly the Israelis arrive and everything is kaput. No assassination of the Queen, no use for the nerve-gas, no annihilation of the entire pseudo-democratic parliamentary cadres in the House of Commons at one fell swoop, no . . .'

In the living-room the telephone interrupted this insane catalogue. Wilt listened to it with relief. So did Gudrun Schautz. The paranoia which was part of her make-up was beginning to assume new proportions in her mind with every shift in Wilt's position.

'I'll answer it,' she said but Wilt glared at her ferociously.

'Informer,' he snarled, 'you've done enough harm already. You will stay where you are. That's your only hope.'

And leaving her to work out this strange logic, Wilt crawled through the kitchen and opened the box.

'Listen you fascist pig swine,' he yelled before Flint could get a word in edgeways, 'don't think you're going to sweet-talk the People's Alternative Army into one of your lying dialogues. We demand—'

'Shut up, Wilt,' snapped the Inspector. Wilt shut up. So the sods knew. In particular, Flint knew. Which would have been good news if he hadn't had a bloody murderess breathing down his neck. 'So there's no use trying to bluff us. For your information, if you want to see your daughters alive again you had better stop trying to poison your little comrades on the ground floor.'

'Trying to what?' asked Wilt, stunned by this new accusation into using his normal voice.

'You heard me. You've been doctoring the water supply and they want it undoctored as of now.'

'Doctoring the . . .' Wilt began before remembering he couldn't talk openly in present company.

'The water supply,' said Flint. 'They've set a deadline for it to be cleared and it runs out in half an hour. And I do mean deadline.'

There was a moment's silence while Wilt tried to think. There must have been something in that bloody hold-all that was poisonous. Perhaps the terrorists carried their own supply of cyanide. He'd have to get the bag out but in the meantime he had to maintain his lunatic stand. He fell back on his earlier approach.

'We make no deals,' he shouted. 'If our demands aren't met by eight in the morning the hostage dies.'

There was the sound of laughter at the other end of the line. 'Pull the other one, Wilt,' said Flint. 'How are you going to kill her? Screw her to death perhaps?'

168

He paused to let this information sink in before continuing, 'We've got every little antic you've been up to on tape. It's going to sound great when we play it back in court.'

'Shit,' said Wilt, this time impersonally.

'Mrs Wilt particularly enjoyed it. Yes, you heard me right. Now then, are you going to clear that water or do you want your daughters to have to drink it?'

'All right, I agree. You have the aircraft waiting on the runway and I don't move from here until the car arrives. One driver and no tricks or the woman dies with me. You understand?'

'No,' said Flint beginning to feel confused himself but Wilt had ended the conversation. He was sitting on the floor trying to think himself out of this new dilemma. He couldn't do anything about the water tank with the Schautz woman watching. He would have to continue his bluff. He went back into the kitchen and found her standing uncertainly by the bathroom door.

'So now you know,' he said.

Gudrun Schautz didn't. 'Why did you say you would kill me?' she asked.

'Why do you think?' said Wilt, plucking up sufficient courage to move towards her with something approximating to menace. 'Because you are an informer? Without you the plan . . .'

But Gudrun Schautz had heard enough. She retreated into the bathroom, slammed the door and bolted it. This little man was insane. The whole situation was insane. Nothing made any sort of sense, and contradiction piled on contradiction so that the outcome was an incomprehensible flux of impressions. She sat on the toilet and tried to think her way through the chaos. If this weird man with his talk of assassinating the Queen was wanted by the police, and everything seemed to point in that direction, however illogically, there was something to be said for seeming to be his hostage. The British police weren't supposed to be fools but they might free her without asking too many awkward questions. It was the only chance she had. And through the door she could hear Wilt muttering to himself alarmingly. He had started to wire the doorhandle again.

When he had finished Wilt climbed back into the attic space and was presently elbow-deep in the water tank. It was certainly a very murky colour and when he finally managed to drag the hold-all out his arm was blue. Wilt laid the bag on the floor and began to rummage through its contents. At the bottom he found a portable typewriter and a large ink pad with a rubber stamp. There was nothing to suggest poison, but the typewriter ribbon and the ink pad had certainly polluted the water. Wilt went back to the kitchen and turned on the tap. 'No wonder the buggers thought they were being doctored,' he muttered and, leaving the tap running, climbed back into the roof space. By the time he had crawled round the back of the tank with the hold-all and hidden it under the fibreglass insulation the dawn was beginning to compete with the floodlights. He emerged, went through to the living-room, lay down on the sofa and wondered what to do next.

18

And so Day Two of the siege of Willington Road began. The sun rose, the floodlights faded, Wilt nodded fitfully in a corner of the attic, Gudrun Schautz lay in the bathroom, Mrs de Frackas sat in the cellar, and the quads huddled together under a pile of sacks in which Eva had once stored 'organic' potatoes. Even the two terrorists snatched some sleep, while in the Communications Centre the Major, installed on a camp bed, snored and twitched in his sleep like a hound dreaming of the hunt. Elsewhere in Mrs de Frackas' house several Anti-Terrorist men had made themselves comfortable. The sergeant in charge of the listening devices was curled on a sofa and Inspector Flint had commandeered the main bedroom. But for all this human inactivity the electronic sensors relayed information to the tapes and via them to the computer and the Psycho-Warfare team, while the field telephone, like some audio-visual Trojan horse, monitored Wilt's breathing and scanned his movements through its TV camera eye.

Only Eva didn't sleep. She lay in a cell in the police station staring at the dim lightbulb in the ceiling and kept the duty sergeant in a state of uncertainty by demanding to see her solicitor. It was a request he didn't know how to refuse. Mrs Wilt was not a criminal and to the best of his knowledge there were no legal grounds for keeping her locked in a cell. Even genuine villains were allowed to see their solicitors, and after fruitlessly trying to contact Inspector Flint the sergeant gave in.

'You can use the telephone in here,' he told her, and discreetly left her in the office to make as many calls as she chose. If Flint didn't like it he could lump it. The duty sergeant wasn't laying his own head on the chopping-block for anyone.

Eva made a great many phone calls. Mavis Mottram was woken at four and was mollified to learn that the only reason Eva hadn't contacted her before was because she was being held illegally by the police.

'I never heard anything so scandalous in my life. You poor thing. Now don't worry we'll have you out of there in no time,' she said, and promptly woke Patrick to tell him to get in touch with the Chief Constable, the local MP and his friends at the BBC.

'I won't have any friends at the Beeb if I call them at half-past four.'

'Nonsense,' said Mavis, 'it will give them plenty of time to get it on the early-morning news.'

The Braintrees were woken too. This time Eva horrified them by describing how she had been assaulted by the police and asked them if they knew anyone who could help. Peter Braintree phoned the secretary of the League of Personal Liberties and, as an afterthought, every national newspaper with the story.

And Eva continued her calls. Mr Gosdyke, the Wilts' solicitor, was dragged from his bed to answer the phone and promised to come to the police station at once.

171

'Don't say anything to anyone,' he advised her, in the firm belief that Mrs Wilt must have committed some crime. Eva ignored his advice. She spoke to the Nyes, the Principal of the Tech and as many people as she could think of, including Dr Scully. She had just finished when the BBC called back and Eva gave a taped interview as the mother of the quadruplets held by the terrorists who was herself being held by the police for no good reason.

From that moment on a crescendo of protest gathered. The Home Secretary was woken by his Permanent Under-Secretary with the news that the BBC was refusing his request not to broadcast the interview in the national interest on the grounds that the illegal detention of the hostages' mother was diametrically oppposed to the national interest. From there the information reached the Police Commissioner, who was held responsible for the activities of the Anti-Terrorist Squad, and even the Ministry of Defence, whose Special Ground Services had assaulted Mrs Wilt in the first place.

Eva hit the radio news at seven and the headlines of every paper in time for the morning rush hour, and by half-past seven the Ipford police station was more obviously besieged by press men, TV cameras, photographers, Eva's friends and onlookers, than the house in Willington Road. Even Mr Gosdyke's scepticism had evaporated in the face of the sergeant's confession that he did not know why Mrs Wilt was in custody.

'Don't ask me what she's supposed to have done,' said the sergeant. 'I was ordered to keep her in the cells by Inspector Flint. If you want any further information, ask him.'

'I intend to,' said Mr Gosdyke. 'Where is he?'

'At the siege. I can try and get him on the phone for you.'

And so it was that Flint, who had finally snatched some sleep with the happy thought that he had at long last got that little bastard Wilt where he wanted him, up to his eyes in a genuine crime, suddenly found that the tables had been turned on him.

'I didn't say arrest her. I said she was to be held in custody under the Terrorism Act.'

'Are you suggesting for one moment that my client is a

terrorist suspect?' demanded Mr Gosdyke. 'Because if you are . . .'

Inspector Flint considered the law on slander and decided he wasn't. 'She was being kept in custody for her own safety,' he equivocated. Mr Gosdyke doubted it.

'Well, having seen the state she's in all I can say is that it's my considered opinion that she would have been safer outside the police station than in it. She has obviously been badly beaten, dragged through the mud, and if I'm any judge of the matter, several hedges into the bargain, has suffered multiple abrasions to the hands and legs and is in a state of nervous exhaustion. Now are you going to allow her to leave or do I have to apply for . . .'

'No,' said Flint hastily, 'of course she can go, but I'm not taking any responsibility for her safety if she comes here.'

'I hardly need any assurance from you on that score,' said Mr Gosdyke, and escorted Eva out of the police station. She was greeted by a barrage of questions and cameras.

'Mrs Wilt, is it correct that the police beat you up?'

'Yes,' said Eva before Mr Gosdyke could interject that she was making no comments.

'Mrs Wilt, what do you intend to do now?'

'I'm going home,' said Eva, but Mr Gosdyke hustled her into the car.

'That's out of the question, my dear. You must have some friends you can stay with for the time being.'

From the crowd Mavis Mottram was trying to make herself heard. Eva ignored her. She had begun thinking about Henry and that awful German girl in bed together, and the last person she wanted to talk to now was Mavis. Besides, at the back of her mind she still blamed Mavis for insisting on going to that stupid seminar. If she had stayed at home none of this would have happened.

'I'm sure the Braintrees won't mind my going there,' she said, and presently she was sitting in their kitchen sipping coffee and telling Betty all about it.

'Are you sure, Eva?' said Betty. 'I mean, it doesn't sound at all like Henry?'

Eva nodded tearfully. 'It did. They have these loudspeaker things all round the house and they can hear everything that's going on inside.'

'I must say I can't understand.'

Nor could Eva. It wasn't simply that it was unlike Henry to be unfaithful; it wasn't Henry at all. Henry never even looked at other women. She had always known he didn't and there had been times when she had been almost irritated by his lack of interest. It somehow deprived her of the little jealousy she was entitled to as his wife, and there was also the suspicion that his lack of interest extended to her too. Now she felt doubly betrayed.

'You'd think he'd be far too worried about the children,' she went on. 'They're downstairs and there he is up in the flat with that creature . . .' Eva broke down and wept openly.

'What you need is a bath and then a good sleep,' said Betty, and Eva allowed herself to be led upstairs to the bathroom. But as she lay in the hot water, instinct and thought combined again. She was going home. She had to, and this time she would go in broad daylight. She got out of the bath, dried herself, and put on the maternity dress which was the only thing Betty Braintree had been able to find that would fit her, and went downstairs. She had made up her mind what to do.

In the temporary conference room which had once been Major-General de Frackas' private den, Inspector Flint, the Major and the members of the Psycho-Warfare team sat looking at a television set which had been placed incongruously in the middle of the Battle of Waterloo. The late Major-General's obsession with toy soldiers and their precise deployment on a large ping-pong table where they had been gathering dust since his death added a surrealist element to the extraordinary sights and sounds being relayed by the TV camera in the field telephone next door. The Wilt alternative had entered a new phase, one in which he had apparently gone clean off his rocker.

'Mad as a March hare,' said the Major as Wilt, horribly distorted by the fish-eye lens, loomed and dwarfed as he strode about the attic mouthing words that made no sense at all. Even Flint found it hard not to accept the verdict.

'What the hell does "Life is prejudicial to Infinity" mean?' he asked Dr Felden, the psychiatrist.

'I need to hear more before I express a definite opinion,' said the doctor.

'I'm damned if I do,' muttered the Major, 'it's like peering into a padded cell.'

On the screen Wilt could be seen shouting something about fighting for the religion of Allah and death to all unbelievers. He then made some extremely disturbing noises which suggested a village idiot having trouble with a fishbone, and disappeared into the kitchen. There was a moment's silence before he began chanting, 'The bells of hell go tingalingaling for you but not for me,' in a frightening falsetto. When he reappeared he was armed with a bread knife and yelling, 'There's a crocodile in the cupboard, mother and it's eating up your coat. Bats and lizards braving blizzards keep the world afloat.' Finally he lay on the bed and giggled.

Flint leant across the sunken road and switched the set off. 'Much more of that and I'll go off my head too,' he muttered. 'All right, you've seen and heard the sod, and I want to know your opinion as to the best way of handling him.'

'Looked at from the standpoint of a coherent political ideology,' said Professor Maerlis, 'I must confess that I find it hard to express an opinion.'

'Good,' said the Major, who still harboured the suspicion that the professor shared the views of the terrorists.

'On the other hand the transcripts of the tapes made last night indicate definite evidence that Mr Wilt has a profound knowledge of terrorist theory and was apparently engaged in a conspiracy to assassinate the Queen. What I don't understand is where the Israelis come in.'

'That could easily be a symptom of paranoia,' said Dr Felden. 'A very typical example of persecution mania.'

'Never mind about the "could be",' said Flint, 'is the bugger mad or not?'

'Difficult to say. In the first place the subject may well be suffering the after-effects of the drugs he was given yesterday before entering the house. I have ascertained from the so-called medical officer who administered it that the concoction consisted of three parts valium, two sodium amytal, a jigger of bromide and what he chose to call a bouquet of laudanum. He couldn't specify the actual quantities involved, but in my opinion it says something for Mr Wilt's constitution that he is still alive.'

'Says something for the canteen coffee that the bugger drank it without noticing,' said Flint. 'Anyway, do we get him on the blower and ask him what he has done with the Schautz woman or not?'

Dr Felden toyed with a lead Napoleon pensively. 'On the whole I am against the idea. If Fräulein Schautz is still alive I wouldn't want to be responsible for introducing the notion of murdering her to a man in Mr Wilt's condition.'

'That's a big help. So when those swine demand her release again I suppose I'll have to tell them she's being held by a lunatic.' And wishing to God the replacement for the head of the Anti-Terrorist Squad would arrive before mass murder began next door, Flint went through to the Communications Centre.

'No go,' he told the sergeant. 'The Idiot Brigade reckon we're dealing with a homicidal maniac.'

It was more or less the reaction that Wilt wanted. He had spent a miserable night pondering his next move. So far he had played a number of roles – a revolutionary terrorist group, a grateful father, a chinless wonder, an erratic lover and a man who had intended to assassinate the Queen – and with each fresh fabrication he had seen Gudrun Schautz's sense of certainty waver. Stoned out of her mind by the drug of revolutionary dogma, she was incapable of adjusting to a world of absurd fantasy. And Wilt's world was absurd; it always had been and as far as he could tell it always would be. It was fantastic and absurd that Bilger had made the bloody film about the crocodile but it was true, and Wilt had spent his adult life surrounded by pimply youths who thought they were God's gift to women, and by lecturers who imagined that they could convert Plasterers and Motor Mechanics into sensitive human beings by forcing them to read *Finnegan's Wake* or instil them with a truly proletarian consciousness by handing out dollops of *Das Kapital*. And Wilt himself had been through the gamut of fantasy, those internal dreams of being a great writer which had been re-awakened by his first glimpse of Irmgard Mueller and, on a previous occasion, the cold-blooded murderer of Eva. And for eighteen years he had lived with a woman who had changed roles almost as frequently as she changed her clothes. With such a wealth of experience behind him Wilt could produce new fantasies at a moment's notice just so long as he wasn't called upon to give them greater credibility by doing anything more practical than gloss them with words. Words were his medium and had been through all the years at the Tech. With Gudrun Schautz locked in the bathroom he was free to use them to his heart's content and her discomfort. Provided those creatures down below didn't start doing anything violent.

But Baggish and Chinanda had their hands full with another form of bizarre behaviour. The quads had woken early to renew their assault on Eva's freezer and stock of bottled fruit, and Mrs de Frackas had given up the unequal battle to keep them moderately clean. She had spent an exceedingly uncomfortable night on the wooden chair and her rheumatism had given her hell. In the end she had been driven to drink, and since the only drink available was Wilt's patented homebrew the results had been remarkable.

From the first appalling mouthful the old lady wondered what the hell had hit her. It wasn't simply that the stuff tasted foul, so foul that she had immediately taken another shot to try to wash her mouth out, it was also extremely potent. Having choked down a second mouthful Mrs de Frackas looked at the bottle with downright disbelief. It was impossible to suppose that anyone had seriously distilled the stuff for human consumption, and for a moment or two she considered the

177

awful possibility that Wilt had, for some diabolical reason of his own, laid up a binful of undiluted paint stripper. It didn't seem likely somehow, but then again what she had just swallowed hadn't seemed likely either. It had seared its way down her gullet with all the virulence of a powerful toilet-cleaner going to work on a neglected U-bend. Mrs de Frackas examined the label and felt reassured. The muck proclaimed itself 'Lager' and while the title was in blatant disregard of the facts, whatever the bottle contained was meant to be drunk. The old lady took another mouthful and instantly forgot her rheumatism. It was impossible to concentrate on two ailments simultaneously.

By the time she had finished the bottle she had difficulty concentrating on anything. The world had suddenly become a delightful place and all it needed to make it even better was more of the same. She swayed back to the wine store and selected a second bottle and was in the process of unscrewing the top when the thing exploded. Doused with beer and holding the neck of the bottle Mrs de Frackas was about to try a third when she caught sight of several larger bottles in the bottom rack. She pulled one out and saw that it had once contained champagne. What it contained now she couldn't imagine but at least it seemed safer to open and less likely to fragment than the beer bottles. She took two bottles out into the cellar and tried to uncork them. It was easier said than done. Wilt had fastened the corks down with Sellotape and what looked like the remnants of a wire coathanger.

'Need some pliers,' she muttered as the quads gathered round with interest.

'That's Daddy's best,' said Josephine. 'He wouldn't like it if you drank it.'

'No dear, I daresay he wouldn't,' said the old lady with a belch that suggested her stomach was of the same opinion.

'He calls it his four-star BB,' said Penelope. 'But Mummy says it ought to be called peepee.'

'Does she?' said Mrs de Frackas with mounting disgust.

'That's because he has to get up in the night when he's drunk it.'

178

Mrs de Frackas relaxed. 'We wouldn't want to do anything that would upset your father,' she said, 'and anyway, champagne needs to be chilled.'

She went back to the bins, returned with two opened bottles that had proved less explosive than the others, and sat down again. The quads were gathered round the freezer but the old lady was too busy to care what they were doing. By the time she had finished the third bottle the Wilt quads were octuplets in her eyes and she was having difficulty focusing. In any case she had begun to understand what Eva had meant about peepee. Wilt's homebrew was making its presence felt. Mrs de Frackas got up, fell over and finally crawled up the steps to the door. The damned thing was locked.

'Let me out,' she shouted, and banged on the door. 'Let me out this inshtant.'

'What you want?' demanded Baggish.

'Never you mind what I want. Itsh what I need that matters and thatsh no concern of yours.'

'Then you stay where you are.'

'I shan't be reshponsible for what happens if I do,' said Mrs de Frackas.

'What you mean?'

'Young man, there are shome things better left unshaid and I don't intend dishcushing them with you.'

Through the door the two terrorists could be heard struggling with slurred English sentences. 'Things better left unshed' had them baffled, while 'not be reshponsible for what happens' sounded faintly ominous, and they had already been alarmed by several popping noises and the crunch of glass from the cellar.

'We want to know what happens if we don't let you out,' said Chinanda finally.

Mrs de Frackas was in no doubt. 'I shall almosht shertainly burst,' she yelled.

'You what?'

'Burst, burst, burst. Like a bomb,' screamed the old lady, now convinced she was in the terminal stage of diuresis. A muttered conversation took place in the kitchen.

'You come out with your hands up,' Chinanda ordered, and unlocked the door before backing away into the hall and aiming his automatic. But Mrs de Frackas was no longer in a condition to obey. She was trying to reach one of several doorknobs and missing. From the bottom of the steps the quads watched in fascination. They were used to Wilt's occasional bouts of booziness but they had never seen anyone paralytically drunk before.

'For Heaven's shake shomeone open the door,' Mrs de Frackas burbled.

'I will,' squealed Samantha and a rush of competing girls fought their way over the old lady for the privilege. By the time Penelope had won and the quads had cascaded over her into the kitchen the old lady had lost all interest in toilets. She lay across the threshold and, raising her head with difficulty, delivered her verdict on the quads.

'Do me a favour, shomeone, and shoot the little shits,' she gurgled before passing out. The terrorists didn't hear her. They knew now what she had meant about a bomb. Two devastating explosions came from the cellar and the air was filled with frozen peas and broad beans. In the freezer Wilt's BB had finally burst.

19

Eva had been busy too. She had spent part of the morning on the phone to Mr Gosdyke and the rest arguing with Mr Symper, the local representative of the League of Personal Liberties. He was a very earnest and concerned young man, and in the normal course of events, would have been dismayed at the outrageous behaviour of the police in putting at risk the lives of a senior citizen and four impressionable children by refusing to meet the legitimate demands of the freedom fighters besieged in Number 9 Willington Road. Instead, Eva's treatment at the hands of the police had put Symper in the extremely uncomfortable position of having to look at the problem from her point of view.

'I do understand the case you're making, Mrs Wilt,' he said forced by her bruised appearance to subdue his bias in favour of radical foreigners, 'but you must admit you are free.'

'Not to enter my own house. I am not at liberty to do that. The police won't let me.'

'Now if you want us to take up your case against the police for infringing your liberty by holding you in custody, we'll ...'

Eva didn't. 'I want to enter my own home.'

'I do sympathize with you, but you see our organization aims to protect the individual from the infringement of her personal liberty by the police and in your case ...'

'They won't let me go home,' said Eva. 'If that isn't infringing my personal liberty I don't know what is.'

'Yes, well I do see that.'

'Then do something about it.'

'I don't really know what I can do about it,' said Mr Symper.

'You knew what to do when the police stopped a container truck of deep-frozen Bangladeshis outside Dover,' said Betty. 'You organized a protest rally and ...'

'That was quite different,' said Mr Symper, bridling. 'The Customs officials had no right to insist that the refrigeration unit be turned on. They were suffering from acute frostbite. And besides, they were in transit.'

'They shouldn't have labelled themselves cod fillets, and anyhow you argued that they were simply coming to join their families in Britain.'

'They were in transit to their families.'

'And so is Eva, or should be,' said Betty. 'If anyone has a right to join her family it's Eva.'

'I suppose we could apply for a court order,' said Mr Symper sighing for less domestic issues, 'that would be the best way.'

'It wouldn't,' said Eva, 'it would be slowest. I am going home now and you are coming with me.'

'I beg your pardon?' said Mr Symper, whose concern didn't extend to becoming a hostage himself.

'You heard me,' said Eva, and loomed over him with a

ferocity that put in question his ardent feminism, but before he could make a plea for his own personal liberty he was being hustled out of the house. A crowd of reporters had gathered there.

'Mrs Wilt,' said a man from the *Snap*, 'our readers would like to hear how it feels as the mother of quads to know that your loved ones are being held hostage.'

Eva's eyes bulged in her head. 'Feel?' she asked. 'You want to know how I feel?'

'That's right,' said the man, licking his ballpen, 'human interest—'

He got no further. Eva's feelings had passed beyond the stage of words or human interest. Only actions could express them. Her hand came up, descended in a karate chop and as he fell her knee caught him in the stomach.

'That's how it feels,' said Eva as he rolled into a foetal position on the flowerbed. 'Tell your readers that.' And she marched the now thoroughly cowed Mr Symper to his car and pushed him in.

'I am going home to my children,' she told the other reporters. 'Mr Symper of the League of Personal Liberties is accompanying me and my solicitor is waiting for us.'

And without another word she got into the driver's seat. Ten minutes later, followed by a small convoy of press cars, they reached the road block in Farringdon Road to find Mr Gosdyke arguing ineffectually with the police sergeant.

'I'm afraid it's no use, Mrs Wilt. The police have orders to let no one through.'

Eva snorted. 'This is a free country,' she said, dragging Mr Symper out of the car with a grip that contradicted her statement. 'If anyone tries to stop me from going home we will take the matter to the courts, to the Ombudsman and to Parliament. Come along, Mr Gosdyke.'

'Now hold it, lady,' said the sergeant, 'my orders . . .'

'I've taken your number,' said Eva, 'and I shall sue you personally for denying me free access to my children.'

And pushing the unwilling Mr Symper before her she marched through the gap in the barbed wire, followed cautiously by

Mr Gosdyke. Behind them a cheer went up from the crowd of reporters. For a moment the sergeant was too stunned to react and by the time he reached for his walkie-talkie the trio had turned the corner into Willington Road. They were stopped half way down by two armed SGS men.

'You've no right to be here,' one of them shouted. 'Don't you know there's a siege on?'

'Yes,' said Eva, 'which is why we're here. I'm Mrs Wilt, this is Mr Symper of the League of Personal Liberties and Mr Gosdyke is here to handle negotiations. Now kindly take us to . . .'

'I don't know anything about this,' said the soldier. 'All I know is that we've got orders to shoot . . .'

'Then shoot me,' said Eva defiantly, 'and see where that gets you.'

The SGS man hesitated. Shooting mothers wasn't included in Queen's Rules and Regulations, and Mr Gosdyke looked too respectable to be a terrorist.

'All right, come this way,' he said, and escorted them into Mrs de Frackas' house to be greeted abusively by Inspector Flint.

'What the fuck's going on?' he yelled. 'I thought I gave orders for you to stay away.'

Eva pushed Mr Gosdyke forward. 'Tell him,' she said.

Mr Gosdyke cleared his throat and looked uncomfortably round the room. 'As Mrs Wilt's legal representative,' he said, 'I have come to inform you that she demands to join her family. Now to the best of my knowledge there is nothing in law to prevent her from entering her own home.'

Inspector Flint goggled at him. 'Nothing?' he spluttered.

'Nothing in law,' said Mr Gosdyke.

'Bugger the law,' shouted Flint. 'You think those sods in there give a tuppenny fuck for the law?'

Mr Gosdyke conceded the point.

'Right,' continued Flint, 'so there's a houseful of armed terrorists who'll blow the heads off her four blasted daughters if anyone so much as goes near the place. That's all. Can't you get that into her thick skull?'

'No,' said Mr Gosdyke bluntly.

The Inspector sagged into a chair and looked balefully at Eva. 'Mrs Wilt,' he said, 'tell me something. You don't by any chance happen to belong to some suicidal religious cult, do you? No? I just wondered. In that case let me explain the situation to you in simple four-letter words that even you will understand. Inside your house there are—'

'I know all that,' said Eva, 'I've heard it over and over again and I don't care. I demand the right to enter my own home.'

'I see. And I suppose you intend walking up to the front door and ringing the bell?'

'I don't,' said Eva, 'I intend to be dropped in.'

'Dropped in?' said Flint with a gleam of incredulous hope in his eyes, 'did you really say "dropped in"?'

'By helicopter,' explained Eva, 'the same way you dropped that telephone in to Henry last night.'

The Inspector held his head in his hands and tried to find words.

'And it's no use your saying you can't,' continued Eva, 'because I've seen it done on telly. I wear a harness and the helicopter . . .'

'Oh my God,' said Flint, closing his eyes to shut out this appalling vision. 'You can't be serious.'

'I can,' said Eva.

'Mrs Wilt, if, and I repeat if, you were to enter the house by the means you have described, will you be good enough to tell me how you think it would help your four daughters?'

'Never you mind.'

'But I do mind, I mind very much. In fact I'll go so far as to say that I mind what happens to your children rather more than you appear to and . . .'

'Then why aren't you doing something about it? And don't say you are, because you aren't. You're sitting in here with all this transistor stuff listening to them being tortured and you like it.'

'Like it? Like it?' yelled the Inspector.

'Yes, like it,' Eva yelled back. 'It gives you a feeling of importance and what's more you've got a dirty mind. You enjoyed listening to Henry in bed with that woman and don't say you didn't.'

Inspector Flint couldn't. Words failed him. The only ones that sprang to mind were obscene and almost certain to lead to an action for slander. Trust this bloody woman to bring her solicitor and the sod from the Personal Liberties mob with her. He rose from his chair and stumbled through to the toy-room, slamming the door behind him. Professor Maerlis, Dr Felden and the Major were sitting watching Wilt pass the time by idly examining his glans penis for signs of incipient gangrene on the television screen. Flint switched the unnerving image off.

'You're not going to believe this,' he mouthed, 'but that bloody Mrs Wilt is demanding that we use the helicopter to swing her through the attic window on the end of a rope so she can join her fucking family.'

'I hope you're not going to allow it,' said Dr Felden. 'After what she threatened to do to her husband last night I hardly think it's advisable.'

'Don't tempt me,' said Flint. 'If I thought I could sit here and watch her tear the little shit limb from limb . . .' He broke off to savour the thought.

'Damned plucky little woman,' said the Major. 'Blowed if I'd choose to swing into that house on the end of a rope. Well, not without a lot of covering fire anyhow. Still, there's something to be said for it.'

'What?' said Flint wondering how the hell anyone could call Mrs Wilt a little woman.

'Diversionary tactics, old man. Can't think of anything more likely to unnerve the buggers than the sight of that woman dangling from a helicopter. Know it would scare the pants off me.'

'I daresay. But since that doesn't happen to be the purpose of the exercise I'd like some more constructive suggestion.'

From the other room Eva could be heard shouting that she'd send a telegram to the Queen if she wasn't allowed to join her family.

'That's all we need,' said Flint. 'We've got the press baying for blood and there hasn't been a decent mass suicide for months. She'll hit the headlines.'

'Certainly hit that window with a hell of a bang,' said the Major practically. 'Then we could rush the sods and—'

'No! Definitely no,' shouted Flint and dashed into the Communications Centre. 'All right, Mrs Wilt, I am going to try to persuade the two terrorists holding your daughters to allow you to join them. If they refuse that's their business. I can't do more.'

He turned to the sergeant on the switchboard. 'Get the two wogs on the phone and let me know when they've finished their Fascist Pig Overture.'

Mr Symper felt called upon to protest. 'I really do think these racialist remarks are quite unnecessary,' he said. 'In fact they are illegal. To call foreigners wogs—'

'I'm not calling foreigners wogs. I'm calling two fucking murderers wogs and don't tell me I shouldn't call them murderers either,' said Flint as Mr Symper tried to interject. 'A murderer is a murderer is a murderer and I've had about as much as I can take.'

So, it seemed, had the two terrorists. There was no preliminary tirade of abuse. 'What do you want?' Chinanda asked.

Flint took the phone. 'I have a proposal to make,' he said. 'Mrs Wilt, the mother of the four children you are holding, has volunteered to come in to look after them. She is unarmed and is prepared to meet any conditions you may choose to make.'

'Say that again,' said Chinanda. The Inspector repeated the message.

'Any conditions?' said Chinanda incredulously.

'Any. You name them, she'll meet them,' said Flint looking at Eva, who nodded.

A muttered conference took place in the kitchen next door made practically inaudible by the squeals of the quads and the occasional moan from Mrs de Frackas. Presently the terrorist came back on the line.

'Here are our conditions. The woman must be naked first of all. You hear me, naked.'

'I hear what you say but I can't say I understand . . .'

'No clothes on. So we see she has no weapons. Right?'

'I'm not sure Mrs Wilt will agree . . .'

'I do,' said Eva adamantly.

'Mrs Wilt agrees,' said Flint with a sigh of disgust.

'Second. Her hands are tied above her head.'

Again Eva nodded.

'Third. Her legs are tied.'

'Her legs are tied?' said Flint. 'How the hell is she going to walk if her legs are tied?'

'Long rope. Half metre between ankles. No running.'

'I see. Yes, Mrs Wilt agrees. Anything else?'

'Yes,' said Chinanda. 'As soon as she comes in, out go the children.'

'I beg your pardon?' said Flint. 'Did I hear you say "Out go the children"? You mean you don't want them?'

'Want them!' yelled Chinanda. 'You think we want to live with four dirty, filthy, disgusting little animals who shit all over the floor and piss . . .'

'No,' said Flint, 'I take your point.'

'So you can take the fucking little fascist shit-machines too,' said Chinanda, and slammed the phone down.

Inspector Flint turned to Eva with a happy smile. 'Mrs Wilt, I didn't say it, but you heard what the man said.'

'And he'll live to regret it,' said Eva with blazing eyes. 'Now, where do I undress?'

'Not in here,' said Flint firmly. 'You can use the bedrooms upstairs. The sergeant here will tie your hands and legs.'

While Eva went up to undress the Inspector consulted the Psycho-Warfare Team. He found them at odds with one another. Professor Maerlis argued that by exchanging four coterminiously conceived siblings for one woman whom the world would scarcely miss, there was propaganda advantage to be gained from the swop. Dr Felden disagreed.

'It's evident that the terrorists are under considerable pressure from the girls,' he said. 'Now, by relieving them of that psychological burden we may well be giving them a morale boost.'

'Never mind about their morale,' said Flint. 'If the bitch goes in she'll be doing me a favour and after that the Major here can mount Operation Slaughterhouse for all I care.'

'Whacko,' said the Major.

Flint went back to the Communications Centre, averted his eyes from the monstrous revelations of Eva in the raw, and turned to Mr Gosdyke.

'Let's get one thing straight, Gosdyke,' he said. 'I want you to understand that I am totally opposed to your client's actions and am not prepared to take responsibility for what happens.'

Mr Gosdyke nodded. 'I quite understand, Inspector, and I would just as soon not be involved myself. Mrs Wilt, I appeal to you . . .'

Eva ignored him. With her hands tied above her head and with her ankles linked by a short length of rope, she was an awesome sight and not a woman with whom anyone would willingly argue.

'I am ready,' she said. 'Tell them I'm coming.'

She hobbled out of the door and down Mrs de Frackas' drive. In the bushes SGS men blanched and thought wistfully of booby traps in South Armagh. Only the Major, surveying the scene from a bedroom window, gave Eva his blessing. 'Makes a chap proud to be British,' he told Dr Felden. 'By God that woman's got some guts.'

'I must say I find that remark in singularly bad taste,' said the doctor, who was studying Eva from a purely physiological point of view.

There was something of a misunderstanding next door. Chinanda, viewing Eva through the letter-box in the Wilts' front door, had just begun to have second thoughts when a waft of vomit hit him from the kitchen. He opened the door and aimed his automatic.

'Get the children,' he shouted to Baggish. 'I'm covering the woman.'

'You're what?' said Baggish, who had just glimpsed the expanse of flesh that was moving towards the house. But there was no need to fetch the children. As Eva reached the doormat they rushed towards her squealing with delight.

'Back,' yelled Baggish, 'back or I fire!'

It was too late. Eva swayed on the doorstep as the quads clutched at her.

'Oh Mummy, you do look funny,' shrieked Samantha, and grabbed her mother's knees. Penelope clambered over the others and flung her arms round Eva's neck. For a moment they swayed uncertainly and then Eva took a step forward, tripped and with a crash fell heavily into the hall. The quads slithered before her across the polished parquet and the hatstand, seismically jolted from the wall, crashed forward against the door and slammed it. The two terrorists stood staring down at their new hostage while Mrs de Frackas raised a drunken head from the kitchen, took one look at the amazing sight and passed out again. Eva heaved herself to her knees. Her hands were still tied above her head but her concern was all for the quads.

'Now don't worry, darlings. Mummy's here,' she said. 'Everything is going to be all right.'

From the safety of the kitchen the two terrorists surveyed the extraordinary scene with dismay. They didn't share her optimism.

'Now what do we do?' asked Baggish. 'Throw the children out the door?'

Chinanda shook his head. He wasn't going within striking distance of this powerful woman. Even with her hands tied above her head there was something dangerous and frightening about Eva, and now she seemed to be edging towards him on bulging knees.

'Stay where you are,' he ordered, and raised his gun. Next to him the telephone rang. He reached for it angrily.

'What do you want now?' he asked Flint.

'I might ask you the same question,' said the Inspector. 'You've got the woman and you said you'd let the children go.'

'If you think I want this fucking woman you're crazy,' Chinanda yelled, 'and the fucking children won't leave her. So now we've got them all.'

What sounded like a chuckle came from Flint. 'Not my fault. We didn't ask for the children. You volunteered to . . .'

'And we didn't ask for this woman,' screamed Chinanda his voice rising hysterically. 'So now we do a deal. You . . .'

'Forget it, Miguel,' said Flint, beginning to enjoy himself. 'Deals are out and for your information you'd be doing me a favour shooting Mrs Wilt. In fact you go right ahead and shoot whoever you want, mate, because the moment you do I'm sending my men in and where they shoot you and Comrade Baggish you won't die in a hurry. You'll be . . .'

'Fascist murderer,' screamed Chinanda, and pulled the trigger of his automatic. Bullets spat holes across a chart on the kitchen wall which had until that moment announced the health-giving properties of any number of alternative herbs, most of them weeds. Eva regarded the damage balefully and the quads sent up a terrible wail.

Even Flint was horrified. 'Did you kill her?' he asked, suddenly conscious that his pension came before personal satisfaction.

Chinanda ignored the question. 'So now we deal. You send Gudrun down and have the jet ready in one hour only. From now on we don't play games.'

He slammed the phone down.

'Shit,' said Flint. 'All right, get me Wilt. I've got news for him.'

20

But Wilt's tactics had changed again. Having run the gamut of roles from chinless wonder to village idiot by way of revolutionary fanatic, which to his mind was merely a more virulent form of the same species, it had slowly dawned on him he was approaching the destabilization of Gudrun Schautz from the wrong angle. The woman was an ideologue, and a German one at that. Behind her a terrible tradition stretched back into the mists of history, a cultural hertitage of solemn, monstrously serious and ponderous *Dichter und Denker*, philosophers, artists, poets and thinkers obsessed with the meaning, significance and process of social and historical development. The word *Weltanschauung* sprang, or at least lumbered, to mind. Wilt had no idea what it meant and doubted if anyone else knew. Something to do with having a world view and about as charming as *Lebensraum* which should have meant living-room but actually signified the occupation of Europe and as much of Russia as Hitler had been able to lay his hands on. And after *Weltanschauung* and *Lebensraum* there came, even less comprehensibly, *Weltschmerz* or world pity which, considering Fräulein Schautz's propensity for putting bullets into unarmed opponents without a qualm, topped the bill for codswallop. And beyond these dread concepts there were the carriers of the virus, Hegel, Kant, Fichte, Schopenhauer, and Nietzsche who had gone clean off his nut from a combination of syphilis, superman and large ladies in helmets trumpeting into theatrical forests at Bayreuth. Wilt had once waded lugubriously through *Thus Spoke Zarathustra* and had come out convinced that either Nietzsche hadn't known what the hell he was on about or, if he had, he had kept it very verbosely to himself. And Nietzsche was sprightly by comparison with Hegel and Schopenhauer, tossing off meaningless maxims with an abandon that was positively joyful. If you wanted the real hard stuff Hegel was your man, while Schopenhauer hit a nadir of gloom that made King Lear sound like an hysterical optimist under the influence of laughing gas. In short, Gudrun Schautz's weak spot was happiness. He could blather on about the horrors of the world until he was blue in the face but she wouldn't bat an eyelid. What was needed to send her reeling was a dose of undiluted good cheer, and Wilt beneath his armour of domestic grumbling was at heart a cheerful man.

And so while Gudrun Schautz cowered in the bathroom and Eva stumbled across the threshold downstairs he bombarded his captive audience with good tiding. The world was a splendid place.

Gudrun Schautz disagreed. 'How can you say that when millions are starving?' she demanded.

'The fact that I can say it means that I'm not starving,' said Wilt, applying the logic he had learnt with Plasterers Two, 'and anyway now that we know they're starving means we can do something about it. Things would be much worse if we didn't know. We couldn't send them food for one thing.'

'And who is sending food?' she asked unwisely.

'To the best of my knowledge the wicked Americans,' said Wilt. 'I'm sure the Russians would if they could grow enough but they don't so they do the next best thing and send them Cubans and tanks to take their minds off their empty stomachs. In any case, not everyone is starving and you've only got to look around you to see what fun it is to be alive.'

Gudrun Schautz's view of the bathroom didn't include fun. It looked uncommonly like a prison cell. But she didn't say so.

'I mean, take me for example,' continued Wilt. 'I have a wonderful wife and four adorable daughters . . .'

A snort from the bathroom indicated that there were limits to the Schautz woman's credulity.

'Well, you may not think so,' said Wilt, 'but I do. And even if I didn't you've got to admit that the quads love life. They may be a trifle exuberant for some people's taste, but no one can say they're unhappy.'

'And Mrs Wilt is a wonderful wife?' said Gudrun Schautz with advanced scepticism.

'As a matter of fact I couldn't ask for a better,' said Wilt. 'You may not believe me but—'

'Believe you? I have heard what she calls you and you are always fighting.'

'Fighting?' said Wilt. 'Of course we have our little differences of opinion, but that is essential for a happy marriage. It's what we British call give and take. In Marxist terms I suppose you'd call it thesis, antithesis and synthesis. And the synthesis in our case is happiness.'

'Happiness,' snorted Gudrun Schautz. 'What is happiness?'

Wilt considered the question and the various ways he could answer it. On the whole it seemed wisest to steer clear of the metaphysical and stick to everyday things. 'In my case it happens to be walking to the Tech on a frosty morning with the sun shining and the ducks waddling and knowing I don't have any committee meetings and teaching and going home by moonlight to a really good supper of beef stew and dumplings and then getting into bed with an interesting book.'

'Bourgeois pig. All you think about is your own comfort.'

'It's not all I think about,' said Wilt, 'but you asked for a definition of happiness and that happens to be mine. If you want me to go on I will.'

Gudrun Schautz didn't but Wilt went on all the same. He spoke of picnics by the river on hot summer days and finding a book he wanted in a secondhand shop and Eva's delight when the garlic she had planted actually managed to show signs of growing and his delight at her delight and decorating the Christmas tree with the quads and waking in the morning with them all over the bed tearing open presents and dancing round the room with toys they had wanted and would probably have forgotten about in a week and ... Simple family pleasures and surprises which this woman would never know but which were the bedrock of Wilt's existence. And as he retold them they took on a new significance for him and soothed present horrors with a balm of decency and Wilt felt himself to be what he truly was, a good man in a quiet and unobtrusive way married to a good woman in a noisy and ebullient way. If nobody else saw him like this he didn't care. It was what he was that mattered and what he was grew out of what he did, and for the life of him Wilt couldn't see that he had ever done anything wrong. If anything he had done a modicum of good.

That wasn't the way Gudrun Schautz viewed things. Hungry, cold and fearful, she heard Wilt tell of simple things with a growing sense of unreality. She had lived too long in a world of bestial actions taken to achieve the ideal society to be able to stand this catechism of domestic pleasures. And the only answers she could give him were to call him a fascist swine and secretly she knew she would be wasting her breath. In the end she stayed silent and Wilt was about to take pity on her and cut short a modified version of the family's holiday in France when the telephone rang.

'All right, Wilt,' said Flint, 'you can forget the travelogue. This is the crunch. Your missus is downstairs with the children and if the Schautz doesn't come down right now you're going to be responsible for a minor massacre.'

'I've heard that one before,' said Wilt. 'And for your information . . .'

'Oh no, you haven't. This time it's for real. And if you don't bring her down, by God, we will. Take a look out the window.' Wilt did. Men were climbing into the helicopter in the field.

'Right,' continued Flint, 'so they'll land on the roof and the first person they'll take out is you. Dead. The Schautz bitch we want alive. Now move.'

'I can't say I like your priorities,' said Wilt, but the Inspector had rung off. Wilt went through the kitchen and untied the bathroom door.

'You can come out now,' he said. 'Your friends downstairs seem to be winning. They want you to join them.'

There was no reply from the bathroom. Wilt tried the door and found it was locked.

'Now listen. You've got to come out. I'm serious. Messrs Baggish and Chinanda are downstairs with my wife and children and the police are prepared to meet their demands.'

Silence suggested that Gudrun Schautz wasn't. Wilt put his ear to the door and listened. Perhaps the wretched creature had escaped somehow or, worse still, committed suicide.

'Are you there?' he asked inanely. A faint whimper reassured him.

'Right. Now then, nobody is going to hurt you. There is absolutely no point in staying in there and . . .' A chair was jammed under the doorhandle on the other side.

'Shit,' said Wilt, and tried to calm himself. 'Please listen to reason. If you don't come out and join them all hell is going to be let loose and someone is going to get hurt. You've got to believe me.'

But Gudrun Schautz had listened to too much unreason

194

already to believe anything. She gibbered faintly in German.

'Yes, well that's a great help,' said Wilt, suddenly conscious that his alternative had gone into overkill. He went back to the living-room and called Flint.

'We've got a problem,' he said before the Inspector stopped him.

'You've got problems, Wilt. Don't include us.'

'Yes, well we've all got problems now,' said Wilt. 'She's in the bathroom and she's locked the door and the way things sound she isn't going to come out.'

'Still your problem,' said Flint. 'You got her in there and you get her out.'

'Now hold on. Can't you persuade those two goons . . .'

'No,' said Flint and ended the discussion. With a weary sigh Wilt went back to the bathroom but the sounds inside didn't suggest that Gudrun Schautz was any more amenable to rational persuasion than before, and after putting his case as forcibly as he could and swearing to God that there were no Israelis downstairs he was driven back to the telephone.

'All I want to know,' said Flint when he answered, 'is whether she's down with Bonnie and Clyde or not. I'm not interested in . . .'

'I'll open the attic door. I'll stand where the buggers can see I'm not armed and they can come up and get her. Now will you kindly put that suggestion to the sods?'

Flint considered the offer in silence for a moment and said he would call back.

'Thank you,' said Wilt and having pulled the bed away from the door lay on it listening to his heart beat. It seemed to be making up for lost time.

Two floors below Chinanda and Baggish were edgy too. Eva's arrival, far from quietening the quads, had aroused their curiosity to new levels of disgusting frankness.

'You've got ever so many wrinkles on your tummy, Mummy,' said Samantha, putting into words what Baggish had already noticed with revulsion. 'How did you get them?'

'Well, before you were born, dear,' said Eva, who had crossed the Rubicon of modesty by hobbling naked into the house. 'Mummy's tummy was much bigger. You see, you were inside it.'

The two terrorists shuddered at the thought. It was bad enough being stuck in a kitchen and hall with those revolting children without being regaled with the physiological intimacies of their pre-natal existence in this extraordinary woman.

'What were we doing inside you?' asked Penelope.

'Growing, dear.'

'What did we eat?'

'You didn't exactly eat.'

'You can't grow unless you eat. You're always telling Josephine she won't grow up big and strong unless she eats her muesli.'

'Don't like muesli,' said Josephine. 'It's got sultanas in it.'

'I know what we ate,' said Samantha with relish, 'blood.'

In the corner by the cellar stairs Mrs de Frackas, in the throes of a stupendous hangover, opened a veined eye.

'I shouldn't be at all surprised,' she mumbled. 'Nearest thing to human vampires I've ever met. Whoever called it baby-sitting? Some damned fool.'

'But we didn't have teeth,' continued Samantha.

'No, dear, you were tied to Mummy by your umbilical cords. And what Mummy ate went through the cord . . .'

'Things can't go through cords, mummy,' said Josephine. 'Cords are string.'

'Knives can go through string,' said Samantha.

Eva looked at her appreciatively. 'Yes, dear so they can . . .'

The discussion was cut short by Baggish. 'Shut up and cover yourself,' he shouted throwing the Mexican rug from the living-room at Eva.

'I don't see how I can with my hands tied,' Eva began, but the telephone was ringing. Chinanda answered.

'No more talking. Either . . .' he said before stopping and listening. Behind him Baggish clutched his sub-machine gun and kept a wary eye on Eva.

'What are they saying?'

196

'That Gudrun won't come down,' said Chinanda. 'They want for us to go up.'

'No way. It's a trap. The police are up there. We know that.'

Chinanda took his hand from the phone. 'No one goes up and Gudrun comes down. Five minutes we give you or . . .'

'I'll go up,' Eva called out: 'The police aren't up there. My husband is. I'll bring them both down.'

The terrorists stared at her. 'Your husband?' they asked in unison. The quads joined in. 'You mean Daddy's in the attic? Oh, Mummy do bring him down. He's going to be ever so cross with Mrs de Frackas. She drank ever such a lot of Daddy's peepee.'

'You can say that again,' moaned the old lady, but Eva ignored the extraordinary statement. She was looking fixedly at the terrorists and willing them to let her go up to the flat.

'I promise you I'll . . .'

'You're lying. You want to go up there to report to the police.'

'I want to go up there to save my children,' said Eva, 'and if you don't believe me tell Inspector Flint that Henry has got to come down now.'

The terrorists moved away down the kitchen and conferred.

'If we can free Gudrun and get rid of this woman and her filthy children it's good,' said Baggish. 'We have the man and the old woman.'

Chinanda disagreed. 'We keep the children. That way the woman does nothing wrong.'

He went back to the phone and repeated Eva's message. 'Five minutes we give you only. The man Wilt comes down . . .'

'Naked,' said Eva, determined to see that Henry shared her discomfort.

'He comes down naked,' Chinanda repeated, 'and with his hands tied . . .'

'He can't tie his own hands,' said Flint practically.

'Gudrun can tie them for him,' answered Chinanda. 'Those are our conditions.'

He put the phone down and sat looking wearily at Eva. The

English were strange people. With women like this, why had they ever given up their Empire? He was roused from his reverie. Mrs de Frackas was getting woozily to her feet.

'Sit down,' he shouted at her but the old lady ignored him. She wobbled across to the sink.

'Why don't I shoot her?' said Baggish. 'That way they'll know we mean what we say.'

Mrs de Frackas squinted at him with bloodshot eyes. 'Young man,' she said, 'with a head like mine you'd be doing me a favour. Just don't miss.' And to emphasize the point she turned her back on him and stuck her bun under the cold tap.

21

In the Communications Centre there was confusion too. Flint was happily relaying the message to Wilt and enjoying his protest that it was bad enough risking death by gunshot but he didn't see why he had to go naked and risk double pneumonia into the bargain and anyway how the hell he was was going to tie his own hands together he hadn't the faintest idea, when he was stopped by the new head of the Anti-Terrorist Squad.

'Hold everything,' the Superintendent told Flint. 'The Idiot Brigade have just come up with a psycho-political profile of Wilt and it looks bad.'

'It's going to look a damned sight worse if the bastard doesn't get down out of that flat in the next three minutes,' said Flint, 'and anyway what the hell is a psycho-political profile?'

'Never mind that now. Just go into a holding pattern with the terrorists on the ground floor.'

Leaving Flint feeling like a flight controller trying to deal with two demented pilots on a collision course, he hurried through to the conference room.

'Right,' he said, 'I've ordered all armed personnel to fall back to lessen the tension. Now do we allow the swop to go ahead or not?'

Dr Felden was in no doubt. 'No,' he said. 'From the data we have accumulated there is no doubt in my mind that Wilt is a latent psychopath with extremely dangerous homicidal tendencies and to let him loose . . .'

'I cannot agree,' said Professor Maerlis. 'The transcripts of the conversations he has been having with the Schautz woman indicate a degree of ideological commitment to post-Marcusian anarchism of the highest possible order. I would go further . . .'

'We haven't time, Professor. In fact we've got precisely two minutes and all I want to know is whether to make the swop.'

'My advice is definitely negative,' said the psychiatrist. 'If we add the subject Wilt together with Gudrun Schautz to the two terrorists holding the children the effect will be explosive.'

'That's a great help,' said the Superintendent. 'We're sitting on a keg of dynamite and . . . yes, Major?'

'I suppose if we got all four of them together on the ground floor we could kill two birds with one stone,' said the Major.

The Superintendent looked at him keenly. He had never understood why the SGS had been called in from the beginning and the Major's lack of obvious logic had him baffled.

'If by that you mean we could slaughter everyone in the house I can't see any reason for going ahead with the exchange. We can do that already. The purpose of the exercise is not to kill anyone at all. I want to know how to avoid a bloodbath, not achieve one.'

But events in the house next door had already moved ahead of him. Far from getting the terrorists into a holding pattern, Flint's message that there was a slight technical hitch had met with an immediate reply that if Wilt didn't come down in exactly one minute he would be the father of triplets. But it had been Eva who had forced Wilt to act.

'Henry Wilt,' she yelled up the stairs, 'if you don't come down this minute I'll . . .'

Flint with his ear glued to the phone heard Wilt's tremulous 'Yes, dear, I'm coming.' He switched on the monitoring device in the field telephone and could hear Wilt stumbling about

199

undressing and presently his faint steps on the staircase. They were followed a moment later by the heavier tread of Eva coming up. Flint went through to the conference room and announced this latest development.

'I thought I told you . . .' began the Superintendent before sitting down heavily. 'So now we're really into a different ball-game.'

The quads had reached much the same conclusion, though they didn't put it like that. As Wilt moved cautiously across the hall into the kitchen they squealed with delight.

'Daddy's got a wigwag, Mummy's got a cunt. Mummy wee-wees down her legs and Daddy out in front,' they chanted to the amazement of the terrorists and the disgust of Mrs de Frackas.

'How utterly revolting,' she said, combining criticism of their language with her verdict on Wilt. She had never liked him with his clothes on: without them she detested him. Not only was this wretch responsible for the lethal concoction that had made her head behave like a sentient ping-pong ball in a mixing bowl, and was now, by the flaming feel of things, busily at work cauterizing her waterworks but he was presenting a full frontal view of that diabolical organ which had once helped to thrust four of the most loathsome little girls she had ever met on to an already suffering world. And all this with a blatant disregard for those social niceties to which she was accustomed. Mrs de Frackas threw caution to the winds.

'If you think for one moment I intend to remain in a house with a naked man you're much mistaken,' she said and headed for the kitchen door.

'Stay where you are,' shouted Baggish, but Mrs de Frackas had lost what little fear she had ever possessed. She kept on going.

'One more move and I fire,' yelled Baggish. Mrs de Frackas snorted derisively and moved. So did Wilt. As the gun came up he hurled himself and the quads who were clutching him out of the line of fire. It was also out of the kitchen. The cellar door

200

stood open. Wilt and his brood shot through it, cascaded down the steps, slid across the pea-strewn floor and ended up in the coal-heap. Above them a shot rang out, a thud, and the cellar door slammed to as Mrs de Frackas crashed against it and slumped to the ground.

Wilt waited no longer. He had no wish to hear any more shots. He scrambled up the pile of coal and heaved with his shoulders against the iron lid of the chute. Beneath his feet the coal slithered but the cover was moving and his head and shoulders were in the open air. The cover slid forward and Wilt crawled out before dragging each quad out and dropping the lid back in place. For a moment he hesitated. To his right were the kitchen windows, to his left the door, but beyond that were the dustbins and more usefully Eva's Organic Compost Collector. For the first time Wilt regarded the bin with gratitude. No matter what it contained it had space for them all and was, thanks to the insistence of the Health Authorities, constructed of alternative wood or concrete. Wilt hesitated long enough to scoop the quads up under his arms and then dashed for the thing and dropped them in before hurling himself on top of them.

'Oh, Daddy, this is fun,' squawked Josephine, raising a face that was largely covered with rotten tomato.

'Shut up,' snarled Wilt and shoved her down into the mess. Then, conscious that anyone opening the kitchen door might see them, he burrowed down into the stinking remains of cabbages, fish ends and the household garbage until it was almost impossible to tell where Wilt and the children began and the compost ended.

'It's ever so warm,' squeaked the indefatigable Josephine from beneath a seasoning of decomposing courgettes.

'It will be a sight warmer if you don't keep your trap shut,' said Wilt wishing to hell he had. His mouth was half-filled with eggshell and something that suggested it had once seen the inside of a vacuum cleaner and should have stayed there. Wilt spat the mixture out and as he did so there came the sound of rapid fire from somewhere within the house. The terrorists

201

were shooting at random into the darkness of the cellar. Wilt stopped spitting and wondered what the hell was going to happen to Eva now.

He had no need to worry. In the attic Eva was busy. She had already used the broken glass of the balcony window to cut the ropes on her hands and had untied her legs. Then she had gone through to the kitchen. As Wilt had passed her on the stairs he had whispered something about the bitch being in the bathroom. Eva had said nothing. She was reserving her comments on his behaviour with the bitch until the children were safe and the way to ensure that was to take Gudrun Schautz downstairs and do what the terrorists wanted. But now as she tried the bathroom door she heard the shot that had felled Mrs de Frackas. It was the signal for all the pent-up fury inside her to let itself loose. If any of the children had been murdered, the vile creature she had invited into her house would die too. And if Eva had to die she would take as many of the terrorists as she could with her. Standing in front of the bathroom door she raised a muscular leg. The next moment a further volley of shots came from below and the sole of the Eva's foot slammed forward. The door tore from its hinges and the lock splintered. Eva kicked again; the door fell back into the bath and Eva Wilt stepped over it. In the corner by the washbasin crouched a woman as naked as Eva herself. They had nothing else in common. Gudrun Schautz's body bore no marks of birth upon it. It was as smooth and synthetically attractive as the centre-page of a girlie magazine and her face mocked its appeal. From a mask of terror and madness her eyes stared blankly, her cheeks were the colour of putty, and her mouth uttered the meaningless sounds of a terrified animal.

But Eva was beyond pity. She moved forward, ponderously implacable, and then with surprising swiftness her hands struck out and clenched in the woman's hair. For a moment Gudrun Schautz struggled before Eva's knee came up. Gasping for breath and doubled over, Gudrun was dragged from the bathroom and thrown to the kitchen floor. Eva pinned her down with a knee between her shoulder blades and twisting her arms behind her tied her wrists with the electric cord before gagging her with a cloth from the sink. Finally she bound her legs together with a strip of towel.

All this Eva did with as little compunction as she would have trussed a chicken for Sunday lunch. A plan had matured in her mind, a plan that seemed almost to have been waiting for this moment, a plan born of desperation and murder. She turned and foraged in the cupboard under the sink and found what she was looking for, the rope fire escape she had had installed when the flat was first built. It was designed to hang from a hook over the balcony window to save lives in an emergency, but she had a different purpose for it now. And as more shots echoed from below she went swiftly to work. She cut the rope in two and fetched an upright chair which she placed in the middle of the bedroom facing the door. Then she dragged the bed over and wedged it on top of the chair before going back to the kitchen and pulling her captive by the ankles across the room on to the balcony. A minute later she was back with the two lengths of rope and had tied them to the legs of the chair, slid them over the hook and, leaving one slack, threaded the other under the woman's arms, wound it round her body and knotted it. The second she coiled neatly on the floor by the chair and, with unconscious expertise, looped the other end into a noose and slipped it over the terrorist's head and around her throat.

Then Gudrun Schautz, who had put the fear of death into so many other innocent people, came to know its terror herself. For a moment she squirmed on the balcony, but Eva was already back in the room and dragging on the rope round her chest. Gudrun Schautz rose sagging to her feet as Eva hauled. Then she was off the ground and level with the railing. Eva tied the rope to the bed and went back to the balcony and hoisted her over the railing. Below lay the patio and oblivion. Finally Eva removed the gag and returned to the chair. But before sitting down she opened the door to the stairs and loosened the rope from the bed. Grasping it in both hands, she played it out until it had run over the balcony rail and seemed taut. Still grasping it, she pushed the bed off the chair and sat down. Then she let go. For a second it felt as if the chair would lift under

203

the strain but her weight held it down. The moment she was shot or rose from the chair it would hurtle away across the room and the murderess now dangling on the makeshift scaffold would drop to her death by hanging. In her own frighteningly domestic way Eva Wilt had reestablished the terrible scales of Justice.

That was hardly the way it looked to the viewers in the Conference Room next door. On the TV screen Eva took on the dimensions of some archetypal Earth Mother and her actions had a symbolic quality surpassing mere reality. Even Dr Felden, whose experience of homicidal maniacs was extensive, was appalled, while Professor Maerlis, witnessing for the first time the awful preparations of a naked hangwoman, was heard to mutter something about a great beast slouching towards Bedlam. But it was the representative of the League of Personal Liberties who reacted most violently. Mr Symper could not believe his eyes.

'Dear God,' he squawked, 'she's going to hang the poor girl. She's out of her mind. Someone must stop her.'

'Can't see why, old boy,' said the Major. 'Always been in favour of capital punishment myself.'

'But it's illegal,' shrieked Mr Symper, and appealed to Mr Gosdyke, but the solicitor had shut his eyes and was considering a plea of diminished responsibility. On the whole he thought it less likely to convince a jury than justified homicide. Self-defence was clearly out. In the view of the wide-angle lens in the field telephone Eva bulked gigantic while Gudrun Schautz had the tiny proportions of one of Major-General de Frackas' toy soldiers. Professor Maerlis as usual took refuge in logic.

'An interesting ideological situation,' he said. 'I cannot think of a clearer example of social polarization. On the one hand we have Mrs Wilt and on the other . . .'

'A headless Kraut by the look of things,' said the Major enthusiastically as Eva, having hauled Gudrun Schautz into the air, shoved her over the balcony railing. 'I don't know what the proper drop for a hanging is but I should have thought forty feet was a bit excessive.'

'Excessive?' squeaked Mr Symper. 'It's positively monstrous. And what's more I take exception to your use of the word "kraut". I shall protest most vehemently to the authorities.'

'Odd bod,' said the Major as the secretary of the League of Personal Liberties rushed from the room. 'Anyone would think Mrs Wilt was the terrorist instead of a devoted mother.'

It was more or less the attitude adopted by Inspector Flint. 'Listen, mate,' he told the distraught Symper, 'you can lead as many protest marches as you fucking well like but don't come yelling at me that Mrs Bloody Wilt is a murderess. You brought her here . . .'

'I didn't know she was going to hang people. I refuse to be party to a private execution.'

'No, well you won't be that. You're an accessory. The bastards on the ground floor have bumped off Wilt and the children by the sound of things. How's that for loss of personal liberties?'

'But they wouldn't have if you had let them go. They . . .'

Flint had heard enough. Much as he had disliked Wilt the thought that this hysterical do-gooder was blaming the police for refusing to give way to the demands of a group of bloodthirsty foreigners was too much for him. He rose from his chair and grabbed Mr Symper by the lapels. 'All right, if that's the way you feel about it I'm sending you next door to persuade the Widow Wilt to come downstairs and let herself be shot by . . .'

'I won't go,' gibbered Mr Symper. 'You've no right . . .'

Flint tightened his grip and was frogmarching him backwards down the hall when Mr Gosdyke interrupted.

'Inspector, something has got to be done immediately. Mrs Wilt is taking the law into her own hands!'

'Good for her,' said Flint. 'This little shit has just volunteered to act as an emissary to our friendly neighbourhood freedom fighters . . .'

'I have done nothing of the sort,' squeaked Mr Symper. 'Mr Gosdyke, I appeal to you to . . .'

The solicitor ignored him. 'Inspector Flint, if you are prepared to give an undertaking that my client will not be held responsible, questioned, taken into custody, charged or placed on remand or in any way proceeded against for what she is evidently about to do . . .'

Flint released the egregious Mr Symper. Years of courtroom procedure told him when he was beaten. He followed Mr Gosdyke into the Conference Room and studied Eva Wilt's astonishing posterior with amazement. Gosdyke's remark about taking the law into her own hands seemed totally inappropriate. She was flattening the damned thing. Flint looked to Dr Felden.

'Mrs Wilt is obviously in an extremely disturbed mental state, Inspector. We must try to reassure her. I suggest you use the telephone . . .'

'No,' said Professor Maerlis. 'Mrs Wilt may appear from this angle to have the proportions of an attenuated gorilla, but even so I doubt if she could reach the telephone without getting off the chair.'

'And what's so wrong with that?' demanded the Major aggressively. 'The Schautz bitch has it coming to her.'

'Perhaps, but we don't want to make a martyr of her. She already has a very considerable political charisma . . .'

'Bugger her charisma,' said Flint, 'she's had the rest of the Wilt family martyred and we can always claim that her death was accidental.'

The Professor looked at him sceptically. 'You could try, I suppose, but I think you'd have some difficulty persuading the media that a woman who has been suspended from a balcony on the end of two ropes, one of which had been expertly knotted round her neck, and who was subsequently hanged and/or decapitated, died in any meaningfully accidental manner. Of course it's up to you but . . .'

'All right, then what the hell do you suggest?'

'Turn a blind eye, old boy,' said the Major. 'After all Mrs Wilt is only human . . .'

'Only?' muttered Dr Felden. 'A clearer example of anthropomorphism . . .'

'And she's got to answer the call of nature sometime.'

'Call of nature?' shouted Flint. 'She's done that already. She's squatting there like a ruddy performing elephant . . .'

'Pee, old boy, pee,' continued the Major. 'She's got to get up to have a pee sooner or later.'

'Pray later than sooner,' said the psychiatrist. 'The thought of that ghastly shape getting off that chair would be too much to bear.'

'Anyway she's probably got a bladder like a barrage balloon,' said Flint. 'Mind you, she can't be any too warm and there's nothing like cold for making one hit the piss-pot.'

'In which case it's curtains for La Schautz,' said the Major. 'Lets us off the hook, what?'

'I can think of happier ways of putting it,' said the Professor, 'and it would still leave us with the problem of Fräulein Schautz's evident martyrdom.'

Flint left them arguing and went out to look for the Superintendent. As he passed through the Communication Centre he was stopped by the sergeant. A series of squeaks and squelches was coming from one of the listening devices.

'It's the boom aimed at the kitchen window,' the sergeant explained.

'Kitchen window?' said Flint incredulously. 'Sounds more like a squad of mice tap-dancing in a septic tank. What the hell are those squeaks?'

'Children,' said the sergeant. 'Hardly likely, I know, but I've yet to hear one mouse tell another to shut its fucking trap. And it's not coming from inside the house. The two wogs have been complaining that they haven't anyone left to shoot. If you want my opinion . . .'

But Flint was already clambering across the rubble of the conservatory in search of the Superintendent. He found him lying in the grass beside the summerhouse at the bottom of the Wilts' garden, studying Gudrun Schautz's anatomy through a pair of binoculars.

'Extraordinary lengths these lunatics will go to gain some publicity,' he said by way of explanation. 'It's a good thing we've kept the TV cameras out of range.'

'She's not up there out of choice,' said Flint. 'It's Mrs Wilt's doing and we've got a chance to take the two swine on the ground floor. They're out of hostages for the time being.'

'Are they really?' said the Superintendent, and transferred his observation to the kitchen windows with some reluctance. A moment later he was refocusing his binoculars on the compost bin.

'Good God,' he muttered, 'I've heard of rapid fermentation but . . . Here, you take a look at that bin by the back door.'

Flint took the binoculars and looked. In close-up he could see what the Superintendent meant by rapid fermentation. The compost was alive. It moved, it heaved, several bean haulms rose and fell, while a beetroot suddenly emerged from the sludge and promptly disappeared again. Finally, and most disconcerting of all, something that resembled a Hallowe'en pumpkin with matted hair peered over the side of the bin.

Flint closed his eyes, opened them again and found himself looking through a mask of decaying vegetable matter at a very familiar face.

22

Five minutes later Wilt was hauled unceremoniously from the compost heap while a dozen armed policemen aimed guns at the kitchen door and windows.

'Bang, bang, you're dead,' squealed Josephine as she was lifted from the mess. A constable bundled her through the hedge and went back for Penelope. Inside the house the terrorists made no move. They were being occupied on the phone by Flint.

'You can forget any deals,' he was saying as the Wilt family were led through the conservatory. 'Either you come out with your hands up and no guns or we're coming in firing, and after the first ten bullets you won't know what hit you . . . Christ, what's that revolting smell?'

'It says it's called Samantha,' said the constable who was carrying the foetid child.

'Well take it away and disinfect the beastly thing,' said Flint, groping for a handkerchief.

'I don't want to be disinfected,' bawled Samantha. Flint turned a weary eye on the group and for a moment had the nightmarish feeling that he was looking at something in an advanced state of decomposition. But the vision faded. He could see now that it was simply Wilt clotted with compost.

'Well, look what the cat dragged in. If it isn't Compost Casanova himself, our beanstalk hero of the hour. I've seen some sickening sights in my time but . . .'

'Charming,' said Wilt. 'Considering what I've just been through I can do without cracks about *nostalgie de la boue*. And what about Eva? She's still in there and if you start shooting . . .'

'Shut up, Wilt,' said Flint, lumbering to his feet. 'For your information, if it weren't for Mrs Wilt's latest enthusiasm for hanging people we'd have been into that house an hour ago.'

'Her enthusiasm for *what*?'

'Someone give him a blanket,' said Flint, 'I've seen enough of this human vegetable to last me a lifetime.' He went into the Conference Room followed by Wilt wrapped rather meagrely in one of Mrs de Frackas' shawls.

'Gentlemen, I'd like you all to meet Mr Henry Wilt,' he told the dumbfounded Psycho-Warfare Team, 'or should I say Comrade Wilt?'

Wilt didn't hear the crack. He was staring at the television screen. 'That's Eva,' he said numbly.

'Yes, well, it takes one to know one, I suppose,' said Flint, 'and on the end of all those ropes is your playmate, Gudrun Schautz. The moment your missus gets up from that chair you're going to find yourself married to the first British female executioner. Now that's fine with me. I'm all in favour of capital punishment and women's lib. Unfortunately these gentlemen don't share my lack of prejudice and home hanging is against the law, so if you don't want to see Mrs Wilt on a charge of justifiable homicide you'd better come up with something quick.' But Wilt sat staring in dismay at the screen. His own alternative terrorism had been tame by comparison with Eva's. She was sitting there calmly waiting to be murdered and had devised a hideous deterrent.

'Can't you call her on the telephone?' he asked finally.

'Use your loaf. The moment she gets off . . .'

'Quite,' said Wilt hastily. 'And I don't suppose there's any way of putting a net or something under Miss Schautz. I mean . . .'

Flint laughed nastily. 'Oh, it's Miss Schautz now, is it? Such modesty. Considering that only a few hours ago you were pork-swording the bitch I must say I find . . .'

'Under duress,' said Wilt. 'You don't think I make a habit of leaping into bed with killers, do you?'

'Wilt,' said Flint, 'what you do in your spare time is no concern of mine. Or wouldn't be if you kept within the limits of the law. Instead of which you fill your house with terrorists and give them lectures in the theory of mass murder.'

'But that was—'

'Don't argue. We've got every word you said on tape. We've built up a psycho . . .'

'Profile,' prompted Dr Felden, studying Wilt in preference to watching Eva on the screen.

'Thank you, doctor. A psycho-profile of you . . .'

'Psycho-political profile,' said Professor Maerlis. 'I would like to hear Mr Wilt explain where he gained such an extensive knowledge of the theory of terrorism.'

Wilt scraped a carrot-peeling from his ear and sighed. It was always the same. No one ever understood him: no one ever would. He was a creature of infinite incomprehensibility and the world was filled with idiots, himself included. And all the time Eva was in danger of being killed and killing. He got wearily to his feet.

'All right, if that's the way you want it I'll go back into the house and put it to those maniacs that . . .'

'Like hell you will,' said Flint. 'You'll stay exactly where you are and come up with a solution to the mess you've got us all into.'

Wilt sat down again. There was no way he could think of to end the stalemate. Happenstance reigned supreme and only chaos could be counted on to determine man's fate.

As if to confirm this opinion there came the sound of a dull rumble from the house next door. It was followed by a violent explosion and the crash of breaking glass.

'My God, the swine have blown themselves up kamikaze-style,' shouted Flint as several toy soldiers toppled on the ping-pong table. He turned and hurried into the Communications Centre with the rest of the Psycho-Warfare Team. Only Wilt remained behind staring fixedly at the television screen. For a moment Eva had seemed to lift from the chair, but she had settled back again and was sitting there as stolidly as ever. From the other room the sergeant could be heard shouting his version of the disaster to Flint.

'I don't know what happened. One moment they were arguing about giving themselves up and claiming we were using poison gas and the next minute the balloon had gone up. I shouldn't think they knew what hit them.'

But Wilt did. With a cheerful smile he stood up and went into the conservatory.

'If you'll just follow me,' he told Flint and the others, 'I can explain everything.'

'Hold it there, Wilt,' said Flint. 'Let's get something straight. Are you by any chance suggesting that you're responsible for that explosion?'

'Only in passing,' said Wilt with the sublime confidence of a man who knew he was telling nothing but the truth, 'only in passing. I don't know if you're at all acquainted with the workings of the bio-loo but—'

'Oh shit,' said Flint.

'Precisely, Inspector. Now shit is converted anaerobically in the bio-loo or, more properly speaking, the alternative toilet, into methane, and methane is a gas which ignites with the greatest of ease in the presence of air. And Eva has been into self-sufficiency in what you may well call a big way. She had dreams of cooking by perpetual motion, or rather by perpetual motions. So the cooker is hooked to the bio-loo and what goes in one end has got to come out the other and vice versa. Take a boiled egg for instance . . .'

Flint looked incredulously at him. 'Boiled eggs?' he shouted. 'Are you seriously telling me that boiled eggs . . . oh no. No, definitely no. We've been through the pork-pie routine before. You're not fooling me this time. I'm going to get to the bottom of this.'

'Anatomically speaking . . .' began Wilt, but Flint was already floundering through the conservatory into the garden. One glance over the fence was enough to convince him that Wilt was right. The few remaining windows on the ground floor of the house were spattered with blobs of stained yellow paper and something else. But it was the stench that hit him which was so convincing. The Inspector groped for his handkerchief. Two extraordinary figures had lurched through the shattered patio windows. As terrorists they were unrecognizable. Chinanda and Baggish had taken the full force of the bio-loo and were perfect examples of the worth of their own ideology.

'Shits in shits' clothing,' murmured Professor Maerlis, gazing in awe at the human excreta that stumbled about the lawn.

'Hold it there,' shouted the head of the Anti-Terrorist Squad as his men aimed revolvers at them, 'we've got you covered.'

'Rather an unnecessary injunction if you ask me,' said Dr Felden. 'I've heard of bullshit baffling brains but I've never realized the destabilizing potential of untreated sewage before.'

But the two terrorists were past caring about the destruction of pseudo-democratic fascism. Their concern was purely personal. They rolled on the ground in a frantic attempt to rid themselves of the filth while above them Gudrun Schautz looked down with an idiot smile.

As Baggish and Chinanda were dragged to their feet by reluctant policemen Wilt entered the house. He passed through the devastated kitchen and stepped over old Mrs de Frackas and climbed the stairs. On the landing he hesitated.

'Eva,' he called, 'it's me, Henry. It's all right. The children are safe. The terrorists are under arrest. Now don't get up from that chair. I'm coming up.'

212

'I warn you if this is some sort of trick I won't be responsible for what happens,' shouted Eva.

Wilt smiled to himself happily. That was the old Eva talking in defiance of all logic. He went up to the attic and stood in the doorway looking at her with open admiration. There was nothing silly about Eva now. Sitting naked and unashamed she possessed a strength he would never have.

'Darling,' he began incautiously before stopping. Eva was studying him with frank disgust.

'Don't you "darling" me, Henry Wilt,' she said. 'And how did you get in that filthy state?'

Wilt looked down at his torso. Now that he came to examine it he was in a filthy state. A piece of celery poked rather ambiguously from Mrs de Frackas' shawl.

'Well, as a matter of fact, I was in the compost heap with the children . . .'

'With the children?' shouted Eva furiously. 'In the compost heap?'

And before Wilt could explain she had risen from the chair. As it shot across the room Wilt hurled himself at the rope, clung to it, was slammed against the opposite wall and finally managed to wedge himself behind a wardrobe.

'For Christ's sake, help me pull her up,' he yelled, 'you can't let the bitch hang.'

Eva put her hands on her hips. 'That's your problem. I'm not doing anything to her. You're holding the rope.'

'Only just. And I suppose you're going to tell me that if I really love you I'll let go. Well, let me tell you . . .'

'Don't bother,' shouted Eva. 'I heard you in bed with her. I know what you got up to.'

'Up to?' yelled Wilt. 'The only way I got anything up was by pretending she was you. I know it seems unlikely . . .'

'Henry Wilt, if you think I'm going to stand here and let you insult me . . .'

'I'm not insulting you. I'm paying you the biggest bloody compliment you've ever received. Without you I don't know what I would have done. And now for goodness sake—'

'I know what you did without me,' shouted Eva, 'you made love to that horrible woman . . .'

'Love?' yelled Wilt. 'That wasn't love. That was war. The bitch battened on to me like a sex-starved barnacle and . . .' But it was too late to explain. The wardrobe was shifting and the next moment Wilt, still gripping the rope, rose slowly into the air and moved toward the hook. Behind him came the chair and presently he was crouched up against the ceiling with his head twisted at a curious angle. Eva looked up at him uncertainly. For a second she hesitated, but she couldn't let him stay there and it was wrong to hang the German girl now that the quads were safe.

Eva grabbed Wilt's legs and began to pull. Outside the police had reached Gudrun Schautz and were cutting her down. As the rope broke Wilt fell from his perch and mingled with portions of the chair.

'Oh my poor darling,' said Eva, her voice suddenly taking on a new and, to Wilt, thoroughly alarming solicitude. It was typical of the bloody woman to practically turn him into a cripple and then be conscience-stricken. As she took him in her arms Wilt groaned and decided the time had come to put the boot in diplomatically. He passed out.

On the patio below Gudrun Schautz was unconscious too. Before she could be more than partially strangled she had been lifted down and now the head of the Anti-Terrorist Squad was giving her the kiss of life rather more passionately than was called for. Flint dragged himself away from this unnatural relationship and cautiously entered the house. A hole in the kitchen floor testified to the destructive force of a ruptured bio-loo. 'Out of their tiny minds,' he muttered behind his handkerchief and slithered through into the hall before climbing the stairs to the attic. The scene that greeted him there confirmed his opinion. The Wilts were clasped in one another's arms. Flint shuddered. He would never understand what these two diabolical people saw in one another. Come to think of it, he didn't want to know. There were some mysteries better left unprobed. He turned back towards his more orderly world where there were no such awful ambiguities and was greeted on the landing by the quads. They were dressed in some clothes they had found in Mrs de Frackas' chest of drawers and wearing hats that had been fashionable before the First World War. As they tried to rush past him Flint stopped them.

'I don't think your mummy and daddy want to be disturbed,' he said, firmly holding to the view that nice children should be spared the sight of their naked parents presumably making love. But the Wilt quads had never been nice.

'What are they doing?' asked Samantha.

Flint swallowed. 'They're . . . er . . . engaged.'

'You mean they're not married?' asked Samantha gleefully adjusting her boa.

'I didn't say that . . .' began Flint.

'Then we're bastards,' squealed Josephine. 'Michael's daddy says if mummies and daddies aren't married their babies are called bastards.'

Flint stared down at the hideously precocious child. 'You can say that again,' he muttered, and went on downstairs. Above him the quads could be heard chanting something about daddies having wigwags and mummies having . . . Flint hurried out of earshot and found the stench in the kitchen a positive relief. Two ambulance men were carrying Mrs de Frackas out on a stretcher. Amazingly she was still alive.

'Bullet lodged in her stays,' said one of the ambulance men. 'Tough old bird. Don't make them like this any more.'

Mrs de Frackas opened a beady eye. 'Are the children still alive?' she asked faintly.

Flint nodded. 'It's all right. They're quite safe. You needn't worry about them.'

'Them?' moaned Mrs de Frackas. 'You can't seriously suppose I'm worried about them. It's the thought that I'll have to live next door to the little savages that . . .'

But the effort to express her horror was too much for her and she sank back on the pillow. Flint followed her out to the ambulance.

'Take me off the drip,' she pleaded as they loaded her inside.

'Can't do that, mum,' said the ambulance man, 'it's against union rules.'

He shut the doors and turned to Flint. 'Suffering from shock, poor old dear. They get like that sometimes. Don't know what they're saying.'

But Flint knew better, and as the ambulance drove away his heart went out to the courageous old lady. He was thinking of asking for a transfer himself.

23

It was the end of term at the Tech. Wilt walked across the common with the frost on the grass, ducks waddling by the river and the sun shining out of a cloudless sky. He had no committee meetings to attend and no teaching to do. About the only cloud on the horizon was the possibility that the Principal might congratulate the Wilt family on their remarkable escape from danger. To avert it Wilt had already intimated to the Vice-Principal that such rank hypocrisy would be in the worst of taste. If the Principal were to express his true feelings he would have to admit that he wished to hell the terrorists had carried out their promises.

Dr Mayfield was certainly of this opinion. The Special Branch had been going through the students in Advanced English For Foreigners with a fine-tooth comb and the Anti-Terrorist Squad had detained two Iraquis for questioning. Even the curriculum had been under scrutiny and Professor Maerlis, ably assisted by Dr Board, had submitted a report condemning the seminars on Contemporary Theories of Revolution and Social Change as positively subversive and inciting to violence. And Dr Board had helped to exonerate Wilt.

'Considering the political lunatics he has to cope with in his department it's a wonder Wilt isn't a raving fascist. Take

Bilger for example . . .' he had told the Special Branch officer in charge of enquiries. The officer had taken Bilger. He had also screened the film and had viewed it with incredulity.

'If this is the sort of filth you encourage your lecturers to produce it's no bloody wonder the country is in the mess it is,' he told the Principal, who had promptly tried to shift the blame to Wilt.

'I always considered the thing a disgrace,' said Wilt, 'and if you'll check the minutes of the Education Committee meeting you'll see I wanted to make the issue public. I think parents have a right to know when their children are being politically indoctrinated.'

And the minutes had proved him right. From that moment Wilt was given a clean ticket. Officially.

But on the domestic front suspicion still lurked. Eva had taken to waking him in the small hours to demand proof that he loved her.

'Of course I do, damn it,' grunted Wilt. 'How many times do I have to tell you?'

'Actions speak louder than words,' retorted Eva snuggling up to him.

'Oh all right,' said Wilt. And the exercise had done him good. It was a leaner, healthier Wilt who walked briskly to the Tech, and the knowledge that he would never have to take this path again buoyed his spirits. They were moving from Willington Road. The removal van had already arrived when he left and this afternoon the home he returned to would be 45 Oakhurst Avenue. The choice of the new house had been Eva's. It was a several steps down the social ladder from Willington Road, but the big house there had bad vibes for her. Wilt deplored the word but agreed. He had always disliked the pretensions of the neighbourhood and Oakhurst Avenue was nicely anonymous.

'At least we'll be away from haute academe and the relicts of Imperial arrogance,' he told Peter Braintree as they sat in The Pig In The Poke after the Principal's pep talk. There had been no mention of Wilt's ordeal and they were celebrating. 'And there's a quiet little pub round the corner so I won't have to brew my own gutrot.'

'Thank heavens for that. But won't Eva pine for the compost heap and all that?'

Wilt drank his beer cheerfully. 'The educative effects of exploding septic tanks have to be seen to be believed,' he said. 'To say that ours revealed the fundamental flaws in the Alternative Society might be going too far but it certainly blew Eva's mind. I've noticed she's taken to medicated toilet paper and it wouldn't surprise me to learn she's making tea with distilled water.'

'But she'll have to find something to occupy her energy.'

Wilt nodded. 'She has. The quads. She's determined to see they don't grow up in the image of Gudrun Schautz. A losing battle, to my way of thinking, but at least I've managed to prise her away from sending them to the Convent. It's remarkable how much better their language has become of late. All in all I have an idea that life is going to be more peaceful from now on.'

But as with so many of Wilt's predictions this one was premature. When, having spent an hour tidying his office, he sauntered contentedly up Oakhurst Avenue it was to find the new house unlit and empty. There was no sign of Eva, the quads or the furniture van. He waited about for an hour and then phoned from a call-box. Eva exploded at the other end.

'Don't blame me,' she shouted, 'the removal men have had to unload the van.'

'Unload the van? What on earth for?'

'Because Josephine hid in the wardrobe and they put that in first, that's why.'

'But they don't have to unload because of that,' said Wilt. 'She wouldn't suffocate and it would teach her a lesson'

'And what about Mrs de Frackas' cat and the Balls' poodle and Jennifer Willis' four pet rabbits . . .'

'The what?' said Wilt.

'She was playing hostages,' shouted Eva, 'and . . .'

But the coin in the phone box ran out. Wilt didn't bother to put another in. He strolled out along the street wondering what it was about his marriage with Eva that turned everyday events into minor catastrophes. He couldn't bring himself to think what sort of time Josephine was having in the wardrobe. Talk about trauma . . . Oh well, there was nothing like experience. As he passed along Oakhurst Avenue towards the pub Wilt suddenly felt pity for his new neighbours. They still had no idea what was going to hit them.

The Great Pursuit

1

When anyone asked Frensic why he took snuff he replied that it was because by rights he should have lived in the eighteenth century. It was, he said, the century best suited to his temperament and way of life, the age of reason, of style, of improvement and expansion and those other characteristics he so manifestly possessed. That he didn't, and happened to know that the eighteenth century hadn't either, only heightened his pleasure at his own affectation and the amazement of his audience and, by way of paradox, justified his claim to be spiritually at home with Sterne, Swift, Smollett, Richardson, Fielding and other giants of the rudimentary novel whose craft Frensic so much admired. Since he was a literary agent who despised nearly all the novels he handled so successfully, Frensic's private eighteenth century was that of Grub Street and Gin Lane and he paid homage to it by affecting an eccentricity and cynicism which earned him a useful reputation and armoured him against the literary pretensions of unsaleable authors. In short he bathed only occasionally, wore woollen vests throughout the summer, ate a great deal more than was good for him, drank port before lunch and took snuff in large quantities so that anyone wishing to deal with him had to prove their hardiness by running the gauntlet of these deplorable habits. He also arrived early for work, read every manuscript that was submitted to him, promptly returned those he couldn't sell and just as promptly sold the others and in general conducted his business with surprising efficiency. Publishers took Frensic's opinions seriously. When Frensic said a book would sell, it sold. He had a nose for a bestseller, an infallible nose.

It was, he liked to think, something he had inherited from his father, a successful wine-merchant whose own nose for a palatable claret at a popular price had paid for that expensive education which, together with Frensic's more metaphysical nose, gave him the edge over his competitors. Not that the connection between a good education and his success as a connoisseur of commercially rewarding literature was direct.

5

He had arrived at his talent circuitously and if his admiration for the eighteenth century, while real, nevertheless concealed an inversion, it was by exactly the same process that he had arrived at his success as a literary agent.

At twenty-one he had come down from Oxford with a second-class degree in English and the ambition to write a great novel. After a year behind the counter of his father's wine shop in Greenwich and at his desk in a room in Blackheath the 'great' had been abandoned. Three more years as an advertising copywriter and the author of a rejected novel about life behind the counter of a wine shop in Greenwich had completed the demolition of his literary ambitions. At twenty-four Frensic hadn't needed his nose to tell him he would never be a novelist. The two dozen literary agents who had refused to handle his work had said so already. On the other hand his experience of them had revealed a profession entirely to his taste. Literary agents, it was obvious, lived interesting, comfortable and thoroughly civilized lives. If they didn't write novels, they met novelists, and Frensic was still idealistic enough to imagine that this was a privilege; they spent their days reading books; they were their own masters, and if his own experience was anything to go by they showed an encouraging lack of literary perspicacity. In addition they seemed to spend a great deal of time eating and drinking and going to parties, and Frensic, whose appearance tended to limit his sensual pleasures to putting things into himself rather than into other people, was something of a gourmet. He had found his vocation.

At twenty-five he opened an office in King Street next to Covent Garden and sufficiently close to Curtis Brown, the largest literary agency in London, to occasion some profitable postal confusion, and advertised his services in the *New Statesman*, whose readers seemed more prone to pursue those literary ambitions he had so recently relinquished. Having done that he sat down and waited for the manuscripts to arrive. He had to wait a long time and he was beginning to wonder just how long his father could be persuaded to pay the rent when the postman delivered two parcels. The first contained a novel by Miss Celia Thwaite of The Old Pumping

Station, Bishop's Stortford and a letter explaining that *Love's Lustre* was Miss Thwaite's first book. Reading it with increasing nausea, Frensic had no reason to doubt her word. The thing was a hodgepodge of romantic drivel and historical inaccuracy and dealt at length with the unconsummated love of a young squire for the wife of an absent-bodied crusader whose obsession with his wife's chastity seemed to reflect an almost pathological fetishism on the part of Miss Thwaite herself. Frensic wrote a polite note explaining that *Love's Lustre* was not a commercial proposition and posted the manuscript back to Bishop's Stortford.

The contents of the second package seemed at first sight to be more promising. Again it was a first novel, this time called *Search for a Lost Childhood* by a Mr P. Piper who gave as his address the Seaview Boarding House, Folkestone. Frensic read the novel and found it perceptive and deeply moving. Mr Piper's childhood had not been a happy one but he wrote discerningly about his unsympathetic parents and his own troubled adolescence in East Finchley. Frensic promptly sent the book to Jonathan Cape and informed Mr Piper that he foresaw an immediate sale followed by critical acclaim. He was wrong. Cape rejected the book. Bodley Head rejected it. Collins rejected it. Every publisher in London rejected it with comments that ranged from the polite to the derisory. Frensic conveyed their opinions in diluted form to Piper and entered into a correspondence with him about ways of improving it to meet the publishers' requirements.

He was just recovering from this blow to his acumen when he received another. A paragraph in *The Bookseller* announced that Miss Celia Thwaite's first novel, *Love's Lustre*, had been sold to Collins for fifty thousand pounds, to an American publisher for a quarter of a million dollars, and that she stood a good chance of winning The Georgette Heyer Memorial Prize for Romantic Fiction. Frensic read the paragraph incredulously and underwent a literary conversion. If publishers were prepared to pay such enormous sums for a book which Frensic's educated taste had told him was romantic trash, then everything he had learnt from F. R Leavis and more directly from his own supervisor at Oxford, Dr Sydney Louth, about the modern novel was entirely false in the world of commercial publishing; worse still it constituted a deadly threat to his own career as a literary agent. From that moment of revelation Frensic's outlook changed. He did not discard his educated standards. He stood them on their head. Any novel that so much as approximated to the criteria laid down by Leavis in *The Great Tradition* and more vehemently by Miss Sydney Louth in her work, *The Moral Novel*, he rejected out of hand as totally unsuitable for publication while those books they would have dismissed as beneath contempt he pushed for all he was worth. By virtue of this remarkable reversal Frensic prospered. By the time he was thirty he had established an enviable reputation among publishers as an agent who recommended only those books that would sell. A novel from Frensic could be relied upon to need no alterations and little editing. It would be exactly eighty thousand words long or, in the case of historical romance where the readers were more voracious, one hundred and fifty thousand. It would start with a bang, continue with more bangs and end happily with an even bigger bang. In short, it would contain all those ingredients that public taste most appreciated.

But if the novels Frensic submitted to publishers needed few changes, those that arrived on his desk from aspiring authors seldom passed his scrutiny without fundamental alteration. Having discovered the ingredients of popular success in *Love's Lustre*, Frensic applied them to every book he handled so that they emerged from the process of rewriting like literary plum puddings or blended wines and incorporated sex, violence, thrills, romance and mystery, with the occasional dollop of significance to give them cultural respectability. Frensic was very keen on cultural respectability. It ensured reviews in the better papers and gave readers the illusion that they were participating in a pilgrimage to a shrine of meaning. What the meaning was remained, necessarily, unclear. It came under the general heading of meaningfulness but without it a section of the public who despised mere escapism would have been lost to Frensic's authors. He therefore always insisted on significance, and while on the whole he lumped it with insight and sensibility as being in any large measure as lethal to a book's chances as a pint of strychnine in a clear soup, in homeopathic doses it had a tonic effect on sales.

So did Sonia Futtle, whom Frensic chose as a partner to handle foreign publishers. She had previously worked for a New York agency and being an American her contacts with US publishers were invaluable. And the American market was extremely profitable. Sales were larger, the percentage from authors' royalties greater, and the incentives offered by Book Clubs enormous. Appropriately for one who was to expand their business in this direction, Sonia Futtle had already expanded personally in most others and was of distinctly unmarriageable proportions. It was this as much as anything that had persuaded Frensic to change the agency's name to Frensic & Futtle and to link his impersonal fortune with hers. Besides, she was an enthusiast for books which dealt with interpersonal relations and Frensic had developed an allergy to interpersonal relationships. He concentrated on less demanding books, thrillers, detective stories, sex when unromantic, historical novels when unsexual, campus novels, science fiction and violence. Sonia Futtle handled romantic sex, historical romance, liberation books whether of women or negroes, adolescent traumas, interpersonal relationships and animals. She was particularly good with animals, and Frensic, who had once almost lost a finger to the heroine of *Otters to Tea*, was happy to leave this side of the business to her. Given the chance he would have relinquished Piper too. But Piper stuck to Frensic as the only agent ever to have offered him the slightest encouragement and Frensic, whose success was in inverse proportion to Piper's failure, reconciled himself to the knowledge that he could never abandon Piper and that Piper would never abandon his confounded *Search for a Lost Childhood*.

Each year he arrived in London with a fresh version of his novel and Frensic took him out to lunch and explained what was wrong with it while Piper argued that a great novel must deal with real people in real situations and could never conform to Frensic's blatantly commercial formula. And each year they would part amicably, Frensic to wonder at the man's incredible perseverance and Piper to start work in a different boarding-house in a different seaside town on a different search for the same lost childhood. And so year after year the novel was partially transformed and the style altered to suit Piper's latest model. For this Frensic had no one to blame but himself. Early in their acquaintance he had rashly recommended Miss Louth's essays in *The Moral Novel* to Piper as something he ought to study and, while Frensic had come to regard her appreciations of the great novelists of the past as pernicious to anyone trying to write a novel today, Piper had adopted her standards as his own. Thanks to Miss Louth he had produced a Lawrence version of *Search for a Lost Childhood*, then a Henry James; James had been superseded by Conrad, then by George Eliot; there had been a Dickens version and even a Thomas Wolfe; and one awful summer a Faulkner. But through them all there stalked the figure of Piper's father, his miserable mother and the self-consciously pubescent Piper himself. Derivation followed derivation but the insights remained implacably trite and the action non-existent. Frensic despaired but remained loyal. To Sonia Futtle his attitude was incomprehensible.

'What do you do it for?' she asked. 'He's never going to make it and those lunches cost a fortune.'

'He is my *memento mori*,' said Frensic cryptically, conscious that the death Piper served to remind him of was his own, the aspiring young novelist he himself had once been and on the betrayal of whose literary ideals the success of Frensic & Futtle depended.

But if Piper occupied one day in his year, a day of atonement, for the rest Frensic pursued his career more profitably. Blessed with an excellent appetite, an impervious liver and an inexpensive source of fine wines from his father's cellars, he was able to entertain lavishly. In the world of publishing this was an immense advantage. While other agents wobbled home from those dinners over which books are conceived, publicized or bought, Frensic went portly on eating, drinking and advocating his novels *ad nauseam* and boasting of his 'finds'. Among the latter was James Jamesforth, a writer whose novels were of such unmitigated success that he was compelled for tax purposes to wander the world like some alcoholic fugitive from fame.

It was thanks to Jamesforth's itinerantly drunken progress from one tax haven to the next that Frensic found himself in the witness box in the High Court of Justice, Queen's Bench Division in the libel case of Mrs Desdemona Humberson *versus* James Jamesforth, author of *Fingers of Hell*, and Pulteney Press, publishers of the said novel. Frensic was in the witness box for two hours and by the time he stepped down he was a shaken man.

2

'Fifteen *thousand* pounds plus costs,' said Sonia Futtle next morning, 'for inadvertent libel? I don't believe it.'

'It's in the paper,' said Frensic handing her *The Times*. 'Next to the bit about the drunken lorry driver who killed two children and got fined a hundred and fifty pounds. Mind you he did lose his licence for three months too.'

'But that's insane. A hundred and fifty pounds for killing two children and fifteen thousand for libelling a woman James didn't even know existed.'

'On a zebra crossing,' said Frensic bitterly. 'Don't forget the zebra crossing.'

'Mad. Stark staring raving mad,' said Sonia. 'You English are out of your minds legally.'

'So's Jamesforth,' said Frensic, 'and you can forget him as one of our authors. He doesn't want to know us.'

'But we didn't do anything. We aren't supposed to check his proofs out. Pulteneys should have done that. They'd have spotted the libel.'

'Like hell they would. How does anyone spot a woman called Desdemona Humberson living in the wilds of Somerset who grows lupins and belongs to the Women's Institute? She's too improbable for words.'

'She's also done very nicely for herself. Fifteen grand for being called a nymphomaniac. It's worth it. I mean if someone called me a raving nymphomaniac I'd be only too glad to accept fifteen—'

'Doubtless,' said Frensic, forestalling a discussion of this highly unlikely eventuality. 'And for fifteen thousand I'd have hired a drunken lorry driver and had her erased on a zebra crossing. Split the difference with the driver and we would have still been to the good. And while I was about it I would have had Mr Galbanum slaughtered too. He should have had more sense than to advise Pulteneys and Jamesforth to fight the case.'

'Well it was innocent libel,' said Sonia. 'James didn't mean to malign the woman.'

'Oh quite. The fact remains that he did and under the Defamation Act of 1952 designed to protect authors and publishers from actions of this sort, innocent libel demands that they show they took reasonable care—'

'Reasonable care? What does that mean?'

'According to that senile old judge it means going to Somerset House and checking to see if anyone called Desdemona was born in 1928 and married a man called Humberson in 1951. Then you go throught the Lupin Growers' Association Handbook looking for Humbersons and if they're not there you have a whack at the Women's Institute and finally the telephone directory for Somerset. Well, they didn't do all that so they got lumbered for fifteen thousand and we've got the reputation of handling authors who libel innocent women. Send your novels to Frensic & Futtle and get sued. We are the pariahs of the publishing world.'

'It can't be as bad as all that. After all, it's the first time it's happened and everyone knows that James is a souse who can't remember where he's been or who he's done.'

'Can't they just. Pulteneys can. Hubert rang up last night to say that we needn't send them any more novels. Once *that* word gets round we are going to have what is euphemistically called a cash flow problem.'

'We're certainly going to have to find someone to replace James,' said Sonia. 'Bestsellers like that don't grow on trees.'

'Nor lupins,' said Frensic and retired to his office.

All in all it was a bad day. The phone rang almost incessantly. Authors demanded to know if they were likely to end up in the

High Court of Justice, Queen's Bench Division, because they had used the names of people they were at school with, and publishers turned down novels they would previously have accepted. Frensic sat and took snuff and tried to remain civil. By five o'clock he was finding it increasingly difficult and when the Literary Editor of the *Sunday Graphic* phoned to ask if Frensic would contribute an article on the iniquities of the British libel laws he was downright rude.

'What do you want me to do?' he shouted. 'Stick my head in a bloody noose and get hauled up for contempt of court? For all I know that blithering idiot Jamesforth is going to appeal against the verdict.'

'On the grounds that you inserted the passage which libelled Mrs Humberson?' the editor asked. 'After all it was suggested by the defence counsel—'

'By God, I'll have you for slander,' shouted Frensic. 'Galbanum had the gall to say that in court where he's protected but if you repeat that in public I'll institute proceedings myself.'

'You'd have a hard time,' said the editor. 'Jamesforth wouldn't make a good witness. He swears you advised him to jack Mrs Humberson up sexwise and when he wouldn't you altered the proofs.'

'That's a downright lie,' yelled Frensic. 'Anyone would think I wrote my authors' novels for them!'

'As a matter of fact a great many people do believe just that,' said the editor. Frensic hurled imprecations and went home with a headache.

If Wednesday was bad, Thursday was no better. Collins rejected William Lonroy's fifth novel *Seventh Heaven* as being too explicit sexually. Triad Press turned down Mary Gold's *Final Fling* for the opposite reason and Cassells even refused *Sammy The Squirrel* on the grounds that it was preoccupied with individual acquisition and lacked community concern. Cape rejected this, Secker rejected that. There were no acceptances. Finallly there was a moment of high drama when an elderly clergyman whose autobiography Frensic had repeatedly refused to handle, explaining each time there wasn't a large reading public for a book that dealt exclusively with parish life in South Croydon, smashed a vase with his umbrella and only consented to leave with his manuscript when Sonia threatened to call the police. By lunchtime Frensic was bordering on hysteria.

'I can't stand it,' he whimpered. The phone rang and Frensic shied. 'If it's for me, tell them I'm not in. I'm having a breakdown. Tell them—'

It was for him. Sonia put her hand over the mouthpiece.

'It's Margot Joseph. She says she's dried up and doesn't think she can finish—'

Frensic fled to the safety of his own office and took his phone off the hook.

'For the rest of the day I'm not in,' he told Sonia when she came through a few minutes later. 'I shall sit here and think.'

'In that case you can read this,' said Sonia and put a parcel on his desk. 'It came this morning. I haven't had time to open it.'

'It's probably a bomb,' said Frensic gloomily and undid the string. But the package contained nothing more threatening than a neatly typed manuscript and an envelope addressed to Mr F. A. Frensic. Frensic glanced at the manuscript and noted with satisfaction that its pages were pristine and its corners unthumbed, a healthy sign which indicated that he was the first recipient and that it hadn't gone the rounds of other agents. Then he looked at the title-page. It said simply PAUSE O MEN FOR THE VIRGIN, A Novel. There was no author's name and no return address. Odd. Frensic opened the envelope and read the letter inside. It was brief and impersonal and mystifying.

> *Cadwalladine & Dimkins*
> *Solicitors*
> *596 St Andrew's Street*
> *Oxford*

Dear Sir,
All communications concerning the possible sale, publication and copyright of the enclosed manuscript should be addressed to this office marked for the Personal Attention of P. Cadwalladine.

*The author, who wishes to remain strictly anonymous, leaves
the matter of terms of sale and choice of a suitable non de plume
and related matters entirely in your hands.
Yours faithfully,
Percy Cadwalladine.*

Frensic read the letter through several times before turning his
attention to the manuscript. It was a very odd letter. An author
who wished to remain strictly anonymous? Left everything
concerning sale and choice of *nom de plume* and related matters entirely in his hands? Considering that all the authors he
had ever dealt with were notoriously egotistical and interfering
there was a lot to be said for one who was so self-effacing.
Positively endearing, in fact. With the silent wish that Mr
Jamesforth had left everything in his hands Frensic turned the
title page of *Pause O Men for the Virgin* and began to read.

He was still reading an hour later, his snuff box open on the
desk and his waistcoat and the creases of his trousers powdered
with snuff. Frensic reached unthinkingly for the box and took
another large pinch and wiped his nose with his third handkerchief. In the next office the phone rang. People climbed the
stairs and knocked on Sonia's door. Traffic rumbled outside in
the street. Frensic was oblivious to these extraneous sounds.
He turned another page and read on.

It was half past six when Sonia Futtle finished for the day and
prepared to leave. The door of Frensic's office was shut and
she hadn't heard him go. She opened it and peered inside.
Frensic was sitting at his desk staring fixedly through the window over the dark roofs of Covent Garden with a slight smile
on his face. It was an attitude she recognized, the posture of
triumphant discovery.

'I don't believe it,' she said standing in the doorway.

'Read it,' said Frensic. 'Don't believe me. Read it for yourself.' His hand flicked dismissively towards the manuscript.

'A good one?'

'A bestseller.'

'Are you sure?'

'Positive.'

15

'And of course it's a novel?'

'One hopes so,' said Frensic, 'fervently.'

'A dirty book,' said Sonia, who recognized the symptoms.

'Dirty,' said Frensic, 'is hardly adequate. The mind that penned – if minds can pen – this odyssey of lust is of a prurience indescribable.' He got up and handed her the manuscript. 'I will value your opinion,' he said with the air of a man who had regained his authority.

But if it was a jaunty Frensic who went home to his flat in Hampstead that night, it was a wary one who came back next morning and wrote a note on Sonia's scratch pad. 'Will discuss the novel with you over lunch. Not to be disturbed.' He went into his office and shut the door.

For the rest of the morning there was little to indicate that Frensic had anything more important on his mind than a vague interest in the antics of the pigeons on the roof opposite. He sat at his desk staring out of the window, occasionally reaching for the phone or jotting something on a piece of paper. For the most part he just sat. But external appearances were misleading. Frensic's mind was on the move, journeying across the internal landscape which he knew so well and in which each publishing house in London was a halt for bargaining, a crossroads where commercial advantages were exchanged, favours given and little debts repaid. And Frensic's route was a devious one. It was not enough to sell a book. Any fool could do that, given the right book. The important thing was to place it in precisely the right spot so that the consequences of its sale would have maximum effect and ramify out to advance his reputation and promote some future advantage. And not his alone but that of his authors. Time entered into these calculations, time and his intuitive assessment of books that had yet to be written, books by established authors which he knew would be unsuccessful and books by new writers whose success would be jeopardized by their lack of reputation. Frensic juggled with intangibles. It was his profession and he was good at it.

Sometimes he sold books for small advances to small firms when the very same book offered to one of the big publishing houses would have earned its author a large advance. On these occasions the present was sacrificed to the future in the knowledge that help given now would be repaid later by the publication of some novel that would never sell more than five hundred copies but which Frensic, for reasons of his own, wished to see in print. Only Frensic knew his own intentions, just as only Frensic knew the identities of those well-reputed novelists who actually earned their living by writing detective stories or soft porn under pseudonyms. It was all a mystery and even Frensic, whose head was filled with abstruse equations involving personalities and tastes, who bought what and why, and all the details of the debts he owed or was owed, knew that he was not privy to every corner of the mystery. There was always luck and of late Frensic's luck had changed. When that happened it paid to walk warily. This morning Frensic walked very warily indeed.

He phoned several friends in the legal profession and assured himself that Cadwalladine & Dimkins, Solicitors, were an old, well-established and highly reputable firm who handled work of the most respectable kind. Only then did he phone Oxford and ask to speak to Mr Cadwalladine about the novel he had sent him. Mr Cadwalladine sounded old-fashioned. No, he was sorry to say, Mr Frensic could not meet the author. His instructions were that absolute anonymity was essential and all matters would have to be referred to Mr Cadwalladine personally. Of course the book was pure fiction. Yes, Mr Frensic could include an extra clause in any contract exonerating the publishers from the financial consequences of a libel action. In any case he had always assumed such a clause to be part of contracts between publishers and authors. Frensic said they were but that he had to be absolutely certain when dealing with an anonymous author. Mr Cadwalladine said he quite understood.

Frensic put the phone down with a new feeling of confidence, and returned less warily to his interior landscape where imaginary negotiations took place. There he retraced his route, stopped at several eminent publishing houses for consideration, and travelled on. What *Pause O Men for the Virgin* needed was a publisher with an excellent reputation to give it the imprimatur of respectability. Frensic narrowed them down and finally made up his mind. It would be a gamble but it would be a gamble that was worth taking. He would have to have Sonia Futtle's opinion first.

She gave it to him over lunch in a little Italian restaurant where Frensic entertained his less important authors.

'A weird book,' she said.

'Quite,' said Frensic.

'But it's got something. Compassionate,' said Sonia, warming to her task.

'I agree.'

'Deeply insightful.'

'Definitely.'

'Good story line.'

'Excellent.'

'Significant,' said Sonia.

Frensic sighed. It was the word he had been waiting for. 'You really think that?'

'I do. I mean it. I think it's really got something. It's good. I really do.'

'Well,' said Frensic doubtfully, 'I may be an anachronism but ...'

'You're role-playing again. Be serious.'

'My dear,' said Frensic, 'I am being serious. If you say that stuff is significant I am delighted. It's what I thought you'd say. It means it will appeal to those intellectual flagellants who can't enjoy a book unless it hurts. That I happen to know that, from a genuinely literary standpoint, it is an abomination is perhaps beside the point but I am entitled to protect my instincts.'

'Instincts? No man had fewer.'

'Literary instincts,' said Frensic. 'And they tell me that this is a bad, pretentious book and that it will sell. It combines a filthy story with an even filthier style.'

'I didn't see anything wrong with the style,' said Sonia.

'Of course you didn't. You're an American and Americans aren't burdened by our classical inheritance. You can't see that there is a world of difference between Dreiser and Mencken or Tom Wolfe and Bellow. That's your prerogative. I find such lack of discrimination invaluable and most reassuring. If you accept sentences endlessly convoluted, spattered with commas and tied into knots with parentheses, unrelated verbs and qualifications of qualifications, and which, to parody, have, if they are to be at all comprehended, to be read at least four times with the aid of a dictionary, who am I to quarrel with you? Your fellow-countrymen, whose rage for self-improvement I have never appreciated, are going to love this book.'

'They may not go such a ball on the story line. I mean it's been done before you know. *Harold and Maude.*'

'But never in such exquisitely nauseating detail,' said Frensic and sipped his wine. 'And not with Lawrentian overtones. Besides that's our trump. Seventeen loves eighty. The liberation of the senile. What could be more significant than that? By the way when is Hutchmeyer due in London?'

'Hutchmeyer? You've got to be kidding,' said Sonia. Frensic held up a piece of ravioli in protest.

'Don't use that expression. I am not a goat.'

'And Hutchmeyer's not the Olympia Press. He's strictly middle-brow. He wouldn't touch this book.'

'He would if we baited the trap right,' said Frensic.

'Trap?' said Sonia suspiciously. 'What trap?'

'I was thinking of a very distinguished London publisher to take the book first,' said Frensic, 'and then you sell the American rights to Hutchmeyer.'

'Who?'

'Corkadales,' said Frensic.

Sonia shook her head. 'Corkadales are far too old and stodgy.'

'Precisely,' said Frensic. 'They are prestigious. They are also broke.'

'They should have dropped half their list years ago,' said Sonia.

'They should have dropped Sir Clarence years ago. You read his obituary?' But Sonia hadn't.

'Most entertaining. And instructive. Tributes galore to his services to Literature, by which they meant he had subsidized more unread poets and novelists than any other publisher in London. The result: they are now broke.'

'In which case they can hardly afford to buy *Pause O Men for the Virgin*.'

'They can hardly afford not to,' said Frensic. 'I had a word with Geoffrey Corkadale at the funeral. He is not following in his father's footsteps. Corkadales are about to emerge from the eighteenth century. Geoffrey is looking for a bestseller. Corkadales will take *Pause* and we will take Hutchmeyer.'

'You think Hutchmeyer is going to be impressed?' said Sonia. 'What the hell have Corkadales got to offer?'

'Distinction,' said Frensic, 'a most distinguished past. The mantelpiece against which Shelley leant, the chair Mrs Gaskell was pregnant in, the carpet Tennyson was sick on. The incunabula of, if not *The Great Tradition*, at least a very important strand of literary history. By accepting this novel for free Corkadales will confer cultural sanctity on it.'

'And you think the author will be satisfied with that? You don't think he'll want money too?'

'He'll get the money from Hutchmeyer. We're going to sting Mr Hutchmeyer for a fortune. Anyhow, this author is unique.'

'I got that from the book,' said Sonia. 'How else is he unique?'

'He doesn't have a name, for one thing,' said Frensic and explained his instructions from Mr Cadwalladine. 'Which leaves us with an entirely free hand,' he said when he finished.

'And the little matter of a pseudonym,' said Sonia. 'I suppose we could kill two birds with one stone and say it was by Peter Piper. That way he'd see his name on the cover of a novel.'

'True,' said Frensic sadly, 'I'm afraid poor Piper is never going to make it any other way.'

'Besides, it would save the expense of his annual lunch and you wouldn't have to go through yet another version of his *Search for a Lost Childhood*. By the way, who is the model this year?'

'Thomas Mann,' said Frensic. 'One dreads the thought of sentences two pages long. You really think it would put an end to his illusions of literary grandeur?'

'Who knows?' said Sonia. 'The very fact of seeing his name

on the cover of a novel and being taken for the author ...'

'It's the only way he's ever going to get into print, I'll stake my reputation on that,' said Frensic.

'So we'll be doing him a favour.'

That afternoon Frensic took the manuscript to Corkadales. On the front under the title Sonia had added 'by Peter Piper'. Frensic spoke long and persuasively to Geoffrey Corkadale and left the office that night well pleased with himself.

A week later the editorial board of Corkadales considered *Pause O Men for the Virgin* in the presence of that past upon which the vestige of their reputation depended. Portraits of dead authors lined the panelled walls of the editorial room. Shelley was not there, nor Mrs Gaskell, but there were lesser notables to take their place. Ranged in glass-covered bookshelves there were first editions, and in some exhibition cases relics of the trade. Quills, Waverley pens, pocket-knives, an ink-bottle Trollope was said to have left in a train, a sandbox used by Southey, and even a scrap of blotting paper which, held up to a mirror, revealed that Henry James had once inexplicably written 'darling'.

In the centre of this museum the Literary Director, Mr Wilberforce, and the Senior Editor, Mr Tate, sat at an oval walnut table observing the weekly rite. They sipped Madeira and nibbled seedcake and looked disapprovingly at the manuscript before them and then at Geoffrey Corkadale. It was difficult to tell which they disliked most. Certainly Geoffrey's suede suit and floral shirt did not fit the atmosphere. Sir Clarence would not have approved. Mr Wilberforce helped himself to some more Madeira and shook his head.

'I cannot agree,' he said. 'I find it wholly incomprehensible that we should even consider lending our name, our great name, to the publication of this ... thing.'

'You didn't like the book?' said Geoffrey.

'Like it? I could hardly bring myself to finish it.'

'Well, we can't hope to please everyone.'

'But we've never touched a book like this before. We have our reputation to consider.'

'Not to mention our overdraft,' said Geoffrey. 'And to be brutally frank, we have to choose between our reputation and bankruptcy.'

'But does it have to be this awful book?' said Mr Tate. 'I mean have you read it?'

Geoffrey nodded. 'As a matter of fact I have. I know that my father didn't make a habit of reading anything later than Meredith but ...'

'Your poor father,' said Mr Wilberforce with feeling, 'must be turning in his grave at the very thought—'

'Where, with any luck, he will shortly be joined by the so-called heroine of this disgusting novel,' said Mr Tate.

Geoffrey rearranged a stray lock of hair. 'Considering that papa was cremated I shouldn't have thought that this turning or her joining him would be very easy,' he murmured. Mr Wilberforce and Mr Tate looked grim. Geoffrey adjusted his smile. 'Your objection then I take it is based on the fact that the romance in this novel is between a seventeen-year-old boy and an eighty-year-old woman?' he said.

'Yes,' said Mr Wilberforce more loudly than was his wont, 'it is. Though how you can bring yourself to use the word "romance" ...'

'The relationship then. The term doesn't matter.'

'It's not the term I'm worried about,' said Mr Tate. 'It's not even the relationship. If it simply stuck to that it wouldn't be so bad. It's the bits in between that get me. I had no idea ... oh well never mind. The whole thing is so awful.'

'It's the bits in between,' said Geoffrey, 'that will sell the book.'

Mr Wilberforce shook his head. 'Personally I'm inclined to think we would run the risk, the gravest risk of being prosecuted for obscenity,' he said, 'and in my view quite rightly.'

'I agree,' said Mr Tate. 'I mean, take the episode where they use the rocking horse and the douche—'

'For God's sake,' squawked Mr Wilberforce. 'It was bad enough having to read it. Do we have to hold a post-mortem?'

'The term is applicable,' said Mr Tate. 'Even the title ...'

'All right,' said Geoffrey, 'I grant you that it's a bit tasteless but—'

'Tasteless? What about the part where he—'

'Don't, Tate, don't, there's a good fellow,' said Mr Wilberforce feebly.

'As I was saying,' continued Geoffrey, 'I'm prepared to admit that that sort of thing isn't everyone's cup of tea ... oh for goodness sake, Wilberforce ... well anyway I can think of half a dozen books like it ...'

'I can't, thank God,' said Mr Tate.

'... which in their time were considered objectionable but—'

'Name me one,' shouted Mr Wilberforce. 'Just name me one to equal this!' His hand shook at the manuscript.

'*Lady Chatterley*,' said Geoffrey.

'Pah,' said Mr Tate. 'By comparison *Chatterley* was pure as the driven snow.'

'Anyway *Chatterley*'s banned,' said Mr Wilberforce.

Geoffrey Corkadale heaved a sigh. 'Oh God,' he muttered, 'someone tell him that the Georgians aren't around any longer.'

'More's the pity,' said Mr Tate. 'We did rather well with some of them. The rot set in with *The Well of Loneliness*.'

'And there's another filthy book,' said Mr Wilberforce, 'but we didn't publish it.'

'The rot set in,' Geoffrey interrupted, 'when Uncle Cuthbert took it into his woolly head to pulp Wilkie's *Ballroom Dancing Made Perfect* and published Fashoda's *Guide to the Edible Fungi* in its place.'

'Fashoda was a bad choice,' Mr Tate agreed. 'I remember the coroner was most uncomplimentary.'

'Let's get back to our present position,' said Geoffrey, 'which from a financial point of view is just as deadly. Now Frensic has offered us this novel and in my view we ought to accept it.'

'We've never had dealings with Frensic before,' said Mr Tate. 'They tell me he drives a hard bargain. How much is he demanding this time?'

'A purely nominal sum.'

'A nominal sum? Frensic? That doesn't sound like him. He usually asks the earth. There must be a snag.'

'The damned book's the snag. Any fool can see that,' said Mr Wilberforce.

23

'Frensic has wider views,' said Geoffrey. 'He foresees a Transatlantic purchase.'

There was an audible sigh from the two old men.

'Ah,' said Mr Tate, 'an American sale. That could make a considerable difference.'

'Exactly,' said Geoffrey, 'and Frensic is convinced that the book has merits the Americans might well appreciate. After all it's not all sex and there are passages with Lawrentian overtones, not to mention references to many important literary figures. The Bloomsbury Group for instance, Virginia Woolf and Middleton Murry. And then there's the philosophy.'

Mr Tate nodded. 'True. True,' he said. 'It's the sort of pot of message Americans might fall for but I don't see what good that is going to do us.'

'Ten per cent of the American royalties,' said Geoffrey. 'That's what good it's going to do us.'

'The author agrees to this?'

'Mr Frensic seems to think so and if the book makes the best-seller lists in the States it will consequently sell wildly over here.'

'If,' said Mr Tate. 'A very big if. Who has he in mind as the American publisher?'

'Hutchmeyer.'

'Ah,' said Mr Tate, 'one begins to see his drift.'

'Hutchmeyer,' said Mr Wilberforce, 'is a rogue and a thief.'

'He is also one of the most successful promoters in American publishing,' said Geoffrey. 'If he decides to buy a book it will sell. And he pays enormous advances.'

Mr Tate nodded. 'I must say I have never understood the working of the American market but it's true they often pay enormous advances and Hutchmeyer is flamboyant. Frensic could well be right. It's a chance I suppose.'

'Our only chance,' said Geoffrey. 'The alternative is to put the firm up for auction.'

Mr Wilberforce poured some more Madeira. 'It seems a terrible comedown,' he said. 'To think that we should have sunk to this ... this pseudo-intellectual pornography.'

'If it keeps us financially solvent ...' said Mr Tate. 'Who is this man Piper anyway?'

'A pervert,' said Mr Wilberforce firmly.

'Frensic tells me he's a young man who has been writing for some time,' said Geoffrey. 'This is his first novel.'

'And hopefully his last,' said Mr Wilberforce. 'Still I suppose it could have been worse. Who was that dreadful creature who had herself castrated and then wrote a book advertising the fact?'

'I should have thought that was an impossibility,' said Geoffrey. 'Castrated herself. Now himself I—'

'You're probably thinking of *In Cold Blood* by someone called McCullers,' said Mr Tate. 'Never did read the book myself but people tell me it was foul.'

'Then we are all agreed,' said Geoffrey to change the subject from one so close to the bone. Mr Tate and Mr Wilberforce nodded sadly.

Frensic greeted their decision without overt enthusiasm.

'We can't be sure of Hutchmeyer yet,' he told Geoffrey over lunch at Wheelers. 'There must be no leaks to the press. If this gets out Hutchmeyer won't bite. I suggest we simply refer to it as *Pause*.'

'It's appropriate,' said Geoffrey. 'It will take at least three months to get the proofs done.'

'That will give us time to work on Hutchmeyer.'

'And you really think there's a chance he will buy?'

'Every chance,' said Frensic. 'Miss Futtle exercises enormous charms for him.'

'Extraordinary,' said Geoffrey with a shudder. 'Still, having read *Pause* there's obviously no accounting for tastes.'

'Sonia is also an excellent saleswoman,' said Frensic. 'She makes a point of asking for very large advances and that always impresses Americans. It shows we have faith in the book.'

'And this fellow Piper agrees to our ten per cent cut?'

Frensic nodded. He had spoken to Mr Cadwalladine. 'The author has left all the terms of the negotiations and sale entirely in my hands,' he said truthfully. And there the matter rested until Hutchmeyer flew into London with his entourage in the first week of February.

3

It was said of Hutchmeyer that he was the most illiterate publisher in the world and that having started life as a fight promoter he had brought his pugilistic gifts to the book trade and had once gone eight rounds with Mailer. It was also said that he never read the books he bought and that the only words he could read were those on cheques and dollar bills. It was said that he owned half the Amazon forest and that when he looked at a tree all he could see was a dustjacket. A great many things were said about Hutchmeyer, most of them unpleasant, and, while each contained an element of truth, added together they amounted to so many inconsistencies that behind them Hutchmeyer could guard the secret of his success. That at least no one doubted. Hutchmeyer was immensely successful. A legend in his own lifetime, he haunted the insomniac thoughts of publishers who had turned down *Love Story* when it was going for a song, had spurned Frederick Forsyth and ignored Ian Fleming and now lay awake cursing their own stupidity. Hutchmeyer himself slept soundly. For a sick man, remarkably soundly. And Hutchmeyer was always sick. If Frensic's success lay in outeating and outdrinking his competitors, Hutchmeyer's was due to his hypochondria. When he hadn't an ulcer or gallstones, he was subject to some intestinal complaint that necessitated a régime of abstinence. Publishers and agents coming to his table found themselves obliged to plough their way through six courses, each richer and more alarmingly indigestible than the last, while Hutchmeyer toyed with a piece of boiled fish, a biscuit and a glass of mineral water. From these culinary encounters Hutchmeyer rose a thinner and richer man while his guests staggered home wondering what the hell had hit them. Nor were they allowed time to recover. Hutchmeyer's peripatetic schedule – London today, New York tomorrow, Los Angeles the day after – had a dual purpose. It provided him with an excuse to insist on speed and avoided prolonged negotiations, and it kept his sales staff on their toes. More than one contract had been signed by an author in the throes of so awful a hangover that he could hardly put pen to paper, let alone read the small print. And the small print in Hutchmeyer's contracts was exceedingly small. Understandably so, since it contained clauses that invalidated almost everything set out in bold type. To add to the hazards of doing business with Hutchmeyer, most of them legal, there was his manner. Hutchmeyer was gross, partly by nature and partly as a reaction to the literary aestheticism he was exposed to. It was one of the qualities he appreciated about Sonia Futtle. No one had ever called her aesthetic.

'You're like a daughter to me,' he said hugging her when she arrived at his suite in the Hilton. 'What's my baby got for me this time?'

'One humdinger,' said Sonia disengaging herself and climbing on to the bicycle exerciser that accompanied Hutchmeyer everywhere. Hutchmeyer selected the lowest chair in the room.

'You don't say. A novel?'

Sonia cycled busily and nodded.

'What's it called?' asked Hutchmeyer for whom first things came first.

'*Pause O Men for the Virgin.*'

'*Pause O Men for the* what?'

'*Virgin,*' said Sonia and cycled more vigorously than ever.

Hutchmeyer glimpsed a thigh. 'Virgin? You mean you've got a religious novel that's hot?'.

'Hot as Hades.'

'Sounds good, a time like this. It fits with the Jesus freaks and Superstar and Zen and how to mend automobiles. And it's women's year so we got The Virgin.'

Sonia stopped peddling. 'Now don't get carried away, Hutch. It's not that kind of virgin.'

'It's not?'

'No way.'

'So there's different kinds of virgin. Sounds interesting. Tell me.' And Sonia Futtle, seated on the bicycle machine, told him while her legs moved up and down with a delicious lethargy that lulled his critical faculties. Hutchmeyer made only token resistance. 'Forget it,' he said when she had finished. 'You can deepsix that crap. Eighty years old and still fucking. That I don't need.'

Sonia climbed off the exerciser and stood in front of him. 'Don't be a dumbcluck, Hutch. Now you listen to me. You're not going to throw this one out. Over my dead body. This book's got class.'

Hutchmeyer smiled happily. This was Fuller Brush talking. The sales pitch. No soft sell. 'Convince me.'

'Right,' said Sonia. 'Who reads? Don't answer. I'll tell you. The kids. Fifteen to twenty-one. They read. They got the time. They got the education. Literacy rate peak is sixteen to twenty. Right?'

'Right,' said Hutchmeyer.

'Right, so we've got a seventeen-year-old boy in the book with an identity crisis.'

'Identity crisises is out. That stuff went the way of all Freud.'

'Sure, but this is different. This boy isn't sick or something.'

'You kidding? Fucking his own grandmother isn't sick?'

'She isn't his grandmother. She's a woman a—'

'Listen baby, I'll tell you something. She's eighty, she's no goddam woman no more. I should know. My wife, Baby, is fifty-eight and she's drybones. What the beauty surgeons have left of her. That woman has had more taken out of her than you'd believe possible. She's got silicon boobs and degreased thighs. She's had four new maidenheads to my knowledge and her face lifted so often I've lost count.'

'And why?' said Sonia. 'Because she wants to stay all woman.'

'All woman she ain't. More spare parts than woman.'

'But she reads. Am I right?'

'Reads? She reads more books than I sell in a month.'

'And that's my point. The young read and the old read. You can kiss the in-betweens goodbye.'

'You tell Baby she's old and you can kiss yourself goodbye. She'd have your fanny for a dishcloth. I mean it.'

'What I'm saying is that you've got literacy peak sixteen to twenty, then a gap and another LP sixty on out. Tell me I'm lying.'

Hutchmeyer shrugged. 'So you're right.'

'And what's this book about?' said Sonia. 'It's—'

'Some crazy kid shacked up with Grandma Moses. It's been

done some place else. Tell me something new. Besides, it's dirty.'

'You're wrong, Hutch, you're so wrong. It's a love story, no shit. They mean something to one another. He needs her and she needs him.'

'Me, I need neither of them.'

'They give one another what they lack alone. He gets maturity, experience, wisdom, the fruit of a lifetime ...'

'Fruit? Fruit? Jesus, you want me to throw up or something?'

'... and she gets youth, vitality, life,' Sonia continued. 'It's great. I mean it. A deep, meaningful book. It's liberationist. It's existentialist. It's ... Remember what *The French Lieutenant's Woman* did? Swept America. And *Pause* is what America's been waiting for. Seventeen loves eighty. Loves, Hutch, L.O.V.E.S. So every senior citizen is going to buy it to find out what they've been missing and the students will go for the philosophomore message. Pitch it right and we can scoop the pool. We get the culture buffs with significance, the weirdos with the porn and the marshmallows with romance. This is the book for the whole family. It could sell by the—'

Hutchmeyer got up and paced the room. 'You know, I think maybe you've got something there,' he said. 'I ask myself "Would Baby buy this story?" and I have to say yes. And what that woman falls for the whole world buys. What price?'

'Two million dollars.'

'Two million ... You've got to be kidding.' Hutchmeyer gaped.

Sonia climbed back on to the bicycle machine. 'Two million. I kid you not.'

'Go jump, baby, go jump. Two million? For a novel? No way.'

'Two million or I go flash my gams at Milenberg.'

'That cheapskate? He couldn't raise two million. You can hawk your pussy all the way to Avenue of the Americas it won't do you no good.'

'American rights, paperback, film, TV, serialization, book clubs ...'

Hutchmeyer yawned. 'Tell me something new. They're mine already.'

'Not on this book they're not.'

'So Milenberg buys. You get no price and I buy him. What's in it for me?'

'Fame,' said Sonia simply, 'Just fame. With this book you're up there with the all-time greats. *Gone With The Wind*, *Forever Amber*, *Valley of The Dolls*, *Dr Zhivago*, *Airport*, *The Carpetbaggers*. You'd make the *Reader's Digest Almanac*.'

'The *Reader's Digest Almanac*?' said Hutchmeyer in an awed voice. 'You really think I could make that?'

'Think? I know. This is a prestige book about life's potentialities. No kitsch. Message like Mary Baker Eddy. A symphony of words. Look who's bought it in London. No fly-by-night firm.'

'Who?' said Hutchmeyer suspiciously.

'Corkadales.'

'Corkadales bought it? The oldest publishing—'

'Not the oldest. Murrays are older,' said Sonia.

'So, old. How much?'

'Fifty thousand pounds,' said Sonia glibly.

Hutchmeyer stared at her. 'Corkadales paid fifty thousand pounds for this book? Fifty grand?'

'Fifty grand. First time off. No hassle.'

'I heard they were in trouble,' said Hutchmeyer. 'Some Arab bought them?'

'No Arab. It's a family firm. So Geoffrey Corkadale paid fifty grand. He knows this book is going to get them out of hock. You think they'd risk that sort of money if they were going to fold?'

'Shit,' said Hutchmeyer, 'somebody's got to have faith in this fucking book ... but two million! No one's ever paid two million for a novel. Robbins a million but ...'

'That's the whole point, Hutch. You think I ask two million for nothing? Am I so dumb? Its the two million makes the book. You pay two million and people know, they've got to read the book to find out what you paid for. *You* know that. You're in a class on your own. Way out in front. And then with the film ...'

'I'd want a cut of the film. No single-figure percentage. Fifty-fifty.'

'Done,' said Sonia. 'You've got yourself a deal. Fifty-fifty on the film it is.'

'The author ... this Piper guy, I'd want him too,' said Hutchmeyer.

'Want him?' said Sonia, sobering. 'Want him for what?'

'To market the product. He's going to be out there up front where the public can see him. The guy who fucks the geriatrics. Public appearances across the States, signings, TV talk shows, interviews, the whole razzamattaz. We'll build him up like he's a genius.'

'I don't think he's going to like that,' said Sonia nervously, 'he's shy and reserved.'

'Shy? He washes his jock in public and he's shy?' said Hutchmeyer. 'For two million he'll chew asses if I tell him.'

'I doubt if he'd agree—'

'Agree he will or there's no deal,' said Hutchmeyer. 'I'm throwing my weight behind his book, he has to too. That's final.'

'OK, if that's the way you want it,' said Sonia.

'That's the way I want it,' said Hutchmeyer. 'Like the way I want you ...'

Sonia made her escape and hurried back to Lanyard Lane with the contract.

She found Frensic looking decidedly edgy. 'Home and dry,' she said, dancing heavily round the room.

'Marvellous,' said Frensic. 'You are brilliant.'

Sonia stopped cavorting. 'With a proviso.'

'Proviso? What proviso?'

'First the good news. He loves the book. He's just wild about it.'

Frensic regarded her cautiously. 'Isn't he being a bit premature? He hasn't had a chance to read the bloody thing yet.'

'I told him about it ... a synopsis and he loved it. He sees it as filling a much-needed gap.'

'A much-needed gap?'

'The generation gap. He feels—'

'Spare me his feelings,' said Frensic. 'A man who can talk about filling much-needed gaps is deficient in ordinary human emotions.'

'He thinks *Pause* will do for youth and age what *Lolita* did for ...'

'Parental responsibility?' suggested Frensic.

'For the middle-aged man,' said Sonia.

'For God's sake, if this is the good news can leprosy be far behind.'

Sonia sank into a chair and smiled. 'Wait till you hear the price.'

'Frensic waited. 'Well?'

'Two million.'

'Two million?' said Frensic trying to keep the quaver out of his voice. 'Pounds or dollars?'

Sonia looked at him reproachfully. 'Frenzy, you are a bastard, an ungrateful bastard. I pull off—'

'My dear, I was merely trying to ascertain the likely extent of the horrors you are about to reveal to me. You spoke of a proviso. Now if your friend from the Mafia had been prepared to pay two million pounds for this verbal hogwash I would have known the time had come to pack up and leave town. What does the swine want?'

'One, he wants to see the Corkadales contract.'

'That's all right. There's nothing wrong with it.'

'Just that it doesn't mention the sum of fifty thousand pounds Corkadales have paid for *Pause*,' said Sonia. 'Otherwise it's just dandy.'

Frensic gaped at her. 'Fifty thousand pounds? They didn't pay—'

'Hutchmeyer needed impressing so I said ...'

'He needs his head read. Corkadales haven't fifty thousand pennies to rub together, let alone pounds.'

'Right. Which he knew. So I told him Geoffrey had staked his personal fortune. Now you know why he wants to see the contract?'

Frensic rubbed his forehead and thought. 'I suppose we could always draw up a new contract and get Geoffrey to sign it *pro tem* and tear it up when Hutchmeyer's seen it,' he said at last. 'Geoffrey won't like it but with his cut of two million ... What's the next problem?'

Sonia hesitated. 'This one you won't like. He insists, but insists, that the author goes to the States for a promotional tour. Senior-citizens-I-have-loved sort of stuff on TV and signings.'

Frensic took out his handkerchief and wiped his face. 'Insists?' he spluttered. 'He can't insist. We've got an author who won't even sign his name to a contract, let alone appear in public, some madman with agoraphobia or its equivalent and Hutchmeyer wants him to parade round America appearing on TV?'

'Insists, Frenzy, insists. Not wants. Either the author goes or the deal is off.'

'Then it's off,' said Frensic. 'The man won't go. You heard what Cadwalladine said. Total anonymity.'

'Not even for two million?'

Frensic shook his head. 'I told Cadwalladine we were going to ask for a large sum and he said money didn't count.'

'But two million isn't money. It's a fortune.'

'I know it is, but . . .'

'Try Cadwalladine again,' said Sonia and handed him the phone. Frensic tried again. At length. Mr Cadwalladine was emphatic. Two million dollars was a fortune but his instructions were that his client's anonymity meant more to him than mere . . .

It was a dispiriting conversation for Frensic.

'What did I tell you,' he said when he had finished. 'We're dealing with some sort of lunatic. Two lunatics. Hutchmeyer being the other.'

'So we're just going to sit back and watch twenty per cent of two million dollars disappear down the plughole and do nothing about it?' said Sonia. Frensic stared miserably across the roofs of Covent Garden and sighed. Twenty per cent of two million came to four hundred thousand dollars, over two hundred thousand pounds. That would have been their commission on the sale. And thanks to James Jamesforth's libel action they had just lost two more valuable authors.

'There must be some way of fixing this,' he muttered. 'Hutchmeyer doesn't know who the author is any more than we do.'

'He does too,' said Sonia. 'It's Peter Piper. His name's on the title-page.'

Frensic looked at her with new appreciation. 'Peter Piper,' he murmured, 'now there's a thought.'

They closed the office for the night and went down to the pub across the road for a drink.

'Now if there were some way we could persuade Piper to act as understudy ...' said Frensic after a large whisky.

'And after all it would be one way of getting his name into print,' said Sonia. 'If the book sells ...'

'Oh it will sell all right. With Hutchmeyer anything sells.'

'Well then, Piper would have got his foot in the publishing door and perhaps we could get someone to ghost *Search* for him.'

Frensic shook his head. 'He'd never stand for that. Piper has principles I'm afraid. On the other hand if Geoffrey could be persuaded to agree to publish *Search for a Lost Childhood* as part of the present contract ... I'm seeing him tonight. He's holding one of his little suppers. Yes I think we may be on to something. Piper would do almost anything to get into print and a trip to the States with all expenses paid ... I think we'll drink to that.'

'Anything is worth trying,' said Sonia. And that night before setting out for Corkadales Frensic returned to the office and drew up two new contracts. One by which Corkadales agreed to pay fifty thousand for *Pause O Men for the Virgin* and the second guaranteeing the publication of Mr Piper's subsequent novel, *Search for a Lost Childhood*. The advance on it was five hundred pounds.

'After all, it's worth the gamble,' said Frensic as he and Sonia locked the office again, 'and I'm prepared to put up five hundred of our money if Geoffrey won't play ball on the advance to Piper. The main thing is to get a copperbottomed guarantee that they will publish *Search*.'

'Geoffrey has ten per cent of two million at stake too,' said Sonia as they separated. 'I should have thought that would be a persuasive argument.'

'I shall do my level best,' said Frensic as he hailed a taxi.

Geoffrey Corkadale's little suppers were what Frensic in a bitchy moment had once called badinageries. One stood around with a drink, later with a plate of cold buffet, and spoke lightly and allusively of books, plays and personalities, few of which one had read, seen or known but which served to provide a catalyst for those epicene encounters which were the real purpose of Geoffrey's little suppers. On the whole Frensic tended to avoid them as frivolous and a little dangerous. They were too androgynous for comfort and besides he disliked running the risk of being discovered talking glibly on a subject he knew absolutely nothing about. He had done that too often as an undergraduate to relish the prospect of continuing it into later life. And the very fact that there were never any women of marriageable propensity, they were either too old or unidentifiable – Frensic had once made a pass at an eminent theatre critic with horrifying consequences – tended to put him off. He preferred parties where there was just the faintest chance that he would meet someone who would make him a wife and at Geoffrey's gatherings the expression was taken literally. And so Frensic usually avoided them and confined his sex life to occasional desultory affairs with women sufficiently in their prime not to resent his lack of passion or charm, and to passionate feelings for young women on tube trains, which feelings he was incapable of expressing between Hampstead and Leicester Square. But this evening he came with a purpose, only to find that the rooms were crowded. Frensic poured himself a drink and mingled in the hope of cornering Geoffrey. It took some time. Geoffrey's elevation to the head of Corkadales lent him an appeal he had previously lacked and Frensic found himself subjected to a scrutiny of his opinion of *The Prancing Nigger* by a poet from Tobago who confessed that he found Firbank both divine and offensive. Frensic said those were his feelings too but that Firbank had been remarkably seminal, and it was only after an hour and by the unintentional stratagem of locking himself in the bathroom that he managed to corner Geoffrey.

'My dear, you are too unkind,' said Geoffrey when Frensic, after hammering on the door, finally freed himself with the help of a jar of skin cleanser. 'You should know we never lock the boys' room. It's so unspontaneous. The chance encounter ...'

'This isn't a chance encounter,' said Frensic, dragging Geoffrey in and shutting the door again. 'I want a word with you. It's important.'

'Just don't lock it again ... oh my God! Sven is obsessively jealous. He goes absolutely berserk. It's his Viking blood.'

'Never mind that,' said Frensic, 'we've had Hutchmeyer's offer. It's substantial.'

'Oh God, business,' said Geoffrey, subsiding on to the lavatory seat. 'How substantial?'

'Two million dollars,' said Frensic.

Geoffrey clutched at the toilet roll for support. 'Two million dollars?' he said weakly. 'You really mean two *million* dollars? You're not pulling my leg?'

'Absolute fact,' said Frensic.

'But that's magnificent! How wonderful. You darling—'

Frensic pushed him roughly back on the seat. 'There's a snag. Two snags, to be precise.'

'Snags? Why must there always be snags? As if life wasn't complicated enough without snags.'

'We had to impress him with the amount you paid for the book,' said Frensic.

'But I hardly paid anything. In fact ...'

'Exactly, but we have had to tell him you paid fifty thousand pounds in advance and he wants to see the contract.'

'Fifty thousand pounds? My dear chap, we couldn't—'

'Quite,' said Frensic, 'you don't have to explain your financial situation to me. You're in ... you've got a cash-flow problem.'

'To put it mildly,' said Geoffrey, twisting a strand of toilet paper between his fingers.

'Which Hutchmeyer is aware of, which is why he wants to see the contract.'

'But what good is that going to do. The contract says ...'

'I have here,' said Frensic fishing in his pocket, 'another contract which will do some good and reassure Hutchmeyer. It says you agree to pay fifty thousand ...'

'Hang on a moment,' said Geoffrey, getting to his feet, 'if you think I'm going to sign a contract that says I'm going to pay you fifty thousand quid you're labouring under a mis-apprehension. I may not be a financial wizard but I can see this one coming.'

'All right,' said Frensic huffily and folded the contract, 'if that's the way you feel about it bang goes the deal.'

'What deal? You've already signed the contract for us to publish the novel.'

'Not your deal. Hutchmeyer's. And with it goes your ten per cent of two million dollars. Now if you want ...'

Geoffrey sat down again. 'You really mean it, don't you?' he said at last.

'Every word,' said Frensic.

'And you really promise that Hutchmeyer has agreed to pay this incredible sum?'

'My word,' said Frensic with as much dignity as the bath-room allowed, 'is my bond.'

Geoffrey looked at him sceptically. 'If what James James-forth says is ... All right. I'm sorry. It's just that this has come as a terrible shock. What do you want me to do?'

'Just sign this contract and I'll write out a personal IOU for fifty thousand pounds. That ought to be a guarantee ...'

They were interrupted by someone hammering on the door. 'Come out of there,' shouted a Scandinavian voice, 'I know what you're doing!'

'Oh Christ, Sven,' said Geoffrey and struggled with the lock. 'Calm yourself, dearest,' he called, 'we were just discussing business.'

Behind him Frensic prudently armed himself with a lavatory brush.

'Business,' yelled the Swede, 'I know your business ...'

The door sprang open and Sven glared wild-eyed into the bathroom.

'What is he doing with that brush?'

'Now, Sven dear, do be reasonable,' said Geoffrey. But Sven hovered between tears and violence.

'How could you, Geoffrey, how could you?'

'He didn't,' said Frensic vehemently.

The Swede looked him up and down. 'And with such a horrid baggy little man too.'

It was Frensic's turn to look wild-eyed. 'Baggy I may be,' he shouted, 'but horrid I am not.'

There was a moment's scuffle and Geoffrey urged the sobbing Sven down the passage. Frensic put his weapon back in its holder and sat on the edge of the bath. By the time Geoffrey returned he had devised new tactics.

'Where were we?' asked Geoffrey.

'Your *petit ami* was calling me a horrid baggy little man,' said Frensic.

'My dear, I'm so sorry but really you can count yourself lucky. Last week he actually struck someone and all the poor man had come to do was mend the bidet.'

'Now about this contract. I'm prepared to make a further concession,' said Frensic. 'You can have Piper's second book, *Search for a Lost Childhood* for a thousand pounds advance . . .'

'His *next* novel? You mean he's working on another?'

'Almost finished it,' said Frensic, 'much better than *Pause*. Now you can have it for practically nothing just so long as you sign this contract for Hutchmeyer.'

'Oh all right,' said Geoffrey, 'I'll just have to trust you.'

'If you don't get it back within the week to tear up you can go to Hutchmeyer and tell him it's a fraud,' said Frensic. 'That's your guarantee.'

And so in the bathroom of Geoffrey Corkadale's house the two contracts were signed. Frensic staggered home exhausted and next morning Sonia showed Hutchmeyer the Corkadale contract. The deal was on.

4

In the Gleneagle Guest House in Exforth Peter Piper's nib described neat black circles and loops on the forty-fifth page of his notebook. Next door Mrs Oakley's vacuum cleaner roared back and forth making it difficult for Piper to concentrate on this his eighth version of his autobiographical novel. The fact that his new attempt was modelled on *The Magic Mountain* did not help. Thomas Mann's tendency to build complex sentences and to elaborate his ironic perceptions with a multitude of exact details did not transfer at all easily to a description of family life in Finchley in 1953 but Piper persisted with the task. It was, he knew, the hallmark of genius to persist and he knew just as certainly that he had genius. Unrecognized genius to be sure but one day, thanks to his capacity for taking infinite pains, the world would acclaim it. And so, in spite of the vacuum cleaner and the cold wind blowing from the sea through the cracks in the window, he wrote.

Around him on the table were the tools of his trade. A notebook in which he put down ideas and phrases which might come in handy, a diary in which he recorded his deepest insights into the nature of existence and a list of each days activities, a tray of fountain pens and a bottle of partially evaporated black ink. The latter was Piper's own invention. Since he was writing for posterity it was essential that what he wrote should last indefinitely and without fading. For a while he had imitated Kipling in the use of Indian ink but it tended to clog his pen and to dry before he could even write one word. The accidental discovery that a bottle of Waterman's Midnight Black left open in a dry room acquired a density surpassing Indian ink while still remaining sufficiently fluid to enable him to write an entire sentence without recourse to his handkerchief had led to his use of evaporated ink. It gleamed on the page with a patina that gave substance to his words, and to ensure that his work had infinite longevity he bought leatherbound ledgers, normally used by old-fashioned firms of accountants or solicitors, and ignoring their various vertical lines, wrote his novels in them. By the time he had filled a ledger it was in its own way a work of art. Piper's handwriting was small and extremely regular and flowed for page after page with hardly a break. Since there was very little conversation in any of his novels, and that only of the meaningful and significant kind requiring long sentences, there were very few pages with broken lines or unfilled spaces. And Piper kept his ledgers. One day, perhaps when he was dead, certainly when his genius was recognized, scholars would trace the course of his development through these encrusted pages. Posterity was not to be ignored.

On the other hand the vacuum cleaner next door and the various intrusions of landladies and cleaners had to be ignored. Piper refused to allow his mornings to be interrupted. It was then that he wrote. After lunch he took a walk along whatever promenade he happened to be living opposite at the time. After tea he wrote again and after supper he read, first what he had written during the day and second from the novel that was serving as his present model. Since he read rather more quickly than he wrote he knew *Hard Times*, *Nostromo*, *The Portrait of A Lady*, *Middlemarch* and *The Magic Mountain* almost off by heart. With *Sons and Lovers* he was word-perfect. By thus confining his reading to only the greatest masters of fiction he ensured that lesser novelists would not exercise a malign influence on his own work.

Besides these few masterpieces he drew inspiration from *The Moral Novel*. It lay on his bedside table and before turning out the light he would read a page or two and mull Miss Louth's adjurations over in his mind. She was particularly keen on 'the placing of characters within an emotional framework, a context as it were of mature and interrelated susceptibilities, which corresponds to the reality of the experience of the novelist in his own time and thus enhances the reality of his fictional creations'. Since Piper's own experience had been limited to eighteen years of family life in Finchley, the death of his parents in a car crash, and ten years of boarding-houses, he found it difficult in his work to provide a context of mature and interrelated susceptibilities. But he did his best and subjected the unsatisfactory marriage of the late Mr and Mrs Piper to the minutest examination in order to imbue them with the maturity and insightfulness Miss Louth demanded. They emerged from his emotional exhumation with feelings they had never felt and insights they had never had. In real life Mr Piper had been a competent plumber. In *Search* he was an insightful one with tuberculosis and a great number of startlingly ambiguous feelings towards his wife. Mrs Piper came out, if anything, rather worse. Modelled on Frau Chauchat out of Isabel Archer she was given to philosophical disquisitions, to slamming doors, to displaying bare shoulders and to private sexual feelings for her son and the man next door which would have horrified her. For her husband she had only contempt mixed with disgust. And finally there was Piper himself, a prodigy of fourteen burdened by a degree of self-knowledge and an insight into his parents' true feelings for one another that would, had he in fact possessed them, have made his presence in the house utterly unbearable. Fortunately for the sanity of the late Mr and Mrs Piper and for the safety of Piper himself, he had at fourteen been a singularly dull child and with none of the perceptions he subsequently claimed for himself. What few feelings he had were concentrated on the person of his English mistress at school, a Miss Pears, who, in an unguarded moment, had complimented little Peter on a short story he had in fact copied almost verbatim from an old copy of *Horizon* he had found in a school cupboard. From this early derived promise Piper had gained his literary ambitions – and from the fatigue of a tanker driver who, four years later, had fallen asleep at the wheel of his lorry, crossed a main road at sixty miles an hour and obliterated Mr and Mrs Piper who were doing thirty on their way to visit friends in Amersham, he had acquired the wherewithal to pursue them. At eighteen he had inherited the house in Finchley, a substantial sum from the insurance company, and his parents' savings. Piper had sold the house, had banked all his capital and, to provide himself with a pecuniary motive to write, had lived off the capital ever since. After ten years and several million unsold words he was practically penniless.

He was therefore delighted to receive a telegram from London which said URGENT SEE YOU RE SALE OF NOVEL ETC ONE THOUSAND POUNDS ADVANCE PLEASE PHONE IMMEDIATELY FRENSIC.

Piper phoned immediately and caught the midday train in

41

a state of wild anticipation. His moment of recognition had arrived at last.

In London Frensic and Sonia were also in a state of anticipation, less wild and with sombe overtones.

'What happens if he refuses?' asked Sonia as Frensic paced his office.

'God alone knows,' said Frensic. 'You heard what Cadwalladine said, "Do what you please but in no way involve my client." So it's Piper or bust.'

'At least I manged to squeeze another twenty-five thousand dollars out of Hutchmeyer for the tour, plus expenses,' said Sonia. 'I should have thought that was a sufficient inducement.'

Frensic had doubts. 'With anyone else,' he said, 'but Piper has principles. For God's sake don't leave a copy of the proofs of *Pause* around where he can see what he's supposed to have written.'

'He's bound to read the book sometime.'

'Yes, but I want him signed up for the tour first and with some of Hutchmeyer's money in his pocket. He won't find it so easy to back out then.'

'And you really think the Corkadales' offer to publish *Search For a Lost Childhood* will grab him?'

'Our trump card,' said Frensic. 'What you've got to realize is that with Piper we are treating a subspecies of lunacy known as *dementia novella* or bibliomania. The symptoms are a wholly irrational urge to get into print. Well, I'm getting Piper into print. I've even got him one thousand pounds which is incredible considering the garbled rubbish he writes. He's being paid twenty-five thousand dollars to make the tour. Now all we've got to do is play our cards right and he'll go. The Corkadales' contract is our ace. I mean, the man would murder his own mother to get *Search* published.'

'I thought you said his parents were dead,' said Sonia.

'They are,' said Frensic. 'To the best of my knowledge the poor fellow has no living relatives. I wouldn't be at all surprised if we aren't his nearest and dearest.'

'It's amazing what twenty per cent commission on two million dollars will do to some people,' said Sonia. 'I've never thought of you in the role of a foster-father.'

It was amazing what the prospect of having his novel published had done to Piper's morale. He arrived in Lanyard Lane wearing the blue suit he kept for formal visits to London and an expression of smug self-satisfaction that alarmed Frensic. He preferred his authors subdued and a little depressed.

'I'd like you to meet Miss Futtle, my partner,' he said when Piper entered. 'She deals with the American side of the business.'

'Charmed,' said Piper bowing slightly, a habit he had derived from Hans Castorp.

'I just adored your book,' said Sonia, 'I think it's marvellous.'

'You did?' said Piper.

'So insightful,' said Sonia, 'so deeply significant.'

In the background Frensic stirred uncomfortably. He would have chosen less brazen tactics and Sonia's accent, borrowed, he suspected, from Georgia in 1861, disturbed him. On the other hand it seemed to affect Piper favourably. He was blushing.

'Very kind of you to say so,' he murmured.

Frensic asserted himself. 'Now, as to the matter of Corkadales' contract to publish *Search*,' he began and looked at his watch. 'Why don't we go down and discuss the whole thing over a drink?'

They went downstairs to the pub across the road and while Frensic bought drinks Sonia continued her assault.

'Corkadales are one of the oldest publishing houses in London. They are terribly prestigious but I just think we've got to do everything to see your work reaches a wide audience.'

'The thing is,' said Frensic, returning with two single gin and tonics for himself and Sonia and a double for Piper, 'that you need exposure. Corkadales will do for a start but their sales record is none too good.'

'It isn't?' said Piper who had never thought of such mundane things as sales.

'They're naturally old-fashioned and if they do take *Search*

– and that's still not entirely certain – are they going to be the best people to push it? That's the question.'

'But I thought you said they'd agreed to buy?' said Piper uncomfortably.

'They've made an offer, a good offer, but are we going to accept it?' said Frensic. 'That's what we have to discuss.'

'Yes,' said Piper. 'Yes, we are.'

Frensic looked questioningly at Sonia. 'The US market?' he asked.

Sonia shook her head.

'If we're going to sell to a US publisher we need someone bigger than Corkadales over here first. Someone with get-up-and-go who's going to promote the book in a big way.'

'My feelings exactly,' said Frensic. 'Corkadales have the prestige but they could kill it stone dead.'

'But ...' began Piper, by now thoroughly disturbed.

'Getting a first novel off the ground in the States isn't easy,' said Sonia. 'And with a new British author it's like ...'

'Trying to sell fireworks in hell?' suggested Frensic, doing his best to avoid Eskimos and ice cream.

'The words from my mouth,' said Sonia. 'They don't want to know.'

'They don't?' said Piper.

Frensic bought another round of drinks. When he returned Sonia was into tactics.

'A British author in the States needs a gimmick. Thrillers are easy. Historical romance better still. Now if *Search* were about Regency beaux, or better still Mary Queen of Scots, we'd have no problem. That sort of stuff they lap up but *Search* is a deeply insight—'

'What about *Pause O Men for the Virgin*?' said Frensic. 'Now there's a book that is going to take America by storm.'

'Absolutely,' said Sonia. 'Or would have done if the author could go to promote it.'

They relapsed into gloomy silence.

'Why can't he go?' asked Piper.

'Too ill,' said Sonia.

'Too reserved and shy,' said Frensic. 'I mean he insists on using a *nom de plume*.'

'A *nom de plume*?' said Piper amazed that an author didn't want his name on the cover of his book.

'It's tragic really,' said Sonia. 'He's having to throw away two million dollars because he can't go.'

'Two million dollars?' said Piper.

'And all because he's got osteo-arthritis and the American publisher insists on his making a promotional tour and he can't do it.'

'But that's terrible,' said Piper.

Frensic and Sonia nodded more gloomily than before.

'And he's got a wife and six children,' said Sonia. Frensic started. The wife and six children weren't in the script.

'How awful,' said Piper.

'And with terminal osteo-arthritis he'll never write another book.' Frensic started again. That wasn't in the script either. But Sonia ploughed on. 'And maybe with that two million dollars he could have taken a new course of drugs ...'

Frensic hurried away for some more drinks. This was really laying it on with a trowel.

'Now if we could only get someone to take his place,' said Sonia looking deeply and significantly into Piper's eyes. 'The fact that he is prepared to use a *nom de plume* and the American publisher doesn't know ...' She left the implications to be absorbed.

'Why can't you tell the American publisher the truth?' he asked.

Frensic, returning this time with two singles and a triple for Piper, intervened. 'Because Hutchmeyer is one of those bastards who would take advantage of the author and drop his price,' he said.

'Who's Hutchmeyer?' asked Piper.

Frensic looked at Sonia. 'You tell him.'

'He just happens to be about the biggest publisher in the States. He sells more books than all the publishers in London and if he buys you you're made.'

'And if he doesn't it's touch and go,' said Frensic.

Sonia took up the running. 'If we could get Hutchmeyer to buy *Search* your problems would be over. You'd have guaranteed sales and enough money to go on writing for ever.'

Piper considered this glorious prospect and sipped his triple gin. This was the ecstasy he had been waiting so many years for, the knowledge that at last he was going to see *Search* in print and if Hutchmeyer could be persuaded to buy it ... ah bliss! An idea grew in his befuddled mind. Sonia saw it dawning and jogged it along.

'If there was only some way of bringing you and Hutchmeyer together,' she said. 'I mean, supposing he thought you had written *Pause* ...'

But Piper was there already. 'Then he'd buy *Search*,' he said and was smitten by immediate doubts. 'But wouldn't the author of the other book mind?'

'Mind?' said Frensic. 'My dear fellow, you would be doing him a favour. He's never going to write another book and if Hutchmeyer refuses to go ahead with the deal ...'

'And all you would have to do is go and take his place on the promotional tour,' said Sonia. 'It's as simple as that.'

Frensic put in his oar. 'And you would be paid twenty-five thousand dollars and all expenses into the bargain.'

'It would be marvellous publicity,' said Sonia. 'Just the sort of break you need.'

Piper absolutely agreed. It *was* just the sort of break he needed. 'But wouldn't it be illegal? Me going around pretending I'd written a book I hadn't?' he asked.

'You'd naturally have the real author's permission. In writing. There would be nothing illegal about it. Hutchmeyer wouldn't have to know, but then he doesn't read the books he buys and he's simply a businessman in books. All he wants is an author to go round signing books and putting in an appearance. In addition to which he has taken an option on the author's second novel.'

'But I thought you said the author couldn't write a second book?' said Piper.

'Exactly,' said Frensic, 'so Hutchmeyer's second book from the same author would be *Search for a Lost Childhood*.'

'You'd be in and made,' said Sonia. 'With Hutchmeyer behind you, you couldn't go wrong.'

They went round the corner to the Italian restaurant and continued the discussion. There was still something bothering

Piper. 'But if Corkadales want to buy *Search* isn't that going to make things difficult. They know the author of this other book.'

Frensic shook his head. 'Not a chance. You see we handled his work for him and he can't come to London so it's all between the three of us. No one else will ever know.'

Piper smiled down into his spaghetti. It was all so simple. He was on the brink of recognition. He looked up into Sonia's face. 'Oh well. All's fair in love and war,' he said, and Sonia smiled back. She raised her glass. 'I'll drink to that,' she murmured.

'To the making of an author,' said Frensic.

They drank. Later that night in Frensic's flat in Hampstead Piper signed two contracts. The first sold *Search for a Lost Childhood* to Corkadales for the advance sum of one thousand pounds. The second stated that as the author of *Pause O Men for the Virgin* he agreed to make a promotional tour of the United States.

'On one condition,' he said as Frensic opened a bottle of champagne to celebrate the occasion.

'What's that?' said Frensic.

'That Miss Futtle comes with me,' said Piper. There was a bang as the champagne cork hit the ceiling. On the sofa Sonia laughed gaily. 'I second that motion,' she said.

Frensic carried it. Later he carried a very drunk Piper through to his spare room and put him to bed.

Piper smiled happily in his sleep.

5

Piper awoke next morning and lay in bed with a feeling of elation. He was going to be published. He was going to America. He was in love. Suddenly everything he had dreamt of had come true in the most miraculous fashion. Piper had no qualms. He got up and washed and looked at himself in the bathroom mirror with a new appreciation of his previously unrecognized gifts. The fact that his sudden good fortune was derived from the misfortune of an author with terminal arthritis no longer disturbed him. His genius deserved a break and this was it. Besides, the long years of frustration had anaesthetized those moral principles which so informed his novels. A chance reading of Benvenuto Cellini's Autobiography helped too. 'One's duty is to one's art,' Piper told his reflection in the bathroom mirror as he shaved, adding that there was a tide in the affairs of men which taken at its flood led on to fortune. Finally there was Sonia Futtle.

Piper's dedication to his art had left him little time for real feelings for real people and that little time he had devoted to avoiding the predatory advances of several of his landladies or to worshipping at a distance attractive young women who stayed at the boarding-houses he frequented. And those girls he had taken out had proved, on acquaintance, to be uninterested in literature. Piper had reserved himself for the great love affair, one that would equal in intensity the affairs he had read about in great novels, a meeting of literary minds. In Sonia Futtle he felt he had found a woman who truly appreciated what he had to offer and one with whom he could enter into a genuine relationship. If anything more was needed to convince him that he need have no hesitation in going to America to promote someone else's work it was the knowledge that Sonia was going with him. Piper finished shaving and went out into the kitchen to find a note from Frensic saying he had gone to the office and telling Piper to make himself at home. Piper made himself at home. He had breakfast and then, taking his diary and bottle of evaporated ink through to Frensic's study, settled down at the desk to write his radiant perceptions of Sonia Futtle in his diary.

But if Piper was radiant, Frensic wasn't. 'This thing could blow up in our faces,' he told Sonia when she arrived. 'We got the poor sod drunk and he signed the contract but what happens if he changes his mind?'

'No way,' said Sonia. 'We make a down-payment on the tour and you take him round to Corkadales this afternoon and get him to sign for *Search*. That way we sew him up good and tight.'

But even that relief was denied him. Half an hour later a telegram was delivered. CLIENT AGREES TO SUBSTITUTION STOP ANONYMITY OVERRIDING CONSIDERATION CADWALLADINE.

'So we're in the clear,' said Sonia. 'I'll confirm Piper for Wednesday and see if the *Guardian* will run a feature on him. You get on to Geoffrey and arrange for Piper to exchange contracts for *Search* this afternoon.'

'That could lead to misunderstandings,' said Frensic. 'Geoffrey happens to think Piper wrote *Pause* and since Piper hasn't read *Pause*, let alone written the thing ...'

'So you take him out to lunch and liquor him up and ...'

'Have you ever considered,' asked Frensic, 'going into the kidnapping business?'

In the event there was no need to liquor Piper up. He arrived in a state of euphoria and installed himself in Sonia's office where he sat gazing at her meaningfully while she telephoned the literary editors of several daily papers to arrange pre-publication interviews with the author of the world's most expensively purchased novel, *Pause O Men for the Virgin*. In the next office Frensic coped with the ordinary business of the day. He phoned Geoffrey Corkadale and made an appointment for Piper in the afternoon, he listened abstractedly to the whining of two authors who were having difficulties with their plots, did his best to assure them that it would all come right in the end and tried to ignore the intimations of his own instincts which were telling him that with the signing up of Piper the firm of Frensic & Futtle had bitten off more than they could chew. Finally when Piper went downstairs to the washroom Frensic managed to have a word with Sonia.

'What gives?' he asked, a lapse into transatlantic brevity that indicated his disturbed state of mind.

'The *Guardian* have agreed to interview him tomorrow and the *Telegraph* say they'll let me—'

'With Piper. Whence the fixed smile and the goggle eyes?'

Sonia smiled. 'Has it ever occurred to you that he might find me attractive?'

'No,' said Frensic. 'No it hasn't.'

Sonia's smile faded. 'Get lost,' she said.

Frensic got lost and considered this new and quite incomprehensible development. It was one of the fixed stars in his firmament of opinions that no one in his right mind could find Sonia Futtle attractive apart from Hutchmeyer, and Hutchmeyer had evidently perverse tastes both in books and in women. That Piper should be in love with her, and at such short notice, intruded a new dimension into the situation – which in his opinion was sufficiently crowded already. Frensic sat down behind his desk and wondered what advantages could be gained from Piper's infatuation.

'At least it gets me off the hook,' he muttered finally and went next door again. But Piper was back in his chair gazing with adoring eyes at Sonia. Frensic retreated and phoned her.

'From now on, he's your pigeon,' he told her. 'You dine, wine him and anything else that pleases you. The man's besotted.'

'Jealousy will get you nowhere,' said Sonia smiling at Piper.

'Right,' said Frensic, 'I want no part of this corruption of the innocent.'

'Squeamish?' said Sonia.

'Extremely,' said Frensic and put down the phone.

'Who was that?' asked Piper.

'Oh just an editor at Heinemann. He's got a crush on me.'

'Hm,' said Piper disgruntledly.

And so while Frensic lunched at his club, a thing he did only when his ego, vanity or virility (such as it was) had taken a bashing in the real world, Sonia swept the besotted Piper off to Wheelers and fed him on dry Martinis, Rhine wine, salmon cutlets and her own brand of expansive charm. By the time they emerged into the street he had told her in so many words that he considered her the first woman in his life to have possessed both the physical and mental attractions which made for a real relationship and one who moreover understood the true nature of the creative literary act. Sonia Futtle was not used to such ardent confessions. The few advances she had had in the past had been expressed less fluently and had largely consisted of inquiries as to whether she would or wouldn't and Piper's technique, borrowed almost entirely from Hans Castorp in *The Magic Mountain* with a bit of Lawrence thrown in for good measure, came as a pleasant surprise. There was an old-fashioned quality about him, she decided, which made a nice change. Besides, Piper, for all his literary ambitions, was personable and not without an angular charm and Sonia could accommodate any amount of angular charm. It was a flushed and flattered Sonia who stood on the pavement and hailed a taxi to take them to Corkadales.

'Just don't shoot your mouth off too much,' she said as they drove across London. 'Geoffrey Corkadale's a fag and he'll do the talking. He'll probably say a whole lot of complimentary things about *Pause O Men for the Virgin* and you just nod.'

Piper nodded. The world was a gay, gay place in which anything was possible and everything permissible. As an accepted author it became him to be modest. In the event he excelled himself at Corkadales. Inspired by the sight of Trollope's inkpot in the glass case he launched into an explanation of his own writing techniques with particular reference to the use of evaporated ink, exchanged contracts for *Search*, and accepted Geoffrey's praise of *Pause* as a first-rate novel with a suitably ironical smile.

'Extraordinary to think he could have written that filthy book,' Geoffrey whispered to Sonia as they were leaving. 'I had expected some long-haired hippie and my dear, this one is out of the Ark.'

'Just shows you can never tell,' said Sonia. 'Anyway you're going to get a lot of excellent publicity for *Pause*. I've got him on the "Books To Be Read" programme.'

'How very clever you are,' said Geoffrey. 'I'm delighted. And the American deal is definitely on?'

'Definitely,' said Sonia.

They took another taxi and drove back towards Lanyard Lane.

'You were marvellous,' she told Piper. 'Just stick to talking about your pens and ink and how you write your books and refuse to discuss their content and we'll have no trouble.'

'Nobody seems to discuss books anyway,' said Piper. 'I thought the conversation would be quite different. More literary.'

He got out in Charing Cross Road and spent the rest of the

afternoon browsing in Foyle's while Sonia went back to the office and reassured Frensic.

'No problems,' she said. 'He had Geoffrey fooled.'

'That's hardly surprising,' said Frensic, 'Geoffrey is a fool. Wait till Eleanor Beazley starts asking him about his portrayal of the sexual psyche of an eighty-year-old woman. That's when the fat's going to be in the fire.'

'She won't. I've told her he never discusses his past work. She's to stick to biographical details and how he works. He's really convincing when he gets on to pens and ink. Did you know he uses evaporated ink and writes in leatherbound ledgers? Isn't that quaint?'

'I'm only surprised he doesn't use a quill,' said Frensic. 'It's in keeping.'

'It's good copy. The *Guardian* interview with Jim Fossie is tomorrow morning and the *Telegraph* wants him for the colour supplement in the afternoon. I tell you this bandwagon is beginning to roll.'

That night, as Frensic made his way back to his flat with Piper, it was clear that the bandwagon had indeed begun to roll. The newsstands announced BRITISH NOVELIST MAKES TWO MILLION IN BIGGEST DEAL EVER.

'Oh what a tangled web we weave when first we practise to deceive,' murmured Frensic and bought a paper. Beside him Piper nursed the large green hardback copy of Thomas Mann's *Doctor Faustus* which he had bought at Foyle's. He was thinking of utilizing its symphonic approach in his third novel.

6

Next morning the bandwagon began to roll in earnest. After a night spent dreaming of Sonia and preparing himself for the ordeal, Piper arrived at the office to discuss his life, literary opinions and methods of work with Jim Fossie of the *Guardian*. Frensic and Sonia hovered anxiously in the background to ensure discretion but there was no need. Whatever Piper's limitations as a writer of novels, as a putative novelist he played his role expertly. He spoke of Literature in the abstract, referred scathingly to one or two eminent contemporary novelists, but for the most part concentrated on the use of evaporated ink and the limitations of the modern fountain pen as an aid to literary creation.

'I believe in craftmanship,' he said, 'the old-fashioned virtues of clarity and legibility.' He told a story about Palmerston's insistence on fine writing by the clerks in the Foreign Office and dismissed the ball-pen with contempt. So obsessive was his concern with calligraphy that Mr Fossie had ended the interview before he realized that no mention had been made of the novel he had come to discuss.

'He's certainly different from any other author I've ever met,' he told Sonia as she saw him out. 'All that stuff about Kipling's notepaper, for God's sake!'

'What do you expect from genius?' said Sonia. 'Some spiel about how brilliant his novel is?'

'And how brilliant is this genius's novel?'

'Two-million-dollars worth. That's the reality value.'

'Some reality,' said Mr Fossie with more percipience than he knew.

Even Frensic, who had anticipated disaster, was impressed. 'If he keeps that up we'll be all right,' he said.

'We're going to be fine,' said Sonia.

After lunch the *Daily Telegraph* photographer insisted, thanks to a chance remark by Piper that he had once lived near the scene of the explosion in *The Secret Agent* in Greenwich Park, on taking his photographs as it were on location.

'It adds dramatic interest,' he said evidently supposing the explosion to have been a real one. They went down on the riverboat from Charing Cross, Piper explaining to the interviewer, Miss Pamela Wildgrove, that Conrad had been a major influence on his work. Miss Wildgrove made a note of the fact. Piper said Dickens had also been an influence. Miss Wildgrove made a note of that fact too. By the time they reached Greenwich her notebook was crammed with influences but Piper's own work had hardly been mentioned.

'I understand *Pause O Men for the Virgin* deals with the love affair between a seventeen-year-old boy and ...' Miss Wildgrove began but Sonia intervened.

'Mr Piper doesn't wish to discuss the content of his novel,' she said hurriedly. 'We're keeping the book under wraps.'

'But surely he's prepared to say ...'

'Let's just say it is a work of major importance and opens new ground in the area of age differentials,' said Sonia and hurried Piper away to be photographed incongruously on the deck of the *Cutty Sark*, in the grounds of the Maritime Museum and by the Observatory. Miss Wildgrove followed disconsolately.

'On the way back stick to ink and your ledgers,' Sonia told Piper and Piper followed her advice with a distinctly nautical flavour while Sonia shepherded her charge back to the office.

'You did very well,' she told him.

'Yes, but hadn't I better read this book I'm supposed to have written? I mean, I don't even know what it's about.'

'You can do that on the boat going over to the States.'

'Boat?' said Piper.

'Much nicer than flying,' said Sonia. 'Hutchmeyer is arranging some big reception for you in New York and it will draw bigger crowds at the dockside. Anyway we've done the interviews and the TV programme isn't till next Wednesday. You can go back to Exforth and pack. Get back here Tuesday afternoon and I'll brief you for the programme. We're leaving from Southampton Thursday.'

'You're wonderful,' said Piper fervently, 'I want you to know that.' He left the office and caught the evening train to Exeter. Sonia sat on in her office and thought wistfully about him. Nobody had ever told her she was wonderful before.

Certainly Frensic didn't next morning. He arrived at the office in a towering rage carrying a copy of the *Guardian*.

'I thought you told me all he was going to talk about was inks and pens,' he shouted at the startled Sonia.

'That's right. He was quite fascinating.'

'Well then kindly explain all this about Graham Greene

being a second-rate hack,' Frensic yelled and thrust the article under her nose. 'That's right. Hack. Graham Greene. A hack. The man's insane!'

Sonia read the article and had to admit that it was a bit extreme.

'Still, it's good publicity,' she said. 'Statements like that will get his name before the public.'

'Get his name before the courts more like,' said Frensic. 'And what about this bit about *The French Lieutenant's Woman* ... Piper hasn't even written one single publishable word and here he is castigating half a dozen eminent novelists. Look what he says about Waugh. Quote "... a very limited imagination and an overrated style ..." unquote. Waugh just happens to have been one of the finest stylists of the century. And "limited imagination" coming from a blithering idiot who hasn't got any imagination at all. I tell you Pandora's box will be a tea-party by comparison with Piper on the loose.'

'He's entitled to his opinions,' said Sonia.

'He isn't entitled to have opinions like these,' said Frensic. 'God knows what Cadwalladine's client will say when he reads what he's supposed to have said, and I shouldn't think Geoffrey Corkadale is too pleased to know he's got an author on his list who thinks Graham Greene is a second-rate hack.' He went into his office and sat miserably wondering what new storm was going to break. His nose was playing all hell with him.

But the storm when it did break came from an unexpected direction. From Piper himself. He returned to the Gleneagle Guest House in Exforth madly in love with Sonia, life, his own newly established reputation as a novelist and his future happiness to find a parcel waiting for him. It contained the proofs of *Pause O Men for the Virgin* and a letter from Geoffrey Corkadale asking him if he would mind correcting them as soon as possible. Piper took the parcel up to his room and settled down to read. He started at nine o'clock at night. By midnight he was wide awake and halfway through. By two o'clock he had finished and had begun a letter to Geoffrey Corkadale stating very precisely what he thought of *Pause O Men for the Virgin* as a novel, as pornography, as an attack on established values both sexual and human. It was a long letter. By six o'clock he had posted it. Only then did he go to bed, exhausted by his own fluent disgust and harbouring feelings for Miss Futtle that were the exact reverse of those he had held for her nine hours earlier. Even then he couldn't sleep but lay awake for several hours before finally dozing off. He woke again after lunch and went for a haggard walk along the beach in a state bordering on the suicidal. He had been tricked, conned, deceived by a woman he had loved and trusted. She had deliberately bribed him into accepting the authorship of a vile, nauseating, pornographic ... He ran out of adjectives. He would never forgive her. After contemplating the ocean bleakly for an hour he returned to the boarding-house, his mind made up. He composed a terse telegram stating that he had no intention of going through with the charade and had no wish to see Miss Futtle ever again. That done he confided his darkest thoughts to his diary, had supper and went to bed.

The following morning the storm broke in London. Frensic arrived in a good mood. Piper's absence from his flat had relieved him of the obligation to play host to a man whose conversation had consisted of the need for a serious approach to fiction and Sonia Futtle's attractions as a woman. Neither topic had been at all to Frensic's taste and Piper's habit at breakfast of reading aloud passages from *Doctor Faustus* to illustrate what he meant by symbolic counterpoint as a literary device had driven Frensic from his own home even earlier than was his custom. With Piper in Exforth he had been spared that particular ordeal but on his arrival at the office he was confronted with fresh horrors. He found Sonia, whitefaced and almost tearful, clutching a telegram, and had been about to ask her what the matter was when the phone rang. Frensic answered it. It was Geoffrey Corkadale. 'I suppose this is your idea of a joke,' he said angrily.

'What is?' said Frensic thinking of the *Guardian* article about Graham Greene.

'This bloody letter,' shouted Geoffrey.

'What letter?'

'This letter from Piper. I suppose you think it's funny to get him to write abusive filth about his own beastly book.'

It was Frensic's turn to shout. 'What about his book?' he yelled.

'What do you mean "What about it"? You know damned well what I mean.'

'I've no idea,' said Frensic.

'He says here he considers it one of the most repulsive pieces of writing it's ever been his misfortune to have to read—'

'Shit,' said Frensic frantically wondering how Piper had got hold of a copy of *Pause*.

'Yes, that too,' said Geoffrey. 'Now where does he say that? Here we are. "If you imagine even momentarily that for motives of commercial cupidity I am prepared to prostitute my albeit so far unknown but not I think inconsiderable talent by assuming even remotely and as it were by proxy responsibility for what in my view and that of any right-minded person can only be described as the pornographic outpourings of verbal excreta ..." There! I knew it was embedded somewhere. Now what do you say to that?'

Frensic stared venomously at Sonia and tried to think of something to say. 'I don't know,' he muttered. 'It sounds odd. How did he get the blasted book?'

'What do you mean "How did he get the book"?' yelled Geoffrey. 'He wrote the thing, didn't he?'

'Yes, I suppose so,' said Frensic edging towards the safety of admitting he didn't know who had written it and that he had been hoodwinked by Piper. It didn't seem a very safe position to adopt.

'What do you mean "You suppose so"? I send him proofs of his own book to correct and I get this abusive letter back. Anyone would think he'd never read the damned thing before. Is the man mad or something?'

'Yes,' said Frensic for whom the suggestion came as a Godsend, 'the strain of the past few weeks ... nervous breakdown. Very highly strung you know. He gets into these states.'

Geoffrey Corkadale's fury abated a little. 'I can't say I'm at all surprised,' he admitted. 'Anyone who can go to bed with an eighty-year-old woman must have something mentally wrong with him. What do you want me to do with these proofs?'

'Send them round to me and I'll see he corrects them,' said Frensic. 'And in future I suggest you deal with Piper through me here. I think I understand him.'

'I'm glad someone does,' said Geoffrey. 'I don't want any more letters like this one.'

Frensic put the phone down and turned on Sonia. 'Right,' he yelled, 'I knew it. I just knew it would happen. You heard what he said?'

Sonia nodded sadly. 'It was our mistake,' she said. 'We should have told them to send the proofs here.'

'Never mind the bloody proofs,' snarled Frensic, 'our mistake was coming up with Piper in the first place. Why Piper? The world is full of normal, sane, financially motivated, healthily commercial authors who would be glad to stick their name to any old trash, and you had to come up with Piper.'

'There's no need to go on about it,' said Sonia. 'Look what he's said in this telegram.'

Frensic looked and slumped into a chair. '"Yours ineluctably Piper"? In a telegram? I wouldn't have believed it ... Well at least he's put us out of our misery though how the hell we're going to explain to Geoffrey that the Hutchmeyer deal is off ...'

'It isn't off,' said Sonia.

'But Piper says—'

'Screw what he says. He's going to the States if I have to carry him. We've paid him good money, we've sold his lousy book and he's under obligation to go. He's not going to back out on that contract now. I'm going down to Exforth to talk with him.'

'Leave well alone,' said Frensic, 'that's my advice. That young man can—' but the phone rang and by the time he had spent ten minutes discussing the new ending of *Final Fling* with Miss Gold, Sonia had left.

'Hell hath no fury ...' he muttered, and returned to his own office.

Piper took his afternoon walk along the promenade like some late migrating bird whose biological clock had let it down. It was summer and he should have gone inland to cheaper climes but the atmosphere of Exforth held him. The little resort was nicely Edwardian and rather prim and served in its old-fashioned way to help bridge the gap between Davos and East Finchley. Thomas Mann, he felt, would have appreciated Exforth with its botanical gardens, its clock golf, its pier and tessellated toilets, its bandstand and its rows of balustraded boarding-houses staring south towards France. There were even some palm trees in the little park that separated the Gleneagle Guest House from the promenade. Piper strolled beneath them and climbed the steps in time for tea.

Instead he found Sonia Futtle waiting for him in the hall. She had driven down at high speed from London, had rehearsed her tactics on the way and a brief encounter with Mrs Oakley on the question of coffee for non-residents had whetted her temper. Besides, Piper had rejected her not only as an agent but as a woman, and as a woman she wasn't to be trifled with.

'Now you just listen to me,' she said in decibels that made it certain that everyone in the guest-house would. 'You can't get out of this so easily. You accepted money and you—'

'For God's sake,' spluttered Piper, 'don't shout like that. What will people think?'

It was a stupid question. In the lounge the residents were staring. It was clear what they thought.

'That you're a man no woman can trust,' bawled Sonia pursuing her advantage, 'that you break your word, that you ...'

But Piper was in flight. As he went down the steps and into the street Sonia followed in full cry.

'You deliberately deceived me. You took advantage of my inexperience to make me believe—'

Piper plunged wildly across the road into the park. 'I deceived you?' he counter-attacked under the palms. 'You told me that book was—'

'No I didn't. I said it was a bestseller. I never said it was good.'

'Good? It's disgusting. It's pure pornography. It debases ...'

'Pornography? You've got to be kidding. So you haven't read anything later than Hemingway you've got this idea any book deals with sex is pornographic.'

'No I don't,' protested Piper, 'what I meant was it undermines the foundations of English literature ...'

'Don't give me that crap. You took advantage of Frenzy's faith in you as a writer. Ten years he's been trying to get you published and now when we finally come up with this deal you throw it back at us.'

'That's not true. I didn't know the book was that bad. I've got my reputation to think of and if my name is on—'

'Your reputation? What about our reputation?' said Sonia as they skirmished past a bus queue on the front. 'You ever thought what you're doing to that?'

Piper shook his head.

'So where's your reputation? As what?'

'As a writer,' said Piper.

Sonia appealed to the bus queue. 'Whoever heard of you?'

Clearly no one had. Piper fled down on to the beach.

'And what is more no one ever will,' shouted Sonia. 'You think Corkadales are going to publish *Search* now? Think again. They'll take you through the courts and break you moneywise and then they'll blacklist you.'

'Blacklist me?' said Piper.

'The blacklist of authors who are never to be published.'

'Corkadales aren't the only publishers,' said Piper now thoroughly confused.

'If you're on the blacklist no one will publish you,' said Sonia inventively. 'You'll be finished. As a writer *finito*.'

Piper stared out at the sea and thought about being *finito* as a writer. It was terrible prospect.

'You really think ...' he began but Sonia had already changed her tactics.

'You told me you loved me,' she sobbed sinking on to the sand close to a middle-aged couple. 'You said we would ...'

'Oh Lord,' said Piper, 'don't go on like that. Not here.'

But Sonia went on, there and elsewhere, combining a public display of private anguish with the threat of legal action if Piper didn't fulfil his part of the bargain and the promise of fame as a writer of genius if he did. Gradually his resolve weakened. The blacklist had hit him hard.

'I suppose I could always write under another name,' he said as they stood at the end of the pier. But Sonia shook her head.

'Darling, you're so naïve,' she said. 'Don't you see that what you write is instantly recognizable. You can't escape your own uniqueness, your own original brilliance ...'

'I suppose not,' said Piper modestly, 'I suppose that's true.'

'Of course it's true. You're not some hack turning books out to order. You're you, Peter Piper. Frenzy has always said there's only one you.'

'He has?' said Piper.

'He's spent more time on you than any other author we handle. He's had faith in you and this is your big opportunity, the chance to break through into fame ...'

'With someone else's awful book,' Piper pointed out.

'So it's someone else's, it might have had to be your own. Like Faulkner with *Sanctuary* and the rape with the corncob.'

'You mean Faulkner didn't write that?' said Piper aghast.

'I mean he did. He had to so he'd get noticed and have the breakthrough. Nobody's bought him before *Sanctuary* and afterwards he was famous. With *Pause* you don't have to do that. You keep your artistic integrity intact.'

'I hadn't thought of it like that,' said Piper.

'And later when you're known as a great novelist you can write your autobiography and set the world straight about *Pause*,' said Sonia.

'So I can,' said Piper.

'Then you'll come?'

'Yes. Yes, I will.'

'Oh, darling.'

They kissed on the end of the pier and the tide, rising gently under the moon, lapped below their feet.

7

Two days later a triumphant if exhausted Sonia walked into the office to announce that she had persuaded Piper to change his mind.

'Brought him back with you?' said Frensic incredulously. 'After that telegram? Good Lord, you must have positively Circean charms for the poor brute. How on earth did you do it?'

'Made a scene and quoted Faulkner,' said Sonia simply.

Frensic was appalled. 'Not Faulkner again. We had him last summer. Even Mann's easier to move to East Finchley. Every time I see a pylon now I ...'

'This was *Sanctuary*.'

Frensic sighed. 'That's better I suppose. Still the thoughts of Mrs Piper ending up in some brothel in Memphis-cum-Golders Green ... And you mean to say he's prepared to go on with the tour? That's incredible.'

'You forget I'm a salesperson,' said Sonia. 'I could sell sun-lamps in the Sahara.'

'I believe you. After that letter he wrote Geoffrey I thought we were done for. And he is quite reconciled to being the author of what he chose to call the most repulsive piece of writing it had ever been his misfortune to have to read?'

'He sees it as a necessary step on the road to recognition,' said Sonia. 'I managed to persuade him it was his duty to sup-press his own critical awareness in order to achieve—'

'Critical awareness my foot,' said Frensic, 'he hasn't got any. Just so long as I don't have to put him up again.'

'He's staying with me,' said Sonia, 'and don't smirk. I just want him where I can reach him.'

Frensic stopped smirking. 'And what is the next event on the agenda?'

'The "Books To Be Read" programme. It will help get him ready for the TV appearances in the States.'

'Quite so,' said Frensic. 'Added to which it has the advantage of getting him committed to the authorship of *Pause* with what is termed the maximum exposure. One can hardly see him backing out after that.'

'Frenzy dear,' said Sonia, 'you are a born worrier. It's going to work out all right.'

'I just hope you're right,' said Frensic, 'but I shall be re-lieved when you leave for the States. There's many a slip 'twixt cup and lip, and—'

'Not this cup and these lips,' said Sonia smugly, 'no way. Piper will go on the box . . .'

'Like a lamb to the slaughter?' suggested Frensic.

It was an apt simile and one that had already occurred to Piper who had begun to have qualms.

'Not that I doubt my love for Sonia,' he confided to his diary which, now that he had moved into Sonia's flat, had taken the place of *Search* as his main mode of self-expression. 'But it is surely arguable that my honesty as an artist is at stake whatever Sonia may say about Villon.'

And in any case Villon's end didn't commend itself to Piper. To calm his conscience he turned once again to the Faulkner interview in *Writers at Work*. Mr Faulkner's view on the artist was most reassuring. 'He is completely amoral,' Piper read, 'in that he will rob, borrow, beg or steal from anybody and everybody to get the work done.' Piper read right through the interview and came to the conclusion that perhaps he had been wrong to abandon his Yoknapatawpha version of *Search* in favour of *The Magic Mountain*. Frensic had disapproved on the grounds that the prose had seemed a bit clotted for the story of adolescence. But then Frensic was so commercial. It had come as a considerable surprise to Piper to learn that Frensic had so much faith in him. He had begun to suspect that Frensic was merely fobbing him off with his annual lunches but Sonia had reassured him. Dear Sonia. She was such a comfort. Piper made an ecstatic note of the fact in his diary and then turned on the television set. It was time he decided what sort of image he wanted to present on the 'Books To Be Read' programme. Sonia said image was very important and with his usual gift for derivation Piper finally adopted Herbert Herbison as his model. Sonia came home that night to find him muttering alliterative clichés to his reflection in her dressing-table mirror.

'You've just got to be yourself,' she told him. 'It's no use trying to copy other people.'

'Myself?' said Piper.

'Natural. Like you are with me.'

'You think it will be all right like that?'

'Darling, it will be fine. I've had a word with Eleanor Beazley and she'll go easy on you. You can tell her all about your work methods and pens and things.'

'Just so long as she doesn't ask me why I wrote that bloody book,' said Piper gloomily.

'You'll be great,' said Sonia confidently. She was still insisting that everything would be just fine when three days later at Shepherd's Bush Piper was led away to be made up for the interview.

For once she was wrong. Even Geoffrey Corkadale, whose authors seldom achieved a circulation sufficient to warrant their appearance on 'Books To Be Read' and who therefore tended to ignore the programme, could see that Piper was, to put it mildly, not himself. He said as much to Frensic who had invited him over for the evening in case the need should arise for a fresh explanation as to who had actually written *Pause O Men for the Virgin*.

'Come to think of it, I don't suppose he is,' said Frensic staring nervously at the image on the screen. Certainly Piper had a stricken look about him as he sat opposite Eleanor Beazley and the title faded.

'Tonight I have in the studio with me Mr Peter Piper,' said Miss Beazley addressing the camera, 'the author of a first novel, *Pause O Men for the Virgin*, which will shortly be published by Corkadales, price £3.95, and which has been bought for the unheard-of sum of ...' (there was a loud thump as Piper kicked the microphone) 'by an American publisher.'

'Unheard-of is about right,' said Frensic. 'We could have done with that bit of publicity.'

Miss Beazley did her best to make good the erasure. She turned to Piper. 'Two million dollars is a very large sum to be paid for a first novel,' she said, 'it must have come as a great shock to you to find yourself ...'

There was another thump as Piper crossed his legs. This time he managed to kick the microphone and spill a glass of water on the table at the same time.

'I'm sorry,' he shouted. Miss Beazley continued to smile expectantly as water dribbled down her leg. 'Yes, it was a great shock.'

'No,' said Piper.

'I wish to God he'd stop twitching like that,' said Geoffrey. 'Anyone would think he'd got St Vitus's dance.'

Miss Beazley smiled solicitously. 'I wonder if you'd care to tell us something about how you came to write the book in the first place?' she asked.

Piper gazed stricken into a million homes. 'I didn't ...' he began, before jerking his leg forward galvanically and knocking the microphone on to the floor. Frensic shut his eyes. Muffled voices came from the set. When he looked again Miss Beazley's insistent smile filled the screen.

'*Pause O Men* is a most unusual book,' she was saying. 'It's a love story about a young man who falls in love with a woman much older than himself. Was this something you had had in mind for a long time? I mean was it a theme that had occupied your attention?'

The face of Piper appeared again. Beads of perspiration were visible on his forehead and his mouth was working uncontrollably. 'Yes,' he bawled finally.

'Christ, I don't think I can stand much more of this,' said Geoffrey. 'The poor fellow looks as though he's going to burst.'

'And did it take you long to write?' asked Miss Beazley.

Again Piper struggled for words, looking desperately round the studio as he did so. Finally he took a sip of water and said 'Yes.'

Frensic mopped his brow with a handkerchief.

'To change the subject,' said the indefatigable Miss Beazley whose smile had a positively demented gaiety about it now, 'I understand that your working methods are very much your own. You were telling me earlier that you always write in longhand?'

'Yes,' said Piper.

'And you grind your own ink?'

Piper ground his teeth and nodded.

'This was an idea you got from Kipling?'

'Yes. *Something Of Myself.* It's in there,' said Piper.

'Methinks I hear the voice of Hutchmeyer speaking,' said Frensic. 'Sew him up good and tight. Tight being the operative word. Good I have doubts about.'

'It's for his own,' said Sonia. 'Name me some other way he's ever going to see *Search* in print.'

Frensic nodded his agreement. 'Geoffrey is going to have a fit when he sees what he's agreed to publish. *The Magic Mountain* in East Finchley. The mind boggles. You should have read Piper's version of *Nostromo*, likewise set in East Finchley.'

'I'll wait for the reviews,' said Sonia. 'In the meantime we'll have made a cool quarter of a million. Pounds, Frenzy, not dollars. Think of that.'

'I have thought of that,' said Frensic. 'I have also thought what will happen if this thing goes wrong. We'll be out of business.'

'It isn't going to go wrong. I've been on the phone to Eleanor Beazley of the "Books To Be Read" programme. She owes me a favour. She's agreed to squeeze Piper into next week's—'

'No,' said Frensic. 'Definitely not. I won't have you rushing Piper—'

'Listen, baby,' said Sonia, 'we've got to strike while the iron's hot. We get Piper on the box saying he wrote *Pause* and he ain't going to back out nohow.'

Frensic regarded her with distaste. 'He ain't going to back out nohow? Charming. We're really getting into Mafia-land now. And kindly don't "baby" me. If there is one expression I abominate it's being called "baby". And as for putting the poor demented Piper on the box, have you thought what effect this is going to have on Cadwalladine and his anonymous client?'

'Cadwalladine has agreed to the substitution in principle,' said Sonia. 'What's he got to complain about?'

'There is a difference between "in principle" and "in practice",' said Frensic. 'What he actually said was that he would consult his client.'

'And has he let you know?'

'Not yet,' said Frensic, 'and in some ways I rather hope he turns the idea down. At least it would put an end once and for all to the internecine strife between my greed and my scruples.'

'At least he's warming up,' said Geoffrey only to have his hopes blighted by Miss Beazley's ignorance of Kipling's auto-biography.

'Something of yourself is in your novel?' she asked hope-fully. Piper glared at her. It was obvious he disliked the ques-tion.

'The ink,' he said, 'it's in *Something Of Myself.*'

Miss Beazley's smile took on a bemused look. 'Is it? The ink?'

'He used to grind it himself,' said Piper, 'or rather he got a boy to grind it for him.'

'A boy? How very interesting,' said Miss Beazley searching for some way out of the maze. Piper refused to help.

'It's blacker if you grind your own Indian ink.'

'I suppose it must be. And you find that using a very black Indian ink helps you to write?'

'No,' said Piper, 'it gums up the nib. I tried diluting it with ordinary ink but it still wouldn't work. It got in the ducts and blocked them up.' He stopped suddenly and stared at Miss Beazley.

'Ducts? It blocks the ducts?' she said, evidently supposing Piper to be referring to some strange conduit of inspiration. 'You mean you found your ...' she groped for a less old-fashioned alternative but gave up the struggle to remain con-temporary, 'you found your muse wouldn't ...'

'Daemon,' said Piper abruptly, still in the role of Kipling.

Miss Beazley took the insult in her stride. 'You were talking about ink,' she said.

'I said it blocked the ducts of the fountain pen. I couldn't write more than one word at a time.'

'That's hardly surprising,' said Geoffrey. 'It would be bloody odd if he could.'

It was evidently a thought that had occurred to Piper too. 'I mean I had to keep stopping and wiping the nib all the time,' he explained. 'So what I do now is I ...' He stopped. 'It sounds silly.'

'It sounds insane,' said Geoffrey but Miss Beazley would have none of it.

'Go on,' she said encouragingly.

'Well, what I do now is I get a bottle of Midnight Black and let it dry out a bit and then when it's sort of gooey if you see what I mean I dip my nib in and ...' Piper faltered to a stop.

'How very interesting,' said Miss Beazley.

'Well at least he's said something even if it wasn't very edifying,' said Geoffrey. Beside him Frensic stared at the set forlornly. He could see now that he should never have allowed himself to be persuaded to agree to the scheme. It was bound to end in disaster. So was the programme. Miss Beazley tried to get back to the book.

'When I read your novel,' she said, 'I was struck by your understanding of the need for a mature woman's sexuality to find expression physically. Would I be wrong to suppose that there is an autobiographical element in your writing?'

Piper goggled at her vindictively. That he should be supposed to have written *Pause O Men for the* beastly *Virgin* was bad enough, to be taken for the main protagonist in the drama of perversion was more than he could bear. Frensic felt for him and cringed in his chair.

'What did you say?' yelled Piper reverting to his earlier explosive mode of expression. This time he combined it with fluency. 'Do you really think I approve of the filthy book?'

'Well naturally I thought ...' Miss Beazley began but Piper swept her objections aside.

'The whole thing's disgusting. A boy and an eighty-year-old woman. It debases the very foundations of English literature. It's a vile monstrous degenerate book and it should never have been published and if you think—'

But viewers of the 'Book To Be Read' programme were never to hear what Piper supposed Miss Beazley to have thought. A figure interposed itself between the camera and the couple in the chairs, a large figure and clearly a very disturbed one that shouted 'Cut! Cut!' and waved its hands horribly in the air.

'God Almighty,' gasped Geoffrey, 'what the hell's going on?'

Frensic said nothing. He shut his eyes to avoid the sight of Sonia Futtle hurling herself about the studio in a frantic attempt to prevent Piper's terrible confession from reaching its enormous audience. There was an even more startling crackle from the TV set. Frensic opened his eyes again in time to catch a glimpse of the microphone in mid-air and then in the silence that followed watched the ensuing chaos. In the understandable belief that a lunatic had somehow got into the studio and was about to attack her, Miss Beazley shot out of her chair and dived for the door. Piper stared wildly round while Sonia, catching her foot in a cable, crashed forward across the glass-topped table and sprawled revealingly on the floor. For a moment she lay there kicking and then the screen went blank and a sign appeared. It said OWING TO CIRCUMSTANCES BEYOND OUR CONTROL TRANSMISSION HAS BEEN TEMPORARILY SUSPENDED. Frensic regarded it balefully. It seemed gratuitous. That circumstances were now beyond anyone's control was perfectly obvious. Thanks to Piper's high-mindedness and Sonia Futtle's ghastly intervention his career as a literary agent was done for. The morning papers would be filled with the exposé of The Author Who Wasn't. Hutchmeyer would cancel the contract and almost certainly sue for damages. The possibilities were endless and all of them awful. Frensic turned to find Geoffrey looking at him curiously.

'That *was* Miss Futtle, wasn't it?' he said.

Frensic nodded dumbly.

'What on earth was she doing hurling herself about like that for? I've never seen anything so extraordinary in my life. A bloody author starts lambasting his own novel. What did he say it was? A vile monstrous degenerate book debasing the very foundations of English literature. And the next thing you know is his own agent behaving like a gargantuan banshee, yelling "Cut!" and hurling mikes about the place. Something out of a nightmare.'

Frensic sought frantically for an explanation. 'I suppose you could call it a happening,' he muttered.

'A happening?'

'You know. a sort of random, inconsequential occurrence,' said Frensic lamely.

'A random ... inconsequential ... ?' said Geoffrey. 'If you

think there aren't going to be any consequences ...'

Frensic tried not to think of them. 'It certainly made it a very memorable interview,' he said.

Geoffrey goggled at him. 'Memorable? I should think it will go down in history.' He stopped and regarded Frensic open-mouthed. 'A happening? You said a happening. Good Lord, you mean to say you put them up to it?'

'I what?' said Frensic.

'Put them up to it. You deliberately stage-managed that shambles. You got Piper to say all those extraordinary things about his own novel and then Miss Futtle bursts in and goes berserk and you've pulled the biggest publicity stunt ...'

Frensic considered this explanation and found it better than the truth. 'I suppose it was rather good publicity,' he said modestly. 'I mean most of those interviews are rather tame.'

Geoffrey helped himself to some more whisky. 'Well I must take my hat off to you,' he said. 'I wouldn't have had the nerve to dream up a thing like that. Mind you, that Eleanor Beazley has had it coming to her for years.'

Frensic began to relax. If only he could get hold of Sonia before she was arrested or whatever they did to people who burst into TV studios and disrupted programmes, and before Piper could do any more damage with his literary high-mindedness, he might be able to save something from the cata-strophe.

In the event there was no need. Sonia and Piper had already left the studio in a hurry followed by Eleanor Beazley's shrill voice uttering threats and imprecations and the programme producer's still shriller promise to take legal action. They fled down the corridor and into a lift and shut the door.

'What did you mean by—' Piper began as they descended.

'Drop dead,' said Sonia. 'If it hadn't been for me you'd have landed us all in it up to the eyeballs, shooting your mouth off like that.'

'Well, she said—'

'The hell with what she said,' shouted Sonia, 'it was what *you* were saying that got to me. Looks great, an author telling half a million viewers that his own novel stinks.'

70

'But it isn't my own novel,' said Piper.

'Oh yes it is. It is now. Wait till you see tomorrow's papers. They're going to have headlines to make you famous. AUTHOR SLAMS OWN NOVEL ON TV. You may not have written *Pause* but you're going to have a hard time proving it.'

'Oh God,' said Piper. 'What are we to do?'

'Get the hell out of here fast,' said Sonia as the lift doors opened. They crossed the foyer and went out to the car. Sonia drove and twenty minutes later they were back at her flat.

'Now pack,' she said. 'We're moving out of here before the press get on to us.'

Piper packed, his mind racing with conflicting emotions. He was saddled with the authorship of a dreadful book, there was no backing out, he was committed to a promotional tour of the States and he was in love with Sonia. When he had finished he made one last attempt at resistance.

'Look, I really don't think I can go on with this,' he said as Sonia lugged her suitcase to the door. 'I mean my nerves can't stand it.'

'You think mine are any better – and what about Frenzy? A shock like that could have killed him. He's got a heart condition.'

'A heart condition?' said Piper. 'I had no idea.'

Nor had Frensic when she phoned him from a call box an hour later.

'I have a what?' he said. 'You wake me in the middle of the night to tell me I've got a heart condition?'

'It was the only way to stop him backing out. That Beazley woman blew his mind.'

'The whole programme blew mine,' said Frensic, 'and to make matters worse I had Geoffrey gibbering beside me all the time too. It's fine experience for a reputable publisher to watch one of his authors describe his own book as a vile degenerate thing. It does something to the soul. And to cap it all Geoffrey thought I'd put you up to rushing on like that screaming "Cut".'

'Put me up to it?' said Sonia. 'I had to do that to stop—'

'*I* know all that but *he* didn't. He thinks it's some sort of publicity stunt.'

'But that's great,' said Sonia. 'Gets us off the hook.'

'Get us on it if you ask me,' said Frensic grimly. 'Anyway where are you? Why the call box?'

'We're going down to Southampton,' said Sonia. 'Now, before he changes his mind again. There's a spare berth on the *QE2* and she's sailing tomorrow. I'm not taking any more chances. We're sailing with her if I have to bribe my way on board. And if that doesn't work I'm going to keep him holed up in a hotel where the press can't get at him until we have him word-perfect on what he's to say about *Pause*.'

'Word-perfect? You make him sound like a performing parrot—'

But Sonia had rung off and was back in the car driving down the road to Southampton.

The next morning a bemused and weary Piper walked unsteadily up the gangway and down to his cabin. Sonia stopped at the Purser's Office. She had a telegram to send to Hutchmeyer.

8

In New York MacMordie, Hutchmeyer's Senior Executive Assistant, brought him the telegram.

'So they're coming early,' said Hutchmeyer. 'Makes no difference. Just got to get this ball moving a bit quicker is all. Now then, MacMordie, I want you to organize the biggest demonstration you can. And I mean the biggest. You got any angles?'

'With a book like that the only angle I've got is Senior Citizens mobbing him like he's the Beatles.'

'Senior Citizens don't mob the Beatles.'

'Okay, so he's Valentino come to life. Whoever. Some great star of the twenties.'

Hutchmeyer nodded. 'That's more like it,' he said. 'The nostalgia angle. But that's not enough. Senior Citizens you don't get much impact.'

'Absolutely none,' said MacMordie. 'Now if this guy Piper was a gay liberationist Jew-baiter with a nigger boyfriend from Cuba called O'Hara I could really call up some muscle. But with a product that screws old women ...'

'MacMordie, how often have I got to tell you what the product is and what the action is are two separate things? There doesn't have to be any connection. You've got to get coverage any way you can.'

'Yes but with a British author nobody's ever heard of and a first-timer who wants to know?'

'I do,' said Hutchmeyer. 'I do and I want a hundred million TV viewers to know too. And I mean know. This guy Piper has to be famous this time next week and I don't care how. You can do what you like just so long as when he steps ashore it's like Lindbergh's flown the Atlantic first time. So you get yourself a pussy posse and every pressure group and lobby you can find and see he gets charisma.'

'Charisma?' said MacMordie doubtfully. 'With the picture we've got of him for the cover you want charisma too? He looks sick or something.'

'So he's sick! Who cares what he looks like? All that matters is he becomes the spinster's prayer overnight. Get Women's Lib involved, and that's a good idea of yours about the fags.'

'We get a lot of little old ladies and the Ms brigade and the gays down on the docks could be we'd have a riot on our hands.'

'That's right,' said Hutchmeyer, 'a riot. Throw the lot at him. A cop gets hurt is good. And some old lady has a coronary, that's good too. She gets pushed in the drink is better still. By the time we've finished with his image this Piper's going to be like he was pied.'

'Pied?' said MacMordie.

'With rats for Chrissake.'

'Rats? You want rats too?'

Hutchmeyer looked at him dolefully. 'Sometimes, MacMordie, I think you've just got to be goddam illiterate,' he snarled. 'Anyone would think you'd never heard of Edgar Allan Poe. And another thing. When Piper's finished stirring the shit publicitywise down here I want him put on the plane up to Maine. Baby wants to meet him.'

'Mrs Hutchmeyer wants to meet this jerk?' said MacMordie.

Hutchmeyer nodded helplessly. 'Right. Like she was crazy for me to get her that guy who wrote about cracking his whip all the time. What the fuck was his name?'

'Portnoy,' said MacMordie. 'We couldn't get him. He wouldn't come.'

'Was that surprising? It was a wonder he could walk after what he'd done to himself. That stuff saps you.'

'We didn't publish him either,' said MacMordie.

'Well there's that too.' Hutchmeyer agreed, 'but we publish this Piper and if Baby wants him she's going to have him. You know something. MacMordie, you'd think at her age and all the operations she's had and being on a diet and all she'd have laid off a bit. I meant can you do it twice a day every goddam day of the year? Well, me neither. But that woman is insatiable. She's going to eat this cuntlapper Piper alive.'

MacMordie made a note to book the company plane for Piper.

'Could be there won't be so much of him to eat by the time the reception committee down here is finished with him,' he said morosely. 'The way you want it things could get rough.'

'The rougher the better. By the time my fucking wife is through with him he's going to know just how rough things can get. You know what that woman's been into now?'

'No,' said MacMordie.

'Bears,' said Hutchmeyer.

'Bears?' said MacMordie. 'You don't mean it. Isn't that a little dangerous? I'd have to be fucking desperate to even think of bears. I knew a woman once who had this German Shepherd but—'

'Not that way,' shouted Hutchmeyer, 'Jesus, MacMordie, we're talking about my wife, not some crazy bitch dog lover. Have some respect please.'

'But you said she was into bears and I thought—'

'The trouble with you, MacMordie, is you don't think. So she's into bears. Doesn't mean the bears are into her for Chrissake. Whoever heard of a woman into anything sexual? It isn't possible.'

'I don't know. I knew a woman once with this—'

'You want to know something, MacMordie, you know some fucking horrible women no kidding. You should get yourself a decent wife.'

'I got a decent wife. I don't go messing no longer. I just don't have the energy.'

'Should eat Wheatgerm and Vitamin E like I do. Helps get it up better than anything. What were we talking about?'

'Bears,' said MacMordie avidly.

'Baby's got this thing about ecology and wildlife. Been reading about animals being human and all. Some guy called Morris wrote a book ...'

'I read that too,' said MacMordie.

'Not that Morris. This Morris worked in a zoo and had a naked ape and writes this book about it. Must have shaved the fucking thing. So Baby reads it and the next thing you know she has bought a lot of bears and things and let them loose round the house. Place is thick with bears and the neighbours start complaining just when I'm applying to join the Yacht Club. I tell you, that woman give me a pain in the ass all the problems she manages to come up with.'

MacMordie looked puzzled. 'If this Morris guy went in for apes how come Mrs Hutchmeyer is into bears?' he asked.

'Whoever heard of a fucking naked ape in the Maine woods? It's impossible. The thing would freeze to death first snowfall and it's got to be natural.'

'Isn't natural having bears in your backyard. Not any place I know.'

'First thing I said to Baby. I said you want an ape it's okay with me but bears is into another ballgame. Know what she said? She said she'd had a naked fucking ape round the house forty years and bears needed protecting. Protecting? Three hundred fifty pounds they weigh and they need protection? Anyone round the place needs protection it's got to be me.'

'What did you do then?' asked MacMordie.

'Got myself a machine-gun and told her the first bear I saw coming into the house I'd blow its fucking head off. So the bears got the message and took to the woods and now it's all fine up there.'

It was all fine at sea too. Piper woke the next morning to find himself in a floating hotel but since his adult life had been spent moving from one boarding-house to another, each with a view of the English Channel, there was nothing very surprising about his new circumstances. True, the luxury he was now enjoying was better than the amenities offered by the Gleneagle Guest House in Exforth, but surroundings meant little to Piper. The main thing in his life was his writing and he continued his routine on the ship. In the morning he wrote at a table in his cabin and after lunch lay with Sonia on the sundeck discussing life, literature and *Pause O Men for the Virgin* in a haze of happiness.

'For the first time in my life I am truly happy,' he confided to his diary and that band of future scholars who would one day study his private life. 'My relationship with Sonia has added a new dimension to my existence and extended my understanding of what it means to be mature. Whether this can be called love only time will tell but is it not enough to know that we interrelate so personally? I can only find it in myself to regret that we have been brought together by so humanly debasing a book as *POMFTV*. But as Thomas Mann would have said with that symbolic irony which is the hallmark of his work "Every cloud has a silver lining", and one can only agree with him. Would that it were otherwise!!! Sonia insists on my re-reading the book so that I can imitate who wrote it. I find this very difficult, both the assumption that I am the author and the need to read what can only influence my own work for the worse. Still, I am persevering with the task and *Search for a Lost Childhood* is coming along as well as can be expected given the exigencies of my present predicament.'

There was a great deal more in the same vein. In the evening Piper insisted on reading what he had written of *Search* aloud to Sonia when she would have preferred to be dancing or playing roulette. Piper disapproved of such frivolities. They were not part of those experiences which made up the significant relationships upon which great literature was founded.

'But shouldn't there be more action?' said Sonia one evening when he had finished reading his day's work. 'I mean nothing ever seems to happen. It's all description and what people think.'

'In the contemplative novel thought is action,' said Piper quoting verbatim from *The Moral Novel*. 'Only the immature mind finds satisfaction in action as an external activity. What we think and feel determines what we are and it is in the essential areness of the human character that the great dramas of life are enacted.'

'Ourness?' said Sonia hopefully.

'Areness,' said Piper. 'Are with an A.'

'Oh.'

'It means essential being. Like *Dasein*.'

'Don't you mean "design"?' said Sonia.

'No,' said Piper, who had once read several sentences from Heidegger, '*Dasein*'s got an A too.'

'You could have fooled me,' said Sonia. 'Still, if you say so.'

'And the novel if it is to justify itself as a mode of inter-communicative art must deal solely with experienced reality. The self-indulgent use of the imagination beyond the parameter of our personal experience demonstrates a superficiality which can only result in the unrealization of our individual potentialities.'

'Isn't that a bit limiting?' said Sonia. 'I mean if all you can write about is what has happened to you you've got to end up describing getting up in the morning and having breakfast and going to work ...'

'Well, that's important too,' said Piper, whose morning's writing had consisted of a description of getting up and having breakfast and going to school. 'The novelist invests these events with his own intrinsic interpretation.'

'But maybe people don't want to read about that sort of thing. They want romance and sex and excitement. They want the unexpected. That's what sells.'

'It may sell,' said Piper, 'but does it matter?'

'It matters if you want to go on writing. You've got to earn your bread. Now *Pause* sells ...'

77

'I can't imagine why,' said Piper. 'I read that chapter you told me to and honestly it's disgusting.'

'So reality isn't all that nice,' said Sonia, wishing that Piper wasn't quite so highminded. 'We live in a crazy world. There are hijackings and killings and violence all over and *Pause* isn't into that. It's about two people who need one another.'

'People like that shouldn't need one another,' said Piper, 'it's unnatural.'

'It's unnatural going to the moon and people still do it. And there are rockets with nuclear warheads pointing at one another ready to blow the world apart and just about everywhere you look there's something unnatural going on.'

'Not in *Search*,' said Piper.

'So what's that got to do with reality?'

'Reality,' said Piper reverting to *The Moral Novel*, 'has to do with the realness of things in an extra-ephemeral context. It is the re-establishment in the human consciousness of traditional values ...'

While Piper quoted on, Sonia sighed and wished that he would establish traditional values like ask her to marry him or even just climb into bed with her one night and make love in a good old-fashioned way. But here again Piper had principles. In bed at night his activities remained firmly literary. He read several pages of *Doctor Faustus* and then turned to *The Moral Novel* as to a breviary. Then he switched off the light and resisted Sonia's charms by falling fast asleep.

Sonia lay awake and wondered if he was queer or she unattractive, came to the conclusion that she was closeted with some kind of dedicated nut and, hopefully, a genius and decided to postpone any discussion of Piper's sexual proclivities to a later date. After all, the main thing was to keep him cool and collected through the publicity tour and if chastity was what Piper wanted, chastity was what he was going to get.

In fact it was Piper himself who raised the issue one afternoon as they lay on the sundeck. He had been thinking about what Sonia had said about his lack of experience and the need for a writer to have it. In Piper's mind experience was equated with observation. He sat up and decided to observe and was just in time to pay close attention to a middle-aged woman climbing out of the swimming bath. Her thighs, he noted, were dimpled. Piper reached for his ledger of Phrases and wrote down, 'Legs indented with the fingerprints of ardent time,' and then as an alternative, 'the hallmarks of past passion.'

'What are?' said Sonia looking over his shoulder.

'The dimples on that woman's legs,' Piper explained, 'the one that's just sitting down.'

Sonia examined the woman critically.

'They turn you on?'

'Certainly not,' said Piper, 'I was merely making a note of the fact. It could come in useful for a book. You said I needed more experience and I'm getting it.'

'That's a hell of a way to get experience,' said Sonia, 'voyeurizing ancient broads.'

'I wasn't voyeurizing anything. I was merely observing. There was nothing sexual about it.'

'I should have known,' said Sonia and lay back in her chair. 'Known what?'

'That there was nothing sexual about it. There never is with you.'

Piper sat and thought about the remark. There was a touch of bitterness about it that disturbed him. Sex. Sex and Sonia. Sex with Sonia. Sex and love. Sex with love and sex without love. Sex in general. A most perplexing subject and one that had for sixteen years upset the even tenor of his days and had produced a wealth of fantasies at variance with his literary principles. The great novels did not deal with sex. They confined themselves to love, and Piper had tried to do the same. He was reserving himself for that great love affair which would unite sex and love in an all-embracing and wholly rewarding totality of passion and sensibility in which the women of his fantasies, those mirages of arms, legs, breasts and buttocks, each particular item serving as the stimulus for a different dream, would merge into the perfect wife. With her because his feelings were on the highest plane he would be perfectly justified in doing the lowest possible things. The gulf that divided the beast in Piper from the angel in his truly beloved would be bridged by the fine flame of their passion, or some such. The great novels said so. Unfortunately they didn't explain how.

Beyond love merged with passion there stretched something: Piper wasn't sure what. Presumably happiness. Anyway marriage would absolve him from the interruptions of his fantasies in which a predatory and beastly Piper prowled the dark streets in search of innocent victims and had his way with them which, considering that Piper had never had his way with anyone and lacked any knowledge of female anatomy, would have landed him either in hospital or in the police courts.

And now in Sonia he seemed to have found a woman who appreciated him and should by rights have been the perfect woman. But there were snags. Piper's perfect woman, culled from the great novels, was a creature who combined purity with deep desires. Piper had no objection to deep desires provided they remained deep. Sonia's didn't. Even Piper could tell that. She emanated a readiness for sex which made things very awkward. For one thing it deprived him of his right to be predatory. You couldn't very well be beastly if the angel you were supposed to be beastly to was being even beastlier than you were. Beastliness was relative. Moreover it required a passivity that Sonia's kisses proved she lacked. Locked occasionally in her arms, Piper felt himself at the mercy of an enormously powerful woman and even Piper with his lack of imagination could not see himself being predatory with her. It was all extremely difficult and Piper, sitting on the sundeck watching the ship's wake widening towards the horizon, was struck once again by the contradiction between Life and Art. To relieve his feelings he opened his ledger and wrote, 'A mature relationship demands the sacrifice of the Ideal in the interests of experience and one must come to terms with the Real.'

That night Piper armed himself to come to terms with the Real. He had two large vodkas before dinner, a bottle of Nuits St Georges, which seemed to be appropriately named for the encounter, during the meal, followed this with a Benedictine with his coffee and finally went down in the elevator breathing alcohol endearments over Sonia.

'Look, you don't have to,' she said as he fondled her on the way down. Piper remained determined.

'Darling, we're two mature people,' he mumbled and walked

unsteadily to the cabin. Sonia went inside and switched on the light. Piper switched it off again.

'I love you,' he said.

'Look, you don't have to appease your conscience,' said Sonia. And anyhow . . .'

Piper breathed heavily and seized her with dedicated passion. The next moment they were on the bed.

'Your breasts, your hair, your lips . . .'

'My period,' said Sonia.

'Your period,' murmured Piper. 'Your skin, your . . .'

'Period,' said Sonia.

Piper stopped. 'What do you mean, your period?' he asked vaguely aware that something was amiss.

'My period period,' said Sonia. 'Get it?'

Piper had got it. With a bound the author by proxy of *Pause O Men for the Virgin* was off the bed and into the bathroom. There were more contradictions between Life and Art than he had ever dreamt of. Like physiological ones.

In the big house overlooking Freshman's Bay in Maine, Baby Hutchmeyer, *née* Sugg, Miss Penobscot 1935, lay languorously on her great waterbed and thought about Piper. Beside her was a copy of *Pause* and a glass of Scotch and Vitamin C. She had read the book three times now, and with each reading she had felt increasingly that here at last was a young author who truly appreciated what an older woman had to offer. Not that Baby was, in most aspects, older. At forty, read fifty-eight, she still had the body of an accident-prone eighteen-year-old and the face of an embalmed twenty-five. In short she had what it takes, the It in question having been taken by Hutchmeyer in the first ten years of their married life and left for the last thirty. What Hutchmeyer had to give by way of attention and bovine passion he bestowed on secretaries stenographers and the occasional stripper in Las Vegas Paris or Tokyo. In return for Baby's complaisancy he gave her money, indulged her enthusiasms whether artistic, social, metaphysical or eco-cultural, and boasted in public about their happy marriage. Baby made do with bronzed young interior decorators and had the house and herself redone more times than was strictly necessary. She frequented hospitals that specialized in cosmetic surgery and Hutchmeyer, arriving home from one of his peripatetic passions, had once failed to recognize her. It was then that the matter of divorce first came up.

'So I don't grab you,' said Baby, 'well you don't grab me either. The last time you had it up was the fall of fifty-five and you were drunk then.'

'I must have been,' said Hutchmeyer and immediately regretted it. Baby pulled the rug from under.

'I've been looking into your affairs,' she said.

'So I have affairs. A man in my position's got to prove his virility. You think I'm going to get financial backing when I need it if I'm too old to screw.'

'You're not too old to screw,' said Baby, 'and I'm not talking about those affairs. I'm talking financial affairs. Now you want a divorce it's all right with me. We split fifty-fifty and the price is twenty million bucks.'

'Are you crazy?' yelled Hutchmeyer. 'No way!'

'Then no divorce. I've done an audit on your books and those are the affairs I'm talking of. Now if you want the Internal Revenue boys and the FBI and the courts to know you've been evading taxes and accepting bribes and handling laundered money for organized crime ...'

Hutchmeyer didn't. 'You go your way I'll go mine,' he said bitterly.

'And just remember,' said Baby, 'that if anything happens to me like I die suddenly and like unnaturally I've stashed photocopies of all your little misdemeanours with my lawyers and in a bank vault too ...'

Hutchmeyer hadn't forgotten it. He had an extra seat belt installed in Baby's Lincoln and saw to it she didn't take any risks. The interior decorators returned and so did actors, painters and anyone else Baby fancied. Even MacMordie got dragged one night into the act and was promply docked a thousand dollars from his salary for what Hutchmeyer lividly called fringe benefits. MacMordie didn't see it that way and had protested to Baby. Hutchmeyer reimbursed him two thousand and apologized.

But for all these side-effects Baby remained unsatisfied. When she wasn't able to find someone or something interesting to do, she read. At first Hutchmeyer had welcomed the move into literacy as an indication that Baby was either growing up or dying down. As usual he was wrong. The strain of self-improvement that had manifested itself in her numerous cosmetic operations combined now with intellectual aspirations to form a fearful hybrid. From being a simple if scarred broad Baby graduated to a well-read woman. The first intimation Hutchmeyer had of this development came when he returned from the Frankfurt Book Fair to find her into *The Idiot*.

'You find it what?' he said when she told him she found it fascinating and relevant. 'Relevant to what?'

'The the spiritual crisis in contemporary society,' said Baby. 'To us.'

'*The Idiot*'s relevant to us?' said Hutchmeyer, scandalized. 'A guy thinks he's Napoleon and icepicks some old dame and that's relevant to us? That is all I need right now. A hole in the head.'

'You've got one. That's *Crime and Punishment*, Dummkopf. For a publisher you know but nothing.'

'I know how to sell books. I don't have to read the goddam things,' said Hutchmeyer. 'Books is for people who don't get satisfaction in doing things. Like vicarious.'

'They teach you things,' said Baby.

'Like what? Having apoplectic fits?' said Hutchmeyer who had finally got his bearings on *The Idiot*.

'Epileptic. A sign of genius. Like Mohammed had them.'

'So now I've got an encyclopedia for a wife,' said Hutchmeyer, 'and with Arabs. What are you going to do? Turn this house into a literary Mecca or something?' And leaving Baby with the germ of this idea he had flown hurriedly to Tokyo and the physical pleasures of a woman who couldn't speak English let alone read it. He came back to find Baby had been into Dostoyevsky and out the other side. She was devouring books with as little discrimination as her bears were now devouring blueberry patches. She hit Ayn Rand with as much fervour as Tolstoy, swept amazingly through Dos Passos, lathered in Lawrence, saunaed in Strindberg and then birched herself with Céline. The list was endless and Hutchmeyer found himself married to a biblionut. To make matters worse Baby got into authors. Hutchmeyer loathed authors. They talked about their books and Hutchmeyer under threat from Baby found himself forced to be relatively polite and apparently interested. Even Baby found them disappointing but since the presence of even one novelist in the house sent Hutchmeyer's blood pressure soaring she was generous in her invitations and continued to live in hopes of finding one who lived in the flesh up to his words on paper. And with Peter Piper and *Pause O Men for the Virgin* she felt sure that here at last was a man and his book without discrepancy. She lay on the waterbed and savoured her expectations. It was such a romantic novel. In a significant sort of way. And different.

Hutchmeyer came through from the bathroom wearing a quite unnecessary truss.

'That thing suits you,' said Baby studying the contraption dispassionately. 'You should wear it more often. It gives you dignity.'

Hutchmeyer glared at her.

'No, I mean it,' Baby continued. 'Like it gives you a supportive role.'

'With you to support I need it,' said Hutchmeyer.

'Well, if you've got a hernia you should have it operated on.'

'Seeing what they've done with you I don't need no operations,' Hutchmeyer said. He glanced at *Pause* and went through to his room.

'You still like that book?' he called out presently.

'First good book you've published in years,' said Baby. 'It's beautiful. An idyll.'

'A what?'

'An idyll. You want me to tell you what an idyll is?'

'No,' said Hutchmeyer, 'I can guess.' He climbed into bed and thought about it. An idyll? Well if she said an idyll, an idyll was what it would be to a million other women. Baby was infallible. Still, an idyll?

9

There was nothing idyllic about the scene that greeted Piper when the ship berthed in New York. Even the fabulous view of the skyline and the Statue of Liberty, which Sonia had promised would send him, didn't. A heavy mist hung over the river and the great buildings only emerged from it as they moved slowly past the Battery and inched into the berth. By that time Piper's attention had been drawn from the view of Manhattan to a large number of people with visibly different backgrounds and opinions who were gathered on the roadway outside the Customs shed.

'Boy, Hutch has really done you proud,' said Sonia as they went down the gangway. There were shouts from the street and a glimpse of banners some of which said ambiguously, 'Welcome To Gay City', and others even more ominously, 'Go Home, Peipmann'.

'Who on earth is Peipmann?' Piper asked.

'Don't ask me,' said Sonia.

'Peipmann?' said the Customs Officer not bothering to open their bags. 'I wouldn't know. There's a million hags and fags out there waiting for him. Some are for lynching him and others for worse. Have a nice trip.'

Sonia hustled Piper away with their luggage through a barrier to where MacMordie was waiting with a crowd of reporters. 'Pleased to make your acquaintance, Mr Piper,' he said. 'Now if you'll just step this way.'

Piper stepped this way and was immediately surrounded by cameramen and reporters who shouted incomprehensible questions.

'Just say "No comment",' shouted MacMordie as Piper tried to explain that he had never been to Russia. 'That way nobody gets the wrong idea.'

'It's a bit late for that, isn't it?' said Sonia. 'Who the hell told these goons he was in the KGB?'

MacMordie grinned with complicity and the swarm with Piper at its centre moved out into the entrance hall. A squad of cops fought their way through the newsmen and escorted

Piper into an elevator. Sonia and MacMordie went down the stairs.

'What in the name of hell gives?' asked Sonia.

'Mr Hutchmeyer's orders,' said MacMordie. 'A riot he asks for, a riot he gets.'

'But you didn't have to say that about him being a hit man for Idi Amin,' said Sonia bitterly. 'Jesus wept!'

At street level it was clear that MacMordie had said a great many other things about Piper, all of them conflicting. A contingent of Survivors of Siberia surged round the entrance chanting, 'Solzhenitsyn Yes. Piperovsky No.' Behind them a band of Arabs for Palestine, acting on the assumption that Piper was an Israeli Minister travelling incognito on an arms-buying mission, battled with Zionists whom MacMordie had alerted to the arrival of Piparfat of the Black September Movement. Farther back a small group of older Jews carried banners denouncing Piepmann but were heavily outnumbered by squads of Irishmen whose information was that O'Piper was a leading member of the IRA.

'Cops are all Irish,' MacMordie explained to Sonia. 'Best to have them on our side.'

'And which goddam side is that?' said Sonia but at that moment the elevator doors opened and an ashen-faced Piper was hustled into public view by his police escort. As the crowd outside surged forward the reporters continued their indefatigable quest for the truth.

'Mr Piper, would you mind just telling us who and what the hell you are?' one of them shouted above the din. But Piper was speechless. His eyes started out of his head and his face was grey.

'Is it true that you personally shot ... ?'

'Can we take it that your government isn't negotiating the purchase of Minutemen rockets?'

'How many people are still in mental ...'

'I know one who soon will be if you don't do something fast,' said Sonia thrusting MacMordie forward. MacMordie launched himself into a fray.

'Mr Piper has nothing to say,' he yelled gratuitously before being hurled to one side by a cop who had just been hit by a bottle of Seven-Up thrown by an Anti-Apartheid protester for whom Van Piper was a White South African racist. Sonia Futtle shoved past him.

'Mr Piper is a famous British novelist,' she bawled but the time had passed for such unequivocal statements. More missiles rained against the wall of the building, banners disintegrated and were used as weapons, and Piper was dragged back into the hall.

'I haven't shot anyone,' he squawked. 'I've never been to Poland.' But no one heard him. There was a crackle of walkie-talkies and an urgent plea for police reinforcements. Outside the Survivors of Siberia had succumbed to the Gay Liberationists who were fighting for their own. A number of middle-aged dragsters broke through the police cordon and swooped on Piper.

'No, I'm nothing of the kind,' he yelled as they tried to rescue him from the cops. 'I'm simply a normal ...' Sonia grabbed a pole which had once held a sign saying 'Golden Oldies Love You', and fended off the falsies of one of Piper's captors.

'Oh no he's not,' she shrieked, 'he's mine!' and dewigged another. Then flailing about her she drove the Gay Liberationists out of the lobby. Behind her Piper and the cops cowered while MacMordie shouted encouragement. In the medley outside Arabs For Palestine and Zionists For Israel momentarily united and completed the demolition of Gay Liberation before joining battle again. By that time Sonia had dragged Piper into the elevator. MacMordie joined them and pressed the button. For the next twenty minutes they went up and down while the struggle for Piparfat, O'Piper and Peipmann raged on outside.

'You've really screwed things up now,' Sonia told Mac-Mordie. 'It takes me all my time to get the poor guy over here and you have to arrange Custer's Last Stand for a welcome.'

In the corner the poor guy was sitting on the floor. Mac-Mordie ignored him. 'The product needed exposure and it's sure getting it. This will hit prime time TV. I wouldn't wonder there aren't news flashes going out now.'

'Great,' said Sonia, 'and what have you got laid on for us next? The *Hindenburg* disaster?'

'So this is going to hit the headlines ...' MacMordie began but there was a low moan from the corner. Something had already hit Piper. His hand was bleeding. Sonia knelt beside him.

'What happened, honey?' she asked. Piper pointed wanly at a frisbee on which were painted the words Gulag Go. The frisbee was edged with razor blades. Sonia turned on Mac-Mordie.

'I suppose that was your idea too,' she yelled. 'Frisbees with razor blades. You could guillotine someone with a thing like that.'

'Me? I didn't have a thing—' MacMordie began but Sonia had stopped the elevator.

'Ambulance! Ambulance,' she shouted, but it was an hour before the police managed to get Piper out of the building. By that time Hutchmeyer's instructions had been carried out. So had a large number of protesters who had been rushed to hospital. The streets were littered with broken glass, smashed banners and tear-gas canisters. As Piper was helped into the ambulance his eyes were streaming tears. He sat nursing his injured hand and the conviction that he had come to a madhouse.

'What did I do wrong?' he asked Sonia pathetically.

'Nothing. Nothing at all.'

'You were great, just great,' said MacMordie appreciatively and studied Piper's wound. 'Pity there's not more blood.'

'What more do you want?' snarled Sonia. 'Two pounds of flesh? Haven't you got enough already?'

'Blood,' said MacMordie. 'Colour TV you can tell the difference from ketchup. This has got to be authentic.' He turned to the nurse. 'You got any whole blood?'

'Whole blood? For a scratch like that you want whole blood?' she said.

'Listen,' said MacMordie, 'this guy's a haemophiliac. You going to let him bleed to death?'

'I am not a haemophiliac,' protested Piper but the siren drowned his voice.

'He needs a transfusion,' shouted MacMordie. 'Give me that blood.'

'Are you out of your fucking mind?' screamed Sonia as Mac-Mordie grappled with the nurse. 'Hasn't he been through enough without you wanting to give him a blood transfusion?'

'I don't want a transfusion,' squeaked Piper frantically. 'I don't need one.'

'Yea but the TV cameras do,' said MacMordie. 'In Technicolor.'

'I will not give the patient ...' said the nurse but MacMordie had grabbed the bottle and was wrestling with the cap.

'You don't even know his blood group,' the nurse yelled as the cap came off.

'No need to,' said MacMordie and emptied most of the bottle over Piper's head.

'Now look what you've done,' bawled Sonia. Piper had passed out.

'Okay, so we resuscitate him,' said MacMordie. 'This is going to make Kildare look like nothing,' and he clamped the oxygen mask over Piper's face. By the time Piper was lifted out of the ambulance on a stretcher he looked like death itself. Under the mask and the blood his face had turned purple. In the excitement nobody had thought to turn the oxygen on.

'Is he still alive?' asked a reporter who had followed the ambulance.

'Who knows?' said MacMordie enthusiastically. Piper was carried into Casualty while a bloodstained Sonia tried to calm the nurse who was having hysterics.

'It was too terrible. Never in my whole life have I known such a thing and in my ambulance too,' she screamed at the TV cameras and reporters before being led away after her patient. As the crimson stretcher with Piper's body was lifted on to a trolley and wheeled away, MacMordie wiped his hands with satisfaction. Around him the TV cameras buzzed. The product had got exposure. Mr Hutchmeyer would be pleased.

Mr Hutchmeyer was. He watched the riot on TV with evident satisfaction and all the fervour of a fight enthusiast.

'That's my boy,' he yelled as a young Zionist flattened an innocent Japanese passenger off the ship with a placard saying 'Remember Lod'. A cop tried to intervene and was promptly felled by something in drag. The picture joggled violently as the cameraman was hit from behind. When it finally steadied it was focused on an elderly woman lying bleeding on the ground.

'Great,' said Hutchmeyer, 'MacMordie's done a great job. That boy's got a real talent for action.'

'That's what you think,' said Baby, who knew better.

'What the hell do you mean by that?' said Hutchmeyer, momentarily diverted. Baby shrugged.

'I just don't like violence is all.'

'Violence? So life is violent. Competitive. That's the way the cookie crumbles.'

Baby studied the screen. 'There's two more cookies just crumbled now,' she said.

'Human nature,' said Hutchmeyer, 'I didn't invent human nature.'

'Just exploit it.'

'Make a living.'

'Make a killing if you ask me,' said Baby. 'That woman's not going to make it.'

'Shit,' said Hutchmeyer.

'Took the word out of my mouth,' said Baby. Hutchmeyer concentrated on the screen and tried to ignore Baby. A police posse with Piper came out of Customs.

'That's him,' said Hutchmeyer. 'The motherfucker looks like he's pissing himself.'

Baby looked and sighed. The haunted Piper was just as she had hoped, young, pale, sensitive and intensely vulnerable. Like Keats at Waterloo she thought.

'Who's the fatso with MacMordie?' she asked as Sonia kneed a Ukrainian who had just spat on her dress.

'That's my girl,' shouted Hutchmeyer enthusiastically. Baby looked at him incredulously.

'You've got to be joking. One bounce with that female Russian shotput and you'd bust your truss.'

'Never mind my goddam truss,' said Hutchmeyer, 'I'm just telling you that that baby there is the greatest little saleswoman in the world.'

'Great she may be,' said Baby, 'little she ain't. That Musdovite doubled up with lover's balls knows that. What's her name?'

'Sonia Futtle,' said Hutchmeyer dreamily.

'I could have guessed,' said Baby, 'she's just futtled an Irishman now. He'll never ride again.'

'Jesus,' said Hutchmeyer and retreated to his study to avoid the disillusionment of Baby's commentary. He put a call through to the New York office for a computer forecast on predicted sales of *Pause O Men for the Virgin* in the light of this great new publicity. Then he got through to Production and ordered another half million copies. Finally a call to Hollywood and a demand for another five per cent in TV serial takings. And all the time his mind was busy with wanton thoughts of Sonia Futtle and some natural way of killing what remained of Miss Penobscot 1935 so that he wouldn't have to part with twenty million dollars to get a divorce. Maybe MacMordie could come up with something. Like fucking her to death. That would be natural. And this Piper guy had a hard-on for old women. Could be there was something there.

In the emergency theatre at the Roosevelt Hospital doctors and surgeons struggled to save Piper's life. The fact that appearances led them to suppose he had bled to death from a head wound while his symptoms were those of suffocation made their task more complicated than it might otherwise have been. The hysterical nurse was no help at all.

'He said he was a bleeder,' she told the chief surgeon who could see that already. 'He said he had to have a transfusion. I didn't want to do it and he said he didn't want one and she told him not to and he got at the blood bank and then he passed out and then they put him on resuscitation and—'

'Put her on sedation,' shouted the surgeon as the nurse was dragged out still screaming. On the operating table Piper was bald. In a desperate attempt to find the site of the wound his hair had been clipped.

'So where the fuck's the haemorrhage?' said the surgeon, shining a light down Piper's left ear in the hope of finding some source for this terrible loss of blood. By the time Piper revived they were none the wiser. The scratch on his hand had been cleansed and covered with a Band-Aid and through a needle in his right wrist he was getting the transfusion he had dreaded. Finally they cut off the supply and Piper got off the table.

'You've had a lucky escape,' said the surgeon. 'I don't know what you're suffering from but you want to take it easy for a while. Maybe the Mayo could come up with an answer. We sure as hell can't.'

Piper wobbled out into the corridor bald as a coot. Sonia burst into tears.

'Oh my God what have they done to you, my darling?' she wailed. MacMordie studied Piper's bald head thoughtfully.

'That doesn't look so good,' he said finally and went into the theatre. 'We've got ourselves a problem,' he told the surgeon.

'No need to tell me. Diagnostically I wouldn't know.'

'Yeah,' said MacMordie, 'it's like that. Now what he needs is bandages round his head. I mean he's famous and there's all those TV guys out there and he's going to come out looking like Kojak and he's an author. That isn't going to improve his image.'

'His image is your problem,' said the surgeon, 'mine just happens to be his illness.'

'You cut his hair all off,' said MacMordie. 'Now how about a whole heap of bandages? Like right across his face and all. This guy needs his anonymity till his hair grows back.'

'No way,' said the surgeon, true to his medical principles.

'A thousand dollars,' said MacMordie and went to fetch Piper. He came reluctantly and clutching Sonia's arm pathetically. By the time he emerged and went outside with Sonia on one side and a nurse on the other only two frightened eyes and his nostrils were visible.

'Mr Piper has nothing to say,' said MacMordie quite unnecessarily. Several million viewers could see that. Piper's bandaged face had no mouth. For them he could have been the invisible man. The cameras zoomed in for close-ups and MacMordie spoke.

'Mr Piper has authorized me to say that he had no idea his great novel *Pause O Men for the Virgin* would arouse the degree of public controversy that has marked the start of his lecture tour of this country . . .'

'His what?' demanded a reporter.

'Mr Piper is Britain's greatest novelist: His novel *Pause O Men for the Virgin* published by Hutchmeyer Press and available at seven dollars ninety—'

'You mean his novel caused all this?' said an interviewer.

MacMordie nodded. '*Pause O Men for the Virgin* is the most controversial novel of this century. Read it and see what has caused this terrible sacrifice on Mr Piper's part ...'

Beside him Piper swayed groggily and had to be helped down the steps to the waiting car.

'Where are you taking him to now?'

'He's being flown to a private clinic for diagnostic treatment,' said MacMordie and the car moved off. In the back seat Piper whimpered through his bandages.

'What's that, darling?' Sonia asked. But Piper's mumble was incomprehensible.

'What was all that about a diagnostic treatment?' Sonia asked MacMordie. 'He doesn't need—'

'Just to throw the press and media off the trail. Mr Hutchmeyer wants you to stay with him at his residence in Maine. We're going to the airport. Mr Hutchmeyer's private plane is waiting.'

'I'll have something to say to Mr Goddam Hutchmeyer when I see him,' said Sonia. 'It's a wonder you didn't get us all killed.'

MacMordie turned in his seat. 'Listen,' he said, 'you try promoting a foreign writer. He's got to have a gimmick like he's won the Nobel Prize or been tortured in the Lubianka or something. Charisma. Now what's this Piper got? Nothing. So we build him up. We have ourselves a little riot, a bit of blood and all and overnight he's charismatic. And with those bandages he's going to be in every home tonight on TV. Sell a million copies on that face alone.'

They drove to the airport and Sonia and Piper climbed aboard *Imprint One*. Only when they had taken off did Sonia remove the bandages from Piper's face.

'We'll have to leave the rest on till your hair starts to grow again,' she said. Piper nodded his bandaged head.

From Maine Hutchmeyer phoned his congratulations to Mac-

Mordie. 'That scene outside the hospital was the greatest,' he said. 'That's going to blow a million viewers' minds. Why we've made a martyr out of him. Like a sacrificial lamb on the altar of great literature. I tell you, MacMordie, for this you get a bonus.'

'It was nothing,' said MacMordie modestly.

'How did he take it?' Hutchmeyer.

'Well he seemed a little confused is all,' said MacMordie. 'He'll get over it.'

'All authors have confused minds,' said Hutchmeyer, 'it's natural with them.'

10

And Piper spent the flight in a confused state of mind. He still wasn't sure what had hit him or why and his mixed reception as O'Piper, Piparfat, Peipmann, Piperovsky *et al* added to the problems already confronting him as the supposititious author of *Pause*. And in any case as a putative genius Piper had assumed so many different identities that past personae compounded those of the present. So did shock, MacMordie's bloodbath, suffocation, resuscitation, and the fact that he was wearing a turban of bandages over an unscathed scalp. He stared out of the window and wondered what Conrad or Lawrence or George Eliot would have done in his position. Apart from the certainty that they wouldn't have been in it, he could think of nothing. And Sonia was no great help. Her mind seemed set on making the financial most from his ordeal.

'Either way we've got him over a barrel,' she said as the plane began to descend over Bangor. 'You're too sick to go through with this tour.'

'I absolutely agree,' said Piper.

Sonia crushed his hopes. 'He won't wear that one,' she said. 'With Hutchmeyer it's the contract counts. You could be on an intravenous drip and you'd still have to make appearances. So we sting him for compensation. Like another twenty-five thousand dollars.'

'I think I would rather go home,' said Piper.

'The way I'm going to play it you'll go home with fifty grand.'

Piper raised objections. 'But won't Mr Hutchmeyer be very cross?'

'Cross? He'll blow his top.'

Piper considered the prospect of Mr Hutchmeyer blowing his top and disliked it. It added yet another awful ingredient to a situation that was already sufficiently alarming. By the time the plane landed he was in a state of acute anxiety and it took all Sonia's coaxing to get him down the steps and into the waiting car. Presently they were speeding through pine forests towards the man whom Frensic in an unguarded moment had spoken of as the Al Capone of the publishing world.

'Now you leave all the talking to me,' said Sonia, 'and just remember that you're a shy introverted author. Modesty is the line to take.'

The car turned down a drive towards a house that had proclaimed itself by the gate as 'The Hutchmeyer Residence'.

'No one can call that modest,' said Piper staring out at the house. It stood in fifty acres of park and garden, birch and pine, an ornate shingle-style monument to the romantic eclecticism of the late nineteenth century as embodied in wood by Peabody and Stearns, Architects. Sprouting towers, dormer windows, turrets with dovecotes, piazzas with oval windows cut in their latticework, convoluted chimneys and angled balconies, the Residence was awe-inspiring. They drove under a porte-cochère into a courtyard already crammed with cars and got out. A moment later the enormous front door opened and a large red-faced man bounded down the steps.

'Sonia baby,' he bawled and hugged her to his Hawaiian shirt, 'and this must be Mr Piper.' He crunched Piper's hand and stared fiercely into his face. 'This is a great honour, Mr Piper, a very great honour to have you with us,' still holding Piper's hand he propelled him up the steps and through the door. Inside, the house was as remarkable as the exterior. A vast hall incorporated a thirteenth-century fireplace, a Renaissance staircase, a minstrels' gallery, an excruciatingly ferocious portrait of Hutchmeyer in the pose of J. P. Morgan as photographed by Steichner, and underfoot a mosaic floor depicting a great many stages in the manufacture of paper. Piper stepped cautiously across falling trees, a log jam and a vat of boiling wood pulp and up several more steps at the top of which stood a woman of breathtaking shape.

'Baby,' said Hutchmeyer, 'I want you to meet Mr Peter Piper. Mr Piper, my wife, Baby.'

'Dear Mr Piper,' murmured Baby huskily, taking his hand and smiling as far as the surgeons had permitted, 'I've been just dying to meet you. I think your novel is just the loveliest book I've been privileged to read.'

Piper gazed into the limpid azure contact lenses of Miss Penobscot 1935 and simpered. 'You're too kind,' he murmured. Baby tucked his hand under her arm and together they went into the piazza lounge.

'Does he always wear a turban?' Hutchmeyer asked Sonia as they followed.

'Only when he gets hit with a frisbee,' said Sonia coldly.

'Only when he gets hit with a frisbee,' bawled Hutchmeyer roaring with laughter. 'You hear that, Baby. Mr Piper only wears a turban when he gets hit with a frisbee. Isn't that the greatest?'

'Edged with razor blades, Hutch. With goddam razor blades!' said Sonia.

'Yeah, well that's different of course,' said Hutchmeyer deflating. 'With razor blades is different.'

Inside the piazza lounge stood a hundred people. They clutched glasses and were talking at the tops of their voices.

'Folks,' bawled Hutchmeyer and stilled the din, 'I want you all to meet Mr Peter Piper, the greatest novelist to come out of England since Frederick Forsyth.'

Piper smiled inanely and shook his head with unaffected modesty. He was not the greatest novelist to come out of England. Not yet. His greatness lay in the future and it was on the point of his tongue to state this clearly when the crowd closed round him eager to make his acquaintance. Baby had chosen her guests with care. Against their geriatric backdrop her own reconstituted charms would stand out all the more alluringly. Cataracts and fallen arches abounded. So did bosoms, as opposed to breasts, dentures, girdles, surgical stockings and the protuberant tracery of varicose veins. And strung round every puckered neck and blotchy wrist were jewels, an armoury of pearls and diamonds and gold that hung and wobbled and glistened to detract the eye from the lost battle with time.

'Oh, Mr Piper, I just want to say how much pleasure ...'

'I can't tell you how much it means to me to ...'

'I think it's fascinating to meet a real ...'

'If you would just sign my copy ...'

'You've done so much to bring people together ...'

With Baby on his arm Piper was swallowed up in the adulating crowd.

'Boy, he's really going over big,' said Hutchmeyer, 'and this is Maine. What's he going to do to the cities?'

'I hate to think,' said Sonia watching anxiously as Piper's turban bobbed among the hairdos.

'Wow them. Zap them. We'll sell two million copies if this is anything to indicate. I got a computer forecast after the welcome he got in New York and—'

'Welcome? You call that riot a welcome?' said Sonia bitterly. 'You could have got us killed.'

'Great copy,' said Hutchmeyer, 'I'm going to give MacMordie a bonus. That boy's got talent. And while we're on the subject let me say I've got a proposition to make to you.'

'I've heard your propositions, Hutch, and the answer is still no.'

'Sure but this is different.' He steered Sonia over to the bar.

By the time he had signed fifty copies of *Pause O Men for the Virgin* and drunk, unthinkingly, four Martinis, Piper's earlier apprehensions had entirely vanished. The enthusiasm with which he was being greeted had the merit that it didn't require him to say anything. He was bombarded from all sides by compliments and opinions. They seemed to come in two sizes. The thin women were intense, the ones with obesity problems cooed. No one expected Piper to contribute more than the favour of his smile. Only one woman broached the subject of his novel and Baby immediately intervened.

'Knock you up, Chloe?' she said. 'Now why should Mr

Piper want to do that? He's got a very tight schedule to meet.'

'So not everyone's had the benefit of a pussy lift,' said Chloe with a hideous wink at Piper. 'Now the way I read it Mr Piper's book is about going into the natural in a big way ...'

But Baby dragged Piper away before he could hear what Chloe had to say about going into the natural in a big way.

'What's a pussy lift?' he asked.

'That Chloe's just a cat,' said Baby, leaving Piper under the happy illusion that pussy lifts were things cats went up and down in. By the time the party broke up Piper was exhausted.

'I've put you in the Boudoir bedroom,' said Baby as she and Sonia escorted him up the Renaissance staircase. 'It's got a wonderful view of the bay.'

Piper went into the Boudoir bedroom and looked around. Originally designed to combine convenience with medieval simplicity, it had been refurbished by Baby with an eye to the supposedly sensual. A heart-shaped bed stood on a carpet of intermingled rainbows which competed for radiance with a furbelowed stool and an Art Deco dressing-table. To complete the ensemble a large and evidently demented Spanish gipsy supported a tasselled lampshade on a bedside table while a black glass chest of drawers gleamed darkly against the Wedgwood blue walls. Piper sat down on the bed and looked up at the great timber rafters. There was a solid craftsmanship about them that contrasted with the ephemeral brilliance of the furnishings. He undressed and brushed his teeth and climbed into bed. Five minutes later he was asleep.

An hour later he was wide awake again. There were voices coming through the wall behind his quilted bedhead. For a moment Piper wondered where on earth he was. The voices soon told him. The Hutchmeyers' bedroom was evidently next to his and their bathroom had a connecting door. During the next half an hour Piper learnt to his disgust that Hutchmeyer wore a truss, that Baby objected to his use of the wash-basin as a urinal, that Hutchmeyer didn't give a damn what she objected to, that Baby's late and unlamented mother, Mrs Sugg, would have done the world a service by having an abortion before Baby was born, and finally that on one traumatic occasion Baby had washed down a sleeping pill with Dentaclene from a glass containing Hutchmeyer's false teeth so would he kindly not leave the things in the medicine cabinet. From these distressing domestic details the conversation veered to personalities. Hutchmeyer thought Sonia mighty attractive. Baby didn't. All Sonia Futtle had got were her hooks into a cute little innocent. It took Piper a moment or two to recognize himself in this description and he was just wondering if he liked being called little and cute when Hutchmeyer riposted by saying he was an asslicking motherfucking Limey who just happened to have written a book that would sell. Piper most definitely didn't like that. He sat up in bed fumbled with the anatomy of the Spanish gipsy and switched the light on. But the Hutchmeyers had warred themselves to sleep.

Piper got out of bed and waded across the carpet to the window. Outside in the darkness he could just make out the shapes of a yacht and a large cruiser lying out at the end of a long narrow jetty. Beyond them across the bay a mountain was silhouetted against the starry sky and the lights of a small town shone faintly. Water slapped on the rocky beach below the house and in any other circumstances Piper would have felt the need to muse on the beauties of nature and their possible use in some future novel. Hutchmeyer's opinion of him had driven such thoughts from his mind. He got out his diary and committed to paper his observations that Hutchmeyer was the epitome of everything that was vulgar, debased, stupid and crassly commercial about modern America and that Baby Hutchmeyer was a woman of sensitivity and beauty, and deserved something better than to be married to a coarse brute. Then he got back into bed, read a chapter of *The Moral Novel* to restore his faith in human nature, and fell asleep.

Breakfast next morning proved a further ordeal. Sonia wasn't up and Hutchmeyer was in his friendliest mood.

'What I like about you is you give your readers a good fuck fantasy,' he told Piper who was trying to make up his mind which breakfast cereal to try.

'Wheatgerm is great for Vitamin E,' said Baby.

'That's for potency,' said Hutchmeyer. 'Piper's potent already, eh Piper? What he needs is roughage.'

'I'm sure he'll get all he needs of roughage from you,' said Baby. Piper poured himself a plateful of Wheatgerm.

'Now like I was saying,' Hutchmeyer continued, 'what readers want is—'

'I'm sure Mr Piper knows already what readers want,' said Baby, 'he doesn't have to hear it over breakfast.'

Hutchmeyer ignored her. 'A guy comes home from work what's he to do? Has himself a beer and watches TV, eats and goes to bed too tired to lay his wife so he reads a book—'

'If he's that tired why does he need to read a book?' asked Baby.

'He's too damned tired to sleep. Needs something to send him off. So he picks up a book and has fantasies he's not in the Bronx but in ... where did you set your book?'

'East Finchley,' said Piper, having trouble with a mouthful of Wheatgerm.

'Devon,' said Baby, 'the book is set in Devon.'

'Devon?' said Hutchmeyer. 'He says it's set in East Finchley, he ought to know for Chrissake. He wrote the goddam thing.'

'It's set in Devon and Oxford,' said Baby stubbornly. 'She has this big house and he—'

'Devon's right,' said Piper, 'I was thinking of my second book.'

Hutchmeyer glowered. 'Yeah, well, wherever. So this guy in the Bronx has fantasies he's in Devon with this old broad who's crazy about him and before he knows it he's asleep.'

'That's a great recommendation,' said Baby, 'and I don't think Mr Piper writes his books with insomniacs in the Bronx in mind. He portrays a developing relationship ...'

'Sure, sure he does but—'

'The hesitations and uncertainties of a young man whose feelings and emotional responses deviate from the socially accepted norms of his socio-sexual age grouping.'

'Right,' said Hutchmeyer, 'no question about it. He's a deviant and—'

'He is not a deviant,' said Baby, 'he is a very gifted adolescent with an identity problem and Gwendolen ...'

While Piper munched his Wheatgerm the battle about his intentions in writing *Pause* raged on. Since Piper hadn't written the book and Hutchmeyer hadn't read it, Baby came out on top. Hutchmeyer retreated to his study and Piper found himself alone with a woman who, for quite the wrong reasons, shared his own opinion that he was a great writer. And cute. Piper had reservations about being called cute by a woman whose own attractions were sufficiently at odds with one another to be disturbing. In the dim light of the party the night before he had supposed her to be thirty-five. Now he was less sure. Beneath her blouse her bra-less breasts pointed to the early twenties. Her hands didn't. Finally there was her face. It had a masklike quality, a lack of anything remotely individual, irregular or out of harmony with the faces of the two-dimensional women he had seen staring so fixedly from the pages of women's magazines like *Vogue*. Taut, impersonal and characterless it held a strange fascination for him, while her limpid azure eyes ... Piper found himself thinking of Yeats's *Sailing to Byzantium* and the artifice of jewelled birds that sang. To steady himself he read the label on the Wheatgerm jar and found that he had just consumed 740 milligrammes of phosphorus, 550 of potassium, together with vast quantities of other essential minerals and every Vitamin B under the sun.

'It seems to have a lot of Vitamin B,' he said, avoiding the allure of those eyes.

'The Bs give you energy,' murmured Baby.

'And As?' asked Piper.

'Vitamin A smooths the mucous membranes,' said Baby and once again Piper was dimly conscious that beneath this dietetic commentary there lurked an undertow of dangerous suggestion. He looked up from the Wheatgerm label and was held once more by that masklike face and limpid azure eyes.

11

Sonia Futtle rose late. Never an early riser, she had slept more heavily than usual. The strain of the previous day had taken its toll. She came downstairs to find the house empty apart from Hutchmeyer who was growling into the telephone in his study. She made herself some coffee and interrupted him.

'Have you seen Peter?' she asked.

'Baby's taken him some place. They'll be back,' said Hutchmeyer. 'Now about that proposition I put to you ...'

'No way. F & F is a good agency. We're doing well. So what would I want to change?'

'It's a Vice-Presidency I'm offering you,' said Hutchmeyer, 'and the offer stays open.'

'The only offer I'm interested in right now,' said Sonia, 'is the one you're going to make my client for all the physical injury and mental suffering and public ridicule he sustained as a result of yesterday's riot you organized at the docks.'

'Physical injury? Mental suffering?' shouted Hutchmeyer incredulously. 'That was the greatest publicity in the world and you want me to make an offer?'

Sonia nodded. 'Compensation. In the region of twenty-five thousand.'

'Twenty-five ... Are you crazy? Two million I give him for that book and you want to take me for another twenty-five grand?'

'I do,' said Sonia. 'There is nothing in the contract that says my client has to be subjected to violence, assault and the attentions of lethal frisbees. Now you organized that caper—'

'Go jump,' said Hutchmeyer.

'In that case I shall advise Mr Piper to cancel the tour.'

'You do that,' shouted Hutchmeyer, 'and I'll sue for non-fulfilment of contract. I'll take him to the cleaners. I'll goddam ...'

'Pay up,' said Sonia taking a seat and crossing her legs provocatively.

'Jesus,' said Hutchmeyer admiringly, 'I'll say this for you, you've got nerve.'

'Not all I got,' said Sonia, exposing a bit more, 'I've got Piper's second novel too.'

'And I have the option on it.'

'If he finishes it, Hutch, if he finishes it. You keep this sort of pressure up on him he's likely to Scott Fitzgerald on you. He's sensitive and—'

'I heard all that already. From Baby. Shy, sensitive, my ass. The sort of stuff he writes he ain't sensitive. Got a hide like a fucking armadillo.'

'Which, since you haven't read it ...' said Sonia.

'I don't have to read it. MacMordie read it and he said it made him almost fetch up and MacMordie don't fetch up easy.'

They wrangled on until lunch, happily embroiled in threat and counter-threat and the financial game of poker which was their real expertise. Not that Hutchmeyer paid up. Sonia had never expected him to, but at least it took his mind off Piper.

The same could not be said for Baby. Their walk along the shore to the studio after breakfast had confirmed her impression that at long last she had met a writer of genius. Piper had talked incessantly about literature and for the most part with an incomprehensibility that Baby found so impressive that she returned to the house feeling that she had undergone a cultural experience of the most profound kind. Piper's impressions were rather different, an amalgam of pleasure at having such an attentive and interested audience and wonder that so perceptive a woman could find the book he was supposed to have written anything less than disgusting. He went up to his room and was about to get out his diary when Sonia entered.

'I hope you've been discreet,' she said. 'That Baby's a ghoul.'

'A ghoul?' said Piper. 'She's a deeply sensitive ...'

'A ghoul in gold lamé pants. So what's she been doing with you all morning?'

'We went for a walk and she told me about her interest in conservation.'

'Well she didn't have to. You've only got to look at her to see she's done a great job. Like on her face.'

'She's very keen on health foods,' said Piper.

'And sandblasting,' said Sonia. 'Next time she smiles take a look at the back of her head.'

'At the back of her head? What on earth for?'

'To see how far the skin stretches. If that woman laughed she'd scalp herself.'

'Well all I can say is that she's a lot better than Hutchmeyer,' said Piper, who hadn't forgotten what he had been called the night before.

'Hutch I can handle,' said Sonia, 'no problems there. I've got him eating out of my hand so don't foul things up by making goo-goo eyes at his wife and blowing your top about things literary.'

'I am not making goo-goo eyes at Mrs Hutchmeyer,' said Piper indignantly, 'I wouldn't dream of doing such a thing.'

'Well she's making them at you, said Sonia. 'And another thing, keep that turban on. It suits you.'

'It may suit me, but it's very uncomfortable.'

It will be a lot more uncomfortable if Hutch finds out you didn't get hit with a frisbee,' said Sonia.

They went down to lunch. Thanks to a call for Hutchmeyer from Hollywood which kept him out of the room for most of the meal it was a lot easier than breakfast. He came in as they were having coffee and looked at Piper suspiciously.

'You heard of a book called *Harold and Maude*?' he asked.

'No,' said Piper.

'Why?' said Sonia.

Hutchmeyer looked at her balefully. 'Why? I'll tell you why,' he said. 'Because *Harold and Maude* just happens to be about an eighteen-year-old who falls in love with an eighty and they've already made the movie. That's why. And I want to know how come no one told me I was buying a novel that had already been written by someone else and—'

'Are you suggesting that Piper's guilty of plagiarism?' said Sonia. 'Because if you are let me—'

'Plagiarism?' yelled Hutchmeyer. 'What plagiarism? I'm saying he stole the goddam story and I've been had for a sucker by some two-bit—'

Hutchmeyer had turned purple and Baby intervened. 'If you're going to stand there and insult Mr Piper,' she said, 'I am not going to sit here and listen to you. Come along, Mr Piper. You and I will leave these two—'

'Stop,' bawled Hutchmeyer, 'I've paid two million dollars and I want to know what Mr Piper has to say about it. Like ...'

'I assure you I have never read *Harold and Maude*,' said Piper, 'I've never even heard of it.'

104

'I can vouch for that,' said Sonia. 'Besides, it's quite different. It's not the same at all . . .'

'Come, Mr Piper,' said Baby and shepherded him out of the room. Behind them Hutchmeyer and Sonia could be heard shouting. Piper staggered across the piazza lounge and sank ashen-faced into a chair.

'I knew it would go wrong,' he muttered.

Baby looked at him curiously. 'What would go wrong, honey?' she asked. Piper shook his head despondently. 'You didn't copy that book, did you?'

'No,' said Piper, 'I've never even heard of it.'

'Then you've got nothing to worry about. Miss Futtle will sort it out with him. They're two of a kind. Now why don't you go and have a rest?'

Piper went dolefully upstairs with her and into his room. Baby went into her bedroom thoughtfully and shut the door. Her intuition was working overtime. She sat on the bed and thought about his words, 'I knew it would go wrong.' Peculiar. What would go wrong? One thing at least was clear in her mind. He had never heard of *Harold and Maude*. That was sincerity speaking. And Baby Hutchmeyer had lived with insincerity long enough to recognize the truth when she heard it. She waited a while and then went along the passage and quietly opened the door of Piper's room. He was sitting with his back to her at the table by the window. At his elbow was a bottle of ink and in front of him a large leatherbound book. He was writing. Baby watched for a minute and then very gently shut the door and went back to the great waterbed inspired. She had just seen true genius at work. Like Balzac. Downstairs there was the rumble of Hutchmeyer and Sonia Futtle in battle. Baby lay back and stared into space, filled with a terrible sense of her own inutility. In the next room a solitary writer strove to convey to her and millions like her the significance of everything he thought and felt, to create a world enhanced by his imagination which would move into the future a thing of beauty and a joy forever. Downstairs those two word-merchants haggled and fought and ultimately marketed his work. And she did nothing. She was a barren creature without use or purpose, self-indulgent and insignificant. She turned her face to a Tretchikoff and presently fell asleep.

She woke an hour later to the sound of voices from the next room. They were faint and indistinct. Sonia and Piper talking. She lay and listened but could distinguish nothing. Then she heard Piper's door shut and their voices in the passage. She got off the bed and crossed to the bathroom and unbolted the door. A moment later she was in Piper's room. The leatherbound book was still there on the table. Baby crossed the room and sat down. When she got up half an hour later Baby Hutchmeyer was a different woman. She went back through the bathroom, locked the door again and sat before her mirror filled with a terrible intention.

Hutchmeyer's intentions were pretty terrible too. After his row with Sonia he had retreated to his study to blast hell out of MacMordie for not telling him about *Harold and Maude* but it was Saturday and MacMordie wasn't available for blasting. Hutchmeyer called his home number and got no reply. He sat back fuming and wondering about Piper. There was something wrong with the guy, something he couldn't put his finger on, something that didn't fit in with his idea of an author who had written about screwing old women, something weird. Hutchmeyer's suspicions were aroused. He'd known a lot of authors and none of them had been like Piper. No way. They had talked about their work all the time. But this Piper ... He'd love to have a talk with him, get him alone and give him a drink or two to loosen him up. But when he came out of his study it was to find Piper screened by women. Baby was down with a fresh dressing of warpaint and Sonia presented him with a book.

'What's that?' said Hutchmeyer recoiling.

'*Harold and Maude*,' said Sonia. 'Peter and I bought it in Bellsworth for you. You can read it and see for yourself—'

Baby laughed shrilly. 'This I must see. Him reading.'

'Shut up,' said Hutchmeyer. He poured a large highball and handed it to Piper. 'Have a highball, Piper.'

'I won't if you don't mind,' said Piper. 'Not tonight.'

'First goddam writer I ever met who doesn't drink,' said Hutchmeyer.

'First real writer you ever met period,' said Baby. 'You think Tolstoy drank?'

'Jesus,' said Hutchmeyer, 'how should I know?'

'That's a lovely yacht out there,' said Sonia to change the subject. 'I didn't know you were a sailing man, Hutch.'

'He isn't,' said Baby before Hutchmeyer could point out that his boat was the finest ocean racer money could buy and that he'd take on any man who said it wasn't. 'It's part of the props. Like the house and the neighbours and—'

'Shut up,' said Hutchmeyer.

Piper left the room and went up to the Boudoir bedroom to confide some more dark thoughts about Hutchmeyer to his diary. When he came down to dinner Hutchmeyer's face was more flushed than usual and his belligerence index was up several points. He had particularly disliked listening to an exposé of his married life by Baby who had, woman-to-woman, discussed with Sonia the symbolic implications of truss-wearing by middle-aged husbands and its relevance to the male menopause. And for once his 'Shut up' hadn't worked. Baby hadn't shut up, she had opened out with further intimate details of his habits so that Hutchmeyer was in the process of telling her to go drown herself when Piper entered the room. Piper wasn't in a mood to put up with Hutchmeyer's lack of chivalry. His years as a bachelor and student of the great novels had infected him with a reverence for Womanhood and very firm views on husbands' attitudes to wives and these didn't include telling them to go drown themselves. Besides, Hutchmeyer's blatant commercialism and his credo that what readers wanted was a good fuck-fantasy had occupied his mind all day. In Piper's opinion what readers wanted was to have their sensibilities extended and fuck-fantasies didn't come into the category of things that extended sensibilities. He went in to dinner determined to make the point. The opportunity occurred early on when Sonia, to change the subject, mentioned *Valley of The Dolls*. Hutchmeyer, glad to escape from the distressing revelations about his private life, said it was a great book.

'I absolutely disagree with you,' said Piper. 'It panders to the public taste for the pornographic.'

Hutchmeyer choked on a piece of cold lobster. 'It does what?' he said when he had recovered.

'It panders to the public taste for pornography,' said Piper, who hadn't read the book but had seen the cover.

'It does, does it?' said Hutchmeyer.

'Yes.'

'And what's wrong with pandering to public taste?'

'It's debasing,' said Piper.

'Debasing?' said Hutchmeyer, eyeing him with mounting fury.

'Absolutely.'

'And what sort of books do you think the public are going to read if you don't give them what they want?'

'Well I think . . .' Piper began before being silenced by a kick under the table from Sonia.

'I think Mr Piper thinks—' said Baby.

'Never mind what you think he thinks,' snarled Hutchmeyer, 'I want to hear what Piper thinks he thinks.' He looked expectantly at Piper.

'I think it is wrong to expose readers to books that are lacking in intellectual content,' said Piper, 'and which are deliberately designed to inflame their imaginations with sexual fantasies that—'

'Inflame their sexual fantasies?' yelled Hutchmeyer, interrupting this quotation from *The Moral Novel*. 'You sit there and tell me you don't hold with books that inflame their readers' sexual fantasies when you've written the filthiest book since *Last Exit*?'

Piper steeled himself. 'Yes, as a matter of fact I do. And as another matter of fact I . . .'

But Sonia had heard enough. With sudden presence of mind she reached for the salt and knocked the waterjug sideways into Piper's lap.

'You ever hear anything like that?' said Hutchmeyer as Baby left the room to fetch a cloth and Piper went upstairs to put on a fresh pair of trousers. 'The guy has the nerve to tell me I got no right to publish . . .'

'Don't listen to him,' said Sonia, 'he's not himself. He's upset.

108

It was that riot yesterday. The blow he got on the head. It's affected him.'

'Affected him? I'll say it has and I'm going to affect the little asshole too. Telling me I'm a goddam pornographer. Why I'll show him ...'

'Why don't you show me your yacht?' said Sonia putting her arms round his neck, a move designed at one and the same time to prevent Hutchmeyer from leaping out of his chair to pursue the retreating Piper and to indicate a new willingness on her part to listen to propositions of all kinds. 'Why don't you and me go out and take a cosy little sail around the bay?'

Hutchmeyer succumbed to the soothing influence. 'Who the hell does he think he is anyhow?' he asked with unconscious acumen. Sonia didn't answer. She clung to his arm and smiled seductively. They went out on to the terrace and down the path to the jetty.

Behind them from the piazza lounge Baby watched them thoughtfully. She knew now that in Piper she had found the man she had been waiting for, an author of real merit and one who, without a drink inside him, could stand up to Hutchmeyer and tell him to his face what he thought of him and his books. One too who appreciated her as a sensitive, intelligent and perceptive woman. She had learnt that from Piper's diary. Piper had expressed himself freely on the subject, just as he had given vent to his opinion that Hutchmeyer was a coarse, crass, stupid and commercially motivated moron. On the other hand there had been several references to *Pause* in the diary that had puzzled her and particularly his statement that it was a disgusting book. It seemed a strangely objective criticism for a novelist to make about his own work and while she didn't agree with him it raised him still further in her estimation. It showed he was never satisfied. He was a truly dedicated writer. And so, standing in the piazza lounge staring through limpid azure contact lenses at the yacht moving slowly away from the jetty, Baby Hutchmeyer was herself filled with a sense of dedication, a maternal dedication amounting to euphoria. The days of useless inactivity were over. From now on she would stand between Piper and the harsh insensitivity of Hutchmeyer and the world. She was happy.

Upstairs Piper was anything but. The first flush of his courage in challenging Hutchmeyer had ebbed away leaving him with the horrible feeling that he was in desperate trouble. He took his wet trousers off and sat on the bed wondering what on earth to do. He should never have left the Gleneagle Guest House in Exforth. He should never have listened to Frensic and Sonia. He should never have come to America. He should never have betrayed his literary principles. As the sunset faded Piper got up and was just looking for another pair of trousers when there was a knock at the door and Baby entered.

'You were wonderful,' she said, 'really wonderul.'

'Kind of you to say so,' said Piper interposing the fur-belowed stool between his trouserless self and Mrs Hutchmeyer and conscious that if anything more was needed to infuriate Mr Hutchmeyer it was to find two of them in this compromising situation.

'And I want you to know I appreciate what you have written about me,' continued Baby.

'Written about you?' said Piper groping in the cupboard.

'In your diary,' said Baby. 'I know I shouldn't have ...'

'What?' squawked Piper from the depths of the cupboard. He found a pair of trousers and struggled into them.

'I just couldn't help it,' said Baby. 'It was lying open on the table and ...'

'Then you know,' said Piper emerging from the cupboard.

'Yes,' said Baby.

'Christ,' said Piper and slumped on to the stool. 'Are you going to tell him?'

Baby shook her head. 'It's between us two.'

Piper considered this and found it only faintly reassuring. 'It's been a terrible strain,' he said finally. 'I mean not being able to talk to anyone about it. Apart from Sonia of course but she's no help.'

'I don't suppose she is,' said Baby who didn't for one moment suppose that Miss Futtle appreciated being told what a deeply sensitive, intelligent and perceptive person another woman was.

110

'Well she wouldn't be,' said Piper, 'I mean it was her idea in the first place.'

'It was?' said Baby.

'She said it would work out all right but I knew I would never be able to keep up the pretence,' continued Piper.

'I think that does you great credit,' said Baby trying desperately to imagine what Miss Futtle had had in mind in persuading Piper to pretend that he ... There was something very screwy about all this. 'Look, why don't we go downstairs and have a drink and you can tell me all about it.'

'I've got to talk to someone,' said Piper, 'but won't they be down there?'

'They've gone out on the yacht. We've got all the privacy in the world.'

They went downstairs to a little corner room with a balcony which hung out over rocks and the water lapping the beach.

'It's my hidey hole,' said Baby indicating the rows of books lining the walls. 'Where I can be myself.' She poured two drinks while Piper looked miserably at the titles. They were as confusing as his own situation and seemed to argue an eclecticism he found surprising. Maupassant leant against Hailey who in turn propped up Tolkien, and Piper, whose self was founded upon a few great writers, couldn't imagine how anyone could be themselves in these surroundings. Besides, there were a large number of detective stories and thrillers and Piper held very strong views on such trite works.

'Now tell me all about it,' said Baby soothingly and settled herself on a sofa. Piper sipped his drink and tried to think where to begin.

'Well you see I've been writing for ten years now,' he said finally, 'and ...'

Dusk deepened into night outside as Piper told his story. Beside him Baby sat enthralled. This was better than books. This was life, life not as she had known it but as she had always wanted it to be. Exciting and mysterious and filled with strange, extraordinary hazards which excited her imagination. She refilled their glasses and Piper, intoxicated by her sympathy, spoke on more fluently than he had ever written. He told the story of his life as an unrecognized genius alone in a garret, in any number of garrets looking out on to the windswept sea, struggling through months and years to express with pen and ink and those exquisite curlicues she had so admired in his notebooks the meaning of life and its deepest significance.

Baby gazed into his face and invested it all with a new romance. Pea-soup fogs returned to London. Gas lamps gleamed on the seafronts as Piper took his nightly stroll along the promenade. Baby drew copiously on her fund of half-remembered novels to add these details. Finally there were villains, tawdry rogues out of Dickens, Fagins of the literary world in the form of Frensic & Futtle of Lanyard Lane who lured the genius from his garret with the false promise of recognition. Lanyard Lane! The very name evoked for Baby a legendary London. And Covent Garden. But best of all there was Piper standing alone on a sea wall with the waves breaking below him staring fixedly out across the English Channel, the wind blowing through his hair. And here in front of her was the man himself with his peaked anxious face and tortured eyes, the living embodiment of undiscovered genius as she had visualized it in Keats and Shelley and all those other poets who had died so young. And between him and the harsh relentless reality of Hutchmeyer and Frensic and Futtle there was only Baby herself. For the first time she felt needed. Without her he would be hounded and persecuted and driven to ... Baby prophesied suicide or madness and certainly a haunted, hunted future, with Piper prey to the commercial rapacity of all those forces which had conspired to compromise him. Baby's imagination raced on into melodrama.

'We can't let it happen,' she said impetuously as Piper ran out of self-pity. He looked at her sorrowfully.

'What can I do?' he asked.

'You've got to get away,' said Baby and turned to the door on to the balcony and flung it open. Piper looked dubiously out into the night. The wind had risen and nature, imitating art or Piper's modicum of art, was hurling waves against the rocks below the house. The gusts caught at the curtains and threw them flapping into the room. Baby stood between them gazing out across the bay. Her mind was inflamed with images from novels. The night escape. The sea lashing at a small boat. A great house blazing in the darkness and two lovers locked in one another's arms. She saw herself in new guises, no longer the disregarded wife of a rich publisher, a creature of habits and surgical artifice, but the heroine of some great novel: *Rebecca, Jane Eyre, Gone With The Wind*. She turned back into the room and Piper was astonished at the intensity of her expression. Her eyes gleamed and her mouth was firm with purpose. 'We will go together,' she said and reached out her hand.

Piper took it cautiously. 'Together?' he said. 'You mean ...'

'Together,' said Baby. 'You and I. Tonight.' And holding Piper's hand she led the way out into the piazza lounge.

12

In the middle of the bay Hutchmeyer wrestled with the helm. His evening had not been a success. It was bad enough to be insulted by one of his own authors, a unique experience for which nothing in twenty-five years in the book trade had prepared him; it was even worse to be out in a yacht in the tail end of a typhoon on a pitch-dark night with a crew that consisted of one cheerfully drunk woman who insisted on enjoying herself.

'This is great,' she shouted as the yacht heaved and a wave broke over the deck, 'England here we come.'

'Oh no we don't,' said Hutchmeyer and put the helm over in order to avoid the possibility that they were heading out into the Atlantic. He stared out into the darkness and then down at the binnacle. At that moment *Romain du Roy* took a terrible turn, water flushed along the rail and into the cockpit. Hutchmeyer clung to the wheel and cursed. Beside him in the darkness Sonia squealed, whether from fear or excitement Hutchmeyer neither knew nor cared. He was wrestling with nautical problems beyond his meagre knowledge. In the dim recesses of his memory he seemed to remember that you shouldn't have sails up in a storm. You rode storms out.

'Hold this,' he yelled to Sonia and waded below into the

113

cabin to find a knife. Another wave broke over the cockpit and into his face as he emerged.

'What are you doing with that thing?' Sonia asked. Hutchmeyer brandished the knife and clung to the rail.

'I'm going to make goddam certain we don't hit land,' he shouted as the yacht scudded forward alarmingly. He crawled along the deck and hacked at every rope he could find. Presently he was writhing in canvas. By the time he had untangled himself they were no longer scudding. The yacht wallowed.

'You shouldn't have done that,' said Sonia, 'I was getting a real high out of that zoom.'

'Well, I wasn't,' said Hutchmeyer, peering into the night. It was impossible to tell where they were. A black sky hung overhead and the lights along both shores seemed to have gone out. Or they had. Out to sea.

'Christ,' said Hutchmeyer dismally. Beside him Sonia played with the wheel happily. There was something exhilarating about being out in a storm on a dark night that appealed to her sense of adventure. It awoke her combative instincts. Something tangible to pit herself against. And besides, Hutchmeyer's despondency was reassuring. At least she had taken his mind off Piper – and off her too. A storm at sea was no scene for seduction. And Hutchmeyer's efforts in that direction had been heavy-handed. Sonia had sought refuge in Scotch. Now as they rose and fell with each successive wave she was cheerfully drunk.

'We'll just have to sit the storm out,' said Hutchmeyer presently but Sonia demanded action.

'Start the motor,' she said.

'What the hell for? We don't know where we are. We could run aground.'

'I want the wind in my hair and the spume in my face,' yelled Sonia.

'Spume?' said Hutchmeyer hoarsely.

'And a man at the helm with his hand on the tiller ...'

'You got a man at the helm,' said Hutchmeyer taking it from her.

The yacht lurched into the wind and waves sucked at the dragging mainsail. Sonia laughed. 'A real man, a he-man, a seaman. A man with salt in his veins and a sail in his heart. Someone to stir the blood.'

'Stir the blood,' muttered Hutchmeyer. 'You'll get all the blood-stirring you want if we hit a rock. I should never have listened to you. Coming out on a night like this.'

'You should have listened to the weather report,' said Sonia, 'that's what you should have listened to. All I said was ...'

'I know what you said. You said, "Let's take a sail round the bay." That's what you said.'

'So we're having a little sail. The challenge of the elements. I think it's just wonderful.'

Hutchmeyer didn't. Wet, cold and bedraggled he clutched the wheel and searched the darkness for some sign of the shore-line. It was nowhere to be seen.

'Challenge of the elements my ass,' he thought bitterly, and wondered why it was that women had so little sense of reality.

It was a thought that would have found an echo in Piper's heart. Baby had changed. From being the deeply perceptive intelligent woman he had described in his diary she had become a quite extraordinarily urgent creature hell-bent on get-ting him out of the house in the middle of a most unsuitably stormy night. To make matters worse she seemed determined to come with him, a course of action calculated in Piper's opinion to put his already strained relations with Mr Hutch-meyer to a test which even flight was hardly likely to mitigate. He made the point to Baby as she led the way through the piazza lounge and into the great hall.

'I mean we can't just walk out together in the middle of the night,' he protested standing on a mosaic vat of boiling wood pulp. Hutchmeyer glowered down from his portrait on the wall.

'Why not?' said Baby, whose sense of the melodramatic seemed to be heightened in these grandiose surroundings. Piper tried to think of a persuasive answer and could only come up with the rather obvious one that Hutchmeyer wouldn't like it. Baby laughed luridly.

'Let him lump it,' she said and before Piper could point out that Hutchmeyer's lumping it was going to be personally disadvantageous and that in any case he would prefer the dangers involved in pulling the wool over Hutchmeyer's eyes as to the authorship of *Pause* to the more terrible ones of running off with his wife, Baby had clutched his hand again and was leading him up the Renaissance staircase.

'Pack your things as quickly as you can,' she said in a whisper as they stood outside the door of the Boudoir bedroom.

'Yes but ...' Piper began whispering involuntarily himself. But Baby had gone. Piper went into his room and switched on the light. His suitcase lay uninvitingly against the wall. Piper shut the door and wondered what on earth to do now. The woman must be demented to think that he was going to ... Piper staggered across the room to the window trying to rid himself of the notion that all this was really happening to him. There was an awful hallucinatory quality about the experience which fitted in with everything that had taken place since he had stepped ashore in New York. Everyone was stark staring mad. What was more they acted out their madness without a moment's hesitation. 'Shoot you as soon as look at you' was the expression that sprang to mind. It certainly sprang to mind five minutes later when Piper, his case still unpacked, opened the door of the Boudoir bedroom and poked his head outside. Baby was coming down the corridor with a large revolver in her hand. Piper shrank back into his room.

'You'd better pack this,' she said .

'Pack it?' said Piper still glowering at the thing.

'Just in case,' said Baby. 'You never know.'

Piper did. He sidled round the bed and shook his head. 'You've got to understand ...' he began but Baby had dived into the drawers of the dressing-table and was piling his underclothes on the bed.

'Don't waste time talking. Get this suitcase,' she said. 'The wind's dying down. They could be back at any moment now.'

Piper looked longingly at the window. If only they would come back now before it was too late. 'I really do think we ought to reconsider this,' he said. Baby stopped emptying the drawers and turned to him. Her taut face was alight with unventured dreams. She was every heroine she had ever read, every woman who had gone off happily to Siberia or followed her man across the Sherman-devastated South. She was more, at once the inspiration and protectress of this unhappy youth. This was her one chance of realization and she was not going to let it escape her. Behind was Hutchmeyer, the years of servitude to boredom and artifice, of surgical restoration and constructed enthusiasms; in front Piper, the knowledge that she was needed, a new life filled with meaning and significance in the service of this young genius. And now at this moment of supreme sacrifice, the culmination of so many years of expectation, he was hesitating. Baby's eyes filled with tears and she raised her arms in supplication.

'Don't you understand what this means?' she asked. Piper gaped at her. He understood only too well what it meant. He was alone in an enormous house with the demented wife of America's richest and most powerful publisher and she was proposing that they should run away together. And if he didn't she would almost certainly tell Hutchmeyer the true story of *Pause* or invent some equally frightful tale about how he had tried to seduce her. And finally there was the gun. It lay on the bed where she had dropped it. Piper glanced at the thing and as he did so Baby took a step forward, the tears that had gathered in her eyes ran down her cheeks and carried with them a contact lens. She fumbled for it on the counterpane and encountered the gun. Piper hesitated no longer. He grabbed the suitcase and plumped it on the bed and the next moment was packing it hastily with his shirts and pants. He didn't stop until everything was in, his ledgers and pens and his bottle of Waterman's Midnight Black. Finally he sat on it and fastened the catches. Only then did he turn towards her. Baby was still groping on the bed.

'I can't find it,' she said, 'I can't find it.'

'Leave it, we don't need a thing like that,' said Piper anxious to avoid any further acquaintance with firearms.

'I must have it,' said Baby, 'I can't get along without it.'

Piper humped the suitcase off the bed and Baby found the contact lens. And the gun. Clutching the one while trying to reinsert the other she followed Piper into the corridor. 'Take your bag down and come back for mine,' she told him and went into her own bedroom. Piper went downstairs, encountered

117

the glowering portrait of Hutchmeyer and came back again. Baby was standing by the great waterbed wearing a mink. Beside her were six large travel bags.

'Look,' said Piper, 'are you sure you really want . . .'

'Yes, oh yes,' said Baby. 'It's what I've always dreamt of doing. Leaving all this . . . this falsehood and starting afresh.'

'But don't you think . . .' Piper began again but Baby was not thinking. With a grand final gesture she picked up the gun and fired it repeatedly into the waterbed. Little spurts of water leapt into the air and the room echoed deafeningly with the shots.

'That's symbolic,' she cried and tossed the gun across the room. But Piper didn't hear her. Grabbing three travel bags in each hand he staggered out of the bedroom and dragged them along the corridor, his ears ringing with the sound of gunfire. He knew now that she was definitely out of her mind and the sight of the expiring waterbed had been another awful reminder of his own mortality. By the time he reached the bottom of the stairs he was panting and puffing. Baby followed him, a wraith in mink.

'Now what?' he asked.

'We'll take the cruiser,' she said.

'The cruiser?'

Baby nodded, her imagination once more inflamed with images from novels. The night flight across the water was essential.

'But won't they . . .' Piper began.

'That way they'll never know where we've gone,' said Baby. 'We'll land down the coast and buy a car.'

'Buy a car?' said Piper. 'But I haven't any money.'

'I have,' said Baby and with Piper lugging the travel bags behind her they went through the lounge and down the path to the jetty. The wind had fallen but still the water was choppy and slapped against the wooden piles and the rocks so that drifts of spray sprang up wetly against Piper's face.

'Put the bags aboard,' said Baby, 'I've got to go back for something.'

Piper hesitated for a moment and stared with mixed feelings out across the bay. He wasn't sure whether he wanted Sonia and Hutchmeyer to heave in sight now or not. But there was no sign of them. In the end he dropped the bags down into the cruiser and waited. Baby returned with a briefcase.

'My alimony,' she explained, 'from the safe.' Clutching her mink to her, she clambered down into the cruiser and went to the controls. Piper followed her unsteadily.

'Low on fuel,' she said. 'We'll need some more.' Presently Piper was trudging back and forth between the cruiser and the fuel store at the far side of the courtyard behind the house. It was dark and occasionally he stumbled.

'Isn't that enough?' he asked after the fifth journey as he handed the cans down to Baby in the cruiser.

'We can't afford to make mistakes,' she replied. 'You wouldn't want us to run out of gas in the middle of the bay.'

Piper set off for the store again. There was no doubt in his mind that he had already made a terrible mistake. He should have listened to Sonia. She had said the woman was a ghoul and she was right. A demented ghoul. And what on earth was he doing in the middle of the night filling a cruiser with cans of petrol? It wasn't an activity even vaguely related with being a novelist. Thomas Mann wouldn't have been found dead doing it. Nor would D. H. Lawrence. Conrad might have, just. Even then it was highly unlikely. Piper consulted *Lord Jim* and found nothing reassuring in it, nothing to justify this insane activity. Yes, insane was the word. Standing in the fuel store with two more cans Piper hesitated. There wasn't a single novelist of any merit who would have done what he was doing. They would all have refused to be party to such a scheme. Which was all very well, but then none of them had been in the awful predicament he was in. True, D. H. Lawrence had run off with Mr Somebody-or-other's wife, Frieda, but presumably of his own accord and because he was in love with the woman. Piper was most certainly not in love with Baby and he wasn't doing this of his own accord. Definitely not. Having consulted these precedents Piper tried to think how to live up to them. After all, he hadn't spent the last ten years of his life being the great novelist for nothing. He would take a moral stand. Which was rather easier said than done. Baby Hutchmeyer wasn't the sort of woman who would understand taking a moral stand. Besides there wasn't time to explain. The best thing to do would be to stay where he was and not go down to the boat again. That would put her in a spot when Hutchmeyer and Sonia got back. She'd have her work cut out explaining what she was doing on board the cruiser with her bags packed and ten five-gallon cans of gasolene stashed around the cabin. At least she wouldn't be able to argue that he had forced her to elope with him – if elope was the right word for running away with another man's wife. Not if he wasn't there. On the other hand there was his suitcase on board too. He would have to get that off. But how? Well of course if he didn't go back down there she would come looking for him and in that case ... Piper peered out of the store and seeing that the courtyard was clear, stole across it to the front door and into the house. Presently he was looking out from behind the lattice of the piazza lounge at the boat. Around him the great wooden house creaked. Piper looked at his watch. It was one o'clock. Where had Sonia and Hutchmeyer got to? They should have been back hours ago.

On board the cruiser Baby was having the same thought about Piper. What was keeping him? She had started the engine and checked the fuel gauge and was ready to go now and he was holding everything up. After ten minutes she became genuinely alarmed.

And with each succeeding minute her alarm grew. The sea was calm now and if he didn't come soon ...

'Genius is so unpredictable,' she muttered finally and climbed back on to the jetty. She went round the house and across the yard to the fuel store and switched on the light. Empty. Two jerry-cans standing in the middle of the floor were mute testimony to Piper's change of heart. Baby went to the door.

'Peter,' she called, her thin voice dying in the night air. Thrice she called and thrice there was no reply.

'Oh heartless boy!' she cried and this time it seemed there was an answer. It came faintly from the house in the form of a crash and a muffled shout. Piper had tripped over an ornamental vase. Baby headed across the court and up the steps to the door. Once inside she called again. In vain. Standing in the centre of the great hall Baby looked up at the portrait of her detested husband and it seemed to her overwrought imagination that a smile played about those gross arrogant lips. He had won again. He would always win and she would always remain the plaything of his idle hours.

'Never!' she shouted in answer to the clichés that fluttered hysterically about her mind and to the portrait's unspoken scorn. She hadn't come this far to be deprived of her right to freedom and romance and significance by a pusillanimous literary genius. She would do something, something symbolic that would stand as a testimony to her independence. From the ashes of the past she would arise anew like some wild phoenix from the ... Flames? Ashes? The symbolism drew her on. It would be an act from which there could be no going back. She would burn her boats. Baby, urged on by heroines of several hundred novels, flew back across the courtyard, opened a jerry-can and a moment later was trailing gasolene back to the house. She sloshed it up the steps, over the threshold, across the manifold activities of the mosaic floor, up more steps into the piazza lounge and across the carpet to the study. Then with the reckless abandon that so became her in her new role she seized a table lighter from the desk and lit it. A sheet of flame engulfed the room, scurried into the lounge, hurtled across the hall and out into the night. Then and only then did Baby turn and open the door to the terrace.

Meanwhile Piper, after his brief contretemps with the ornamental vase, was busy on the cruiser. He had heard her call and had seized his opportunity to retrieve his suitcase. He ran down the path to the jetty and clambered aboard. Above him the huge house loomed dark with derived menace. Its towers and turrets, culled from Ruskin and Morris and distilled into shingle through the architectural extravagance of Peabody and Stearns, merged with the lowering sky. Only behind the lattice of the piazza were there lights and these were dim. So was the interior of the cruiser. Piper fumbled about among the travel bags and jerry-cans for his suitcase. Where the hell had it got to? He found it finally under the mink coat and was just disentangling it when he was stopped by a sudden roar from the house and the flicker of flames. Dropping the coat he stumbled to the cabin door and looked out dumbfounded.

The Hutchmeyer Residence was ablaze. Flames shot up across the windows of Hutchmeyer's study. More flames danced behind the latticework. There was a crash of breaking glass as windows shattered in the heat and almost simultaneously from behind the house a mushroom of flame billowed up into the sky followed by the most appalling explosion. Piper gaped, transfixed by the enormity of what was happening. And as he gaped a slim figure detached itself from the shadows of the house and ran across the terrace towards him. It was Baby. The bloody woman must have ... but Piper had no time to follow this obvious train of thought to its conclusion. As Baby ran towards him another train appeared round the side of the house, a train of flames that danced and skipped, held for a moment and then flickered on along the trail of gasolene Piper had left from the fuel store. Piper watched it coming and then, with a presence of mind that was wholly his own and owed nothing to *The Moral Novel*, he clambered on to the jetty and wrestled with the ropes that held the cruiser.

'We've got to get away before that fire ...' he yelled to Baby as she rushed along the jetty towards him. Baby looked over her shoulder at the fuse.

'Oh my God,' she shrieked. The dancing flames were scurrying closer. She leapt down into the boat and into the cabin.

'It's too late,' shouted Piper. The flames were licking along the jetty now. They would reach the boat with its cargo of gas and then ... Piper dropped the line and ran. In the cabin of the cruiser, Baby struggled to find her alimony, grabbed the mink, dropped it again, and finally found the case she was looking for. She turned back towards the door but the flames had reached the end of the jetty and as she looked they leapt the gap. There was no hope. Baby turned to the controls, put the throttle full on, and as the cruiser surged forward, she scrambled out of the cabin and, still clutching the briefcase, dived over the side. Behind her the cruiser gathered speed. Flames flickered somewhere inside to mark its progress and then seemed to die down. Finally it disappeared into the darkness of the bay, the roar of its motor drowned by the much more powerful roar of the blazing house. Baby swam ashore and stumbled up the rocky beach. Piper was standing on the lawn staring in horror at the house. The flames had reached the upper storeys now, they glowed behind windows briefly, there was the crash of breaking glass as more windows splintered and then great gusts of flame shot out to lick up the sides of the shingle. Within minutes the entire façade was ablaze. Baby stood beside Piper proudly.

'There goes my past,' she murmured. Piper turned to look at her. Her hair straggled down her head and her face was naked of its pancake mask. Only her eyes seemed real and in the reflected glow Piper could see that they shone with a demented joy.

'You're out of your tiny mind,' he said with uncharacteristic frankness. Baby's fingers tightened on his arm.

'I did it all for you,' she said. 'You understand that, don't you? We have to plunge into the future unfettered by the past. We have to commit ourselves irrevocably by some free act and make an existential choice.'

'Existential choice?' shrieked Piper. The flames had reached the decorative dovecotes now and the heat was intense. 'You call setting fire to your own house an existential choice? That's not an existential choice, that's a bloody crime, that is.'

Baby smiled happily at him. 'You must read Genet, darling,' she murmured and still gripping his arm pulled him away across the lawn towards the trees. In the distance there came the wail of sirens. Piper hurried. They had just reached the edge of the forest when the night air was split by another series of explosions. Far out across the bay the cruiser had exploded. Twice. And silhouetted against the second ball of flame Piper seemed to glimpse the mast of a yacht.

'Oh my God,' he muttered.

'Oh my darling,' murmured Baby in response and turned her face to his.

13

Hutchmeyer was in a foul temper. He had been insulted by an author, he had proved himself an inept yachtsman, had lost his sails, and finally his virility had been put in doubt by Sonia Futtle's refusal to take his overtures seriously.

'O come on now, Hutch baby,' she had said, 'put it away. This is no time to be proving your manhood. Okay, so you're a man and I'm a woman. I heard you. And I don't doubt you. I really don't. You've got to believe me, I don't. Now you just put your clothes back on again and ...'

'They're wet,' said Hutchmeyer. 'They're soaking wet. You want me to catch my death of pneumonia or something?'

Sonia shook her head. 'Let's just get on back to the house and you can be nice and dry in no time at all.'

'Yeah, well you just tell me how I'm going to get us back home with the mainsail in the water. So all we do is go round in circles. That's what we do. Aw come on, honey ...'

But Sonia wouldn't. She went up on deck and looked across the water. In the cabin doorway Hutchmeyer, pinkly naked and shivering, made one last plea. 'You're all woman,' he said, 'you know that. All woman. I got a real respect for you. I mean we've got ...'

'A wife,' said Sonia bluntly, 'that's what you've got. And I've got a fiancé.'

'You've got a what?' said Hutchmeyer.

'You heard me. A fiancé. Name of Peter Piper.'

'That little—' but Hutchmeyer got no further. His attention had been drawn to the shoreline. He could see it now quite clearly. By the light of a blazing house.

'Look at that,' said Sonia, 'somebody's having one hell of a house-warming.'

Hutchmeyer grabbed the binoculars and peered through them. 'What do you mean "somebody"?' he yelled a moment later. 'That's no somebody. That's my house!'

'That was your house,' said Sonia practically, before the full implications of the blaze dawned on her, 'oh my God!'

'You're damn right,' Hutchmeyer snarled and hurled himself at the starter. The marine engine turned over and the yacht began to move. Hutchmeyer wrestled with the wheel and tried to maintain course for the holocaust that had been his home. Over the port gunwale the mainsail acted as a a trawl and the *Romain du Roy* veered to the left. Naked and panting, Hutchmeyer fought to compensate but it was no good.

'I'll have to ditch the sail,' he shouted and at that moment a dark shape appeared silhouetted against the blaze. It was the cruiser. Travelling at speed towards them she too had begun to burn. 'My God, the bastard's going to ram us,' he yelled but the next moment the cruiser proved him wrong. She exploded. First the jerry-cans in the cabin blew up and portions of the cruiser cavorted into the air; second what remained of the hull careered towards them and the main fuel tanks blew. A ball of flame ballooned out and from it there appeared a dark oblong lump which arced through the air and fell with a terrible crash through the foredeck of the yacht. The *Romain de Roy* lifted her stern out of the water, slumped back and began to settle. Sonia, clinging to the rail, stared around her. The hull of the cruiser was sinking with a hissing noise. Hutchmeyer had disappeared and a second later Sonia was in the water as the yacht keeled over, tilted and sank. Sonia swam away from the wreckage. Fifty yards away the sea was alight with flaming fuel from the cruiser and by this eerie light she saw Hutchmeyer in the water behind her. He was clinging to a piece of wood.

'Are you okay?' she called.

Hutchmeyer whimpered. It was obvious that he was not okay. Sonia swam over to him and trod water.

'Help, help,' squawked Hutchmeyer.

'Take it easy,' said Sonia, 'just don't panic. You can swim, can't you?'

Hutchmeyer's eyes goggled in his head. 'Swim? What do you mean "swim"? Of course I can swim. What do you think I'm doing?'

'So you're okay,' said Sonia. 'Now all we got to do is swim ashore . . .'

But Hutchmeyer was gurgling again. 'Swim ashore? I can't swim that far. I'll drown. I'll never make it. I'll . . .'

Sonia left him and headed towards the floating wreckage.

125

Maybe she could find a lifejacket. Instead she found a number of empty jerry-cans. She swam back with one to Hutchmeyer.

'Hang on to this,' she told him. Hutchmeyer exchanged his piece of wood for the can and clung to it. Sonia swam off again and collected two more jerry-cans. She also found a piece of rope. Tying the cans together she looped the rope round Hutchmeyer's waist and knotted it.

'That way you can't drown,' she said. 'Now you just stay right here and everything is going to be just fine.'

Hutchmeyer, balancing on his raft of cans, stared at her maniacally. 'Fine?' he shrieked. 'Fine? My house is being burnt, some crazy swine tries to murder me with a fireboat, my beautiful yacht is sunk underneath me and everything is just fine?'

But Sonia was already out of earshot, swimming for the shore with a steady sidestroke that would not tire her. All her thoughts were centred on Piper. He had been in the house when she left and now all that was left of the house ... She turned over and looked across the water. The house still bulked large upon the horizon, a yellow, ruddy mass from which sparks flew continually upwards, and as she watched a great flame leapt up. The roof had evidently collapsed. Sonia turned on her side and swam on. She had to get back to find out what had happened. Perhaps poor darling Peter had had another of his accidents. She prepared herself for the worst while taking refuge in the maternal excuse that he was accident-prone before recognizing that Piper's accidents had not after all been of his making. It had been MacMordie who had arranged the riot on their arrival in New York. She could hardly blame Piper for that. If anyone was to blame it had been ...

Sonia shut out the thought of her own culpability by wondering about the boat that had careered out of the darkness at them and exploded. Hutchmeyer had said someone had tried to murder him. It seemed an extraordinary notion but then again it was extraordinary that his house had caught fire. Put these two events together and it argued an organized and premeditated action. In that case Piper was not responsible. Nothing he had ever done had been organized and premeditated.

He was plain accident-prone. With this reassuring thought Sonia reached the beach and clambered ashore. For several minutes she lay on the ground to get her strength back and as she lay there another dreadful possibility crossed her mind. If Hutchmeyer had been right and someone had really tried to murder him it was all too likely that finding Piper and Baby alone in the house they had first ... Sonia staggered to her feet and set off through the trees towards the fire. She had to find out what had happened. And supposing it had been an accident there was still the chance that the shock of being present when the great house ignited had caused Piper to blurt out to someone that he wasn't the real author of *Pause*. In which case the fat would really be in the fire. If the fat wasn't already. It was the first question she put to a fireman she found dousing a blazing bush in the garden.

'Well if there was he's roasted to a cinder,' he said. 'Some crazy guy loosed off a whole lot of shots when we got here but the roof fell in and he hasn't fired since.'

'Shots?' said Sonia. 'You did say shots?'

'With a machine-gun,' said the firemen, 'from the basement. But like I said the roof fell in and he hasn't fired no more.'

Sonia looked at the glowing mass. Heat waves gusted into her face. Someone firing a machine-gun from the basement? It didn't make sense. Nothing made sense. Unless of course you accepted Hutchmeyer's theory that someone had deliberately set out to murder him.

'And you're quite sure nobody escaped?' she asked.

The fireman shook his head.

'Nobody,' he said. 'We were the first truck to get here and apart from the shooting there hasn't anything come out of there. And the guy who did the shooting just has to be a goner.'

So was Sonia. For a moment she tried to steady herself and then she collapsed. The firemen hoisted her over his shoulder and carried her to an ambulance. Half an hour later Sonia Futtle was fast asleep in hospital. She had been heavily sedated.

Hutchmeyer on the other hand was wide awake. He sat naked except for the jerry-cans in the back of the Coastguard launch that had rescued him and tried to explain what he had been doing in the middle of the bay at two o'clock in the morning. The Coastguard didn't appear to believe him.

'Okay, Mr Hutchmeyer, so you weren't on board your cruiser when she bombed out ...'

'My cruiser?' yelled Hutchmeyer. 'That wasn't my cruiser. I was on board my yacht.'

The Coastguard regarded him sceptically and pointed to a piece of wreckage on the deck. Hutchmeyer stared at it. The words *Folio Three* were clearly visible, painted on the wood.

'*Folio Three*'s my boat,' he muttered.

'Thought it just might be,' said the Coastguard. 'Still if you say you weren't on her ...'

'On her? On her? Whoever was on that boat is barbecued duck by now. Do I look like I was ...'

Nobody said anything and presently the launch bumped into the shore below what remained of the Hutchmeyer Residence and Hutchmeyer was helped ashore, wrapped in a blanket. In single file they made their way through the woods to the drive where a dozen police cars, fire trucks and ambulances were gathered.

'Found Mr Hutchmeyer floating out there with these,' the Coastguard told the Police Chief and indicated the jerry-cans. 'Thought you might be interested.'

Police Chief Greensleeves looked at Hutchmeyer, at the jerry-cans, and back again. He was obviously very interested.

'And this,' said the Coastguard and produced the piece of wood with *Folio Three* written on it.

Police Chief Greensleeves studied the name. '*Folio Three* eh? Mean anything to you, Mr Hutchmeyer?'

Huddled in the blanket Hutchmeyer was staring at the glowing ruins of his house.

'I said, does *Folio Three* mean anything to you, Mr Hutchmeyer?' the Police Chief repeated and followed Hutchmeyer's gaze speculatively.

'Of course it does,' said Hutchmeyer, 'it's my cruiser.'

'Mind telling us what you were going out on your cruiser this time of the night?'

'I wasn't on my cruiser. I was on my yacht.'

'*Folio Three* is a cruiser,' said the Coastguard officiously.

'I know it's a cruiser,' said Hutchmeyer. 'What I'm saying is that I wasn't on it when the explosion occurred.'

'Which explosion, Mr Hutchmeyer?' said Greensleeves.

'What do you mean "which explosion"? How many explosions have there been tonight?'

Police Chief Greensleeves looked back at the house. 'That's a good question,' he said, 'a very good question. It's a question I keep asking myself. Like how come nobody calls the Fire Department to say the house is burning until it's too late. And when we get here how come somebody is so anxious we don't put the fire out they open up with a heavy machine-gun from the basement and blast all hell out of a fire truck.'

'Somebody opened fire from the basement?' said Hutchmeyer incredulously.

'That's what I said. With a goddam machine-gun, heavy calibre.'

Hutchmeyer looked unhappily at the ground. 'Well I can explain that,' he began and stopped.

'You can explain it? I'd be glad to hear your explanation, Mr Hutchmeyer.'

'I keep a machine-gun in the romper room.'

'You keep a heavy-calibre machine-gun in the romper room? Like to tell me why you keep a machine-gun in the romper room?'

Hutchmeyer swallowed unhappily. He didn't like to at all. 'For protection,' he muttered finally.

'For protection? Against what?'

'Bears,' said Hutchmeyer.

'Bears, Mr Hutchmeyer? Did I hear you say "bears"?'

Hutchmeyer looked round desperately and tried to think of a reasonable answer. In the end he told the truth. 'You see one time my wife was into bears and I . . .' he tailed off miserably.

Police Chief Greensleeves studied him with even keener interest. 'Mrs Hutchmeyer was into bears? Did I hear you say Mrs Hutchmeyer was into bears?'

But Hutchmeyer had had enough. 'Don't keep asking me if that's what you heard,' he shouted. 'If I say Mrs Hutchmeyer was into bears she was into goddam bears. Ask the neighbours. They'll tell you.'

'We sure will,' said Chief Greensleeves. 'So you go out and buy yourself some artillery? To shoot bears?'

'I didn't shoot bears. I just had the gun in case I had to.'

'And I suppose you didn't shoot up fire trucks either?'

'Of course I didn't. Why the hell should I want to do a thing like that?'

'I wouldn't know, Mr Hutchmeyer, any more than I'd know what you were doing in the middle of the bay in the raw with a heap of empty gas-cans tied round you and your house is on fire and nobody has called the Fire Department.'

'Nobody called ... You mean my wife didn't call ...' Hutchmeyer gaped at Greensleeves.

'Your wife? You mean you didn't have your wife with you out in the bay on board your cruiser?'

'Certainly not,' said Hutchmeyer, 'I've told you already I wasn't on my cruiser My cruiser tried to ram me on my yacht and blew up and ...'

'So where's Mrs Hutchmeyer?'

Hutchmeyer looked around desperately. 'I've no idea,' he said.

'Okay, take him down the station,' said the Police Chief, 'we'll go into this thing more thoroughly down there.' Hutchmeyer was bundled into the back of the police car and presently they were on their way into Bellsworth. By the time they reached the station Hutchmeyer was in an advanced state of shock.

So was Piper. The fire, the exploding cruiser, the arrival of the fire engines and police cars with their wailing sirens and finally the rapid machine-gun fire from the romper room had all served to undermine what little power of self-assertion he had ever possessed. As the firemen ran for cover and the police dropped to the ground he allowed himself to be led away through the woods by Baby. They hurried along a path and came out in the garden of another large house. People were standing outside the front door gazing at the smoke and flames roaring into the air over the trees. Baby hesitated a moment and then, taking advantage of the cover of some bushes, dragged Piper along below the house and into the woods on the other side.

'Where are we going?' Piper asked after another half mile. 'I mean we can't just walk away like this as if nothing had happened.'

'You want to go back?' hissed Baby.

Piper said he didn't.

'Right, so we've got to get some mileage,' said Baby. They went on and passed three more houses. After two miles Piper protested again.

'They're bound to wonder what's become of us,' he said.

'Let them wonder,' said Baby.

'I don't see that's going to do us any good,' said Piper. 'They are going to find out you deliberately set fire to the house and then there's the cruiser. It's got all my things on it.'

'It had all your things on it. Right now they're not on it any more. They're either at the bottom of the bay or they're floating around alongside my mink. When they find them you know what they're going to think?'

'No,' said Piper.

Baby giggled. 'They're going to think we went with them.'

'Went with them?'

'Like we're dead,' said Baby with another sinister giggle. Piper didn't see anything to laugh about. Death even by proxy wasn't a joke and besides he had lost his passport. It had been in the suitcase with his precious ledgers.

'Right, so they'll know you're dead,' said Baby when he pointed this out to her. 'Like I said, we have to make a break with the past. So we've made it. Completely. We're *free*. We can go anywhere and do anything. We've broken the fetters of circumstance.'

'You may see it that way,' said Piper, 'I can't say I do. As far as I'm concerned the fetters of circumstance happen to be a lot stronger than they ever were before all this happened.'

'Oh you're just a pessimist,' said Baby. 'I mean you've got to look on the bright side.'

Piper did. Even the bay was lit up by the conflagration and a number of boats had gathered offshore to watch the blaze.

'And just how do you think you're going to explain all this?' he said, forgetting for the moment that he was free and that there was no going back. Baby turned on him violently.

'Who's to explain to?' she demanded. 'We're dead. Get it, dead. We don't exist in the world where that happened. That's past history. It hasn't got anything to do with us. We belong to the future.'

'Well someone's going to have to explain it,' said Piper, 'I mean you can't just go round burning houses down and exploding boats and hope that people aren't going to ask questions. And what happens when they don't find our bodies at the bottom of the bay?'

'They'll think we floated out to sea or the sharks got us or something. That's not our problem what they think. We've got our new lives to live.'

'Fat chance there's going to be of that,' said Piper, not to be consoled. But Baby was undismayed. Grasping Piper's hand she led the way on through the woods.

'Dual destiny, here we come,' she said gaily. Behind her Piper groaned. Dual destiny with this demented woman was the last thing he wanted. Presently they came out of the woods again. In front of them stood another large house. Its windows were dark and there was no sign of life.

'We'll hole up here until the heat's off,' said Baby using a vernacular that Piper had previously only heard in B-movies.

'What about the people who live here?' he asked. 'Aren't they going to mind if we just move in?'

'They won't know. This is the Van der Hoogens' house and they're away on a world tour. We'll be as safe as houses.'

Piper groaned again. In the light of what had just happened at the Hutchmeyer house the saying seemed singularly inappropriate. They crossed the grass and went round a gravel path to the side door.

'They always leave the key in the glasshouse,' said Baby. 'You just stay here and I'll go get it. She went off and Piper stood uncertainly by the door. Now if ever was his chance to escape. But he didn't take it. He had lived too long in the shadow of other authors' identities to be able now to act on his own behalf. By the time Baby returned he was shaking. A reaction to his predicament had set in. He wobbled into the house after her. Baby locked the door behind them.

In Hampstead Frensic got up early. It was Sunday, the day before publication, and the reviews of *Pause O Men for the Virgin* should be in the papers. He walked up the hill to the newsagent and bought them all, even the *News of The World* which didn't review books but would be consoling reading if the reviews were bad in the others or, worse still, non-existent. Then, savouring his self-restraint, he strolled back to his flat without glancing at them on the way and put the kettle on for breakfast. He would have toast and marmalade and go through the papers as he ate. He was just making coffee when the telephone rang. It was Geoffrey Corkadale.

'You've seen the reviews?' he asked excitedly. Frensic said he hadn't.

'I've only just got up,' he said, piqued that Geoffrey had robbed him of the pleasure of reading the evidently excellent coverage. 'I gather from your tone that they're good.'

'Good? They're raves, absolute raves. Listen to what Frieda Gormley has to say in *The Times*, "The first serious novel to attempt the disentanglement of the social complicity surrounding the sexual taboo that has for so long separated youth from age. Of its kind *Pause O Men for the Virgin* is a masterpiece."'

'Gormless bitch,' muttered Frensic.

'Isn't that splendid?' said Geoffrey.

'It's senseless,' said Frensic. 'If *Pause* is the first novel to attempt the disentanglement of complicity, and Lord alone knows how anyone does that, it can't be "of its kind". It hasn't got any kind. The bloody book is unique.'

'That's in the *Observer*,' said Geoffrey not to be discouraged, 'Sheila Shelmerdine says, "*Pause O Men* blah blah blah moves us by the very intensity of its literary merits while at the same time demonstrating a compassionate concern for the elderly and the socially isolated. This unique novel attempts to unfathom those aspects of life which for too long have been ignored by those whose business it is to advance the frontiers of social sensibility. A lovely book and one that deserves the widest readership." What do you think of that?'

133

'Frankly,' said Frensic, 'I regard it as unmitigated tosh but I'm delighted that Miss Shelmerdine has said it all the same. I always said it would be a money-spinner.'

'You did, you most certainly did,' said Geoffrey, 'I have to hand it to you, you've been absolutely right.'

'Well we'll have to see about that,' said Frensic before Geoffrey could become too effusive. 'Reviews aren't everything. People have yet to buy the book. Still, it augurs well for American sales. Is there anything else?'

'There's a rather nasty piece by Octavian Dorr.'

'Oh good,' said Frensic. 'He's usually to the point and I like his style.'

'I don't,' said Geoffrey. 'He's far too personal for my taste and he should stick to the book. That's what he's paid for. Instead he has made some rather odious comparisons. Still I suppose he has given us some quotable quotes for the jacket of Piper's next book and that's the main thing.'

'Quite,' said Frensic and turned with relish to Octavian Dorr's column in the *Sunday Telegraph*, 'I just hope we do as well with the weeklies.'

He put the phone down, made some toast and settled down with Octavian Dorr whose piece was headed 'Permissive Senility'. It began, 'It is appropriate that the publishers of *Pause O Men for the Virgin* by Peter Piper should have printed their first book during the reign of Catherine The Great. The so-called heroine of this their latest has many of the less attractive characteristics of that Empress of Russia. In particular a fondness amounting to sexual mania for the favours of young men and partiality for indiscretion that was, to say the least, regrettable. The same can be said for the publishers, Corkadales . . .'

Frensic could see exactly why Geoffrey had hated the review. Frensic found it entirely to his taste. It was long and strident and while it castigated the author, the publisher and the public whose appetite for perverse eroticism made the sale of such novels profitable, and then went on to blame society in general for the decline in literary values, it nevertheless drew attention to the book. Mr Dorr might deplore perverse eroticism but he also helped to sell it. Frensic finished the review with a sigh of relief and turned to the others. Their praise, the presumptuous pap of progressive opinion, earnest, humourless and sickeningly well-meaning, had given *Pause* the imprimatur of respectability Frensic had hoped for. The novel was being taken seriously and if the weeklies followed suit there was nothing to worry about.

'Significance is all,' Frensic murmured and helped his nose to snuff. 'Prime the pump with meaningful hogwash.'

He settled back in his chair and wondered if there was anything he could do to ensure that *Pause* got the maximum publicity. Some nice big sensational story for the daily papers ...

14

In the event Frensic had no need to worry. Five hours to the west the sensational story of Piper's death at sea was beginning to break. So was Hutchmeyer. He sat in the police chief's office and stared at the chief and told his story for the tenth time to an incredulous audience. It was empty gasolene cans that were fouling things up for him.

'Like I've told you, Miss Futtle tied them to me to keep me afloat while she went to get help.'

'She went to get help, Mr Hutchmeyer? You let a little lady go and get help ...'

'She wasn't little,' said Hutchmeyer 'she's goddam large.'

Chief Greensleeves shook his head sorrowfully at this lack of chivalry. 'So you were out in the middle of the bay with this Miss Futtle. What was Mrs Hutchmeyer doing all this time?'

'How the hell would I know? Setting fire to my hou ...' Hutchmeyer stopped himself.

'That's mighty interesting,' said Greensleeves. 'So you're telling us Mrs Hutchmeyer is an arsonist.'

'No I'm not,' shouted Hutchmeyer, 'all I know is—' He was interrupted by a lieutenant who came in with a suitcase and several articles of clothing, all sodden.

'Coastguards found these out in the wreckage,' he said and held a coat up for inspection. Hutchmeyer stared at it in horror.

'That's Baby's,' he said. 'Mink. Cost a fortune.'

'And this?' asked the lieutenant indicating the suitcase.

Hutchmeyer shrugged. The lieutenant opened the case and removed a passport.

Greensleeves took it from him. 'British,' he said. 'British passport in the name of Piper, Peter Piper. The name mean anything to you?'

Hutchmeyer nodded. 'He's an author.'

'Friend of yours?'

'One of my authors. I wouldn't call him a friend.'

'Friend of Mrs Hutchmeyer maybe?' Hutchmeyer ground his teeth.

'Didn't hear that, Mr Hutchmeyer. Did you say something?'

'No,' said Hutchmeyer.

Chief Greensleeves scratched his head thoughtfully. 'Seems like we've got ourselves another little problem here,' he said finally. 'Your cruiser blows out of the water like she's been dynamited and when we go look see what do we find? A mink coat that's Mrs Hutchmeyer's and a bag that belongs to a Mr Piper who just happens to be her friend. You think there's any connection?'

'What do you mean "any connection"?' said Hutchmeyer.

'Like they was on that cruiser when she blew?'

'How the hell would I know where they were? All I know is that whoever was on that cruiser tried to kill me.'

'Interesting you say that,' said Chief Greensleeves, 'very interesting.'

'I don't see anything interesting about it.'

'Couldn't be the other way round, could it?'

'Could what be the other way round?' said Hutchmeyer.

'That you killed them?'

'I did what?' shouted Hutchmeyer and let go his blanket. 'Are you accusing me of—'

'Just asking questions, Mr Hutchmeyer. There's no need for you getting excited.'

But Hutchmeyer was out of his chair. 'My house burns

down, my cruiser blows up, my yacht's sunk under me, I'm in the water drowning some hours and you sit there and suggest I killed my ... why you fat bastard I'll have my lawyers sue you for everything you've got. I'll—'

'Sit down and shut up,' bawled Greensleeves. 'Now you just listen to me. Fat bastard I may be but no New York mobster's going to tell me. We know all about you, Mr Hutchmeyer. We don't just sit on our asses and watch you move in and buy up good real estate with money that could be laundered for the Mafia and we don't know about it. This isn't Hicksville and it isn't New York. This is Maine and you don't carry any weight round here. And we don't like your sort moving in and buying us up. We may be a poor state but we ain't dumb. Now, are you going to tell us what really happened with your wife and her fancy friend or are we going to have to drag the bay and sift the ashes of your house till we find them?'

Hutchmeyer slumped nakedly back into his chair, appalled at the glimpse he had just been given of his social standing in Frenchman's Bay. Like Piper, he knew now that he should never have come to Maine. He was more than ever convinced of his mistake when the lieutenant came in with Baby's travel bags and pocket book.

'There's a whole lot of money in the bag,' he told Greensleeves. The Chief pawed through it and extracted a wad of wet notes. 'Seems like Mrs Hutchmeyer was going some place with a lot of dollars when she died,' he said. 'So now we've really got ourselves a problem. Mrs Hutchmeyer on that cruiser with her friend, Mr Piper. Both got baggage with them and money. And then "Bam" their cruiser explodes just like that. I reckon we're going to have to send divers down to see if they can find the bodies.'

'Have to start quick,' said the lieutenant. 'The way the tide's running they could be out to sea by now.'

'So we start now,' said Greensleeves and went out into the lobby where some reporters were waiting.

'Got any theory?' they asked.

Greensleeves shook his head. 'We got two people missing presumed drowned. Mrs Baby Hutchmeyer and a Mr Piper. He's a British author. That's all for now.'

'What about this Miss Futtle? 'said the lieutenant. 'She's missing too.'

'And what about the house being burnt down?'

'We're waiting for a report on that,' said Greensleeves.

'But you do suspect deliberate arson?'

Greensleeves shrugged. 'You put all these things together and work out what I suspect,' he said and pressed on. Five minutes later the wires were buzzing with the news that Peter Piper, the famous author, was dead in bizarre circumstances.

In the Van der Hoogen mansion the victims of the tragedy listened to the news of their deaths on a transistor in the gloom of a bedroom on the top floor. Part of the gloom resulted from the shutters on the windows and part, from Piper's point of view, from the prospect that his death opened up before him. It was bad enough being an author by proxy, but being a corpse by proxy was awful beyond belief. Baby on the other hand greeted the news gaily.

'We've made it,' she said. 'They're not even going to come looking for us. You heard what they said. With the tide running the skindivers aren't expecting to find the bodies.'

Piper looked miserably round the bedroom. 'It's all very well you talking,' he said. 'What you don't seem to understand is that I don't have an identity. I've lost my passport and all my work. How on earth am I going to get back to England? I can't go to the Embassy and ask for another passport. And the moment I appear in public I'm going to be arrested for arson and boat-burning and attempted murder. You've landed us in a ghastly mess.'

'I've freed you from the past. You can be anyone you want to be now.'

'All I want to be is myself,' said Piper.

Baby looked at him dubiously. 'From what you told me last night you weren't yourself before,' she said, 'I mean what sort of self were you being the author of a book you didn't write?'

'At least I knew what I wasn't. Now I don't even know that.'

'You're not a dead body. That's one good thing.'

'I might just as well be,' said Piper looking lugubriously at the sheeted forms of the furniture as if they were so many shrouds cloaking those different authors he had so happily aspired to be. The dim light filtering through the shutted windows added to the impression that he was sitting in a tomb, the sepulchre of his literary ambitions. A sense of profound melancholy settled on him and with it the imagery of *The Flying Dutchman* doomed to wander the seas until such day ... but for Piper there would be no release. He had been party to a crime, a whole number of crimes, and even if he went to the police now they wouldn't believe him. Why should they? Was it likely that a rich woman like Baby would burn down her own home and blow up an expensive cruiser and sink her husband's yacht? And even if she admitted that she was to blame for the whole thing, there would still be a trial and Hutchmeyer's lawyers would want to know why his suitcase had been on the boat. And finally the fact that he hadn't written *Pause* would come out and then everyone would suspect ... not even suspect, they would be certain he was a fraud and after the Hutchmeyer money. And Baby had stolen a quarter of a million dollars from the safe in Hutchmeyer's study. Piper shook his head hopelessly and looked up to find her watching him with interest.

'No way, baby,' she said evidently reading his mind. 'It's dual destiny for us now. You try anything and I'll turn myself in and say you forced me.'

But Piper was past trying anything. 'What are we going to do now?' he asked. 'I mean we can't just sit here in someone else's house for ever.'

'Two days, maybe three,' said Baby, 'then we'll move on.'

'How? Just how are we going to move on?'

'Simple,' said Baby, 'I'll call for a cab and we'll take a flight from Bangor. No problems. They won't be looking for us on dry land ...'

She was interrupted by a crunch on the drive. Piper went to the shutters and looked down. A police car had stopped outside.

'The cops,' Piper whispered. 'You said they wouldn't be looking for us.'

Baby joined him at the window. A bell chimed eerily two floors below. 'They're merely checking the Van der Hoogens to

139

ask if they heard anything suspicious last night,' she said. 'They'll go away again.' Piper stared down at the two policemen. All he had to do now was to call out and ... but Baby's fingers tightened on his arm and Piper made no sound. Presently after wandering round outside the house the two cops got back into their car and drove away.

'What did I tell you?' said Baby, 'no problems. I'll go down to the kitchen and get us something to eat.'

Left to himself Piper paced the dim room and wondered why he hadn't called out to those two policemen. The simple, obvious reasons no longer sufficed. If he had called out it would have been some proof that he'd had nothing to do with the fire ... at least an indication of innocence. But he had made no move. Why not? He had had a chance to escape from this mess and he hadn't taken it. Not through fear only but more alarmingly out of a willingness, almost a desire, to remain alone in this empty house with an extraordinary woman. What sort of terrible complicity was it that had prevented him? Baby was mad. He had no doubt in his mind about that and yet she exercised a weird fascination for him. He had never met anyone in his life before like her. She was oblivious of the ordinary conventions that ordered other people's lives and she could look calmly down at the police and say 'They will go away again' as if they were simply neighbours paying a social call. And they had. And he had done what she had expected and would go on doing it, even to the point of being anyone he wanted in this circumscribed freedom she had created round him by her actions. Anyone he wanted? He could only think of other authors but none had been in his predicament, and without a model to guide him Piper was thrown back on his own limited resources. And on Baby's. He would become what she wanted. That was the truth of the matter. Piper glimpsed the attraction she held for him. She knew what he was. She had said so last night before everything had started to go wrong. She had said he was a literary genius and she had meant it. For the first time he had met someone who knew what he really was and having found her he couldn't let her go. Exhausted by this frightening realization Piper lay down on the bed and closed his eyes and when Baby came upstairs with a tray she found him fast asleep. She looked at him fondly and then putting the tray down, took a sheet from a chair and covered him with it. Under the shroud Piper slept on.

In the police station Hutchmeyer would have done the same if they had let him. Instead, still naked beneath the blanket, he was subjected to interminable questions about his relations with his wife and with Miss Futtle and what Piper meant to Mrs Hutchmeyer and finally why he had chosen a particularly stormy night to go sailing in the bay.

'You usually go sailing without checking the weather?'

'Look I told you we just went out for a sail. We weren't figuring on going places, we just got up . . .'

'From the dinner table and said, "Let's just you and me . . ." '

'Miss Futtle suggested it,' said Hutchmeyer.

'Oh she did, did she? And what did Mrs Hutchmeyer have to say about you going sailing with another woman?'

'Miss Futtle isn't another woman. Not that sort of other woman. She's a literary agent. We do business together.'

'Naked on a yacht in the middle of a mini-hurricane you do business together? What sort of business?'

'We weren't doing business on the yacht. It was a social occasion.'

'Kind of thought it was. I mean naked and all.'

'I wasn't naked to begin with. I just got wet so I took my clothes off.'

'You just got wet so you took your clothes off? Are you sure that was the only reason you were naked?'

'Of course I'm sure. Look, no sooner had we got out there than the wind blew up . . .'

'And the house blew up. And your cruiser blew up. And Mrs Hutchmeyer blew up and this Mr Piper . . .' Hutchmeyer blew up.

'Okay, Mr Hutchmeyer, if that's the way you want it,' said Greensleeves as Hutchmeyer was pinned back into his chair. 'Now we're really going to get tough.'

He was interrupted by a sergeant who whispered in his ear. Greensleeves sighed. 'You're sure?'

'That's what she says. Been up at the hospital all day.'

Greensleeves went out and looked at Sonia. 'Miss Futtle? You say you're Miss Futtle?'

Sonia nodded. 'Yes,' she said. The police chief could see that Hutchmeyer had been telling the truth after all. Miss Futtle was not a little lady, not by a long way.

'Okay, we'll take your statement in here,' he said and took her into another office. For two hours Sonia made her statement. When Greensleeves came out he had an entirely new theory. Miss Futtle had been most cooperative.

'Right,' he said to Huchmeyer, 'now we'd like you to tell us just what happened down in New York when Piper arrived. We understand you arranged a kind of riot for him.'

Hutchmeyer looked wildly round. 'Now wait a minute. That was just a publicity stunt. I mean ...'

'And what I mean,' said Greensleeves, 'is that you set this Mr Piper up for a target for every crazy pressure group going. Arabs, Jews, Gays, the IRA, the blacks, old women, you name it, you let them loose on the guy and you call that a publicity stunt?'

Hutchmeyer tried to think. 'Are you telling me that one of those groups did this thing?' he asked.

'I'm not telling you anything, Mr Hutchmeyer. I'm asking.'

'Asking what?'

'Asking you if you think it was so goddam clever setting Mr Piper up for a target when the poor guy hadn't done anything worse than write a book for you? Doesn't seem you did yourself or him a favour the way things have worked out, does it?'

'I didn't think anything like this ...'

Greensleeves leant forward. 'Now I'm just telling you something for your own good, Mr Hutchmeyer. You're going to get the hell out of here and not come back. Not if you know what's good for you. And next time you dream up a publicity stunt for one of your authors you'd better get him a goddam bodyguard first.'

Hutchmeyer staggered out of the office.

'I need some clothes,' he said.

'Well you're not going to get any back at your house. It's all burnt down.'

On a bench Sonia Futtle was weeping.

'What's the matter with her?' said Hutchmeyer.

'She's all broken up with this Piper's dying,' said Greensleeves, 'and it kind of surprises me you aren't grief-stricken about the late Mrs Hutchmeyer.'

'I am,' said Hutchmeyer, 'I just don't show my feelings is all.'

'So I noticed,' said Greensleeves. 'Well you'd better go comfort your alibi. We'll send out some clothes.'

Hutchmeyer crossed to the bench in his blanket. 'I'm sorry ...' he began but Sonia was on her feet.

'Sorry?' she shrieked, 'you murdered my darling Peter and now you say you're sorry?'

'Murdered him?' said Hutchmeyer. 'All I did was ...'

Greensleeves left them to it and sent out for some clothes. 'We can forget this case,' he told the lieutenant, 'this is Federal stuff. Terrorists in Maine. I mean who the hell would believe it?'

'You don't think it was the Mafia then?'

'What's it matter who it was? We aren't going to get anywhere to solving it is all I know. The FBI can handle this case. I know when I'm out of my depth.'

In the end Hutchmeyer, dressed in a dark suit that didn't fit him properly, and the still inconsolable Sonia were driven to the airport and took the company plane to New York.

They landed to find that MacMordie had laid on the media. Hutchmeyer lumbered down the steps and made a statement.

'Gentlemen,' he said brokenly, 'this has been a double tragedy for me. I have lost the most wonderful, warm-hearted little wife a man ever had. Forty years of happy marriage lie ...' He broke off to blow his nose. 'It's just terrible. I can't express the full depths of my feelings.'

'Peter Piper was a young novelist of unsurpassed brilliance. His passing has been a great blow to the world of letters.' He paraded his handkerchief again and was prompted by MacMordie.

'Say something about his novel,' he whispered.

Hutchmeyer stopped sniffing and said something about *Pause O Men for the Virgin* published by Hutchmeyer Press price seven dollars ninety and available at all ... Behind him Sonia wept audibly and had to be escorted to the waiting car. She was still weeping when they drove off.

'A terrible tragedy,' said Hutchmeyer, still under the influence of his own oratory, 'really terrible.'

He was interrupted by Sonia who was pummelling Mac-Mordie.

'Murderer,' she screamed, 'it was all your fault. You told all those crazy terrorists he was in the KGB and the IRA and a homosexual and now look what's happened!'

'What the hell's going on?' yelled McMordie, 'I didn't do ...'

'The fucking cops up in Maine think it was the Symbionese Liberation Army or The Minutemen or someone,' said Hutchmeyer, 'so now we've got another problem.'

'I can see that,' said MacMordie as Sonia blacked his eye. Finally, refusing Hutchmeyer's offer of hospitality, she insisted on being driven to the Gramercy Park Hotel.

'Don't worry,' said Hutchmeyer as she got out, 'I'm going to see that Baby and Piper go to their Maker with all the trimmings. Flowers, a cortège, a bronze casket ...'

'Two,' said MacMordie, 'I mean they wouldn't fit ...'

Sonia turned on them. 'They're dead,' she screamed. 'Dead. Doesn't that mean anything to you? Haven't you any consciences? They were real people, real living people and now they're dead and all you can talk about is funerals and caskets and—'

'Well we've got to recover the bodies first,' said MacMordie practically, 'I mean there's no use talking about caskets, we don't have no bodies.'

'Why don't you just shut your mouth?' Hutchmeyer told him, but Sonia had fled into the hotel.

They drove on in silence.

For a while Hutchmeyer had considered firing MacMordie but he changed his mind. After all he had never liked the great wooden house in Maine and with Baby dead ...

'It was a terrible experience,' he said, 'a terrible loss.'

'It must have been,' said MacMordie, 'all that loveliness gone to waste.'

'It was a showhouse, part of the American heritage. People

144

used to come up from Boston just to look at it.'

'I was thinking of Mrs Hutchmeyer,' said MacMordie. Hutchmeyer looked at him nastily.

'I might have expected that from you, MacMordie. At a time like this you have to think about sex.'

'I wasn't thinking sex,' said MacMordie, 'she was a remarkable woman characterwise.'

'You can say that again,' said Hutchmeyer. 'I want her memory embalmed in books. She was a great book-lover you know. I want a leather-bound edition of *Pause O Men for the Virgin* printed with gold letters. We'll call it the Baby Hutchmeyer Memorial Edition.'

'I'll see to it,' said MacMordie.

And so while Hutchmeyer resumed his role as publisher Sonia Futtle lay weeping on her bed in the Gramercy Park. She was consumed by guilt and grief. The one man who had ever loved her was dead and it was all her fault. She looked at the telephone and thought of calling Frensic but it would be the middle of the night in England. Instead she sent a telegram. PETER PRESUMED DEAD DROWNED MRS HUTCHMEYER DITTO POLICE INVESTIGATING CRIME WILL CALL WHEN CAN SONIA.

15

Frensic arrived in Lanyard Lane next morning in fine fettle. The world was a splendid place, the sun was shining, the people would shortly be in the shops buying *Pause* and best of all Hutchmeyer's cheque for two million dollars was nestling happily in the F & F bank account. It had arrived the previous week and all that needed to be done now was to subtract four hundred thousand dollars commission and transfer the remainder to Mr Cadwalladine and his strange client. Frensic would see to it this morning. He collected his mail from the box and stumped upstairs to his office. There he seated himself at his desk, took his first pinch of Bureau for the day and went through the letters in front of him. It was near the bottom of the pile that he came upon the telegram.

'Telegrams, really!' he muttered to himself in criticism of the extravagant hurry of an insistent author and opened it. A moment later Frensic's rosy view of the world had disintegrated, to be replaced by fragmentary and terrible images that rose from the cryptic words on the form. Piper dead? Presumed drowned? Mrs Hutchmeyer ditto? Each staccato message became a question in his mind as he tried to cope with the information. It was a minute before Frensic could realize the full import of the thing and even then he doubted and took refuge in disbelief. Piper couldn't be dead. In Frensic's comfortable little world death was something your authors wrote about. It was unreal and remote, a fabrication, not something that happened. But there, in these few words unadorned by punctuation marks and typed on crooked strips of paper, death intruded. Piper was dead. So was Mrs Hutchmeyer but Frensic accorded her no interest. She wasn't his responsibility. Piper was. Frensic had persuaded him to go to his death. And POLICE INVESTIGATING CRIME robbed him of even the consolation that there had been an accident. Crime and death suggested murder and to be confronted with Piper's murder added to Frensic's sense of horror. He sagged in his chair ashen with shock.

It was some time before he could bring himself to read the telegram again. But it still said the same thing. Piper dead. Frensic wiped his face with his handkerchief and tried to imagine what had happened. This time PRESUMED DROWNED held his attention. If Piper was dead why was there the presumption that he had drowned? Surely they knew how he had died. And why couldn't Sonia call? WILL CALL WHEN CAN added a new dimension of mystery to the message. Where could she be if she couldn't phone straightaway? Frensic visualized her lying hurt in a hospital but if that was the case she would have said so. He reached for the phone to put a call through to Hutchmeyer Press before realizing that New York was five hours behind London time and there would be no one in the office yet. He would have to wait until two o'clock. He sat staring at the telegram and tried to think practically. If the police were investigating the crime it was almost certain they would follow their inquiries into Piper's past. Frensic foresaw them discovering that Piper hadn't in fact written *Pause*. From that it would follow that ... my God, Hutchmeyer would get to know and there'd be the devil to pay. Or, more precisely, Hutchmeyer. The man would demand the return of his two million dollars. He might even sue for breach of contract or fraud. Thank God the money was still in the bank. Frensic sighed with relief.

To take his mind off the dreadful possibilities inherent in the telegram he went through to Sonia's office and looked in the filing cabinet for the letter from Mr Cadwalladine authorizing Piper to represent the author on the American tour. He took it out and studied it carefully before putting it back. At least he was covered there. If there was any trouble with Hutchmeyer Mr Cadwalladine and his client were party to the deception. And if the two million had to be refunded they would be in no position to grumble. By concentrating on these eventualities Frensic held at bay his sense of guilt and transferred it to the anonymous author. Piper's death was his fault. If the wretched man had not hidden behind a *nom de plume* Piper would still be alive. As the morning wore on and he sat unable to work at anything else Frensic's feeling of grievance grew. He had been fond of Piper in an odd sort of way. And now he was dead. Frensic sat miserably at his desk looking out over the roofs of Covent Garden and mourned Piper's passing. The poor fellow had been one of nature's victims, or rather one of literature's victims. Pathetic. A man who couldn't write to save his life ...

The phrase brought Frensic up with a start. It was too apt. Piper was dead and he had never really lived. His existence had been one long battle to get into print and he had failed. What was it that drove men like him to try to write, what fixation with the printed word held them at their desks year after year? All over the world there were thousands of other Pipers sitting at this very moment in front of blank pages which they would presently fill with words that no one would ever read but which in their naïve conceit they considered to have some deep significance. The thought added to Frensic's melancholy. It was all his fault. He should have had the courage and good sense to tell Piper that he would never be a novelist. Instead he had encouraged him. If he had told him Piper would still be alive, he might even have found his true vocation as a bank clerk or plumber, have married and settled down – whatever that meant. Anyway, he wouldn't have spent those forlorn years in forlorn guest-houses in forlorn seaside resorts living by proxy the lives of Conrad and Lawrence and Henry James, the shadowy ghost of those dead authors he had revered. Even Piper's death had been by way of being a proxy one as the author of a novel he hadn't written. And somewhere the man who should have died was living undisturbed.

Frensic reached for the phone. The bastard wasn't going to go on living undisturbed. Mr Cadwalladine could relay a message to him. He dialled Oxford.

'I'm afraid I've got some rather bad news for you,' he said when Mr Cadwalladine came on the line.

'Bad news? I don't understand,' said Mr Cadwalladine.

'It concerns the young man who went to America as the supposed author of that novel you sent me,' said Frensic.

Mr Cadwalladine coughed uncomfortably. 'Has he ... er ... done something indiscreet?' he asked.

'You could put it like that,' said Frensic. 'The fact of the matter is that we are likely to have some problems with the police.' Mr Cadwalladine made more uncomfortable noises which Frensic relished. 'Yes, the police,' he continued. 'They may be making inquiries shortly.'

'Inquiries?' said Mr Cadwalladine, now definitely alarmed. 'What sort of inquiries?'

'I can't be too certain at the moment but I thought I had better let you and your client know that he is dead,' said Frensic.

'Dead?' croaked Mr Cadwalladine.

'Dead,' said Frensic.

'Good Lord. How very unfortunate.'

'Quite,' said Frensic. 'Though from Piper's point of view "unfortunate" seems rather too mild a word, particularly as he appears to have been murdered.'

This time there was no mistaking Mr Cadwalladine's alarm

'Murdered?' he gasped, 'You did say "murdered"?'

'That's exactly what I said. Murdered.'

'Good God,' said Mr Cadwalladine. 'How very dreadful.'

Frensic said nothing and allowed Mr Cadwalladine to dwell on the dreadfulness of it all.

'I don't quite know what to say,' Mr Cadwalladine muttered finally.

Frensic pressed home his advantage. 'In that case if you will just give me the name and address of your client I will convey the news to him myself.'

Mr Cadwalladine made negative noises. 'There's no need for that. I shall let him know.'

'As you wish,' said Frensic. 'And while you're about it you had also better let him know that he will have to wait for his American advance.'

'Wait for his American advance? You're surely not suggesting . . .'

'I am not suggesting anything. I am merely drawing your attention to the fact that Mr Hutchmeyer was not privy to the substitution of Mr Piper for your anonymous client and, that being the case, if the police should unearth our little deception in the course of their inquiries . . . you take my point?'

Mr Cadwalladine did. 'You think Mr . . . er . . . Hutchmeyer might . . . er . . . demand restitution?'

'Or sue,' said Frensic bluntly, 'in which case it would be as well to be in a position to refund the entire sum at once.'

'Oh definitely,' said Mr Cadwalladine for whom the prospect of being sued evidently held very few attractions. 'I leave the matter entirely in your hands.'

Frensic ended the conversation with a sigh. Now that he had passed some of the responsibility on to Mr Cadwalladine and his damned client he felt a little better. He took a pinch of snuff and was savouring it when the phone rang. It was Sonia Futtle calling from New York. She sounded extremely distressed.

'Oh Frenzy, I'm sorry,' she said, 'it's all my fault. If it hadn't been for me this would never have happened.'

'What do you mean your fault?' said Frensic. 'You don't mean you . . .'

'I should never have brought him over here. He was so happy ...' she broke off and there was the sound of sobs.

Frensic gulped. 'For God's sake tell me what's happened,' he said.

'The police think it was murder,' said Sonia and sobbed again.

'I gathered that from your telegram. But I still don't know what happened. I mean how did he die?'

'Nobody knows,' said Sonia, 'that's what's so awful. They're dragging the bay and going through the ashes of the house and ...'

'The ashes of the house?' said Frensic, trying desperately to square a burnt house with Piper's presumed death by drowning.

'You see Hutch and I went out in his yacht and a storm blew up and then the house caught fire and someone fired at the firemen and Hutch's cruiser tried to ram us and exploded and we were nearly killed and ...'

It was a confused and disjointed account and Frensic, sitting with the phone pressed hard to his ear, tried in vain to form a coherent picture of what had occurred. In the end he was left with a series of chaotic images, an insane jigsaw puzzle in which, though the pieces all fitted, the final picture made no sense at all. A huge wooden house blazing into the night sky. Someone inside this inferno fending off firemen with a heavy machine-gun. Bears. Hutchmeyer and Sonia on a yacht in a hurricane. Cruisers hurtling across the bay and finally, most bizarre of all, Piper being blown to Kingdom Come in the company of Mrs Hutchmeyer wearing a mink coat. It was like a glimpse of hell.

'Have they no idea who did it?' he asked.

'Only some terrorist group,' said Sonia. Frensic swallowed.

'Terrorist group? Why should a terrorist group want to kill poor Piper?'

'Well because of all the publicity he got in that riot in New York,' said Sonia. 'You see when we landed ...'

She told the story of their arrival and Frensic listened in horror. 'You mean Hutchmeyer deliberately provoked a riot? The man's mad.'

150

'He wanted to get maximum publicity,' Sonia explained.

'Well he's certainly succeeded,' said Frensic.

But Sonia was sobbing again. 'You're just callous,' she wept. 'You don't seem to see what this means ...'

'I do,' said Frensic, 'it means the police are going to start looking into Piper's background and ...'

'That we're to blame,' cried Sonia, 'we sent him over and we are the ones—'

'Now hold it,' said Frensic, 'if I'd known Hutchmeyer was going to rent a riot for his welcome I would never have consented to his going. And as for terrorists ...'

'The police aren't absolutely certain it was terrorists. They thought at first that Hutchmeyer had murdered him.'

'That's more like it,' said Frensic. 'From what you've told me it's nothing more than the truth. He's an accessory before the fact. If he hadn't ...'

'And then they seemed to think the Mafia could be involved.'

Frensic swallowed again. This was even worse. 'The Mafia? What would the Mafia want to kill Piper for? The poor little sod hadn't ...'

'Not Piper. Hutchmeyer.'

'You mean the Mafia were trying to kill Hutchmeyer?' said Frensic wistfully.

'I don't know what I mean,' said Sonia, 'I'm telling you what I heard the police say and they mentioned that Hutchmeyer had had dealings with organized crime.'

'If the Mafia wanted to kill Hutchmeyer why did they pick on Piper?'

'Because Hutch and I were out on the yacht and Peter and Baby ...'

'What baby?' said Frensic desperately incorporating this new and grisly ingredient into an already cluttered crimescape.

'Baby Hutchmeyer.'

'Baby Hutchmeyer? I didn't know the swine had any ...'

'Not that sort of baby. Mrs Hutchmeyer. She was called Baby.'

'Good God,' said Frensic.

'There's no need to be so heartless. You sound as if you didn't care.'

'Care?' said Frensic. 'Of course I care. This is absolutely frightful. And you say the Mafia ...'

'No I didn't. I said that's what the police said. They thought it was some sort of attempt to intimidate Hutchmeyer.'

'And has it?' asked Frensic trying to extract a morsel of comfort from the situation.

'No,' said Sonia, 'he's out for blood. He says he's going to sue them.'

Frensic was horrified. 'Sue them? What do you mean "sue them"? You can't sue the Mafia and anyway ...'

'Not them. The police.'

'Hutchmeyer's going to sue the police?' said Frensic now totally out of his depth.

'Well first off they accused him of doing it. They held him for hours and grilled him. They didn't believe his story that he was out on the yacht with me. And then the gas-cans didn't help.'

'Gas-can? What gas-can?'

'The ones I tied round his waist.'

'You tied gas-cans round Hutchmeyer's waist?' said Frensic.

'I had to. To stop him from drowning.'

Frensic considered the logic of this remark and found it wanting. 'I should have thought ...' he began before deciding there was nothing to be gained by regretting that Hutchmeyer hadn't been left to drown. It would have saved a lot of trouble.

'What are you going to do now?' he asked finally.

'I don't know,' said Sonia, 'I've got to wait around. The police are still making inquiries and I've lost all my clothes ... and oh Frenzy it's all so horrible.' She broke down again and wept. Frensic tried to think of something to cheer her up.

'You'll be interested to hear that the reviews in the Sunday papers were all good,' he said but Sonia's grief was not assuaged.

'How can you talk about reviews at a time like this?' she said. 'You just don't care is all.'

'My dear I do. I most certainly do,' said Frensic, 'it's a tragedy for all of us. I've just been speaking to Mr Cadwalladine and explaining that in the light of what has happened his client will have to wait for his money.'

'Money? Money? Is that all you think about, money? My darling Peter is dead and ...'

Frensic listened to a diatribe against himself, Hutchmeyer and someone called MacMordie, all of whom in Sonia's opinion thought only about money. 'I understand your feelings,' he said when she paused for breath, 'but money does come into this business and if Hutchmeyer finds out that Piper wasn't the author of *Pause* ...'

But the phone had gone dead. Frensic looked at it reproachfully and replaced the receiver. All he could hope now was that Sonia kept her wits about her and that the police didn't carry their investigations too far into Piper's past history.

In New York Hutchmeyer's feelings were just the reverse. In his opinion the police were a bunch of half-wits who couldn't investigate anything properly. He had already been in touch with his lawyers only to be advised that there was no chance of suing Chief Greensleeves for wrongful arrest because he hadn't been arrested.

'That bastard held me for hours with nothing on but a blanket,' Hutchmeyer protested. 'They grilled me under hot lamps and you tell me I've got no comeback. There ought to be a law protecting innocent citizens against that kind of victimization.'

'Now if you could show they'd roughed you up a bit we could maybe do something but as it is ...'

Having failed to get satisfaction from his own lawyers Hutchmeyer turned his attention to the insurance company and got even less comfort there. Mr Synstrom of the Claims Department visited him and expressed doubts.

'What do you mean you don't necessarily go along with the police theory that some crazy terrorists did this thing?' Hutchmeyer demanded.

Mr Synstrom's eyes glinted behind silver-rimmed spectacles. 'Three and a half million dollars is a lot of money,' he said.

'Of course it is,' said Hutchmeyer, 'and I've been paying my premiums and that's a lot of money too. So what are you telling me?'

Mr Synstrom consulted his briefcase. 'The Coastguard recovered six suitcases belonging to Mrs Hutchmeyer. That's one. They contained all her jewellery and her best clothing. That's two. Three is that Mr Piper's suitcase was on board that boat and we've checked it contained all his clothes too.'

'So what?' said Hutchmeyer.

'So if this is a political murder it seems peculiar that the terrorists made them pack their bags first and loaded them aboard the cruiser and then set fire to the boat and arsoned the house. That doesn't fit the profile of terrorist acts of crime. It looks like something else again.'

Hutchmeyer glared at him. 'If you're suggesting I blew myself up in my own yacht and bumped my wife and most promising author ...'

'I'm not suggesting anything,' Mr Synstrom said, 'all I'm saying is that we've got to go into this thing a lot deeper.'

'Yeah, well you do that,' said Hutchmeyer, 'and when you've finished I want my money.'

'Don't worry,' said Mr Synstrom, 'we'll get to the bottom of this thing. With three and a half million at stake we've incentive.'

He got up and made for the door. 'Oh and by the way it may interest you to know that whoever arsoned your house knew exactly where everything was. Like the fuel store. This could have been an inside job.'

He left Hutchmeyer with the uncomfortable notion that if the cops were morons, Mr Synstrom and his investigators weren't. An inside job? Hutchmeyer thought about the words. And all Baby's jewellery on board. Maybe ... just supposing she *had* been going to run off with that jerk Piper? Hutchmeyer permitted himself the luxury of a smile. If that was the case the bitch had got what was coming to her. Just so long as those incriminating documents she had deposited with her lawyers didn't suddenly turn up. That wasn't such a pleasant prospect. Why couldn't Baby have gone some simpler way, like a coronary?'

16

In Maine the Van der Hoogens' mansion was shuttered and shrouded and empty. As Baby had promised their departure had passed unnoticed. Leaving Piper alone in the dim twilight of the house she had simply walked into Bellsworth and bought a car, a secondhand estate.

'We'll ditch it in New York and buy something different,' she said as they drove south. 'We don't want to leave any trail behind us.'

Piper, lying on the floor in the back, did not share her confidence. 'That's all very well,' he grumbled, 'but they're still going to be looking for us when they don't find our bodies out in the bay. I mean it stands to reason.'

But Baby drove on unperturbed. 'They'll reckon we were washed out to sea by the tide,' she said. 'That's what would have happened if we had really drowned. Besides I heard in Bellsworth they picked up your passport and my jewels in the bags they found. They've got to believe we're dead. A woman like me doesn't part with pearls and diamonds until the good Lord sends for her.'

Piper lay on the floor and found some sense in this argument. Certainly Frensic & Futtle would believe he was dead and without his passport and his ledgers ... 'Did they find my notebooks too?' he asked.

'Didn't mention them but if they got your passport, and they did, it's even money your notebooks were with them.'

'I don't know what I'm going to do without my notebooks,' said Piper, 'they contained my life's work.'

He lay back and watched the tops of the trees flashing past and the blue sky beyond, and thought about his life's work. He would never finish *Search for a Lost Childhood* now. He would never be recognized as a literary genius. All his hopes had been destroyed in the blaze and its aftermath. He would go through what remained of his existence on earth posthumously famous as the author of *Pause O Men for the Virgin*. It was an intolerable thought and provoked in him a growing determination to put the record straight. There had to be some way of issuing a disclaimer. But disclaimers from beyond the grave were not easy to fabricate. He could hardly write to *The Times Literary Supplement* pointing out that he hadn't in fact written *Pause* but that its authorship had been foisted on to him by Frensic & Futtle for their own dubious ends.. Letters signed 'the late Peter Piper' ... No, that was definitely out. On the other hand it was insufferable to go down in literary history as a pornographer. Piper wrestled with the problem and finally fell asleep.

When he woke they had crossed the state line and were in Vermont. That night they booked into a small motel on the shores of Lake Champlain as Mr and Mrs Castorp. Baby signed the register while Piper carried two empty suitcases purloined from the Van der Hoogen mansion into the cabin.

'We'll have to buy some clothes and things tomorrow,' said Baby. But Piper was not concerned with such material details. He stood at the window staring out and tried to adjust himself to the extraordinary notion that to all intents and purposes he was married to this crazy woman.

'You realize we are never going to be able to separate,' he said at last.

'I don't see why not,' said Baby from the depths of the shower.

'Well for one simple reason I haven't got an identity and can't get a job,' said Piper, 'and for another you've got all the money and if either of us gets picked up by the police we'll go to prison for the rest of our lives.'

'You worry too much,' said Baby. 'This is the land of opportunity. We'll go some place nobody will think of looking and begin all over again.

'Such as where?'

Baby emerged from the shower. 'Like the South. The Deep South,' she said. 'That's one place Hutchmeyer is never going to come. He's got this thing about the Ku Klux Klan. South of the Mason-Dixon he's never been.'

'And what the hell am I going to do in the Deep South?' asked Piper.

'You could always try your hand at writing Southern novels.

Hutch may not go South but he certainly publishes a lot of novels about it. They usually have this man with a whip and a girl cringing on the cover. Surefire bestsellers.'

'Sounds just my sort of book,' said Piper grimly and took a shower himself.

'You could always write it under a pseudonym.'

'Thanks to you I'd bloody well have to.'

As night fell outside the cabin Piper crawled into bed and lay thinking about the future. In the twin bed beside him Baby sighed.

'It's great to be with a man who doesn't pee in the washbasin,' she murmured. Piper resisted the invitation without difficulty.

The next morning they moved on again, following back roads and driving slowly and always south. And always Piper's mind nagged away at the problem of how to resume his interrupted career.

In Scranton, where Baby traded the estate for a new Ford, Piper took the opportunity to buy two new ledgers, a bottle of Higgins Ink and an Esterbrook pen.

'If I can't do anything else I can at least keep a diary,' he explained to Baby.

'A diary? You don't even look at the landscape and we eat in McDonalds so what's to put in a diary?'

'I was thinking of writing it retrospectively. As a form of vindication. I would—'

'Vindication? And how can you write a diary retrospectively?'

'Well I'd start with how I was approached by Frensic to come to the States and then work my way forward day by day with the voyage across and everything. That way it would look authentic.'

Baby slowed the car and pulled into a rest area. 'Let's just get this straight. You write the diary backwards ...'

'Yes, I think it was April the 10th Frensic sent me the telegram ...'

'Go on. You start 10 April and then what?'

'Well then I'd write how I didn't want to do it and how they persuaded me and promised to get *Search* published and everything.'

'And where would you finish?'

'Finish?' said Piper. 'I wasn't thinking of finishing. I'd just go on and . . .'

'So what about the fire and all?' said Baby.

'Well I would put that in too. I'd have to.'

'And how it started by accident, I suppose?'

'Well, no I wouldn't say that. I mean it didn't did it?'

Baby looked at him and shook her head. 'So you'd put in how I started it and sent the cruiser out to blow up Hutchmeyer and the Futtle? Is that it?'

'I suppose so,' said Piper. 'I mean that's what did happen and . . .'

'And that's what you call vindication. Well you can forget it. No way. You want to vindicate yourself that's fine with me but you don't implicate me at the same time. Dual destiny I said and dual destiny I meant.'

'It's all very well for you to talk,' said Piper morosely, 'you're not lumbered with the reputation of having written that filthy novel and I am . . .'

'I'm just lumbered with a genius is all,' said Baby and started the car again. Piper sat slumped in his seat and sulked.

'The only thing I know how to do is write,' he grumbled, 'and you won't let me.'

'I didn't say that,' said Baby, 'I just said no retrospective diaries. Dead men tell no tales. Not in diaries they don't and anyhow I don't see why you feel so strongly about *Pause*. I thought it was a great book.'

'You would,' said Piper.

'The thing that really has me puzzled is who did write it. I mean they had to have some real good reason for staying under cover.'

'You've only got to read the beastly book to see that,' said Piper. 'All that sex for one thing. And now everyone's going to think I did it.'

'And if you had written the book you would have cut out all the sex?' said Baby.

'Of course. That would be the first thing and then ...'

'Without the sex the book wouldn't have sold. That much I do know about the book trade.'

'So much the better,' said Piper. 'It debases human values. That is what that book does.'

'In that case you should rewrite it the way you think it ought to have been written ...' and amazed at this sudden inspiration she lapsed into thoughtful silence.

Twenty miles farther on they entered a small town. Baby parked the car and went into a supermarket. When she returned she was holding a copy of *Pause O Men for the Virgin*.

'They're selling like wild-fire,' she said and handed him the book.

Piper looked at his photograph on the back cover. It had been taken in those halcyon days in London when he had been in love with Sonia and the inane face that smiled up at him seemed to be that of a stranger. 'What am I supposed to do with this?' he asked. Baby smiled.

'Write it.'

'Write it?' said Piper. 'But it's already been—'

'Not the way you would have written it, and you're the author.'

'I'm bloody well not.'

'Honey, somewhere out there in the great wide world there is a man who wrote that book. Now he knows it, and Frensic knows it and that Futtle bitch knows it and you and I know it. That's the lot. Hutch doesn't.'

'Thank God,' said Piper.

'Right. And if that's the way you feel, just imagine the way Frensic & Futtle must be feeling now. Two million Hutch paid for that novel. That's a lot of money.'

'It's a ludicrous sum,' said Piper. 'Did you know that Conrad only got—'

'No and I'm not interested. Right now what interests me is what happens when you rewrite this novel in your own beautiful handwriting and Frensic gets the manuscript.'

'Frensic gets ...' Piper began but Baby silenced him.

'Your manuscript,' she said, 'from beyond the grave.'

'My manuscript from beyond the grave? He'll do his nut.'

'Right first time, and we follow that up with a demand for the advance and full royalties,' said Baby.

'Well, then he'll know I'm still alive,' Piper protested. 'He'll go straight to the police and ...'

'He does that he's going to have a lot of explaining to do to Hutch and everyone. Hutch will set his legal hound-dogs on him. Yes sir, we've got Messrs Frensic & Futtle right where we want them.'

'You are mad,' said Piper, 'stark staring mad. If you seriously think I'm going to rewrite this awful ...'

'You were the one who wanted to retrieve your reputation,' said Baby as they drove out of town. 'And this is the only way you can.'

'I wish I could see how.'

'I'll show you,' said Baby. 'Leave it to momma.'

That evening in another motel room Piper opened his ledger, arranged his pen and ink as methodically as they had once been arranged in the Gleneagle Guest House and with a copy of *Pause* propped up in front of him began to write. At the top of the page he wrote 'Chapter One', and underneath, 'The house stood on a knoll. Surrounded by three elms, a beech and a deodar whose horizontal branches gave it the air ...'

Behind him Baby relaxed on a bed with a contented smile. 'Don't make too many alterations this draft,' she said. 'We've got to make it look really authentic.'

Piper stopped writing. 'I thought the whole point of the exercise was to retrieve my lost reputation by rewriting the thing ...'

'You can do that with the second draft,' said Baby. 'This one is to light a fire under Frensic & Futtle. So stay with the text.'

Piper picked up his pen again and stayed with the text. He made several alterations per page and then crossed them out and added the originals from the book. Occasionally Baby got up and looked over his shoulder and was satisfied.

'This is really going to blow Frensic's mind,' she said but Piper hardly heard her. He had resumed his old existence and with it his identity. And so he wrote on obsessively, lost once more in a world of someone else's imagining and as he wrote he foresaw the alterations he would make in the second draft, the draft that would save his reputation. He was still copying at midnight when Baby had gone to bed. Finally at one, tired but vaguely satisfied, Piper brushed his teeth and climbed into bed too. In the morning he would start again.

But in the morning they were on the road again and it was not until late afternoon that Baby pulled into a Howard Johnson's in Beanville, South Carolina, and Piper was able to start work again.

While Piper started his life again as a peripatetic and derivative novelist Sonia Futtle mourned his passing with a passion that did her credit and disconcerted Hutchmeyer.

'What do you mean she won't attend the funeral?' he yelled at MacMordie when he was told that Miss Futtle sent her regrets but was not prepared to take part in a farce simply to promote the sales of *Pause*.

'She says without bodies in the coffins . . .' MacMordie began before being silenced by an apoplectic Hutchmeyer. 'Where the fuck does she think I'm going to get the bodies from? The cops can't get them. The insurance investigators can't get them. The fucking coastguard divers can't get them. And I'm supposed to go find the things? By this time they're way out in the Atlantic some place or the sharks have got them.'

'But I thought you said they were weighted down like with concrete,' said MacMordie, 'and if they are . . .'

'Never mind what I said, MacMordie. What I'm saying now is we've got to think positive about Baby and Piper.'

'Isn't that a bit difficult? Them being dead and missing and all. I mean . . .'

'And I mean we've got a promotional set-up here that can put *Pause* right up the charts.'

'The computer says sales are good already.'

'Good? Good's not enough. They've got to be terrific. Now the way I see it we've got an opportunity for building this Piper guy up with a reputation like . . . Who was that bastard got himself knocked off in a car smash?'

'Well there've been so many it's a little difficult to ...'

'In Hollywood. Famous guy.'

'James Dean,' said MacMordie.

'Not him. A writer. Wrote a great book about insects.'

'Insects?' said MacMordie. 'You mean like ants. I read a great book about ants once ...'

'Not ants for Chrissake. Things with long legs like grasshoppers. Eat every goddam thing for miles.'

'Oh, locusts. *The Day of the Locust*. A great movie. They had this one scene where there's a guy jumping up and down on this little kid and—'

'I don't want to know about that movie, MacMordie. Who wrote the book?'

'West,' said MacMordie, 'Nathanael West. Only his real name was Weinstein.'

'So who cares what his real name was? Nobody's ever heard of him and he gets himself killed in a pile-up and suddenly he's famous. With Piper we've got it even better. I mean we've got mystery. Maybe mobsters. House burning, boats exploding, the guy's in love with old women and suddenly it's all happening to him.'

'Past tense,' said MacMordie.

'Damn right, and that's what I want on him. His past. A full run-down on him, where he lived, what he did, the women he loved ...'

'Like Miss Futtle?' said MacMordie tactlessly.

'No,' yelled Hutchmeyer, 'not like Miss Futtle. She won't even come to the poor guy's funeral. Other women. With what he put in that book there've got to be other women.'

'With what he put in that book they'll have maybe died by now. I mean the heroine was eighty and he was seventeen. This Piper was twenty-eight, thirty so it's got to have been eleven years ago which would put her up in the nineties and around that age they tend to forget things.'

'Jesus, do I have to tell you everything? Fabricate, MacMordie, fabricate. Call London and speak to Frensic and get the press cuttings. There's bound to be something there we can use.'

162

MacMordie left the room and put through the call to London. He returned twenty minutes later with the news that Frensic was being uncooperative.

'He says he doesn't know anything,' he told a glowering Hutchmeyer. 'Seems this Piper just sent in the book, Frensic read it, sent it to Corkadales, they liked it and bought and that's about the sum total. No background. Nothing.'

'There's got to be something. He was born some place, wasn't he? And his mother ...'

'No relatives. Parents dead in a car smash. I mean it's like he never had an existence.'

'Shit,' said Hutchmeyer.

Which was more or less the word that sprang to Frensic's mind as he put the phone down after MacMordie's call. It was bad enough losing an author who hadn't written a book without having demands for background material on his life. The next thing would be the press, some damned woman reporter hot on the trail of Piper's tragic childhood. Frensic went into Sonia's office and hunted through the filing cabinet for Piper's correspondence. It was, as he expected, voluminous. Frensic took the file back to his desk and sat there wondering what to do with the thing. His first inclination to burn it was dissipated by the realization that if Piper had written scores of letters to him from almost as many different boarding-houses over the years, he had replied as often. The copies of Frensic's replies were there in the file. The originals were presumably still in safe keeping somewhere. With an aunt? Or some ghastly boarding-house keeper? Frensic sat and sweated. He had told MacMordie that Piper had no relatives, but what if it turned out that he had an entire lineage of avaricious aunts, uncles and cousins anxious to cash in on royalties? And what about a will? Knowing Piper as well as he did, Frensic thought it unlikely he had made one. In which case the matter of his legacy might well end up in the courts and then ... Frensic foresaw appalling consequences. On the one hand the anonymous author demanding his advance, and on the other ... And in the middle the firm of Frensic & Futtle being dragged through the mud, exposed as the perpetrators of fraud, sued by Hutch-

163

meyer, sued by Piper's relatives, forced to pay enormous damages and vast legal costs and finally bankrupted. And all because some demented client of Cadwalladine had insisted on preserving his anonymity.

Having reached this ghastly conclusion Frensic took the file back to the cabinet, re-labelled it Mr Smith as a mild precaution against intruding eyes and tried to think of some defence. The only one seemed to be that he had merely acted on the instructions of Mr Cadwalladine and since Cadwalladine & Dimkins were eminently respectable solicitors they would be as anxious to avoid a legal scandal as he was. And so presumably would the genuine author. It was small consolation. Let Hutchmeyer get a whiff of the impersonation and all hell would be let loose. And finally there was Sonia, who, if her attitude on the phone had been anything to go by, was in a highly emotional state and likely to say something rash. Frensic reached for the phone and dialled International to put through a call to the Gramercy Park Hotel. It was time Sonia Futtle came back to England. When he got through it was to learn that Miss Futtle had already left, and should, according to the desk clerk, be in mid-Atlantic.

' "Is" and "above",' corrected Frensic before realizing that there was something to be said for American usage.

That afternoon Sonia landed at Heathrow and took a taxi straight to Lanyard Lane. She found Frensic in a mood of apparently deep mourning.

'I blame myself,' he said, forestalling her lament, 'I should never have allowed poor Piper to have jeopardized his career by going over in the first place. Our only consolation must be that his name as a novelist has been made. It is doubtful if he would ever have written a better book had he lived.'

'But he didn't write this one,' said Sonia.

Frensic nodded. 'I know. I know,' he murmured, 'but at least it established his reputation. He would have appreciated the irony. He was a great admirer of Thomas Mann you know. Our best memorial to him must be silence.'

Having thus pre-empted Sonia's recriminations Frensic allowed her to work off her feelings by telling the story of the

164

night of the tragedy and Hutchmeyer's subsequent reaction. At the end he was none the wiser.

'It all seems most peculiar,' he said when she had finished. 'One can only suppose that whoever did it made a terrible mistake and got the wrong person. Now if Hutchmeyer had been murdered ...'

'I would have been murdered too,' said Sonia through her tears.

'We must be grateful for small mercies,' said Frensic.

Next morning Sonia Futtle resumed her duties in the office. A fresh batch of animal stories had come in during her absence and while Frensic congratulated himself on his tactics and sat at his desk silently praying that there would be no further repercussions Sonia busied herself with *Bernie the Beaver*. It needed a bit of rewriting but the story had promise.

17

In a cabin in the Smoky Mountains Piper held the same opinion about *Pause*. He sat out on the stoop and looked down at the lake where Baby was swimming and had to admit that his first impression of the novel had been wrong. He had been misled by the passages of explicit sex. But now that he had copied it out word for word he could see that the essential structure of the story was sound. In fact there were large sections of the book which dealt meaningfully with matters of great significance. Subtract the age difference between Gwendolen and Anthony, the narrator, and eradicate the pornography and *Pause O Men for the Virgin* had the makings of great literature. It examined in considerable depth the meaning of life, the writer's role in contemporary society, the anonymity of the individual in the urban collective and the need to return to the values of earlier, more civilized times. It was particularly good on the miseries of adolescence and the satisfaction to be found in the craftsmanship of furniture-making. 'Gwendolen ran her fingers along the gnarled and knotted oak with a sensual touch that belied her years. "The hardiness of time has tamed the wildness of the wood," she said. "You will carve against the grain and give form to what has been formless and insensate." ' Piper nodded approvingly. Passages like that had genuine merit and better still they served as an inspiration to him. He too would cut against the grain of this novel and give form to it, so that in the revised version the grossness of the bestseller would be eliminated, and the sexual addenda which defiled the very essence of the book would be removed and it would stand as a monument to his literary gifts. Posthumously perhaps, but at least his reputation would be retrieved. In years to come critics would compare the two versions and deduce from his deletions than in its earlier uncommercial form the original intentions of the author had been of the highest literary quality and that the novel had subsequently been altered to meet the demands of Frensic and Hutchmeyer and their perverse view of public taste. The blame for the bestseller would lie with them and he would be exonerated. More, he would be acclaimed. He closed the ledger and stood up as Baby came out of the water and walked up the beach to the cabin.

'Finished?' she asked. Piper nodded.

'I shall start the second version tomorrow,' he said.

'While you're doing that I'll take the first down into Ashville and get it copied. The sooner Frensic gets it the sooner we're going to light a fire under him.'

'I wish you wouldn't use that expression,' said Piper, 'lighting fires. And anyway where are you going to mail it from? They could trace us from the postmark.'

'We shan't be here from the day after tomorrow. We rented the cabin for a week. I'll drive down to Charlotte and catch a flight to New York and mail it there. I'll be back tomorrow night and we move on the day after.'

'I wish we didn't have to move all the time,' said Piper, 'I like it here. There's been nobody to bother us and I've had time to write. Why can't we just stay on?'

'Because this isn't the Deep South,' said Baby, 'and when I said Deep I meant it. There are places down Alabama, Mississippi, that just nobody has ever heard of and I want to see them.'

'And from what I've read about Mississippi they aren't partial to strangers,' said Piper, 'they are going to ask questions.'

'You've read too many Faulkners,' said Baby, 'and where we're going a quarter of a million dollars buys a lot of answers.'

She went inside and changed. After lunch Piper swam in the lake and walked along the shore, his mind filled with possible changes he was going to make in *Pause Two*. Already he had decided to change the title. He would call it *Work in Regress*. There was a touch of *Finnegans Wake* about it which appealed to his sense of the literary. And after all Joyce had worked and reworked his novels over and over again with no thought for their commercial worth. And in exile from his native land. For a moment Piper saw himself following in Joyce's footsteps, incognito and endlessly revising the same book, with the difference that he could never emerge from obscurity into fame in his own lifetime. Unless of course his work was of such an indisputable genius that the little matter of the fire and the burning boats and even his apparent death would become part of the mystique of a great author. Yes, greatness would absolve him. Piper turned and hurried back along the shore to the cabin. He would start work at once on *Work in Regress*. But when he got back he found that Baby had already taken the car and his first manuscript and driven into Ashville. There was a note for him on the table. It said simply, 'Gone today. Here tomorrow. Stay with it. Baby.'

Piper stayed with it. He spent the afternoon with a pen going through *Pause* changing all references to age. Gwendolen lost fifty-five years and became twenty-five and Anthony gained ten which made him twenty-seven. And in between times Piper scored out all those references to peculiar sexual activities which had ensured the book's popular appeal. He did this with particular vigour and by the time he had finished was filled with a sense of righteousness which he conveyed to his notebook of Ideas. 'The commercialization of sex as a thing to be bought and sold is at the root of the present debasement of civilization. In my writing I have striven to eradicate the

Thingness of sex and to encapsulate the essential relationship of humanity.' Finally he made himself supper and went to bed.

In the morning he was up early and at his table on the stoop. In front of him the first page of his new ledger lay blank and empty waiting for his imprint. He dipped his pen in the ink-bottle and began to write. 'The house stood on a knoll. Surrounded by three elms, a beech and a ...' Piper stopped. He wasn't sure what a deodar was and he had no dictionary to help him. He changed it to 'oak' and stopped again. Did oak have horizontal branches? Presumably some oaks did. Details like that didn't matter. The essential thing was to get down to an analysis of the relationship between Gwendolen and the narrator. Great books didn't bother with trees. They were about people, what people felt about people and what they thought about them. Insight was what really mattered and trees didn't contribute to insight. The deodar might just as well stay where it was. He crossed out 'oak' and put 'deodar' above it He continued the description for half a page and then hit another problem. How could the narrator, Anthony, be on holiday from school when he was now twenty-seven. Unless of course he was a schoolmaster in which case he would have to teach something and that meant knowing about it. Piper tried to remember his own schooldays and a model on which to base Anthony, but the masters at his school had been nondescript men and had left little impression on him. There was only Miss Pears and she had been a mistress.

Piper put down his pen and thought about Miss Pears. Now if she had been a man ... or if she were Gwendolen and he was Anthony ... and if instead of being twenty-seven Anthony had been fourteen ... or better still if his parents had lived in a house on a knoll surrounded by three elms, a beech and a ... Piper stood up and paced the stoop, his mind alive with new inspiration. It had suddenly come to him that from the raw material of *Pause O Men for the Virgin* it might be possible to distil the essence of *Search for a Lost Childhood*. Or if not distil, at least amalgamate the two. There would have to be considerable alterations. After all tuberculotic plumbers didn't live on knolls. On the other hand his father hadn't actually had tuberculosis. He had got it from Lawrence and Thomas Mann.

And a love affair between a schoolboy and his teacher was a very natural occurrence, provided of course that it didn't become physical. Yes, that was it. He would write *Work in Regress* as *Search*. He sat down at the table and picked up his pen and began to copy. There was no need now to worry about changing the main shape of the story. The deodar and the house on the knoll and all the descriptions of houses and places could remain the same. The new ingredient would be the addition of his troubled adolescence and the presence of his tormented parents. And Miss Pears as Gwendolen, his mentor, adviser and teacher with whom he would develop a significant relationship, meaningfully sexual and without sex.

And so once more the words formed indelibly black upon the page with all the old elegance of shape that had so satisfied him in the past. Below him the lake shone in the summer sunlight and a breeze ruffled the trees around the cabin, but Piper was oblivious to his surroundings. He had picked up the thread of his existence where it had broken in the Gleneagle Guest House in Exforth and was back into *Search*.

When Baby returned that evening from her flight to New York with the copy of his first manuscript now safely mailed to Frensic & Futtle, Lanyard Lane, London, she found Piper his old self. The trauma of the fire and their flight had been forgotten.

'You see, what I am doing is combining my own novel with *Pause*,' he explained as she poured herself a drink. 'Instead of Gwendolen being ...'

'Tell me about it in the morning,' said Baby. 'Right now I've had a tiring day and tomorrow we've got to be on the road again.'

'I see you've bought another car,' said Piper looking out at a red Pontiac.

'Air-conditioned and with South Carolina plates. Anyone thinks they're going to come looking for us, they're going to have a hard time. I didn't even trade in this time. Sold the Ford in Beanville and took a Greyhound to Charlotte and bought this in Ashville on the way back. We'll change again farther south. We're covering our tracks.'

'Not by sending copies of *Pause* to Frensic, we aren't,' said Piper, 'I mean he's bound to know I haven't died.'

'That reminds me. I sent him a telegram in your name.'

'You did what?' squawked Piper.

'Sent him a telegram.'

'Saying what?'

'Just, quote Transfer advance royalties care of First National Bank of New York account-number 478776 love Piper unquote.'

'But I haven't got an account . . .'

'You have now, honey. I opened one for you and made the first deposit. One thousand dollars. Now when Frensic gets that birthday greeting—'

'Birthday greeting? You send a telegram demanding money and you call that a birthday greeting?'

'Had to delay it somehow till he'd had time to read the original of *Pause*,' said Baby, 'so I said he had a birthday on the 19th and they're holding it over.'

'Christ,' said Piper, 'some damned birthday greeting. I suppose you realize he's got a heart condition? I mean shocks like this could kill him.'

'Makes two of you,' said Baby. 'He's effectively killed you . . .'

'He did nothing of the sort. You were the one to sign my death certificate and end my career as a novelist.'

Baby finished her drink and sighed. 'There's gratitude for you. Your career as a novelist is just about to begin.'

'Posthumously,' said Piper bitterly.

'Well, better late than never,' said Baby, and took herself off to bed.

The next morning the red Pontiac left the cabin and wound up the curving mountain road in the direction of Tennessee.

'We'll go west as far as Memphis,' said Baby, 'and ditch the car there and double back by Greyhound to Chattanooga. I've always wanted to see the Choo Choo.'

Piper said nothing. He had just realized how he had met Miss Pears/Gwendolen. It had been one summer holiday when his parents had taken him down to Exforth and instead of sitting on the beach with them he had gone to the public library

170

and there ... The house no longer stood on a knoll. It was at the top of the hill by the cliffs and its windows stared out to sea. Perhaps that wasn't such a good idea. Not in the second version. No, he would leave it where it was and concentrate on relationships. In that way there would be more consistency between *Pause* and *Work in Regress*, more authenticity. But in the third revision he would work on the setting and the house would stand on the cliffs above Exforth. And with each succeeding draft he would approximate a little more closely to that great novel on which he had been working for ten years. Piper smiled to himself at this realization. As the author of *Pause O Men for the Virgin* he had been given the fame he had always sought, had had fame forced upon him, and now by slow, persistent rewriting of that book he would reproduce the literary masterpiece that had been his life's work. And there was absolutely nothing Frensic could do about it.

That night they slept in separate motels in Memphis and next morning met at the bus depot and took the Greyhound to Nashville. The red Pontiac had gone. Piper didn't even bother to inquire how Baby had disposed of it. He had more important things on his mind. What, for instance, would happen if Frensic produced the real original manuscript of *Pause* and admitted that he had sent Piper to America as the substitute author?

'Two million dollars,' said Baby succinctly when he put this possibility to her.

'I don't see what they have to do with it,' said Piper.

'That's the price of the risk he took playing people poker with Hutch. You stake two million on a bluff you've got to have good reasons.'

'I can't imagine what they are.'

Baby smiled. 'Like who the real writer is. And don't give me that crap about a guy with six children and terminal arthritis. There's no such thing.'

'There isn't?' said Piper.

'No way. So we've got Frensic willing to risk his reputation as a literary agent for a percentage of two million and an author who goes along with him to preserve his precious anonymity from disclosure. That adds up to one hell of a weird set of circumstances. And Hutch hears what's going on he's going to murder them.'

'If Hutchmeyer hears what we've been doing he isn't going to be exactly pleased,' said Piper gloomily.

'Yes but we aren't there and Frensic is. In Lanyard Lane and by now he's got to be sweating.'

And Frensic was. The arrival of a large packet mailed in New York and addressed Personal, Frederick Frensic, had excited his curiosity only mildly. Arriving early at the office he had taken it upstairs with him and had opened several letters before turning his attention to the package. But from that moment onwards he had sat petrified staring at its contents. In front of him lay, neatly Xeroxed, sheet after sheet of Piper's unmistakable handwriting and just as equally unmistakably the original manuscript of *Pause O Men for the Virgin*. Which was impossible. Píper hadn't written the bloody book. He couldn't have. It was out of the question. And anyway why should anyone send him Xeroxed copies of a manuscript? The manuscript. Frensic rummaged through the pages and noted the corrections. The damned thing *was* the manuscript of *Pause*. And it was in Piper's handwriting. Frensic got up from his desk and went through to the filing cabinet and brought back the file now marked Mr Smith and compared the handwriting of Piper's letters with that of the manuscript. No doubt about it. He even reached for a magnifying glass and studied the letters through it. Identical. Christ. What the hell was going on? Frensic felt most peculiar. Some sort of waking nightmare had taken hold of him. Piper had written *Pause*? The obstacles in the way of such a supposition were insuperable. The little bugger couldn't have written anything and if he had ... even if he quite miraculously had, what about Mr Cadwalladine and his anonymous client? Why should Piper have sent him the typed copy of the book through a solicitor in Oxford? And anyway the sod was dead. Or was he? No, he was definitely dead, drowned, murdered ... Sonia's grief had been too real for disbelief. Piper was dead. Which brought him full circle to the question, who had sent this post-mortem manuscript? From

New York? Frensic looked at the postmark. New York. And why Xeroxed? There had to be a reason. Frensic grabbed the package and rummaged inside it in the hope that it might contain some clue like a covering letter. But the package was empty. He turned to the outside. The address was typed. Frensic turned the packet over in search of a return address but there was nothing there. He turned back to the pages and read several more. There could be no doubting the authenticity of the writing. The corrections on every page were conclusive. They had been there in exactly the same form in every annual copy of *Search for a Lost Childhood*, a sentence scratched neatly out and a new one written in above. Worst of all, there were even the spelling mistakes. Piper had always spelt necessary with two cs and parallel with two Rs, and here they were once again as final proof that the little maniac had actually penned the book which had gone to print with his name on the title-page. But the decision to use his name hadn't been Piper's. He had only been consulted when the book had already been sold ...

Frensic's thoughts spiralled. He tried to remember who had suggested Piper. Was it Sonia, or had he himself...? He couldn't recall and Sonia wasn't there to help him. She had gone down to Somerset to interview the author of *Bernie the* blasted *Beaver* and to ask for amendments in his opus. Beavers, even voluble beavers, didn't say 'Jesus wept' and 'Bloody hell', not if they wanted to get into print as children's bestsellers. Frensic did, several times, as he stared at the pages in front of him. Pulling himself together with an effort, he reached for the phone. This time Mr Cadwalladine was going to come clean about his client. But the telephone beat Frensic to it. It rang. Frensic cursed and picked up the receiver.

'Frensic & Futtle, Literary Agents ...' he began before being stopped by the operator.

'Is that Mr Frensic, Mr Frederick Frensic?'

'Yes,' said Frensic irritably. He had never liked his Christian name.

'I have a birthday greeting for you,' said the operator.

'For me?' said Frensic. 'But it isn't my birthday.'

But already a taped voice was crooning 'Happy Birthday To

You, Happy Birthday, Dear Frederick, Happy Birthday To You.'

Frensic held the receiver away from his ear. 'I tell you it isn't my bloody birthday,' he shouted at the recording. The operator came back on the line.

'The greetings telegram reads TRANSFER ADVANCE ROYALTIES CARE OF FIRST NATIONAL BANK OF NEW YORK ACCOUNT NUMBER FOUR SEVEN EIGHT SEVEN SEVEN SIX LOVE PIPER. I will repeat that. TRANSFER . . .' Frensic sat and listened. He was beginning to shake.

'Would you like that account number repeated once again?' asked the operator.

'No,' said Frensic. 'Yes.' He grabbed a pencil with an unsteady hand and wrote the message down.

'Thank you,' he said without thinking as he finished.

'You're welcome,' said the operator. The line went dead.

'Like hell I am,' said Frensic and put the phone down. He stared for a moment at the word 'Piper' and then groped his way across the room to the cubicle in which Sonia made coffee and washed the cups. There was a bottle of brandy there, kept for emergency resuscitation of rejected authors. 'Rejected?' Frensic muttered as he filled a tumbler. 'More like resurrected.' He drank half the tumbler and went back to his desk feeling little better. The nightmare quality of the manuscript had doubled now with the telegram but it was no longer incomprehensible. He was being blackmailed. 'Transfer advance royalties . . .' Frensic suddenly felt faint. He got out of his chair and lay down on the floor and shut his eyes.

After twenty minutes he got to his feet. Mr Cadwalladine was going to learn that it didn't pay to tangle with Frensic & Futtle. There was no point in phoning the wretched man again. Stronger measures were needed now. He would have the bastard squealing the name of his client and there would be an end to all this talk of professional confidentiality. The situation was desperate and desperate remedies were called for. Frensic went downstairs and out into the street. Half an hour later, armed with a parcel that contained sandals, dark glasses, a lightweight tropical suit and a Panama hat, he returned to the office. All that was needed now was an ambulance-chasing libel lawyer. Frensic spent the rest of the morning going through *Pause* for a suitable identity and then phoned Ridley, Coverup, Makeweight and Jones, Solicitors of Ponsett House. Their reputation as shysters in cases of libel was second to none. Mr Makeweight would see Professor Facit at four.

At five to four, Frensic, armed with a copy of *Pause O Men for the Virgin* and peering dimly through his tinted glasses, sat in the waiting-room and looked down at his sandals. He was rather proud of them. If anything distinguished him from Frensic, the literary agent, it was, he felt, those awful sandals.

'Mr Makeweight will see you now,' said the receptionist. Frensic got up and went down the passage to the door marked Mr Makeweight and entered. An air of respectable legal fustiness clung to the room. It didn't to Mr Makeweight. Small, dark and effusive, he was rather too quick for the furnishings. Frensic shook hands and sat down. Mr Makeweight regarded him expectantly. 'I understand you are concerned with a passage in a novel,' he said.

Frensic put the copy of *Pause* on the desk.

'Well, I am rather,' he said hesitantly. 'You see ... well it's been drawn to my attention by some of my colleagues who read novels – I am not a novel-reader myself you understand – but they have pointed out ... well I'm sure it must be a coincidence ... and they have certainly found it very funny that ...'

'That a character in this novel resembles you in certain ways?' said Mr Makeweight, cutting through Frensic's hesitations.

'Well I wouldn't like to say that he resembles me ... I mean the crimes he commits ...'

'Crimes?' said Mr Makeweight, taking the bait. 'A character resembling you commits crimes? In this novel?'

'It's the name you see. Facit,' said Frensic leaning forward to open *Pause* at the page he had marked. 'If you read the passage in question you will see what I mean.'

Mr Makeweight read three pages and looked up with a concern that masked his delight. 'Dear me,' he said, 'I do see what you mean. These are exceedingly serious allegations.'

'Well they are, aren't they?' said Frensic pathetically. 'And my appointment as Professor of Moral Sciences at Wabash

175

has yet to be confirmed and, quite frankly, if it were thought for one moment ...'

'I take your point,' said Mr Makeweight. 'Your career would be put in jeopardy.'

'Ruined,' said Frensic.

Mr Makeweight selected a cigar happily. 'And I suppose we can take it that you have never ... that these allegations are quite without foundation. You have never for instance seduced one of your male students?'

'Mr Makeweight,' said Frensic indignantly.

'Quite so. And you have never had intercourse with a fourteen-year-old girl after dosing her lemonade with a barbiturate?'

'Certainly not. The very idea revolts me. And besides I'm not sure I would know how to.'

Mr Makeweight regarded him critically. 'No, I daresay you wouldn't,' he said finally. 'And there is no truth in the accusation that you habitually fail students who reject your sexual overtures?'

'I don't make sexual overtures to students, Mr Makeweight. As a matter of fact I am neither on the examining board nor do I give tutorials. I am not part of the University. I am over here on a sabbatical and engaged in private research.'

'I see,' said Mr Makeweight, and made a note on his pad.

'And what makes it so much more embarrassing,' said Frensic, 'is that at one time I did have lodgings in De Frytville Avenue.'

Mr Makeweight made a note of that too. 'Extraordinary,' he said, 'quite extraordinary. The resemblance would seem to be almost exact. I think, Professor Facit, in fact I do more, I know that ... provided of course that you haven't committed any of these unnatural acts ... I take it you have never kept a Pekinese ... no. Well as I say, provided you haven't and indeed even if you have, I can tell you now that you have grounds for taking action against the author and publishers of this disgraceful novel. I should estimate the damages to be in the region of ... well to tell the truth I shouldn't be at all surprised if they don't constitute a record in the history of libel actions.

'Oh dear,' said Frensic, feigning a mixture of anxiety and avarice, 'I was rather hoping it might be possible to avoid a court case. The publicity, you understand.'

Mr Makeweight quite understood. 'We'll just have to see how the publishers respond,' he said. 'Corkadales aren't a wealthy firm of course but they'll be insured against libel.'

'I hope that doesn't mean the author won't have to ...'

'Oh he'll pay all right, Professor Facit. Over the years. The insurance company will see to that. A more deliberate case of malicious libel I have never come across.'

'Someone told me that the author, Mr Piper, has made a fortune out of the book in America,' said Frensic.

'In that case I think he will have to part with it,' said Mr Makeweight.

'And if you could expedite the matter I would be most grateful. My appointment at Wabash ...'

Mr Makeweight assured him that he would put the matter in hand at once and Frensic, having given his address as the Randolph Hotel, Oxford, left the office well pleased. Mr Cadwalladine was about to get the shock of his life.

So was Geoffrey Corkadale. Frensic had only just returned to Lanyard Lane and was divesting himself of the disgusting sandals and the tropical suit when the phone rang. Geoffrey was in a state bordering on hysteria. Frensic held the phone away from his ear and listened to a torrent of abuse.

'My dear Geoffrey,' he said when the publisher ran out of epithets. 'What have I done to deserve this outburst?'

'Done?' yelled Corkadale. 'Done? You've done for this firm for one thing. You and that damnable Piper ...'

De mortuis nil nisi ...' Frensic began.

'And what about the bloody living?' screamed Geoffrey. 'And don't tell me he didn't speak ill of this Professor Facit knowing full well that the swine was alive because ...'

'What swine?' said Frensic.

'Professor Facit. The man in the book who did those awful things ...'

'Wasn't he the character with satyriasis who ...'

'Was?' bawled Geoffrey. 'Was? The bloody maniac is.'

177

'Is what?' said Frensic.

'Is! Is! The man's alive and he's filing a libel action against us.'

'Dear me. How very unfortunate.'

'Unfortunate? It's catastrophic. He's gone to Ridley, Cover-up, Makeweight and ...'

'Oh no,' said Frensic, 'but they're absolute rogues.'

'Rogues? They're bloodsuckers. Leeches. They'd get blood out of a stone and with all this filth in the book about Professor Facit they've got a watertight case. They're dunning us for millions. We're finished. We'll never ...'

'The man you want to speak to is a Mr Cadwalladine,' said Frensic. 'He acted for Piper. I'll give you his telephone number.'

'What good is that going to do? It's deliberate libel ...'

But Frensic was already dictating Mr Cadwalladine's telephone number and with apologies because he had a client in the room next door he put the phone down on Geoffrey's ravings. Then he changed out of the tropical suit, phoned the Randolph and booked a room in the name of Professor Facit and waited. Mr Cadwalladine was bound to call and when he did Frensic was going to be ready and waiting. In the meantime he sought further inspiration by studying Piper's telegram. 'Transfer advance royalties care of account number 478776.' And the little bastard was supposed to be dead. What in God's name was going on? And what on earth was he going to tell Sonia? And where did Hutchmeyer fit into all this? According to Sonia the police had grilled him for hours and Hutchmeyer had come out of the experience a shaken man, and had even threatened to sue the police. That didn't sound like the action of a man who ... Frensic put the notion of Hutchmeyer kidnapping Piper and demanding his money back by proxy as too improbable for words. If Hutchmeyer had known that Piper hadn't written *Pause* he would have sued. But Piper apparently had written *Pause*. The proof was there in front of him in the copy of the manuscript. Well he would have to screw the truth out of Cadwalladine and with Mr Makeweight in the wings demanding enormous damages, Mr Cadbloodywalladine was going to have to come clean.

He did. 'I don't know who the author of this awful book is,' he admitted in faltering tones when he rang up half an hour later.

'You don't know?' said Frensic, faltering incredulously himself. 'You must know. You sent me the book in the first place. You gave me the authorization to send Piper to the States. If you didn't know you had no right ...' Mr Cadwalladine made negative noises. 'But I've got a letter here from you saying ...'

'I know you have,' said Mr Cadwalladine faintly. 'The author gave his consent and ...'

'But you've just said you don't know who the bloody author is,' shouted Frensic, 'and now you tell me he gave his consent. His written consent?'

'Yes,' said Mr Cadwalladine.

'In that case you've got to know who he is.'

'But I don't,' said Mr Cadwalladine. 'You see I've always dealt with him through Lloyds Bank.'

Frensic's mind boggled. 'Lloyds Bank?' he muttered. 'You did say Lloyds Bank?'

'Yes. Care of the manager. It's such a very respectable bank and I never for one moment supposed ...'

He left the sentence unfinished. There was no need to end it. Frensic was already ahead of him. 'So what you're saying is that whoever wrote this bloody novel sent the thing to you by way of Lloyds Bank in Oxford and that whenever you've wanted to correspond with him you've had to do so through the bank. Is that right?'

'Precisely,' said Mr Cadwalladine, 'and now that this frightful libel case has come up I think I know why. It puts me in a dreadful situation. My reputation ...'

'Stuff your reputation,' shouted Frensic, 'what about mine? I've been acting in good faith on behalf of a client who doesn't exist and on your instructions and now we've got a murder on our hands and ...'

'This terrible libel action,' said Mr Cadwalladine. 'Mr Corkadale told me that the damages are bound to amount to something astronomical.'

But Frensic wasn't listening. If Mr Cadwalladine's client had to correspond with him through Lloyds Bank the bastard must have something to hide. Unless of course it was Piper. Frensic groped for a clue. 'When the novel first came to you there must have been a covering letter.'

'The manuscript came from a typing agency,' said Mr Cadwalladine. 'The covering letter was sent a few days earlier via Lloyds Bank.'

'With a signature?' said Frensic.

'The signature of the bank manager,' said Mr Cadwalladine.

'That's all I need,' said Frensic. 'What is his name?'

Mr Cadwalladine hesitated. 'I don't think ...' he began but Frensic lost patience.

'Damn your scruples, man,' he snarled, 'the name of the bank manager and quick.'

'The late Mr Bygraves,' said Mr Cadwalladine sadly.

'The what?'

'The late Mr Bygraves. He died of a heart attack climbing Snowdon at Easter.'

Frensic slumped in his chair. 'He had a heart attack climbing Snowdon,' he muttered.

'So you see, I don't think he's going to be able to help us very much,' continued Mr Cadwalladine, 'and anyway banks are very reticent about disclosing the names of their clients. You have to have a warrant, you know.'

Frensic did know. It was one of the few things about banks he had previously admired. But there was something else that Mr Cadwalladine had said earlier ... something about a typing agency. 'You said the manuscript came from a typing agency,' he said. 'Have you any idea which one?'

'No. But I daresay I could find out if you'll give me time.' Frensic sat holding the receiver while Mr Cadwalladine found out. 'It's the Cynthia Bogden Typing Service,' he told Frensic at long last. He sounded distinctly subdued.

'Now we're getting somewhere,' said Frensic. 'Ring her up and ask where ...'

'I'd rather not,' said Mr Cadwalladine.

'You'd rather not? Here we are in the middle of a libel action which is probably going to cost you your reputation and ...'

'It's not that,' interrupted Mr Cadwalladine. 'You see, I handled the divorce case ...'

'Well that's all right . . .'

'I was acting for her ex-husband,' said Mr Cadwalladine. 'I don't think she'd appreciate my . . .'

'Oh all right, I'll do it,' said Frensic. 'Give me her number.' He wrote it down, replaced the receiver and dialled again.

'The Cynthia Bogden Typing Service,' said a voice, coyly professional.

'I'm trying to trace the owner of a manuscript that was typed by your agency . . .' Frensic began but the voice cut him short.

'We do not divulge the names of our clients,' it said.

'But I'm only asking because a friend of mine . . .'

'Under no circumstances are we prepared to confide confidential information of the sort . . .'

'Perhaps if I spoke to Mrs Bogden,' said Frensic.

'You are,' said the voice and rang off. Frensic sat at his desk and cursed.

'Confidential information my foot,' he said and slammed the phone down. He sat thinking dark thoughts about Mrs Bogden for a while and then called Mr Cadwalladine again.

'This Bogden woman,' he said, 'how old is she?'

'Around forty-five,' said Mr Cadwalladine, 'why do you ask?'

'Never mind,' said Frensic.

That evening, having left a note on Sonia Futtle's desk saying that urgent business would keep him out of town for a day or two, Frensic travelled by train to Oxford. He was wearing a lightweight tropical suit, dark glasses and a Panama hat. The sandals were in his dustbin at home. He carried with him in a suitcase the Xeroxed manuscript of *Pause*, a letter written by Piper and a pair of striped pyjamas. Dressed in the last he climbed into bed at eleven in the Randolph Hotel. His room had been booked for Professor Facit.

18

In Chattanooga Baby had fulfilled her ambition. She had seen the Choo Choo. Installed in Pullman Car Number Nine, she lay on the brass bedstead and stared out of the window at the illuminated fountain playing across the tracks. Above the main building of the station tube lighting emblazoned the night sky with the words Hilton Choo Choo and below, in what had once been the waiting-room, dinner was being served. Beside the restaurant there was a crafts shop and in front of them both stood huge locomotives of a bygone era, their cow-catchers freshly painted and their smokestacks gleaming as if in anticipation of some great journey. In fact they were going nowhere. Their fireboxes were cold and empty and their pistons would never move again. Only in the imagination of those who stayed the night in the ornate and divided Pullman cars, now motel bedrooms, was it still possible to entertain the illusion that they would presently pull out of the station and begin the long haul north or west. The place was part museum, part fantasy and wholly commercial. At the entrance to the car park uniformed guards sat in a small cabin watching the television screen on which each platform and each dark corner of the station was displayed for the protection of the guests. Outside the perimeter of the station Chattanooga spread dark and seedy with boarded hotel windows and derelict buildings, a victim of the shopping precincts beyond the ring of suburbs.

But Baby wasn't thinking about Chattanooga or even the Choo Choo. They had joined the illusions of her retarded youth. Age had caught up with her and she felt tired and empty of hope. All the romance of life had gone. Piper had seen to that. Travelling day after day with a self-confessed genius whose thoughts were centred on literary immortality to the exclusion of all else had given Baby a new insight into the monotony of Piper's mind. By comparison Hutchmeyer's obsession with money and power and wheeling and dealing now seemed positively healthy. Piper evinced no interest in the countryside nor the towns they passed through and the fact that they were now in, or at least on the frontier of, the Deep South and that wild country of Baby's soft-corn imagination appeared to mean nothing to him. He had hardly glanced at the locomotives drawn up in the station and seemed only surprised that they weren't travelling anywhere on them. Once that had been impressed on him he had retreated to his stateroom and had started work again on his second version of *Pause*.

'For a great novelist you've just got to be the least observant,' Baby said when they met in the restaurant for dinner. 'I mean don't you ever look around and wonder what it's all about.'

Piper looked around. 'Seems an odd place to put a restaurant,' he said. 'Still, it's nice and cool.'

'That just happens to be the air-conditioning,' said Baby irritably.

'Oh, is that what it is,' said Piper. 'I wondered.'

'He wondered. And what about all the people who have sat right here waiting to take the train north to New York and Detroit and Chicago to make their fortunes instead of scratching a living from a patch of dirt? Doesn't that mean anything to you?'

'There don't seem many of them about,' said Piper looking idly at a woman with an obesity problem and tartan shorts, 'and anyway I thought you said the trains weren't running any more.'

'Oh my God,' said Baby, 'I sometimes wonder what century you're living in. And I suppose it doesn't mean a thing to you that there was a battle here in the Civil War?'

'No,' said Piper. 'Battles don't figure in great literature.'

'They don't? What about *Gone With The Wind* and *War and Peace*? I suppose they aren't great literature.'

'Not English literature,' said Piper. 'What matters in English literature is the relationships people have with one another.'

Baby dug into her steak. 'And people don't relate to one another in battles? Is that it?'

Piper nodded.

'So when one guy kills another that's not relating in a way that matters?'

'Only transitorily,' said Piper.

'And when Sherman's troops go looting and burning and

raping their way from Atlanta to the sea and leave behind them homeless families and burning mansions that isn't altering relationships either so you don't write about it?'

'The best novelists wouldn't,' said Piper. 'It didn't happen to them and therefore they couldn't.'

'Couldn't what?'

'Write about it.'

'Are you telling me a writer can only write what has really happened to him? Is that what you're saying?' said Baby with a new edge to her voice.

'Yes,' said Piper, 'you see it would be outside the range of his experience and therefore ...'

He spoke at length from *The Moral Novel* while Baby slowly chewed her way through her steak and thought dark thoughts about Piper's theory.

'In that case you're going to need a lot more experience is all I can say.'

Piper pricked up his ears. 'Now wait a minute,' he said, 'if you think I want to be involved in any more house-burning and boat-exploding and that sort of thing—'

'I wasn't thinking of that sort of experience. I mean things like burning houses don't count do they? It's relationships that matter. What you need is experience in relating.'

Piper ate uneasily. The conversation had taken a distasteful turn. They finished their meal in silence. Afterwards Piper returned to his stateroom and wrote five hundred more words about his tortured adolescence and his feeling for Gwendolen/Miss Pears. Finally he turned out the electric oil lamp that hung above his brass bedstead and undressed. In the next compartment Baby readied herself for Piper's first lesson in relationships. She put on a very little nightdress and a great deal of perfume and opened the door to Piper's stateroom.

'For God's sake,' squawked Piper as she climbed into bed with him.

'This is where it all begins, baby,' said Baby, 'relationship-wise.'

'No, it doesn't,' said Piper. 'It's—'

Baby's hand closed over his mouth and her voice whispered in his ear.

184

'And don't think you're going to get out of here. They've got TV cameras on every platform and you go hobbling out there in the raw the guards are going to want to know what's been going on.'

'But I'm not in the raw,' said Piper as Baby's hand left his mouth.

'You soon will be, honey,' Baby whispered as her hands deftly untied his pyjamas.

'Please,' said Piper plaintively.

'I aim to, honey, I aim to,' said Baby. She lifted her night-dress and her great breasts dug into Piper's chest. For the next two hours the brass bedstead heaved and creaked as Baby Hutchmeyer, née Sugg, Miss Penobscot 1935, put all the expertise of her years to work on Piper. And in spite of himself and his invocation of the precepts in *The Moral Novel*, Piper was for the first time lost to the world of letters and moved by an inchoate passion. He writhed beneath her, he pounded on top, his mouth sucked at her silicon breasts and slithered across the minute scars on her stomach. All the time Baby's fingers caressed and dug and scratched and squeezed until Piper's back was torn and his buttocks marked by the curve of her nails and all the time Baby stared into the dimness of the stateroom dispassionately and wondered at her own boredom. 'Youth must have its fling,' she thought to herself as Piper hurled himself into her yet again. But she was no longer young, and flinging without feeling was not her scene. There was more to life than fucking. Much more, and she was going to find it.

In Oxford Frensic was up and about and finding it when Baby returned to her own compartment and left Piper sleeping exhaustedly next door. Frensic had got up early and had breakfasted before eight. By half-past he had found the Cynthia Bogden Typing Service in Fenet Street. With what he hoped was the expectant look of an American tourist he haunted the church opposite and sat in one of the pews staring back through the open door at the entrance to the Bogden Bureau. If he knew anything about middle-aged women who were divorced and ran their own businesses, Miss Bogden would be the first to arrive in the morning and the last to leave at night. By quarter past nine Frensic certainly hoped so. The trail of women he had seen entering the office were not at all to his taste but at least the first to arrive had been the most presentable. She had been a large woman but Frensic's brief glimpse had told him that her legs were good and that if Mr Cadwalladine had been right about her being forty-five she didn't look it. Frensic left the church and pondered his next step. There was no point in going into the Agency and asking Miss Bogden point blank who had sent her *Pause*. Her tone the previous day had indicated that more subtle tactics were necessary.

Frensic made his next move. He found a flower shop and went inside. Twenty minutes later two dozen red roses were delivered to the Bogden Typing Service with a note which said simply, 'To Miss Bogden from an Admirer.' Frensic had thought of adding 'ardent' but had decided against it. Two dozen expensive red roses argued an ardency by themselves. Miss Bodgen or more properly Mrs Bogden, and the reversion indicated a romantic direction to that lady's thoughts, would supply the adjective. Frensic wandered round Oxford, had coffee in the Ship and lunch back at the Randolph. Then, gauging that enough time had elapsed for Miss Bogden to have digested the implications of the roses, he went to Professor Facit's room and phoned the Agency. As before, Miss Bogden answered. Frensic took a deep breath, swallowed and presently heard himself asking with an agony of unaffected coyness if she would do him the honour and privilege of having dinner with him at the Elizabeth. There was a sibilant pause before Miss Bogden replied.

'Do I know you?' she asked archly. Frensic squirmed.

'An admirer,' he murmured.

'Oo,' said Miss Bogden. There was another pause while she observed the proprieties of hesitation.

'Roses,' said Frensic garrottedly.

'Are you quite sure? I mean it's rather unusual . . .'

Frensic silently agreed that it was. 'It's just that . . .' he began and then took the plunge, 'I haven't had the nerve before and . . .' The garrotte tightened.

Miss Bogden on the other hand breathed sympathy. 'Better late than never,' she said softly.

'That's what I thought,' said Frensic who didn't.

'And you did say the Elizabeth?'

'Yes,' said Frensic, 'shall we say eight in the bar?'

'How will I know you?'

'I know you,' said Frensic and giggled involuntarily. Miss Bogden took it as a compliment.

'You haven't told me your name.'

Frensic hesitated. He couldn't use his own and Facit was in *Pause*. It had to be someone else. 'Corkadale,' he muttered finally, 'Geoffrey Corkadale.'

'Not *the* Geoffrey Corkadale?' said Miss Bogden.

'Yes,' stammered Frensic hoping to hell that Geoffrey's epicene reputation hadn't reached her ears. It hadn't. Miss Bogden cooed.

'Well in that case . . .' She left the rest unsaid.

'Till eight,' said Frensic.

'Till eight,' echoed Miss Bogden. Frensic put the phone down and sat limply on the bed.

Then he lay down and had a long nap. He woke at four and went downstairs. There was one last thing to do. He didn't know Miss Bogden and there must be no mistake. He made his way to Fenet Street and stationed himself in the church. He was there at five-thirty when the trail of awful women came out of the office. Frensic sighed with relief. None of them was carrying a bunch of red roses. Finally the large woman appeared and locked the door. She clutched roses to her ample bosom and hurried off down the street. Frensic emerged from the church and watched her go. Miss Bogden was definitely well preserved. From her permed head to her pink shoes by way of a turquoise costume there was a tastelessness about the woman that was almost inspired. Frensic went back to the hotel and had a stiff gin. Then he had another, took a bath and rehearsed various approaches that seemed likely to elicit from Miss Bogden the name of the author of *Pause*.

On the other side of Oxford, Cynthia Bogden prepared herself for the evening with the same thoroughness with which she did everything. It had been some years since her divorce and to be asked to dine at the Elizabeth by a publisher augured well. So did the roses, carefully arranged in a vase, and the nervousness of her admirer. There had been nothing brash about the voice on the telephone. It had been an educated voice and Corkadales were most respectable publishers. And in any case Cynthia Bogden was in need of admirers. She selected her most seductive costume, sprayed herself in various places with various aerosols, fixed her face and set out prepared to be wined, dined and, not to put too fine a point on it, fucked. She entered the foyer of the Elizabeth exuding an uncertain hauteur and was somewhat startled when a short baggy man sidled up to her and took her hand.

'Miss Bogden,' he murmured, 'your fond admirer.'

Miss Bogden looked down at her fond admirer dubiously. She was still looking down at him half an hour and three pink gins later as they made their way to the table Frensic had reserved in the farthest corner of the restaurant. He held her chair for her and then, conscious that perhaps he hadn't come as far up to her expectations as he might have done, threw himself into the part of fond admirer with a desperate gallantry and inventiveness that surprised them both.

'I first glimpsed you a year ago when I was up for a conference,' he told her having ordered the wine waiter to bring them a bottle of not too dry champagne, 'I saw you in the street and followed you to your office.'

'You should have introduced yourself,' said Miss Bogden.

Frensic blushed convincingly. 'I was too shy,' he murmured, 'and besides I thought you were ...'

'Married?' said Miss Bogden helpfully.

'Exactly,' said Frensic, 'or shall we say attached. A woman as ... er ... beautiful ... er ...'

It was Miss Bogden's turn to blush. Frensic plunged on. 'I was overcome. Your charm, your air of quiet reserve, your ... how shall I put it ...' There was no need to put it. While Frensic burrowed into an avocado pear, Cynthia Bogden savoured a shrimp. Baggy this little man might be but he was clearly a gentleman and a man of the world. Champagne at twelve pounds a bottle was sufficient indication of his honourable intentions. When Frensic ordered a second, Miss Bogden protested feebly.

'Special occasion,' said Frensic wondering if he wasn't overdoing things a bit, 'and besides we have something to celebrate.'

'We do?'

'Our meeting for one thing,' said Frensic, 'and the success of a mutual venture.'

'Mutual venture?' said Miss Bogden, her thoughts veering sharply to the altar.

'Something we both had a hand in,' continued Frensic, 'I mean we don't usually publish that sort of book but I must say it's been a great success.'

Miss Bogden's thoughts turned away from the altar. Frensic helped himself to more champagne. 'We're a very traditional publishing house,' he said, 'but *Pause O Men for the Virgin* is what the public demands these days.'

'It was rather awful, wasn't it?' said Miss Bogden, 'I typed it myself you know.'

'Really?' said Frensic.

'Well I didn't like my girls having to do it and the author was so peculiar about it.'

'Was he?'

'I had to phone up ever so often,' said Miss Bogden. 'But you don't want to hear about that.'

Frensic did but Miss Bogden was adamant. 'We mustn't spoil our first evening talking shop,' she said and in spite of more champagne and a large Cointreau all Frensic's attempts to steer the conversation back to the subject failed. Miss Bogden wanted to hear about Corkadales. The name seemed to appeal to her.

'Why don't you come back to my place?' she asked as they walked beside the river after dinner. 'For a nightcap.'

'That's frightfully kind of you,' said Frensic prepared to pursue his quarry to the bitter end. 'Are you sure I wouldn't be imposing on you?'

'I'd like that,' said Miss Bogden with a giggle and took his arm, 'to be imposed on by you.' She steered him to the car-park and a light blue MG. Frensic gaped at the car. It did not accord with his notion of what a forty-five-year-old head of a typing bureau should drive and besides he was unused to bucket seats. Frensic squeezed in and was forced to allow Miss Bogden to fasten his safety belt. Then they drove rather faster than he liked along the Banbury Road and into a hinterland of semi-detached houses. Miss Bogden lived at 33 Viewpark Avenue, a mixture of pebbledash and Tudor. She pulled up in front of the garage. Frensic fumbled for the catch of his safety belt but Cynthia Bogden was there before him and leaning expectantly. Frensic nerved himself for the inevitable and took her in his arms. It was a long kiss and a passionate one, made even less enjoyable for Frensic by the presence of the gear lever in his right kidney. By the time they had finished and climbed out of the car he was having third and fourth thoughts about the whole enterprise. But there was too much at stake to falter now. Frensic followed her into the house. Miss Bogden switched on the hall light.

'Would you like a drinkie?' she asked.

'No,' said Frensic with a fervour that came largely from the conviction that she would offer him cooking sherry. Miss Bogden took his refusal as a compliment and once more they grappled, this time in the company of a hat stand. Then taking his hand she led the way upstairs.

'The you-know-what's in there,' she said helpfully. Frensic staggered into the bathroom and shut the door. He spent several minutes staring at his reflection in the mirror and wondering why it was that only the most predatory women found him attractive and wishing to hell they didn't and then, having promised himself that he would never again be rude about Geoffrey Corkadale's preferences, he came out and went into the bedroom. Cynthia Bogden's bedroom was pink. The curtains were pink, the carpet pink, the padded and quilted bedhead pink and the lampshade beside it pink. And finally there was a pink Frensic wrestling with the intricacies of Cynthia Bogden's pink underwear while muttering pinkish endearments in her pink ear.

An hour later Frensic was no longer pink. Against the pink sheets he was puce and having palpitations to boot. His efforts to get into her good books among other less savoury things had done something to his circulatory system and Miss Bogden's sexual skills, nurtured in a justifiably broken marriage and gleaned, Frensic suspected, from some frightful manual on how to make sex an adventure, had led him to contortions which would have defied the imaginations of his most sexually obsessed authors. As he lay panting, alternately thanking God it was all over and wondering if he was going to have a coronary, Cynthia bent her permed head over him.

'Satisfied?' she asked. Frensic stared at her and nodded frantically. Any other answer would have invited suicide.

'And now we'll have a little drinkie,' she said and skipping to Frensic's amazement lightly off the bed she went downstairs and returned with a bottle of whisky. She sat down on the edge of the bed and poured two tots.

'To us,' she said. Frensic drank deeply and held out his glass for more. Cynthia smiled and handed him the bottle.

In New York Hutchmeyer was having problems too. They were of a different sort to Frensic's but since they involved three and a half million dollars the effect was much the same. 'What do you mean they aren't prepared to pay?' he yelled at MacMordie who had reported that the insurance company were holding back on compensation. 'They got to pay. I mean why should I insure my property if they aren't going to pay when it's arsonized?'

'I don't know,' said MacMordie, 'I'm just telling you what Mr Synstrom said.'

'Get me Synstrom,' yelled Hutchmeyer. MacMordie got Synstrom. He came up to Huchmeyer's office and sat blandly regarding the great publisher through steel-rimmed glasses.

'Now I don't know what you're trying to get at—' Hutchmeyer began.

'The truth,' said Mr Synstrom. 'Just the plain truth.'

'That's okay by me,' said Hutchmeyer, 'just so long as you pay up when you've got it.'

'The thing is, Mr Hutchmeyer, we know how that fire started.'

'How?'

'Someone deliberately lit the house with a can of gasolene. And that someone was your wife . . .'

'You know that?'

'Mr Hutchmeyer, we've got analysts who can figure out the nail varnish your wife was wearing when she opened that safe and took out that quarter of a million dollars you had stashed there.'

Hutchmeyer eyed him suspiciously. 'You can?' he said.

'Sure. And we know too she loaded that cruiser of yours with fifty gallons of gasolene. She and that Piper. He carried the cans down and we've got their prints.'

'What the hell would she do that for?'

'We thought you might have the answer to that one,' said Mr Synstrom.

'Me? I was out in the middle of the goddam bay. How should I know what was going on back at my house?'

'We wouldn't know that, Mr Hutchmeyer. Just seems a kind of coincidence you go sailing with Miss Futtle in a storm and your wife is setting out to burn your house down and fake her own death.'

Hutchmeyer paled. 'Fake her own death? Did you say ...'

My Synstrom nodded. 'We call it the Stonehouse syndrome in the trade,' he said. 'It happens every once in a while someone wants the world to think they're dead so they disappear and leave their nearest and dearest to claim the insurance. Now you've put in a claim for three and a half million dollars and we've got no proof your wife isn't alive some place.'

Hutchmeyer stared miserably at him. He was considering the awful possibility that Baby was still around and with her she was carrying all that evidence of his tax evasions, bribes and illegal dealings that could send him to prison. By comparison the forfeiture of three and a half million dollars was peanuts.

'I just can't believe she'd do a thing like that,' he said finally. 'I mean we had a happy marriage. No problems. I gave her everything she asked for ...'

'Like young men?' said Mr Synstrom.

'No, not like young men,' shouted Hutchmeyer, and felt his pulse.

'Now this Piper writer was a young man,' said Mr Synstrom.

'and from what we've heard Mrs Hutchmeyer had a taste for ...'

'Are you accusing my wife of ... My God, I'll ...'

'We're not accusing anyone of anything, Mr Hutchmeyer. Like I've said we're trying to get at the truth.'

'And are you telling me that my wife, my own dear little Baby, filled that cruiser with gasolene and deliberately tried to murder me by aiming it at my yacht in the middle of—'

'That's exactly what I'm saying. Mind you, that could have been an accident,' said Mr Synstrom, 'the cruiser blowing up where she did.'

'Yeah, well from where I was standing it didn't look like an accident. You can believe it didn't,' said Huchmeyer. 'You want to have a cruiser come out of the night straight for you before you go round making allegations like you've just done.'

Mr Synstrom got to his feet. 'So you still want us to continue with our investigations?' he said.

Hutchmeyer hesitated. If Baby was still alive the last thing he wanted was investigations. 'I just don't believe my Baby would have done a thing like that is all,' he said.

Mr Synstrom sat down again. 'If she did and we can prove it I'm afraid Mrs Hutchmeyer would stand trial. Arson, attempted murder, defrauding an insurance company. And then there's Mr Piper. He's an accessory. Bestselling author, I hear. I guess he could always get a job in the prison library. Make a sensational trial too. Now if you don't want all of that ...'

Hutchmeyer didn't want any of that. Sensational trials with Baby in the box pleading that ... Oh no! Definitely not. And *Pause* was selling by the hundred thousand, had passed the million mark and with the movie of the book in production the computer was overheating with the stupendous forecasts. Sensational trials were out.

'What's the alternative?' he asked.

Mr Synstrom leant forward. 'We could come to an arrangement,' he said.

'We could,' Hutchmeyer agreed, 'but that still leaves the cops ...'

Mr Synstrom shook his head. 'They're sitting around waiting to see what we come up with. Now the way I see it . . .'

By the time he had finished Hutchmeyer saw it that way too. The insurance company would announce that the claim had been met in full and in return Hutchmeyer would write a disclaimer. Hutchmeyer did. Three and a half million dollars was worth every cent for keeping Baby 'dead'.

'What happens if you're right and she turns up out of the blue?' Hutchmeyer asked as Synstrom got up to leave.

'Then you've really got problems,' he said. 'That's what I'd say.'

He left and Hutchmeyer sat back and considered those problems. The only consolation he could find was that if Baby was still alive she had problems too. Like coming back to life and going to prison. She wasn't fool enough to do that. Which left Hutchmeyer free to go his own way. He could even marry again. His thoughts turned to Sonia Futtle. Now there was a *real* woman.

19

Two thousand miles to the south Baby's problems had taken on a new dimension. Her attempt to give Piper the experience he needed relationshipwise had succeeded too well and where before he had thrown himself into *Work in Regress* he now insisted on throwing himself into her as well. The years of his celibacy were over and Piper was making up for them in a hurry. As he lay each night kissing her reinforced breasts and gripping her degreased thighs Piper experienced an ecstasy he could never have found with another woman. Baby's artificiality was entirely to his taste. Lacking so many original parts she had none of those natural physiological disadvantages he had found in Sonia. She had, as it were, been expurgated and Piper, himself in the process of expurgating *Pause*, derived enormous satisfaction from the fact that with Baby he could act out the role he had been assigned as a narrator in the book

194

and with a woman who if she was much older than him didn't look it. And Baby's response added to his pleasure. She combined lack of fervour with sexual expertise so that he didn't feel threatened by her passion. She was simply there to be enjoyed and didn't interfere with his writing by demanding his constant attention. Finally her intimate knowledge of the novel meant that she could respond word-perfect to his cues. When he murmured, 'Darling, we're being so heuristically creative,' at the penultimate moment of ecstasy, Baby, feeling nothing, could reply, 'Constating, my baby,' in unison with her prototype the ancient Gwendolen on page 185, and thus maintain quite literally the fiction that was the essential core of Piper's being.

But if Baby met Piper's requirements as the ideal lover the reverse was not true. Baby found it unflattering to know that she was merely a stand-in for a figment of his imagination and not even his own imagination but that for the real author of *Pause*. Knowing this, Piper's ardour took on an almost ghoulish quality so that Baby, staring over his shoulder at the ceiling, had the horrid feeling that she might just as well not have been present. At such moments she saw herself as something that had coalesced from the pages of *Pause*, a phantom of the opus which was Piper's pretentious name for what he was now doing in *Work in Regress* and intended to continue in another version. Her future seemed destined to be the recipient of his derived feelings, a sexual artefact compiled from words upon pages to be ejaculated into and then set aside while he put pen to paper. Even the routine of their days had altered. Piper insisted on writing each morning and driving through the heat of the day and stopping early at a motel so that he could read to her what he had written that morning and then relate.

'Can't you just say "fuck" once in a while?' Baby asked one evening at a motel in Tuscaloosa. 'I mean that's what we're doing so why not name it right?'

But Piper wouldn't. The word wasn't in *Pause* and 'relating' was an approved term in *The Moral Novel*.

'What I feel for you ...' he began but Baby stopped him.

'So I read the original. I don't need to see the movie.'

'As I was saying,' said Piper, 'what I feel for you is ...'

'Zero,' said Baby, 'absolute zero. You've got more feelings towards that inkbottle you're always sticking your pen in than you have towards me.'

'Well, I like that . . .' said Piper.

'I don't,' said Baby and there was a new note of desperation in her voice. For a moment she thought of leaving Piper there in the motel and going off on her own. But the moment passed. She was tied by the irrevocable act of the fire and her disappearance to this literary mongol whose notion of great writing was to step backwards in time in futile imitation of novelists long dead. Worst of all, she saw in Piper's obsession with past glories a mirror-image of herself. For forty years she too had waged a war with time and had by surgical recession maintained the outward appearance of the foolish beauty who had been Miss Penobscot 1935. They had so much in common and Piper served to remind her of her own stupidity. All that was gone now, the longing to be young again and the sense of knowing she was still sexually attractive. Only death remained and the certainty that when she died there would be no call for the embalmer. She had seen to that in advance.

She had seen to more than that. She had already died by fire, by water, by the bizarre circumstances of her own romantic madness. Which gave her something more in common with Piper. They were both nonentities moving in a limbo of monotonous motels, he with his ledgers and her body but she with nothing more than a sense of meaninglessness and a desperate futility. That night while Piper related, Baby, inanimate beneath him, made up her mind. They would leave the beaten track of motels and drive down dirt roads into the hinterland of the Deep South. What happened to them there would be beyond her choosing.

What was happening to Frensic was definitely beyond his choosing. He sat at the Formica-topped table in Cynthia Bogden's kitchen and tried to eat his cornflakes and forget what had occurred towards dawn. Driven frantic by Cynthia's omnivorous sexuality he had proposed to the woman. It had seemed in his whisky-sodden state the only defence against a fatal coronary and a means of getting her to tell him who had sent her *Pause*. But Miss Bogden had been too overwhelmed to discuss minor matters of that sort in the middle of the night. In the end Frensic had snatched a few hours sleep and had been woken by a radiant Cynthia with a cup of tea. Frensic had staggered through to the bathroom and had shaved with someone else's razor and had come down to breakfast determined to force the issue. But Miss Bogden's thoughts were confined to their wedding day.

'Shall we have a church wedding?' she asked as Frensic toyed biliously with a boiled egg.

'What? Oh. Yes.'

'I've always wanted a church wedding.'

'So have I,' said Frensic with as much enthusiasm as if she had suggested a crematorium. He savaged the egg and decided on the direct approach. 'By the way did you ever meet the author of *Pause O Men for the Virgin*?'

Miss Bogden dragged her thoughts away from aisles, altars and Mendelssohn. 'No,' she said, 'the manuscript came by post.'

'By post?' said Frensic, dropping his spoon. 'Isn't that rather unusual?'

'You're not eating your egg,' said Miss Bogden. Frensic took a spoonful of egg into his dry mouth.

'Where did it come from?'

'Lloyds Bank,' said Miss Bogden and poured herself another cup of tea. 'Another cup for you?'

Frensic nodded. He needed something to wash the egg down with. 'Lloyds Bank?' he said finally. 'But there must have been words you couldn't read. What did you do then?'

'Oh I just rang up and asked.'

'You phoned? You mean you phoned Lloyds Bank and they'd ...'

'Oh you are silly, Geoffrey,' said Miss Bogden, 'I didn't phone Lloyds Bank. I had this other number.'

'What other number?'

'The one I had to ring, silly,' said Miss Bogden and looked at her watch. 'Oh look at the time. It's almost nine. You've made me late, you naughty boy.' And she rushed out of the kitchen. When she returned she was dressed for the day. 'You can call a taxi when you're ready,' she said, 'and we'll meet at the office.' She kissed Frensic passionately on his egg-filled mouth and went out.

Frensic got to his feet and spat the egg into the sink and turned the tap on. Then he took a pinch of snuff, helped himself to some more tea and tried to think. A phone number she had to ring? The whole business became more extraordinary the further he delved into it. And for once delved was the right word. In looking for the source of *Pause* he had dug himself ... Frensic shuddered. Dug was the right word too. In the plural it was exact. He went through to the lavatory and sat there miserably for ten minutes trying to concentrate on his next move. A phone number? An author who insisted on making corrections by telephone? There was an insanity about all this that made his own actions over the past few days look positively rational. And there was absolutely nothing rational about proposing to Miss Cynthia Bogden. Frensic finished his business in the lavatory and came out. On a small table in the hall stood a telephone. Frensic crossed to it and looked through Miss Bogden's private list of numbers but there was nothing there to indicate the author. Frensic returned to the kitchen, made himself a cup of instant coffee, took some more snuff and finally telephoned for a taxi.

It came at ten and at half-past Frensic shuffled into the Typing Agency. Miss Bogden was waiting for him. So were twelve awful women sitting at typewriters.

'Girls,' Miss Bogden called euphemistically as Frensic peered anxiously into the office, 'I want you all to meet my fiancé, Mr Geoffrey Corkadale.'

The women all rose from the seats and gaggled congratulations on Frensic while Miss Bogden suppurated happiness.

'And now the ring,' she said when the congratulations died down. She led the way out of the office and Frensic followed. The bloody woman would want a ring. Just so long as it wasn't too expensive. It was.

'I think I like the solitaire,' she told the jeweller in the Broad. Frensic flinched at the price and was about to put his entire scheme in jeopardy when he was struck by a brilliant thought. After all, what was five hundred pounds when his entire future was at stake?

198

'Oughtn't we to have it engraved?' he said as Cynthia put it on her finger and admired its brilliance.

'What with?' she cooed.

Frensic simpered. 'Something secret,' he whispered, 'something we two alone will understand. A *code d'amour*.'

'Oh you are awful,' said Miss Bogden. 'Fancy thinking of something like that.' Frensic glanced at the jeweller uncomfortably and applied his lips to the perm again.

'A code of love,' he explained.

'A code of love?' echoed Miss Bogden. 'What sort of code?'

'A number,' said Frensic, and paused. 'Some number that only we would know had brought us together.'

'You mean . . . ?'

'Exactly,' said Frensic forestalling any alternatives, 'after all, you typed the book and I published it.'

'Couldn't we just have Till Death Do Us Part?'

'Too much like the TV series,' said Frensic who had very much earlier intentions. He was saved by the jeweller.

'You'd never get that inside the ring. Not Till Death Do Us Part. Too many letters.'

'But you could do numbers?' said Frensic.

'Depends how many.'

Frensic looked inquiringly at Miss Bogden. 'Five,' she said after a moment's hesitation.

'Five,' said Frensic. 'Five teeny weeny little numbers that are our code of love, our own, our very own itsy bitsy secret.' It was his last desperate act of heroism. Miss Bogden succumbed. For a moment she had . . . but no, a man who could in the presence of an austere jeweller By Appointment to Her Majesty talk openly about five teeny weeny itsy bitsy numbers that were their code of love, such a man was above suspicion.

'Two oh three five seven,' she simpered.

'Two oh three five seven,' said Frensic loudly. 'You're quite sure? We don't want to make any mistakes.'

'Of course I'm sure,' said Miss Bogden, 'I'm not in the habit of making mistakes.'

'Right,' said Frensic plucking the ring from her finger and handing it to the jeweller, 'stick them on the inside of the thing. I'll be back to collect it this afternoon,' and taking Miss

Bogden firmly by the arm he steered her towards the door.

'Excuse me, sir,' said the jeweller, 'but if you don't mind ...'

'Mind what?' said Frensic.

'I would prefer it if you paid now sir. With engraving, you understand, we have to ...'

Frensic understood all too well. He released Miss Bogden and sidled back to the counter.

'Er ... well ...' he began but Miss Bogden was still between him and the door. This was no time for half-measures. Frensic took out his cheque book.

'I'll be with you in a moment, dear,' he called. 'You just go over the road and look at dresses.'

Cynthia Bogden obeyed her instincts and stayed where she was.

'You do have a cheque card, sir?' said the jeweller.

Frensic looked at him gratefully. 'As a matter of fact, I don't. Not on me.'

'Then I'm afraid it will have to be cash, sir.'

'Cash?' said Frensic. 'In that case ...'

'We'll go to the bank,' said Miss Bogden firmly. They went to the bank in the High Street. Miss Bogden seated herself while Frensic conferred at the counter.

'Five hundred pounds?' said the teller. 'We'll have to have proof of identity and telephone your own branch.'

Frensic glanced at Miss Bogden and lowered his voice. 'Frensic,' he said nervously, 'Frederick Frensic, Glass Walk, Hampstead but my business account is with the branch in Covent Garden.'

'We'll call you when we have confirmation,' said the teller.

Frensic blanched. 'I'd be grateful if you didn't ...' he began.

'Didn't what?'

'Never mind,' said Frensic and went back to Miss Bogden. He had to get her out of the bank before that blasted teller started hollering for Mr Frensic.

'This is going to take some time, darling. Why don't you toddle back to ...'

'But I've taken the day off and I thought ...'

'Taken the day off?' said Frensic. If this sort of stress went on much longer it would take years off. 'But ...'

'But what?' said Miss Bogden.

'But I'm supposed to be meeting an author for lunch. Professor Dubrowitz. From Warsaw. He's only over for the day and ...' He hustled her out of the bank promising to come to the office just as soon as he could. Then with a sigh of relief he went back and collected five hundred pounds.

'Now for the nearest telephone,' he said to himself as he pocketed the money and descended the steps. Cynthia Bogden was still there.

'But ...' Frensic began and gave up. With Miss Bogden there were no buts.

'I thought we'd just go and get the ring first,' she said taking his arm, 'then you can go and have lunch with your boring old professor.'

They went back to the jewellers and Frensic paid £500. Only then did Miss Bogden allow him to escape.

'Call me as soon as you've finished,' she said pecking his cheek. Frensic promised to and hurried off to the main post office. In a foul temper he dialled 23507.

'The Bombay Duck Restaurant,' said an Indian who was unlikely to have written *Pause*. Frensic slammed the phone down and tried another combination of the digits in the ring. This time he got MacLoughlin's Fish Emporium. Then he ran out of change. He went across to the main counter and handed over a five-pound note for a 6½p stamp and returned with a pocketful of coins. The phone booth was occupied. Frensic stood beside it looking belligerent while an apparently subnormal youth plighted his acned troth to a girl who giggled audibly. Frensic spent the time trying to remember the exact number and by the time the youth had finished he had got it. Frensic went in and dialled 20357. There was a long pause and the sound of the ringing tone before anyone answered. Frensic plunged a coin into the machine.

'Yes,' said a thin querulous voice, 'who is it?'

Frensic hesitated a moment and then coarsened his voice. 'This is the General Post Office, telephone faults department,' he said. 'We are trying to trace a crossed connection in a junction box. If you would just give me your name and address.'

'A fault?' said the voice. 'We haven't had any faults.'

'You soon will have. There's a burst water main and we need your name and address.'

'But I thought you said you had a crossed connection?' said the voice peevishly. 'Now you say there's a water main ...'

'Madam,' said Frensic officiously, 'the burst water main is affecting the junction box and we need your help to locate it. Now if you will be so good as to give me your name and address ...' There was a long pause during which Frensic gnawed a nail.

'Oh well if you must,' said the voice at long last, 'the name is Dr Louth and the address is 44 Cowpasture Gardens ... Hello, are you there?'

But Frensic was miles away in a world of terrible conjecture. Without another word he replaced the receiver and staggered out into the street.

In Lanyard Lane Sonia sat at her typewriter and stared at the calendar. She had returned from Somerset, satisfied that Bernie the Beaver would use less forceful language in future, to find two messages for her. The first was from Frensic saying that he would be out of town on business for a few days and would she mind coping. That was queer enough. Frensic usually left fuller explanations and a telephone number where she could call him in case of emergencies. The second message was even more peculiar and in the shape of a long telegram from Hutchmeyer: POLICE ESTABLISHED DEATHS PIPER AND BABY ACCIDENTAL NO RESPONSIBILITY TERRORISTS RUNNING AWAY WITH EACH OTHER CRAZY ABOUT YOU ARRIVING THURSDAY ALL MY LOVE HUTCHMEYER.

Sonia studied the message and found it at first incomprehensible. Deaths accidental? No responsibility terrorists running away with each other? What on earth did it mean? For a moment she hesitated and then dialled International and was put through to New York and Hutchmeyer Press. She got MacMordie.

'He's in Brasilia right now,' he said.

'What's all this business about Piper's death being accidental?' she asked.

'That's the theory the police have come up with,' said Mac-Mordie, 'like they were eloping some place with all that fuel on board when she blew.'

'Eloping? Piper and that bitch eloping? In the middle of the night with a cabin cruiser? Somebody's out of their mind.'

'I wouldn't know,' said MacMordie, 'all I'm saying is what the cops and the insurance company have come up with. And that Piper had this big thing for old women. I mean take his book. It shows.'

'Like hell it does,' said Sonia before recalling that Mac-Mordie didn't know Piper hadn't written it.

'If you don't believe me, call the cops in Maine or the insurers. They'll tell you.'

Sonia called the insurers. They were more likely to come up with the truth. They had money at stake. She was put through to Mr Synstrom.

'And you really believe he was running off with Mrs Hutchmeyer and it was all an accident?' she said when he had given his version of the event. 'I mean you're not having me on?'

'This is the Claims Department,' said Mr Synstrom firmly. 'We don't have people on. It's not our line of business.'

'Well it sounds crazy to me,' said Sonia, 'she was old enough to be his mother.'

'If you want further delineation of the circumstances surrounding the accident I suggest you speak to the Maine State police,' said Mr Synstrom and ended the conversation.

Sonia sat stunned by this new development. That Piper had preferred that awful old hag ... From being in love with his memory one minute she was out of it the next. Piper had betrayed her and with the knowledge there came a new sense of bitterness and reality. In life, now that she came to think about it, he had been a bit dreary and her love had been less for him as a man than for his aptitude as a husband. Given the chance she could have made something of him. Even before his death she had made him famous as an author and had he lived they would have gone on to greater things. It was not for nothing that Brahms was her favourite composer. There would have been little Pipers, each to be helped towards a suitable career by a woman who was at the same time a mother and a literary agent. That dream had ended. Piper had died with a surgically preserved bitch in a mink coat.

Sonia looked at the telegram again. It had a new message for her now. Piper was not the only man ever to have found her attractive. There was still Hutchmeyer, a widowed Hutchmeyer whose wife had stolen her darling from her. There was a fine irony in the thought that by her action, Baby had made it possible for Hutchmeyer to marry again. And marry her he would. It was marriage or nothing. There would be no messing.

Sonia reached for a sheet of paper and put it in the typewriter. Frenzy would have to be told. Poor old Frenzy, she would miss him but wedlock called and she must respond. She would explain her reasons and then leave. It seemed the best thing to do. There would be no recriminations and in a way she was sacrificing herself for him. But where on earth had he got to, and why?

20

Frensic was in Blackwell's bookshop. Half hidden among the stacks of English literary criticism he stood with a copy of *The Great Pursuit* in his hand and *Pause* propped up on the shelf in front of him. *The Great Pursuit* was Dr Sydney Louth's latest, a collection of essays dedicated to F. R. Leavis and a monument to a lifetime's execration of the shallow, the obscene, the immature and the non-significant in English literature. Generations of undergraduates had sat mesmerized by the turgid inelegance of her style while she denounced the modern novel, the contemporary world and the values of a sick and dying civilization. Frensic had been among those undergraduates and had imbibed the truisms on which Dr Louth's reputation as a scholar and a critic had been founded. She had praised the obviously great and cursed the rest and for that simple formula she was known as a great scholar. And all this in language which was the antithesis of the stylistic brilliance of the writers she praised. But it was her anathema which had stuck in Frensic's mind, those bitter graceless curses she had heaped on other critics and those who disagreed with her. By her denunciations she had implanted the inhibitions which had spoilt Frensic and so many others like him who had wanted to write. To appease her he had adopted the grotesque syntax of her lectures and essays. By their style Louthians were instantly recognizable. And by their sterility.

For three decades her influence on English literature had been malignant. And all her imprecations on the present had been hallowed by the great past which had she been a living influence at the time would never have existed. Like some religious fanatic she had consecrated the already sacred and had bred an intellectual intolerance that denied a living to the less than best. There were only saints in Dr Louth's calendar, saints and devils who failed the test of greatness. Hardy, Forster, Galsworthy, Moore and Meredith, even Peacock, consigned to outer darkness and oblivion because they did not measure up to Conrad or Henry James. And what about poor Trollope and Thackeray? More devils. The less than best. And Fielding ... The list was endless. And for the present generation the only hope of salvation was to genuflect to her opinions and learn by rote the answers to her literary catechism. And this arid bitch had written *Pause O Men for the Virgin*. Frensic inverted the title and found it wholly appropriate. Dr Louth had given birth to nothing. The stillborn opinions in *The Moral Novel* and now *The Great Pursuit* would moulder and decompose upon the shelves a few more years and be forgotten. And she had known it and had written *Pause* to seek an anonymous immortality. The clues were there to be seen. Frensic wondered how he could have missed them. On page 269 of *Pause*: 'And so inexorably their livingness became lovingness, a rhythmic lovingness that placed them within a new dimension of feeling so that the really real became an ...' Frensic shut the book before he came to 'apprehended totality'. How many times in his youth had he heard her use those fearful words? And used them himself in his essays for her. That 'placed' too was proof enough but followed by so many meaningless abstractions and a 'really real' it was conclusive. He thrust both books under his arm and went to the counter to pay for them. There were no doubts left, and everything was explained, the obsessive precautions to preserve the author's anonymity, the readiness to allow Piper to act as substitute ... But now Piper was claiming to have written *Pause*.

Frensic walked more slowly across the Parks deep in thought. Two authors for the same book? And Piper had been a devotee of Dr Louth. *The Moral Novel* was his scripture. In which case he could well have ... No. Miss Bogden had not been lying. Frensic increased his pace and strode beside the river towards Cowpasture Gardens. Dr Louth was going to learn that she had made a bad mistake in sending her manuscript to one of her former pupils. Because that was what it was all about. In her conceit she had chosen Frensic out of a hundred other agents. The irony of her gesture would have appealed to her. She had never had much time for him. 'A mediocre mind' she had once written at the end of one of his essays. Frensic had never forgiven her. He was going to get his revenge.

He left the parks and entered Cowpasture Gardens. Dr Louth's house stood at the far end, a large Victorian mansion with an air of deliberate desuetude as if the inhabitants were too committed intellectually to notice overgrown borders and untended lawns. And there had been, Frensic recalled, cats.

There were still cats. Two sat on a window-ledge and watched as Frensic walked to the front door and rang the bell. He stood waiting and looked around. If anything the garden had regressed still further towards the pastoral which Dr Louth had so extolled in literature. And the Monkey Puzzle tree stood there as unclimbable as ever. How often had he looked out of the window at that Monkey Puzzle tree while Dr Louth intoned the need for a mature moral purpose in all art. Frensic was about to fall into a nostalgic reverie when the door opened and Miss Christian peered out at him uncertainly.

'If you're from the telephone people ...' she began but Frensic shook his head.

'My name is ...' he hesitated as he tried to recall a favoured pupil. 'Bartlett. I was a student of hers in 1955.'

Miss Christian pursed her lips. 'She isn't seeing anyone,' she said.

Frensic smiled. 'I just wanted to pay my respects. I've always regarded her as the greatest influence in my development. Seminal you know.'

Miss Christian savoured 'seminal'. It was the password. 'In 1955?'

'The year she published *The Intuitive Felicity*,' said Frensic to bring out the bouquet of that vintage.

'So it was. It seems so long ago now,' said Miss Christian and opened the door wider. Frensic stepped into the dark hall where the stained-glass windows on the stairs added to the air of sanctity. Two more cats sat on chairs.

'What did you say your name was?' said Miss Christian.

'Bartlett,' said Frensic. (Bartlett had got a First.)

'Ah, yes, Bartlett,' said Miss Christian. 'I'll just go and ask her if she will see you.'

She went away down a threadworn passage to the study. Frensic stood and gritted his teeth against the odour of cats and the almost palpable atmosphere of intellectual high-mindedness and moral intensity. On the whole he preferred the cats.

Miss Christian shuffled back. 'She will see you,' she said. 'She seldom sees visitors now but she will see you. You know the way.'

Frensic nodded. He knew the way. He went down the length of worn carpet and opened the door.

Inside the study it was 1955. In twenty years nothing had changed. Dr Sydney Louth sat in an armchair beside a small fire, a pile of papers on her lap, a cigarette tilted on the lip of an ashtray and a cup of cold half-finished tea on the table at her elbow. She did not look up as Frensic entered. That was an old habit, too, the mark of an inner concentration so profound that to disturb it was the highest privilege. A red ballpen wriggled illegibly in the margin of the essay. Frensic took his seat opposite her and waited. There were advantages to be gained from her arrogance. He laid the copy of *Pause*, still in its Blackwell's wrapping, on his knees and studied the bowed head and busy hand. It was all exactly as he had remembered it. Then the hand stopped writing, dropped the ballpen and reached for the cigarette.

'Bartlett, dear Bartlett,' she said and looked up. She stared at him dimly and Frensic stared back. He had been wrong. Things had changed. The face he looked at was not the face he remembered. Then it had been smooth and slightly plump. Now it was swollen and corrugated. A plexus of dropsical wrinkles bagged under the eyes and scored her cheeks, and from the lip of this reticulated mask there hung the cigarette. Only the expression in the eyes remained the same, dimmer but burning with the certainty of her own rightness.

The conviction faded as Frensic watched. 'I thought ...' she began and looked at him more closely, 'Miss Christian precisely said ...'

'Frensic. You were my supervisor in 1955,' said Frensic.

'Frensic?' The eyes filled with conjecture now. 'But you said Bartlett ...'

'A little deceit,' said Frensic, 'to guarantee this interview. I'm a literary agent now. Frensic & Futtle. You won't have heard of us.'

But Dr Louth had. The eyes flickered. 'No. I'm afraid I haven't.'

Frensic hesitated and chose a circuitous approach. 'And since ... well ... since you were my supervisor I was wondering, well, if you would consider ... I mean it would be a great favour to ask ...' Frensic paraded deference.

'What do you want?' said Dr Louth.

Frensic unwrapped the packet on his lap. 'You see we have a novel and if you would write a piece ...'

'A novel?' The eyes behind the wrinkles glinted at the wrapping paper. 'What novel?'

'This,' said Frensic, and passed her *Pause O Men for the Virgin*. For a moment Dr Louth stared at the book and the cigarette slouched on her lip. Then she cringed in her chair.

'That?' she whispered. The cigarette dropped from her lip and smouldered on the essay on her lap. 'That?'

Frensic nodded and leaning forward removed the cigarette and put the book down. 'It seemed your sort of book,' he said.

'My sort of book?'

Frensic sat back in his chair. The centre of power had

passed to him. 'Since you wrote it,' he said, 'I thought it only fair ...'

'How did you know?' She was staring at him with a new intensity. There was no high moral purpose in that intensity now. Only fear and hatred. Frensic basked in it. He crossed his legs and looked out at the Monkey Puzzle tree. He had climbed it.

'Mainly through the style,' he said, 'and to be perfectly frank, by critical analysis. You used the same words too often in your books and I placed them. You taught me that, you see.'

There was a long pause while Dr Louth lit another cigarette. 'And you expect me to review it?' she said at last.

'Not really,' said Frensic, 'it's unethical for an author to review her own work. I just wanted to discuss how best we could announce the news to the world.'

'What news?'

'That Dr Sydney Louth, the eminent critic, had written both *Pause* and *The Great Pursuit*. I thought an article in *The Times Literary Supplement* would do to start the controversy raging. After all, it's not every day that a scholar produces a bestseller, particularly the sort of book she has spent her life denouncing as obscene ...'

'I forbid it,' Dr Louth gasped. 'As my agent ...'

'As your agent it is my business to see that the book sells. And I can assure you that the literary scandal the announcement will provoke in circles where your name has previously been revered ...'

'No,' said Dr Louth, 'that must never happen.'

'You're thinking of your reputation?' inquired Frensic gently. Dr Louth did not reply.

'You should have thought of that before. As it is you have placed me in a very awkward situation. I have a reputation to maintain too.'

'Your reputation? What sort of reputation is that?' She spat the words at him.

Frensic leant forward. 'An immaculate one,' he snarled, 'beyond your comprehension.'

Dr Louth tried to smile. 'Grub Street,' she muttered.

'Yes, Grub Street,' said Frensic, 'and proud of it. Where people write without hypocrisy for money.'

'Lucre, filthy lucre.'

Frensic grinned. 'And what did you write for?'

The mask looked at him venomously. 'To prove that I could,' she said, 'that I could write the sort of trash that sells. They thought I couldn't. A sterile critic, impotent, an academic. I proved them wrong.' Her voice rose.

Frensic shrugged. 'Hardly,' he said. 'Your name is not upon the title-page. Until it is no one will ever know.'

'No one must ever know.'

'But I intend to tell them,' said Frensic. 'It will make fascinating reading. The anonymous author, Lloyds Bank, the Typing Service, Mr Cadwalladine, Corkadales, your American publisher ...'

'You mustn't,' she whimpered, 'no one must ever know. I tell you I forbid it.'

'It's no longer in your hands,' said Frensic, 'it's in mine and I will not sully them with your hypocrisy. Besides I have another client.'

'Another client?'

'The scapegoat Piper who went to America for you. He has a reputation, too, you know.'

Dr Louth sniggered. 'Like yours, immaculate I suppose.'

'In conception, yes,' said Frensic.

'But which he was prepared to put in jeopardy for money.'

'If you like. He wanted to write and he needed the money. You, I take it, don't. You mentioned lucre, filthy lucre. I am prepared to bargain.'

'Blackmail,' snapped Dr Louth and stubbed out her cigarette.

Frensic looked at her with a new disgust. 'For a moral coward who hides behind a *nom de plume* your language is imprecise. Had you come to me in the first place I would not have engaged Piper but since you chose anonymity at the expense of honesty I am now in the position of having to choose between two authors.'

'Two? Why two?'

'Because Piper claims he wrote the book.'

'Let him claim. He accepted the onus, let him bear it.'

'He also claims the money.'

Dr Louth glared at the smouldering fire. 'He has been paid,' she said finally. 'What more does he want?'

'Everything,' said Frensic.

'And you're prepared to let him have it?'

'Yes,' said Frensic. 'My reputation is at stake too. If there's a scandal I will suffer.'

'A scandal,' Dr Louth shook her head. 'There must be no scandal.'

'But there will be,' said Frensic. 'You see, Piper is dead.'

Dr Louth shivered suddenly. 'Dead? But you said just now ...'

'There is the estate to be wound up. It will go to court and with two million dollars ... Need I say more?'

Dr Louth shook her head. 'What do you want me to do?' she asked.

Frensic relaxed. The crisis was over. He had broken the bitch. 'Write a letter to me denying that you ever wrote the book. Now.'

'Will that suffice?'

'To begin with,' said Frensic. Dr Louth got up and crossed to her desk. For a minute or two she sat there writing. When she had finished she handed Frensic the letter. He read it through and was satisfied.

'And now the manuscript,' he said, 'the original manuscript in your own handwriting and any copies you may have made.'

'No,' she said, 'I will destroy it.'

'We will destroy it,' said Frensic, 'before I leave.'

Dr Louth turned back to the desk and unlocked a drawer and took out a box. She crossed to her chair by the fire and sat down. Then she opened the box and took the pages out. Frensic glanced at the top one. It began 'The house stood on a knoll. Surrounded by three elms, a beech and a deodar whose horizontal branches ...' He was looking at the original of *Pause*. A moment later the page was on the fire and blazing up into the chimney. Frensic sat and watched as one by one the pages flared up, crinkled to black so that the words upon them stood out like white lace, broke and caught in the draught and were swept up the chimney. And as they blazed Frensic seemed to catch out of the corner of his eye the gleam of tears in the runnels of Dr Louth's cheeks. For a moment he faltered. The woman was cremating her own work. Trash she had called it and yet she was crying over it now. He would never understand writers and the contradictory impulses that were the source of their invention.

As the last page disappeared he got up. She was still huddled over the grate. For a second time Frensic was tempted to ask her why she had written the book. To prove her critics wrong. That wasn't the answer. There was more to it than that, the sex, the ardent love affair . . . He would never learn from her. He left the room quietly and went down the passage to the front door. Outside the air was filled with small black flakes falling from the chimney and near the gate a young cat jumped up clawing at a fragment which danced in the breeze.

Frensic took a deep breath of fresh air and hurried down the road. He had his things to collect from the hotel and then a train to catch to London.

Somewhere south of Tuscaloosa Baby dropped the road map out of the window of the car. It fluttered behind them in the dust and was gone. As usual Piper noticed nothing. His mind was intent on *Work In Regress*. He had reached page 178 and the book was going well. In another fortnight of hard work he would have finished it. And then he would start the third revision, the one in which not only the characters were changed but the setting of every scene. He had decided to call it *Postscript to a Childhood* as a precursor to his final, commercially unadulterated novel *Search for a Lost Childhood* which was to be considered in retrospect as the very first draft of *Pause* by those same critics who had acclaimed that obnoxious novel. In this way his reputation would have been rescued from the oblivion of facile success and scholars would be able to trace the insidious influence of Frensic's commercial recommendations upon his original talent. Piper smiled to himself at his own ingenuity. And after all there could be other yet-to-be-discovered novels. He would go on writing 'posthumously' and every few years another novel would turn up on Frensic's desk to be released to the world. There was nothing Frensic could do about it. Baby was right. By deceiving Hutchmeyer Frensic & Futtle had made themselves vulnerable. Frensic would have to do what he was told. Piper closed his eyes and lay back in his seat contentedly. Half an hour later he opened them again and sat up. The car, a Ford that Baby had bought in Rossville, was lurching on a bad road surface. Piper looked out and saw they were driving along a road built on an embankment. On either side tall trees stood in dark water.

'Where are we?' he asked.

'I've no idea,' said Baby.

'No idea? You've got to know where we are heading.'

'Into the sticks is all I know. And when we get some place we'll find out.'

Piper looked down at the dark water beneath the trees. The forest had a sinister quality to it that he didn't like. Always before they had travelled along homely, cheerful roads with only the occasional stretch of kudzu vine crawling across trees and banks to suggest wild natural growth. But this was different. There were no billboards, no houses, no gas stations, none of those amenities which had signified civilization. This was a wilderness.

'And what happens if when we do get some place there isn't a motel?' he asked.

'Then we'll have to make do with what there is,' said Baby, 'I told you we were coming to the Deep South and this is where it's at.'

'Where what's at?' said Piper staring down at the black water and thinking of alligators.

'That's what I've come to find out,' said Baby enigmatically and braked the car to a standstill at a crossroads. Piper peered through the windshield at a sign. Its faded letters said BIBLIOPOLIS 15 MILES.

'Looks like your kind of town,' said Baby and turned the car on to the side road. Presently the dark water forest thinned and they came out into an open landscape with lush meadows hazy

213

with heat where cattle grazed in long grass and clumps of trees stood apart. There was something almost English about this scenery, an English parkland gone to seed, luxuriant yet immanent with half-remembered possibilities. Everywhere the distance faded into haze blurring the horizon. Piper, looking across the meadows, felt easier in his mind. There was a sense of domesticity here that was reassuring. Occasionally they passed a wooden shack part-hidden by vegetation and seemingly unoccupied. And finally there was Bibliopolis itself, a small town, almost a hamlet, with a river running sluggishly beside an abandoned quay. Baby drove down to the riverside and stopped. There was no bridge. On the far side an ancient rope ferry provided the only means of crossing.

'Okay, go ring the bell,' said Baby. Piper got out and rang a bell that hung from a post.

'Harder,' said Baby as Piper pulled on the rope. Presently a man appeared on the far shore and the ferry began to move across.

'You wanting something?' said the man when the ferry grounded.

'We're looking for somewhere to stay,' said Baby. The man peered at the licence plate on the Ford and seemed reassured. It read Georgia.

'There ain't no motel in Bibliopolis,' said the man. 'You'd best go back to Selma.'

'There must be somewhere,' said Baby as the man still hesitated.

'Mrs Mathervitie's Tourist Home,' said the man and stepped aside. Baby drove on to the ferry and got out.

'Is this the Alabama river?' she asked. The man shook his head.

'The Ptomaine River, ma'am,' he said and pulled on the rope.

'And that?' asked Baby, pointing to a large dilapidated mansion that was evidently ante-bellum.

'That's Pellagra. Nobody lives there now. They all died off.'

Piper sat in the car and stared gloomily at the sluggish river. The trees along its bank were veiled with Spanish moss like

214

widows' weeds and the dilapidated mansion below the town put him in mind of Miss Havisham. But Baby, when she got back into the car and drove off the ferry, was clearly elated by the atmosphere.

'I told you this was where it's at,' she said triumphantly. 'And now for Mrs Mathervitie's Tourist Home.'

They drove down a tree-lined street and stopped outside a house. A signboard said Welcome. Mrs Mathervitie was less effusive. Sitting in the shadow of a porch she watched them get out of the car.

'You folks looking for some place?' she asked, her glasses glinting in the sunset.

'Mrs Mathervitie's Tourist Home,' said Baby.

'Selling or staying? Cos if it's cosmetics I ain't in the market.'

'Staying,' said Baby.

Mrs Mathervitie studied them critically with the air of a connoisseur of irregular relationships.

'I only got singles,' she said and spat into the hub of a sun flower, 'no doubles.'

'Praise be the Lord,' said Baby involuntarily.

'Amen,' said Mrs Mathervitie.

They went into the house and down a passage.

'This is yourn,' said Mrs Mathervitie to Piper and opened a door. The room looked out on to a patch of corn. On the wall there was an oleograph of Christ scourging the money-lenders from the Temple and a cardboard sign that decreed NO BROWNBAGGING. Piper looked at it dubiously. It seemed a thoroughly unnecessary injunction.

'Well?' said Mrs Mathervitie.

'Very nice,' said Piper who had spotted a row of books on a shelf. He looked at them and found they were all Bibles.

'Good Lord,' he muttered.

'Amen,' said Mrs Mathervitie and went off with Baby down the passage leaving Piper to consider the sinister implications of NO BROWNBAGGING. By the time they returned he was no nearer a solution to the riddle.

'The Reverend and I are happy to accept your hospitality,' said Baby. 'Aren't we, Reverend?'

'What?' said Piper. Mrs Mathervitie was looking at him with new interest.

'I was just telling Mrs Mathervitie how interested you are in American religion,' said Baby. Piper swallowed and tried to think what to say.

'Yes,' seemed the safest.

There was an extremely awkward silence broken finally by Mrs Mathervitie's business sense.

'Ten dollars a day. Seven with prayers. Providence is extra.'

'Yes, well I suppose it would be,' said Piper.

'Meaning?' said Mrs Mathervitie.

'That the good Lord will provide,' interjected Baby before Piper's slight hysteria could manifest itself again.

'Amen,' said Mrs Mathervitie. 'Well which is it to be? With prayers or without?'

'With,' said Baby.

'Fourteen dollars,' said Mrs Mathervitie, 'in advance.'

'Pay now and pray later?' said Piper hopefully.

Mrs Mathervitie's eyes gleamed coldly. 'For a preacher ...' she began but Baby intervened. 'The Reverend means we should pray without ceasing.'

'Amen,' said Mrs Mathervitie and knelt on the linoleum.

Baby followed her example. Piper looked down at them in astonishment.

'Dear God,'. he muttered.

'Amen,' said Mrs Mathervitie and Baby in unison.

'Say the good words, Reverend,' said Baby.

'For Christ's sake,' said Piper for inspiration. He didn't know any prayers and as for good words ... On the floor Mrs Mathervitie twitched dangerously. Piper found the good words. They came from *The Moral Novel*.

'It is our duty not to enjoy but to appreciate,' he intoned, 'Not to be entertained but to be edified, not to read that we may escape the responsibilities of life but that, through reading, we may more properly understand what it is that we are and do and that born anew in the vicarious experience of others we may extend our awareness and our sensibilities and so enriched by how we read we may be better human beings.'

'Amen,' said Mrs Mathervitie fervently.

'Amen,' said Baby.

'Amen,' said Piper and sat down on the bed. Mrs Mathervitie got to her feet.

'I thank you for those good words, Reverend,' she said and left the room.

'What the hell was all that about?' said Piper when her footsteps had faded. Baby stood up and raised a finger to her lips.

'No cussing. No browbagging.'

'And that's another thing ...' Piper began but Mrs Mathervitie's footsteps came down the passage again.

'Conventicle's at eight,' she said poking her head round the door. 'Doesn't do to be late.'

Piper regarded her biliously. 'Conventicle?'

'Conventicle of the Seventh Day Church of The Servants of God,' said Mrs Mathervitie. 'You said you wanted prayers.'

'The Reverend and I will be right with you,' said Baby. Mrs Mathervitie removed her head. Baby took Piper's arm and pushed him towards the door.

'Good God, you've really landed us—'

'Amen,' said Baby as they went out into the passage. Mrs Mathervitie was waiting on the porch.

'The Church is in the town square,' she said as they climbed into the Ford and presently they were driving down the darkened street where the Spanish moss looked even more sinister to Piper. By the time they stopped outside a small wooden church in the square he was in a state of panic.

'They won't want me to pray again, will they?' he whispered to Baby as they climbed the steps to the church. From inside there came the sound of a hymn.

'We're late,' said Mrs Mathervitie and hurried them down the aisle. The church was crowded but a row of seats at the very front was empty. A moment later Piper found himself clutching a hymnbook and singing an extraordinary hymn called 'Telephoning To Glory'.

When the hymn ended there was a scuffling of feet and the congregation knelt and the preacher launched into prayer.

'Oh Lord we is all sinners,' he declared.

'Oh Lord we is all sinners,' bawled Mrs Mathervitie and the rest of the congregation.

'Oh Lord we is all sinners waiting to be saved,' continued the preacher.

'Waiting to be saved. Waiting to be saved.'

'From the fires of hell and the snares of Satan.'

'From the fires of hell and the snares of Satan.'

Beside Piper Mrs Mathervitie had begun to quiver. 'Hallelujah,' she cried.

When the prayer ended a large black woman who was standing beside the piano began 'Washed In The Blood Of The Lamb' and from there it was but a short step to 'Jericho' and finally a hymn which went 'Servants of the Lord we Pledge our Faith in Thee' with a chorus of 'Faith, Faith, Faith in The Lord, Faith in Jesus is Mightier than the Sword'. Much to his own amazement Piper sang as loudly as anyone and the enthusiasm began to get to him. By this time Mrs Mathervitie was stomping her foot while several other women were clapping their hands. They sang the hymn twice and then went straight into another about Eve and The Apple. As the reverberations died away the preacher raised his hands.

'Brothers and sisters . . .' he began, only to be interrupted.

'Bring on the serpents,' shouted someone at the back.

The preacher lowered his hands. 'Serpents night's Saturday,' he said. 'You know that.'

But the cry 'Bring on the serpents,' was taken up and the large black lady struck up 'Faith in The Lord and the Snakes won't Bite, Them's has Faith is Saved all Right.'

'Snakes?' said Piper to Mrs Mathervitie, 'I thought you said this was Servants of The Lord.'

'Snakes is Saturday,' said Mrs Mathervitie looking decidedly alarmed herself. 'I only come Thursdays. I don't hold with serpentizing.'

'Serpentizing?' said Piper suddenly alive to what was about to happen, 'Jesus Wept.' Beside him Baby was already weeping but Piper was too concerned for his own safety to bother about her. A sack was brought down the aisle by a tall gaunt man. It was a large sack, a large sack which writhed. So did

Piper. A moment later he had shot out of his seat and was heading for the door only to find his way blocked by a number of other people who evidently shared his lack of enthusiasm for being confined in a small church with a sackful of poisonous snakes. A hand shoved him aside and Piper fell back into his seat again. 'Let's get the hell out of here,' he shouted to Baby but she was looking with rapt attention at the pianist, a small thin man who was thumping away on the keys with a fervour that was possibly due to what looked like a small boa constrictor which had twined itself round his neck. Behind the piano the large black lady was using two rattlesnakes as maracas and singing 'Bibliopolis we hold Thee Dear, Snakes Infest us we don't Fear' – which certainly didn't apply to Piper. He was about to make another dash for the door when something slithered across his feet. It was Mrs Mathervitie. Piper sat petrified and moaned. Beside him Baby was moaning too. There was a strange seraphic look on her face. At that moment the man with the sack lifted from it a snake with red and yellow bands across its body.

'The Coral,' someone hissed. The strains of 'Bibliopolis we Hold Thee Dear' faded abruptly. In the silence that followed Baby got to her feet and moved hypnotically forward. By the dim light of the candles she looked majestic and beautiful. She took the snake from the man and held it aloft and her arm became a caduceus, the symbol of medicine. Then, turning to face the congregation, she tore her blouse to the waist and exposed two voluptuously pointed breasts. There was another gasp of horror. Naked breasts were out in Bibliopolis. On the other hand the coral snake was in. As Baby lowered her arm the outraged snake sank its fangs into six inches of plastic silicon. For ten seconds it writhed there before Baby detached it and offered it the other breast. But the coral had had enough. So had Piper. With a groan he joined Mrs Mathervitie on the floor. Baby, triumphantly topless, tossed the coral into the sack and turned to the pianist.

'Launch into the deep, brother,' she cried.

And once again the little church reverberated to the strains of 'Bibliopolis we hold Thee Dear, Snakes Infest us we don't Fear.'

21

In his Hampstead flat Frensic lay in his morning bath and twiddled the hot tap with his big toe to maintain an even temperature. A good night's sleep had helped to undo the ravages of Cynthia Bogden's passion and he was in no hurry to go to the office. He had things to think about. It was all very well congratulating himself for his subtlety in unearthing the genuine author of *Pause* and forcing her to renounce all rights in the book but there were still problems to be faced. The first of these concerned the continuing existence of Piper and his inordinate claim to be paid for a novel he hadn't written. On the face of it this seemed a minor problem. Frensic could now go ahead and deposit the two million dollars less his own and Corkadales' commissions in account number 478776 in the First National Bank of New York. This seemed at first sight the sensible thing to do. Pay Piper and be rid of the rogue. On the other hand it was succumbing to blackmail and blackmailers tended to renew their demands. Give in once and he would have to give in again and again and in any case transferring the money to New York would necessitate explaining to Sonia that Piper wasn't dead. One whiff of that and she'd be off after him like a scalded cat. Perhaps he might be able to fudge the issue and tell her that Mr Cadwalladine's client had given instructions for the royalties to be paid in this way.

But beyond all these technical problems there lay the suspicion that Piper hadn't come up with this conspiracy to defraud on his own initiative. Ten years of the recurrent *Search for a Lost Childhood* was proof enough that Piper lacked any imagination at all and whoever had dreamt this devious plot up had a remarkably powerful imagination. Frensic's suspicions centred on Mrs Baby Hutchmeyer. If Piper, who was supposed to have died with her, was still alive there was every reason to believe that Baby Hutchmeyer had survived with him. Frensic tried to analyse the psychology of Hutchmeyer's wife. To have endured forty years of marriage to that monster argued either masochism or resilience beyond the ordinary. And then to burn an enormous house to the ground, blow up a cruiser and sink a yacht, all of them belonging to her husband and all in a matter of twenty minutes ... Clearly the woman was insane and couldn't be relied upon. At any moment she might resurrect herself and drag from his temporary grave the wretched Piper. What would follow this momentous event blew Frensic's mind. Hutchmeyer would go litigiously berserk and sue everyone in sight. Piper would be dragged through the courts and the entire story of his substitution for the real author would be announced to the world. Frensic got out of the bath and dried himself to ward off the spectre of Piper in the witness box.

And as he dressed the problem became more and more complicated. Even if Baby Hutchmeyer didn't decide to go in for self-exhumation there was every chance that she would be discovered by some nosey reporter who might at this very moment be hungrily tracking her down. What the hell would happen if Piper told the truth? Frensic tried to foresee the outcome of his revelations, and was just making himself some coffee when he remembered the manuscript. The manuscript in Piper's handwriting. Or at least the copy. That was the way out. He could always deny Piper's allegation that he hadn't written *Pause* and produce that manuscript copy as proof. And even if the psychotic Baby backed Piper up, nobody would believe her. Frensic sighed with relief. He had found a way out of the dilemma. After breakfast he walked up the hill to the tube station and caught a train in a thoroughly good mood. He was a clever fellow and it would take more than the benighted Piper and Baby Hutchmeyer to put one across him.

He arrived at Lanyard Lane to find the office locked. That was odd. Sonia Futtle should have been back from Bernie the Beaver the previous day. Frensic unlocked the door and went in. No sign of Sonia. He crossed to his desk and there lying neatly separated from the rest of the mail was an envelope. It was addressed in Sonia's handwriting to him. Frensic sat down and opened it. Inside was a long letter which began 'Dearest Frenzy' and ended, 'Your loving Sonia.' In between these endearments Sonia explained with a wealth of nauseating sentimentality and self-deception how Hutchmeyer had asked her to marry him and why she had accepted. Frensic was flabbergasted. And only a week before the girl had been crying her eyes out over Piper. Frensic took out his snuff box and red spotted handkerchief and thanked God he was still a bachelor. The ways and wiles of women were quite beyond him.

They were quite beyond Geoffrey Corkadale too. He was still in a state of nervous agitation over the threatened libel suit of Professor Facit versus the author, publisher and printer of *Pause O Men for the Virgin* when he received a telephone call from Miss Bogden.

'I did what?' he asked with a mixture of total incredulity and disgust. 'And stop calling me darling. I don't know you from a bar of soap.'

'But Geoffrey sweetheart,' said Miss Bogden, 'you were so passionate, so manly ...'

'I was not!' shouted Geoffrey. 'You've got the wrong number. You can't say these things.'

Miss Bogden could and did. In detail. Geoffrey Corkadale curdled.

'Stop,' he yelled, 'I don't know what the hell has been going on but if you think for one moment that I spent the night before last in your beastly arms ... dear God ... you must be out of your bloody mind.'

'And I suppose you didn't ask me to marry you,' screamed Miss Bogden, 'and buy me an engagement ring and ...'

Geoffrey slammed the phone down to shut out this appalling catalogue. The situation was sufficiently desperate on the legal front without demented women claiming he had asked them to marry him. Then, to forestall any resumption of Miss Bogden's accusations, he left the office and made his way to his solicitors to discuss a possible defence in the libel action.

They were singularly unhelpful. 'It isn't as if the defamation of Professor Facit was accidental,' they told him. 'This man Piper evidently set out with deliberate malice to ruin the reputation of the Professor. There can be no other explanation. In our opinion the author is entirely culpable.'

'He also happens to be dead,' said Geoffrey.

'In that case it rather looks as though you are going to have to bear the entire costs of this action and, frankly, we would advise you to settle.'

Geoffrey Corkadale left the solicitors' office in despair. It was all that bloody man Frensic's fault. He should have known better than to have dealt with a literary agent who had already been involved in one disastrous libel action. Frensic was libel-prone. There was no other way of looking at it. Geoffrey took a cab to Lanyard Lane. He was going to tell Frensic what he thought of him. He found Frensic in an unusually affable mood.

'My dear Geoffrey, how very nice to see you,' he said.

'I haven't come to exchange compliments,' said Geoffrey, 'I've come to tell you that you've landed me in the most appalling mess and ...'

Frensic raised a hand.

'You mean Professor Facit? Oh I shouldn't worry too much ...'

'Worry too much? I've got every right to worry and as for too much, with bankruptcy staring me in the face just how much is too much?'

'I've been making some private inquiries,' said Frensic, 'in Oxford.'

'You have?' said Geoffrey. 'You don't mean to say he actually did do all those frightful things? That ghastly Pekinese for instance?'

'I mean,' said Frensic pontifically, 'that no one in Oxford has ever heard of a Professor Facit. I've checked with the Lodging House Syndicate and the university library and they had no records of any Professor Facit ever having applied for a ticket to use the library. And as for his statement that he once lived in De Frytville Avenue, it's quite untrue.'

'Good Lord,' said Geoffrey, 'if nobody up there has ever heard of him ...'

'It rather looks as if Messrs Ridley, Coverup, Makeweight and Jones have just tried to ambulance-chase once too often and are hoist with their own petard.'

'My dear fellow, this calls for a celebration,' said Geoffrey. 'And you mean to say you went up there and found all this out ..'

But Frensic was modesty itself. 'You see, I knew Piper pretty well. After all he had been sending me stuff for years,' he said as they went downstairs, 'and he wasn't the sort of fellow to set out to libel someone deliberately.'

'But I thought you told me that *Pause* was his first book,' said Geoffrey.

Frensic regretted his indiscretion. 'His first *real* book,' he said. 'The rest was just ... well, a bit derivative. Not the sort of stuff I could ever have sold.'

They strolled across to Wheeler's for lunch. 'Talking of Oxford,' said Geoffrey when they had ordered, 'I had the most extraordinary phone call this morning from some lunatic woman called Bogden.'

'Really?' said Frensic, spilling dry Martini down his shirt front. 'What did she want?'

'She claimed I'd asked her to marry me. It was absolutely awful.'

'It must have been,' said Frensic, finishing his drink and ordering another kind. 'Mind you, some women will go to any lengths ...'

'From what I could gather I was the one to have gone to any lengths. Said I'd bought her an engagement ring.'

'I hope you told her to go to hell,' said Frensic, 'and talking of marriages I've got some news too. Sonia Futtle is going to marry Hutchmeyer.'

'Marry Hutchmeyer?' said Geoffrey. 'But the man's only just lost his wife. You'd think he'd have the decency to wait a bit before sticking his head in the noose again.'

'An apt metaphor,' said Frensic with a smile, and raised his glass.

His worries were over. He had just realized that in marrying Hutchmeyer Sonia had acted more wisely than she knew. She had effectively spiked the enemy's guns. A bigamous Hutchmeyer was no threat, and besides, a man who could find Sonia physically attractive must be besotted and a besotted Hutch would never believe his new wife had once been party to a conspiracy to deceive him. All that remained was to implicate Piper financially. After an excellent lunch Frensic walked back to Lanyard Lane and thence to the bank. There he subtracted Corkadales' ten per cent and his own commission and despatched one million four hundred thousand dollars to account number 478776 in the First National Bank of New York. He had honoured his side of the contract. Frensic went home by taxi. He was a rich and happy man.

So was Hutchmeyer. Sonia's whirlwind acceptance of his whirlwind proposal had taken him by surprise. The thighs that had over the years so entranced him were his at last. Her ample body was entirely to his taste. It bore no scars, none of the surgical modifications that in Baby's case had served to remind him of his faithlessness and the artificiality of their relationship. With Sonia he could be himself. There was no need to assert himself by peeing in the washbasin every night or to prove his virility by badgering strange girls in Rome and Paris and Las Vegas. He could relapse into domestic happiness with a woman who had energy enough for both of them. They were married in Cannes and that night as Hutchmeyer lay supine between those hustling thighs he gazed up at her breasts and knew that this was for real. Sonia smiled down at his contented face and was contented herself. She was a married woman at long last.

And married to a rich man. The next night Hutchmeyer celebrated by losing forty grand at Monte Carlo and then, in memory of the good fortune that had brought them together, chartered a vast yacht with an experienced skipper and a competent crew. They cruised in the Aegean. They explored the ruins of ancient Greece and, more profitably, a deal involving supertankers which were going cheap. And finally they flew back to New York for the première of the film, *Pause*.

There in the darkness, garlanded with diamonds, Sonia finally broke down and wept. Beside her Hutchmeyer understood. It was a deeply moving movie with fashionable radicals playing Gwendolen and Anthony and combined *Lost Horizon*, *Sunset Boulevard* and *Deep Throat* with *Tom Jones*. Under MacMordie's financial tutelage the critics raved. And all the time the profits from the novel poured in. The movie boosted sales and there was even talk of a Broadway musical with Maria Callas in the leading role. To keep sales moving ever upwards Hutchmeyer consulted the computer and ordered a new cover for the book with the result that people who had bought the book before found themselves buying it yet again. After the musical some would doubtless buy it a third time. The Book Club sales were enormous and the leather-bound Baby Hutchmeyer Memorial edition with gold tooling sold out in a week. All over the country *Pause* left its mark. Elderly women emerged from the seclusion of bridge clubs and beauty parlours to inveigle young men into bed. The vasectomy index fell rapidly. And finally, to crown Hutchmeyer's success, Sonia announced that she was pregnant.

In Bibliopolis, Alabama, things had changed too. The funeral of the victims of the unscheduled serpentizing took place among the live oaks that bordered the Ptomaine River. There were seven in all, though only two from snake bite. Three had been crushed in the stampede for the door. The Reverend Gideon had succumbed to heart failure, and Mrs Mathervitie to outraged shock on awakening from her faint to find Baby standing topless in the pulpit. Out of this terrible infestation Baby emerged with a remarkable reputation. It was due as much to the perfection of her breasts as to their immunity; taken together the two were irresistible. Never before had Bibliopolis witnessed so complete a demonstration of faith, and in the absence of the late Reverend Gideon Baby was offered the ministry. She accepted gratefully. It put an end to Piper's sexual depredations, and besides she had found her forte. From the pulpit she could denounce the sins of the flesh with a relish that endeared her to the womenfolk and excited the men, and having spent so much of her life in Hutchmeyer's company she could speak about hell from experience. Above all she was free to be what remained of herself. And so as the coffins were lowered into the ground the Reverend Hutchmeyer led the congregation in 'Shall we Gather by the River' and the little population of Bibliopolis bowed their heads and raised their voices. Even the snakes, hissing as they were emptied from the sack into the Ptomaine, had benefited. Baby had abolished serpentizing in a long sermon about Eve and The Apple in which she had pointed out that they were creatures of Satan. The relatives of the deceased tended to agree. And finally there was the problem of Piper. Having found her faith Baby felt obliged to the man who had so fortuitously led her to it.

With the advance royalties from *Pause* she restored Pellagra House to its ante-bellum glory and installed Piper there to continue work on his third version, *Postscript to a Lost Childhood*. As the days passed into weeks and the weeks into months, Piper wrote steadily on and resumed the routine of his life at the Gleneagle Guest House. In the afternoons he walked by the banks of the Ptomaine and in the evening read passages from *The Moral Novel* and the great classics it commended. With so much money at his disposal Piper had ordered them all. They lined the shelves of his study at Pellagra, icons of that literary religion to which he had dedicated his life. Jane Austen, Conrad, George Eliot, Dickens, Henry James, Lawrence, Mann, they were all there to spur him on. His one sorrow was that the only woman he could ever love was sexually inaccessible. As preacher Baby had made it plain she could no longer sleep with him.

'You'll just have to sublimate,' she told him. Piper tried to sublimate but the yearning remained as constant as his ambition to become a great novelist.

'It's no good,' he said, 'I keep thinking about you all the time. You are so beautiful, so pure, so ... so ...'

'You've too much time on your hands,' said Baby. 'Now if you had something more to do ...'

'Such as?'

Baby looked at the beautiful script upon the page. 'Like you could teach people to write,' she said.

'I can't even write myself,' said Piper. It was one of his self-pitying days.

'But you can. Look at the way you form your "f"s and this lovely tail to your "y". If you can't teach people to write, who can?'

'Oh you mean "write",' said Piper, 'I suppose I could do that. But who would want to learn?'

'Lots of people. You'd be surprised. When I was a girl there were schools of penmanship in almost every town. You'd be doing something useful.'

227

'Useful?' said Piper, attenuating that word with melancholy. 'All I want to do is—'

'Write,' said Baby, hurriedly forestalling his sexual suggestion. 'Well, this way you can combine artistry with education. You can hold classes every afternoon and it will take your mind off yourself.'

'My mind isn't on myself. It's on you. I love you . . .'

'We must all love one another,' said Baby sententiously and left.

A week later the School of Penmanship opened and instead of brooding all afternoon by the sluggish waters of the Ptomaine River, Piper stood in front of his pupils and taught them to write beautifully. The classes were mostly of children but later adults came too and sat there pens in hand and bottles of Higgins Eternal Evaporated Ink at the ready while Piper explained that a diagonal ligature required an upstroke and that a wavy serif was obtrusive. Over the months his reputation grew and with it there came theory. To visitors from as far away as Selma and Meridian Piper expounded the doctrine of the word made perfect. He called it Logosophy, and won adherents. It was as if the process by which he had failed as a novelist had reversed itself in his Writing. In the old days of his obsession with the great novel theory had preceded and indeed pre-empted practice. What *The Moral Novel* had condemned Piper had avoided. With penmanship Piper was his own practitioner and theorist. But still the old ambition to see his novel in print remained and as each newly expurgated version of *Pause* was finished he mailed it to Frensic. At first he sent it to New York to be readdressed and forwarded to Lanyard Lane but as the months passed his confidence in his new life grew and with it forgetfulness and he sent it direct. And every month he ordered *Books & Bookmen* and *The Times Literary Supplement* and scanned the lists of new novels only to be disappointed. *Search for a Lost Childhood* was never there.

Finally, late one night when the moon was full, he decided on a fresh approach and taking up his pen wrote to Frensic. His letter was blunt and to the point. Unless Frensic & Futtle as his literary agents were prepared to guarantee that his novel was published he would be forced to ask some other literary agent to handle his work in future.

'In fact I am seriously considering sending my manuscript direct to Corkadales,' he wrote. 'As you will remember I signed a contract with them to publish my second novel and I can see no good reason why this specific agreement should be negated. Yours sincerely, Peter Piper.'

22

'The man must be out of his bloody mind,' muttered Frensic a week later. 'I can see no reason why this arrangement should be negated.' Frensic could. 'The sod can't seriously suppose I can go round to Corkadales and force them to publish a book by a corpse.'

But it was evident from the tone of the letter that Piper supposed exactly that. Over the months Frensic had received four Xeroxed and altered drafts of Piper's novel and had consigned them to a filing cabinet which he kept carefully locked. If Piper wanted to waste his own time reworking the damned book until every element that had made *Pause* the least bit readable had been eliminated he was welcome to do so. Frensic felt under no obligation to hawk his rubbish round publishing houses. But the threat to deal direct with Corkadales was, to put it mildly, a different kettle of fish. Piper was dead and buried and he was being well paid for it. Every month Frensic saw that the proceeds from the sale of *Pause* went into account number 478776, and wondered at the extraordinary inefficiency of the American tax system that didn't seem to mind that a taxpayer was supposedly dead. Doubtless Piper paid his taxes promptly or perhaps Baby Hutchmeyer had made complicated accountancy arrangements for his royalties to be laundered. That was none of Frensic's business. He took his commission and paid the rest over. But it was certainly his business when Piper made threats about going to Corkadales or another agent. That arrangement had definitely to be negated.

Frensic turned the letter over and studied the postmark on the envelope. It came from a place called Bibliopolis, Alabama. 'Just the sort of idiotic town Piper would choose,' he thought miserably and wondered how to reply. Or whether he should reply at all. Perhaps the best thing would be to ignore the threat. He certainly had no intention of committing to paper any words that could be used in court to prove that he knew of Piper's continued afterdeath. 'The next thing he'll come up with is a request for me to go and see him and discuss the matter. And fat chance there is of that.' Frensic had had his fill of pursuing phantom authors.

Miss Bogden on the other hand had not given up her pursuit of the man who had asked her to marry him. After the terrible telephone conversation she had had with Geoffrey Corkadale she had wept briefly, had made up her face, and had continued business as usual. For several weeks she had lived in hope that he would phone again, or that another bunch of red roses would suddenly appear, but those hopes had dwindled. Only the diamond solitaire gleaming on her finger kept her spirits up – that and the need to maintain the fiction before her staff that the engagement was still on. To that end she invented long weekends with her fiancé and reasons for the delayed wedding. But as weeks became months Cynthia's disappointment turned to determination. She had been had, and while being had was in some respects better than not being had at all, being made to look foolish in the eyes of her staff was infuriating. Miss Bogden applied her mind to the problem of finding her fiancé. While his disappearance was proof that he hadn't wanted her, the five hundred pounds he had spent on the ring was indication that he had wanted something else. Again Miss Bogden's business sense told her that the favours she had bestowed bodywise on her lover during the night hardly merited the expense of the engagement ring. Only a madman would make such a quixotic gesture and her pride refused the notion that the one man to propose to her since her divorce had been off his head.

No, there had to be another motive and as she recalled the events of those splendid twenty-four hours it slowly dawned on her that the one consistent theme had been the novel *Pause O Men for the Virgin*. In the first place her fiancé had posed as Geoffrey Corkadale, in the second he had reverted to the question of the typescript too frequently for it to be coincidental, and thirdly there had been the *code d'amour*. And the *code d'amour* had been the telephone number she had had to call for information while typing the novel. Cynthia Bogden called the number again but there was no reply, and when a week later she tried again the line had been disconnected. She looked up the name Piper in the phone directory but no one of that name had the number 20357. She called Directory Enquiries and asked for the address and name of the number but was refused the information. Defeated in that direction, she turned to another. Her instructions had been to forward the completed typescript to Cadwalladine & Dimkins, Solicitors and to return the handwritten draft to Lloyds Bank. Miss Bogden phoned Mr Cadwalladine and was puzzled by his apparent inability to remember having received the typescript. 'We may have done,' he said, 'but I'm afraid we handle so much business that ...'

Miss Bogden pressed him further and was finally told that it was unethical for solicitors to disclose confidential information. Miss Bogden was not satisfied with this answer. With each rebuttal her determination grew and was reinforced by the snide inquiries of her girls. Her mind worked slowly but it worked steadily too. She followed the line from the bank to her typing service and from there to Mr Cadwalladine and from Mr Cadwalladine to Corkadales, the publishers. The secrecy with which the entire transaction had been surrounded intrigued her too. An author who had to be contacted by phone, a solicitor ... With less flair than Frensic, but with as much perseverance, she followed the trail as far as she could, and late one evening she realized the full implications of Mr Cadwalladine's refusal to tell her where the typescript had been sent. And yet Corkadales had published the book. There had to be someone in between Cadwalladine and Corkadales and that someone was almost certainly a literary agent. That night Cynthia Bogden lay awake filled with a sense of discovery. She had found the missing link in the chain. The next morning she was up early and at the office at half past eight. At nine she telephoned Corkadales and asked to speak to the editor who had handled *Pause*. The editor wasn't in. She called again at ten. He still hadn't arrived. It was only at a quarter to eleven that she got through to him and by then she had had time to devise her approach. It was a straightforward one.

'I run a typing bureau,' she said, 'and I have typed a novel for a friend who is anxious to send it to a good literary agent and I wondered if ...'

'I'm afraid we can't advise you on that sort of thing,' said Mr Tate.

'Oh I do understand that,' said Miss Bogden sweetly, 'but you published that wonderful novel *Pause O Men for the Virgin* and my friend wanted to send her novel to the same agent. It would be so good of you if you could ...'

Responding to flattery Mr Tate did.

'Frensic & Futtle of Lanyard Lane?' she repeated.

'Well, Frensic now,' said Mr Tate, 'Miss Futtle is no longer there.'

Nor was Miss Bogden. She had put the phone down and was picking it up to dial Directory Enquiries. A few minutes later she had Frensic's number. Her intuition told her that she was getting close to home. She sat for a while staring into the depths of the solitaire for inspiration. Should she phone or ... Mr Cadwalladine's refusal to say where the manuscript had gone persuaded her. She got up from her typewriter, asked her senior 'girl' to take over for the day, drove to the station and caught the 11.15 to London. Two hours later she walked down Lanyard Lane to Number 36 and climbed the stairs to Frensic's office.

It was fortunate for Frensic that he was lunching with a promising new author in the Italian restaurant round the corner when Miss Bogden arrived. They came out at two-fifteen and walked back to the office. As they climbed the stairs Frensic stopped on the first landing.

'You go on up,' he said, 'I'll be with you in a moment.' He went into the lavatory and shut the door. The promising new author climbed the second flight. Frensic finished his business and came out and he was about to go on up when he heard a voice.

'Are you Mr Frensic?' it asked. Frensic stopped in his tracks.

'Me?' said the promising young author with a laugh. 'No I'm here with a book. Mr Frensic's downstairs. He'll be up in a minute.'

But Frensic wasn't. He shot down to the ground floor again and out into the street. That ghastly woman had tracked him down. What the hell to do now? He went back to the Italian restaurant and sat in a corner. How on earth had she managed to find him? Had that Cadbloodywalladine ... Never mind how. The thing was what to do about it. He couldn't sit in the restaurant all day and he was no more going to confront Miss Bogden than fly. Fly? The word took on a new significance for him. If he didn't turn up at the office the promising young author would ... To hell with promising young authors. He had asked that dreadful woman to marry him and ... Frensic signalled to a waiter.

'A piece of paper please.' He scribbled a note of apology to the author, saying he had been taken ill and handed it with a five pound note to the waiter, asking him to deliver it for him. As the man went out Frensic followed and hailed a taxi. 'Glass Walk, Hampstead,' he said and got in. Not that going home would do him any good. Miss Bogden's tracking powers would soon lead her there. All right, he wouldn't answer the door. But what then? A woman with the perseverance of Miss Bogden, a woman of forty-five who had painstakingly worked her way towards her quarry over the months ... such a woman held terrors for him. She wouldn't stop now. By the time he reached his flat he was panic-stricken. He went inside and locked and bolted the door. Then he sat down in his study and tried to think. He was interrupted by the phone. Unthinkingly he picked it up. 'Frensic here,' he said.

'Cynthia here,' said that pebbledashed voice. Frensic slammed the phone down. A moment later, to prevent her calling again, he picked it up and dialled Geoffrey's number.

'Geoffrey, my dear fellow,' he said when Corkadale answered, 'I wonder if ...'

But Geoffrey didn't let him finish. 'I've been trying to get hold of you all afternoon,' he said. 'I've had the most extraordinary manuscript sent to me. You're not going to believe this but there's some lunatic in a place called of all things Bibliopolis ... I mean can you beat that? Bibliopolis, Alabama ... Well anyway he calmly announces that he is our late Peter Piper and will we kindly quote fulfil the obligations incurred in my contract unquote and publish his novel, *Search for a Lost Childhood*. I mean it's incredible and the signature ...'

'Geoffrey dear,' said Frensic lapsing into the affectionate as a prophylactic against Miss Bogden's feminine charms and as a means of preparing Corkadale for the worst, 'I wonder if you would do me a favour ...'

He spoke fluently for five minutes and rang off. With amazing rapidity he packed two suitcases, telephoned for a taxi, left a note for the milkman cancelling his two pints a day, took his chequebook, his passport and a briefcase containing copies of all Piper's manuscripts, and half an hour later was carrying his belongings into Geoffrey Corkadale's house. Behind him the flat in Glass Walk was locked and when Cynthia Bogden arrived and rang the bell there was no reply. Frensic was sitting in Geoffrey Corkadale's withdrawing-room sipping a large brandy and implicating his host in the plot to deceive Hutchmeyer. Geoffrey stared at him with bulging eyes.

'You mean you deliberately lied to Hutchmeyer and to me for that matter and told him that this Piper madman had written the book?' he said.

'I had to,' said Frensic miserably. 'If I hadn't, the whole deal would have fallen through. Hutchmeyer would have backed out and where would we have been then?'

'We wouldn't be in the ghastly position we are now, that I do know.'

'You'd have gone out of business,' said Frensic. '*Pause* saved you. You've done very nicely out of the book and I've sent you others. Corkadales is a name to be reckoned with now.'

'Well, I suppose that's true,' said Geoffrey, slightly mollified, 'but it's going to be a name that will stink if it gets out that Piper is still alive and didn't write ...'

'It isn't going to get out,' said Frensic, 'I promise you that.'

Geoffrey looked at him doubtfully. 'Your promises ...' he began.

'You'll just have to trust me,' said Frensic.

'Trust you? After this? You can rest assured that if there's one thing I'm not going to do ...'

'You'll have to. Remember that contract you signed? The one saying you had paid fifty thousand pounds advance for *Pause*?'

'You tore that up,' said Geoffrey, 'I saw you do it.'

Frensic nodded. 'But Hutchmeyer didn't,' he said. 'He had photocopies made and if this thing comes to court you're going to have a hard time explaining why you signed two contracts with the same author for the same book. It isn't going to look good, Geoffrey, not good at all.'

Geoffrey could see that. He sat down.

'What do you want?' he asked.

'A bed for the night,' said Frensic, 'and tomorrow morning I shall go to the American Embassy for a visa.'

'I can't see why you've got to spend the night here,' said Geoffrey.

'You would if you saw her,' said Frensic man-to-man. Geoffrey poured him another brandy.

'I'll have to explain to Sven,' he said, 'he's obsessively jealous. By the way, who *did* write *Pause*?' But Frensic shook his head. 'I can't tell you. There are some thing it's best for you not to know. Just let's say the late Peter Piper.'

'The late?' said Geoffrey with a shudder. 'It's a curious expression to apply to the living.'

'It's a curious expression to apply to the dead,' said Frensic, 'It seems to suggest that they may yet turn up. Better late than never.'

'I wish I could share your optimism,' said Geoffrey.

Next morning, after a restless night in a strange bed, Frensic went to the American Embassy and got his visa. He visited his bank and he bought a return ticket to Florida. That night he left Heathrow. He spent the crossing in a drunken stupor and boarded the flight from Miami to Atlanta next day feeling hot, ill and filled with foreboding. To delay matters he spent the next night in a hotel and studied a map of Alabama. It was a detailed map but he couldn't find Bibliopolis. He tried the desk clerk but the man had never heard of it.

'You'd best go to Selma and ask there,' he told Frensic. Frensic caught the Greyhound to Selma and inquired at the Post Office.

'The sticks. A wide place in the road over Mississippi way,' he was told. 'Swamp country on the Ptomaine River. Take Route 80 about a hundred miles and go north. Are you from New England?'

'Old England,' said Frensic, 'why do you ask?'

'Just that they don't take too kindly to Northern strangers in those parts. Damn Yankees they call them. They're still living in the past.'

'So is the man I want to see,' said Frensic and went out to rent a car. The man at the office increased his apprehension.

'You're going out along Blood Alley you want to take care,' he said.

'Blood Alley?' said Frensic anxiously.

'That what they call Route 80 through to Meridian. That road's seen a whole heap of deaths.'

'Isn't there a more direct route to Bibliopolis?'

'You can go through the backwoods but you could get lost. Blood Alley's your best route.'

Frensic hesitated. 'I don't supose I could hire a driver?' he asked.

'Too late now,' said the man, 'Saturday afternoon this time everyone's gone home and tomorrow being Sunday ...'

Frensic left the office and drove to a motel. He wasn't going to drive to Bibliopolis along Blood Alley at nightfall. He would go in the morning.

Next day he was up early and on the road. The sun shone down out of a cloudless sky and the day was bright and beautiful. Frensic wasn't. The desperate resolution with which he had left London had faded and with each mile westward it diminished still further. Woods closed in on the road and by the time he reached the sign with the faded inscription BIBLIOPOLIS 15 MILES he almost turned back. But a pinch of

236

snuff and the thought of what would happen if Piper continued his campaign of literary revival gave him the courage he needed. Frensic turned right and followed the dirt road into the woods, trying not to look at the black water and the trees strangled with vines. And, like Piper those many months before, he was relieved when he came to the meadows and the cattle grazing in the long grass. But still the abandoned shacks depressed him and the occasional glimpse of the river, a brown slurry in the distance fringed by veiled trees, did nothing for his morale. The Ptomaine looked aptly named. Finally the road veered down to the left and across the water Frensic looked at Bibliopolis. A wide place in the road, the girl in Selma had called it, but she had quite evidently never seen it. Besides, the road stopped at the river. The little town huddled round the square and looked old and unchanged from some time in the nineteenth century. And the ferry which presently moved towards him with an old man pulling on the rope was from some bygone age. Frensic thought he knew now why Bibliopolis was said to be in the sticks. By the Styx would have done as well. Frensic drove the car carefully on to the ferry and got out.

'I'm looking for a man called Piper,' he told the ferryman.

The man nodded. 'Guessed you might be,' he said. 'They come from all over to hear him preach. And if it isn't him it's the Reverend Baby up at the Church.'

'Preach?' said Frensic, 'Mr Piper preaches?'

'Sure does. Preaching and teaching the good word.'

Frensic raised his eyebrows. Piper as preacher was a new one to him. 'Where will I find him?' he asked.

'Down Pellagra.'

'Down with pellagra?' said Frensic hopefully.

'At Pellagra,' said the old man, 'the house.' He nodded in the direction of a large house fronted by tall white columns. 'There's Pellagra. Used to be the Stopes's place but they all died off.'

'Hardly surprising,' said Frensic, his intellectual compass spinning between vitamin deficiency, advocates of birth control, the Monkey Trial and Yoknapatawpha County. He gave the man a dollar and drove down the drive to an open gate. On one side a sign in large italic said THE PIPER SCHOOL OF PEN-

MANSHIP while on the other an inscribed finger pointed to the CHURCH OF THE GREAT PURSUIT. Frensic stopped the car and stared at the enormous finger. The Church of The Great Pursuit? The Church of ... There could be no doubting that he had come to the right place. But what sort of religious mania was Piper suffering from now? He drove on and parked beside several other cars in front of the large white building with a wrought-iron balcony extending forward to the columns from the first-floor rooms. Frensic got out and walked up the steps to the front door. It was open. Frensic peered into the hall. A door to the left had painted on it THE SCRIPTORIUM while from a room on the right there came the drone of an insistent voice. Frensic crossed the marble floor and listened. There was no mistaking that voice. It was Piper's, but the old hesitant quality had gone and in its place there was a new strident intensity. If the voice was familiar, so were the words.

'And we must not (the "must" here presupposing explicitly a sustained seriousness of purpose and an undeviating moral duty) allow ourselves to be deluded by the seeming naïvety so frequently ascribed by other less perceptive critics to the presentation of Little Nell. Sentiment not sentimentality as we must understand it is cognizant ...'

Frensic shyed away from the door. He knew now what the Church of The Great Pursuit had for its gospel. Piper was reading aloud from Dr Louth's essay 'How We must Aproach *The Old Curiosity Shop*'. Even his religion was derived. Frensic found a chair and sat down filled with a mounting anger. 'The unoriginal little sod,' he muttered, and cursed Dr Louth into the bargain. The apotheosis of that dreadful woman, the cause of all his troubles, was taking place here in the heart of the Bible belt. Frensic's anger turned to fury. The Bible belt! Bibliopolis and the Bible. And instead of that magnificent prose, Piper was disseminating her graceless style, her angular inverted syntax, her arid puritanism and her denunciations against pleasure and the joy of reading. And all this from a man who couldn't write to save his soul! For a moment Frensic felt that he was at the heart of a great conspiracy against life. But that was paranoia. There had been no conscious purpose in the circumstances that had led to Piper's missionary zeal. Only the accident of literary mutation which had turned Frensic himself from a would-be novelist into a successful agent and, by the way of *The Moral Novel*, had mutilated what little talent for writing Piper might once have possessed. And now like some carrier of literary death he was passing the infection on. By the time the droning voice stopped and the little congregation filed out, their faces taut with moral intensity, and made their way to the cars, Frensic was in a murderous mood.

He crossed the hall and entered the Church of The Great Pursuit. Piper was putting the book away with all the reverence of a priest handling the Host. Frensic stood in the doorway and waited. He had come a long way for this moment. Piper shut the cupboard and turned. The look of reverence faded from his face.

'You,' he said faintly.

'Who else?' said Frensic loudly to exorcize the atmosphere of sanctity that pervaded the room. 'Or were you expecting Conrad?'

Piper's face paled. 'What do you want?'

'Want?' said Frensic and sat down in one of the pews and took a pinch of snuff. 'Just to put an end to this bloody game of hide-and-seek.' He wiped his nose with a red handkerchief.

Piper hesitated and then headed for the door. 'We can't talk in here,' he muttered.

'Why not?' said Frensic. 'It seems as good a place as any.'

'You wouldn't understand,' said Piper and went out. Frensic blew his nose coarsely and then followed.

'For a horrid little blackmailer you've got a hell of a lot of pretensions,' he said as they stood in the hall, 'all that crap in there about *The Old Curiosity Shop*.'

'It isn't crap.' said Piper, 'and don't call me a blackmailer. You started this. And that's the truth.'

'Truth?' said Frensic with a nasty laugh. 'If you want the truth you're going to get it. That's what I've come here for.' He looked across at the door marked SCRIPTORIUM. 'What's in there?'

'That's where I teach people to write,' said Piper.

Frensic stared at him and laughed again. 'You're joking,' he said and opened the door. Inside the room was filled with desks, desks on which stood bottles of ink and pens, and each desk tilted at an angle. On the walls were framed examples of script and, in front, a blackboard. Frensic glanced round.

'Charming. The Scriptorium. And I suppose you've got a Plagiarium too?'

'A what?' said Piper.

'A special room for plagiarism. Or do you combine the process in here? I mean there's nothing like going the whole hog. How do you go about it? Do you give each student a bestseller to alter and then flog it as your own work?'

'Coming from you, that's a dirty crack,' said Piper. 'I do all my own writing in my study. Down here I teach my students how to write. Not what.'

'How? You teach them how to write?' He picked up a bottle of ink and shook it. The sludge moved slowly. 'Still on the evaporated ink, I see.'

'It gives the greatest density,' said Piper but Frensic had put the bottle down and turned back to the door.

'And where's your study?' he asked. Piper led the way slowly upstairs and opened another door. Frensic stepped inside. The walls were lined with shelves and a big desk stood in front of a window which looked out across the drive towards the river. Frensic studied the books. They were bound in calf. Dickens, Conrad, James ...

'The old testament,' he said and reached for *Middlemarch*. Piper took it brusquely from him and put it back.

'This year's model?' asked Frensic.

'A world, a universe beyond your tawdry imagination,' said Piper angrily. Frensic shrugged. There was a pathos about Piper's tenseness that was weakening his resolve. Frensic steeled himself to be coarse.

'Bloody cosy little billet you've got yourself here,' he said, seating himself at the desk and putting his feet up. Behind him Piper's face whitened at the sacrilege. 'Curator of a museum, counterfeiter of other people's novels, a bit of blackmail on the side – and what do you do about sex?' He hesitated and picked up a paperknife for safety's sake. If he was going to put the boot in there was no knowing what Piper might do. 'Screw the late Mrs Hutchmeyer?'

240

There was a hiss behind him and Frensic swung round. Piper was facing him with his pinched face and narrow eyes blazing with hatred. Frensic's grip tightened on the paperknife. He was frightened but the thing had to be done. He had come too far to go back now.

'It's none of my business, I daresay,' he said as Piper stared, 'but necrophilia seems to be your forte. First you rob dead authors, then you put the bite on me for two million dollars, what do you do to the late Mrs Hutch—'

'Don't you dare say it,' shouted Piper, his voice shrill with fury.

'Why not?' said Frensic. 'There's nothing like confession for cleansing the soul.'

'It isn't true,' said Piper. His breathing was audible.

Frensic smiled cynically. 'What isn't? The truth will out, as the saying goes. That's why I'm here.' He stood up with assumed menace and Piper shrank back.

'Stop it. Stop it. I don't want to hear any more. Just go away and leave me alone.'

Frensic shook his head. 'And have you send me yet another manuscript and tell me to sell it? Oh no, those days are over. You're going to learn the truth if I have to ram it down your snivelling—'

Piper covered his ears with his hands. 'I won't,' he shouted, 'I won't listen to you.'

Frensic reached in his pocket and took out Dr Louth's letter. 'You don't have to listen. Just read this.'

He thrust the letter forward and Piper took it. Frensic sat down in the chair. The crisis was over. He was no longer afraid. Piper might be mad but his madness was self-directed and held no threat for Frensic. He watched him read the letter with a new sense of pity. He was looking at a nonentity, the archetypal author for whom only words had any reality, and one who couldn't write. Piper finished the letter and looked up.

'What does it mean?' he asked.

'What it doesn't say,' said Frensic. 'That the great Dr Louth wrote *Pause*. That's what it means.'

Piper looked down at the letter again. 'But it says here she didn't.'

Frensic smiled. 'Quite. And why should she have written that? Ask yourself that question. Why deny what nobody had ever supposed?'

'I don't understand,' said Piper, 'it doesn't make sense.'

'It does if you accept that she was being blackmailed,' said Frensic.

'Blackmailed? But by whom?'

Frensic helped himself to snuff. 'By you. You threatened me and I threatened her.'

'But . . .' Piper wrestled with this incomprehensible sequence. It was beyond his simple philosophy.

'You threatened to expose me and I passed the message on,' said Frensic. 'Dr Sydney Louth paid two million dollars not to be revealed as the author of *Pause*. The price of her sacred reputation.'

Piper's eyes were glazed. 'I don't believe you,' he muttered.

'Don't,' said Frensic. 'Believe what you bloody well like. All you've got to do is resurrect yourself and tell Hutchmeyer you're still alive and kicking and the media will do the rest. It will all come out. My role, your role, the whole damned story and at the end of it, your Dr Louth with her reputation as a critic in ruins. The bitch will be the laughing-stock of the literary world. Mind you, you'll be in prison. And I dare say I'll be bankrupt too, but at least I won't have to put up with the impossible task of trying to sell your rotten *Search for a Lost Childhood*. That'll be some compensation.'

Piper sat down limply in a chair.

'Well?' said Frensic, but Piper simply shook his head. Frensic took the letter from him and turned to the window. He had called the little sod's bluff. There would be no more threats, no more manuscripts. Piper was broken. It was time to leave. Frensic stared out at the dark river and the forest beyond, a strange foreign landscape, dangerously lush, and far from the comfortable little world he had come to protect. He crossed to the door and went down the broad staircase and across the hall. All that was needed now was to get home as quickly as possible.

But when he got into his rented car and drove down the

drive to the ferry it was to find the pontoon on the far side of the river and no one to bring it across. Frensic rang the bell but nobody answered. He stood in the bright sunlight and waited. There was a stillness in the air and only the sound of the black river slurping against the bank below him. Frensic got back into the car and drove into the square. Here too there was nobody in sight. Dark shadows under the tin roofs that served as awnings to the shop fronts, the white-painted church, a wooden bench at the foot of the statue in the middle of the square, blank windows. Frensic got out of his car and looked round. The clock on the courthouse stood at midday. Presumably everyone was at lunch, but there was still a sense of unnatural desolation which disturbed him and back beyond the river the forest, an undomesticated tangle of trees and underbush, made a close horizon above which the sky was an empty blue. Frensic walked round the square and then got back into the car. Perhaps if he tried the ferry again ... But it was still there across the water and when Frensic tried to pull on the rope there was no movement. He rang the bell again. There was no echo and his sense of unease redoubled. Finally leaving the car in the road he walked along the bank of the river following a little path. He would wait a while until the lunch hour was over and then try again. But the path led under live oaks hung with Spanish moss and ended in the cemetery. Frensic looked for a moment at the gravestones and then turned back.

Perhaps if he drove west he would find a road out of town on that side which would lead him back to Route 80. Blood Alley had an almost cheerful ring to it now. But he had no map in the car and after driving down a number of side streets that ended in culs-de-sac or uninviting tracks into the woods he turned back. Perhaps the ferry would be open now. He looked at his watch. It was two o'clock and people would be out and about again.

They were. As he drove into the little square a group of gaunt men standing on the sidewalk outside the courthouse moved across the road. Frensic stopped the car and stared unhappily through the windshield. The gaunt men had holsters on their belts and the gauntest of them all wore a star on his chest. He walked round the car to the side window and leant in. Frensic studied his yellow teeth.

'Your name Frensic?' he asked, Frensic nodded. 'Judge wants to see you,' continued the man. 'You going to come quietly or . . . ?' Frensic came quietly and with the little group behind him climbed the steps to the courthouse. Inside it was cool and dark. Frensic hesitated but the tall man pointed to a door.

'Judge is in chambers,' he said. 'Go on in.'

Frensic went in. Behind a large desk sat Baby Hutchmeyer. She was dressed in a long black robe and above it her face, always unnaturally taut, was now unpleasantly white. Frensic, staring down at her, had no doubt about her identity.

'Mrs Hutchmeyer . . .' he began, 'the late Mrs Hutchmeyer?'

'Judge Hutchmeyer to you,' said Baby, 'and we won't have anything more about the late unless you want to end up the late Mr Frensic right soon.'

Frensic swallowed and glanced over his shoulder. The sheriff was standing with his back against the door and the gun on his belt glinted obtrusively.

'May I ask what the meaning of this is?' he asked after a moment's significant silence. 'Bringing me here like this and . . .'

The judge looked across at the sheriff. 'What have you got on him so far?' she asked.

'Uttering threats and menaces,' said the sheriff. 'Possession of an unauthorized firearm. Spare tyre stashed with heroin. Blackmail. You name it, Judge, he's got it.'

Frensic groped for a chair. 'Heroin?' he gasped. 'What do you mean heroin? I haven't a single grain of heroin.'

'You think not?' said Baby. 'Herb'll show you, won't you, Herb?'

Behind Frensic the sheriff nodded. 'Got the automobile round at the garage dismantling it right now,' he said, 'you want proof we'll show it to you.'

But Frensic was in no need of proof. He sat stunned in the chair and stared at Baby's white face. 'What do you want?' he asked finally.

'Justice,' said Baby succinctly.

'Justice,' muttered Frensic, 'you talk about justice and . . .'

'You want to make a statement now or reserve your defence for court tomorrow?' said Baby.

Frensic glanced over his shoulder again. 'I'd like to make a statement now. In private,' he said.

Baby nodded to the sheriff. 'Wait outside, Herb,' she said, 'and stay close. Any trouble in here and ...'

'There won't be any trouble in here,' said Frensic hastily, 'I can assure you of that.'

Baby waved his assurances and Herb aside. As the door closed Frensic took out his handkerchief and mopped his face.

'Right,' said Baby, 'so you want to make a statement.'

Frensic leant forward. It was in his mind to say 'You can't do this to me,' but the cliché culled from so many of his authors didn't seem appropriate. She *could* do this to him. He was in Bibliopolis and Bibliopolis was off the map of civilization.

'What do you want me to do?' he asked faintly.

Judge Baby swung her chair and leant back. 'Coming from you, Mr Frensic, that's an interesting question,' she said. 'You come into this little town and you start uttering threats and menaces against one of our citizens and you want me to tell you what I want you to do.'

'I didn't utter threats and menaces,' said Frensic, 'I came to tell Piper to stop sending me his manuscripts. And if anyone's been uttering threats it's him, not me.'

Baby shook her head. 'If that's your defence I can tell you right off nobody in Bibliopolis is going to believe you. Mr Piper is the most peaceful non-violent citizen around these parts.'

'Well, he may be around these parts,' said Frensic, 'but from where I'm sitting in London ...'

'You ain't sitting in London now,' said Baby, 'you're sitting right here in my chambers and shaking like a hound dog pissing peach pits.'

Frensic considered the simile and found it disagreeable. 'You'd be shaking if you'd been accused of having a spare tyre filled with heroin,' he said.

Baby nodded. 'You could be right at that,' she said. 'I can give you life for that. Throw in the threats and menaces, the firearm and the blackmail and it could all add up to life plus ninety-nine years. You had better consider that before you say anything more.'

Frensic considered it and found he was shaking even harder. Hound dogs having problems with peach pits were no comparison. 'You can't mean it,' he gasped.

Baby smiled. 'You'd better believe I mean it. The warden of the penitentiary's a deacon in my church. You wouldn't have to do the ninety-nine years. Like life would be three months and you wouldn't last in the chain gang. They got snakes and things to make it natural death. You've seen our little cemetery?'

Frensic nodded, 'So we've got a little plot marked out already,' said Baby. 'It wouldn't have no headstone. No name like Frensic. Just a little mound and nobody would ever know. So that's your choice.'

'What is?' said Frensic when he could find his voice.

'Like life plus ninety-nine or you do what I tell you.'

'I think I'll do what you tell me,' said Frensic for whom this was no choice at all.

'Right,' said Baby, 'so first you make a full confession.'

'Confession?' said Frensic. 'What sort of confession?'

'Just that you wrote *Pause O Men for the Virgin* and palmed it off on Mr Piper and hoodwinked Hutch and instigated Miss Futtle to arsonize the house and—'

'No,' cried Frensic, 'never. I'd rather ...' He stopped. He wouldn't rather. There was a look on Baby's face that told him that. 'I don't see why I've got to confess to all those things,' he said.

Baby relaxed. 'You took his good name away from him. Now you're going to give it back to him.'

'His good name?' said Frensic.

'By putting it on the cover of that dirty novel,' said Baby.

'He didn't have any sort of name till we did that,' said Frensic, 'he never published anything and now he's so-called dead he isn't going to.'

'Oh yes, he is,' said Baby leaning forward. 'You're going to give him your name. Like *Search for a Lost Childhood* by Frederick Frensic.'

Frensic stared at her. The woman was mad as a March hare.

246

'*Search* by me?' he said. 'You don't understand. I've hawked that blasted book around every publisher in London and no one wants to know. It's unreadable.'

Baby smiled. Unpleasantly.

'That's your problem. You're going to get it published and you're going to get all his future books published under your own name. It's that or the chain gang.'

She glanced significantly out of the window at the horizon of trees and the empty sky and Frensic following her glance gazed into a terrible future and an early death. He'd have to humour her. 'All right,' he said, 'I'll do my best.'

'You'll do better than that. You'll do exactly what I say.' She took a sheet of paper from a drawer and handed him a pen. 'Now write,' she said.

Frensic hitched his chair foward and began to write very shakily. By the time he had finished he had confessed to having evaded British income tax by paying two million dollars plus royalties into account number 478776 in the First National Bank of New York and to having incited his partner, the former Miss Futtle, to arsonize the Hutchmeyer residence. The whole statement was such an amalgam of things he had done and things he hadn't that, cross-examined by a competent lawyer, he would never be able to disentangle himself. Baby read it through and witnessed his signature. Then she called Herb in and he witnessed it too.

'That should keep you on the straight and narrow,' she said as the sheriff left the room. 'One squeak out of you and one attempt to evade your obligation to publish Mr Piper's novels and this goes straight to Hutchmeyer, the insurance company, the FBI and the tax authorities, and you can wipe that smile off your face.' But Frensic wasn't smiling. He had developed a nervous tic. 'Because if you think you can worm your way out of this by going to the authorities yourself and telling them to look me up in Bibliopolis you can forget it. I've got friends round here and no one talks if I say no. You understand that?'

Frensic nodded. 'I quite understand,' he said.

Baby stood up and took off her robe. 'Well, just in case you don't, you're going to be saved,' she said. They went out into the hall where the group of gaunt men waited.

'We've got a convert, boys,' she said. 'See you all in Church.'

Frensic sat in the front row of the little Church of The Servants of The Lord. Before him, radiant and serene, Baby conducted the service. The church was packed and Herb sat next to Frensic and shared his hymnbook with him. They sang 'Telephoning to Glory' and 'Rock of Ages' and 'Shall we Gather by the River', and with Herb's nudging Frensic sang as loudly as the rest. Finally Baby delivered a virulent sermon on the text 'Behold a man gluttonous, and a winebibber, a friend of publishers and sinners,' her gaze fixed pointedly on Frensic throughout, and the congregation launched into 'Bibliopolis we Hold Thee Dear'. It was time for Frensic to be saved. He moved shakily forward and knelt. Snakes might no longer infest Bibliopolis, but Frensic was still petrified. Above him Baby's face was radiant. She had triumphed once again.

'Swear by the Lord to keep the covenant,' she said. And Frensic swore.

He was still swearing an hour later as he sat in his car and the ferry crossed the river. Frensic glanced across at Pellagra. The light was burning on the upper floor. Piper was doubtless at work on some terrible novel that Frensic would have to sell under his own name. He drove off the ferry recklessly and the hired car bucketed down the dirt road and the headlights picked out the dark water gleaming beneath the entwined trees. After Bibliopolis the grim landscape held no menace for him. It was a natural world full of natural dangers and Frensic could cope with them. With Baby Hutchmeyer there had been no coping. Frensic swore again.

In his study in Pellagra Piper sat silently at his desk. He was not writing. He was looking at the guarantee Frensic had written promising to publish *Search for a Lost Childhood* even at his own expense. Piper was going to be published at long last. Never mind that the name on the cover would be Frensic. One day the world would learn the truth. Or better still, perhaps, would be an unanswered question. After all who knew who Shakespeare was or who had written *Hamlet*? No one.

23

Nine months later *Search for a Lost Childhood* by Frederick Frensic, published by Corkadales, price £3.90, came out in Britain. In America it was published by Hutchmeyer Press. Frensic had had to apply some direct pressure in both direc- and it was only the threat of exposure that had persuaded Geoffrey to accept the book. Sonia had been influenced by feelings of loyalty, and Hutchmeyer had needed no urging. The sound of a familiar female voice on the telephone had sufficed. And so the review copies had gone out with Frensic's name on the title-page and the dust jacket. A short biography at the back said he had once been a literary agent. He was one no longer. The name on the door of the office in Lanyard Lane still lingered but the office was empty and Frensic had moved from Glass Walk to a cottage in Sussex without a tele- phone.

There, safe from Mrs Bogden, he was Piper's amanuensis. Day after day he typed out the manuscripts Piper sent him and night after night lurked in the corner of the village pub and drowned his sorrows. His friends in London saw him sel- dom. From necessity he visited Geoffrey and occasionally went out to lunch with him. But for the most part he spent his days at his typewriter, cultivated his garden and went for long walks sunk in melancholy thought.

Not that his thoughts were always depressed. There remained a deep core of deviousness in Frensic which nagged at the problem of his predicament and sought ways to escape. But none came to mind. His imagination had been anaesthetized by his terrible experience and each day Piper's dreary prose re- inforced the effect. Distilled from so many sources, it acted on Frensic's literary nerve and kept him in a state of disorienta- tion so that he had no sooner recognized a sentence from Mann than he was flung a chunk of Faulkner to be followed by a *mot* from Proust or a slice of *Middlemarch*. After such a paragraph Frensic would get up and reel into the garden to escape his associations by mowing the lawn. At night before going to sleep he would excise the memory of Bibliopolis by reading a page or two of *The Wind in the Willows* and wish he could potter about in boats like the Water Rat. Anything to escape the ordeal he had been set.

And now it was Sunday and the reviews of *Search* would be in the papers. In spite of himself Frensic was drawn to the little shop in the village to buy the *Sunday Times* and the *Observer*. He bought them both and didn't wait until he got home to read the worst. It was best to get the agony over and done with. He stood in the lane and opened the *Sunday Times Review* and turned to the book page and there it was. At the top of the list. Frensic leant againt a gatepost and read the review as he read his world turned topsy-turvy once again. Linda Gormley 'loved' the book and devoted two columns to its praise. She called it 'the most honest and original appraisal of the adolescent trauma I have read for a very long time'. Frensic stared at the words in disbelief. Then he rummaged in the *Observer*. It was the same there. 'For a first novel it has not only freshness but a deeply intuitive insight into family relationships ... a masterpiece ...' Frensic shut the paper hurriedly. A masterpiece? He looked again. The word was still there, and further down there was even worse. 'If one can say of a novel that it is a great work of genius ...' Frensic clutched the gatepost. He felt weak. *Search for a Lost Childhood* was being acclaimed. He staggered on up the lane with a fresh sense of loss. His nose, his infallible nose, had betrayed him. Piper had been right all along. Either that or the plague of *The Moral Novel* had spread and the days of the novel of entertainment were over, supplanted by the religion of literature. People no longer read for pleasure. If they liked *Search* they couldn't. There wasn't an ounce of enjoyment to be got from the book. Frensic had painstakingly (and the word was precise) typed the manuscript out page by ghastly page and from those pages there had emanated a whining self-pity, an arrogantly self-directed sycophancy that had sickened him. And this wretched puke of words was what the reviewers calleld originality and freshness and a work of genius. Genius! Frensic spat the word. It had lost all meaning.

And as he lumbered up the lane the full portent of the book's success hit him. He would have to go through life bearing the stigma of being known as the author of a book he hadn't written. His friends would congratulate him ... For one awful moment Frensic contemplated suicide but his sense of irony saved him. He knew now how Piper had felt when he had discovered what Frensic had foisted on him with *Pause*. 'Hoist with his own petard' sprang to mind and he acknowledged Piper's triumphant revenge. The thought brought Frensic to a standstill. He had been made to look a fool and if the world now considered him a genius, one day they would learn the truth and the laughter would never cease. It was a threat he had used against Dr Louth and it had been turned against him. Frensic's fury at the thought spurred his deviousness to work. Standing in the lane between the hedgerows he saw his escape. He would turn the tables on them yet. Out of the accumulated experience of the thousand commercially successful novels he had sold he could surely concoct a story that would contain every ingredient Piper and his mentor, Dr Louth, would most detest. It would have sex, violence, sentimentality, romance – and all this without an ounce of significance. It would be a rattling good yarn, a successor to *Pause*, and on the dust jacket in bold type there would be Peter Piper's name. No, that was wrong. Piper was a mere pawn in the game. Behind him there lay a far deadlier enemy to literature. Dr Sydney Louth.

Frensic quickened his pace and hurried across the little wooden bridge that led to his cottage. Presently he was sitting at his typewriter and had inserted a sheet of paper. First he needed a title. His fingers hammered on the keys and the words appeared. 'AN IMMORAL NOVEL by DR SYDNEY LOUTH. CHAPTER ONE'. Frensic typed on and his mind flickered with fresh subtleties. He would incorporate her graceless style. And her ideas. It would be a grotesque pastiche of everything she had ever written and with it all there would be a story so sickly and vile as to deny every precept of *The Moral Novel*. He would stand the bitch on her head and shake her till her teeth rattled. And there was nothing she could do about it. As her agent, Frensic was safe. Only the truth could hurt him and she was in no position to tell the truth. Frensic stopped typing at the thought and stared into the distance. There was no need to concoct a story.

The truth was far more deadly. He would tell the history of The Great Pur̄uit just as it had happened. His name would be mud but it was mud already in his own eyes with the success of *Search* and besides he owed a duty to English literature. To hell with English literature. To Grub Street and all those writers without pretensions who wrote for a living. A living? The ambiguity of the world held him for a moment. Who wrote for a living and the living too. Frensic tore the sheet from the typewriter and started again.

He would call it THE GREAT PURSUIT. A TRUE STORY by Frederick Frensic. The living deserved the truth, and a story, and he would give them both. He would dedicate the book to Grub Street. It had a good old eighteenth-century ring to it. Frensic's nose twitched. He knew he had just begun to write a book that would sell. And if they wanted to sue, let them. He would publish and be damned.

In Bibliopolis the publication of *Search* made no impression on Piper. He had lost his faith. It had gone with Frensic's visit and the revelation that Dr Sydney Louth had written *Pause*. It had taken some time for the truth to sink in and he had gone on writing and rewriting for a few months almost automatically. But in the end he knew that Frensic had not lied. He had written to Dr Louth and had had no reply. Piper closed the Church of The Great Tradition. Only the School of Penmanship remained and with it the doctrine of logosophy. The age of the great novel was over. It remained only to commemorate it in manuscript. And so while Baby preached the need to imitate Christ, Piper too returned to traditional virtues in everything. Already he had abolished pens and his pupils had moved back to quills. They were more natural than nibs. They needed cutting, they were the original tools of his craft and they stood as reminders of that golden age when books were written by hand and to be a copyist was to belong to an honourable profession.

And so that Sunday morning Piper sat in the Scriptorium and dipped his quill in Higgins Eternal Evaporated Ink and began to write: 'My father's family name being Pirrip, and my Christian name Philip, my infant tongue could make of both names nothing longer or more explicit than Piper ...' He stopped. That wasn't right. It should have been Pip. But after a moment's hesitation he dipped his quill again and continued.

After all in a thousand years who the dickens would care who had written *Great Expectations*? Only a few scholars who could still read English. The printed works would have perished by then. Only Piper's own parchment manuscripts bound in the thickest leather and filled with his perfect hieroglyphic handwriting and gold illuminated lettering would stand the test of time and lie in the museums of the world, mute testimony to his dedication to literature, and to his craftsmanship. And when he had finished Dickens, he would start on Henry James and write *his* novels out in longhand too. There was a lifetime's work ahead of him just copying the great tradition out in Higgins Eternal Ink. The name of Piper would be literally immortal yet ...

Douglas Reeman £4.99

Special Limited Edition

The Iron Pirate
In Danger's Hour

Two bestselling naval adventures for the price of one!

Classic World War Two adventure from master storyteller
Douglas Reeman

From the summer of 1944, from the killing grounds of the
Atlantic and the Baltic, two electrifying bestsellers from the
master storyteller of the sea.

The Iron Pirate is the story of Germany's last hope in the
seaborne war – the crack heavy cruiser *Prinz Luitpold*. The
men who hunted with her. And those who would see her
destroyed . . .

And from the deadly waters of the Channel and the
Mediterranean, *In Danger's Hour* tells of the unsung heroes
of the 'little ships'. As D-Day approaches, fleet
minesweeper *HMS Rob Roy* faces her most dangerous
mission yet: a deadly challenge that will test captain and
crew to the limits of endurance – and beyond . . .

'Vivid naval action at its most authentic'

Sunday Times

Dick Francis £4.99

Special Limited Edition

Reflex
Comeback

Two champion thrillers for the price of one!

'Dick Francis at his brilliant best'

Sporting Life

A veterinary surgeon with a string of bloody accidents to his name . . .

. . . a murdered photographer, ready to send shockwaves through the racing world with a legacy from beyond the grave.

From the undisputed champion of the racing crime thriller, two more classic tales of murder, mystery and intrigue – set against the colourful background of the Sport of Queens. *Reflex*, a fast-moving story of corruption and greed, was one of Dick Francis's earliest triumphs. *Comeback*, set among the Gloucestershire raceyards the former jockey knows so well, is the master's 30th consecutive Number 1 bestseller.

'Still the best bet for a winning read'

Mail on Sunday

'The finish had me sweating. The Gold Cup is tame by comparison'

Evening Standard

Elizabeth Jane Howard £4.99

Special Limited Edition

The Long View
The Sea Change

Two Beautiful stories for the price of one!

Loyalty . . . Passion . . . Discovery . . .

Elizabeth Jane Howard, bestselling author of The Cazalet
Chronicle, dissects love, marriage and relationships in two
revealing – and wonderfully entertaining – full length
novels.

The Long View
Elizabeth Jane Howard's acclaimed fictional portrait of a
contemporary marriage – ingeniously constructed to give a
very real view of the shifting relationship between two
people.

'If artistry lies in heightened awareness, this is it'
The Times

The Sea Change
A classic story of compulsion – deftly unravelling the
complex interactions between two men and two women
whose lives become entangled in London, New York, and
finally on a remote and mysterious Greek island.

Beautifully written and richly perceptive'
Daily Telegraph

Rumer Godden £6.99

Special Limited Edition

COROMANDEL SEA CHANGE
THE GREENGAGE SUMMER
THE RIVER

Three classics for the price of one!

Rumer Godden's genius for storytelling has captivated
readers all over the world for nearly four decades.
Acclaimed as 'one of the finest of living English novelists'
Orville Prescott, her stories have a timelessness and a
haunting simplicity that have earned them the status of
modern classics.

Now in one anthology, three of Rumer Godden's best-loved
novels will delight her many fans and new readers alike.
Included are *Coromandel Sea Change*, Rumer Godden's
first Number 1 bestseller of the 1990's, a captivating love
story set in Southern India at election time; *The Greengage
Summer*, an evocative portrait of love and deceit in rural
France which became a memorable film starring Kenneth
More and Susannah York; and *The River*, a beautiful tribute
to India and childhood, made into a film by the great
French director Jean Renoir.

'Sheer enjoyment'

Guardian

'The miracle is Godden's genius for storytelling'
Evening Standard

'The prose is as simple and luminous as the fantasy it
elaborates'

Independent on Sunday

Tama Janowitz £4.99

Special Limited Edition

AMERICAN DAD
SLAVES OF NEW YORK

Two cult classics for the price of one!

When Tama Janowitz first hit the Big Apple in the 1980s
her fearless, quirky and totally original talent for satire,
ensured that no artistes, residents, freaks, urban guerillas
or all-round poseurs who stalk that area of gilt-edged real
estate – Manhattan – escaped unnoticed. In her own
merciless, irreverent style Tama Janowitz ensures that no
reputation survives intact!

Slaves of New York is her classic comedy of life on the
island of dreams which was captured for posterity in the
Hendler-Merchant Ivory film. It's joined here by Tama
Janowitz's hilarious first novel, *American Dad*; an
irresistibly outrageous portrait of postmodern American
family life.

'The shrewd observation, the skewed invention . . . are the
gifts of a singular talent'
Jay McInerney, New York Times

'Laugh out loud funny and wonderfully sharp'
Washington Post

'So savagely witty, so acerbic, so piercingly accurate . . .
Tama Janowitz has a merciless eye for absurdity'
Los Angeles Herald

Kathy Lette £4.99

Special Limited Edition

THE LLAMA PARLOUR
GIRLS' NIGHT OUT

Two bestsellers for the price of one!

From the beer-halls of Sydney to the bars at the Groucho –
beware and make way for the irrepressible, irresistible,
insatiable Kathy Lette . . .

The Llama Parlour
Kathy Lette's bestselling first novel: the book that launched
a thousand quips. In Hollywood, Kat is sure she can smell
love in the air – but her mate, Tash, assures her it's only car
exhaust . . .

'The best one-liners you're likely to see in print all year'
Guardian

Girls' Night Out
In twelve brilliantly funny short stories, Kathy Lette reveals the
secrets women tell each other when men aren't around . . .

'Written in fresh blood from the war between the sexes'
Los Angeles Times

'Utterly outrageous, irreverent and screamingly funny . . . I
squirmed and cried and laughed'
Jilly Cooper

All Pan Books are available at your local bookshop or newsagent, or can be ordered direct from the publisher. Indicate the number of copies required and fill in the form below.

Send to: Macmillan General Books C.S.
Book Service By Post
PO Box 29, Douglas I-O-M
IM99 1BQ

or phone: 01624 675137, quoting title, author and credit card number.

or fax: 01624 670923, quoting title, author, and credit card number.

Please enclose a remittance* to the value of the cover price plus 75 pence per book for post and packing. Overseas customers please allow £1.00 per copy for post and packing.

*Payment may be made in sterling by UK personal cheque, Eurocheque, postal order, sterling draft or international money order, made payable to Book Service By Post.

Alternatively by Access/Visa/MasterCard

Card No. ☐☐☐☐☐☐☐☐☐☐☐☐☐☐☐☐☐☐

Expiry Date ☐☐☐☐☐☐☐☐☐☐☐☐☐☐☐☐☐☐

Signature _____

Applicable only in the UK and BFPO addresses.

While every effort is made to keep prices low, it is sometimes necessary to increase prices at short notice. Pan Books reserve the right to show on covers and charge new retail prices which may differ from those advertised in the text or elsewhere.

NAME AND ADDRESS IN BLOCK CAPITAL LETTERS PLEASE

Name _____

Address _____

_____

_____

_____

3/95

Please allow 28 days for delivery.
Please tick box if you do not wish to receive any additional information. ☐